DRY BONES THAT DREAM
&
THE HANGING VALLEY

Peter Robinson grew up in Yorkshire and now lives in Toronto.

His Inspector Banks series has won numerous awards in Britain, Europe, the United States and Canada. There are now fifteen novels published by Pan Macmillan in the series; *Aftermath*, the twelfth, was a *Sunday Times* bestseller.

PETER ROBINSON

DRY BONES THAT DREAM
&
THE HANGING VALLEY

INSPECTOR BANKS MYSTERIES

PAN BOOKS

Dry Bones That Dream first published 1995 by Constable
First published by Pan Books 2003
The Hanging Valley first published 1989 by Penguin Books Canada
First published by Pan Books 2002

This omnibus first published 2011 by Pan Books
an imprint of Pan Macmillan, a division of Macmillan Publishers Limited
Pan Macmillan, 20 New Wharf Road, London N1 9RR
Basingstoke and Oxford
Associated companies throughout the world
www.panmacmillan.com

ISBN 978-0-330-54549-5

1 3 5 7 9 8 6 4 2

A CIP catalogue record for this book is available from
the British Library.

Typeset by SX Composing DTP, Rayleigh, Essex
Printed in the UK by CPI Mackays, Chatham ME5 8TD

DRY BONES THAT DREAM

For Sheila

Dry bones that dream are bitter.
They dream and darken our sun.

W. B. Yeats
The Dreaming of the Bones

1

ONE

The uniformed constable lifted the tape and waved Detective Chief Inspector Banks through the gate at two forty-seven in the morning.

Banks's headlights danced over the scene as he drove into the bumpy farmyard and came to a halt. To his left stood the squat, solid house itself, with its walls of thick limestone and mossy, flagstone roof. Lights shone in both the upstairs and downstairs windows. To his right, a high stone wall buttressed a copse that straggled up the daleside, where the trees became lost in darkness. Straight ahead stood the barn.

A group of officers had gathered around the open doors, inside which a ball of light seemed to be moving. They looked like the cast of a fifties sci-fi film gazing in awe on an alien spaceship or lifeform.

When Banks arrived, they parted in silence to let him through. As he entered, he noticed one young PC leaning against the outside wall dribbling vomit on his size twelves. Inside, the scene looked like a film set.

Peter Darby, the police photographer, was busy videotaping, and the source of the light was attached to the top of his camera. It created an eerie chiaroscuro and sudden, sickening illuminations as it swept around the barn's interior. All he needed, Banks thought, was for someone to yell 'Action!' and the place would suddenly be full of sound and motion.

But no amount of yelling would breathe life back into the grotesque shape on the floor, by which a whey-faced young police surgeon, Dr Burns, squatted with a black notebook in his hand.

At first, the position of the body reminded Banks of a parody of Moslem prayer: the kneeling man bent forward from the waist, arms stretched out in front, bum in the air, forehead touching the ground, perhaps facing Mecca. His fists were clenched in the dirt, and Banks noticed the glint of a gold cufflink, initialled 'KAR', as Darby's light flashed on it.

But there was no forehead to touch the ground. Above the charcoal suit jacket, the bloodsoaked collar of the man's shirt protruded about an inch, and after that came nothing but a dark, coagulated mass of bone and tissue spread out on the dirt like an oil stain: a shotgun wound, by the look of it. Patches of blood, bone and brain matter stuck to the whitewashed stone walls in abstract-expressionist patterns. Darby's roving light caught what looked like a fragment of skull sprouting a tuft of fair hair beside a rusty hoe.

Banks felt the bile rise in his throat. He could still smell the gunpowder, reminiscent of a childhood bonfire night, mixed with the stink of urine and faeces and the rancid raw meat smell of sudden violent death.

'What time did the call come in?' he asked the PC beside him.

'One thirty-eight, sir. PC Carstairs from Relton was first on the scene. He's still puking up out front.'

Banks nodded. 'Do we know who the victim was?'

'DC Gay checked his wallet, sir. Name's Keith Roth-well. That's the name of the bloke who lived here, all

2

right.' He pointed over to the house. 'Arkbeck Farm, it's called.'

'A farmer?'

'Nay, sir. Accountant. Some sort of businessman, any road.' One of the constables found a light switch and turned on the bare bulb, which became a foundation for the brighter light of Darby's video camera. Most regions didn't use video because it was hard to get good enough quality, but Peter Darby was a hardware junkie, forever experimenting.

Banks turned his attention back to the scene. The place looked as if it had once been a large stone Yorkshire barn, with double doors and a hayloft, called a 'field house' in those parts. Originally, it would have been used to keep the cows inside between November and May, and to store fodder, but Rothwell seemed to have converted it into a garage.

To Banks's right, a silver-grey BMW, parked at a slight angle, took up about half the space. Beyond the car, against the far wall, a number of metal shelf units held all the tools and potions one would associate with car care: anti-freeze, wax polish, oily rags, screwdrivers, spanners. Rothwell had retained the rural look in the other half of the garage. He had even hung old farm implements on the whitewashed stone wall: a mucking rake, a hay knife, a draining scoop and a Tom spade, among others, all suitably rusted.

As he stood there, Banks tried to picture what might have happened. The victim had clearly been kneeling, perhaps praying or pleading for his life. It certainly didn't look as if he had tried to escape. Why had he submitted so easily? Not much choice, probably, Banks thought. You usually don't argue when someone is pointing a shotgun at you. But still . . . would a man simply kneel there, brace himself and wait for his executioner to pull the trigger?

Banks turned and left the barn. Outside, he met Detective Sergeant Philip Richmond and Detective Constable Susan Gay coming from around the back.

'Nothing there, sir, far as I can tell,' said Richmond, a large torch in his hand. Susan, beside him, looked pale in the glow from the barn entrance.

'All right?' Banks asked her.

'I'm okay now, sir. I was sick, though.'

Richmond looked the same as ever. His sang-froid was legendary around the place, so much so that Banks sometimes wondered if he had any feelings at all or whether he had come to resemble one of those computers he spent most of his time with.

'Anyone know what happened?' Banks asked.

'PC Carstairs had a quick word with the victim's wife when he first got here,' said Susan. 'All she could tell him was that a couple of men were waiting when she got home and they took her husband outside and shot him.' She shrugged. 'Then she became hysterical. I believe she's under sedation now, sir. I fished his wallet from his pocket, anyway,' she went on, holding up a plastic bag. 'Says his name's—'

'Yes, I know,' said Banks. 'Have we got an Exhibits Officer yet?'

'No, sir,' Susan answered, then both she and Phil Richmond looked away. Exhibits Officer was one of the least popular jobs in an investigation. It meant keeping track of every piece of possible evidence and preserving a record of continuity. It usually went to whoever was in the doghouse at the time.

'Get young Farnley on the job, then,' Banks said. PC

Farnley hadn't offended anyone or cocked up a case, but he lacked imagination and had a general reputation around the station as a crashing golf bore.

Clearly relieved, Richmond and Susan wandered off towards the Scene of Crime team, who had just pulled into the farmyard in a large van. As they piled out in their white boiler suits, they looked like a team of government scientists sent to examine the alien landing spot. Pretty soon, Banks thought, if they weren't all careful, there would be a giant spider or a huge gooey blob rolling around the Yorkshire Dales gobbling up everyone in sight.

The night was cool and still, the air moist, tinged with a hint of manure. Banks still felt half asleep, despite the shock of what he had seen in the garage. Maybe he was dreaming. No. He thought of Sandra, warm at home in bed, and sighed.

Detective Superintendent Gristhorpe's arrival at about three-thirty brought him out of his reverie. Gristhorpe limped over from his car. He wore an old donkey-jacket over his shirt, and he clearly hadn't bothered to shave or comb his unruly thatch of grey hair.

'Bloody hell, Alan,' he said by way of greeting, 'tha looks like Columbo.'

There's the pot calling the kettle black, Banks thought. Still, the super was right. He had thrown on an old rain-coat over his shirt and trousers because he knew the night would be chilly.

After Banks had explained what he had found out so far, Gristhorpe took a quick look in the barn, questioned PC Carstairs, the first officer at the scene, then rejoined Banks, his usually ruddy, pockmarked face a little paler. 'Let's go in the house, shall we, Alan?' he said. 'I hear PC

Weaver's brewing up. He should be able to give us some background.'

They walked across the dirt yard. Above them, the stars shone cold and bright like chips of ice on black velvet.

The farmhouse was cosy and warm inside, a welcome change from the cool night and the gruesome scene in the barn. It had been renovated according to the yuppie idea of the real rustic look, with exposed beams and rough stone walls in an open, split-level living room, all earthy browns and greens. The remains of a log fire glowed in the stone hearth, and beside it stood a pair of antique andirons and a matching rack holding poker and tongs.

In front of the fire, Banks noticed two hardbacked chairs facing one another. One of them had fallen over, or had been pushed on its side. Beside both of them lay coils of rope. One of the chair seats looked wet.

Banks and Gristhorpe walked through into the ultra-modern kitchen, which looked like something from a colour supplement, where PC Weaver was pouring boiling water into a large red teapot.

'Nearly ready, sir,' he said when he saw the CID officers. 'I'll just let it mash a couple of minutes.'

The kitchen walls were done in bright red and white patterned tiles, and every available inch of space had been used to wedge fitted microwave, oven, fridge, dishwasher, cupboards and the like. It also boasted a central island unit, complete with tall pine stools. Banks and Gristhorpe sat down.

'How's his wife?' Gristhorpe asked.

'There's a wife and daughter here, sir,' said Weaver. 'The doctor's seen them. They're both unharmed, but they're suffering from shock. Hardly surprising when you consider they found the body. They're upstairs with WPC

Smithies. Apparently there's also a son rambling around America somewhere.'

'Who was this Rothwell bloke?' Banks asked. 'He must have had a bob or two. Anything missing?'

'We don't know yet, sir,' Weaver said. He looked around the bright kitchen. 'But I see what you mean. He was some sort of financial whizz-kid, I think. These new-fangled kitchens don't come cheap, I can tell you. The wife's got in the habit of leaving the *Mail on Sunday* supplement open at some design or another. Her way of dropping hints, like, and about as subtle as a blow on the head with a hammer. The price of them makes me cringe. I tell her the one we've got is perfectly all right, but she—'

As he talked, Weaver began to pour the tea into the row of cups and mugs he had arranged. But after filling the second one, he stopped and stared at the door. Banks and Gristhorpe followed his gaze and saw a young girl standing there, her slight figure framed in the doorway. She rubbed her eyes and stretched.

'Hello,' she said. 'Are you the detectives? I'd like to talk to you. My name's Alison Rothwell and someone just killed my father.'

TWO

She was about fifteen, Banks guessed, but she made no attempt to make herself look older, as many teenagers do. She wore a baggy, grey sweatshirt advertising an American football team, and a blue tracksuit bottom with a white stripe down each side. Apart from the bruiselike pouches under her light blue eyes, her complexion was pale. Her mousy blonde hair was parted in the centre and hung in uncombed strands over her shoulders. Her mouth, with its pale, thin lips, was too small for her oval face.

'Can I have some tea, please?' she asked. Banks noticed she had a slight lisp.

PC Weaver looked for direction. 'Go ahead, lad,' Gristhorpe told him. 'Give the lass some tea.' Then he turned to Alison Rothwell. 'Are you sure you wouldn't rather be upstairs with your mum, love?'

Alison shook her head. 'Mum'll be all right. She's asleep and there's a policewoman sitting by her. I can't sleep. It keeps going round in my mind, what happened. I want to tell you about it now. Can I?'

'Of course.' Gristhorpe asked PC Weaver to stay and take notes. He introduced Banks and himself, then pulled out a stool for her. Alison gave them a sad, shy smile and sat down, holding the mug of tea to her chest with both hands as if she needed its heat. Gristhorpe indicated subtly that Banks should do the questioning.

'Are you sure you feel up to this?' Banks asked her first.

Alison nodded. 'I think so.'

'Would you like to tell us what happened, then?'

Alison took a deep breath. Her eyes focused on something Banks couldn't see.

'It was just after dark,' she began. 'About ten o'clock, quarter past or thereabouts. I was reading. I thought I heard a sound out in the yard.'

'What kind of sound?' Banks asked.

'I . . . I don't know. Just as if someone was out there. A thud, like someone bumping into something or something falling on the ground.'

'Carry on.'

Alison hugged her cup even closer. 'At first I didn't pay

it any mind. I carried on reading, then I heard another sound, a sort of scraping, maybe ten minutes later.'

'Then what did you do?' Banks asked.

'I turned the yard light on and looked out of the window, but I couldn't see anything.'

'Did you have the television on, some music?'

'No. That's why I could hear the sounds outside so clearly. Usually it's so quiet and peaceful up here. All you can hear at night is the wind through the trees, and sometimes a lost sheep baa-ing, or a curlew up on the moors.'

'Weren't you scared being by yourself?'

'No. I like it. Even when I heard the noise I just thought it might be a stray dog or a sheep or something.'

'Where were your parents at this time?'

'They were out. It's their wedding anniversary. Their twenty-first. They went out to dinner in Eastvale.'

'You didn't want to go with them?'

'No. Well . . . I mean, it was *their* anniversary, wasn't it?' She turned up her nose. 'Besides, I don't like fancy restaurants. And I don't like Italian food. Anyway, it's not as if it was *Home Alone* or something. I *am* nearly sixteen, you know. And it was my choice. I'd rather stay home and read. I don't mind being by myself.'

Perhaps, Banks guessed, they hadn't invited her. 'Carry on,' he said. 'After you turned the yard light on, what did you do?'

'When I couldn't see anything, I just sort of brushed it off. Then I heard another noise, like a stone or something, hitting the wall. I was fed up of being disturbed by then, so I decided to go out and see what it was.'

'You still weren't frightened?'

'A bit, maybe, by then. But not *really* scared. I still

thought it was probably an animal or something like that, maybe a fox. We get them sometimes.'

'Then what happened?'

'I opened the front door, and as soon as I stepped out, someone grabbed me and dragged me back inside and tied me to the chair. Then they put a rag in my mouth and put tape over it. I couldn't swallow properly. It was all dry and it tasted of salt and oil.'

Banks noticed her knuckles had turned white around the mug. He worried she would crush it. 'How many of them were there, Alison?' he asked.

'Two.'

'Do you remember anything about them?'

She shook her head. 'They were both dressed all in black, except one of them had white trainers on. The other had some sort of suede slip-ons, brown I think.'

'You didn't see their faces?'

Alison hooked her feet over the crossbar. 'No, they had balaclavas on, black ones. But they weren't like the ones you'd buy to keep you warm. They were just made of cotton or some other thin material. They had little slits for the eyes and slits just under the nose so they could breathe.'

Banks noticed that she had turned paler. 'Are you all right, Alison?' he asked. 'Do you want to stop now and rest?'

Alison shook her head. Her teeth were clenched. 'No. I'll be all right. Just let me . . .' She sipped some tea and seemed to relax a little.

'How tall were they?' Banks asked.

'One was about as big as you.' She looked at Banks, who at only five foot nine was quite small for a policeman – just over regulation height, in fact. 'But he was fatter. Not really fat, but just not, you know, wiry . . . like you. The other was a few inches taller, maybe six foot, and quite thin.'

'You're doing really well, Alison,' Banks said. 'Was there anything else about them?'

'No. I can't remember.'

'Did either of them speak?'

'When he dragged me back inside, the smaller one said, "Keep quiet and do as you're told and we won't hurt you."'

'Did you notice his accent?'

'Not really. It sounded ordinary. I mean, not foreign or anything.'

'Local?'

'Yorkshire, yes. But not Dales. Maybe Leeds or something. You know how it sounds different, more citified?'

'Good. You're doing just fine. What happened next?'

'They tied me to the chair with some rope and just sat and watched television. First the news was on, then some horrible American film about a psycho slashing women. They seemed to like that. One of them kept laughing when a woman got killed, as if it was funny.'

'You heard them laugh?'

'Just one of them, the tall one. The other one told him to shut up. He sounded like he was in charge.'

'The smaller one?'

'Yes.'

'That's all he said: "Shut up"?'

'Yes.'

'Was there anything unusual about the taller man's laugh?'

'I . . . I don't . . . I can't remember.' Alison wiped a tear from her eye with the sleeve of her sweatshirt. 'It was just a laugh, that's all.'

'It's all right. Don't worry about it. Did they harm you in any way?'

Alison reddened and looked down into her half-empty

mug. 'The smaller one came over to me when I was tied up, and he put his hand on my breast. But the other one made him stop. It was the only time he said anything.'

'How did he make him stop? What did he do?'

'He just said not to, that it wasn't part of the deal.'

'Did he use those exact words, Alison? Did he say, "It's not part of the deal"?'

'Yes. I think so. I mean, I'm not completely sure, but it was something like that. The smaller man didn't seem to like it, being told what to do by the other, but he left me alone after that.'

'Did you see any kind of weapon?' Banks asked.

'Yes. The kind of gun that farmers have, with two barrels. A shotgun.'

'Who had it?'

'The smaller man, the one in charge.'

'Did you hear a car at any time?'

'No. Only when Mum and Dad came home. I mean, I heard cars go by on the road sometimes, you know, the one that goes through Relton and right over the moors into the next dale. But I didn't hear anyone coming or going along our driveway.'

'What happened when your parents came home?'

Alison paused and swirled the tea in the bottom of her mug as if she were trying to see into her future. 'It must have been about half past eleven or later. The men waited behind the door and the tall one grabbed Mum while the other put his gun to Dad's neck. I tried to scream and warn them, honest I did, but the rag in my mouth . . . I just couldn't make a sound . . .' She ran her sleeve across her eyes again and sniffled. Banks gestured to PC Weaver, who found a box of tissues on the window-sill and brought them over.

'Thank you,' Alison said. 'I'm sorry.'

'You don't have to go on if you don't want,' Banks said. 'It can wait till tomorrow.'

'No. I've started. I want to. Besides, there's not much more to tell. They tied Mum up the same as me and we sat there facing each other. Then they went outside with Dad. Then we heard the bang.'

'How long between the time they went out and the shot?'

Alison shook her head dreamily. She held the mug up close to her throat. The sleeves of her sweatshirt had slipped down, and Banks could see the raw, red lines where the rope had cut into her flesh. 'I don't know. It seemed like a long time. But all I can remember is we just sat looking at each other, Mum and me, and we didn't know what was happening. I remember a night-bird calling somewhere. Not a curlew. I don't know what it was. And it seemed like forever, like time just stretched out and Mum and I got really scared now looking at one another not knowing what was going on. Then we heard the explosion and . . . and it was like it all snapped and I saw something die in Mum's eyes, it was so, so . . .' Alison dropped the mug, which clipped the corner of the table then fell and spilled without breaking on the floor. The sobs seemed to start deep inside her, then she began to shake and wail.

Banks went over and put his arms around her, and she clung on to him for dear life, sobbing against his chest.

THREE

'It looks like his office,' Banks said, when Gristhorpe turned on the light in the last upstairs room.

Two large desks formed an L-shape. On one of them stood a computer and a laser printer, and on a small table next to them stood a fax machine with a basket attached at the front for collecting the cut-off sheets. At the back of the computer desk, a hutch stood against the wall. The compartments were full of boxes of disks and software manuals, mostly for word processing, spreadsheets and accounting programmes, along with some for standard utilities.

The other desk stood in front of the window, which framed a view of the farmyard. Scene of Crime officers were still going about their business down there: taking samples of just about everything in sight, measuring distances, trying to get casts of footprints, sifting soil. In the barn, their bright arc lamps had replaced Darby's roving light.

This was the desk where Rothwell dealt with handwritten correspondence and phone calls, Banks guessed. There was a blotter, which looked new – no handy wrong-way-around clues scrawled there – a jam jar full of pens and pencils, a blank scratch-pad, an electronic adding machine of the kind that produces a printed tape of its calculations and an appointment calendar open at the day of the murder, 12 May.

The only things written there were 'Dr Hunter' beside the 10:00 a.m. slot, 'Make dinner reservation: Mario's, 8:30 p.m.' Below that, and written in capitals all across the afternoon, 'FLOWERS?' Banks had noticed a vase full of fresh flowers in the living room. An anniversary present? Sad when touching gestures like that outlive the giver. He thought of Sandra again, and suddenly he wanted very much to be near her, to bridge the distance that had grown between them, to hold her and feel her warmth. He shivered.

'All right, Alan?' Gristhorpe asked.

'Fine. Someone just walked over my grave.'

'Look at all this.' Gristhorpe pointed to the two metal filing cabinets and the heavy-duty shelves that took up the room's only long, unbroken wall. 'Business records, by the looks of it. Someone's going to have to sift through it.' He looked towards the computer and grimaced. 'We'd better get Phil to have a look at this lot tomorrow,' he said. 'I wouldn't trust myself to turn the bloody thing on without blowing it up.'

Banks grinned. He was aware of Gristhorpe's Luddite attitude towards computers. He quite liked them, himself. Of course, he had only the most rudimentary skills and never seemed to be able to do anything right, but Phil Richmond, 'Phil the Hacker' as he was known around the station, ought to be able to tell them a thing or two about Rothwell's system.

Finding nothing else of immediate interest in the office, they walked out to the rear of the house, which faced north, and stood in the back garden, the hems of their trousers damp with dew. It was after five now, close to dawn. A pale sun was slowly rising in the east behind a veil of thin cloud that had appeared over the last couple of hours, mauve on the horizon, but giving the rest of the sky a light grey wash and the landscape the look of a water-colour. A few birds sang, and occasionally the sound of a farm vehicle starting up broke the silence. The air smelled moist and fresh.

It was certainly a *garden* they stood in, and not just a backyard. Someone – Rothwell? His wife? – had planted rows of vegetables – beans, cabbage, lettuce, all neatly marked – a small area of herbs and a strawberry patch. At the far end, beyond a dry-stone wall, the land fell away steeply to a beck that coursed down the daleside until it fed into the River Swain at Fortford.

The village of Fortford, about a mile down the hillside, was just waking up. Below the exposed foundations of the Roman fort on its knoll to the east, the cottages with their flagstone roofs huddled around the green and the square-towered church. Already, smoke drifted from some of the chimneys as farm labourers and shopkeepers prepared themselves for the coming day. Country folk were early risers.

The whitewashed front of the sixteenth-century Rose and Crown glowed pink in the early light. Even in there, someone would soon be in the kitchen, making bacon and eggs for the paying guests, especially for the ramblers, who liked to be off early. At the thought of food, his stomach rumbled. He knew Ian Falkland, the landlord of the Rose and Crown, and thought it might not be a bad idea to have a chat with him about Keith Rothwell. Though he was an expatriate Londoner, like Banks, Ian knew most of the local dalesfolk, and, given his line of work, he picked up a fair amount of gossip.

Finally, Banks turned to Gristhorpe and broke the silence. 'They certainly seemed to know what was what, didn't they?' he said. 'I don't imagine it was a lucky guess that the girl was in the house alone.'

'You're thinking along the same lines as I am, aren't you, Alan?' said Gristhorpe. 'An execution. A hit. Call it what you will.'

Banks nodded. 'I can't see any other lines to think along yet. Everything points to it. The way they came in and waited, the position of the body, the coolness, the professionalism of it all. Even the way one of them said touching the girl wasn't part of the deal. It was all planned. Yes, I think it was an execution. It certainly wasn't a robbery or a random killing. They hadn't been through the house, as far as we could tell. Everything seems in order. And if it was a robbery, they'd no need to kill him, especially that way. The question is why? Why should anyone want to execute an accountant?'

'Hmm,' said Gristhorpe. 'Unhappy client, maybe? Someone he turned in to the Inland Revenue?' Nearby, a peewit sensed their closeness to its ground nest and started buzzing them, piping its high-pitched call. 'One of the things we have to do is find out how *honest* an accountant our Mr Rothwell was,' Gristhorpe went on. 'But let's not speculate too much yet, Alan. We don't know if there's anything missing, for a start. Rothwell might have had a million in gold bullion hidden away in his garage for all we know. But you're right about the execution angle. And that means we could be dealing with something very big, big enough to contract a murder for.'

'Sir?'

At that moment, one of the SOC officers came into the garden through the back door.

Gristhorpe turned. 'Yes?'

'We've found something, sir. In the garage. I think you'd both better come and have a look for yourselves.'

FOUR

They followed the officer back to the brightly lit garage. Rothwell's body had, mercifully, been taken to the morgue, where Dr Glendenning, the Home Office pathologist, would get to work on it as soon as he could. Two men from the SOC team stood by the barn door. One was holding something with a pair of tweezers and the other was peering at it closely.

'What is it?' Banks asked.

'It's wadding, sir. From the shotgun,' said the SOCO with the tweezers. 'You see, sir, you can buy commercially made shotgun cartridges, but you can also reload the shells at home. Plenty of farmers and recreational shooters do it. Saves money.'

'Is that what this bloke did?' Banks asked.

'Looks like it, sir.'

'To save money? Typical Yorkshireman. Like a Scotsman stripped of his generosity.'

'Cheeky southern bastard,' said Gristhorpe, then turned to the SOCO. 'Go on, lad.'

'Well, sir, I don't know how much you know about shotguns, but they take cartridges, not bullets.'

Banks knew that much, at least, and he suspected that Gristhorpe, from Dales farming stock, knew a heck of a lot more. But they usually found it best to let the SOCOs show off a bit.

'We're listening,' said Gristhorpe.

Emboldened by that, the officer went on. 'A shotgun shell's made up of a primer, a charge of gunpowder and the pellets, or shot. There's no slug and there's no rifling in the barrel, so you can't get any characteristic markings to trace back to the weapon. Except from the shell, of course, which bears the imprint of the firing and loading mechanisms. But we don't have a shell. What we do have is this.' He held up the wadding. 'Commercial wadding is usually made of either paper or plastic, and you can sometimes trace the shell's manufacturer through it. But this isn't commercial.'

'What exactly is it?' asked Banks, reaching out.

The SOCO passed him the tweezers and said, 'Don't know for certain yet, but it looks like something from a colour magazine. And luckily, it's not too badly burned inside, only charred around the edges. It's tightly packed, but we'll get it unfolded and straightened out when we get it to the lab, then maybe we'll be able to tell you the name, date and page number.'

'Then all we'll have to do is check the list of subscribers,' said Banks, 'and it'll lead us straight to our killer. Dream on.'

The SOCO laughed. 'We're not miracle workers, sir.'

'Has anyone got a magnifying glass?' Banks asked the assembly at large. 'And I don't want any bloody cracks about Sherlock Holmes.'

One of the SOCOs passed him a glass, the rectangular kind that came with the tiny-print, two-volume edition of the *Oxford English Dictionary*. Banks held up the wadding and examined it through the glass.

What he saw was an irregularly shaped wad of crumpled paper, no more than about an inch across at its widest point. At first he couldn't make out anything but the blackened edge of the wadded paper, but it certainly looked as if it were from some kind of magazine. He looked more closely, turning the wadding this way and that, holding it closer and farther, then finally the disembodied shapes coalesced into something recognizable. 'Bloody hell,' he muttered, letting his arm fall slowly to his side.

'What is it, Alan?' Gristhorpe asked.

Banks handed him the glass. 'You'd better have a look for yourself,' he said. 'You won't believe me.'

Banks stood back and watched Gristhorpe scrutinize

the wadding, knowing that it would be only a matter of moments before he noticed, as Banks had done, part of a pink tongue licking a dribble of semen from the tip of an erect penis.

2

ONE

Traditional police wisdom has it that if a case doesn't yield leads in the first twenty-four hours, then everyone is in for a long, tough haul. In practice, of course, the period doesn't always turn out to be twenty-four hours; it can be twenty-three, nine, fourteen, or even forty-eight. That's the problem: when do you scale down your efforts? The answer, Banks reminded himself as he dragged his weary bones into the 'Boardroom' of Eastvale Divisional Police Headquarters at ten o'clock that morning, is that you don't.

The Suzy Lamplugh case was a good example. It started as a missing-persons report. One lunch-time, a young woman left the estate agent's office in Fulham, where she worked, and disappeared. Only after over a year's intensive detective work, which resulted in more than six hundred sworn statements, thousands of interviews, 26,000 index cards and nobody knew how many man-hours, was the investigation wound down. Suzy Lamplugh was never found, either alive or dead.

By the time Banks arrived at the station, Superintendent Gristhorpe had appointed Phil Richmond Office Manager and asked him to set up the Murder Room, where all information regarding the Keith Rothwell case would be carefully indexed, cross-referenced and filed. At first,

Gristhorpe thought it should be established in Fortford or Relton, close to the scene, but later decided that they had better facilities at the Eastvale station. It was only about seven miles from Fortford, anyway.

Richmond was also the only one among them who had training in the use of the HOLMES computer system – acronym for the Home Office Major Enquiry System, with a superfluous 'L' for effect. HOLMES wasn't without its problems, especially as not all the country's police forces used the same computer languages. Still, if no developments occurred before long, Richmond's skill might prove useful.

Gristhorpe had also given a brief press conference first thing in the morning. The sooner photographs of Keith Rothwell and descriptions of the killers, balaclavas and all, were sitting beside the public's breakfast plates or flashing on their TV screens, the sooner information would start to come in. The news was too late for that morning's papers, but it would make local radio and television, the *Yorkshire Evening Post* and tomorrow's national dailies.

Of course, Gristhorpe had given hardly any details about the murder itself. At first, he had even resisted the idea of releasing Rothwell's name. After all, there had been no formal identification, and they didn't have his fingerprints on file for comparison. On the other hand, there was little doubt as to what had happened, and they were hardly going to drag Alison or her mother along to the mortuary to identify the remains.

Gristhorpe had also been in touch with the anti-terrorist squad at Scotland Yard. Yorkshire was far from a stranger to IRA action. People still remembered the M62 bomb in 1974, when a coach carrying British servicemen and their families was blown up, killing eleven and wounding fourteen. Many even claimed to have heard the explosion from as far away as Leeds and Bradford. More recently, two policemen had been shot by IRA members during a routine traffic check on the A1.

The anti-terrorist squad would be able to tell Gristhorpe whether Rothwell had any connections, however tenuous, that would make him a target. As an accountant, he could, for example, have been handling money for a terrorist group. In addition, forensic information and details of the *modus operandi* would be made known to the squad, who would see if the information matched anything on file.

While Gristhorpe handled the news media and Richmond set up the Murder Room, Banks and Susan Gay had conducted a breakfast-time house-to-house of Relton and Fortford – including a visit to the Rose and Crown and a generous breakfast from Ian Falkland – trying to find out a bit about Rothwell, and whether anyone had seen or heard anything unusual on the night of the murder.

Gristhorpe, Richmond and Susan Gay were already in the room when Banks arrived and poured himself a large black coffee. The conference room was nicknamed the 'Boardroom' because of its well-polished, heavy oval table and ten stiff-backed chairs, not to mention the coarse-textured burgundy wallpaper, which gave the room a constant aura of semi-darkness, and the large oil painting (in ornate gilt frame) of one of Eastvale's most successful nineteenth-century wool merchants, looking decidedly sober and stiff in his tight-fitting suit and starched collar.

'Right,' said Gristhorpe, 'time to get up to date. Alan?'

Banks slipped a few sheets of paper from his briefcase and rubbed his eyes. 'Not much so far, I'm afraid. Rothwell was trained as an accountant. At least we've got that much confirmed. Some of the locals in Relton and Fortford knew him, but not well. Apparently, he was a quiet sort of bloke. Kept himself to himself.'

'Who did he work for?'

'Self-employed. We got this from Ian Falkland, landlord of the Rose and Crown in Fortford. He said Rothwell used to drop by now and then for a quick jar before dinner. Never had more than a couple of halves. Well-liked, quiet, decent sort of chap. Anyway, he used to work for Hatchard and Pratt, the Eastvale firm, until he started his own business. Falkland used him for the pub's accounts. I gather Rothwell saved him a bob or two from the Inland Revenue.' Banks scratched the small scar by his right eye. 'There's a bit more to it than that, though,' he went on. 'Falkland got the impression that Rothwell owned a few businesses as well, and that accountancy was becoming more of a sideline for him. We couldn't get any more than that, but we'll be having a close look at his office today.'

Gristhorpe nodded.

'And that's about it,' Banks said. 'The Rothwell family had been living at Arkbeck Farm for almost five years. They used to live in Eastvale.' He looked at his watch. 'I'm going out to Arkbeck Farm again after this meeting. I'm hoping Mrs Rothwell will have recovered enough to tell us something about what happened.'

'Good. Any leads on the two men?'

'Not yet, but Susan spoke to someone who thinks he saw a car.'

Gristhorpe looked at Susan.

'That's right, sir,' she said. 'It was around sunset last night, before it got completely dark. A retired school-teacher from Fortford was coming back home after visiting his daughter in Pateley Bridge. He said he liked to take the lonely roads over the moors.'

'Where did he see this car?'

'At the edge of the moors above Relton, sir. It was parked in a turn-off, just a dip by the side of the road. I think it used to be an old drovers' track, but it's not used any more, and only the bit by the road is clear. The rest has been taken over by moorland. Anyway, sir, the thing is that the way the road curves in a wide semicircle around the farm, this spot would only be about a quarter of a mile away on foot. Remember that copse opposite the farmhouse? Well, it's the same one that straggles up the daleside as far as this turn-off. It would provide excellent cover if someone wanted to get to the farm without being seen, and Alison wouldn't have heard the car approaching if it had been parked way up on the road.'

'Sounds promising,' said Gristhorpe. 'Did the witness notice anything about the car?'

'Yes, sir. He said it looked like an old Escort. It was a light colour. For some reason he thought pale blue. And there was either rust or mud or grass around the lower chassis.'

'It's hardly the bloody stretch-limousine you associate with hit men, is it?' Gristhorpe said.

'More of a Yorkshire version,' said Banks.

Gristhorpe laughed. 'Aye. Better follow it up, then, Susan. Get a description of the car out. I don't suppose your retired schoolteacher happened to see two men dressed in black carrying a shotgun, did he?'

Susan grinned. 'No, sir.'

'Rothwell didn't do any farming himself, did he?' Gristhorpe asked Banks.

'No. Only that vegetable patch we saw at the back. He rented out the rest of his land to neighbouring farmers. There's a fellow I know farms up near Relton I want to talk to. Pat Clifford. He should know if there were any problems in that area.'

'Good,' said Gristhorpe. 'As you know, a lot of locals don't like newcomers buying up empty farms and not using them properly.'

Gristhorpe, Banks knew, had lived in the farmhouse above Lyndgarth all his life. Perhaps he had even been born there. He had sold off most of the land after his parents died and kept only enough for a small garden and for his chief off-duty indulgence, a dry-stone wall he worked on periodically, which went nowhere and fenced nothing in.

'Anyway,' Gristhorpe went on, 'there's been some bad feeling. I can't see a local farmer hiring a couple of killers – people like to take care of their own around these parts – but stranger things have happened. And remember: shotguns are common as cow-clap around farms. Anything on that wadding yet?'

Banks shook his head. 'The lab's still working on it. I've already asked West Yorkshire to make a few inquiries at the kind of places that sell that sort of magazine. I talked to Ken Blackstone at Milltgarth in Leeds. He's a DI there and an old mate.'

'Good,' said Gristhorpe, then turned to Richmond. 'Phil, why don't you go up to Arkbeck Farm with Alan and have a look at Rothwell's computer before you get bogged down managing the office?'

'Yes, sir. Do you think we should have it brought in after I've had a quick look?'

Gristhorpe nodded. 'Aye, good idea.' He scratched his pockmarked cheek. 'Look, Phil, I know you're supposed to be leaving us for the Yard at the end of the week, but—'

'It's all right, sir,' Richmond said. 'I understand. I'll stick around as long as you need me.'

'Good lad. Susan, did you find anything interesting in the appointment book?'

Susan Gay shook her head. 'Not yet, sir. He had a doctor's appointment for yesterday morning with Dr Hunter. I called the office and it appears he kept it. Routine physical. No problems. I'm working my way through. He didn't write much down – or maybe he kept it on computer – but there's a few names to check out, mostly local businesses. I must say, though, sir, he didn't exactly have a full appointment book. There are plenty of empty days.'

'Maybe he didn't need the money. Maybe he could afford to pick and choose. Have a word with someone at his old firm, Hatchard and Pratt. They're just on Market Street. They might be able to tell us something about his background.' Gristhorpe looked at his watch. 'Okay, we've all got plenty to do, better get to it.'

TWO

'I'm afraid my mother's still in bed,' Alison told Banks at Arkbeck Farm. 'I told her you were here . . .' She shrugged.

That was odd, Banks thought. Surely a mother would want to comfort her daughter and protect her from prying policemen? 'Have you remembered anything else?' he asked.

Alison Rothwell looked worn out and worried to death. She wore her hair, unwashed and a little greasy, tied back, emphasizing her broad forehead, a plain white T-shirt and stonewashed designer jeans. She sat with her legs tucked under her, and as she talked, she fiddled with a ring on the little finger of her right hand. 'I don't know,' she said. The lisp made her sound like a little girl.

They sat in a small, cheerful room at the back of the house with ivory-painted walls and Wedgwood blue upholstery. A bookcase stood against one wall, mostly full of paperbacks, their spines a riot of orange, green and black. Against the wall opposite stood an upright piano with a highly lacquered cherry-wood finish. On top of it stood an untidy pile of sheet music. WPC Smithies, who had stayed with the Rothwells, sat discreetly in a corner, notebook open. Phil Richmond was upstairs in Keith Rothwell's study, clicking away on the computer.

The large bay window, open about a foot to let in the birdsongs and fresh air, looked out over Fortford and the dale beyond. It was a familiar enough view to Banks. He had seen it from 'Maggie's Farm' on the other side of Relton, and from the house of a man called Adam Harkness on the valley bottom. The sight never failed to impress, though, even on a dull day like today, with the grey-brown ruins of Devraulx Abbey poking through the trees of its grounds, the village of Lyndgarth clustered around its lop-sided green and, towering over the patchwork of pale green fields and dry-stone walls that rose steeply to the heights, the forbidding line of Aldington Edge, a long limestone scar streaked with fissures from top to bottom like gleaming skeleton's teeth.

'I know it's painful to remember,' Banks went on, 'but we need all the help we can get if we're to catch these men.'

'I know. I'm sorry.'

'Do you remember hearing any sounds between the time they went outside and when you heard the bang?'

Alison frowned. 'I don't think so.'

'No sounds of a struggle, or screaming?'

'No. It was all so quiet. That's what I remember.'

'No talking?'

'I didn't hear any.'

'And you don't know how long they were out there before the explosion?'

'No. I was scared and I was worried. Mum was sitting facing me. I could see how frightened she was, but I couldn't do anything. I just felt so powerless.'

'When it was all over, did you hear any sounds then?'

'I don't think so.'

'Try to remember. Did you hear what direction they went off in?'

'No.'

'Any sounds of a car?'

She paused. 'I think I heard a car door shut, but I can't be sure. I mean, I didn't hear it drive away, but I think I kept sort of drifting in and out. I think I heard a sound like the slam of a car door in the distance.'

'Do you know which direction it came from?'

'Farther up the daleside, I think. Relton way.'

'Good. Now, can you remember anything else about the men?'

'One of them, the one who touched me. I've been thinking about it. He had big brown eyes, a sort of light hazel colour, and watery. There's a word for it. Like a dog.'

'Spaniel?'

'Yes. That's it. Spaniel eyes. Or puppy dog. He had puppy-dog eyes. But they're usually . . . you know, they usually make you feel sorry for the person, but these didn't. They were cruel.'

'Did either of the men say anything else?'

'No.'

'Did they go anywhere else in the house? Any other rooms?'

'No.'

'Did you see them take anything at all?'

Alison shook her head.

'When your father saw them and later went outside with them, how did he seem?'

'What do you mean?'

'Was he surprised?'

'When he first came in and they grabbed him, yes.'

'But after?'

'I . . . I don't know. He didn't do anything or say anything. He just stood there.'

'Do you think he recognized the men?'

'How could he? They were all covered up.'

'Did he seem surprised after the immediate shock had worn off?'

'I don't think he did, no. Just . . . resigned.'

'Was he expecting them?'

'I . . . I don't know. I don't think so.'

'Do you think he knew them, knew why they were there?'

'How could he?'

She spoke with such disbelief that Banks wondered if she had noticed that her father really *wasn't* so shocked or surprised and it confused her. 'Do you think he knew what was happening?' he pressed. 'Why it was happening?'

'Maybe. No. I don't know. He couldn't possibly, could he?' She screwed up her eyes. 'I can't see it that clearly. I don't want to see it clearly.'

'All right, Alison. It's all right. I'm sorry, but I have to ask.'

'I know. I don't mean to be a cry-baby.' She rubbed her bare arm over her eyes.

'You're being very brave. Just one more question

about what happened and then we'll move on. Okay?'

'Okay.'

'Did your father go quietly or did they have to force him?'

'No, he just walked out with them. He didn't say anything.'

'Did he look frightened?'

'He didn't look anything.' She reddened. 'And he didn't *do* anything. He just left Mum and me all tied up and let them take him and . . . and kill him like an animal.'

'All right, Alison, calm down. How did you get free from the chair after they'd gone?'

Alison sniffled and blew her nose. 'It was a long time,' she said finally. 'Hours maybe. Some of the time I just sat there, but not really there, if you know what I mean. I think Mum had fainted. They'd really tied us tight and I couldn't feel my hands properly.'

As she spoke, she rubbed at her wrists, still ringed by the burn marks. 'In the end, I tipped my chair and crawled over near the table where my mother's sewing basket was. I knew there were scissors in there. I had to rub my hands for a long time, so they could feel properly, and I don't know how . . . but in the end I cut the rope, then I untied Mum.' She shifted her position. 'I'm worried about Mum. She's not herself. She doesn't want to eat. What's going to happen to her?'

'I'm all right, Alison, dear. There's no need to worry.'

The voice came from the doorway, and Banks turned for his first glance of Mrs Rothwell. She was a tall woman with short grey hair and fine-boned, angular features, the small nose perhaps just a little too sharply chiselled. There seemed an unusually wide space, Banks thought, between her nose and her thin upper lip, which gave her tilted head a haughty, imperious aspect. Banks could see where Alison got her small mouth from.

Her chestnut-brown eyes looked dull. Tranquillizers prescribed by Dr Burns, Banks guessed. They would help to explain her listless movements, too. Her skin was pale, as if drained of blood, though Banks could tell she had put some make-up on. In fact, she had made a great effort to look her best. She wore black silk slacks over her thin, boyish hips, and a cable-knit jumper in a rainbow pattern, which looked to Banks's untutored eye like an exclusive design. At least he had never seen one like it before. Even in her sedated grief, there was something controlled, commanding and attention-demanding about her, a kind of tightly reined-in power.

She sat down in the other armchair, crossed her legs and clasped her hands on her lap. Banks noticed the chunky rings on her fingers: diamond clusters, a large ruby and a broad gold wedding band.

Banks introduced himself and expressed his condolences. She inclined her head slightly in acceptance.

'I'm afraid I have some difficult questions for you, Mrs Rothwell,' he said.

'Not about last night,' she said, one bejewelled hand going to her throat. 'I can't talk about it. I feel faint, my voice goes and I just can't talk.'

'Mummy,' said Alison. 'I've told him about . . . about that. Haven't I?' And she looked at Banks as if daring him to disagree.

'Yes,' he said. 'Actually, it wasn't that I wanted to ask about specifically. It's just that we need more information on your husband's movements and activities. Can you help?'

She nodded. 'I'm sorry, Chief Inspector. I'm not usually

such a mess.' She touched her hair. 'I must look dreadful.'

Banks murmured a compliment. 'Did your husband have any enemies that you knew of?' he asked.

'No. None at all. But then he didn't bore me with the details of his business. I really had no idea what kind of people he dealt with.' Her accent, Banks noticed, was Eastvale filtered through elocution lessons. *Elocution lessons*. He hadn't thought people took those in this day and age.

'So he never brought his business home, so to speak?'

'No.'

'Did he travel much?'

'Do you mean abroad?'

'Anywhere.'

'Well, he did go abroad now and then, on business, and of course, we'd holiday in Mexico, Hawaii or Bermuda. He also travelled a lot locally in the course of business. He was away a lot.'

'Where did he go?'

'Oh, all over. Leeds, Manchester, Liverpool, Birmingham, Bristol. Sometimes to London, Europe. He had a very important job. He was a brilliant financial analyst, much in demand. He could pick and choose his clients, could Keith, he didn't have to take just any old thing that came along.'

'You mentioned financial analysis. What exactly did he do?'

She picked at the wool on her sleeve with long, bony fingers. 'As I said, he didn't tell me much about work, not about the details, anyway. He qualified as a chartered accountant, of course, but that was only part of it. He had a genius for figures. He advised people what to do with their money, helped businesses out of difficulties. I suppose he was a kind of troubleshooter, if you like. A very exclusive one. He didn't need any new clients and people only found out about him by word of mouth.'

That all sounded sufficiently vague to be suspicious to Banks. On the other hand, what did *he* do? Investigate crimes, yes. But to do so, he chatted with locals over a pint, interviewed bereaved relatives, pored over fingerprints and blood samples. It would all sound rather nebulous and aimless to an outsider.

'And you never met any of his business associates?'

'We had people for dinner occasionally, but we never talked business.'

'Maybe, if you have a moment later, you could make a list of those you entertained most frequently?'

She raised her eyebrows. 'If you want.'

'Now, Mrs Rothwell,' Banks said, wishing he could have a cigarette in what was obviously a non-smoking household, 'this next question may strike you as rather indelicate, but were there any problems in the family?'

'Of course not. We're a happy family. Aren't we, Alison?'

Alison looked at Banks. 'Yes, Mother,' she said.

Banks turned back to Mrs Rothwell. 'Had your husband been behaving at all unusually recently?' he asked. 'Had you noticed any changes in him?'

She frowned. 'He *had* been a bit edgy, tense, a bit more preoccupied and secretive than usual. I mean, he was always quiet, but he'd been even more so.'

'For how long?'

She shrugged. 'Two or three weeks.'

'But he never told you what was wrong?'

'No.'

'Did you ask?'

'My husband didn't appreciate people prying into his private business affairs, Chief Inspector.'

'Not even his wife?'

'I assumed that if and when he wanted to tell me, he would do so.'

'What did you talk about over dinner yesterday?'

She shrugged. 'Just the usual things. The children, the house extension we wanted to have done . . . I don't know, really. What do *you* talk about when you're out for dinner with *your* wife?'

Good question, Banks thought. It had been so long since he and Sandra had gone out to dinner together that he couldn't remember what they talked about. 'Did you have any idea what he might have been worried about?' he asked.

'No. I suppose it was one of the usual business problems. Keith really cared about his clients.'

'What business problems? I thought he didn't talk to you about business.'

'He didn't, Chief Inspector. Please don't twist what I say. He just made the occasional offhand comment. You know, maybe he'd read something in the *Financial Times* or something and make a comment. I never understood what he meant. Anyway, I think one of the companies he was trying to help was sinking fast. Things like that always upset him.'

'Do you know which company?'

'No. It'll be on his computer. He put everything on that computer.' Suddenly, Mrs Rothwell put the back of one ringed hand to her forehead in what seemed to Banks a gesture from a nineteenth-century melodrama. Her forehead looked clammy. 'I'm afraid I can't talk any more,' she whispered. 'I feel a bit faint and dizzy. I . . . Alison.'

Alison helped her up and they left the room. Banks glanced over at WPC Smithies. 'Have you picked up anything at all from them?' he asked.

'Sorry, sir,' she said. 'Nothing. I'll tell you one thing, though, they're a weird pair. It's an odd family. I think they're both retreating from reality, in their own ways, trying to deny what happened, or *how* it happened. But you can see that for yourself.'

'Yes.'

Banks listened to a clock tick on the mantelpiece. It was one of those timepieces with all its brass and silver innards showing inside a glass dome.

A couple of minutes later, Alison came back. 'I'm sorry,' she said. 'Mummy's still weak and in shock. The doctor gave her some pills.'

'That's understandable, Alison,' said Banks. 'I'd almost finished, anyway. Just one last question. Do you know where your brother is? We'll have to get in touch with him.'

Alison picked up a postcard from the top of the piano, gave it to Banks and sat down again.

The card showed the San Francisco Golden Gate Bridge, which looked orange to Banks. He flipped it over. Post-marked two weeks ago, it read,

Dear Ali,

Love California, and San Francisco is a *great* city, but it's time to move on. I'm even getting used to driving on the wrong side of the road! This sightseeing's a tiring business so I'm off to Florida for a couple of weeks just lying in the sun. Ah, what bliss! Also to check out the motion picture conservatory in Sarasota. I'm driving down the coast highway and flying to Tampa from LA on Sunday. More news when I get there. Love to Mum,

Tom

'How long has he been gone?'

'Six weeks. Just over. He left on the thirty-first of March.'

'What does he do? What was that about a motion picture conservatory?'

Alison gave a brief smile. 'He wants to work in films. He worked in a video shop and saved up. He's hoping to go to film college in America and learn how to become a director.'

'How old is he?'

'Twenty-one.'

Banks stood up. 'All right, Alison,' he said. 'Thanks very much for all your help. WPC Smithies will be staying here for a while, so if you need anyone . . . And I'll ask the doctor to pay your mother another visit.'

'Thank you. Please don't worry about us.'

Banks looked in on Richmond, who sat bathed in the bluish glow of Rothwell's monitor, oblivious to the world, then went out to his car and lit a cigarette. He rolled the window down and listened to the birds as he smoked. Birds aside, it was bloody quiet up here. How, he wondered, could a teenager like Alison stand the isolation? As WPC Smithies had said, the Rothwells were an odd family.

As he drove along the bumpy track to the Relton road, he slipped in a tape of Dr John playing solo New Orleans piano music. He had developed a craving for piano music – *any* kind of piano music – recently. He was even think-ing of taking piano lessons; he wanted to learn how to play *everything* – classical, jazz, blues. The only thing that held him back was that he felt too old to embark on such a venture. His forty-first birthday was coming up in a couple of weeks.

In Relton, a couple of old ladies holding shopping

baskets stood chatting outside the butcher's shop, probably about the murder.

Banks thought again about Alison Rothwell and her mother as he pulled up outside the Black Sheep. What were they holding back? And what was it that bothered him? No matter what Mrs Rothwell and Alison had said, there was something wrong in that family, and he had a hunch that Tom Rothwell might know what it was. The sooner they contacted him the better.

THREE

Laurence Pratt delved deep in his bottom drawer and pulled out a bottle of Courvoisier VSOP and two snifters.

'I'm sorry,' he apologized to DC Susan Gay, who sat opposite him at the broad teak desk. 'It's not that I'm a secret tippler. I keep it for emergencies, and I'm afraid what you've just told me most definitely constitutes one. You'll join me?'

'No, thank you.'

'Not on duty?'

'Sometimes,' Susan said. 'But not today.'

'Very well.' He poured himself a generous measure, swirled it and took a sip. A little colour came back to his cheeks. 'Ah . . . that's better.'

'If we could get back to Mr Rothwell, sir?'

'Yes. Yes, of course. But you must understand Miss, Miss . . .?'

'Gay, sir. DC Gay.'

She saw the inadvertent smile flash across his face. People often smiled like that when she introduced herself. 'Gay' had been a perfectly good name when she was a kid

– her nickname for a while had been 'Happy' Gay – but now its meaning was no longer the same. One clever bugger had actually asked, 'Did you say AC or DC Gay?' She comforted herself with the thought that he was doing three to five in Strangeways, thanks largely to her court evidence.

'Yes,' he went on, a frown quickly displacing the smile. 'I'd heard about Keith's death, of course, on the radio this lunchtime, but they didn't say *how* it happened. That's a bit of a shock, to be honest. You see, I knew Keith quite well. I'm only about three years older than he, and we worked here together for some years.'

'He left the firm five years ago, is that right?'

'About right. A big move like that takes quite a bit of planning, quite a bit of organizing. There were client files to be transferred, that sort of thing. And he had the house to think of, too.'

'He was a partner?'

'Yes. My father, Jeremiah Pratt, was one of the founders of the firm. He's retired now.'

'I understand the family used to live in Eastvale, is that right?'

'Yes. Quite a nice house out towards the York roundabout, Catterick Street.'

'Why did they move?'

'Mary always fancied living in the country. I don't know why. She wasn't any kind of nature girl. I think perhaps she wanted to play Lady of the Manor.'

'Oh? Why's that?'

Pratt shrugged. 'Just her nature.'

'What about her husband?'

'Keith didn't mind. I should imagine he liked the solitude. I don't mean he was exactly antisocial, but he was never a great mixer, not lately, anyway. He travelled a lot, too.'

Pratt was in his mid-forties, Susan guessed, which did indeed make him just a few years older than Keith Rothwell. Quite good-looking, with a strong jaw and grey eyes, he wore his white shirt with the sleeves rolled up and his mauve and green tie clipped with what looked like a silver American dollar sign. His hairline was receding and what hair remained was grey at the temples. He wore black-framed glasses, which sat about halfway down his nose.

'Did you ever visit him there?'

'Yes. My wife and I dined with the Rothwells on several occasions.'

'Were you friends?'

Pratt took another sip of cognac, put his hand out and waggled it from side to side. 'Hmm. Somewhere between friends and colleagues, I'd say.'

'Why did he leave Hatchard and Pratt?'

Pratt broke eye contact and looked into the liquid he swirled in his snifter. 'Ambition, maybe? Straightforward accountancy bored him. He was fond of abstractions, very good with figures. He certainly had a flair for financial management. Very creative.'

'Does that imply fraudulent?'

Pratt looked up at her. She couldn't read his expression. 'I resent that implication,' he said.

'Was there any bad feeling?'

'I don't know what you mean.'

'When he left the firm. Had there been any arguments, any problems?'

'Good lord, this was five years ago!'

'Even so.'

Pratt adopted a stiffer tone. 'No, of course there hadn't.

40

Everything was perfectly amicable. We were sorry to lose him, of course, but . . .'

'He wasn't fired or anything?'

'No.'

'Did he take any clients with him?'

Pratt shuffled in his chair. 'There will always be clients who feel they owe their loyalty to an individual member of the firm rather than to the firm as a whole.'

'Are you sure this didn't cause bad feeling?'

'No, of course not. While it's unprofessional to solicit clients and woo them away, most firms *do* accept that they will lose some business whenever a popular member leaves to set up on his own. Say, for example, you visit a particular dentist in a group practice. You feel comfortable with him. He understands how you feel about dentists, you feel safe with him. If he left and set up on his own, would you go with him or stay and take your chances?'

Susan smiled. 'I see what you mean. Do you think you could provide me with a list of names of the clients he took?'

Pratt chewed his lower lip for a moment, as if debating the ethics of such a request, then said, 'I don't see why not. You could find out from his records anyway.'

'Thank you. He must have made a fair bit of money somehow,' Susan said. 'How did he do it?'

Pratt, who if truth be told, Susan thought, suppressing a giggle, might not be entirely happy about *his* name, either, made a steeple of his hairy hands. 'The same way we all do, I assume,' he said. 'Hard work. Good investments. Excellent service. Arkbeck Farm was in pretty poor shape when they bought it, you know. It didn't cost a fortune, and he'd no trouble arranging a fair mortgage. He put a lot into that house over the years.'

Susan looked at her notes and frowned as if she were having trouble reading or understanding them. 'I understand Mr Rothwell actually owned a number of businesses. Do you know anything about this?'

Pratt shook his head. 'Not really. I understand he was interested in property development. As I said, Keith was an astute businessman.'

'Did Mrs Rothwell work?'

'Mary? Good heavens, no! Well, not in the sense that she went out and made money. Mary was a housewife all the way. Well, perhaps "house manager" or "lady of leisure" would be a more appropriate term, as she didn't actually do the work herself. Except for the garden. You must have seen Arkbeck, how clean it is, how well appointed?'

'I'm afraid I had other things on my mind when I was there, sir,' Susan said, 'but I know what you mean.'

Pratt nodded. 'For Mary,' he went on, 'everything centred around the home, the family and the immediate community. Everything had to be just so, to look just right, and it had to be *seen* to look that way. I imagine she was a hard taskmaster, or should that be taskmistress? Of course, she didn't spend *all* her time in the house. There were the Women's Institute, the Church committees, the good works and the charities. Mary kept very busy, I can assure you.'

'Good works? Charities?' There was something positively Victorian about this. Susan pictured an earnest woman striding from hovel to hovel in a flurry of garments, long dress trailing in the mud, distributing alms to the peasants and preaching self-improvement.

'Yes. She collected for a number of good causes. You know, the RSPCA, NSPCC, cancer, heart foundation and the like. Nothing political – I mean, no ban the bomb or anything – and nothing controversial, like AIDS research. Just the basics. She was the boss's daughter, after all. She had certain Conservative standards to keep up.'

'The boss's daughter?'

'Yes, didn't you know? Her maiden name was Mary Hatchard. She was old man Hatchard's daughter. He's dead now, of course.'

'So Keith Rothwell married the boss's daughter,' Susan mused aloud. 'I don't suppose that did his career any harm?'

'No, it didn't. But that was more good luck than good management, if you ask me. Keith didn't just marry the boss's daughter, he got her pregnant first, with Tom, as it turns out, *then* he married her.'

'How did that go over?'

Pratt paused and picked up a paperclip. 'Not very well at first. Old man Hatchard was mad as hell. He kept the lid on it pretty well, of course, and after he'd had time to consider it, I think he was glad to get her off his hands. He could hardly have her married to a mere junior, though, so Keith came up pretty quickly through the ranks to full partner.'

Pratt twisted the paperclip. He seemed to be enjoying this game, Susan thought. He was holding back, toying with her. She had a sense that if she didn't ask exactly the right questions, she wouldn't get the answers she needed. The problem was, she didn't know what the right questions were.

They sat in his office over Winston's Tobacconists, looking out on north Market Street, and Susan could hear the muted traffic sounds through the double-glazing. 'Look,' Pratt went on, 'I realize I'm the one being questioned, but could you tell me how Mary is? And Alison? I do regard myself as something of a friend of the family, and if there's anything I can do . . .'

'Thank you, sir. I'll make sure they know. Can you think of any reason anyone might have for killing Mr Rothwell?'

'No, I can't. Not in the way you described.'

'What do you mean?'

'Well, I suppose I could imagine a burglar, say, perhaps killing someone who got in the way. You read about it in the papers, especially these days. Or an accident, some kids joyriding. But this . . .? It sounds like an assassination to me.'

'When was the last time you saw him?'

'About a month ago. No, earlier. In March, I think. Shortly after St Patrick's Day. The wife and I went for dinner. Mary's a splendid cook.'

'Did they entertain frequently?'

'Not that I know of. They had occasional small dinner parties, maximum six people. Keith didn't like socializing much, but Mary loved to show off the house, especially if she'd acquired a new piece of furniture or something. So they compromised. Last time it was the kitchen we had to admire. They used to have a country-style one, Aga and all, but someone started poking fun at "Aga-louts" in the papers, so Mary got annoyed and went for the modern look.'

'I see. What about the son, Tom? What do you know of him?'

'Tom? He's travelling in America, I understand. Good for him. Nothing like travel when you're young, before you get too tied down. Tom was always a cheerful and polite kid as far as I was concerned.'

'No trouble?'

'Not in any real sense, no. I mean, he wasn't into drugs or any of that weird stuff. At worst I'd say he was a bit uncertain about what he wanted to do with his life, and his father was perhaps just a little impatient.'

'In what way?'

'He wanted Tom to go into business or law. Something solid and respectable like that.'

'And Tom?'

'Tom's the artsy type. But he's a bright lad. With his personality he could go almost anywhere. He just doesn't know where yet. After he left school, he drifted a bit. Still is doing, it seems.'

'Would you say there was friction between them?'

'You can't be suggesting—'

'I'm not suggesting anything.' Susan leaned back in the chair. 'Look, Mr Pratt, as far as we know Tom Rothwell is somewhere in the USA. We're trying to find him, but it could take time. The reason I'm asking you all these questions is because we need to know *everything* about Keith Rothwell.'

'Yes, of course. I'm sorry. But what with the shock of Keith's death and you asking about Tom . . .'

Susan leaned forward again. 'Is there any reason,' she asked, 'why you should think I was putting forward Tom as a suspect?'

'Stop trying to read between the lines. There's nothing written there. It was just the way you were asking about him, that's all. Tom and his father had the usual father–son arguments, but nothing more.'

'Where did Tom get the money for a trip to America?'

'What? I don't know. Saved up, I suppose.'

'You say you last saw Keith Rothwell in March?'

'Yes.'

'Have you spoken with him at all since then?'

'No.'

'Did he seem in any way different from usual then? Worried about anything? Nervous?'

'No, not that I can remember. It was a perfectly normal evening. Mary cooked duck *à l'orange*. Tom dropped in briefly, all excited about his trip. Alison stayed in her room.'

'Did she usually do that?'

'Alison's a sweet child, but she's a real loner, very secretive. Takes after her father. She's a bit of a bookworm, too.'

'What did you talk about that evening?'

'Oh, I can't remember. The usual stuff. Politics. Europe. The economy. Holiday plans.'

'Who else was there?'

'Just us, this time.'

'And Mr Rothwell said nothing that caused you any concern?'

'No. He was quiet.'

'Unusually so?'

'He was usually quiet.'

'Secretive?'

Pratt swivelled his chair and gazed out of the window at the upper storey of the Victorian community centre. Susan followed his gaze. She was surprised to see a number of gargoyles there she had never noticed before.

When he spoke again, Pratt still didn't look at Susan. She could see him only in profile. 'I've always felt that about him, yes,' he said. 'That's why I hesitated to call him a *close* friend. There was always something in reserve.' He turned to face Susan again and placed his hands, palms down, on the desk. 'Oh, years ago we'd let loose once in a while, go get blind drunk and not give a damn. Sometimes we'd go fishing together. But over time, Keith sort of reined himself in, cut himself off. I don't really know how to explain this. It was just a feeling. Keith was a very private person . . . well, lots of people are . . . But the thing was, I had no idea what he lived for.'

'Did he suffer from depression? Did you think—'

Pratt waved a hand. 'No. No, you're getting me wrong. He wasn't suicidal. That's not what I meant.'

'Can you try and explain?'

'I'll try. It's hard, though. I mean, I'd be hard pushed to say what I live for, too. There's the wife and kids, of course, my pride and joy. And we like to go hang-gliding over Semerwater on suitable weekends. I collect antiques, I love cricket and we like to explore new places on our holidays. See what I mean? None of that's what I actually *live for,* but it's all part of it.' He took off his glasses and rubbed the back of his hand over his eyes and the bridge of his nose, then put them back on again. 'I know, I'm getting too philosophical. But I told you it was hard to explain.'

Susan smiled. 'I'm still listening.'

'Well, all those are just *things*, aren't they? Possessions or activities. Things we do, things we care about. But there's something behind them all that ties them all together into *my* life, who I am, what I am. With Keith, you never knew. He was a cipher. For example, I'm sure he loved his family, but he never really showed it or spoke much about it. I don't know what really *mattered* to him. He never talked about hobbies or anything like that. I don't know what he did in his spare time. It's more than being private or secretive, it's as if there was a dimension *missing*, a man with a hole in the middle.' He scratched his temple. 'This is ridiculous. Please forgive me. Keith was a perfectly nice bloke. Wouldn't hurt a fly. But you never really knew what gripped him about life, what his *dream* was. I mean, mine's a villa in Portugal, but a dream doesn't have to be a thing, does it? I don't know . . . maybe he valued abstractions too much.'

He paused, as if he had run out of breath and ideas. Susan didn't really know what to jot down, but she finally settled for 'dimension missing . . . interests and concerns elusive'. It would do. She had a good memory for conversations and could recount verbatim most of what Pratt had said, if Banks wished to hear it.

'Let's get back to Mr Rothwell's work with your firm. Is there anything you can tell me about his . . . style . . . shall we say, his business practices?'

'You want to know if Keith was a crook, don't you?'

She did, of course, though that wasn't why she was asking. Still, she thought, never look a gift-horse in the mouth. She gave him a 'you caught me at it' smile. 'Well, was he?'

'Of course not.'

'Oh, come on, Mr Pratt. Surely in your business you must sail a little close to the wind at times?'

'I resent that remark, especially coming from a police-man.'

Susan let that one slip by. '*Touché*,' she said. Pratt seemed pleased enough with himself. Let him feel he's winning, she thought, then he'll tell you anyway, just to show he holds the power to do so. She was still sure he was holding something back. 'But seriously, Mr Pratt,' she went on, 'I'm not just playing games, bandying insults. If there was anything at all unusual in Mr Rothwell's business dealings, I hardly need tell you it could have a bearing on his murder.'

'Hmm.' Pratt swirled the rest of the brandy and tossed it back. He put the snifter in his 'Out' tray, no doubt for the secretary to take and wash. 'I stand by what I said,' he went on. 'Keith Rothwell never did anything truly *illegal* that I knew of. Certainly nothing that could be relevant to his death.'

'But . . .?'

He sighed. 'Well, maybe I wasn't *entirely* truthful earlier. I suppose I'd better tell you about it, hadn't I? You're bound to find out somehow.'

Susan turned her page. 'I'm listening,' she said.

3

ONE

The Black Sheep was the closest Swainsdale had to a well kept secret. Most tourists were put off by the pub's external shabbiness. Those who prided themselves on not judging a book by its cover would, more often than not, pop their heads around the door, see the even shabbier interior and leave.

The renowned surliness of the landlord, Larry Grafton, kept them away in droves, too. There was a rumour that Larry had once refused to serve an American tourist with a Glenmorangie and ginger, objecting to the utter lack of taste that led her to ask for such a concoction. Banks believed it.

Larry was Dales born and bred, not one of the new landlords up from London. So many were recent immigrants these days, like Ian Falkland in the Rose and Crown. That was a tourist pub if ever there was one, Banks thought, probably selling more lager and lime, pork scratchings and microwaved curries than anything else.

The Black Sheep didn't advertise its pub grub, but anyone who knew about it could get as thick and fresh a ham and piccalilli sandwich as ever they'd want from Elsie, Larry's wife. And on some days, if her arthritis hadn't been bothering her too much and she felt like cooking, she could do you a fry-up so good you could feel your arteries hardening as you ate.

As usual, the public bar was empty apart from one table of old men playing dominoes and a couple of young farm-hands reading the sports news in the *Daily Mirror*.

As Banks had expected, Pat Clifford also stood propping up the bar. Pat was a hard, stout man with a round head, stubble for hair and a rough, red face burned by the sun and whipped by the wind and rain for fifty years.

'Hello, stranger,' said Pat, as Banks stood next to him. 'Long time, no see.'

Banks apologized for his absence and brought up the subject of Keith Rothwell.

'So tha only comes when tha wants summat, is that it?' Pat said. But he said it with a smile, and over the years Banks had learned that Yorkshire folk often take the sting out of their criticisms that way. They put a sting *in* their compliments, too, on those rare occasions they get around to giving any.

In this case, Banks guessed that Pat wasn't mortally offended at his protracted absence; he only wanted to make a point of it, let Banks know his feelings, and then get on with things. Banks acknowledged his culpability with a mild protest about the pressures of work, as expected, then listened to a minute or so of Pat's complaining about how the elderly and isolated were neglected by all and sundry.

When Pat's glass was empty, an event which occurred with alarming immediacy at the end of the diatribe, Banks's offer to buy him another was grudgingly accepted. Pat took a couple of sips, put the glass down on the bar and wiped his lips with the back of his grimy hand.

'He came in once or twice, did Mr Rothwell. Local, like. Nobody objected.'

'How often?'

'Once a week, mebbe. Sometimes twice. Larry—?' And he asked the landlord the same question. Larry, who hardly had a charabanc full of thirsty customers to serve, came over and stood with them. He still treated Banks with a certain amount of disdain – after all, Banks was a southerner *and* a copper – but he showed respect, too.

Banks had never tried *too* hard to fit in, to pretend he was one of the crowd like some of the other incomers. He knew there was nothing annoyed a Dalesman so much as pretentiousness, airs and graces, and that there was nothing more contemptible or condescending than a south-erner appropriating Dales speech and ways, playing the expert on a place he had only just come to. Banks kept his distance, kept his counsel, and in return he was accorded that particular Yorkshire brand of grudging acceptance.

'Just at lunchtimes, like,' Larry said. 'Never saw him of an evening. He'd come in for one of Elsie's sandwiches and always drink half a pint. Just one half, mind you.'

'Did he talk much?'

Larry drifted off to dry some glasses and Pat picked up the threads. 'Nay. He weren't much of chatterbox, weren't Mr Rothwell. Bit of a dry stick, if you ask me.'

'What do you mean? Was he stuck-up?'

'No-o. Just had nowt to talk abaht, that's all.' He tapped the side of his nose. 'If you listen as much as I do,' he said, 'you soon find out what interests people. There's not much when it comes down to it, tha knows.' He started counting on the stubby fingers that stuck out of his cut-off gloves. 'Telly, that's number one. Sport – number two. And sex. That's number three. After that there's nobbut money and weather left.'

52

Banks smiled. 'What about politics?' he asked.

Pat pulled a face. 'Only when them daft buggers in t'Common Market 'ave been up to summat with their Common Agricultural Policy.' Then he grinned, showing stained, crooked teeth. 'Aye, I suppose that's often enough these days,' he admitted, counting it off. 'Politics. Number four.'

'And what did Mr Rothwell talk about when he was here?' Banks asked.

'Nowt. That's what I'm telling thee, lad. Oh, I s'pose seeing as he was an accountant, he was interested in money, but he kept that to himself. He'd be standing there, all right, just where you are, munching on his sandwich, supping his half-pint, and nodding in all the right places, but he never had owt to say. It seemed to me as if he were really somewhere else. And he didn't know *Neighbours* from *Coronation Street*, if you ask me – or Leeds United from Northampton.'

'There's not a lot of difference as far as their performances go over the last few weeks, if you ask me, Pat.'

Pat grunted.

'So you didn't really know Keith Rothwell?' Banks asked.

'No. Nobody did.'

'That's right, Mr Banks,' added Larry as he stood by them to pull a pint. 'He said he came for the company, what with working alone at home and all that, but I reckon as he came to get away from that there wife of his.' Then he was gone, bearing the pint.

Banks turned to Pat. 'What did he mean?'

'Ah, take no notice of him,' Pat said with a dismissive wave in Grafton's direction. 'Mebbe he was a bit henpecked, at that. It must be hard working at home when the wife's around all the time. Never get a minute's peace, you wouldn't. But Larry's lass, Cathy, did for Mrs Rothwell now and again, like, and she says she were a bit of an interfering mistress, if you know what I mean. Standing over young Cathy while she worked and saying that weren't done right, or that needed a bit more elbow grease. I nobbut met Mrs Rothwell once or twice, but my Grace speaks well of her, and that's enough for me.'

Banks thought he might have a word with Larry's lass, Cathy. He noticed Pat's empty glass. 'Another?'

'Oh, aye. Thank you very much.' Banks bought him a pint, but decided to forgo a second himself, much as the idea appealed. 'There were one time, when I comes to think on it,' Pat said, 'that Mr Rothwell seemed a bit odd.'

'When was this?'

'Abaht two or three weeks ago. He came in one lunch-time, as usual, like, but he must have had a couple of pints, not 'alves. Anyroad, he got quite chatty, told a couple of jokes and we all had a good chuckle, didn't we, Larry?'

'Aye,' shouted Larry from down the bar.

That sounded odd to Banks. According to Mrs Rothwell, her husband had been tense and edgy over the past three weeks. If he could chat and laugh at the Black Sheep, then maybe the problem had been at home. 'Is that all?' he asked.

'*All*? Well, it were summat for us to see him enjoying himself for once. I'd say that were enough, wouldn't you?'

'Did he say anything unusual?'

'No. He just acted like an ordinary person. An ordinary *happy* person.'

'As if he'd received some good news or something?'

'He didn't say owt about that.'

Banks gave up and moved on. 'I know there's been a bit of ill feeling among the hill-farmers about incomers lately,' he said. 'Did any of it spill over to Mr Rothwell?'

Pat sniffed. 'You wouldn't understand, Mr Banks,' he said softly, offering an unfiltered cigarette. Banks refused it and lit a Silk Cut. 'It's not that there's any ill feeling, as such. We just don't know where we stand, how to plan for the future. One day the government says this, the next day it's something else. Agricultural Policy . . . Europe . . . grugh.' He spat on the floor to show his feelings. Either nobody noticed or the practice was perfectly welcome in the Black Sheep, another reason why people stayed away. 'It needs years of experience to do it right, does hill-farming,' Pat went on. 'Continuity, passed on from father to son. When too many farms fall to weekenders and holiday-makers, pasture gets abused, walls get neglected. Live and let live, that's what I say. But we want some respect and some understanding. And right now we're not getting any.'

'But what about the incomers?'

'Aye, hold thy horses, lad, I'm getting to them. We're not bloody park keepers, tha knows. We don't graft for hours on end in all t'weather God sends keeping stone walls in good repair because we think they look picturesque, tha knows. They're to keep old Harry Cobb's sheep off my pasture and to make sure there's no hanky-panky between his breed and mine.'

Banks nodded. 'Fair enough, Pat. But how deep did the feeling go? Keith Rothwell bought that farm five years ago, or thereabouts. I've seen what he's done to it, and it's not a farm any more.'

'Aye, well at least Mr Rothwell's a Swainsdale lad, even if he did come from Eastvale. Nay, there were no problems.

He sold off his land – I got some of it, and so did Frank Rowbottom. If you're thinking me or Frank did it, then . . .'

'No, nothing like that,' Banks said. 'I just wanted to get a sense of how Rothwell fitted in with the local scene, if he did.'

'Well, he did and he didn't,' said Pat. 'He was here and he wasn't, and that's all I can tell thee. He could tell a joke well enough when he put his mind to it, though.' Pat chuckled at the memory.

As puzzled as he was before, Banks said goodbye and went outside. On the way back, he slipped in a cassette of Busoni's Bach transcriptions. The precise, ordered music had no influence on the chaos of his thoughts.

TWO

Back in his office, Banks first glanced at Dr Glendenning's post-mortem notes. Generally, there was no such thing as a preliminary post-mortem report, but Dr Glendenning usually condescended to send over the main points in layman's language as quickly as possible. He also liked to appear at the scene, but this time he had been staying overnight with friends in Harrogate.

There was nothing in the notes that Banks hadn't expected. Rothwell hadn't been poisoned before he was shot; the stomach contents revealed only pasta and red wine. Dr Glendenning gave cause of death as a shotgun wound to the occipital region, the back of the head, most likely a contact wound given the massive damage to bone and tissue. He also noted that it was lucky they already knew who the victim was, as there wasn't enough connected bone or tissue left to reconstruct the face, and though the tooth fragments could probably be collected and analysed, it would take a bloody long time. The blood group was 'O', which matched that supplied by Rothwell's doctor, as well as that of about half the population.

Rothwell had most likely been killed in the place and position they found him, Dr Glendenning pointed out, because what blood remained had collected as purplish hypostasis around the upper chest and the ragged edges of the neck. He estimated time of death between eleven and one the previous night.

A cadaveric spasm had caused Rothwell to grab and hold on to a handful of dust at the moment of death, and Banks thought of the T. S. Eliot quotation, 'I will show you fear in a handful of dust', which he had come across as the title of an Evelyn Waugh novel.

Rothwell had been in generally good shape, Dr Glendenning said, and the only evidence of any ill health was an appendix scar. Rothwell's doctor, Dr Hunter, was able to verify that Rothwell had had his appendix removed just over three years ago.

When Banks had finished, he phoned Sandra to say he didn't know when he would be home. She said that didn't surprise her. Then he went over to the window and looked down on the cobbled market square, most of which was covered by parked cars. The gold hands against the blue face of the church clock stood at a quarter to four.

Banks lit a cigarette and watched the local merchants taking deliveries and the tourists snapping pictures of the ancient market cross and the Norman church front. It was fine enough weather out there, sports-jacket warm, but the grey wash that had come at dawn still obscured the sunshine. On Banks's *Dalesman* calendar, the May photograph showed a field of brilliant pink and purple flowers below Great Shunner Fell in Swaledale. So far, the real May had been struggling against showers and cool temperatures.

Sitting at his rattly metal desk, Banks next opened the envelope of Rothwell's pocket contents and spread them out in front of him.

There were a few business cards in a leather slipcase, describing Rothwell as a 'Financial Consultant'. In his wallet were three credit cards, including an American Express Gold; the receipt from Mario's on the night of his anniversary dinner; receipts from Austick's bookshop, a computer supplies shop and two restaurants, all from Leeds, and all dated the previous week; and photos of Alison and Mary Rothwell. Happy families indeed. In cash, Rothwell had a hundred and five pounds in his wallet, in new twenties and one crumpled old fiver.

Other pockets revealed a handkerchief, good quality silk and monogrammed 'KAR', like the cufflinks on the body, BMW keys, house keys, a small pack of Rennies, two buttons, a gold Cross fountain pen, an empty leather-bound notebook and – horror of horrors – a packet of ten Benson and Hedges, six of which had been smoked.

Banks felt a surge of respect for the late Keith Rothwell. But perhaps the cigarettes helped to explain something, too. Banks was certain that Mary Rothwell would never have permitted her husband to pollute the house with his filthy habit. Smoking, then, could be the main reason he liked to sneak off to the Black Sheep or the Rose and Crown every now and then. It certainly wasn't drinking. A secret smoker, then? Or did she know? He found no gold lighter, only a sulphurous old box of Pilot matches; and Rothwell was the kind of person who put his spent matches back in the box facing the opposite direction from the live ones.

It was almost six when the phone rang: Vic Manson

calling from the forensic lab. Vic spent almost as much time with the Scene of Crime team from North Yorkshire Headquarters, in Northallerton, as he did at the lab, and though Banks knew Vic was a fingerprints expert, he sometimes wasn't sure exactly what he did or where he really worked.

'What have you got for us?' Banks asked.

'Hold your horses.'

'Social call, is it, then?'

'Not exactly.'

'Then what?'

'The wadding, for a start.'

'What about it?'

'We managed to get some more of the paper unfolded. It wasn't too badly burned inside. Anyway, the document analysts say it's good magazine quality, probably German. No prints. Nothing but blurs. It's not your common-or-garden girlie magazine, but it's not hardcore perversion either. The fullest picture we could get seemed to be a shaved vagina with a finger touching the clitoris. Bright red nail varnish. The fingernail, that is.'

'That must be the other side of what I saw,' said Banks. 'Does it help?'

'It might do. Apparently there are people who have a fetish about shaved vaginas. It's something to go on, anyway.'

Banks sighed. 'Or maybe our killer's just got a warped sense of humour. We can check with the PNC, anyway, see if there's been any similar incidents. What about the weapon?'

'Twelve-gauge, double-barrel. Judging by the amount of shot we've collected, the bastard who did it must have used both of them.'

'Anything from the house?'

'No prints, if that's what you mean. They wore gloves. And there was nothing special about the rope they used to tie up the wife and daughter, either. By the way, remember one of the chairs was wet, the one overturned by the table?'

'Yes.'

'It was urine. The poor lass must have been so scared she pissed herself.'

Banks swallowed. That was Alison's chair. She was the one who had eventually made her way to the sewing basket and toppled her chair. 'Any footprints?' he asked.

'We're still working on it, but don't hold your breath. The ground had pretty much dried out after last week's rain.'

'Okay, Vic, thanks for calling. Keep at it and keep me informed, okay?'

'Will do.'

After he had hung up, Banks lit another cigarette and walked over to the window again. Most of the tourists were getting in their cars, removing the crook-locks and driving home. The cobbles, cross and church front looked slate grey in the dull afternoon light. At the far side of the square, the El Toro coffee bar and Joplin's newsagent's seemed to be doing good business.

Banks thought of Alison, who had shown so much courage in telling them about what had happened at Arkbeck Farm. Someone had scared her so much she had sat in her own urine, probably for hours. The idea of her indignity and humiliation made him angry. He vowed he would find whoever was responsible for doing that to her and make damn sure they suffered.

THREE

The Queen's Arms was always busy at six o'clock on a Friday, and it was only through good luck and quick reflexes that Banks and Susan Gay managed to grab a copper-topped table by the window when a party of cashiers from the NatWest Bank gathered their things and left.

As happened so often in the Dales, the weather had changed dramatically over a very short period. A light breeze had sprung up and blown away the clouds. Now, the early evening sunlight glowed through the red and amber panes and shot bright rays through the clear ones, lighting on a foaming glass of ale and highlighting the smoke swirling in the air.

The sunlight and smoke reminded Banks of the effect the projection camera created at the cinema when smoking was allowed there. As kids, he and his friends used to put their money together for a packet of five Woodbines, then go to the morning matinee at the Palace: a Three Stooges short, a Buck Rogers or Flash Gordon serial and a black-and-white Western, maybe a Hopalong Cassidy. Slumped down in their seats, they would smoke 'wild woodies' until they felt sick. He smiled at the memory and reached for a Silk Cut.

Conversation and laughter ebbed and flowed all around them, and the general mood was ebullient. After all, it was the weekend. For most people in the pub, there would be no work until Monday morning. They could go off shopping to York or Leeds, wallpaper the bedroom, visit Aunt Maisie in Skipton or just lounge around and watch football or racing on telly. It was Cup Final day tomorrow, Banks remembered. Fat chance he'd get of watching it.

The best he could hope was that he would get home before too late tonight and spend some time with Sandra. It was the ideal opportunity for a bit of bridge-building. Tracy was away in France on a school exchange, and Brian was at Portsmouth Polytechnic, so they had the house to themselves for once. He would be too late for a shared dinner, but maybe a nice bottle of claret, a few Chopin 'Nocturnes', candlelight . . . then, who knew what might follow?

It was a nice fantasy. But right now he was waiting for Gristhorpe and Richmond, here to combine the pleasure of a pint and a steak-and-kidney pud with the business of swapping notes and fishing for leads at an informal meeting.

Once in a while, through the laughter and the arguments, Banks heard the Rothwell case mentioned. 'Did you hear about that terrible murder up near Relton . . .?' 'Hear about that bloke got shot out in the dale? I heard they blew his head right off his shoulders . . .' By now, of course, everyone had had a chance to read the *Yorkshire Evening Post*, and people were only too willing to embroider on the scant details the newspaper gave. Rumour and fantasy were rife. What Gristhorpe hadn't told the media so far was that Rothwell had been executed 'gangland' style, and that the weapon used was a shotgun.

The best the press could manage so far was 'LOCAL BUSINESSMAN MURDERED . . . Not more than a mile above the peaceful Swainsdale village of Fortford, a mild-mannered accountant was shot to death in his own garage in the early hours of this morning . . .' There followed an appeal for information about 'two men in black' and a photograph of Keith Rothwell, looking exactly like a mild-mannered accountant, with his thinning fair hair combed back, showing the slight widow's peak, his high forehead, slightly prissy lips and the wire-rimmed glasses. The glasses, Banks knew, had been found shattered to pieces along with the other wreckage of Rothwell's skull.

Banks waved to Gristhorpe and Richmond, who nudged their way through the crowd to join them at the table. While he was on his feet, Richmond went to get a round of drinks and put in the food orders.

'At least we don't have to worry about civilians over-hearing classified information,' Gristhorpe said as he sat down and scraped his stool forward along the worn stone flagging. 'I can hardly even hear myself think.'

When Richmond got back with the tray of drinks, Gristhorpe said, 'Right, Phil, tell us what you found.'

They huddled close around the table. Richmond took a sip of his St Clements. 'There are several items that have been either encrypted or assigned passwords,' he said. 'Some are complete directories, and one's just a document file in a directory. He's called it "LETTER".'

'Can you get access?' Gristhorpe asked.

'Not easily, no, sir. Not unless you type the password at the prompt. Believe me, I've tried every trick and all I've got for my pains is gibberish.'

'All right.' Gristhorpe coughed and waved away Banks's smoke with an exaggerated gesture. 'Let's assume he had some special reason for keeping these items secret. That means we're definitely interested. You said you couldn't gain access easily, but is there a way?'

Richmond cleared his throat. 'Well, yes there is. Actually, there are two ways.'

'Come on, then, lad. Don't keep us in suspense.'

'We could bring in an expert. I mean a *real* expert, like someone who writes the programmes.'

'Aye, and the other option?'

'Well, it's not much known, for obvious reasons, but I went to a seminar once and the lecturer told me something that struck me as very odd.'

'What?'

'Well, there's a company that sells bypass programmes for various software security systems.'

'That would probably be cheaper and quicker, wouldn't it?' said Gristhorpe. 'Can you get hold of a copy?'

'Yes, sir. But it's not cheap. Actually, it's quite expensive.'

'How much?'

'About two hundred quid.'

Gristhorpe whistled between his teeth, then he said, 'We don't have a lot of choice, do we? Go ahead, order one.'

'I already have done, sir.'

'And?'

'They're based in Akron, Ohio, but they told me there's a distributor in Taunton, Devon, who has some in stock. It could take a while to get it up here.'

'Tell the buggers to send it by courier, then. We might as well be hung for a sheep as a lamb. Lord knows what the DCC will have to say come accounting time.'

'Maybe if it helps us solve the case,' Banks chipped in, 'he'll increase our budget.'

Gristhorpe laughed. 'In a pig's arse, he will. Go on, Phil.'

'That's all, really,' said Richmond. 'In the meantime, I'll keep trying and see what I can do. People sometimes write their passwords down in case they forget them. If Rothwell did, the only problem is finding out *where* and in what form.'

'Interesting,' Banks said. 'I've got one of those plastic cards, the ones you use to get money at the hole in the wall. I keep the number written in my address book disguised as part of a telephone number in case I forget it.'

'Exactly,' said Richmond.

'Short of trying every name and number in Rothwell's address book,' Gristhorpe said, 'is there any quick way of doing this?'

'I don't think so, sir,' Richmond said. 'But often the password is a name the user has strong affinities with.'

'"Rosebud"?' Banks suggested.

'Right,' said Richmond. 'That sort of thing. Maybe something from his childhood.'

'"Woodbines",' said Banks. 'Sorry, Phil, just thinking out loud.'

'But it could be anything. The name of a family member, for example. Or a random arrangement of letters, spaces, numbers and punctuation marks. It doesn't have to make any sense at all.'

'Bloody hell.' Gristhorpe ran his hand through his unruly thatch of grey hair.

'All I can say is leave it with me, sir. I'll do what I can. And I'll ask the software distributor to put a rush on it.'

'All right. Susan? Anything from Hatchard and Pratt?'

Susan leaned forward to make herself heard. Just as she was about to start, Cyril called out their food number, and Richmond and Banks went through to bring back the trays. After a few mouthfuls, Susan started again. 'Yes,' she said, dabbing at the side of her mouth with a napkin. 'As it turns out, Rothwell was asked to leave the firm.'

'Asked to leave?' Gristhorpe echoed. 'Does that mean fired?'

'Not exactly, sir. He was a partner. You can't just fire

partners. He was also married to the boss's daughter. Mary Rothwell's maiden name is Hatchard. He was asked to resign. They didn't want a fuss.'

'Interesting,' said Gristhorpe. 'What was it all about, then?'

Susan ate another mouthful of her Cornish pasty, then washed it down with a sip of Britvic orange and pushed her plate aside. 'Laurence Pratt was reluctant to tell me about it,' she said, 'but I think he knew he'd be in more trouble if we found out some other way. It seems Rothwell was caught padding the time sheets. It's not a rare fiddle, according to Pratt. And he doesn't regard it as strictly illegal, but it *is* unethical, and it's bad luck for anyone who gets caught. Rothwell got off lucky.'

'What happened?' asked Gristhorpe.

'This was about five years ago. Rothwell was doing a lot of work for a large company. Pratt wouldn't tell me who it was, but I don't think that really matters. The point is that Pratt's father was looking over the billings and noticed that Rothwell had doubled up on his hours here and there, at times he couldn't have been working on their account because he'd been on another job, or out of town.'

'What did he do? Isn't there some regulatory board he should have been reported to?'

'Yes, sir, there is. But, remember, Rothwell was married to Hatchard's daughter, Mary. They'd been together nearly sixteen years by then, had two kids. Old man Hatchard would hardly want his son-in-law struck off and his family name dragged through the mud, which is probably what would have happened if Rothwell had been reported. I also got the impression that it might have been Mary's demands that set Rothwell padding his accounts in the first place. Nothing was directly stated, you understand, sir, just hinted. Imagine the headlines: "Accountant fired for padding books to keep boss's daughter in the manner to which she was accustomed." Hardly bears thinking about, does it? Anyway, Laurence Pratt and Rothwell were quite close friends then, so Pratt interceded and stuck up for him. Rothwell was lucky. He had a lot going for him. And there's another reason they didn't want a hue and cry.'

'Which is?'

'Confidence and confidentiality, sir. If it got out to the large company that Rothwell was fiddling, then it would put the partnership in an awkward position. Much better they don't find out and Rothwell simply decides to move on. Keep it in the family. They'd never question the bills, or miss the money.'

'I see.' Gristhorpe rubbed his whiskery chin.

'It's something that could have led to a motive, isn't it, sir? Greed, dishonesty.'

'Aye,' said Gristhorpe. 'It is that. Which makes me think even more that these secret files might prove interesting reading.' He tapped the tabletop. 'Good work, Susan. Let's make Rothwell's business affairs a major line of inquiry. I'll get in touch with the Fraud Squad. I've heard from the anti-terrorist squad, by the way, and they've come up with nothing so far. They want to be kept up to date, of course, but I think we can rule out Rothwell dealing arms or money to the IRA. Anything to add, Alan?'

'I think we should follow up on the wadding. There could be a porn connection.'

'Rothwell in the porn business?'

'It's possible. After all, he had plenty of money, didn't he? He must have got it from somewhere. I'm not suggesting he was a front player, one who got his hands dirty.

Maybe he just made some investments or handled finances. Take the lid off that can of worms – video nasties, prostitution and the like – and it wouldn't surprise me to find murder. Perhaps the wadding was a kind of signature, a symbol.'

'It sounds a bit too fanciful to me,' said Gristhorpe, 'but I take your point. It's all tied together, anyway, isn't it? If he was in the porn business, then that makes porn part of his business affairs. We'll follow up on it.'

'DS Hatchley's coming back on Monday,' said Banks. 'I think he'd be a good man for the job. Remember he spent a while working on the Vice Squad for West Yorkshire? Besides, he'd enjoy it.'

Gristhorpe snorted. 'I suppose he would. But keep him on a tight leash. He's like a bloody bull in a china shop.'

Banks grinned. He knew that Gristhorpe and Hatchley didn't get along. Jim Hatchley was a big, bluff, burly, boozy, roast-beef sort of Yorkshireman, a rugby prop forward until cigarettes and drink took their toll. More at home playing darts in the public bar than chatting in the lounge, he was the kind of person everyone under-estimated, and that often worked to the advantage of the Eastvale CID. And he also had a valuable, countywide network of lowlife, quasi-criminal informers that nobody had been able to penetrate.

'The Rothwells are an interesting family,' Banks went on after a sip of Theakston's. 'Mrs Rothwell assured me everything was fine and dandy on the domestic front, but methought the lady did protest too much. I wonder how much communication there really was between them all. It's nothing I can put my finger on, but there's something bothering me. I think the son, Tom, might have something to do with it.'

'I got that impression, too,' said Susan. 'It all looks fine on the surface, but I'd like to know what life at Arkbeck Farm was like. After I'd talked to Laurence Pratt, I got to thinking that if Tom was the reason Keith and Mary Rothwell had to get married, and Rothwell was unhappy in his marriage, then he might blame Tom. Irrational, of course, but things happen like that.'

'I'd leave the psychology to Jenny Fuller,' said Gristhorpe.

Susan reddened.

'Susan's right,' said Banks. 'The sooner we find Tom Rothwell, the better.'

Gristhorpe shrugged. 'It's up to the Florida police now. We've passed on all the information we've got. Come on, Alan, surely you don't think the wife and daughter had anything to do with it?'

'It would be hard to believe, wouldn't it? On the other hand, we've only *their* word for what happened. Nobody else saw the two men in black. What if Alison and her mother *did* want rid of Rothwell for some reason?'

'Next you'll be telling me the wife and daughter were making porno films for Rothwell. You talked to Alison. You could see the lass was upset.'

'Alison might not have had anything to do with it.'

'You mean Mrs Rothwell? Wasn't she in shock?'

'So I'm told. I didn't get to see her until late this morning. That gave her plenty of time to compose herself, work up an act.'

'But the SOC team went through the place as thoroughly as they usually do, hayloft and all. They couldn't find any traces of a weapon.'

'I'm not saying she shot him.'

'What then? She hired a couple of killers to do it for her?'

'I don't know. She could certainly afford it. I suppose I'm playing devil's advocate, trying to look at it from all angles. I still maintain they're an odd family. Alison was genuinely terrified, I know that. But there's something not quite right about them all, and I'd like to know what that is. I knew when I drove away from Arkbeck Farm that something I'd seen there was bothering me, nagging away, but I didn't know what it was until a short while ago.'

'And?' asked Gristhorpe.

'It was Tom's postcard from California. It was addressed to Alison – he called her Ali – and at the end he wrote, "Love to Mum". There was no mention of his father.'

'Hmm,' said Gristhorpe. 'It doesn't have to mean anything.'

'Maybe not. But that's not all. When I looked through Rothwell's wallet a while back, I found photos of Mary and Alison, but none of Tom. Not one.'

4

ONE

A good night's sleep is supposed to refresh you, not make you feel as if you're recovering from a bloody anaesthetic, thought Banks miserably on Saturday morning. Never a morning person at the best of times, he sat over his second cup of black coffee and a slice of wholewheat toast and Seville marmalade, newspaper propped up in front of him, trying to muster enough energy to get going. As a background to the radio traffic reports, he could hear Sandra having a shower upstairs. Banks hated the contraption – he always seemed to get a lukewarm dribble rather than a hot shower – but Sandra and Tracy swore by it. Banks preferred a long, hot bath with a little quiet background music and a good book.

After catching up with paperwork, he hadn't got home until almost eleven the previous night. He wished Sandra had been angry that they'd had to miss the claret, the Chopin and the candlelight, but she hadn't seemed to care. He didn't know whether she was pretending or she *really* didn't care. In fact, she said she'd just got back from a reception at the community centre herself. It was getting to be par for the course. They had seen so little of one another lately that they were fast becoming strangers. It seemed to Banks that what had been a strength in their relationship – their natural independence – was quickly becoming a threat.

And while Sandra had slept like a log, Banks had tossed and turned all night beside her, worried about the Rothwell case, with only brief, fitful periods of sleep full of shifting images: the pornographic wadding, the headless corpse. Now it was eight-thirty the next morning, and his eyes felt like sandpaper, his brain stuffed with cotton wool.

The national dailies and radio news carried stories on the Keith Rothwell killing – sandwiched between a blood-thirsty put-down of riots on a Caribbean island, where another dictator was nearing the end of his reign of terror, and a male Member of Parliament caught *in flagrante delicto* with a sixteen-year-old rentboy on Clapham Common. It probably wouldn't have even made the papers if it had happened somewhere a bit more up-market, like Hampstead Heath, Banks thought.

The Rothwell murder would be on television too, no doubt, amidst all the speculation on that afternoon's Cup Final, but Banks had never been able to bring himself to turn the thing on during daylight hours.

Now, hints were appearing in the media that the killing was more than a run-of-the-mill domestic disagreement or a burglary gone wrong. According to the radio, Scotland Yard, Interpol and the FBI had been called in. That, Banks reflected, was a slight exaggeration. The Americans had been asked to help trace Tom Rothwell, though as far as Banks knew it was the Florida State Police, not the FBI. Interpol was something the reporters always threw in for good measure, these days, and Scotland Yard was an outright lie.

Banks scanned the *Yorkshire Post* and the *Independent* reports to see if either newspaper knew more than the police. Sometimes they did, and it could be damned embarrassing all round. Not this time, though. To them,

Rothwell was as much the 'quiet, unassuming local accountant and businessman' as he was to the rest of the world.

'More coffee?'

Banks looked up to see Sandra standing at the machine in her navy-blue bathrobe, wet hair hanging over the terry-cloth at her shoulders. He hadn't heard her come down.

'Please.' He held his cup out.

Sandra poured, then put some bread in the toaster and picked up the *Yorkshire Post*. After she had read about Rothwell, she whistled. 'Is this what kept you out so late last night?'

'Hmm,' murmured Banks.

The toast popped up. Sandra put the paper down and went to see to it. 'I've met her a couple of times, you know,' she said over her shoulder, buttering toast.

Banks folded the *Independent* and looked at Sandra's profile. When it was wet, her hair looked darker, of course, but one of the things Banks found attractive about her was the contrast between her blonde hair and black eyebrows. This time, when he looked at her, he felt an ache deep inside. 'Who?' he asked.

'Mrs Rothwell. Mary Rothwell.'

'How on earth did you come across her?'

'At the gallery.'

Sandra ran the local gallery in the Eastvale community centre, where she organized art and photography exhibitions.

'I didn't know she was the artistic type.'

'She's not really. I think for her it was just the thing to do. Women's Institute sort of stuff, you know, organize cultural outings.' Sandra sat down with her toast and wrinkled her nose.

Banks laughed, sensing a definite thaw in the cold war. 'Snob.'

'What! Me?' She hit him lightly with the folded news-paper.

'Anyway,' Banks said, 'the poor woman's on tranquil-lizers. Both she and her daughter saw Rothwell's body before they called us, and you can take my word for it, that's enough to give anyone the heebie-jeebies.'

'How's the daughter?'

'Alison? Not quite so bad, at least not on the surface.' Banks shrugged. 'More resilient, maybe, or she could just be repressing it more. Tina Smithies says she's worried they're both losing touch.' He looked at his watch. 'I'd better go.'

Sandra followed him to the door and leaned against the banister. She nibbled her toast as she watched him put on his light grey sports jacket and pick up his briefcase. 'I can't say I know her well enough to get any kind of impression,' she said, holding her dressing gown at the collar when Banks opened the door, 'but I did sense that she's the kind who . . . well, she puts on a few airs and graces. Not so much as to be a complete pseud, but you can tell there's a touch of the Lady Muck about her. Imperious. And she likes people to know she's not short of a bob or two. You know, she flashes her rings, jewellery, stuff like that. She also struck me as being a very *cold* woman, I don't know why. All sharp edges, like a drawer full of kitchen knives.'

Banks leaned against the door jamb. 'It's a bloody strange family altogether,' he said.

Sandra shrugged. 'Just thought I'd put in my two penn'orth. I don't suppose you know when you'll be back?'

'No. Sorry, got to dash.' Banks risked a quick kiss on the lips. They tasted of strawberry jam.

'Can you leave me the car, today?' Sandra called after him. 'There's a watercolour exhibition I want to see in Ripon. One of our locals is exhibiting. I don't know when I'll be back, either.'

'Okay,' said Banks, wincing at the barb. He could always sign a car out of the pool if he needed one. It wouldn't have a cassette deck, but then this was hardly the best of all possible worlds, was it? At least it should have a radio. He set off determined, after a miserable night, not to let things get him down.

It was a beautiful morning. Calendar weather. May, as he knew it, had finally arrived. The sky was a cloudless blue, apart from a few high milky swirls, and even this early in the morning the temperature seemed to have risen a few notches since yesterday. Banks wouldn't be surprised if it were shirt-sleeves weather before the day was out.

As he walked, he plugged in his earphones and switched on the Walkman in his briefcase. The tape started at the jazzy 'Forlane' section of Ravel's *Le Tombeau de Couperin*. Not bad for a walk to work on a fine spring morning.

It was only about a mile to the station along Market Street, and Banks liked the way the townscape changed almost yard by yard as he walked. At his end of town, the road was broad, and the area was much like the outer part of any town centre: the main road with its garage, supermarket, school, zebra crossings and roundabouts, surrounded by residential streets of tall Victorian houses, most of them converted to student flats, all with names like Mafeking Avenue, Sebastopol Terrace, Crimea Close and Waterloo Road, and a strong smell of petrol and diesel fumes pervading the air.

But the closer Market Street got to the actual market-place, the more it narrowed and turned into a tourist attraction with its overhanging first-floor bays, where people could almost shake hands with someone across the street; the magnifying-glass windows of twee souvenir shops; an expensive walkers' gear shop with orange Goretex clothing hanging by the doorway and a stand of walking sticks out on the pavement; a Waterstone's bookshop, the street's most recent addition; the mingled aromas from Hambleton's Tea and Coffee Emporium and Farleigh's bakery across the street; an Oddbins wine shop; the Golden Grill café; and a newsagent's with a rack of newspapers out front, some of them folded over at Rothwell's grainy photograph, and a display of local guides and Ordnance Survey maps in the window. This narrow part of Market Street was always jammed with honking traffic too – mostly visitors and delivery vans.

Halfway through the 'Menuet' section, Banks arrived at the station, a three-storey, Tudor-fronted building facing the market square. First he called in at the Murder Room and talked to Phil Richmond. The Florida State Police had tracked down the car rental company Tom Rothwell had used at Tampa airport. At least it was a start. Now the police had a licence number to look for among the millions of cars parked at the thousands of Florida hotels, motels and beach clubs.

The PNC reported nothing doing on the use of porno-graphic wadding at other crime scenes.

Gristhorpe was in a meeting with Inspector Macmillan of the Fraud Squad, and Susan Gay was in her hutch phoning around the list of Rothwell's clients Laurence Pratt had given her. Banks poured a coffee and went to his office.

He opened his window and sniffed the air, then lit a cigarette and stood looking down on the early tourists in their bright anoraks and cagoules milling about the cobbled square. It was ten past nine on a Saturday morning, market-day in Eastvale, and the vendors at their canvas-covered stalls, like the old wild-west wagon trains, hawked everything from flat caps and multi-pocketed fishing jackets to burglar alarms, spark plugs and non-stick ovenware. The cheese van was there, as usual, and Banks thought he might nip out and buy a wedge of Coverdale or Wensleydale Blue if he got the chance. If.

Banks mulled over what Sandra had told him about Mary Rothwell. So far, he had an impression of her as an ostentatious and overbearing woman who put too much value on appearances, and of Keith Rothwell as an unassuming, yet sly and greedy, man, easily prey to temptation. Greed, as Susan Gay had remarked, is often a way of making dangerous enemies, and a habit of secrecy is a damn good way of making things difficult for the police. But did the greed originate in Rothwell himself, or had he felt pushed into it by the demands of his wife?

There had certainly been hints in what both Ian Falkland and Larry Grafton had said that Rothwell had been something of a henpecked husband, escaping to the pub for a half-pint and a quiet smoke whenever he could.

In Banks's experience, such people often developed rich and secret fantasy lives, which sometimes imposed on reality with messy and unpredictable results. Keith Rothwell had supplied his wife and children with all the conveniences and many of the luxuries they wanted. What did he get out of it? What did he have going for himself? Nobody seemed to know or care what made him tick.

Banks moved away from the window and stubbed out

his cigarette. There was at least one thing he could do right now, he thought, reaching for a pen and notepad. 'WANTED,' he wrote, 'male Caucasian, about five feet nine, slight paunch, large wet brown eyes, commonly described as "spaniel" or "puppy dog" eyes, fondness for shotguns, can't keep his hands off young girls and probably has a taste for pornography of the shaved pussy variety.' He could just imagine the laughter and the nudge-nudges in police stations around the country as that went out over the PNC.

Just as he was about to start working on a revised version, the phone rang and Sergeant Rowe put him through to a distraught woman asking for the ubiquitous 'someone in charge'.

'Can I help you?' Banks asked her.

'They said they'd put me through to someone in charge. Are you in charge?'

'Depends what you mean,' said Banks. 'In charge of what? What's it about?'

'The man in the paper this morning, the one who was killed.'

Suddenly Banks pricked up his ears. Was he mistaken, or was she sobbing as she spoke? 'Yes,' he said. 'Go on.'

'I knew him.'

'You knew Keith Rothwell?'

'No, no—' She sobbed again then came back on the line. 'You've got it wrong. That's not his name. His name is Robert. Robert Calvert. That's who he is. You've got it all wrong. Is Robert really dead?'

The back of his neck tingling, Banks gripped his pen tight between his fingers. 'I think we'd better have a talk, love,' he said. 'The sooner, the better. Would you like to give me your name and address?'

TWO

Susan Gay drove the unmarked police Fiesta to Leeds, with Banks beside her tapping his fingers on his knees. It wasn't because of her driving. Ordinarily, he would enjoy such a trip and take his time if there were no rush, but today he was anxious to interview the woman who had phoned, Pamela Jeffreys.

He wasn't smoking, either, and that also made him jittery. He refrained in deference to Susan, though she magnanimously said it was okay if he opened the windows. There wasn't much worse, in his experience, than trying to enjoy a cigarette in a car next to a non-smoker with a force nine gale blowing all around you, no matter how good the weather.

As Banks had hoped, though the car had no cassette player, it did have a radio, and he was able to lose himself in a Poulenc chamber concert on Radio Three as he considered the implications of what he had just heard.

'How are we going to play this, sir?' Susan asked as she turned on to the Inner Ring Road and went into the yellow-lit tunnel.

Banks dragged himself out of a passage in the 'Sextet' where a sense of sadness seemed to pervade the levity of the woodwinds. 'By ear,' he said.

They had already called DI Ken Blackstone, out of courtesy for intruding on his patch, and Ken had found nothing on Pamela Jeffreys in records. Hardly surprising, Banks thought, as there was no reason to suppose she was a criminal. He glanced out of the window and saw they were crossing the bridge over the River Aire and the Leeds–Liverpool Canal. The dirty, sluggish water looked especially vile in the bright sunlight.

'Do we tell her anything?' Susan asked.

'If she's read the papers, she'll know almost as much about Keith Rothwell's life as we do. Whether she'll believe it or not is another matter.'

'What do you think it's all about?'

'I haven't a clue. We'll soon find out.'

Susan negotiated the large roundabout on Wellington Road. Above them, the dark, medieval fortress of Armley Jail loomed on its hill. Susan veered right at the junction with Tong Road, passed the disused Crown bingo hall, the medical centre and the New Wortley Cemetery and headed towards Armley. It was an area of waste ground and boarded-up shopfronts, with the high black spire of St Bartholomew's visible above the decay. She slowed to look at the street names, found Wesley Road, turned right, then right again and looked for the address Pamela Jeffreys had given.

'This is it, sir,' she said finally, pulling into a street of terraced back-to-backs, nicely done up, each with a postage-stamp lawn behind a privet hedge, some with new frosted-glass or wood-panel doors and dormer windows. 'Number twenty, twenty-four . . . Here it is.' She pulled up outside number twenty-eight.

The row of houses stood across the street from some allotments behind a low stone wall, where a number of retired or unemployed men worked their patches, stopping now and then to chat. Someone had rested a transistor radio on the wall, and Banks could hear the preamble to the Cup Final commentary. Not far down the street was an old chapel which, according to the sign, had been converted into a Sikh temple. They walked down the path to number twenty-eight and rang the doorbell.

The woman who opened the door had clearly been

crying, but it didn't mar her looks one bit, Banks thought. Perhaps the whites of her almond eyes were a little too red and the glossy blue-black hair could have done with a good brushing, but there was no denying that she was a woman of exceptional beauty.

Northern Indian, Banks guessed, or perhaps from Bangladesh or Pakistan, she had skin the colour of burnished gold, with high cheekbones, full, finely drawn lips and a figure that wouldn't be out of place in *Playboy*, revealed to great advantage by skin-tight ice-blue jeans and a jade-green T-shirt tucked in at her narrow waist. Around her neck, she wore a necklace of many-coloured glass beads. She also wore a gold stud in her left nostril. She looked to be in her mid-twenties.

Her fingers, Banks noticed as she raised her hand to push the door shut, were long and tapered, with clear nails cut very short. A spiral gold bracelet slipped down her slim wrist over her forearm. On the other wrist, she wore a simple Timex with a black plastic strap. She had only one ring, and that was a gold band on the middle finger of her right hand. Light down covered her bare brown arms.

The living room was arranged for comfort. A small three-piece suite with burgundy velour upholstery formed a semicircle around a thick glass coffee table in front of the fireplace, which may once have housed a real coal fire but now was given over to an electric one with three elements and a fake flaming-coals effect. On the coffee table, the new Mary Wesley paperback lay open, face down beside a copy of the *Radio Times* and an earthenware mug half full of milky tea.

A few family photographs in gilt frames stood on the mantelpiece. On the wall above the fire hung a print of Ganesh, the elephant god, in a brightly coloured, primitive style. In the corner by the front window stood a television with a video on a shelf underneath. The only other furniture in the room was a mini stereo system and several racks of compact discs, a glass-fronted cabinet of crystalware and a small bookcase mostly full of modern fiction and books about music.

But it was the far end of the room that caught Banks's interest, for there stood a music stand, with some sheet music on it, and beside that, on a chair, lay what he first took to be an oversized violin, but quickly recognized as a viola.

The woman sat on the sofa, curling her legs up beside her, and Banks and Susan took the armchairs.

'Are you a musician?' Banks asked.

'Yes,' she said.

'Professional?'

'Uh-huh. I'm with the Northern Philharmonia, and I do a bit of chamber work on the side. Why?'

'Just curious.' Banks was impressed. The English Northern Philharmonia played for Opera North, among other things, and was widely regarded as one of the best opera orchestras in the country. He had been to see Opera North's superb production of *La Bohème* recently and must have heard Pamela Jeffreys play.

'Ms Jeffreys,' he began, after a brief silence. 'I must admit that your phone call has us a bit confused.'

'Not half as much as that rubbish in the newspaper has *me* confused.' She had no Indian accent at all, just West Yorkshire with a cultured, university edge.

Banks slipped a recent good-quality photograph of Keith Rothwell from his briefcase and passed it to her. 'Is this the man we're talking about?'

'Yes. I think this is Robert, though he looks a bit stiff

here.' She handed it back. 'There's a mistake, isn't there? It must be someone who looks just like him, that's it.'

'What exactly was your relationship?'

She fiddled with her necklace. 'We're friends. Maybe we were more than that, at one time, but now we're just friends.'

'Were you lovers?'

'Yes. For a while.'

'For how long?'

'Three or four months.'

'Until when?'

'Six months ago.'

'So you've known him for about ten months altogether?'

'Yes.'

'How did you meet?'

'In a pub. The Boulevard, on Westgate, actually. I was with some friends. Robert was by himself. We just got talking, like you do.'

'Have you seen him since you stopped being lovers?'

'Yes. I told you. We remained friends. We don't see each other as often, of course, but we still go out every now and then, purely platonic. I like Robert. He's good fun to be with, even when we stopped being lovers. Look, what's all this in—'

'When did you last see him, Ms Jeffreys?'

'Pamela. Please call me Pamela. Let me see . . . it must have been a month or more ago. Look, is this some mistake, or what?'

'We don't know yet, Pamela,' Susan Gay said. 'We really don't, love. You'll help us best get it sorted out if you answer Chief Inspector Banks's questions.'

Pamela nodded.

PETER ROBINSON

'Was there anything unusual about Mr . . . about Robert the last time you saw him?' Banks asked.

'No.'

'He didn't say anything, tell you about anything that was worrying him?'

'No. Robert never seemed to worry about anything. Except he hated being called Bob.'

'So there was nothing at all different about him?'

'Well, I wouldn't say that.'

'Oh?'

'It's just a guess, like.'

'What was it?'

'I think he'd met someone else. Another woman. I think he was in love.'

Banks swallowed, hardly able to believe what he was hearing. This couldn't be dull, dry, mild-mannered Keith Rothwell. Surely Rothwell wasn't the kind of man to have a wife and children in Swainsdale and a beautiful girl-friend like Pamela Jeffreys in Leeds, whom he could simply dump for yet *another* woman?

'Don't get me wrong,' Pamela went on. 'I'm not bitter or anything. We had a good time, and it was never anything more. We didn't lie to each other. Neither of us wanted to get too involved. And one thing Robert doesn't do is mess you around. That's why we can still be friends. But he made it clear it was over between us – at least in *that* way – and I got the impression it was because he'd found someone else.'

'Did you ever see this woman?'

'No.'

'Did he ever speak of her?'

'No. I just *knew*. A woman can tell about these things, that's all.'

84

'Did you ask him about her?'

'I broached the subject once or twice.'

'What happened?'

'He changed it.' She smiled. 'He has a way.'

'How often did you see each other?'

'When we were going out?'

'Yes.'

'Just once or twice a week. Mostly late in the week, weekends sometimes. He travels a lot on business. Anyway, he's usually at home every week at some time, at least for a day or two.'

'What's his business?'

'Dunno. That's another thing he never said much about. I can't say I was really that interested, either. I mean, it's boring, isn't it, talking about business. I liked going out with Robert because he was fun. He could leave his work at home.'

'Did he smoke?'

'What an odd question. Yes, as a matter of fact. Not much, though.'

'What brand?'

'Benson and Hedges. I don't mind people smoking.'

Encouraged, Banks slipped his Silk Cut out of his pocket. Pamela smiled and brought him a glass ashtray. 'What was he like?' Banks asked. 'What kind of things did you used to do together?'

Pamela looked at Banks with a glint of naughty humour in her eyes and raised her eyebrows. Banks felt himself flush. 'I mean where did you used to go?' he said quickly.

'Yeah, I know. Hmmm . . . Well, we'd go out for dinner about once a week. Brasserie 44 – you know, down by the river – or La Grillade, until it moved. He likes good food. Let's see . . . sometimes we'd go to concerts at the Town

Hall, if I wasn't playing, of course, but he's not very fond of classical music, to be honest. Prefers that dreadful trad jazz. And sometimes we'd just stay in, order a pizza or a curry and watch telly if there was something good on. Or rent a video. He likes oldies. *Casablanca*, *The Maltese Falcon*, that kind of thing. So do I. Let me see . . . we'd go to Napoleon's every once in a while—'

'Napoleon's?'

'Yeah. You know, the casino. And he took me to the races a couple of times – once at Pontefract and once at Doncaster. That's about it, really. Oh, and we went dancing now and then. Quite fleet on his feet is Robert.'

Banks coughed and stubbed out his cigarette. 'Dancing? The casino?'

'Yes. He loves a flutter, does Robert. It worried me sometimes the way he'd go through a hundred or more some nights.' She shrugged. 'But it wasn't my place to say, was it? I mean it wasn't as if we were *married* or anything, or even living together. And he seemed to have plenty of money. Not that that's what interested me about him.' She pulled at her necklace again. 'Can't you tell me what's going on, Chief Inspector? It's not the same person that was murdered, is it? I was so upset when I saw the paper this morning. Tell me it's a case of mistaken identity.'

Banks shook his head. 'I don't know. Maybe he had a double. Did he ever say anything about being married?'

'No, never.'

'Did he have an appendix scar?'

This time, Pamela blushed. 'Yes,' she said. 'Yes, he did. But so do lots of other people. I had mine out when I was sixteen.'

'When you spent time together,' Banks said, 'did he

always come here, to your house? Didn't you ever visit him at his hotel?'

She frowned. 'Hotel? What hotel?'

'The one he stayed at when he was in town, I assume. Did you always meet here?'

'Of course not. Sometimes he came here, certainly. I've nothing to be ashamed of, and I don't care what the neighbours say. Bloody racists, some of them. You know, my mum and dad came over to Shipley to work in the woollen mills in 1952. *Nineteen fifty-two.* They even changed their name from Jaffrey to Jeffreys because it sounded more English. Can you believe it? I was born here, brought up here, went to school and university here and some of them still call me a bleeding Paki.' She shrugged. 'What can you do? Anyway, you were saying?'

'I was asking why you never saw him at his hotel.'

'Oh, that's easy. I don't know what you're talking about. You see, it *can't* be the same person, can it? That proves it.' She leaned forward quickly and clapped her hands. The bracelet spiralled. 'You see, Robert didn't stay at any hotel. Sometimes he came here, yes, but not always. Other times I went to his place. His flat. He's got a flat in Headingley.'

THREE

Banks turned the Yale key in the lock and the three of them stood on the threshold of Robert Calvert's Headingley flat. It was in the nice part of Headingley, more West Park, Banks noted, not the scruffy part around Hyde Park that was honeycombed with student bedsits.

It hadn't been easy getting in. Pamela Jeffreys didn't

have a key, so they had to ask one of the tenants in the building to direct them to the agency that handled rentals. Naturally, it was closed at four o'clock on a Saturday afternoon, so then they had to get hold of one of the staff at home and arrange for her to come in, grumbling all the way, open up the office and give them a spare key.

And no, she told them, she had never met Robert Calvert. The man was a model tenant; he paid his rent on time, and that was all that mattered. One of the secretaries probably handed him the key, but he'd had the place about eighteen months and turnover in secretaries was pretty high. However, if Banks wanted to come back on Monday morning . . . Still, Banks reflected as they stood at the front door, all in all it had taken only about an hour and a half from the first time they had heard of the place, so that wasn't bad going.

'Better not touch anything,' Banks said as they stood in the hallway. 'Which is the living room?' he asked Pamela.

'That one, on the left.'

The door was ajar and Banks nudged it open with his elbow. The bottom of the door rubbed over the fitted beige carpet. Susan Gay and Pamela walked in behind him.

'There's only this room, a bedroom, kitchen and bathroom,' Pamela said. 'It's not very big, but it's cosy.'

The living room was certainly not the kind of place Banks could imagine Mary Rothwell caring much for. Equipped with all the usual stuff – TV, video, stereo, a few jazz compact discs, books, armchairs, gas fireplace – it smelled of stale smoke and had that comfortable, lived-in feel Banks had never sensed at Arkbeck Farm. Perhaps it was something to do with the old magazines – mostly jazz and racing – strewn over the scratched coffee table, the overflowing ashtray, the worn upholstery on the armchair by the fire or the framed photographs of a younger-looking Rothwell on the mantelpiece. On the wall hung a framed print of Monet's *Waterloo Bridge, Grey Day*.

They went into the bedroom and found the same mess. The bed was unmade, and discarded socks, underpants and shirts lay on the floor beside it.

There was also a small desk against one wall, on which stood a jar of pens and pencils, a roll of Sellotape and a stapler, in addition to several sheets of paper, some of them scrawled all over with numbers. 'Is this the kind of thing you're looking for?' Pamela asked.

Carefully, Banks opened the drawer and found a wallet. Without disturbing anything, he could see, through the transparent plastic holder inside, credit cards in the name of Robert Calvert. He put it back.

A couple of suits hung in the wardrobe, along with shirts, ties, casual jackets and trousers. Banks felt in the pockets and found nothing but pennies, sales slips, a couple of felt-tip pens, matches, betting slips and some fluff.

As wood doesn't usually yield fingerprints, he didn't have to be too careful opening cupboards and drawers. Calvert's dresser contained the usual jumble of jeans, jumpers, socks and underwear. A packet of condoms lay forlornly next to a passport and a selection of Dutch, French, Greek and Swiss small change in the drawer of the bedside table. The passport was in the name of Robert Calvert. There were no entry or exit stamps, but then there wouldn't be if he did most of his travelling in Europe, as the coins seemed to indicate. On the bedside table was a shaded reading lamp and a copy of the *Economist*.

The kitchen was certainly compact, and by the sparsity of the fridge's contents, it looked as if Calvert did most of his eating out. A small wine rack stood on the counter. Banks checked the contents: a white Burgundy, Veuve Clicquot Champagne, a Rioja.

Calvert's bathroom was clean and tidy. His medicine cabinet revealed only the barest of essentials: paracetamol tablets, Aspro, Milk of Magnesia, Alka Seltzer, Fisherman's Friend, Elastoplast, cotton swabs, hydrogen peroxide, Old Spice deodorant and shaving cream, a packet of orange disposable razors, toothbrush and a half-used tube of Colgate. Calvert had squeezed it in the middle, Banks noticed, not from bottom to top. Could this be the same man who returned his used matches to the box?

'Come on,' Banks said. 'We'd better use a call-box. I don't want to risk smudging any prints there may be on the telephone.'

'What's going on?' Pamela asked as they walked down the street.

'I'm sorry,' Susan said to her. 'We really don't know. We're not just putting you off. We're as confused as you are. If we can find some of Robert's fingerprints in the flat, then we can check them against our files and find out once and for all if it's the same man.'

'But it just *can't* be,' Pamela said. 'I'm sure of it.'

A pub on the main road advertised a beer garden at the back, and as they were all thirsty, Banks suggested he might as well make the call from there.

He phoned the station and Phil Richmond said he would arrange to get Vic Manson to the flat as soon as possible.

That done, he ordered the drinks and discovered from the barman that Arsenal had won the FA Cup. Good for them, Banks thought. When he had lived in London, he had been an Arsenal supporter, though he always had a soft spot for Peterborough United, his home-town team, struggling as they were near the bottom of the First Division.

The beer garden was quiet. They sat at a heavy wooden bench beside a bowling green and sipped their drinks. Two old men in white were playing on the green, and occasionally the clack of the bowls disturbed the silence. Banks and Susan shared salted roast peanuts and cheese-and-onion crisps, as neither had eaten since breakfast. The sun felt warm on the back of Banks's neck.

'You can go home whenever you want,' Banks told Pamela as she took off the tan suede jacket she had put on to go out. 'We have to stay here, but we'll pay for a taxi. I'm sorry we had to ruin your day for you.'

Pamela squinted in the sun, reached into her bag and pulled out a pair of large pink-rimmed sunglasses. 'It's all right,' she said, picking up her gin and tonic. 'I know it wasn't Robert they were talking about in the paper. Who was this man, this Keith Rothwell?'

'He was an accountant who got murdered,' Banks told her. 'We can't really say much more than that. Did you ever hear the name before?'

Pamela shook her head. 'The papers said he was married.'

'Yes.'

'Robert didn't act like a married man.'

'What do you mean?'

'Guilt. Secrecy. Fleeting visits. Furtive phone calls. The usual stuff. There was none of that with Robert. We went about quite openly. He wasn't tied down. He was a dreamer. Besides, you just *know*.' She took her glasses off and squinted at Banks. 'I'll bet you're married, aren't you?'

'Yes,' said Banks, and saw, he hoped, a hint of disappointment in her eyes.

'Told you.' She put her sunglasses on again.

Banks noticed Susan grinning behind her glass of lemonade. He gave her a dirty look. A clack of bowls came from the green and one of the old men did a little dance of victory.

'So, you see,' Pamela went on. 'It can't be the same man. If I'm sure of one thing, it's that Robert Calvert definitely wasn't a married man with a family.'

Banks picked up his pint and raised it in a toast. 'I hope you're right,' he said, looking at her brave smile and remembering the scene in Rothwell's garage only two nights ago. 'I sincerely hope you're right.'

5

ONE

There was always something sad about an empty farm-yard, Banks thought as he got out of the car in front of Arkbeck Farm again. There should be chickens squawking all over the place, the occasional wandering cow, maybe a barking sheepdog or two.

He thought of the nest egg he had held at his Uncle Len's farm in Gloucestershire on childhood family visits. They used it to encourage hens to lay, he remembered, and when his Aunt Chloe had handed it to him in the coop, it had still felt warm. Banks also remembered the smells of hay and cow dung, the shiny metal milk churns sitting by the roadside waiting to be picked up.

As he rang the doorbell, he doubted that the Rothwells felt the same way about empty farmyards. The place seemed to suit Alison's introspective nature; her father had no doubt appreciated the seclusion and the protection from prying eyes and questions it offered; and Mary Rothwell . . . well, Banks could hardly imagine her mucking out the byre or feeding the pigs. He couldn't imagine her handing a child a warm porcelain egg, either.

'Do come in,' Mary Rothwell said, opening the door. Banks followed her to the split level living room. Today she wore a white shirt that buttoned on the 'man's' side and a loose grey skirt that reached her ankles. Alison lay sprawled on the sofa reading.

On the way to Arkbeck Farm, he had considered what to say to them regarding his talk with Pamela Jeffreys in Leeds, but he hadn't come up with any clear plan. Vic Manson hadn't got back to him yet about the prints, so he still couldn't be absolutely certain that Robert Calvert and Keith Rothwell were the same person. Best play it by ear, he decided.

'How are you doing?' he asked Mary Rothwell.

'Could be worse,' she replied. He noticed her eyes were baggy under the make-up. 'I haven't been sleeping well, despite the pills, and I'm a mass of nerves, but if I keep myself busy, time passes. I have the funeral to organize. Please, sit down.'

Banks had come partly to explain that a van was on its way to pick up Keith Rothwell's computer disks and business files and spirit them off to the Fraud Squad's headquarters in Northallerton, where a team of suits would pore over them for months, maybe years, costing the taxpayers millions. He didn't put it like that, of course. Just as he had finished explaining, he heard the van pull up out front.

He went to the front door and directed the men to Rothwell's office, then returned to the living room, shutting the door firmly behind him. It was dark in the room, and a little chilly, despite the fine weather outside. 'They shouldn't bother us,' he said. 'Perhaps a little music?'

Mary Rothwell nodded and turned on the radio. Engelbert Humperdinck came on, singing 'Release Me'. Banks often regretted that humans hadn't been born with the capacity to close their ears as they did their eyes. He did his best, anyway, and reflected that it was all in a good cause, blanking out the sounds of Keith Rothwell's office being dismantled and carried away.

'Have you found Tom?' Mary Rothwell said, sitting

down. She sat at the edge of the armchair, Banks noticed, and twisted her hands in her lap, a mass of gold and precious stones. She seemed so stiff he wished someone would give her a massage. Her skin, he felt, would be brittle as lacquered hair to the touch.

Banks explained that they had tracked down the car rental agency he had used and that it wouldn't be long before someone spotted the car.

'He should be home,' she said. 'We need him. There's the funeral . . . all the arrangements . . .'

'We're doing our best, Mrs Rothwell.'

'Of course. I didn't mean to imply anything.'

'It's all right. Are you up to answering a few more questions?'

'I suppose so. As long as you don't want to talk about what I went through the other night. I couldn't bear that.' Her eyes moved in the direction of the garage and Banks could see the fear and horror flood into them.

'No, not that.' She would have to talk about it sometime, Banks almost told her, but not now, not yet. 'It's Mr Rothwell I want to talk about. We need a better idea of how he spent his time.'

'Well, it's hard to say, really,' she began. 'When he was here, he was up in his office most of the time. I could hear him clicking away on the computer.'

'Did you ever hear him on the phone?'

'He had his own line up there. I didn't listen in, if that's what you mean.'

'No, I didn't mean that. But sometimes you just can't help overhearing something, anything.'

'No. He always kept the door shut. I could hear his voice, like I could hear the keyboard, but it was muffled, even if I was passing by the office.'

'So you never knew who he was talking to or what he was saying?'

'No.'

'Did he have many calls in the days leading up to his death?'

'Not so much as I noticed. No more than usual. I could always hear it ring, you see, even from downstairs.' She stood up. 'Would you like a cup of tea? I can—'

'Not at the moment, thank you,' Banks said. He didn't want her crossing the path of the removal team. For one thing, it would upset and distract her, and for another she would start telling them off about trailing dirt in and out.

She walked over to the fireplace, straightened a porcelain figurine, then came and sat down in the same position. Alison went on reading her book. It was *Villette*, by Charlotte Brontë, Banks noticed. Surely a bit heavy for a fifteen-year-old?

'I understand your husband would drop in at the Black Sheep or the Rose and Crown now and then?' Banks asked.

'Yes. He wasn't much of a drinker, but he liked to get out of the house for an hour or so. You do when you work at home, don't you? You get to feel all cooped up. He'd usually walk there and back. It was good exercise. Businessmen often don't exercise enough, do they, living such sedentary lives, but Keith believed in keeping in good shape. He swam regularly, too, in Eastvale, and he would sometimes go for long runs.' She started picking pieces of imaginary lint from her skirt. Banks heard a thud from the staircase, and this time he couldn't stop her from dashing to the door and yanking it open.

'Watch what you're doing, you clumsy little man!' she said. 'Just look at this. You've gouged a hole in my wall.

96

The plaster's fallen off. You'll have to pay for that, you know. I'll be talking to your superior.' She popped her head back around the door and said, 'I'll make that tea now, shall I?' then disappeared into the kitchen.

Banks, still sitting, noticed Alison look up and raise her eyes. 'She's been like this since yesterday,' she said. 'Can't sit still. It's even worse than usual.'

'She's upset,' Banks said. 'It's her way of dealing with it.'

'Or *not* dealing with it. I saw him too, you know. Do you think I can forget so easily?'

'You've got to talk to each other,' Banks said. He noticed the book was shaking in her hands and she was making an effort to keep it still.

'If Tom doesn't come home soon, I'm going to run away,' she said. 'I can't stand it any longer. She's always going on about something or other and running about like a headless chi—' She put her hand to her mouth. 'My God, what a thing to say. I'm awful, aren't I? Oh, I hope Tom comes back soon. He must or I'll go mad. We'll both go mad.'

A bit melodramatic, Banks thought, but perhaps to be expected from a young girl on a steady diet of Charlotte Brontë.

Mary Rothwell came in bearing a tea tray and wearing a brave smile. Alison picked up her book again and lapsed into moody silence while her mother poured the tea into delicate china cups with hand-painted roses on the sides and gold around the rims. Banks always felt clumsy and nervous drinking from such fine china; he was afraid he would drop the cup or break off the flimsy handle while lifting it to his mouth.

'Why are they taking all Keith's files anyway?' Mary Rothwell asked.

'We're beginning to think that your husband might have been involved in some shady financial dealings,' Banks explained. 'And they could have something to do with his murder.'

'Shady?' She said it as Lady Bracknell said, 'A handbag?'

'He might not have known what he was involved in,' Banks lied. 'It's just a line of inquiry we have to follow.'

'I can assure you that my husband was as honest as the day is long.'

'Mrs Rothwell, can you tell me *anything* about what your husband did when he was travelling on business?'

'How would I know? I wasn't there.'

'Which hotels did he stay in? You must have phoned him.'

'No. He phoned me occasionally. He told me it was better that way for his tax expenses.' She shrugged. 'Well, *he* was the businessman. I've already told you he travelled all over the place.'

'You never went with him?'

'No, of course not. I have an aversion to lengthy car rides. Besides, they were business trips. One doesn't take one's spouse on business trips.'

'So you've no idea what he got up to in Leeds or wherever?'

She put down her cup. 'Are you implying something, Chief Inspector? Keith didn't "get up to" anything.'

Banks was dying for a cigarette. He finished the weak tea and put his cup and saucer down gently on the coffee table. 'Do you know if your husband was much of a gambler?' he asked.

'Gambler?' She laughed. 'Good heavens, no. Keith never even bet on the Grand National, and most people do that, don't they? No, money for my husband was too hard earned to be frittered away like that. Keith had a poor childhood, you know, and one learns the value of money quite early on.'

'What sort of childhood?'

'His father was a small shopkeeper, and they suffered terribly when the supermarkets started to become popular. He eventually went bankrupt. Keith didn't like to talk about it.'

Banks remembered the cigarettes he had found among the contents of Rothwell's pockets. 'Did you know that your husband smoked?' he asked.

'One minor weakness,' Mary Rothwell said, turning up her nose. 'It's a smelly and unpleasant habit, as well as a possibly fatal one. I certainly wouldn't let him do it in the house, and I was always trying to persuade him to stop.'

I'll bet you were, Banks thought. 'Have you ever heard of a woman called Pamela Jeffreys?' he asked.

Mary Rothwell frowned. For the first time, she sat back in the chair and gripped its arms with both hands. 'No. Why?' Banks saw suspicion and apprehension in her eyes.

Outside, the van door closed and the engine revved up. Banks noticed Mrs Rothwell glance towards the window. 'They're finished,' he said. 'What about Robert Calvert? Does the name mean anything to you?'

She shook her head. 'No, nothing. Look, what's this all about? Are these the people you think killed Keith? Are these the ones who got him involved in this criminal scheme you were talking about?'

Banks sighed. 'I don't know,' he said. 'Maybe, but I don't know.'

'Why don't you go and arrest *them* instead of bothering us?'

Banks didn't think he was likely to get anything else out of Mary Rothwell, or out of Alison. He stood up. 'I'm sorry we had to bother you,' he said. 'We'll be in touch as soon as we track down your son. And please let us know if you hear from him first. Don't worry, I'll see myself out.' And he left.

Maybe she hadn't heard of Pamela Jeffreys, he thought as he got in the car, but he was certain that she suspected her husband might have been seeing another woman. It was there in her eyes, in the whiteness of her knuckles.

He slipped a Thelonious Monk tape in the deck and set off for his next appointment. As the edgy, repetitive figure at the opening of 'Raise Four' almost pushed his ears to the limits of endurance, he wondered how long Mary Rothwell would be able to maintain her thinly lacquered surface before the cracks started to show.

TWO

'Well, now, if it ain't Mr Banks again,' said Larry Grafton when Banks walked into the Black Sheep that lunchtime with the *Sunday Times* folded under his arm. 'Twice in one week. We are honoured. What can we do for you this time?'

'You could start with a pint of best bitter and follow it with a plate of your Elsie's delightful roast beef and Yorkshire pud. And you could cut the bloody sarcasm.'

Grafton laughed and started pulling. Elsie's Sunday lunches were another well-kept secret, and only a privileged few got to taste them. Banks didn't fool himself that he was an accepted member of the élite; he knew damn well that publicans liked to keep on the good side of the law.

100

'And,' he said, when Larry handed him his pint, 'I'd like a word with your Cathy, if I might.'

'About the Rothwells, is it?'

'Yes.'

'Aye. Well she's just having her dinner. I'll send her through when she's done.'

'Thanks.'

Banks took his drink and sat by the tiled fireplace. Before he sat, he glanced at the collection of butterflies pinned to a board in a glass case on the wall. The pub wasn't as busy as most on a Sunday lunchtime. Of course, there was no sandwich board outside advertising 'Tradilional Sunday Lunch'.

Bank's roast beef and Yorkshires came, as good as ever. Not for the first time, he reflected that Elsie's was the only roast beef in Yorkshire, apart from Sandra's, that was pink in the middle. As he ate, he propped the paper against a bottle of HP sauce and began to read an analysis of the growing political unrest on an obscure Caribbean island, feeling an irrational rage grow in him as he read. Christ, how he loathed these tinpot dictators, the ones who stuffed their maws with the best of everything while their subjects starved, who tortured and murdered anyone who dared to complain.

Just as he had picked up the books supplement, he noticed a tourist couple walk in and look around. They went to the bar and the man asked Larry Grafton what food he offered.

'Nowt,' said Grafton. 'We don't do food.'

The man looked towards Banks. 'But he's got some.'

'Last plate.'

The man looked at his watch. 'But it's only twelve-thirty.'

Grafton shrugged.

'Besides, you said you don't do food. You're contra-dicting yourself. You heard him, didn't you, darling?'

His wife said nothing; she just stood there looking embarrassed. He had the kind of upper-class accent that expects immediate subservience, but he obviously didn't know there could be nothing more calculated to get right up a Yorkshireman's nose.

'Look,' said Grafton, 'does tha want a drink or doesn't tha?'

'We want food,' the man said.

His wife tugged at his sleeve. 'Come on, darling,' she whispered just in Banks's range of hearing. 'Don't cause a fuss. Let's go. There are plenty of other pubs.'

'But I—' The man glared petulantly at Grafton, who stared back stone-faced, then followed his wife's advice.

'Really,' Banks heard him say on his way out, 'you'd think these people didn't want to make an honest living. They're supposed to be in the service industry.'

Larry Grafton winked at Banks and ambled off to serve one of the locals. Banks reflected that maybe the tourist was right. What the hell was wrong with Larry Grafton? Nowt so queer as folk, he decided, and went back to his roast beef. A couple of minutes later, when he had just finished, Cathy Grafton came from the back and joined him. He folded up his newspaper, pushed his empty plate aside and lit a cigarette.

Cathy was a plump girl of about sixteen with a fringe and a blotchy complexion, as if she had been sitting too close to the fire too long. She also had the longest, curliest and most beautiful eyelashes Banks had ever seen.

'Dad says you want to talk to me,' she said, wedging herself into a chair. Her accent was thick, and Banks had to listen closely to understand everything she said, even though he had been in Swainsdale for four years.

'You helped Mary Rothwell do the housework at Arkbeck Farm, didn't you?'

'Aye. I do for a few folk around here. I know I should be paying more mind to school, like, but Mum says we need t'money.'

Banks smiled. Not surprising, given the way Grafton scared business away. 'What was it like, working at Arkbeck?' he asked.

Cathy frowned. 'What do you mean?'

'Did you like working there?'

'It were all reet.'

'How about Mary Rothwell? Did you get along well with her?'

Cathy wouldn't meet his eyes. She shifted in her chair and looked down at the scored table.

'Cathy?'

'I heard. It's just I was always told not to speak ill.'

'Of the dead? Mary Rothwell isn't dead.'

'No. Of me employer.'

'Am I to take it that you *didn't* get along, then?'

'Take it as you will, Mr Banks.'

'Cathy, this could be very important. Mr Rothwell was killed, you know.'

'Aye, I know. It's got nowt to do with *her*, though, does it?'

'We still need to know all we can about the family.'

Cathy contemplated the table for a while longer. More locals came in. One or two looked in Banks's direction nudged their friends and raised their eyebrows.

'She were just bossy, that's all,' Cathy said at last.

'Mary Rothwell was?'

'Aye. She'd stand over you while you were working, with her arms folded, like this, and tell you you'd missed a bit or you weren't polishing hard enough. I used to hate doing for her. Will I still have to, do you think?'

'I don't know,' Banks said. 'What about Alison?'

'What about her?'

'You're about the same age, surely you must have had things in common, things to talk about. Pop stars and the like.'

Cathy emitted a loud snort. 'Little Miss La-di-da,' she sneered, then shook her head. 'No, I can't say as we did. She always had her nose stuck in a book.'

'You never chatted with her?'

'No. Every time she saw me she turned up her nose. Stuck-up little madam.'

'How did the family members get along with one another?'

'I weren't there often enough to notice. Not when they was all together, like.'

'But you must have some idea, from your observations?'

'They didn't say much. It were a quiet house. He were in his office, when he were at home, like, and I were never allowed up there.'

'Who cleaned it?'

'Dunno. Maybe he did it himself. I know he didn't like people to go in. Look, Mr Banks, I've got to get back and help me mum. Is there anything else?'

'Did you notice any changes in the family recently? Did they behave any differently?'

'Not so far as I could tell.'

'What about Tom, the son? Did you know him?'

'He were t'best of the lot,' Cathy said without hesita-

tion. 'Always had a smile and a good-morning for you.'
She blushed.

'He's been away for a while now. Did you notice any
changes before he left?'

'They used to argue.'

'Who did?'

'Him and his father.'

'What about?'

'How would I know? I didn't listen. Sometimes you
couldn't help but hear.'

'Hear what?'

'Just their voices, when they were shouting, like.'

'Did you ever hear what they were arguing about?'

'Once t'door were open a bit, and I heard his dad
mention a name then say something like, "I'm disappointed in you." He said "shame", too.'

'What was a shame?'

'No. Just the word. I just heard the word "shame",
that's all. I could tell Mr Rothwell were very angry, but he
sounded cold, you know.'

'Did he say why he was disappointed?'

She shook her head.

'What was the name he mentioned?'

'Sounded like Aston or Afton or summat like that.'

'Did you hear what Tom said back?'

'He said, "You're a right one to talk about being
disappointed in *me*."'

'Did you hear anything more?'

'No.' The chair scraped along the stone flags as she
stood up. 'I've got to go, really. Me mum'll kill me.' And
she hurried back behind the bar with surprising agility.

THREE

'Vic Manson matched prints from the Calvert flat with the ones from the body,' Gristhorpe explained back at the station later that afternoon. 'There were a couple of other sets, too, mostly smudged, not on file.'

It was hot, and Banks was standing by the open window of his office. Gristhorpe sat with his feet up on the desk.

'So Rothwell was Calvert and Calvert was Rothwell,' Banks said.

'It certainly looks that way, aye.'

Banks leaned against the window frame and shook his head. 'I still can't believe it. All right, so we know Rothwell had a secretive side to his nature, and he was greedy, or desperate for cash, to the point of dishonesty once. But this Calvert sounds to me like some sort of playboy. If you could have heard Pamela Jeffreys. Casinos, races, dancing . . . bloody hell. And you should have seen her, the one he chucked over.'

'So you've told me already, two or three times at least,' Gristhorpe said with a smile. 'A proper bobby-dazzler by the sound of her. I'll take your word for it.'

'Well, she dazzled this bobby, anyway,' said Banks, sitting opposite Gristhorpe. He sighed. 'I suppose we just have to accept it: Rothwell led a double life. Like Alec Guinness in that film about the ship's captain.'

'*The Captain's Paradise?*'

'That's the one. The question we have to ask ourselves now is what, if anything, does that fact have to do with his murder?'

'Has the girlfriend dazzled you so much you haven't considered she might have a part to play?'

'The thought's crossed my mind once or twice, yes. I just can't see how. Apparently Roth . . . Calvert found *another* woman five or six months ago. Pamela Jeffreys seemed to think he'd fallen in love. It's her we need to find, but she hasn't come forward yet.'

'There's always jealousy as a motive, then.'

'I don't think so. It's *possible*, though. Maybe Mary Rothwell found out about him and arranged a hit.'

'I was thinking more about this Pamela Jeffreys.'

'Couldn't afford it. She's a classical musician. Besides, she didn't really strike me as the jealous type. She said Calvert was just fun to be with. They never made any commitments.'

'She could be lying.'

'I suppose so.'

'And don't forget the possible porn connection. If Rothwell was mixed up with beautiful women, even under another identity, who knows?'

Banks couldn't believe it, but he didn't bother protesting to Gristhorpe. 'I'll have to talk to her again anyway,' he said.

'Poor you.'

'What did the Fraud Squad have to say?'

Gristhorpe scratched his hooked nose. 'Funny lot, aren't they?' he said. 'I spent a good part of this morning with DI Macmillan. Used to be in banking. Boring little bugger, but you should have seen his eyes light up when he heard about the locked files. Anyway, they've had a quick look at the stuff from Arkbeck Farm, and Macmillan and I had another chat about an hour ago. They haven't much to go on, yet, of course, and they're as anxious as young Phil for that bypass software, but Macmillan's even more excited now.'

'Where has the software got to, by the way?'

'On its way, according to Phil. Apparently they were out of stock but they managed to scrounge around.'

'Sorry. What did Macmillan have to say?'

'Well, he said he won't know anything for certain until they manage to open some of those locked directories. He thinks that's where the really interesting stuff is. But even some of the written documents in the filing cabinets gave him enough to suspect Rothwell was heavily into money-laundering or betting-tax evasion. Apparently, there was a fair bit of cryptic correspondence with foreign banks: Lichtenstein, Netherlands, Antilles, Jersey, Switzerland, the Cayman Islands, among others. Dead giveaway, Macmillan said.'

'Tax havens,' said Banks. 'Isn't that what they are?'

Gristhorpe held up a finger. 'Aha! That was my first thought, too. But they're only tax havens because they have strict secrecy policies and a very flexible attitude towards whom they take on as their clients.'

'In other words,' offered Banks, 'if you want to deposit a lot of money with them, they'll take it, no questions asked?'

'That's about it, aye. Within the law, of course. They do insist that they verify the money's source is legal. When it comes down to it, though, banks are basically run on greed, aren't they?'

'I won't argue with that. So Keith Rothwell was putting a lot of money in foreign banks?'

'Macmillan thought he might have been acting for a third party. He could hardly have made that much money himself. It's a very complicated business. As I said, either he was involved in aiding and abetting some pretty serious tax evasion, or he was part of a money-laundering scheme. There are still more questions than answers.'

'Did Macmillan tell you how this money-laundering business works?' Banks asked.

'Aye, a bit. According to him, it's basically simple. It's only in the application it gets complicated. What happens is that somebody gets hold of a lot of money illegally, and he wants it to look legal so he can live off it without raising any suspicions.' Gristhorpe paused.

'Go on,' Banks urged.

Gristhorpe ran his hand through his hair. 'Well, that's about it, really. I told you it was basically simple. Macmillan said it would take forever to explain all the technicalities of doing it. As far as legal money is concerned, he said, you can either earn it, borrow it or receive it as a gift. When you've laundered your dirty money, it has to look like it came to you one of those ways.'

'I assume we're talking about drug money here,' Banks said. 'Or the profits from some sort of organized crime – prostitution, pornography, loan sharks?'

Gristhorpe nodded. 'You know as well as I do, Alan, that the top cats in the drug trade pull in enormous wads of cash every day. You can't just walk into a showroom and buy a Rolls in cash without raising a few eyebrows, and the last thing you want is any attention from the police or the Inland Revenue.'

Banks walked over to the window again and lit a cigarette. Most of the cars were gone from the cobbled square now and the hush of an early Sunday evening had fallen over the town. A young woman in jeans and a red T-shirt struck a pose by the ancient market cross as her male companion took a photograph, then they got into a blue Nissan Micra and drove off.

'What's in it for the launderer?' Banks asked.

'According to Macmillan, he'd get maybe four per cent for laundering the safer sort of funds and up to ten per cent for seriously dirty money.'

'Per cent of what?'

'Depends,' said Gristhorpe. 'On a cursory glance, Macmillan estimated about between four and six million quid. He said that was conservative.'

'Over how long?'

'That's four to six a year, Alan.'

'Jesus Christ!'

'Money worth murdering for, isn't it? In addition to Rothwell's legitimate earnings as a financial consultant, if he were in this money-laundering racket he also stood to earn, let's say five per cent of five million a year, to make it easy. How much is that?'

'Quarter of a million quid.'

'Aye, my arithmetic was never among the best. Well, no wonder the bugger could afford a BMW and a new kitchen.' He rubbed his hands together. 'And that's about it. Macmillan said they'll start putting a financial profile together first thing in the morning: bank accounts, credit cards, building societies, Inland Revenue, loans, investments, the lot. He said they shouldn't have any trouble getting a warrant from the judge, given the circumstances. He's also getting in touch with the Yard. This is big, Alan.'

'What about Calvert?' Banks asked.

'Well, they'll have to cover him too, now, won't they?'

A sharp knock at the door was immediately followed by Phil Richmond holding a small package. 'I've got it,' he said, an excited light in his eyes. 'The bypass software. Give me a few minutes to study the manual and we'll see what we can do.'

They all followed him to the computer room, once a

cupboard for storing cleaning materials, and stood around tensely in the cramped space while he booted up and consulted the instructions. All Rothwell's computer gear and records were with the Fraud Squad, but Richmond had made back-up disks of the relevant files.

Susan Gay popped her head around the door and, finding no room left inside, stood in the doorway. Banks watched as Richmond went through a series of commands. Dialogue boxes appeared and disappeared; drive lights flashed on and off; the machine buzzed and hummed. Banks noticed Gristhorpe chewing on his thumbnail.

'Got it,' Richmond said. Then a locked file called SUMMARY.924 came to the screen:

Halcyon Props.	16/9/92	82062	C.I.	Ibk.	GCA
Mercury Exps.	18/9/92	49876	Jsy.Cbk	PA	
Jupiter Pds.	23/9/92	47650	Lst.	Zbk	SA
Marryat Dvpts.	4/10/92	76980	N.A.Kbk	PA	
(end 1st shpt)					
Neptune Hlds	6/11/92	65734	Jsy. Cbk	SPA	
City Ents	13/11/92	32450	Sw.	Nbk	LRA
Harbour Trst.	21/11/92	23443	BVI. Hbk	DTFA	
Sunland Props	29/11/92	85443	B.	Gbk	RDA

'What the hell is all that about?' Banks asked.

'It looks like financial records for the last quarter of 1992,' Gristhorpe said. 'Companies, banks, dates, maybe numbered accounts. Keep going, Phil. Try that "LETTER" file you mentioned.'

Richmond highlighted the locked file, tapped at the keyboard again, and the file appeared unscrambled, for all to see.

It was a letter, dated 1 May and addressed to a Mr

Daniel Clegg, Solicitor, of Park Square, Leeds, and on first glance, it seemed innocuous enough:

Dear Mr Clegg,

In the light of certain information that has recently come to my attention, I regret that we must terminate our association.

Yours faithfully,
Keith Rothwell

'That's it?' Gristhorpe asked. 'Are you sure you didn't lose anything?'

Richmond returned to the keyboard to check, then shook his head. 'No, sir. That's it.'

Banks backed towards the door. 'Interesting,' he said. 'I wonder what "information" that was?' He looked at Gristhorpe, who said, 'Get it printed out, will you, Phil, before it disappears into the bloody ether.'

6

ONE

In Park Square on that fine Monday morning in May, with the pink and white blossom still on the trees, Banks could easily have imagined himself a Regency dandy out for a stroll while composing a satire upon the Prince's latest folly.

Opposite the Town Hall and the Court Centre, but hidden behind Westgate, Park Square is one of the few examples of elegant, late eighteenth-century Leeds remaining. Unlike most of the fashionable West End squares, it survived Benjamin Gott's Bean Ing Mills, an enormous steam-powered woollen factory which literally smoked out the middle classes and sent them scurrying north to the fresher air of Headingley, Chapel Allerton and Round-hay, away from the soot and smoke carried over the town on the prevailing westerly winds.

Banks faced the terrace of nicely restored two- and three-storey Georgian houses, built of red brick and yellow sandstone, with their black iron railings, Queen Anne pediments and classical-style doorways with columns and entablatures. Very impressive, he thought, finding the right house. As expected, it was just the kind of place to have several polished brass nameplates beside the door, one of which read 'Daniel Clegg, Solicitor'.

A list on the wall inside the open front door told him

that the office he wanted was on the first floor. He walked up, saw the name on the frosted-glass door, then knocked and entered.

He found himself in a dim anteroom that smelled vaguely of paint, where a woman sat behind a desk sorting through a stack of letters. When he came in, he noticed a look of fear flash through her eyes, quickly replaced by one of suspicion. 'Can I help you?' she asked, as if she didn't really want to.

She was about thirty, Banks guessed, with curly brown hair, a thin, olive-complexioned face and a rather long nose. Her pale green eyes were pink around the rims. She wore a loose fawn cardigan over her white blouse, despite the heat. Banks introduced himself and showed his card. 'I'd like to see Mr Clegg,' he said. 'Is he around?'

'He's not here.'

'Do you know when he'll be back?'

'No.' It sounded like 'dough.'

'Do you know where he is?'

'No.'

'What's your name?'

'Elizabeth. Elizabeth Moorhead. I'm Mr Clegg's secretary. Everyone calls me Betty.' She took a crumpled paper tissue from the sleeve of her cardigan and blew her nose. 'Cold,' she said. 'Godda cold. In May. Can you believe it? I hate summer colds.'

'I'd like to see Mr Clegg, Betty,' Banks said again. 'Is there a problem?'

'I should say so.'

'Can I help?'

She drew back a bit, as if still deciding whether to trust him. 'What do you want him for?'

Banks hesitated for a moment, then told her. At least he

would get some kind of reaction. 'I wanted to ask a few questions about Keith Rothwell.'

Her brow wrinkled in a frown. 'Mr Rothwell? Yes, of course. Poor Mr Rothwell. He and Mr Clegg had some business together now and then. I read about him in the papers. It was terrible what happened.'

'Did you know him well?'

'Mr Rothwell? No, not at all, not really. But he'd been here, in this office. I mean, I knew him to say hello to.'

'When did you see him last?'

'Just last week, it was. Tuesday or Wednesday, I think. He was standing right there where you are now. Isn't it terrible?'

Banks agreed that it was. 'Can you try and remember which day it was? It could be important.'

She muttered to herself about appointments and flipped through a heavy book on her desk. Finally, she said, 'It was Wednesday, just before I finished for the day at five. Mr Rothwell didn't have an appointment, but I remember because it was just after Mr Hoskins left, a client. Mr Rothwell had to wait out here a few moments and we chatted about how lovely the gardens are at this time of year.'

'That's all you talked about?'

'Yes.'

'Then what?'

'Then Mr Clegg came out and they went off.'

'Do you know where?'

'No, but I think they went for a drink. They had business to discuss.'

So Rothwell had visited Clegg in Leeds the day before his murder, almost two weeks after the letter ending their association. Why? It certainly hadn't been noted in his

PETER ROBINSON

appointment book. 'How did Mr Rothwell seem?' he
asked.

'No different from usual.'

'And Mr Clegg?'

'Fine. Why are you asking?'

'Did you notice any tension between them?'

'No.'

'Has anything odd been happening around here lately?
Has Mr Clegg received any strange messages, for example?'

'No-o.' Some hesitation there. He would get back to it
later.

Banks glanced around the small, tidy anteroom. 'Does
everything go through you? Mail, phone calls?'

'Most things, yes. But Mr Clegg has a private line, too.'

'I see. How did he react to the news of Mr Rothwell's
death?'

She studied Banks closely, then appeared to decide to
trust him. She sighed and rested her hands on the desk,
palms down. 'That's just the problem,' she said. 'I don't
know. I haven't seen him since. He's not here. I mean,
he's not just out of the office right now, but he's disappeared. Into thin air.'

'Disappeared? Have you told the local police?'

She shook her head. 'I wouldn't want to look a fool.'

'Has he done anything like this before?'

'No. Never. But if he *has* just gone off . . . you know.
With a woman or something . . . I mean he *could* have,
couldn't he?'

'When did you last see him?'

'Last Thursday. He left the office about half past five
and that was the last I saw of him. He didn't come in to
work on Friday morning.'

'Have you tried to call him at home?'

'Yes, but all I got was the answering machine.'

'Did he say anything about a business trip?' Banks asked.

'No. And he usually tells me if he's going to be away for any length of time.'

'Do you know what kind of business relationship Mr Clegg had with Keith Rothwell?'

'No. I'm only his secretary. Mr Clegg didn't take me into his confidence. All I know is that Mr Rothwell came to the office now and then and sometimes they'd go out to lunch together, or for drinks after work. I knew Mr Rothwell was an accountant, so I supposed it would be something to do with tax. Mr Clegg specializes in tax law, you see. I'm sorry I can't be of more help.'

'Maybe you can be. It seems a bit of a coincidence, doesn't it, Mr Rothwell getting killed and Mr Clegg disappearing around the same time?'

She shrugged. 'I didn't hear about Mr Rothwell's death until Saturday. I just never thought . . .'

'Have you ever heard of someone called Robert Calvert?'

'No.'

'Are you sure? Did Mr Clegg never mention the name?'

'No. He wasn't a client. I'm sure I'd remember.'

'Why didn't you get in touch with the police when you realized Mr Clegg had disappeared and you heard about Mr Rothwell's murder?'

'Why should I? Mr Clegg had a lot of clients. He knew a lot of businessmen.'

'But they don't usually get murdered.'

She sneezed. 'No. As I said, it's tragic what happened, but I don't see how as it connects with Mr Clegg.'

'Maybe it does, and maybe it doesn't,' Banks said. 'But don't you think that's for us to decide?'

'I don't know what you mean.' She reached for the tissue again. This time it disintegrated when she blew her nose. She dropped it in the waste-paper bin and took a fresh one from the box on her desk.

Banks regarded her closely. He didn't think she was lying or evading the issue; she simply didn't understand what he was getting at. He sometimes expected everyone to view the world with the same suspicious mind and jaundiced eye as he did. Besides, she didn't know about the letter Rothwell had left in the locked file.

He sat on the edge of the desk. 'Right, Betty, let's go back a bit. When I came in, you were frightened. Why?'

She paused for a moment, then said, 'I thought you might be one of them again.'

'One of whom?'

'On Saturday morning I was here doing some filing and two men came in and started asking questions about Mr Clegg. They weren't very nice.'

'Is that what you were thinking of when I asked you earlier if anything odd had been going on?'

'Yes.'

'Why didn't you tell me then?'

'It . . . I . . . I didn't connect it. You've got me all confused.'

'All right, Betty, take it easy. Did they hurt you?'

'Of course not. Or I certainly *would* have called the police. You see, sometimes in this business you get people who are . . . well, less than polite. They get upset about money and sometimes they don't care who they take it out on.'

'And these men were just rude?'

'Yes. Well, just a bit brusque, really. Nothing unusual.

I mean, I'm only a secretary, right? I'm not important. They can afford to be short with me.'

'So what bothered you? Why does it stick in your mind? Why were you frightened? Did they threaten you?'

'Not in so many words. But I got the impression that they were testing me to see what I knew. I think they realized early on that I didn't know anything. If they'd thought differently, I'm sure they would have hurt me. Don't ask me how I know. I could just feel it. There was something about them, some sort of coldness in their eyes, as if they'd done terrible things, or witnessed terrible things.' She shivered. 'I don't know. I can't explain. They were the kind of people you look away from when they make eye contact.'

'What did they want to know about?'

'Where Mr Clegg was.'

'That's all?'

'Yes. I asked them why they wanted to know, but they just said they had important business with him. I'd never seen them before, and I'm sure I'd know if they were new clients.'

'Did they leave their names?'

'No.'

'What did they look like?'

'Just ordinary businessmen, really. One was black and the other white. They both wore dark suits, white shirts, ties. I can't remember what colours.'

'What about their height?'

'Both about the same. Around six foot, I'd say. But the white one was burly. You know, he had thick shoulders and a round chest, like a wrestler or something. He had very fair hair, but he was going bald on top. He tried to disguise it by growing the hair at the side longer and combing it right over, but I just think that looks silly, don't you? The black man was thin and fit-looking. More like a runner than a wrestler. He did most of the talking.'

Banks got her to describe them in as much detail as she could and took notes. They certainly didn't match Alison Rothwell's description of the two men in black who had tied her up and killed her father. 'What about their accents?' he asked.

'Not local. The black one sounded a bit cultured, well educated, and the other didn't speak much. I think he had a slight foreign accent, though I couldn't swear to it and I can't tell you where from.'

'You've done fine, Betty.'

'I have?'

Banks nodded.

'There's something else,' she said. 'When I came in this morning, I got the impression that someone had been in the place since then. Again, I can't say why, and I certainly couldn't prove it, but in this job you develop a feel for the way things should be – you know, files, documents, that sort of thing – and you can just tell if something's out of place without knowing what it really is, if you follow my drift.'

'Were there any signs of forced entry?'

'No. Nothing obvious, nothing like that. Not that it would be difficult to get in here. It's hardly the Tower of London. I locked myself out once when Mr Clegg was away on business and I just slipped my Visa card in the door and opened it.' She put her hand to her mouth. 'Oops. I don't suppose I should be telling you that, should I?'

Banks smiled. 'It's all right, Betty. I've had to get into my car with a coat-hanger more than once. Was anything missing?'

'Not so far as I can tell. It's pretty secure inside. There's a good, strong safe and it doesn't look as if anyone tried to tamper with it.'

'Could it have been Mr Clegg?'

'I suppose so. He sometimes comes in on a Sunday if there's something important in progress.' Then she shook her head. 'But no. If it had been Mr Clegg I'd have known. Things would have looked different. They looked the same, but not quite the same, if you know what I mean.'

'As if someone had messed things up and tried to restore them to the way they were originally?'

'Yes.'

'Do you employ a cleaning lady?'

'Yes, but she comes Thursday evenings. It can't have been her.'

'Did she arrive as usual last Thursday?'

'Yes.'

'May I have a look in the office?'

Betty got up, took a key from her drawer and opened Clegg's door for him. He stood on the threshold and saw a small office with shelves of law books, box files and filing cabinets. Clegg also had a computer and stacks of disks on a desk at right angles to the one on which he did his other paperwork. The window, closed and locked, Banks noticed, looked out over the central square with its neatly cut grass, shady trees and people sitting on benches. The office was hot and stuffy.

Certainly nothing *looked* out of the ordinary. Banks was careful not to disturb anything. Soon, the Fraud Squad would be here to pore over the books and look for whatever the link was between Rothwell and Clegg.

'Better keep it locked,' he told Betty on his way out.

'There'll be more police here this afternoon, most likely. May I use the phone?'

Betty nodded.

Banks phoned Ken Blackstone at Millgarth and told him briefly what the situation was. Ken said he'd send a car over right away. Next he phoned Superintendent Gristhorpe in Eastvale and reported his findings. Gristhorpe said he'd get in touch with the Fraud Squad and see if they could co-ordinate with West Yorkshire.

He turned back to Betty. 'You'll be all right here,' he said. 'I'll wait until the locals arrive. They'll need you to answer more questions. Just tell them everything you told me. What's your address, in case I need to get in touch?'

She gave him the address of her flat in Burmantofts. 'What do you think has happened?' she asked, reaching for her tissue again.

Banks shook his head.

'You don't think anything's happened to him, do you?'

'It's probably nothing,' Banks said, without conviction. 'Don't worry, we'll get to the bottom of it.'

'It's just that Melissa will be so upset.'

'Who's Melissa?'

'Oh, didn't you know? It's Mrs Clegg. His wife.'

TWO

After a hurried bowl of vegetable soup in the Golden Grill, Susan Gay walked out into the street, with its familiar smells and noises: petrol fumes, of course; car horns; fresh coffee; bread from the bakery; a busker playing a flute by the church doors.

In the cobbled market square, she noticed an impromptu

evangelist set up his soapbox and start rabbiting on about judgment and sin. It made her feel vaguely guilty just hearing him, and as she went into the station, she contemplated asking one of the uniforms to go out and move him on. There must be a law against it somewhere on the books. Disturbing the peace of an overworked DC?

Charity prevailed, and she went up to her office. It faced the car park out back, so she wouldn't have to listen to him there.

First, she took out the blue file cards she liked to make notes on and pinned them to the cork-board over her desk. It was the same board, she remembered, that Sergeant Hatchley had used for his pin-ups of page-three girls with vacuous smiles and enormous breasts. Now Hatchley was due back any moment. What a thought.

Then, after she had made another appointment to talk to Laurence Pratt, she luxuriated in the empty office, stretching like a cat, feeling as if she were in a deep, warm bubble-bath. Out of the window she could see the maintenance men with their shirtsleeves rolled up washing the patrol cars in the large car park. Sun glinted on their rings and watch-straps and on the shiny chrome they polished; it spread rainbows of oily sheen on the bright wind-screens.

One of the men, in particular, caught her eye: well-muscled, but not overbearingly so, with a lock of blond hair that slipped over his eye and bounced as he rubbed the bonnet in long, slow strokes. The telephone broke into her fantasy. She picked it up. 'Hello. Eastvale CID. Can I help you?'

'To whom am I speaking?'

'Detective Constable Susan Gay.'

'Is the superintendent there?'

'I'm afraid not.'

'And Chief Inspector Banks?'

'Out of the office. Can I help you? What's this about?'

'I suppose you'll have to do. My name is Mary Rothwell. I've just had a call from my son, Tom.'

'You have? Where is he?'

'He's still in Florida. A hotel in Lido Key, wherever that is. Apparently the British newspapers are a couple of days late over there, and he's just read about his father's murder. It's only eight in the morning there. He can't get a flight back until this evening. Anyway, he said he should get into Manchester at about seven o'clock tomorrow morning. I'm going to meet him at the airport and bring him home.'

'That's good news, Mrs Rothwell,' Susan said. 'You do know we'd like to talk to him?'

'Yes. Though I can't imagine why. You'll pass the message on to the Chief Inspector, will you?'

'Yes.'

'Good. And by the way, I've made funeral arrangements for Wednesday. That *is* still all right, isn't it?'

'Of course.'

'Very well.'

'Is there anything else, Mrs Rothwell?'

'No.'

'Goodbye, then. We'll be in touch.'

Susan hung up and stared into space for a moment, thinking what an odd woman Mary Rothwell was. Imperious, highly strung and businesslike. Probably a real Tartar to live with. But was she a murderess?

Though it would take the Fraud Squad a long time to work out exactly how much Rothwell was worth – and to separate the legal from the illegal money – it was bound to be a fortune. Money worth killing for. The problem was, though Susan could imagine Mary Rothwell being cold-blooded enough to have her husband killed, she could not imagine her having it done in such a bloody, dramatic way.

The image of the kneeling, headless corpse came back to her and she tasted the vegetable soup rise in her throat. No, she thought, if the wife were responsible, Rothwell would have been disposed of in a neat, sanitary way – poison, perhaps – and he certainly wouldn't have made such a mess on the garage floor. What was the phrase? *You don't shit on your own doorstep.* It was too close to home for Mary; it would probably taint Arkbeck Farm for her for ever.

Still, there was a lot of money involved. Susan had seen Rothwell's solicitor that morning, and, according to him, Rothwell had owned, or part-owned, about fifteen businesses, from a shipping company registered in the Bahamas to a dry cleaner's in Wigan, not to mention various properties dotted around England, Spain, Portugal and France. Of course, the solicitor assured her, they were all legitimate. She suspected, however, that some had served as fronts for Rothwell's illegal activities.

As Susan was wondering if Robert Calvert's money would now simply get lumped in with Keith Rothwell's, she became aware of a large shadow cast over her desk by a figure in the doorway.

She looked up, startled, right into the smiling face of Detective Sergeant Jim Hatchley. So soon? she thought, with a sinking feeling in the pit of her stomach. Now she knew there really was no God.

'Hello, love,' said Hatchley, lighting a cigarette. 'I see you've taken my pin-ups down. We'll have to do something about that now I'm back to stay.'

THREE

At one-thirty, the hot, smoky pub was still packed with local clerks and shopkeepers on their lunch break. When Banks had phoned Pamela Jeffreys before leaving for Leeds that morning, she had suggested they meet in the pub across from the hall in West Leeds, where she was rehearsing with a string quartet. There was no beer garden, she said, but the curry of the day was usually excellent. Though he had to admit to feeling excitement at the thought of seeing Pamela again, this wasn't a meeting Banks was looking forward to.

She hadn't arrived yet, so Banks got himself a pint of shandy at the bar – just the thing for a hot day – and managed to grab a small table in the corner by the dartboard, fortunately not in use. There, he mulled over Daniel Clegg's disappearance and the mysterious goons Betty Moorhead had seen.

There was no end of trouble a lawyer could get himself into, Banks speculated. Especially if he were a bit crooked to start with. So maybe there was no connection between Clegg's disappearance and Rothwell's murder. But there were too many coincidences – the letter, the timing, the shady accounts – and Banks didn't like coincidences. Which meant that there were two sets of goons on the loose: the ones who killed Rothwell, and the ones who scared Clegg's secretary. But did they work for the same person?

He was saved from bashing his head against a brick wall any longer by the arrival of Pamela Jeffreys, looking gorgeous in black leggings and a long white T-shirt with the Opera North logo on front. She had her hair tied back and wore black-rimmed glasses. As she sat down, she smiled at him. 'The professional musician's look,' she said. 'Keeps my hair out of my eyes so I can read the music.'

'Would you like a drink?' Banks asked.

'Just a grapefruit juice with an ice-cube, please, if they've got any. I have to play through "Death and the Maiden" again this afternoon.'

While he was at the bar, Banks also ordered two curries of the day.

'What's been happening?' Pamela asked when he got back.

'Plenty,' said Banks, hoping to avoid the issue of Calvert's identity for as long as possible. 'But I've no idea how it all adds up. First off, have you ever heard of a man called Daniel Clegg?'

She shook her head. 'No, I can't say as I have.'

'He's a solicitor.'

'He's not mine. Actually, I don't have one.'

'Are you sure Robert never mentioned him?'

'No, and I think I'd remember. But I already told you, he never talked about his work, and I never asked. What do I know or care about business?' She looked at him over the top of her glass as she sipped her grapefruit juice, thin black eyebrows raised.

'Did you ever introduce Robert to any of your friends?'

'No. He never seemed really interested in going to parties or having dinner with people or anything, so I never pushed it. They probably wouldn't have got on very well anyway. Most of my friends are young and artsy, Robert's more mature. Why?'

'Did you ever meet anyone he knew when you were out together, say in a restaurant or at the casino?'

'No, not that I can recall.'

'So you didn't have much of a social life together?'

'No, we didn't. Just a bit of gambling, the occasional day at the races, then it was mostly concerts or a video and a pizza. That was a bit of a problem, really. Robert was a lot of fun, but he didn't like crowds. I'm a bit more of a social butterfly, myself.'

'I don't mean to embarrass you,' Banks said slowly, 'but did Robert show any interest in pornography? Did he like to take photographs, make videos? Anything like that?'

She looked at him open-mouthed, then burst out laughing. 'Sorry, sorry,' she said, patting her chest. 'You know, most girls might be insulted if you suggested they moonlighted in video nasties, but it's so absurd I can't help but laugh.'

'So the answer's no?'

'Don't look so embarrassed. Of course it's no, you silly man. The very thought of it . . .' She laughed again and Banks felt himself blush.

Their curries came and they tucked in. They were, as Pamela had said, delicious: delicately spiced rather than hot, with plenty of chunks of tender beef. They exchanged small talk over the food, edging away from the embarrassing topic Banks had brought up earlier. When they had finished, Pamela went for more drinks and Banks lit a cigarette. Was she going to ask now, he wondered, or was he going to have to bring it up? Maybe she was avoiding the moment, too.

Finally, she asked. 'Did you find out anything? You know, about Robert and this Rothwell fellow.' Very casual, but Banks could sense the apprehension in her voice.

He scraped the end of his cigarette on the rim of the red

metal ashtray and avoided her eyes. A group at the next table burst into laughter at a joke one of them had told.

'Well?'

He looked up. 'It looks very much as if Robert Calvert and Keith Rothwell were the same person,' he said. 'We found fingerprints that matched. I'm sorry.'

For a while she said nothing. Banks could see her beautiful almond eyes fill slowly with tears. 'Shit,' she said, shaking her head and reaching in her bag for a tissue. 'Sorry, this is stupid of me. I don't know why I'm crying. We were just friends really. Can we . . . I mean . . .' She gestured around.

'Of course.' Banks took her arm and they left the pub. Fifty yards along the main road was a park. Pamela looked at her watch and said, 'I've still got a while yet, if you don't mind walking a bit.'

'Not at all.'

They walked past a playground where children screamed with delight as the swings went higher and higher and the roundabout spun faster and faster. A small wading-pool had been filled with water because of the warm weather and more children played there, splashing one another, squealing and shouting, all under their mother's or father's watchful eyes. Nobody let their kids play out alone these days, as they used to do when he was a child, Banks noticed. Being in his job, knowing what he knew, he didn't blame them.

Pamela seemed lost in her silent grief, head bowed, walking slowly. 'It's crazy,' she said at last. 'I hardly knew Robert and things had cooled off between us anyway, and here I am behaving like this.'

Banks could think of nothing to say. He was aware of the warmth of her arm in his and of her scent: jasmine, he thought. What the hell did he think he was doing, walking arm in arm in the park with a beautiful suspect? What if someone saw him? But what could he do? The contact seemed to form an important link between Pamela and something real, something she could hold on to while the rest of her world shifted under her feet like fine sand. And he couldn't deny that the touch of her skin meant something to him, too.

'I was wrong about him, wasn't I?' she went on. 'Dead wrong. He was married, you say? Kids?'

'A son and a daughter.'

'I should know. I read it in the paper but it didn't sink in because I was so *sure* it couldn't have been him. Robert seemed so . . . such a free spirit.'

'Maybe he was.'

She glanced sideways at him. 'What do you mean?'

They stopped at an ice-cream van and Banks bought two cornets. 'It was a different life he lived with you,' he said. 'I can't begin to understand a man like that. It's not that he had a split personality or anything, just that he was capable of existing in very different ways.'

'What ways?' Pamela stuck out her pink tongue and licked the ice-cream.

'The people in Swainsdale knew him as a quiet, unassuming sort of bloke. Bit of a dry stick really.'

'Robert?' she gasped. 'A dry stick?'

'Not Robert. Keith Rothwell. The hard-working, clean-living accountant. The man who put his spent matches back in the box in the opposite direction to the unused ones.'

'But Robert was so alive. He was fun to be with. We laughed a lot. We dreamed. We danced.'

Banks smiled sadly. 'There you are, then. Keith Rothwell probably had two left feet.'

DRY BONES THAT DREAM

'Are you saying it *wasn't* the same man?'

'I don't know what I'm saying. Just that your memories of Robert Calvert won't change, shouldn't change. He's who he was to you, what he meant to you. Don't let this poison it for you. On the other hand, I need to know who killed Keith Rothwell, and it looks as if there might be a connection.'

She put her arm in his again and they walked on. There was hardly any breeze at all, but they passed a boy trying to fly a red-and-green kite. He couldn't seem to get it more than about twenty feet off the ground before it came flopping down again.

'What do you mean, a connection?' Pamela asked, shifting her gaze from the kite back to Banks.

'Maybe something in his life as Robert Calvert spilled over into his life as Keith Rothwell. Are you sure you didn't know he was married, you didn't suspect it?'

She shook her head. 'No. I've been a right bloody fool, haven't I? Muggins again.'

'But you were sure he'd found a new girlfriend?'

'Ninety-nine per cent certain, yes.'

'How did you feel about that?'

'What?'

'His new girlfriend. How did you feel about her? On the one hand you tell me you shouldn't be so upset, you hardly knew Robert Calvert, and your relationship had cooled off anyway. On the other hand, it seems to me from what you say and the way you behave that you were extremely fond of him. Maybe in love with him. What's the truth? How did you really feel when someone else came along and stole him from you? Surely you must have felt hurt, angry, jealous?'

Pamela pulled back her arm and stepped aside from

131

him, an expression of pain and anger shadowing her face. She dropped her ice-cream. It splattered on the Tarmac path. 'What's that got to do with anything? What are you saying? What are you getting at? First you imply that I'm some kind of porn actress, and now you're implying that I killed Robert out of jealousy?'

'No,' said Banks quickly. 'No, nothing like that.'

But she was already backing away from him, hands held up, palms out, as if to ward him off.

'Yes, you are. How could you even . . .? I thought you . . .'

Banks stepped towards her. 'That's not what I mean, Pamela. I'm just—'

But she turned and started to run away.

'Wait!' Banks called after her. 'Please, stop.'

One or two people gave him suspicious looks. As he set off walking quickly after her, a child's coloured ball rolled in front of him, and he had to pull up sharply to avoid knocking into its diminutive owner, whose large father, fast approaching from the nearest bench, didn't seem at all happy about things.

Pamela reached the park exit and dashed across the road, dodging her way through the traffic, back towards the hall. Banks stood there looking after her, the sweat beading on his brow. The remains of his ice-cream had started to melt and drip over the flesh between his thumb and first finger.

'Shit,' he cursed under his breath. Then louder, 'Shit!'

The little boy looked up, puzzled, and his father loomed closer.

7

ONE

The Merrion Centre was one of the first indoor shopping malls in Britain. Built on the northern edge of Leeds city centre in 1964, it now seems something of an antique, a monument to the heady sixties days of slum clearance, tower blocks and council estates.

Covered on top, but open to the wind at the sides, it also suffers competition from a number of more recent, fully enclosed, central shopping centres, such as the St John's Centre, directly across Merrion Street, and the plush dark green and brass luxury of the Schofields Centre, right on The Headrow.

Still, the Merrion Centre does have a large Morrison's supermarket, Le Phonographique discothèque – the longest-surviving disco in Leeds – a number of small speciality shops, a couple of pubs, a flea market and the Classical Record Shop, which is how Banks had come to know the place quite well. And on a warm, windless May afternoon it can be pleasant enough.

Banks found Clegg's Wines and Spirits easily enough. He had phoned Melissa Clegg an hour or so earlier, still smarting over his acrimonious parting with Pamela Jeffreys in the park, and she had told him she could spare a little time to talk. It was odd, he thought, that she hadn't seemed overly curious about his call. He had said that it concerned her husband, yet she had asked for no details.

He opened the door and found himself in a small shop cluttered with bottles and cases. There were a couple of bins of specials on the floor by the door – mostly Bulgarian, Romanian and South African varietals, and some yellow 'marked down' cards on a few of the racks that lined the walls to his right and left, including a Rioja, a Côtes du Rhône and a claret.

Banks looked at the racks and thought he might take something home for dinner, assuming that he and Sandra ever got the chance to sit down to dinner together again, and assuming that she wanted to. Perhaps they could have that wine, candlelight and Chopin evening he had had to cancel when the Rothwell inquiry got in the way.

Behind the counter ranged the bottles of single malt Scotch: Knockando, Blair Athol, Talisker, Glendronach. Evocative names, but he mustn't look too closely. He had a weakness for single malt that Sandra said hit them too hard in the pocket. Besides, he still had a drop of Laphroaig left at home.

The spotty young man behind the counter smiled. 'Can I help you, sir?' He wore a candy-striped shirt with the sleeves rolled up and his tie loose at the neck, the way Banks always wore his own when he could get away with it. His black hair had so much gel or mousse on that it looked like an oil slick.

'Boss around?' Banks asked, showing his card.

'In the back.' He lifted up the counter flap and Banks went through. Stepping over and around cases of wine, he walked along a narrow corridor, then saw on his left a tiny office with the door open. A woman sat at the desk talking on the phone. It sounded to Banks as if she were complaining over non-delivery of several cases of Hungarian Pinot Noir.

When she saw him, she waved him in and pointed to a chair piled high with papers. Banks moved them to the edge of the desk and she grinned at him over the mouthpiece. There were no windows, and it was stuffy in the back room, despite the whirring fan. The office smelled of freshly cut wood. Banks took his jacket off and hung it over the back of the chair. He could feel the steady draught of the fan on the left side of his face.

Finally, she put the phone down and rolled her eyes. 'Some suppliers . . .'

She was wearing a yellow sun-dress with thin straps that left most of her nicely tanned and freckled shoulders and throat bare. About forty, Banks guessed, she looked as if she watched what she ate and exercised regularly, tennis probably. Her straight blonde hair, parted in the middle, hung just above her shoulders, framing a heart-shaped face with high cheek-bones. It was a cheerful face, one to which a smile was no stranger, and the youthful, uneven fringe suited her. But Banks also noticed marks of stress and strain in the wrinkles under her blue-grey eyes and around her slightly puckered mouth. A pair of no-nonsense glasses with tortoiseshell frames dangled on a cord around her neck.

'Your phone call piqued my curiosity,' she said, leaning back in her chair and linking her hands behind her head. Banks noticed the shadow of stubble under her arms. 'What has Danny-boy been up to now?'

'I'm sorry?' said Banks. 'I don't follow.'

'Didn't Betty tell you?'

'Tell me what?'

'Oh, God, that woman. Gormless. About Danny and

me. We're separated. Have been for about two years now. It was all perfectly amicable, of course.'

Of course, Banks thought. How often had he heard that? If it was all so bloody amicable, he wondered, then why aren't you still together? 'I didn't know,' he said.

'Then I'm sorry you're probably on a wild goose chase.' She changed her position, resting her hands on the desk and playing with a rubber band. There were no rings on her fingers. 'Anyway, I'm still intrigued,' she said. 'I *am* still fond of Danny. I would be concerned if I thought anything had happened to him. It hasn't, has it?'

'Do you still see one another?'

'From time to time.'

'When did you last see him?'

'Hmm . . .' She pursed her lips and thought. 'A couple of months ago. We had lunch together at Whitelocks.'

'How did he seem?'

'Fine.' She stretched the rubber band tight. 'Look, you've got me worried. All this interest in Danny all of a sudden. First those clients of his. Now you.'

Banks pricked up his ears. 'What clients?'

'On Saturday. Saturday afternoon. Just a couple of businessmen wondering if I knew where he was.'

'Did they know you were separated?'

'Yes. They said it was a long shot and they were sorry to bother me but they'd had an appointment scheduled with him that morning and he hadn't shown up. He'd mentioned me and the shop at some time or other, of course. He often does, by way of sending me business. What a sweetheart. Anyway, they asked if I had any idea where he was, if he'd suddenly decided to go away for the weekend. As if I'd know. It all seemed innocent enough. Is something wrong?'

'What did they look like?'

She described the same two men who had visited Betty
Moorhead. It wouldn't have been difficult for them to find
out about Melissa's shop – perhaps even Betty had told
them – and if they were looking for Clegg, it was reasonable to assume that his ex-wife might know where he was.
She must have convinced them quickly that she neither
knew nor cared.

The rubber band snapped. 'Look,' she said, 'I've a right
to know if something's happened to Danny, haven't I?'

'We don't know if anything has happened to him,'
Banks said. 'He's just gone missing.'

She breathed a sigh of relief. 'So that's all.'

Banks frowned. 'His secretary seems worried enough.
She says it's unusual.'

'Oh, Betty's a nice enough girl, but she is a bit of an
alarmist. Danny always did have an eye for the ladies.
That's one reason we're no longer together. I should
imagine if he's gone missing, then something came up, so
to speak.' She grinned, showing slightly overlapping front
teeth.

'Wouldn't he at least let his secretary know where he
was?'

'I'll admit that is a bit unusual. While Danny was never
exactly tied to his desk, he didn't like to be too far from the
action. You know the type, always on his car phone to
the office. Who knows? Maybe he's having a mid-life
crisis. Maybe he and his bit of crumpet have gone somewhere where there are no telephones. He's such a
romantic, is Danny.'

The phone rang and Mrs Clegg excused herself for a
moment. Banks caught her half of the conversation about

an order of *méthode champenoise*. A couple of minutes later she put the phone down. 'Sorry. Where were we?'

'Mrs Clegg, we think your husband might have been mixed up in some shady dealings and that might have had something to do with his disappearance.'

She laughed. 'Shady dealings? That hardly surprises me.'

'Do you know anything about his business activities?'

'No. But dishonest in love . . .' She let the thought trail, then shrugged. 'Danny never was one of the most ethical, or faithful, of people. Careful, usually, yes, but hardly ethical.'

'Would you say he was the type to get mixed up in something illegal?'

She thought for a moment, frowning, then answered. 'Yes. Yes, I think so. If he thought the returns were high enough.'

'Is he a greedy man?'

'No-o. Not in so many words, no. I wouldn't call him greedy. He just likes to get what he wants. Women. Money. Whatever. It's more a matter of power, manipulation. He just likes to win.'

'What about the risk?'

She tipped her head to one side. 'There's always *some* risk, isn't there, Chief Inspector? If something's worth having. Danny's not a coward, if that's what you mean.'

'Did you know Keith Rothwell?'

'Yes. Not well, but I had met him. Poor man. I read about him in the paper. Terrible. You're not suggesting there's any link between his murder and Danny's disappearance, are you?'

She's quicker on the ball than Betty Moorhead, Banks thought. 'We don't know. I don't suppose you'd be in a position to enlighten us about their business dealings?'

'Sorry. No. I haven't seen Keith since Danny and I split up. Even then I'd just bump into him at the office now and then, or when he helped with my taxes.'

'So you've no idea what kinds of dealings they were involved in?'

'No. As I said, Keith Rothwell did my accounts a couple of times – you know, the wine business – when Dan and I were together, before things became awkward and our personal life got in the way. He was a damn good accountant. He saved me a lot of money from the Inland Revenue – all above board. Now, it doesn't take a Sherlock Holmes to figure out that if the two of them were in business together it probably involved tax havens of one kind or another, and that they both probably did quite well from it.'

'Have you ever heard of a man called Robert Calvert?'

'Calvert? No. I can't say I have. Should I have? Look, I'm really sorry I can't help you, Chief Inspector. And I certainly didn't mean to sound callous at all. But knowing Danny, I'm sure he's popped off to Paris for the weekend with some floozie or other and just got too overexcited to remember to let anyone know. He'll turn up.'

Banks stood up. 'I hope you're right, Mrs Clegg. And if he gets in touch, please let us know.' He gave her his card. She stood up as he left the office. He turned in the doorway and smiled. 'One more thing.'

'Yes.'

'Could you recommend a decent claret for dinner, not too pricey?'

'Of course. If you're not absolutely stuck on Bordeaux, try a bottle of the Château de la Liquière. It's from Faugères, in Languedoc. Very popular region these days.

Lots of character.' She smiled. 'And you can even afford it on a policeman's salary.'

After Banks thanked her, he made his way back down the corridor, dodging the wine cases, and bought the bottle she had suggested. Not an entirely wasted visit, he thought. At least he'd got a decent bottle of wine out of it. And then there was the Classical Record Shop just around the corner. He couldn't pass so closely without going in. Besides, he needed balm for his wounds. He was still feeling annoyed with himself after the way he had messed things up with Pamela Jeffreys. The new CD of the Khachaturian Piano Concerto, if they had it, might just help make him feel better.

As he walked outside with his bottle of wine, he felt a large hand clap down on his shoulder.

'Well, if it isn't my old mate, Banksy,' a voice said in his ear.

Banks spun round and saw the source of the voice: Detective Superintendent Richard 'Dirty Dick' Burgess, from Scotland Yard. What the hell was he doing here?

'I hope you haven't been accepting bribes,' Burgess said, pointing to the wine. Then he put his arm around Banks's shoulders. 'Come on,' he said. 'We need to go somewhere and have a little chat.'

TWO

Laurence Pratt was waiting in his office, again with his shirtsleeves rolled up, black-framed glasses about halfway down his nose, fingers forming a steeple on the neat desk in front of him. His white shirt was more dazzling than any Susan had seen in a detergent advert. Susan felt stifled. The temperature outside was in the twenties, and the window was closed.

Pratt seemed less easy in his manner this time, Susan observed, and she guessed it was because he had given too much away on her last visit. This was going to be a tough one, she thought, taking her notebook and pen out of her handbag. They had discovered a lot more about Keith Rothwell since Friday, and this time, *she* didn't want to give too much away.

Susan opened her notebook, resisting the impulse to fan her face with it, and unclipped her pen. 'The last time I talked to you, Mr Pratt,' she began, 'you told me you saw the Rothwells for the last time in March.'

'That's right. Carla and I were out to Arkbeck for dinner. Duck *à l'orange*, if I remember correctly.'

'And the new kitchen.'

'Ah, yes. We all admired the new kitchen.'

'Can you be a bit more precise about the date?'

Pratt frowned and pulled at his lower lip. 'Not exactly. It was just after St Patrick's Day, I think. Hang on a sec.' He fished in his briefcase by the side of the desk and pulled out a Filofax. 'Be lost without it,' he grinned. 'Even in the computer age. I mean, you don't want to turn the computer on every time you need an address, do you?' As he talked, he flipped through the pages. 'Ah, there it is.' He held up the open page for Susan to see. '19 March. Dinner with Keith and Mary.'

'And you said Tom dropped in to talk about his trip?'

'Yes.'

'From where?'

'What? Oh, I see. From his room, I suppose. At least I think he'd been up there. He just came in to say hello while we were having cocktails. Is he back from America, by the way?'

No harm in telling a family friend that, Susan thought. 'He's on his way,' she said. 'What was the atmosphere like between Tom and his father that night?'

'They didn't talk, as I remember.'

'Did you notice any antagonism or tension between them?'

'I wouldn't say that, no. I told you before that their relationship was strained because Tom drifted off the course his father had set for him.'

'Was anything said about that on the night you were there?'

'No, I'm certain of it. They didn't talk to one another at all. Tom was excited about going to America. I think he'd been upstairs poring over a map, planning his route.'

'And Keith Rothwell said nothing during your little chat?'

'No. He just sat there rather po-faced. Now you mention it, that *was* a bit odd. I mean, you'd hardly call old Keith a live wire these days, but he'd usually take a bit more interest than he did that night. Especially as his son was off on a big adventure.'

'So his behaviour *was* strange?'

'A little unusual, on reflection, yes.'

'What about Tom? Did he say anything to or about his father?'

Pratt shook his head slowly. Susan noticed a few beads of sweat around his temples where his hairline was receding. She could feel her own sweat tickling her ribs as it slid down her side. So much for the expensive extra-dry, long-lasting anti-perspirant she had put on after her morning shower. This didn't happen to the high-powered women executives and airline pilots in the television adverts. On the other hand, *they* didn't have to deal with the return of Sergeant Hatchley. It had taken her a good five minutes to stop shaking after he had left the office.

She asked Pratt to open the window. He complied, but it didn't do much good. The air outside was still and hot. Even the gargoyles on the upper walls of the community centre looked grumpy and sweaty.

'Did Mr Rothwell ever express any interest in pornography?'

Pratt raised his eyebrows. 'Good lord. How do you mean? As a business venture or for personal consumption?'

'Either.'

'Not in my presence. As I said, I don't know about the extent of his business interests, but he always struck me as rather . . . say . . . sexless. When we were younger, of course, we'd chase the lasses, but since his marriage . . .'

'Have you ever met a solicitor called Daniel Clegg?'

'No. The name doesn't sound familiar. Are you sure he practises in Eastvale?'

'You've never met him?'

'I told you, I've never even heard of him. Why do you ask? Is there some—'

'Did Mr Rothwell ever mention him?'

'Is there some connection?'

'Did Mr Rothwell ever mention him?'

Pratt stared at Susan for about fifteen long seconds, then said, 'No, not that I recall.'

Susan ran the back of her hand across her moist brow. She was beginning to feel a little dizzy. 'What about Robert Calvert?'

'Never heard of him, either. Is this another business

colleague of Keith's? I told you we never talked about his business. He played his cards close to his chest.'

'Did he ever mention a woman called Pamela Jeffreys?'

Pratt raised an eyebrow. 'A woman? Keith? Another woman? Good lord, no. I told you he didn't strike me as the type. Not these days, anyway. Besides, Mary would have killed him. Oh, my God . . .'

'It's all right, Mr Pratt,' Susan said. 'Slip of the tongue. Jealous type, is she?'

He pushed his glasses back up to the bridge of his nose. 'Mary? Well, I'd guess so, yes.'

'But you don't know for certain?'

'No. It's just the impression she gives. How everything centred around Keith, the house, the family. If anything came along to jeopardize that, threaten it, then she'd be a formidable enemy. Possessive, selfish, I'd say, definitely. Is that the same thing?'

Susan closed her notebook and stood up. 'Thank you, Mr Pratt. Thank you very much. Again, you've been most helpful.' Then she hurried out of the hot, stuffy office before she fainted.

THREE

They walked down to Stumps, under the museum, and made their way to the bar, where Burgess ordered a pint of McEwan's lager and Banks a pint of bitter. It wasn't Theakston's, but it would have to do.

As it was a warm day, they took their drinks outside and found a free table. There was a broad, tiled area between the museum-library complex and the buses roaring by on The Headrow, and pedestrians hurried back and forth, some heading for the Court Centre or the Town Hall and some taking short-cuts to Calverley Street and the Civic Hall. A group of people stood playing chess with oversize figures on a board drawn on the tiles. Scaffolding covered the front of one of the nineteenth-century buildings across The Headrow, Banks noticed. Another renovation.

Banks felt both puzzled and apprehensive at Burgess's arrival on the scene. The last time they had locked horns was over the killing of a policeman at an anti-government demonstration in Eastvale back in the Thatcher era.

Burgess had fitted in just fine back then. An East Ender, son of a barrow boy, he had fought his way up from the bottom with a fierce mixture of ego, ambition, cunning and a total disregard for the rules most people played by. He also felt no sympathy for those who had been unable to do likewise. Now, at about Banks's age, he was a Detective Superintendent working for a Scotland Yard department that was not quite Special Branch and not quite M15, but close enough to both to give Banks the willies.

In a period when a fully functioning human heart was regarded as a severe disability, he had been one of the new, golden breed of working-class Conservatives, up there in the firmament of the new Britain alongside the bright young things in the City, the insider traders and their like. Cops and criminals: it didn't seem to make a lot of difference, as long as you were successful. But then, it never did to some people.

Nobody could gainsay Burgess's abilities – intelligence and physical courage being foremost among them – but 'The end justifies the means' could have been written just for him. The 'end' was some vague sort of loyalty to what-ever the people in power wanted done for the preservation of order, as long as the people in power weren't liberals or socialists, of course; and as for the 'means', the sky was the limit.

Maybe he had changed, Banks wondered. After all the recent inquiries and commissions, a policeman could surely no longer walk into a pub, pick up the first group of Irish people he saw and throw them in jail as terrorists, could he? Or walk down the Brixton Road and arrest the first black person he saw running? According to the public-relations people, today's policeman was a cross between Santa Claus and a hotel manager.

On the other hand, perhaps that was only according to the PR people: truth in advertising, *caveat emptor* and the rest. Besides, if there was one thing not likely to make the slightest impression on Burgess's obsidian consciousness, it was political correctness.

Banks lit a cigarette and held out his lighter as Burgess fired up one of his Tom Thumb cigars. He was still in good shape, though filling out a bit around the belly. He had a square jaw and slightly crooked teeth. His black, slicked-back hair was turning silver at the temples and sideboards, and the bags under his seen-it-all grey eyes looked as if they had taken on a bit more weight since Banks had last seen him. About six feet tall, casually dressed in a black leather jacket, open-neck shirt and grey cords, he was still handsome enough to turn the heads of a few thirtyish women, and had a reputation as something of a rake. It wasn't entirely unfounded, Banks had discovered the last time they worked together.

Banks reached for his pint. 'To what do I owe the honour?' he asked. He had never dignified Burgess with the 'sir' his rank demanded, and he was damned if he was about to start now.

Burgess swigged some lager, swished it around his mouth and swallowed.

'Well?' said Banks. 'Enough bloody theatrics, for Christ's sake.'

'I don't suppose you'd believe me if I said I'd missed you?'

'Get on with it.'

'Right. Thought not. Ever heard of a place called St Corona?'

'Of course. It's a Caribbean island, been in the news a bit lately.'

'Clever boy. That's the one. Population about four point eight million. Area about seven thousand square miles. Chief resources: bauxite, limestone, aluminium, sugar cane, plus various fruits and spices, fish and a bit of gold, silver and nickel. A lot of tourism, too, or there used to be.'

'So you've been studying *Whitaker's Almanack*,' said Banks. 'Now what the bloody hell is this all about?'

A tipsy youth bumped into the table and spilled some of Burgess's lager. The youth stopped to apologize, but the look Burgess gave him sent him stumbling off into the bright afternoon sunlight before he could get the words out.

'Fucking lager lout,' Burgess muttered, wiping the beer off the table-top with a handkerchief. 'Gone to the dogs, this country. Where was I? Oh, yes. St Corona. Imports just about everything you need to live, including the machinery to make it. Lots of television sets, radios, fridges, washing machines.' He paused and whistled between his teeth as a young redhead in a mini-skirt walked by. 'Now *that's* not bad,' he said. 'Which reminds me, have you rogered that young redhead in Eastvale yet?

You know, the psychologist.' He flicked the stub of his cigar towards the gutter; it hit the wall just above with a shower of sparks.

Burgess meant Jenny Fuller, as he knew damn well. Banks managed a smile, remembering what happened the last time those two met. 'St Corona,' he said. 'You were saying?'

Burgess pouted. 'You're no fun. Know who the president is?'

'What is this, bloody *Mastermind*? Martin Churchill. Now, if you've got something to tell me, get it off your chest and let me go home. It's been a long day.'

'Back to that lovely wife of yours, eh? Sandra, isn't it? All right, all right. St Corona is a republic, and you're right, Martin Churchill is president for life. Good name for the job, don't you think?'

'I've read about him.'

'Yes, well, the poor sod's a bit beleaguered these days, what with the opposition parties raking up the muck and the independence and liberation movements going from strength to strength.' He sighed. 'I don't know. It seems people just don't believe in a good old benevolent dictatorship any more.'

'Benevolent, my arse,' said Banks. 'He's been bleeding the country dry for ten years and now they're closing in on him. What am I supposed to do, cry?'

Burgess glared at Banks through squinting eyes. 'Still the bloody pinko, huh? Still the limp-wristed, knee-jerking liberal?' He sighed. 'Somehow, Banks, I hadn't expected you to change. That's partly why I'm here. Anyway, whatever you or I might think about it, the powers that be decided it was a good idea to have a stable government in that part of the world, someone we could trust. Of course, it doesn't seem quite so important now, with the Russkies swapping their rusty old atomic warheads for turnips, but other threats exist. Anyway, Britain, France, Canada, the States and a few others pumped millions into St Corona over the years, so you can estimate how important it is to us.'

Banks listened intently. There could be no rushing Burgess; he would get where he was going in his own sweet time.

'Churchill's finished,' Burgess went on with a sweeping hand gesture. 'It's just a matter of time. Weeks . . . months. He knows it. We know it. The only thing now is for him to get out alive with his family while he still can and take up life in exile.'

'And he wants to come here?'

Burgess looked around at the chess players and The Headrow. 'Well, I don't think he's got the north of England in mind specifically, but you're on the right track. Maybe a nice little retirement villa in Devon or Cornwall, the English Riviera. Somewhere where the weather's nice. Cultivate his herbaceous borders. Live out his days in the contemplation of nature. Prepare himself for the life hereafter. Make his peace with the Almighty. That kind of thing. Somewhere he won't do any more harm.'

Burgess lit another little cigar and spat out a flake of loose tobacco. 'The Yanks have said no, but then they've got a good record of turning their backs on their mates. The French are dithering and jabbering and waving their arms about, as usual. They'd probably sneak him in the back door like the good little hypocrites they are, if they had any real incentive left. And the Canadians . . . well, they're just too fucking moral for their own good. The bottom line, Banks, is that there's a lot of pressure on our government to take him in, as quietly as possible, of course.'

'Sneak him in the back door, you mean, like the hypocritical French?'

'If you like.'

'His human rights record is appalling,' Banks said. 'The infant mortality rate in St Corona is over fifteen per cent, for a start. Life expectancy isn't much more than fifty for a man and sixty for a woman.'

'Oh, dear, dear. You've been reading the *Guardian* again, haven't you, Banks?'

'And other papers. The story's the same.'

'Well, you should know better than to believe all you read in the papers, shouldn't you?' Burgess looked around conspiratorially and lowered his voice. Nobody seemed in the least bit interested in them. Laughter and fragments of conversation filled the air. 'Have you ever wondered,' he said, 'why women always seem to have a higher life expectancy rate than men? Don't they have as many bad habits as we do? Maybe they just don't work as hard, don't suffer as much stress? Maybe it's all that slimming and aerobics, eh? Maybe there's something in it.

'Anyway, back to Mr Churchill's predicament. And this is classified, by the way. There are some people in power who want him here, who feel we owe him, and there are some who don't, who feel he's a lowlife scumbag and deserves to die as slowly and painfully as possible.' As usual, Burgess liked to show off his American slang. He went to the States often, on 'courses'.

'Oh, come off it,' said Banks. 'If they want him here it's not out of any sense of duty, it's because he's got something they want, or because he's got something on them.'

Burgess scratched his cheek. 'Cynic,' he said. 'But you're partly right. He's not a nice man. As far as I can gather he's a glutton, a boor, a murderer and a rapist, sodomy preferred. But that's not the issue at all. The problem is that we educated him, made him what he is. Eton and Cambridge. He read law there. Did you know that? He went through school and university with a lot of important people, Banks. Cabinet ministers, bankers, power brokers, backroom boys. You know how people can behave indiscreetly when they're young? Do things they wouldn't want to come back and haunt them when they're in the public eye? And we're talking about people who have the power to loosen the government purse strings now and then, whenever St Corona asks for more aid. And rumour has it that he's also got quite a nice little savings account that won't do our economy any harm at all.'

'Let me guess,' said Banks. 'Laundered money?'

Burgess raised his eyebrows. 'Well, of course. Which brings me to the murder of Keith Rothwell. You are senior field investigator, I understand?'

'Yes.'

'That's why I thought I'd better deal with you in person. I know you, Banks. You're still a pinko liberal, as you've proved time and time again. In fact, as soon as they told me you were on the case, I thought, "Oh, fuck, we're in trouble." You've no respect for the venerable institutions of government, or for the necessity of secrecy in some of their workings. You've got no respect for tradition and you don't give a toss about preserving the natural order of things. You probably don't even stand up for "God Save the Queen". In short, you're a bloody bolshie trouble-maker and a menace to national security.'

Banks smiled. 'Thanks for the compliment,' he said. 'But I wouldn't go quite *that* far.'

Burgess grinned. 'Maybe I exaggerate. But you get my point?'

'Loud and clear.'

'Good. That's why I'm going to tell you something very, very important and very, very secret, and I'm going to trust you with it. We've been keeping an eye on the St Corona situation, and anything that could possibly have to do with Martin Churchill gets flagged. Now, we just got a report from your Fraud Squad late yesterday evening that they found something on Keith Rothwell's computer that indicates he may have been laundering money for Martin Churchill. Lots of trips to the Channel Islands and the Caribbean. Some very dodgy bank accounts. Some very dodgy banks, too, for that matter. Anyway, there's a pattern and a time period that matches exactly the sort of thing we've been looking for. We've known this was going on for some time, but until now we hadn't a clue who was doing it. There's no proof it was Rothwell, yet – the Fraud Squad still has a lot of work to do, chasing down trans-actions and what have you – but if I'm right, then we're talking about a lot of money. Something in the region of thirty or forty million pounds over three or four years. Mostly money that was originally provided as aid by leading western nations. It's the same kind of thing Baby Doc did in Haiti.'

'And you think this might have something to do with Rothwell's murder?'

Burgess shook his head. 'I don't really know, but the odds are that there's some kind of connection, don't you think? Especially considering the way he was killed. I mean, it was hardly a domestic, was it?'

'Possibly,' Banks agreed. 'Do you have any leads on the killers?'

'No more than you. I'm only *suggesting* that Churchill might be behind them.'

'And if he is?'

'Watch your back.'

Banks thought about that for a moment. He wasn't sure who constituted the greatest threat to his exposed back, Churchill or Burgess. 'I must say this is pretty quick work on your part,' he said.

Burgess shrugged. 'Like I said, orders to flag. When I called your station, Superintendent Gristhorpe told me where you were. I missed you at the solicitor's office, but the secretary told me you were coming here.'

'What's Daniel Clegg's connection with all this?'

'We don't know yet. We don't even know if there is one. I only just found out about his disappearance. It's early days yet.'

'Two other men have been looking for him, too. One black, one white. Are they your lot?'

Burgess frowned. 'No, they're nothing to do with me.'

'Know anything about them?'

'No.'

He was lying, Banks was certain. 'So why are you here?' he asked. 'What do you want me to do?'

'Nothing. Just carry on as normal. I simply wanted to warn you to tread very carefully, that's all, that things might be more complicated than they appear on the surface. And to let you know there's help available if you want it, of course. Naturally, if you get close to uncovering the killers' identities, I'd be interested in talking to them.'

'Why?'

'Because I'm interested in everything to do with Martin

Churchill, as I told you.' Burgess looked at his watch. 'Good lord, is that the time already?' he said, then knocked back the rest of his pint, winked and stood up. 'Got to be off now. Be seeing you.' And he strutted off over the square towards Park Row.

Banks lit a cigarette and brooded over the meeting as he finished his pint, wondering what the hell the bastard was up to. He didn't trust Burgess as far as he could throw him, and he was convinced that all that stuff about offering help and giving a friendly warning was rubbish. Burgess was up to something.

At a guess, he wanted to be one of the first to get to the killers so he could find a way of hushing them up. The last thing he would want was a big story about Churchill hiring assassins to murder a Yorkshire accountant splashed all over the press. Churchill might well be up to much worse things on St Corona, but this was England, after all.

Still, no matter what Burgess suspected, and whether or not Martin Churchill was behind it all, Banks still had two killers to find, locals by the sound of them, and he wasn't going to do that by sitting around in Stumps fretting about Dirty Dick Burgess.

FOUR

Banks didn't expect to find anything new in Calvert's Headingley flat, but for some reason he felt the need to revisit the place after he had picked up the Khachaturian compact disc.

West Yorkshire police had talked to the other tenants, who all said they knew nothing about Mr Calvert or Keith Rothwell: they never really saw much of him; he was out a lot; and, yes, now you mention it, there was a resemblance, but it was only a newspaper photo and Mr Calvert didn't look quite the same; besides, Calvert wasn't an Eastvale accountant, was he? He lived in Leeds. Couldn't argue with that. Banks headed upstairs.

The only immediate difference he noticed was the thin layer of fingerprint powder on surfaces of metal or glass: around the gas fireplace, on the glass-topped coffee table and the TV set.

This time, Banks examined the books more closely. There weren't many, and most of them were the usual bestseller list paperbacks: Tom Clancy, Clive Cussler, Ken Follett, Robert Ludlum. There was also some espionage fiction – Len Deighton, John le Carré, Adam Hall, Ian Fleming – plus a couple of Agatha Christies and an oddly out-of-place copy of *Middlemarch*, which looked unread. Hardly surprising, Banks thought, having given up on even the television adaptation. The only other books were Palgrave's *Golden Treasury*, the first part of William Manchester's Churchill biography and a *Concise Oxford Dictionary*.

The small compact disc collection concentrated entirely on jazz, mostly Kenny Ball, Acker Bilk and a few collections of big-band music. Banks noticed some decent stuff: Louis, Bix, Johnny Dodds, Bud Powell. On the whole, though, judging from the Monet print over the fireplace, the Palgrave and the music, Robert Calvert had agreed with Philip Larkin about the evils of Parker, Pound and Picasso.

In the bedroom, all the papers had been removed from the desk, as had the wallet with the Calvert identification and credit card. The Fraud Squad would be working already on Calvert's financial profile, now they knew that he and Rothwell were one and the same. The magazines and coins were still there, the bed still unmade.

Why had Rothwell *needed* Calvert? Banks wondered. Simple escapism? According to what everyone said, he was a different person altogether at Arkbeck Farm and in the wider community of Swainsdale. Most people there spoke of him as a rather dull chap, maybe a bit henpecked.

Then there was Robert Calvert, the dancing, gambling, laughing, fun-loving Lothario and dreamer. The man who had attracted and bedded the beautiful Pamela Jeffreys. The man who squeezed his toothpaste tube in the middle.

So which was the real Keith Rothwell? Both or neither? In a sense, Banks guessed, he needed both worlds. Did that make him a Jekyll and Hyde figure? Did it mean he was mad? Banks didn't think so.

He remembered Susan's account of her interview with Laurence Pratt, in which Pratt had indicated that Rothwell had changed over the years, cut himself off, penned himself in. Perhaps he had once been the kind of person who liked gambling, dancing and drinking. Then he had been pushed into marriage with the boss's daughter, and marriage had changed him. It happened often enough; people settled down. But, for some reason, Rothwell had felt the need for an outlet, one that would not interfere with his family life, or with his local image as a respectable, decent citizen.

Banks could think of one good reason why it was important for Rothwell to maintain this fiction: Rothwell was a crook. He certainly didn't want to draw attention to himself by high living. As Calvert, he could relive his youth as much as he wished and enjoy the proceeds of his money-laundering. Perfect.

Did Mary Rothwell know about her husband's other life? She had probably suspected something was wrong time and time again over the last few years, but denied and repressed the suspicions in order to maintain the illusion of happy, affluent family values in the community. She probably needed to believe in the lies as much as her husband needed to live them.

But you can only maintain an illusion for so long, Banks thought, then cracks appear and the truth seeps in. You can ignore that for a long time, too, but ultimately the wound begins to fester and infect everything. That's when the bad things start to happen. Did Alison know? Or Tom? It would be interesting to meet the lad.

He looked through the wardrobe and dresser drawers again. Most of Calvert's clothes were still there, though the condoms had gone. Genuine scientific testing, Banks wondered, or a Scene of Crime officer with a hot date and no time to get to the chemist's?

He looked under chairs, under the bed, on top of the wardrobe, in the cistern, and in all the usual hiding places before he realized that Vic Manson and his lads had probably already done most of that, even though the flat wasn't a crime scene *per se*, and that he didn't know what he was looking for anyway. He paused by the front window, which looked out onto a tree-lined side street off Otley Road.

Fool, he told himself. He had been looking for Keith Rothwell in Robert Calvert's flat. But he wasn't there. He wasn't anywhere; he was just a slab of chilled meat waiting for a man with his collar on the wrong way around to chant a few meaningless words that might just ease the living's fear of death until the next time it touched too close to home for comfort.

As he glanced out of the window, he glimpsed two men in suits across the street looking up at him. They were partially obscured by trees, but he could see that one was black, the other white.

He hurried down to the street. When he got there, nobody was about except a young man washing his car three houses down.

Banks approached him and showed his identification. The man wiped the sweat off his brow and looked up at Banks, shielding his eyes from the glare. Sunlight winked on the bubbles in his bucket of soapy water.

'Did you see a couple of blokes in business suits pass by a few minutes ago?' Banks asked.

'Yeah,' said the man. 'Yeah, I did. I thought it was a bit odd the way they stopped and looked up at that house. To be honest, though, the way they were dressed I thought they were probably coppers.'

Banks thanked him and went back to the car. So he wasn't getting paranoid. How did the saying go? Just because you think they're out there following you, it doesn't mean they aren't.

8

ONE

Tom Rothwell resembled his father more than his mother, Banks thought, sitting opposite him in the split-level living room at Arkbeck Farm the following morning. Though his hair was darker and longer, he had the same thin oval face and slightly curved nose and the same grey eyes as Banks had seen in the photograph. His sulky mouth, though, owed more to early Elvis Presley, and was no doubt more a result of artifice than nature.

His light brown hair fell charmingly over one eye and hung in natural waves over his ears and the collar of his blue denim shirt. Both knees of his jeans were torn, and the unlaced white trainers on his feet were scuffed and dirty.

The best of the lot, Cathy Grafton had said, and it wasn't hard to guess why a rather plain girl like her would value a smile and a kind word from a handsome lad like Tom.

But right from the start Banks sensed something else about him, an aura of affected arrogance, as if he were condescending from a great intellectual and moral height to answer such stupid questions as those relating to his father's murder.

It was rebellious youth, in part, and Banks certainly understood that. Also, Tom seemed to exhibit that mix of

vanity and overconfidence that Banks had often encount-
ered in the wealthy. In addition there was a hell of a lot of
the wariness and subterfuge that he usually associated
with someone hiding a guilty secret. Tom's body language
said it all: long legs stretched out, crossed at the ankles,
arms folded high on his chest, eyes anywhere but on the
questioner. Susan Gay sat in the background to take notes.
Banks wondered what she thought about Tom.

'Did you have any problems getting a flight?' Banks
asked.

'No. But I had to change at some dreary place in
Carolina, and then again in New York.'

'I know you must be tired. I remember from my trip to
Toronto, the jet lag's much worse flying home.'

'I'm all right. I slept a little on the plane.'

'I can never seem to manage that.'

Tom said nothing. Banks wished that Alison and Mary
Rothwell weren't flanking Tom on the sofa. And again the
room felt dark and cold around him. Though it had
windows, they were set or angled in such a way that they
didn't let in much natural light. And they were all closed.

'I imagine you're upset about your father, too,' he said.

'Naturally.'

'We wanted to talk to you so soon,' Banks said,
'because we hoped you might be able to tell us something
about your father, something that might help lead us to his
killers.'

'How would I know anything? I've been out of the
country since the end of March.'

'It's possible,' Banks said, weighing his words carefully, 'that the roots of the crime lie farther back than that.'

'That's ridiculous. You lot have far too much imagination for your own good.'

'Oh? What do *you* think happened?'

Tom curled his lip and looked at the carpet. 'It was clearly a robbery gone wrong. Or a kidnap attempt. Dad *was* quite well off, you know.'

Banks scratched the scar beside his right eye. 'Kidnapping, eh? We'd never thought of that. Can you explain?'

'Well, that's your job, isn't it? But it's hardly difficult to see how it could have been a kidnap attempt gone wrong. My father obviously wouldn't co-operate, so they had to kill him.'

'Why not just knock him out and take him away?'

Tom shrugged. 'Perhaps the gun went off by accident.'

'Then why not take the body and pretend he was still alive till they got the money?'

'How would I know? You're supposed to be the professionals. I only said that's what it *might* have been. I also suggested a bungled robbery.'

'Look, Tom, this is a pointless game we're playing. Believe me, we've covered all the possibilities, and it wasn't a kidnap attempt or a bungled burglary. I realize how difficult it is for the family to accept that a member may have been involved in something illegal, but all the evidence points that way.'

'Absurd,' spat Mary Rothwell. 'Keith was an honest businessman, a good person. And if you persist in spreading these vicious rumours, we'll have to contact our solicitor.'

'Mrs Rothwell,' Banks said, 'I'm trying to talk to your son. I'd appreciate it if you would keep quiet.' More than once he had thought about breaking the news that her husband led another existence as Robert Calvert, but he held back. In the first place, it would be cruel, and in the second, Gristhorpe said the Chief Constable wanted it kept from the press and family, if possible, at least until they developed a few more leads on the case.

Mary Rothwell glared at him, lips pressed so tight they were white around the edges.

Banks turned back to Tom. 'Were you close to your father?'

'Close enough. He wasn't . . .' Tom turned up his nose. 'He wasn't a clinging, emotional sort of person.'

'But you were on good terms?'

'Yes, of course.'

'Then you might know something that could help us.'

'I still don't see how, but if I can be of any use . . . Ask away.'

'Did he ever mention a man called Martin Churchill?'

'Churchill? No.'

'Do you know who he is?'

'That chap in the Caribbean?'

'Yes.'

'Are you serious?' Tom looked puzzled. 'You are, aren't you? The answer's no, of course he didn't. Why would he?'

'Did you ever see your father with two well-dressed men, both about six feet tall, one black, one white?'

Tom frowned. 'No. Look, I'm sorry but I don't know what you're talking about.'

'Did he ever talk to you about business?'

'No.'

'Did you ever meet any of his business associates?'

'Only if they came over to dinner. And even then, I wasn't generally invited.' Tom looked at his mother. 'I had to find something else to do for the evening. Which usually wasn't much trouble.' He glanced over at Susan, and Banks sensed a softening in his expression as he did so. He seemed interested in her presence, curious about her.

The radio had been playing a request programme quietly in the background, and Banks suddenly picked out the haunting chorus of Delibes' *'Viens, Mallika . . . Dôme épais'*, popularized as the 'Flower Duet' by a television advert. Even trivialization couldn't mar its beauty and clarity. After pausing for a moment, he went on.

'When did you leave for your holiday?'

'March,' he said. 'The thirty-first. But I don't see—'

'What about your job?'

'What job?'

'The one in the video shop in Eastvale.'

'Oh, that. I packed it in.'

'What kind of videos did they deal in?'

'All sorts. Why?'

'Under-the-counter stuff?'

'Oh, come off it, Chief Inspector. Suddenly my father's a crook and I'm a porn merchant? You should be writing for television.' Alison looked up from her book and giggled. Tom smiled at her, obviously pleased with his insolence. 'It was called Monster Videos, that place in the arcade by the bus station. Ask them if you don't believe me.'

'Why did you leave?' Banks pressed on.

'Not that it's any of your business, but it was hardly a fast track to a career.'

'Is that what you want?'

'I'm going to film school in the States.'

'I see.'

'I want to be a movie director.'

'Was that what your father wanted?'

'I don't see that what *he* wanted has anything to do with it.'

It was there, the rancour, Banks thought. Time to push a little harder. 'It's just that I understood you had a falling out over your career choice. I gather he wanted you to become an accountant or a lawyer but he thought you preferred to be an idle, shiftless sod.'

'How dare you?' Mary Rothwell jumped to her feet.

'It's all right, Mother,' Tom sneered. 'Sit down. It's all part of their game. They only say things like that to needle you into saying something you'll regret. Just ignore it.' He looked at Susan again, as if expecting her to defend Banks, but she said nothing. He seemed disappointed.

Mary Rothwell sat down again slowly. Alison, at the other side of Tom, glanced up from *Villette* again for a couple of seconds, raised the corners of her lips in what passed for a smile, then went back to her book.

'Well?' said Banks.

'Well what?'

'What is it that I might needle you into regretting you said?'

'Clever. It was just a figure of speech.'

'All right. Did you and your father have such an argument?'

'You must know as well as I do,' Tom said, 'that fathers and sons have their disagreements. Sure, Dad wanted me to follow in his footsteps, but I had my own ideas. He's not big on the arts, isn't Dad, except when it's good for business to get tickets for the opera or the theatre or something to impress his clients.'

'Where did you travel in America?'

'All over. New York. Chicago. Los Angeles. San Francisco. Miami. Tampa.'

'How did you get around?'

'Plane and car rental. Where is this—'

'Did you visit the Caribbean? St Corona?'

'No, I didn't.'

'How did you finance the trip?'

'What?'

'You heard me. You were over there a month and a half, and you'd still be there now if it weren't for your father's death. All that travelling costs money. You can't have earned that much working in a video shop, especially one that only deals in legal stuff. How could you afford a lengthy trip to America?'

Tom shifted uncomfortably. 'My parents helped me out.'

Banks noticed a confused look flit across Mary Rothwell's face.

'Did you?' Banks asked her.

'Why, yes, of course.'

He could tell from the hesitation that she knew nothing about it. 'Do you mean your father helped you?' he asked Tom.

'He was the one with all the money, wasn't he?'

'So your father financed your trip. How?'

'What do you mean?'

'How did he finance it? Cash? Cheque?'

'He got me the ticket, some travellers' cheques and a supplementary card on his American Express Gold account. You can check the records, if you haven't done already.'

Banks whistled between his teeth. 'American Express Gold, eh? Not bad.' Judging by the look on Mary Rothwell's face, it was news to her. Alison didn't seem to care. She turned a page without looking up. 'Why would he do that?' Banks asked.

'I'm his son. It's the kind of thing parents do, isn't it? Why not?'

Banks had never spent so much on Brian and Tracy, but

then he had never been able to afford it. 'Was he usually so generous?' he asked.

'He was never mean.'

Banks paused. When the silence had made Tom restless, he went on. 'Just before you went away, you had an argument with your father in which he expressed great disappointment in you. Now, I know why that is. You've just told me you didn't want to follow the career he set out for you. But you also expressed disappointment in him. Why did you do that?'

'I don't remember any argument.'

'Come on, Tom. You can do better than that.'

Tom looked at Susan again, and Banks noticed a plea for help in his eyes. He looked left and right for support, too, but found none. His mother seemed lost in thought and Alison was still deep in her Charlotte Brontë.

'I'm telling you,' Tom said, 'I don't know what you're talking about.'

'Why were you disappointed in your father, Tom?'

Tom reddened. 'I wasn't. I don't know what you mean.'

'Did you find out something incriminating about his business dealings?'

'Is *that* what you think?'

'You'd better tell me, Tom. It could help us a lot. What was he up to?'

Tom seemed to relax. 'Nothing. *I* don't know. You're way off beam.'

'Does the name Aston or Afton mean anything to you?'

Banks was sure he saw a flicker of recognition behind Tom's eyes. Recognition and fear. 'No,' Tom said. 'Never heard of him.'

Banks decided they would get nothing more out of this situation, not with the whole family closing ranks. It would be best to leave it for now. No doubt, when Banks and Susan left, the Rothwells would fall into an argument, for Mary Rothwell wasn't looking at all pleased with the return of her prodigal son. Tom could stew over whatever it was that confused him. Plenty of time.

It was a gorgeous morning in the dale. Banks put a Bill Evans solo piano tape in the cassette player as he drove through Fortford, gold and green in the soft, slanting light. To their left, the lush fields of the Leas were full of butter-cups, and here and there the fishermen sat, still as statues, lines arcing down into the River Swain.

'What do you think?' he asked Susan.

'He's lying, sir.'

'That's obvious enough. But why? What about?'

'I don't know. Everything. I just got a strange feeling.'

'Me, too. Next time, I think it might be a good idea if you talked to him alone.'

'Maybe I can catch him after the funeral?'

'You were thinking of going? Damn!'

Half a mile before the road widened at the outskirts of Eastvale, a farmer was moving his sheep across from one pasture to another. There was nothing to be done. They simply had to stop until the sheep had gone.

'Stupid creatures,' Banks said.

'I think they're rather cute, in a silly way,' Susan said. 'Anyway, I thought I might go. You never know, the murderers might turn up to pay their respects, like they do in books.'

Banks laughed. 'Do you know that actually happened to me once?' he said.

'What?'

'It did. Honest. Down in London. There was a feud between two families, the Kinghorns and the Franklins –

none of them exactly intellectual giants – been going on for years. Anyway, old man Franklin gets shot in broad daylight, and there's half a dozen witnesses say they saw Billy Kinghorn, the eldest son, do it. Only trouble is, Billy does a bunk. Until the funeral, that is. Then there he is, young Billy, black tie, armband and all, face as long as a wet Sunday, come to pay his last respects.'

'What happened?'

'We nabbed him.'

Susan laughed. The sheep kept wandering all over the road, despite the ministrations of an inept collie, which looked a bit too long in the tooth for such exacting work.

'I thought there had to be a reason for going,' Susan said. 'Anyway, I quite like funerals. My Auntie Mavis died when I was six and my mum and dad took me to the funeral. It was very impressive, the hymns, the readings. I couldn't understand a word of it at that age, of course, but it certainly sounded important. Anyway, when we got outside I asked my mum where Auntie Mavis was and she sniffled a bit then said, "In Heaven." I asked her where that was and she pointed up at the sky. It was a beautiful blue sky, a bit like today, and there was only one cloud in it, a fluffy white one that looked like a teddy bear. From then on I always thought when people died they became clouds in a perfect blue sky. I don't know . . . it made me feel happy, somehow. I mean, I know funerals are solemn occasions, but I don't seem to mind them so much after that.'

The last sheep finally found the gate and scrambled through. The farmer held up his hand in thanks, as if Banks had had any option but to wait, and closed the gate behind him. Banks set off.

'Rather you than me,' he said. 'I can't stand them. Anyway, see if you can take young Tom aside, take him for a drink or something. I've a feeling he really wants to tell us what he knows. Did you notice the way he kept looking at you?'

'Yes.'

'Think he fancies you?'

'No,' Susan said, after a pause for thought. 'No. Somehow, I don't think it was that at all.'

TWO

Banks crunched the last pickled onion of his ploughman's lunch and swilled it down with a mouthful of Theakston's bitter, then he lit a cigarette. He would have to resort to a Polo mint if he found himself interviewing anyone in the afternoon. Superintendent Gristhorpe sat opposite him in the Queen's Arms, cradling a half-pint. It was the first time they had been able to get together since Banks had met Burgess.

'So,' Gristhorpe said, 'according to Burgess, Rothwell was laundering money for Martin Churchill?'

'Looks that way,' said Banks. 'He said he couldn't be certain but I don't think he'd come all the way up here if he wasn't, do you?'

'Knowing how little Burgess thinks of the north, no. But I still don't think we should overlook the possibility of Rothwell's involvement in some other kind of organized crime, most likely drugs, prostitution or porn. Even if he were laundering money for Churchill, he could have been into something else dirty too. We can't assume it was the Churchill link that got him killed until we know a hell of a lot more.'

'I agree,' said Banks.

'Better do as Burgess says and watch your back, though.'

'Don't worry, sir, I will.'

'Anyway,' Gristhorpe went on, 'I've just had a meeting with Inspector Macmillan, and he tells me that Daniel Clegg acted as Robert Calvert's reference for his bank account and his credit card in Leeds. The account has about twenty thousand in it. Interesting, isn't it?'

'Play money,' Banks said.

'Aye. I wouldn't mind that much to play with, myself. Anyway, according to Inspector Macmillan, the bank employees didn't recognize Rothwell's picture as Calvert because they hardly saw him. He used a busy branch in the city centre, and the only person who did make the connection when Macmillan pushed it said Calvert looked and dressed so differently she wouldn't have known.'

'Thank the lord for Pamela Jeffreys, then.'

'Aye, or we might never have known. What does his family have to say?'

Banks sighed and put the edge of his hand to his throat. 'I've had it up to here with the bloody Rothwells,' he said. 'They give a whole new meaning to "dysfunctional". There's the victim laundering illegal money and leading a double life just for a hobby. There's the daughter, who'd rather bury her face in a book than face reality now that the shock and the tiredness have worn off. There's the son with more than a few guilty secrets hidden away. And then, watching over them all, there's the Queen Bee, who just wants to keep up the usual upper-middle-class appearances and swears the sun shone out of her husband's arse.'

'What do you expect her to do, Alan? Her world's fallen apart. She must be having a hell of a job just holding things together. Have a bit more bloody compassion, lad.'

Banks took a drag at his cigarette, and blew the smoke out slowly. 'You're right,' he said. 'I'm sorry. I've just had it with the bloody Rothwells, that's all. What do they know? It's hard to tell. I think the wife suspects something weird was going on, but she doesn't know what and she doesn't want to know. She denies it, especially to herself.'

'Could they have any involvement?'

'I've thought about it,' Banks said, 'and I've discussed it with Susan. In the final analysis, I don't really think so. Mary Rothwell might well hit out at anything that threatens her comfortable world, and if she thought her husband were profiting from porn, for example, I can't just see her sitting still and accepting it.' He shook his head. 'But not this way. This brings her exactly the kind of attention she *doesn't* want. I don't know how she'd deal with him – Susan guessed poison, maybe, or an accident – but it wouldn't be like this.'

'Hmm. Try this for size,' said Gristhorpe. 'One: let's assume that Rothwell and Clegg are in the money-laundering business together, for Martin Churchill or whoever.'

Banks nodded. 'It makes sense, Clegg being a tax specialist and all.'

'And we'll leave Robert Calvert out of it, as, say, just a personal aberration on Rothwell's part, at least for the moment. A red herring, right?'

'Okay.'

'Something goes wrong. Rothwell finds out something that makes him want to get out of it, so he writes to Clegg ending their association.'

'And,' said Banks, 'Churchill, or whoever it is they're working for, doesn't like this at all.'

'Makes sense, doesn't it?'

'So far. Keep going.'

'Rothwell gets scared. Either he's been cheating on his masters, and they've found out, or they're afraid he's getting nervous and is going to blow the whistle. So what do they do?'

'Take out a contract.'

'Right. And that's the end of Rothwell.'

Gristhorpe paused as a couple of office-workers on a lunch break brushed past them and sat down at the next table. Cyril's cash register rang up another sale.

'He could have been cheating on them to finance his life as Calvert,' said Banks. 'I know we were going to leave him out of the equation, but it fits. He had twenty grand in the bank, you say, and he liked to gamble, according to Pamela Jeffreys.'

'True, but let's stick to the simple line. What's important is that Rothwell has become a liability, or a threat, and his masters want him dead. They've got enough money to be able to pay for the privilege without getting their own hands dirty. Which brings us to Mr Daniel Clegg. The killers had a fair bit of information about Rothwell. They seemed to know that he and his wife would be out celebrating their wedding anniversary, for example. Clegg could probably have told them that. They knew Rothwell had a daughter, too, and that she would be at home. She wasn't "part of the deal", remember? And they knew where he lived, the layout, everything.'

'Clegg?'

Gristhorpe nodded. 'Let's put it this way. If Rothwell were laundering money for someone, there'd be little, if any, contact between him and his masters, wouldn't there?'

'That would seem to be one point of a laundering operation,' Banks agreed. 'Certainly Tom Rothwell seemed genuinely puzzled when I brought up Martin Churchill.'

'Right. And Clegg was the only other person we suspect was involved, and he had information about Rothwell's personal life.'

'So you reckon Clegg was behind it?'

'It's a theory, isn't it? They weren't exactly friends, Alan. Not according to what you've told me. They were business colleagues. Different thing. It was a matter of you scratch my back, I'll scratch yours. Strange bedfellows, maybe. And crooked too. It's an odd thing is a professional gone bad. They talk about bent coppers, but what about bent lawyers, bent accountants, bent doctors? If push came to shove, would you expect one crooked business-man to stick up for another?'

'So you think Clegg was not just involved in the laundering business but in Rothwell's murder, too?'

'Aye. He could be our link.'

'And his disappearance?'

'Scarpered. He knew what was coming, knew when. Maybe they paid him well. It doesn't matter whether he was scared of us or them, the result was the same. He took his money and ran, collected two hundred pounds when he passed go, didn't go to jail. Then his bosses couldn't get in touch with him, so they sent their two goons to find him. The timing's right.'

'What about this scenario,' Banks offered. 'Maybe Churchill had Clegg killed, too. With Rothwell gone, Clegg might just be a nuisance who knew too much, a loose cannon on the deck. If Churchill is planning on coming here, maybe he wanted a clean break.'

Gristhorpe took a sip of his beer. 'Possible, I'll grant you.'

'You know, it's just struck me,' said Banks, 'but do we know if Clegg ever practised criminal law?'

'Seems to be the only kind he practised,' replied Gristhorpe, then held up his hand and grinned as Banks groaned. 'All right, all right, Alan. I promise. No more bad lawyer jokes. As far as we know he didn't. He's a solicitor, not a barrister, so he didn't represent clients in court. But people might have come to him, and he could have referred them. Why?'

'I was just wondering where a man like Clegg might meet a killer for hire.'

'Local Conservative Club, probably,' said Gristhorpe. 'But I see what you mean. It's a loose end we've got to pursue. If we assume Clegg was involved in arranging for Rothwell's murder, then we can look through his contacts and his activities to find a link with a couple of likely assassins. We've got that and the wadding. Not very much, is it?'

'No,' said Banks. 'What if Clegg's dead?'

'Nothing changes. West Yorkshire police keep looking for a body and we keep nosing around asking questions. We could get in touch with Interpol, see if he's holed up somewhere in Spain.' He looked at his watch. 'Look, Alan, I'd better get finished and be off. I've got another meeting with the Chief Constable this afternoon.'

'Okay. I'll be over in a minute.'

Gristhorpe nodded and left, but no sooner had Banks started to let his imagination work on Clegg meeting two hired guns in a smoky saloon than the superintendent poked his head around the door again. 'They think they've found the killers' car,' he said. 'Abandoned near Leeds city centre. Ken Blackstone asks if you want to go and have a look.'

Banks nodded. 'All roads lead to Leeds,' he sighed. 'I might as well bloody move there.' And he followed Gristhorpe out.

9

ONE

A tape of Satie's piano music, especially the 'Trois Gymnopédies', kept Banks calm on his way to Leeds, even though the A1 was busy with juggernauts and commercial travellers driving too fast. He found the car park without too much difficulty; it was an old school playground surrounded by the rubble of demolished buildings just north of the city centre.

'Cheers, Alan,' said Detective Inspector Ken Blackstone. 'You look like a bloody villain with those sunglasses on. How's it going?'

'Can't complain.' Banks shook his hand and took off the dark glasses. He had met Blackstone at a number of courses and functions, and the two of them had always got along well enough. 'And how's West Yorkshire CID?'

'Overworked, as usual. Bit of a bugger, isn't it?' said Blackstone. 'The weather, I mean.'

Banks scratched the scar beside his right eye. Sometimes when it itched, it was trying to tell him something; other times, like this, it was just the heat. 'I remember an American once told me that all we English do is complain about the weather,' he said. 'It's either too hot or too cold for us, too wet or too dry.'

Blackstone laughed. 'True. Still, the station could do with a few of those air-conditioner thingies the Yanks use.

It's hotter indoors than out. Sends the crime figures up, you know, a heat wave. Natives get restless.'

A light breeze had sprung up from the west, but it did nothing to quell the warmth of the sun. Banks took off his sports jacket and slung it over his shoulder as they walked across the soft tarmac to the abandoned car. His tie hung askew, as usual, and his top shirt button was open so he could breathe easily. He could feel the sweat sticking his white cotton shirt to his back. This weather was following a pattern he recognized; it would get hotter and hazier until it ended in a storm.

'What have you got?' he asked.

'You'll see in a minute.' Despite the weather, Ken Blackstone looked cool as usual. He wore a lightweight navy-blue suit with a grey herringbone pattern, a crisp white shirt with a stiff collar and a garish silk tie, secured by a gold tie-clip in the shape of a pair of handcuffs. Banks was willing to bet that his top button was fastened.

Blackstone was tall and slim with light brown hair, thin on top but curly over the ears, and a pale complexion, definitely not the sun-worshipping kind. His Cupid's bow lips and wire-rimmed glasses made him look about thirty, when he was, in fact, closer to Banks's age. He had a long, dour sort of face and spoke with a local accent tempered by three years at Bath University, where he had studied art history.

Blackstone had, in fact, become something of an expert on art fraud after his degree, and he often found himself called in to help out when something of that nature happened. In addition, he was a fair landscape artist himself, and his work had been exhibited several times. Banks remembered Blackstone and Sandra getting into a long conversation about the Pre-Raphaelites at a colleague's wedding once, and remembered the stirrings of jealousy he had felt. Though he was eager to learn, read, look and listen as much as his time allowed, Banks was always aware of his working-class background and his lack of a true formal education.

They arrived at a car guarded by two hot-looking uniformed constables and Banks stood back to survey it. Ancient, but not old enough to attract attention as an antique, the light blue Ford Escort was rusted around the bottom of the chassis and had spider-leg cracks on the passenger side of the windscreen. It matched the description, as far as that went.

'How long's it been here?' Banks asked.

'Don't know,' said Blackstone. 'Our lads didn't notice it until last night. When they ran the number they found it was stolen.'

Banks knelt by the front tyre. Flat. There was plenty of soil and gravel lodged in the grooves. They could have it analysed and at least discover if it came from around Arkbeck Farm. He looked through the grimy window. The beige upholstery was dirty, cracked and split. A McDonald's coffee cup lay crushed on the floor at the driver's side, but apart from that he could see nothing else inside.

'We've looked in the boot,' said Blackstone. 'Nothing. Not even a jack or a spare tyre. I've arranged for it to be taken to our police garage for a thorough forensic examination, but I thought you'd like a look at it *in situ* first.'

'Thanks,' said Banks. 'I don't expect we'll get any prints, if they were pros, but you never know. Who's the lucky owner?'

'Bloke called Ronald Hamilton.'

'When did he report it missing?'

Blackstone paused before answering. 'Friday morning.

Said he left it in the street as usual after he got in about five or six in the evening and it was gone when he went out at ten the next morning. Thought it was maybe kids joy-riding. There's been a lot of it on the estate lately. It's not the safest place in the city. He lives on the Raynville estate in Bramley. Ring any bells?'

Banks shook his head. Pamela Jeffreys lived in Armley, which wasn't far away, and Daniel Clegg lived in Chapel Allerton, a fair distance in both miles and manners. Most likely the killers had picked it at random a good distance from where they lived. 'That's four days ago, Ken,' said Banks. 'And nobody spotted it before last night?'

Again, Blackstone hesitated. 'Hamilton's an unem-ployed labourer,' he said finally. 'He's got at least one wife and three kids that we know of, and lately he's been having a few problems with the social. He's also got a record. Dealing. Aggravated assault.'

'You thought he'd arranged to have it nicked for the insurance?'

Blackstone smiled. 'Something like that. I wasn't involved personally. I don't know what you lot do, but here in the big city we don't send detective inspectors out on routine traffic incidents.'

Banks ignored the sarcasm. It was just Blackstone's manner. 'So your lads didn't exactly put a rush on it?'

'That's right.' Blackstone glanced towards the horizon and sighed. 'Any idea, Alan, how many car crimes we've got in the city now? You yokels wouldn't believe it. So when some scurvy knave comes on with a story about a beat-up old Escort, you think he'd have to pay somebody to steal that piece of shit. So let the fucking insurance company pay. They can afford it. In the meantime we've got joyriding kids, real villains and organized gangs of car thieves to deal with. I'm not making excuses, Alan.'

'Yeah, I know.' Banks leaned against a red Orion. The metal burned through his shirt, so he stood up straight again.

'Didn't you once tell me you came up from the Met for a peaceful time in rural Yorkshire?' Blackstone asked.

Banks smiled. 'I did.'

'Getting it?'

'I can only suppose it's got proportionately worse down there.'

Blackstone laughed. 'Indeed. Business is booming.'

'Have you talked to Hamilton?'

'Yes. This morning. He knows nothing. Believe me, he's so scared of the police he'd sell his own mother down the tubes if he thought we were after her.' Blackstone made an expression of distaste. 'You know the type, Alan, belligerent one minute, yelling that you're picking on him because he's black, then arse-licking the next. Makes you want to puke.'

'Where's he from?'

'Jamaica. He's legit; we checked. Been here ten years.'

'What's his story?'

'Saw nothing, heard nothing, knows nothing. To tell you the truth, I got the impression he'd driven back from the pub after a skinful then settled in front of the telly with a few cans of lager while his wife fed the kiddies and put them to bed. After that he probably passed out. Whole bloody place smelled of shitty nappies and roll-ups and worse. We could probably do him for possession if it was worth our while. At ten the next morning he staggers out to go and sign on, finds his car missing and, bob's your uncle, does the outraged citizen routine on the local bobby, who's got more sense, thank the lord.'

Blackstone stood, slightly hunched, with his hands in his pockets, and kicked at small stones on the tarmac. You could see your face in his shoes.

'Do me a favour, Ken, and have another go at him. You said he was done for dealing?'

'Uh-huh. Small stuff. Mostly cannabis, a little coke.'

'It's probably just a coincidence that the car used belongs to a drug dealer, but pull his record and have another go at him all the same. Find out who his suppliers are. And see if he has any connections with St Corona. Friends, family, whatever. There might be a drug connection or a Caribbean connection in Rothwell's murder, and it's a remote possibility that Mr Hamilton might have done some work for the organization behind it, whoever they are.'

'You mean he might have *loaned* his car?'

'It's possible. I doubt it. I think we're dealing with cleverer crooks than that, but we'd look like the rear end of a pantomime horse if we didn't check it out.'

'Will do.'

'Have you questioned the neighbours?'

'We're doing a house-to-house. Nothing so far. Nobody sees anything on these estates.'

'So that's that?'

'Looks like it. For the moment, anyway.'

'No car-park attendant?'

'No.' Blackstone pointed to the rubble. 'As you can see, it's just an old schoolyard with weeds growing through the tarmac. The school was knocked down months ago.'

Banks looked around. To the south-west he could see the large dome of the Town Hall and the built-up city centre; to the west stood the high white obelisk of the university's Brotherton Library, and the rest of the horizon seemed circled with blocks of flats and crooked terraces of back-to-backs poking through the surrounding rubble like charred vertebrae. 'I could use a break on this, Ken,' Banks said.

'Aye. We'll give it our best. Hey up, the lads have come to pick up the car.'

Banks watched the police tow-team tie a line to the Escort. 'I'd better be off,' he said. 'You'll let me know?'

'Just a minute,' said Blackstone. 'What are your plans?'

'I'm checking into the Holiday Inn. For tonight, at least. There's a couple of people I want to talk to again in connection with Clegg and Rothwell – Clegg's secretary and his ex-wife, for a start. I'd like to get a clearer idea of their relationship now we've got a bit more to go on.'

'Holiday Inn? Well, la-di-da. Isn't that a bit posh for a humble copper?'

Banks laughed. 'I could do with a bit of luxury. Maybe they'll give me the sack when they see my expenses. These days we can't even afford to do half the forensic tests we need.'

'Tell me about it. Anyway, if you're going to be sticking around, I'd appreciate it if we could have a chat. There seems to be a lot going on here I don't know about.'

'There's a lot I don't know about, too.'

'Still . . . I'd appreciate it if you would fill me in.'

'No problem.'

Blackstone hesitated and shifted from foot to foot. 'Look,' he said, 'I'd like to invite you over for a bit of home-cooking but Connie left a couple of months ago.'

'I'm sorry to hear that,' said Banks. 'I didn't know.'

'Yeah, well, it happens, right? Comes with the territory. Still taking care of that lovely wife of yours?'

'You wouldn't think so by the amount of time we've spent together lately.'

'I know what you mean. That was one of the problems. She said we were living such separate lives we might as well make it official. Anyway, I'm not much of a cook myself. Besides, Connie got the house and I'm in a rather small bachelor flat for the moment. But there's a decent Indian restaurant on Eastgate, near the station, if you fancy it? It's called the Shabab. About half past six, seven o'clock? We might have something on Hamilton and the car by then, too.'

'All right,' said Banks. 'You're on. Make it seven o'clock.'

'And, Alan,' said Blackstone as Banks walked away, 'you watch yourself. Hotels give married men strange ideas sometimes. I suppose it's the anonymity and the distance from home, if you know what I mean. Anyway, there's some seem to act as if the normal vows of marriage don't apply in hotels.'

Banks knew what Blackstone meant, and he felt guilty as an image of Pamela Jeffreys flashed unbidden through his mind.

TWO

Susan Gay heard Sergeant Hatchley burp before she had even opened the office door after more fruitless interviews with Rothwell's legitimate clients. She felt apprehension churn in her stomach like a badly digested meal. She could not work with Hatchley; she just couldn't.

Hatchley sat at his desk, smoking. The small, stifling room stank of stale beer and pickled onions. The warped window was open about as far as it would go, but that didn't help much. If this oppressive weather didn't end soon, Susan felt she would scream.

And, by God, he's repulsive, she thought. There was his sheer bulk, for a start – a rugby prop forward gone to fat. Then there was his face: brick-red complexion, white eyelashes and piggy eyes; straw hair, thinning a bit at the top; a smattering of freckles over a broad-bridged nose; fleshy lips; tobacco-stained teeth. To cap it all, he wore a shiny, wrinkled blue suit, and his red neck bulged over his tight shirt collar.

From the corner of her eye, Susan noticed the coloured picture on the cork-board: long blonde hair, exposed skin. Without even stopping to think, she walked over and pulled it down so hard the drawing-pin shot right across the room.

'Oy!' said Hatchley. 'What the hell do you think you're playing at?'

'I'm not playing at anything,' Susan said, waving the picture at him. 'With all respect, sir, I don't care if you are my senior officer, I won't bloody well have it!'

A hint of a smile came to Hatchley's eyes. 'Calm down, lass,' he said. 'You've got steam coming out of your ears. Maybe you're being a bit hasty?'

'No, I'm not. It's offensive. I don't see why I should have to work with this kind of thing stuck to the walls. You might think it's funny, but I don't. *Sir.*'

'Susan. Look at it.'

'No. Why—'

'Susan!'

Slowly, Susan turned the picture over and looked at it. There, in all her maternal innocence, Carol Hatchley, with her long blonde hair hanging over her shoulders, held her naked, newborn baby to her breast, which was covered well beyond the point of modesty by a flesh-tone T-shirt. Susan felt herself blush. All she had seen were the

woman's face, hair and a lot of skin colour. 'I . . . I thought
. . .' She could think of nothing else to say.

'I know what you thought,' said Hatchley. 'You thought
my daughter's head was a tit. You *could* apologize.'

Susan felt such a fool she couldn't even bring herself to
do that.

'All right,' Hatchley said, putting his feet up on the
desk, 'then you can listen to me. Now, nobody's ever
going to convince me that looking at a nice pair of
knockers is wrong. Since time immemorial, since our
ancestors scratched images on cave walls, men have
enjoyed looking at women's tits. They're beautiful things,
nothing dirty or pornographic about them at all.'

'But they're private,' Susan blurted out. 'Don't you
understand? They're a woman's private parts. You don't
see pictures of men's privates all over the place, do you?
You wouldn't like people staring at yours, would you?'

'Susan, love, if I thought it would make you happy I'd
drop my trousers right now. But that's not the point. What
I'm saying is it's my opinion that there's nowt wrong in
admiring a nice pair of bristols. A lot of people agree with
me, too. But you don't like it.' He held up his large hand.
'All right, now I might not be the most sensitive bloke in
Christendom, and I certainly reserve my right to disagree
with you, but I'm not that much of a monster that I'd use
my rank to expose you to something you feel offends you
day in, day out, however wrongheaded I think you are. I
respect your opinion. I don't agree with you, and I never
will, but I respect it. I can live without.

'And another thing. I know you're a bugger about
smoking. I'll try and cut down on the cigarettes in the
office, too. But don't expect miracles, and don't expect it's
going to be all bloody give and no take on my part. You

don't like my smoke. I don't like your perfume. It makes my nose itch and it's probably rotting my lungs as we speak. But for better or for worse, lass, we've got to work together, and we've got to do it in the same damn little cubby-hole for the time being. Mebbe one day we'll have separate offices. Myself, I can hardly wait. But for now, let's just keep the window open and make a bit of an effort to get along, all right?'

Susan nodded. She felt all the wind go out of her sails. She swallowed. 'All right. Sorry, sir.'

Hatchley swung his legs to the floor and rubbed his hands together. 'We'll say no more, then. Now, about that wadding?'

'Yes, sir?'

Hatchley burped again and put his hamlike hand to his mouth. 'Shaved pussies. Smooth and shiny as a baby's bottom.'

'Yes, sir.' Susan felt herself blush again and hated herself for it. Hatchley smiled at her. He seemed to be enjoying himself. Her spirits sank. She had thought for a moment that he might be getting serious about the case, but here he was simply creating another opportunity to embarrass her.

'Aye. Now, I know that's not a lot to go on, but at least we know it's not kiddie porn or the bum brigade. And we've got penetration and a clear image of "a penis in an excited state", as it says in the book, so this is definitely under-the-counter stuff.'

'True, sir.'

'And as far as I can tell,' he went on, 'there's no sign of dogs or cats, either.'

'Sir, can you get to the point?' Susan couldn't keep the impatience out of her voice.

'Hold your horses, lass.' He started to laugh. 'Get that? No animals. Hold your horses? Never mind. The point is, shaved pussies aren't exactly ten a penny, though if we'd come up with something *really* kinky it would have made my job a lot easier. I mean, there aren't many people sell photos of Rottweilers bonking thirteen-year-old girls that we don't know about.'

'I still don't see what you're getting at, sir,' said Susan, a little calmer. She should have known that, if anyone was, Hatchley would be an expert on pornography. 'Surely most of that stuff is sent through the mail from abroad, or from London?'

'Not all of it. There's a fair chance it was bought under the counter somewhere. When I did my stint on Vice with West Yorkshire a few years back, I made one or two useful contacts. Now, if we're assuming these lads were at all local, the odds are they're from the city, as there aren't that many killers-for-hire living in rural areas. Too exposed. That means Leeds, Bradford, Manchester, maybe Newcastle or Liverpool at a stretch. Now if the boss thinks this Clegg chap from Leeds was involved, then Leeds is as good a choice as any, agreed?'

Susan nodded. 'Yes. The daughter, Alison, thought the man had a Leeds accent. She could be wrong about that, of course. Not everyone's accurate on voices. I don't reckon I could tell the difference. But it looks like they've found the car used for the job there. Anyway, as I've already told you, West Yorkshire's got some men asking around. Have had for days.'

'Well, you know how I hate sitting idle,' Hatchley said. 'Guess where I've been this lunchtime.'

'The Queen's Arms, sir?'

Hatchley smiled. 'Not far off. We'll make a detective of

you yet, lass. I've been having drinks with an old informer of mine in The Oak, that's what.' He touched the side of his nose. 'Lives in Eastvale now, but he used to live in Leeds. Gone straight. See, I thought I probably remembered a few purveyors of this kind of porn – if they're still around, that is – and it's odds on that some wet-behind-the-ears young pansy DC fresh from university doesn't even know they exist. There aren't as many as you think, you know, at least not selling shaved pussy porn. It *is* something of a specialist taste. Anyway, there's still plenty prefer the friendly old corner shop to the impersonal supermarket, if you get my drift. I'm not talking about sex shops – I imagine they've all been checked already – just regular newsagents that sell a bit of imported stuff from under the counter along with their *Woman's Weekly*s and gardening magazines. Harmless enough. Hardly any reason for our lads to be interested, really. So I asked my old friend.'

'And?'

'Yes. They're still in business, still selling the same kind of stuff to the same old customers. Some of them, anyway. A couple have retired, some have moved on, and one's dead. Heart attack. Not business-related. The point is, I knew these blokes were a bit bent, but I left them alone. In exchange, they'd pass on the odd tip if anyone came hawking really serious stuff, like kiddie porn or snuff films. Live and let live. Now, what I propose is that you and me go to Leeds and ask a few questions of our own.' He looked at his watch. 'Tomorrow, of course. Don't worry, I'll arrange permission from the super and from West Yorkshire CID. Are you game?'

Susan was aware of her jaw dropping. He made sense, all right, and that was the problem. She was about to go on a porn hunt with Sergeant Hatchley, she could feel it in her bones. But it could pay off. If it led to the owner of the wadding, that would be feathers in both their caps. She swallowed.

'It's a hell of a long shot,' she said.

Hatchley shrugged. 'Nothing ventured, nothing gained. What do you say?'

Susan thought for a moment. 'All right,' she said. 'But *you*'ve got to convince Superintendent Gristhorpe.'

'Right, lass,' Hatchley beamed, rubbing his hands together. 'You're on.'

Oh my God, thought Susan, with that sinking feeling. *A porn hunt.* What have I let myself in for?

THREE

By the looks of it, the heat had drawn one or two refugees from the Magistrates Court over to Park Square. Two skinheads, stripped to the waist, dozed on the grass under a tree. One, lying on his back, had tattoos up and down his arms and scars criss-crossing his abdomen, old knife wounds by the look of them; the other, on his stomach, boasted a giant butterfly tattoo between his shoulder-blades.

In Clegg's office, Betty Moorhead was still holding the fort and fighting off her cold.

'Oh, Mr Banks,' she said when he entered the ante-room. 'It's nice to see a friendly face. There's been nothing but police coming and going since you were last here, and nobody will tell me anything.'

Had she forgotten he was a policeman, too? he wondered. Or was it just that he had been the first to arrive and she had somehow latched on to him as a lifeline?

'Some men in suits took most of his papers,' she went on, 'and there's been others asking questions all day. They've got someone keeping an eye on the building as well, in case those two men come back. Then there was that man from Scotland Yard. I don't know what's what. They all had identification cards, of course, but I don't know whether I'm coming or going.'

Banks smiled. 'Don't worry, Betty,' he said. 'I know it sounds complicated, but we're all working together.'

She nodded and pulled a tissue from the box in front of her and blew her nose; it looked red-raw from rubbing. 'Is there any news of Mr Clegg?' she asked.

'Nothing yet. We're still looking.'

'Did you talk to Melissa?'

'Yes.'

'How is she?'

Banks didn't really know what to say. He wasn't used to giving out information, just digging it up, but Betty Moorhead was obviously concerned. 'She didn't seem unduly worried,' he said. 'She's sure he'll turn up.'

Betty's expression brightened. 'Well, then,' she said. 'There you are.'

'Do you mind if I ask a few more questions?'

'Oh, no. I'd be happy to be of help.'

'Good.' Banks perched at the edge of her desk and looked around the room. 'Sitting here,' he said, 'you'd see everyone who called on Mr Clegg, wouldn't you? Everyone who came in and out of his office.'

'Yes.'

'And if people phoned, you'd speak to them first?'

'Well, yes. But I did tell you Mr Clegg has a private line.'

'Did he receive many calls on it?'

'I can't say, really. I heard it ring once in a while, but I was usually too busy to pay attention. I'm certain he didn't give the number out to just anyone.'

'So you didn't unintentionally overhear any of the conversations?'

'I know what you're getting at,' she said, 'and you can stop right there. I'm not that sort of a secretary.'

'What sort?'

'The sort that listens in on her boss's conversations. Besides,' she added with a smile, 'the walls are too thick. These are old houses, solidly built. You can't hear what's being said in Mr Clegg's office with the door shut.'

'Even if two people are having a conversation in there?'

'Even then.'

'Or arguing?'

'Not that it happened often, but you can only hear the raised voices, not what they're saying.'

'Did you ever hear Mr Clegg arguing with Mr Rothwell?'

'I don't remember. I don't think so. I mean if they ever did, it would certainly have been a rarity. Normally they were all cordial and businesslike.'

'Mr Clegg specializes in tax law, doesn't he?'

'Yes.'

'How many clients does he have?'

'That's very hard to say. I mean, there are regular clients, and then people you just do a bit of work for now and then.'

'Roughly? Fifty? A hundred?'

'Closer to a hundred, I'd say.'

'Any new ones?'

'He's been too busy to take on much new work this year.'

'So there's been no new clients in, say, the past three months?'

'Not really, no. He's done a bit of extra work for friends of friends here and there, but nothing major.'

'What I'm getting at,' Banks said, leaning forward, 'is whether there's been anyone new visiting him often or phoning in the past two or three months.'

'Not visiting, no. There's been a few funny phone calls, though.'

'What do you mean, funny?'

'Well, abrupt. I mean, I know I told you people are sometimes rude and brusque, but usually they at least tell you what they want. Since you were here last, I've been thinking, trying to remember, you know, if there was anything odd. My head's so stuffed up I can hardly think straight, but I remembered the phone calls. I told the other policeman, too.'

'That's okay. Tell me. What did this brusque caller say?'

'I don't know if it was the same person each time, and it only happened two or three times. It was about a month ago.'

'Over what time period?'

'What? Oh, just a couple of days.'

'What did he say? I assume it was a *he*?'

'Yes. He'd just say, "Clegg?" And if I said Mr Clegg was out or busy, he'd hang up.'

'I see what you mean. What kind of voice did he have?'

'I couldn't say. That's all I ever heard him say. It just sounded ordinary, but clipped, impatient, in a hurry.'

'And this happened two or three times over a couple of days?'

'Yes.'

'You never heard the voice again?'

'I never had that sort of call again, if that's what you mean.'

'Nobody visited the office who sounded like the man?'

She sneezed, then blew her nose. 'No. But I told you, I don't think I would recognize it.'

'It wasn't anything like one of the men who came around asking questions?'

'I don't know. I don't think so. I'm sorry.'

'That's all right.'

'What's going on?'

'We don't know,' Banks lied. He was testing Gristhorpe's theory about Clegg's involvement in Rothwell's murder, but he didn't want Betty Moorhead to realize he suspected her boss of such a crime. Certainly the odd phone calls *could* have been from someone giving him orders, or from the people he hired to do the job. The timing was about right. 'Do you think Mr Clegg might have given this caller his private number?'

She nodded. 'That's what must have happened. The first two times, Mr Clegg was out or with a client. The third time, I put the caller through, and he never called me again.'

'And you're sure you never put a face to the voice?'

'No.'

Banks stood up and walked around the small room. Well-tended potted plants stood on the shelf by the small window at the back that looked out on to narrow Park Cross Street. Clegg had obviously been careful where Betty Moorhead was concerned. If he had been mixed up with hired killers and Caribbean dictators, he had been careful to keep them at arm's length. He turned back to Betty. 'Is there anything else you can tell me about Mr Clegg?'

'I don't know what you mean.'

'How would you describe him as a person?'

'Well, I wouldn't know.'

'You never socialized?'

She blushed. 'Certainly not.'

'Had he been depressed lately?'

'No.'

'Did Mr Clegg have many women calling on him?'

'Not as far as I know. What are you suggesting?'

'Did you ever see or hear mention of a woman called Pamela Jeffreys? An Asian woman.'

She looked puzzled. 'No. She wasn't a client.'

'Did he have a girlfriend?'

'I wouldn't know. He kept his private life private.'

Banks decided to give up. Melissa Clegg might know a bit more about her husband's conquests, or Ken Blackstone's men would question his colleagues and perhaps come up with something. It was after five and he was tired of running around in circles. Betty Moorhead clearly didn't know anything else, or if she did she didn't realize its importance. Getting at information like that was like target practice in the dark.

Why not just accept Gristhorpe's theory that Clegg had arranged for Rothwell to be killed, and that they hadn't a hope in hell of finding either Clegg or the killers? And what could they do to Martin Churchill, if indeed he was behind it all? Banks didn't like the feeling of impotence this case was beginning to engender.

On the walk back to his hotel, Banks picked up a half-bottle of Bell's. It would be cheaper than using the minibar in his room. As he threaded his way among the office workers leaving the British Telecom Building for their bus stops on Wellington Street, Banks wished he could just go home and forget about the whole Clegg-Rothwell-Calvert mess.

After leaving Blackstone at the car park, he had phoned Pamela Jeffreys at home, half hoping she might be free for a drink that evening, but he had only got her answering machine. She was probably playing with the orchestra or something. He had left a message anyway, telling her which hotel he was staying at, and now he was feeling guilty. He remembered Blackstone's warning about hotels.

On the surface, he wanted to apologize for their misunderstanding yesterday, but if truth be told, he had let himself get a bit too carried away with his fantasies. Would he do anything if he had the chance? If she agreed to come back to his hotel room for a nightcap, would he try to seduce her? Would he make love to her if she were willing? He didn't know.

He remembered his attraction to Jenny Fuller, a professor of psychology who occasionally helped with cases, and wondered what his life would be like now if he had given in to his desires then. Would he have told Sandra? Would they still be together? Would he and Jenny still be friends? No answer came.

Rather glumly, he recalled the bit at the beginning of the Trollope biography he was reading, where Trollope considers the dreary sermons persuading people to turn their backs on worldly pleasure in the hope of heaven to come and asks, if such is really the case, then 'Why are women so lovely?' That set him thinking again about Pamela's shapely, golden body, her bright personality and her passion for music. Well, at least he had a curry with Ken Blackstone to look forward to, and time for a shower and a rest before that. He thought he might even check out the hotel's Health and Leisure Club, maybe have a swim, take a sauna or a whirlpool.

There were no messages. Banks went straight up to his room, took off his shoes and flopped on the bed. He phoned Sandra, who wasn't in, then called the Eastvale station again and spoke to Susan Gay. Nothing new, except that she sounded depressed.

•

After a brisk shower, much better than the tepid dribble at home, he poured himself a small Scotch and put the television on while he dried off and dressed. He caught the end of the international news and heard that the St Corona riots had been put down swiftly and brutally by Martin Churchill's forces. And Burgess wanted to give the man a retirement villa in Cornwall?

After that, he was only half paying attention to the local news, but at one point, he saw a house he recognized and heard the reporter say, '. . . when she failed to report for rehearsals today. Police are still at the scene and so far have refused to comment . . .'

It was Pamela Jeffreys's house, and outside it stood two patrol cars and an ambulance. Stunned, Banks sat on the side of the bed and tossed back his Scotch, then he got his jacket out of the cupboard and left the room so fast he forgot to turn off the television.

10

ONE

It was hard to imagine that anything terrible could happen on such a fine spring evening, but the activity around the little terrace house in Armley indicated that evil made no allowances for the weather.

Three police cars were parked at angles in front of the house. Beyond the line of white tape, reporters badgered the PCs on guard duty, one of whom jotted down Banks's name and rank before he let him through. Neighbours stood on their doorsteps or by privet hedges and gazed in silence, arms folded, faces grim, and the people working their allotments stopped to watch the spectacle. A small crowd also stood gawping from the steps of the Sikh Temple down the street.

Banks stood on the threshold of the living room. Whatever had happened here, it had been extremely violent: the glass coffee table had been smashed in two; the three-piece suite had been slashed and the stuffing ripped out; books lay torn all over the carpet, pages reduced to confetti; the glass front of the cocktail cabinet was shattered and the crystal-ware itself lay in bright shards; the music stand lay on the floor with the splintered pieces and broken bow of Pamela's viola beside it; even the print of Ganesh over the fireplace had been taken from its frame and torn up. Worst of all, though, was the broad dark stain on the cream carpet. Blood.

One of the officers cracked a racist joke about Ganesh and another laughed. The elephant god was supposed to be the god of good beginnings, Banks remembered. Upstairs, someone was whistling 'Lara's Theme' from *Doctor Zhivago*.

'Who the hell are you?'

Banks turned to face the plain-clothes man coming out of the wreckage of the kitchen.

'Press?' he went on before Banks had time to answer. 'You're not allowed in. You ought to bloody well know that. Bugger off.' He grabbed Banks's arm and steered him towards the door. 'What does that fucking useless PC think he's up to, letting you in? I'll have his bloody balls for Christmas tree decorations.'

'Hang on.' Banks finally managed to get a word in and jerk his arm free of the man's grasp. He showed his card. The man relaxed.

'Oh. Sorry, sir,' he said. 'Detective Sergeant Waltham. I wasn't to know.' Then he frowned. 'What's North Yorkshire want with this one, if you don't mind my asking?'

He was in his early thirties, perhaps a few pounds overweight, about three inches taller than Banks, with curly ginger hair. He had a prominent chin, a ruddy complexion and curious catlike green eyes. He wore a dark brown suit, white shirt and plain green tie. Behind him stood a scruffy-looking youth in a leather jacket. Probably his DC, Banks guessed.

'First things first,' said Banks. 'What happened to the woman who lives here?'

'Pamela Jeffreys. Know her?'

'What happened to her? Is she still alive?'

'Oh, aye, sir. Just. Someone worked her over a treat.

Broken ribs, broken nose, broken fingers. Multiple lacerations, contusions. In fact, multiple just about everything. And it looks as if she broke her leg when she fell. She was in a coma when we found her. First officer on the scene thought she was dead.'

Banks felt a wave of fear and anger surge through his stomach, bringing the bile to his throat. 'When did it happen?' he asked.

'We're not sure, sir. There's a clock upstairs was smashed at twenty past nine, but that doesn't necessarily mean anything. A bit too Agatha Christie, if you ask me. Doc thinks last night, but we're still interviewing the neighbours.'

'So you think she lay there for nearly twenty-four hours?'

'Could be, sir. The doctor said she'd have bled to death if she hadn't been a good clotter.'

Banks swallowed. 'Raped?'

Waltham shook his head. 'Doc says no signs of sexual assault. When we found her she was fully clothed, no signs of interference. Some consolation, eh?'

'Who found her?'

'One of her musician friends got worried when she didn't show up for rehearsals this morning. Some sort of string quartet or something. Apparently she'd been a bit upset lately. He said she was usually reliable and had never missed a day before. He phoned the house several times during the day and only got her answering machine. After work he drove by and knocked. Still no answer. Then he had a butcher's through the window. After that, he phoned the local police. He's in the clear.'

Banks said nothing. DS Waltham leaned against the banister. The scruffy DC squeezed by them and went upstairs. In the front room, someone laughed out loud again.

Waltham coughed behind his hand. 'Er, look, sir, is there something we should know? There'll have to be questions, of course, but we can be as discreet as anyone if we have to be. What with you showing up here and . . .'

'And what, Sergeant?'

'Well, I recognize your voice from her answering machine. It *was* you, wasn't it?'

Banks sighed. 'Yes, yes it was. But no, there's nothing you need to be discreet about. There is probably a lot you should know. Shit.' He looked at his watch. Almost seven. 'Look, Sergeant, I'd clean forgot I'm supposed to be meeting DI Blackstone for dinner.'

'*Our* DI Blackstone, sir?'

'Yes. Know him?'

'Yes, sir.'

'Do you think you can get one of the PCs to page him or track him down? It's the Shabab on Eastgate.'

Waltham smiled. 'I know it. Very popular with the lads at Millgarth. I'll see to it, sir.'

He went to the door and spoke to one of the uniformed constables, then came back. 'He's on his way. Look, sir, PC O'Brien there just told me there's an old geezer across the street thinks he might have seen something. Want to come over?'

'Yes. Very much.' Banks followed him down the path and through the small crowd. One or two reporters shouted for comments, but Waltham just waved them aside. PC O'Brien stood by the low, dark stone wall that ran by the allotments, talking to a painfully thin old man wearing a grubby, collarless shirt. Behind them, other allotment workers stood in a semicircle, watching, some of them leaning on shovels or rakes. Very Yorkshire Gothic, Banks thought.

'Mr Judd, sir,' O'Brien said, introducing Waltham, who, in turn, introduced Banks. 'He was working his allotment last night just before dark.' Waltham nodded and O'Brien walked off. 'Keep those bloody reporters at bay, will you, please, O'Brien?' Waltham called after him.

Banks sat on the wall and took out his cigarettes. He offered them around. Waltham declined, but Mr Judd accepted one. 'Might as well, lad,' he croaked, tapping his chest. 'Too late to worry about my health now.'

He did look ill, Banks thought. Sallow flesh hung off the bones of his face above his scrawny neck with its turkey-flaps and puckered skin, like a surgery scar, around his Adam's apple. The whites of his eyes had a yellow cast, but the dark blue pupils glinted with intelligence. Mr Judd, Banks decided, was a man whose observations he could trust. He sat by and let Waltham do the questioning.

'What time were you out here?' Waltham asked.

'From seven o'clock till about half past nine,' said Judd. 'This time of year I always come out of an evening after tea for a bit of peace, weather permitting. The wife likes to watch telly, but I've no patience with it, myself. Nowt but daft buggers acting like daft buggers.' He took a deep draw on the cigarette. Banks noticed him flinch with pain.

'Were you the only one working here?' Waltham asked.

'Aye. T'others had all gone home by then.'

'Can you tell us what you saw?'

'Aye, well it must have been close to knocking-off time. It were getting dark, I remember that. And this car pulled up outside Miss Jeffreys's house. Dark and shiny, it were. Black.'

'Do you know what make?'

DRY BONES THAT DREAM

'No, sorry, lad. I wouldn't know a Mini from an Aston Martin these days, to tell you the truth, especially since we've been getting all these foreign cars. It weren't a big one, though.'

Waltham smiled. 'Okay. Go on.'

'Well, two men gets out and walks up the path.'

'What did they look like?'

'Hard to say, really. They were both wearing suits. And one of them was a darkie, but that's nowt to write home about these days, is it?'

'One of the men was black?'

'Aye.'

'What happened next?'

Judd went through a minor coughing fit and spat a ball of red-green phlegm on the earth beside him. 'I packed up and went home. The wife needs a bit of help getting up the apples and pears to bed these days. She can't walk as well as she used to.'

'Did you see Miss Jeffreys open the door and let the men in?'

'I can't say I was watching that closely. One minute they were on the doorstep, next they were gone. But the car was still there.'

'Did you hear anything?'

'No. Too far away.' He shrugged. 'I thought nothing of it. Insurance men, most like. That's what they looked like. Or maybe those religious folks, Jehovah's Witnesses.'

'So you didn't see them leave?'

'No. I'd gone home by then.'

'Where do you live?'

Judd pointed across the street. 'Over there. Number fourteen.' It was five houses down from Pamela Jeffreys's. 'Been there forty years or more, now. A right dump it was

201

when we first moved in. Damp walls, no indoor toilets, no bathroom. Had it done up over the years, though, bit by bit.'

Waltham paused and looked at Banks, who indicated he would like to ask one or two questions. Waltham, Banks noted, had been a patient interviewer, not pushy, rude and condescending towards the old, like some. Maybe it was because he had a DCI watching over his shoulder. And maybe that was being uncharitable.

'Did you know Miss Jeffreys at all?' Banks asked.

Judd shook his head. 'Can't say as I did.'

'But you knew her to say hello to?'

'Oh, aye. She was a right nice lass, if you ask me. And a bonny one, too.' He winked. 'Always said hello if she passed me in the street. Always carrying that violin case. I used to ask her if she were in t'mafia and had a machine-gun in it, just joking, like.'

'But you never stopped and chatted?'

'Not apart from that and the odd comment about the weather. What would an old codger like me have to say to a young lass like her? Besides, people round here tend to keep themselves to themselves these days.' He coughed and spat again. 'It didn't used to be that way, tha knows. When Eunice and I first came here there used to be a community. We'd have bloody great big bonfires out in the street on Guy Fawkes night – it were still just cobbles, then, none of this Tarmac – and everyone came out. Eunice would make parkin and treacle-toffee. We'd wrap taties in foil and put 'em in t'fire to bake. But it's all changed. People died, moved away. See that there Sikh Temple?' He pointed down the street. 'It used to be a Congregationalist Chapel. Everyone went there on a Sunday morning. They had Monday whist drives, too, and a youth club, Boys'

Brigade and Girl Guides for the young uns. Pantos at Christmas.

'Oh, aye, it's all changed. People coming and going. We've got indoor toilets now, but nobody talks to anyone. Not that I've owt against Pakis, like. As I said, she was a nice lass. I saw them taking her out on that stretcher an hour or so back.' He shook his head slowly. 'Nowadays you keep your door locked tight. Will she be all right?'

'We don't know,' Banks said. 'We're keeping our fingers crossed. Did she have many visitors?'

'I didn't keep a lookout. I suppose you mean boy-friends?'

'Anyone. Male or female.'

'I never saw any women call, not by themselves. Her mum and dad came now and then. At least, I assumed it was her mum and dad. And there was one bloke used to visit quite regularly a few months back. Used to park outside our house sometimes. And don't ask me what kind of car he drove. I can't even remember the colour. But he stopped coming. Hasn't been anyone since, not that I've noticed.'

'What did this man look like?'

'Ordinary really. Fair hair, glasses, a bit taller than thee.'

Keith Rothwell – or Robert Calvert, Banks thought. 'Anyone else?'

Judd shook his head then smiled. 'Only you and that young woman, t'other day.'

Banks felt Waltham turn and stare at him. If Judd had seen Banks and Susan visit Pamela Jeffreys on Saturday, then he obviously didn't miss much – morning, afternoon or evening. Banks thanked him.

'We'll get someone to take a statement soon, Mr Judd,' said Waltham.

'All right, son,' said the old man, turning back to his allotment. 'I won't be going anywhere except my final resting place, and that'll be a few months off, God willing. I only wish I could have been more help.'

'You did fine,' said Banks.

'What the bloody hell was all that about, sir?' Waltham asked as they walked away. 'You didn't tell me you'd been here before.'

Banks noticed Ken Blackstone getting out of a dark blue Peugeot opposite the Sikh Temple. 'Didn't have time,' he said to Waltham, moving away. 'Later, Sergeant. I'll explain it all later.'

TWO

Banks and Blackstone sat in an Indian restaurant near Woodhouse Moor, a short drive across the Aire valley from Pamela Jeffreys's house, drinking lager and nibbling at pakoras and onion bhajis as they waited for their main courses. Being close to the university, the place was full of students. The aroma was tantalizing – cumin, coriander, cloves, cinnamon, mingled with other spices Banks couldn't put a name to. 'Not exactly the Shabab,' Blackstone had said, 'but not bad.' A Yorkshire compliment.

In the brief time they had been there, Banks had explained as succinctly as he could what the hell was going on – at least to the extent that he understood it himself.

'So why do you think they beat up the girl?' Blackstone asked.

'They must have thought she knew where Daniel Clegg was, or that she was hiding something for him. They ripped her place up pretty thoroughly.'

'And you think they're working for Martin Churchill?'

'Burgess thinks so. It's possible.'

'Do you think it was the same two who visited Clegg's secretary and his ex-wife?'

'Yes. I'm certain of it.'

'But they didn't beat up either of them, or search their places. Why not?'

'I don't know. Maybe they were getting desperate by the time they got to Pamela. Let's face it, they'd found out nothing so far. They must have been frustrated. They felt they'd done enough pussyfooting around and it was time for business. Either that or they phoned their boss and he told them to push harder. They also probably thought she was lying or holding out on them for some reason, maybe something in her manner. I don't know. Perhaps they're just racists.'

Banks shook his head, feeling a sudden ache and rage. He couldn't seem to banish the image of Pamela Jeffreys at the hands of her torturers: her terror, her agony, the smashed viola. And would her broken fingers ever heal enough for her to play again? But he didn't know Blackstone well enough to talk openly about his feelings. 'They'd been polite but pushy earlier,' he said. 'Maybe they just ran out of patience.'

The main course arrived: a plate of steaming chapatis, chicken bhuna and goat vindaloo, along with a selection of chutneys and raita. They shared out the dishes and started to eat, using the chapatis to shovel mouthfuls of food and mop up the sauce. Blackstone ordered a couple more lagers and a jug of ice-water.

'There is another explanation,' Blackstone said between mouthfuls.

'What?'

'That she *did* know something. That she was involved in the double-cross, or whatever it was. From the quick look I got at her house, I'd agree there's no doubt they were looking for something. DS Waltham suggested the same thing.'

'Don't think I haven't considered it,' Banks said, carefully piling a heap of the hot vindaloo on a scrap of chapati. 'But I'm sure she didn't even know Clegg.'

'That's only what she told you, remember.'

'Nobody else contradicted her, Ken. Not Melissa Clegg, not the secretary, not even Mr Judd.'

'Oh, come on, Alan. The old man can't have seen everything. Nor could the secretary or the ex-wife have *known* everything. Maybe Clegg never visited her at her home. They could have had some clandestine relationship, met in secret.'

'Why the need for secrecy? Neither of them was married.'

'Perhaps because they were involved in some funny business – not necessarily of a sexual nature – and it wouldn't be good to be seen together. Maybe she was involved in whatever scam Clegg and Rothwell had going?'

Banks shook his head. 'Clegg was a lawyer, Rothwell a financial whizz-kid and Pamela Jeffreys is a classical musician. It just doesn't fit.'

'They *could* have had business interests in common, though.'

'True. Anything's possible. But remember, Pamela Jeffreys knew *Robert Calvert*. She told me they met by chance in a pub. She'd never heard of Keith Rothwell until after his murder, when his photo appeared in the papers. She had no reason to lie. She was even putting herself in an awkward situation by calling us. She needn't have done so. We hadn't heard of Robert Calvert and might never have done if it weren't for her. Usually people want to stay as far away from a murder investigation as they can get. You know that, Ken. Until we find out differently, we have to assume that Calvert was a persona invented by Rothwell, with Clegg's help, solely for pleasure.'

Blackstone swallowed a mouthful of bhuna. 'I sometimes think I could do with one of those myself,' he said.

Banks laughed. 'Calvert helped Rothwell express another side of his nature, a side he couldn't indulge at home. Or perhaps it helped him be the way he used to be, relive something he'd lost. As Calvert, he'd have fun gambling and womanizing, and probably subsidizing himself with his illicit earnings from the money-laundering. And Pamela Jeffreys wasn't his only conquest, you know. There were no doubt others before her, and she was convinced that he'd met someone else, someone he'd really fallen for.'

'That would upset the apple-cart, wouldn't it?' said Blackstone.

Banks stopped chewing for a moment.

'Alan?' Blackstone said. 'Alan, are you all right? I know the curry's hot, but . . .'

'What? Oh, yes. It was just something you said, that's all. I'm surprised I never thought of it before.'

'What?'

'If *Calvert* really did do it, you know, fall in love, the real thing, with all the bells and whistles, then what would happen to Rothwell?'

'I don't get you. It's the same person, isn't it?'

'Yes and no. What I mean is, how could he go on living his Rothwell life, the one we assumed was his *real* life, at Arkbeck Farm with Mary, Alison and Tom? Forgive me, I'm just thinking out loud, going nowhere. It doesn't matter.'

'I do see what you mean,' said Blackstone. 'It would bugger up everything, wouldn't it?'

'Hmm.' Banks finished his meal and washed away some of the spicy heat with a swig of watery lager. His lips still burned, though, and he felt prickles of sweat on his scalp. The signs of a good curry.

'Did the suspects in the Jeffreys beating know about Rothwell?' Blackstone asked.

Banks shook his head. 'Don't know. They haven't been seen locally, and they certainly don't match the daughter's description of his killers.'

'How old is she?'

'Alison? Fifteen.'

'She didn't see their faces. Could she be wrong?'

'It's possible, but not that wrong, I don't think. Nothing matches.'

'Just a thought. I mean, if Rothwell and Clegg were in the laundering business together, and whoever they were working for sent a couple of goons to find Clegg and whatever money he's made off with, you'd think they'd start with Rothwell's family, wouldn't you?'

'Perhaps. But we've been keeping too close a watch. They wouldn't dare show up within twenty miles of Arkbeck Farm.'

'And another thing: if they killed Rothwell, why did they use different people to chase down Clegg? It seems a bit excessive, doesn't it?'

'Again,' said Banks, 'I can only guess. I think some of what's been happening took them by surprise. It's possible that they asked Clegg to get rid of Rothwell and he hired his own men. As you know, we're looking into what connections he might have had with criminal types.'

Blackstone nodded. 'I see,' he said. 'Then Clegg became a problem and they had to send their own men?'

'Something like that.'

'Makes sense. Clegg was a bit of a ladies' man, you know, according to my DC who talked to his colleagues,' Blackstone said.

'Yes. His estranged wife, Melissa, suggested as much. Did he have a girlfriend?'

'Yes. Apparently nothing serious since he split up with his wife. Prefers to play the field. Recently he's been seeing a receptionist from Norwich Insurance. Name of Marci Lapwing, if you can believe that. Aspiring actress. DC Gaitskill had a word with her this morning. Says she's a bit of a bimbo with obvious attractions. But he's a bit of an arsehole himself, is Gaitskill, so I'd take it with a pinch of salt. Anyway, they saw each other the Saturday before Clegg's disappearance. They went for dinner, then to a nightclub in Harehills. She spent the night with him and he took her home – that's Seacroft – after a pub lunch out at the Red Lion in Burnsall on Sunday afternoon. She hasn't seen or heard from him since.'

'Is she telling the truth?'

'Gaitskill says so. I'd trust him on that.'

'Okay. Thanks, Ken.'

'Clegg had a reserved parking space at the back of the Court Centre. According to what we could find out, he used to eat at a little trattoria on The Headrow after work on Thursdays. The waiters there remember him, all right. Nothing odd about his behaviour. He left about six-thirty or a quarter to seven last Thursday, heading west, towards where his car was parked, and that's the last sighting we have.'

'The car?'

'Red Jag. Gone. We've put it out over the PNC along with this.' Blackstone took a photograph from his briefcase and slid it over the tablecloth. It showed the head and shoulders of a man in his early forties, with determined blue eyes, a slightly crooked nose, fair hair and a mouth that had a cruel twist to its left side.

'Clegg?'

Blackstone nodded and put the photograph back in his briefcase. 'We've also been through Clegg's house in Chapel Allerton. Nothing. Whatever he was up to, he kept it at the office.'

'Anything on Hamilton and the other car?'

'The boffins are still working on the car. I pulled Hamilton's record myself and we had another chat with him at the station this afternoon.' He shook his head. 'I can't see it, Alan. The man's as thick as two short planks. I don't think he's even *heard* of St Corona, and he's strictly small fry on the drugs scene. By the time he gets his stuff to sell, it's been stepped on by just about every dealer in the city.'

'It was just a thought. Thanks for giving it a try.'

'No problem. We'll have another shot in a day or two, just in case. And we'll keep a discreet eye on him. Look, back to what I was saying before. How do you think the goons knew about Pamela Jeffreys if she wasn't involved?'

Banks felt the anger flare up inside him again, but he held it in check. 'That's all too easy,' he said. 'Remember, they were also following me around yesterday. I think they started at Clegg's office first thing yesterday morning and one, or both of them, stayed on my tail until I spotted them outside Calvert's flat that evening. They didn't know who the hell I was, and the only other person I met that they hadn't talked to already was Pamela Jeffreys. They must have thought we were in it together. I met her near the hall where she was rehearsing, and either one of them hung around to follow her home, or they found out some other way who she was and where she lived.

'She must have looked like their best lead so far. They thought she had some connection with Clegg and that she knew where he was or was holding something for him. Clegg has obviously got something they want. Most likely money. If he was laundering for their boss, then it looks like he might have skipped with a bundle. Either that or he's got some sort of evidence for blackmail – books, bank account records. And that's probably what they were looking for when they tore her place apart. Back to square one. The goons worked Pamela over because they thought she knew something, or had something of theirs. She didn't. And I blame myself. I should have bloody well known I was putting her at risk.'

'Come off it, Alan. How could you know?'

Banks shrugged and tapped out a cigarette. He was the only smoker in the entire restaurant and had to ask the waiter specially for an ashtray. It was getting like that these days, he noted glumly. He'd have to stop sometime soon; he knew he was only postponing the inevitable. He had thought about getting a nicotine patch, then quickly dismissed the idea. It was the feel of the cigarette between his fingers he wanted, the sharp intake of tobacco smoke into the lungs, not some slow oozing of poison through his skin into his blood. Pity about the health problems.

He felt rather like St Augustine must have felt when he wrote in his *Confessions*: 'Give me chastity and continency – but not yet!'

'You know what really pisses me off?' Banks said after he had lit the cigarette. 'Dirty Dick Burgess was following me around that day, too, and it wouldn't surprise me at all if he'd seen them outside Melissa Clegg's shop.'

'How would he know who they are?'

'Oh, I think he knows them, all right.'

'Even so, what could he have done? They hadn't broken any laws.'

Banks shrugged. 'I suppose not. It's too bloody late now, anyway,' he said. 'Let's just hope they don't go back to see Betty Moorhead and Melissa Clegg.'

'Don't worry. Charlie Waltham will have them both covered by now. He's a good bloke, Alan. And he'll have descriptions of Mutt and Jeff out, too. They won't get far.'

'I hope not,' said Banks. 'I bloody hope not. I'd like a few minutes alone with them in a quiet cell.'

THREE

Back at the hotel, Banks felt caged. Anger burned inside him like the hot Indian spices, but it would take more than Rennies to quell it. What a bloody fool he'd been to do nothing when he realized he had been followed. He had practically signed Pamela Jeffreys's death warrant, and it was through no virtue of his that she had survived her ordeal. So far.

He poured himself a shot of Bell's and turned to the television. Nothing but a nature programme, a silly comedy, an interview with a has-been politician and an old Dirty Harry movie. He watched Clint Eastwood for a while. He had never much enjoyed cop films or cop programmes on television, but watching right here and now, he could identify with Dirty Harry tracking down the villains and dealing with them in his own way. He had meant what he said to Blackstone. A few minutes alone with Pamela Jeffreys's attackers and they would know what police brutality was all about.

But he hated himself when he felt that way. Luckily, it was rare. After all, policemen are only human, he reminded himself. They have their loyalties, their lusts, their prejudices, their agonies, their tempers. The problem was that they have to keep these emotions in check to do their jobs properly.

'You go home and puke in your own time if you want to get anywhere in this job, lad,' one of his early mentors had told him at a grisly crime scene. 'You don't do it all over the corpse. And you go home and punch holes in your own wall, not in the child molester's face.'

Unable to concentrate, even on Dirty Harry, he turned off the television. He couldn't stand up, couldn't sit down, didn't know what he wanted to do. And all the time, the anger and pain churned inside him, and he couldn't find a way to get them out.

He picked up the phone and dialled the code for Eastvale, then put it down before he started dialling his own number. He wanted to talk to Sandra, but he didn't think he could explain his feelings to her right now, especially the way they'd been drifting apart of late. God knew, under normal circumstances she was an understanding wife, but this would be pushing it a bit far: a woman he had lusted after, fantasized about, gets beaten within a hair's breadth of her life, and he's whipping himself over it. No, he couldn't explain that to Sandra.

And it wasn't just a fantasy. Had things turned out differently, he would have phoned Pamela Jeffreys again and would probably be having dinner or drinks with her right now, plucking up the courage to ask her up to his hotel room, Bell's at the ready. Well, he would never know the outcome now; his virtue hadn't even been put to the test. Hadn't St Augustine said something about that, too, or was that someone else?

He phoned the hospital, and after a bit of officious rank-pulling, actually got a doctor on the line. Yes, Ms Jeffreys was stable but still in intensive care . . . no, she was still unconscious . . . there was no way of telling when or if she would come round . . . no idea yet if there was any permanent damage. He didn't feel any better when he hung up.

It was just after nine-thirty. He knocked back the rest of the glass of Scotch, grabbed his sports jacket and went out. Maybe a walk would help, or the anonymous comfort of a crowded pub, not that he expected Leeds city centre on a Tuesday evening to be the West End.

He walked along Wellington Street past the National Express coach station and the tall Royal Mail Building to City Square, which was deserted except for the silent nymphs, who stood bearing their torches around the central statue of the Black Prince on his horse. From somewhere along Boar Lane, a drunk shouted in the night; a bottle smashed and a woman laughed loudly.

Banks crossed City Square. He walked fast, trying to burn off some of his rage, and soon found himself in the empty Bond Street Centre with only his reflection in the shop windows he passed.

His memories of Leeds's city centre were vague, but he was sure that somewhere among the jungle of refurbished Victorian arcades and modern shopping centres there were a number of pubs down the dingy back alleys that riddled the heart of the old city centre.

And he was right.

The first one he found was an old brass, mirrors and dark wood Tetley's house with a fair-sized crowd and a jukebox at tolerable volume. He ordered a pint and stood sideways at the bar, just watching people chat and laugh. It was mostly a young crowd. Only kids seemed to venture into the city centres at night these days. Perhaps that was why their parents and grandparents stayed away. The pubs in Armley and Bramley, in Headingley and Kirkstall, would be full of locals of all age groups mixed together.

As he leaned against the bar, drinking and smoking, nobody paid him any attention. Banks had always been pleased that he didn't stand out as an obvious policeman. There'd be no mistaking Hatchley or Ken Blackstone no matter how 'off duty' they were, but Banks could fit in almost anywhere without attracting too much attention. Over the years, he had found it a useful quality. It wasn't only that he didn't look like a copper, whatever that meant, but for some reason his presence didn't set off the usual warning bells. At the same time, he didn't like to sit or stand with his back to the door, and he didn't miss much.

He finished his pint quickly and ordered another one, lighting up again. He was smoking too much, he realized, and he would feel it in the morning. But that was the morning. In the meantime, it gave him something to do with his hands, which, left to their own devices, curled and hardened into fists.

His second pint went down easily, too. The ebb and flow of conversation washed over him. Loudest was a group of two middle-aged couples sitting behind the engraved smoked glass and dark wood at the side of the door. The only people over twenty-five, apart from Banks and the bar staff, they had all had a bit too much to drink. The men were on pints of bitter, and the women on oddly coloured concoctions with umbrellas sticking out of them and bits of fruit floating around. By the sound of things, they were celebrating the engagement of one couple's daughter, who wasn't present, and this brought forth all the old, blue jokes Banks had ever heard in his life.

'There's these three women,' said one of the men. 'The prostitute, the nymphomaniac and the wife. After sex, the prostitute says, "That's it, then," all businesslike. The nympho says, "That's *it*?" And the wife says, "Beige. I think the ceiling should be beige."'

They howled with laughter. One of the women, a rather blowsy peroxide blonde, like a late-period Diana Dors, with too much make-up and unfocused eyes, looked over and winked at Banks. He winked back and she nudged her friend. They both started to laugh. A man Banks assumed to be her husband popped his head around the divide and said, 'Tha's welcome to her, lad, but I'll warn thee, she'll have thee worn out in a week. Bloody insatiable, she is.' She hit him playfully and they all laughed so much they had tears in their eyes. Banks laughed with them, then turned away. The barmaid raised her eyebrows and drew a finger across her throat. Banks drank up and moved on.

Outside, he noticed that the evening had turned a little cooler and dark clouds were fast covering the stars. There was an electric edge to the air that presaged a storm. As if he didn't feel tense and wound up enough already without the bloody weather conspiring against him, too.

The next pub, down another alley off Briggate, was busier. Groups of young people stood about outside, leaning against the wall or sitting on the wooden benches. The place danced with long shadows like something out of an old Orson Welles film. Banks took his pint out into the narrow, whitewashed alley and rested it on a ledge at elbow level, like a bar.

He thought of his last meeting with Pamela Jeffreys. She had run off in tears and he had stood there like an idiot in the park watching his ice-cream melt. He had wanted to apologize for treating her feelings so shoddily, but at the same time another part of him, the professional side, knew he had had to ask, and knew an apology would never be completely genuine. Still, he was only human; susceptible to beauty, he found her attractive, and he liked her warm, open personality, her enthusiasm for life and her sense of humour. Her connection with music also excited him. How much of that would she have left when she came out of hospital? If she came out.

Now, slurping his ale in a back alley in Leeds, he considered again what Blackstone had suggested about her involvement in the affair, but he didn't think Pamela Jeffreys was that good an actress. She had liked Calvert; they had had simple fun together, with no demands, no strings attached, no deep commitment. And what was wrong with that? She may have felt hurt when he found someone else – after all, nobody likes rejection – but she had liked him enough to swallow her pride and remain friends. She was young; she had energy enough to deal with a few hard knocks. If she had been jealous enough for murder, she would have killed Robert Calvert, probably in his Leeds flat, and if she had been involved in the laundering operation with Rothwell and Clegg, she wouldn't have phoned the Eastvale station and told them about Calvert.

It was close to eleven; most of the people had gone home. Banks ordered one more for the road, as he would be walking beside it, not driving on it. He was glad he had taken a little time out. The drink had helped douse his anger, or at least dampen it for a while. He was also rational enough to know that tomorrow he would be the professional again and nobody would ever know about his complex, knotted feelings of lust and guilt for Pamela Jeffreys.

He drained his glass, put his cigarettes back in his jacket pocket and set off down the alley. It was long and narrow, rough whitewashed stone on both sides, and lit only by a single high bulb behind wire mesh. When he was a couple of yards from the end, two men walked in from the street and blocked the exit. One of them asked Banks for a light.

Contrary to what one sees on television, detectives rarely find themselves in situations where immediate physical violence is threatened. Banks couldn't remember the last time he had been in a fight, but he didn't stop to try to remember. A number of thoughts flashed through his mind at once, but so quickly that an observer would not have seen him hesitate for a second.

First, he knew that they underestimated him; he was neither as drunk nor as unfit as they probably believed. Secondly, he had learned an important lesson from school-yard fights: you go in first, fast, dirty and hard. Real violence doesn't take place in slow motion, like a Sam Peckinpah film; it's usually over before anyone realizes it has begun.

Before they could make their move, Banks took a step closer, pretended to fumble for matches, then grabbed the nearest one by his shirt-front and nutted him hard on the bridge of the nose. The man put his hands over his face and went down on his knees groaning as blood dripped down his shirt-front.

The other hesitated a moment to glance down at his

friend. Mistake. Banks grabbed him by the arm, whirled him around and slammed him into the wall. Before the man could get his breath back, Banks punched him in the stomach, and as he bent forward in pain, brought his knee up into the man's face. He felt cheekbone or teeth smash against his kneecap. The man fell, putting his hands to his mouth to stem the flow of blood and vomit.

His mate had clambered to his feet by now and he threw himself at Banks, knocking him hard into the wall and banging the side of his head against the rough stone. He got in a couple of close body punches, but before he could gain any further advantage, Banks pushed him back far enough to start throwing quick jabs at his already broken nose. In the sickly light of the alley, Banks could see blood smeared over his attacker's face, almost closing one eye and dripping down his chin. The man backed off and slumped against the wall.

By this time, the other was back wobbling on his feet, and Banks went for him. He aimed one sharp blow to the head after the other, splitting an eyebrow, a lip, jarring a tooth loose. The other stumbled away towards the exit. There was no fight left in either of them, but Banks couldn't stop. He kept slugging away at the man in front of him, feeling the anger in him explode and pour out. When the man tried to protect his face with his hands, Banks pummelled his exposed stomach and ribs.

The man backed away, begging Banks to stop hitting him. His friend, swaying at the alley's exit now, yelled, 'Come on, Kev, run for it! He's a fucking maniac! He'll fucking kill us both!' And they both staggered off towards Commercial Street.

Banks watched them go. There was no one else around, thank God. The whole debacle couldn't have taken more than a couple of minutes. When they were out of sight, Banks fell back against the whitewashed wall, shaking, sweating, panting. He took several deep breaths, smoothed his clothes and headed back to the hotel.

11

ONE

The storm broke in the middle of the night. Banks lay in the dark in his strange hotel bed tossing and turning as lightning flashed and thunder first rumbled in the distance then cracked so loudly overhead that the windows rattled.

Once unbound, the shape of his rage was fluid; it could be as easily warped and twisted into fanciful images by sleep as it had been channelled into violence earlier. He kept waking from one nightmare and drifting back into another. Rain lashed against the windows, and in the background something hissed constantly, the way something always hisses in hotel rooms.

In the worst nightmare, the one he remembered the most clearly, he was talking on the telephone to a woman who had dialled his number by mistake. She sounded disoriented, and the longer she spoke the longer the spaces stretched between her words. Finally, silence took over completely. Banks called hello a few times, then hung up. As soon as he had done so, he was stricken by panic. The woman was committing suicide. He knew it. She had taken an overdose of pills and fallen into a coma while she was still on the line. He didn't know her name or her telephone number. If he had kept the line open and not hung up, he would have been able to trace her and save her life.

He awoke feeling guilty and depressed. And it wasn't only his soul that hurt. His head pounded from too much whisky and from the 'Glasgow handshake' he had given one of his attackers, his chest felt tight from smoking, his knuckles ached and his side felt sore where he had been slammed into the wall. His mouth tasted as dry as the bottom of a budgie's cage and as sour as month-old milk. When he got up to go to the toilet, he felt a stabbing pain shoot through his kneecap and found himself limping. He felt about ninety. He took three extra-strength Panadols from his traveller's survival kit and washed them down with two glasses of cold water.

It was four twenty-three a.m. by the red square numbers of the digital clock. Cars hissed by through the puddles in the road. Around the edges of the curtains, he could see the sickly amber glow of the street-lights and the occasional flash of distant lightning as the storm passed over to the north.

He didn't want to be awake, but he couldn't seem to get back to sleep. All he could do was lie there feeling sorry for himself, remembering what a bloody fool he had been. What had started as a simple bit of childish self-indulgence, drowning his sorrows in drink, had turned into a full-blown exhibition of idiocy, and both his skinned knuckles and the empty Scotch bottle on the bedside table were evidence enough of that.

After the fracas, he had dashed back to the hotel and hurried straight up to his room before anyone could notice his bloody knuckles or torn jacket. Once safe inside, he had poured himself a stiff drink to stop the shakes. Lying on the bed watching television until the programmes ended for the night, he had poured another, then another. Soon, the half-bottle was empty and he had fallen asleep.

Now it was time to pay. He had heard once that guilt and shame contributed to the pain of hangovers, and at four thirty-two that morning, he certainly believed it.

Christ, it was so bloody easy to slide down one's thoughts into the pit of misery and self-recrimination at four thirty-two a.m. At four thirty-two, if you feel ill, you just *know* you have cancer; at four thirty-two, if you feel depressed, suicide seems the only way out. Four thirty-two is the perfect time for fear and self-loathing, the time of the dark night of the soul.

But it wouldn't do, he told himself. Feeling sorry for himself just wouldn't bloody well do. So he wasn't perfect. He had contemplated committing adultery. So what? He wasn't the first and he wouldn't be the last. He felt responsible for Pamela Jeffreys's injuries. Maybe, just *maybe*, he should have acted differently when he knew he was being followed – put a guard on everyone he had talked to – but it was a big maybe. He wasn't God almighty; he couldn't anticipate everything.

Most detective work was pissing about in the dark, anyway, waiting for the light to grow slowly, as it was doing now outside. On rare occasions, the truth hit you quick as a lightning flash. But they were very rare occasions indeed. Even then, before the lightning hit you, you had spent months looking for the right place to stand.

So last night, in the alley, he had lost it. So what? Two yobbos had tried to mug him and he had gone wild on them, plastered them all over the walls. Most of it was a blur now, but he remembered enough to embarrass him.

They had just been kids, really, early twenties at most, out looking for aggro. But one had been black and one white, like the men who had put Pamela Jeffreys in hospital. Banks knew in his mind that they weren't the same ones, but when the bubble of his anger burst and the fury unleashed itself, when the blood started to flow, they were the ones he was lashing out at. No wonder they ran away shitting bricks. There was nothing rational about it; blinded by rage, he had thought he was hurting the people he really wanted to hurt. He had taken out his anger on two unwary substitutes. They had simply been in the wrong place at the wrong time.

Still, he told himself, they bloody well deserved it, bleeding amateurs. At least he might have discouraged two apprentice muggers from their chosen career. And nobody would ever know what happened. *They* certainly wouldn't say anything. After all, he *hadn't* killed them; they had managed to run away and lick their wounds. They would survive to fight again another day, if they got back the bottle. It wasn't the worst thing he had ever done. And soon, surely, that feeling of being a total fucking idiot would go away and he could get on with his life.

He dozed briefly and woke again at five forty-one. Not quite as bad as four thirty-two, he thought, at first glance. He got up and looked outside at the grey morning. The road and pavement were still awash with puddles. Green double-decker buses were already running people to work, splashing up the water where it had collected in the gutters. Banks was on the fifth floor, and he could see the grey sky streaked with blood and milk behind the majestic dome of the Town Hall. Already, dim shadows were shuffling out of the Salvation Army shelter opposite.

Banks made a cup of instant coffee with the electric kettle and sachet provided and took it back to bed with him. He turned on the bedside light and picked up the copy of Evelyn Waugh's *Sword of Honour* trilogy he had brought with him. Guy Crouchback's misadventures should cheer him up a bit. At least he didn't have that much misfortune.

He would put last night behind him, he decided, sipping the weak Nescafé. A man was allowed his mistakes; he had just better not cling to them or they would drag him down to the bottom of the abyss.

TWO

At nine o'clock that morning, Susan Gay sat alone on the second pew from the back of the small nondenominational chapel at Eastvale Crematorium. It was cool inside, thanks to a large fan below the western stained-glass window, and the lighting was suitably dimmed. The place smelled of shoe polish, not the usual musty hymn books she associated with chapels.

The service went briskly enough. The rent-a-vicar said a few words about Keith Rothwell's devotion to his family and his dedication to hard work, then he read Psalm 51. Susan thought it particularly apt, all that guff about being cleansed of sin. 'Bloodguiltiness' was a word she hadn't heard before, and it made her give a little shudder without knowing why. The mention of 'burnt offering' brought the unwelcome image of Rothwell's corpse, the head a black mess, as if it had indeed been burned, but 'Wash me; and I shall be whiter than snow' almost made her laugh out loud. It brought to mind an old television advert for detergent, then Rothwell's money-laundering.

After the vicar read a bit from Revelation about a new heaven and a new earth and all sorrow, pain and death disappearing, it was all over.

The Rothwells, all suitably dressed in shades of black

for the occasion, sat in the front row. Throughout the ceremony, Mary sat stiffly, Alison kept glancing around her at the stained-glass and the font and Tom sat hunched over. As far as Susan could tell from behind, nobody reached for a handkerchief.

When she watched them walk out into the sunlight, she could tell she was right: dry eyes; not a tear in sight; Mary Rothwell doing her stiff-upper-lip routine, bearing her loss and grief with dignity.

Everyone ignored Susan except Tom, who approached her and said, 'You're the detective who was at our house when I got back from the States, aren't you?'

'Yes. DC Susan Gay, in case you've forgotten.'

'I hadn't forgotten. What are you doing here?'

'I'd like a word with you, if you can spare a few minutes.'

Tom took a silver pocket-watch from his waistcoat and looked at it. Susan saw it was attached by a chain to one of his belt loops. Somehow, it seemed like a very affected gesture in one so young. Maybe it had impressed the Americans. He slipped it back in his pocket. 'All right,' he said. 'But I can't come just now. Everyone's going back to Mr Pratt's for coffee and cake. I'll have to show up.'

'Of course. How about an hour?'

'Okay.'

'Look, it's a fine morning,' Susan said. 'How about that café by the river, the one near the pre-Roman site?'

'I know it.'

Susan busied herself with paperwork back at the station for three quarters of an hour, then set off to keep her appointment.

The River Swain was flowing swiftly, still high after the spring thaw. On the grass by the bank, the owner of the small café had stuck a couple of rickety white tables and chairs. Susan bought a can of Coke for Tom and a pot of tea for herself and they sat by the water. Two weeping willows framed the rolling farmland beyond. Right across, in the centre of the view, was a field of bright yellow rape.

Flies buzzed around her head, and Susan kept fanning them away. 'How was it?' she asked.

Tom shrugged. 'I hate those kinds of social gatherings,' he said. 'And Laurence Pratt gets on my nerves.'

Susan smiled. At least they had something in common. She let the silence stretch as she looked closely at the youth sitting opposite her. Wavy brown hair fell over his ears about halfway down his neck. He was tanned, slender, handsome and he looked as good now in his mourning suit as he had in torn jeans and a denim shirt. The more she let herself simply feel his presence, the more she was sure she was right about him.

He shifted in his chair. 'Look,' he said, 'I'm sorry about the other day. I was rude, I know. But I was tired, upset.'

'I understand,' Susan said. 'It's just that I got the impression there was something you wanted to tell me.'

Tom looked away over the river. His face was scrunched up in a frown, or maybe the sun was in his eyes. 'You know, don't you?' he asked. 'You can tell.'

'That you're homosexual? I have a strong suspicion, yes.'

'Am I that obvious?'

Susan laughed. 'Maybe not to everyone. Remember, I'm a detective.'

Tom managed a weak smile. 'Funny thing, that, isn't it?' he said. 'You'd think it would be men who'd guess.'

'I don't know. Women are used to responding to men in certain ways. They can tell when something's . . .'

'Wrong?'

'I was going to say missing, but even that's not right.'

'Different, then?'

'That'll do. Look, I'm not judging you, Tom. You mustn't think that. It's really none of my business, unless your sexual preference connects somehow with your father's murder.'

'I can't see how it does.'

'You're probably right. Tell me about this Aston, or Afton, then. When Chief Inspector Banks mentioned the name, you assumed it was a man. Why?'

'Because I didn't assume. I know damn well who he is. His name's Ashton. Bloody Clive Ashton. How could I forget?'

'Who is he?'

'He's the son of one of my father's clients – Lionel Ashton. We were at a party together once. I made a mistake.'

'You made advances towards him?'

'Yes.'

'And they weren't welcome?'

Tom gave a dry laugh. 'Obviously not. He told his father.'

'And?'

'And his father told my father. And my father told me I was disgusting, sick, *queer*, and that I should see about getting myself cured. That's the exact word he used, *cured*. He said it would kill Mum if she ever found out.'

'And he suggested you take off to America for a while, at his expense?'

'Yes. But that came a bit later. First we let it lie while we figured out what was best.'

'What did you do in the meantime?'

Tom looked at her, tilted his can back and finished his Coke. His Adam's apple bobbed up and down. Susan turned away and watched a family of ducks drift by on the Swain. Tom wiped his lips with the back of his hand, then said, 'I followed him.'

She turned back towards him. 'You followed your father? Why?'

'Because I thought he was up to something. He was away so often. He was always so remote, like he wasn't really with us even when he was at home. I thought he was doing damage to the family.'

'He wasn't always like that?'

Tom shook his head. 'No. Believe it or not, Dad used to have a bit of life about him. I'm sorry, I didn't intend to make a bad joke.'

'I know. How long had he been behaving this way?'

'Hard to say. It was gradual, like. But this past couple of years it was getting worse. You could hardly talk to him.' He shrugged.

'Was that the only reason you followed him, because you thought he was up to something?'

'I don't know. Maybe I wanted to get something on *him*. Revenge, I don't know. Find out what *his* guilty secret was.'

'And did you?'

Tom took a deep breath, held it for a moment, then let it out loudly with a nervous laugh. 'This is harder than I thought. Okay. Here goes. Yes. I saw my father with another woman.' He said it fast, staccato-style. 'There, that's it. I said it.'

Susan paused a moment to take the information in, then asked, 'When?'

'Sometime in February.'

'Where?'

'Leeds. In a pub. They were sitting together at a table in the Guildford, on The Headrow. They were holding hands. Christ.' His eyes were glassy with gathering tears. He rubbed the backs of his hands over them and collected himself. 'Do you know what that feels like?' he asked. 'Seeing your old man with another woman. No, of course you don't. It was like a kick in the balls. Sorry.'

'That's all right. Did your father see you?'

'No. I kept myself well enough hidden. Not that they had eyes for anyone but each other.'

'What happened next?'

'Nothing. I left. I was so upset I just got in the van and drove around the countryside for a while. I remember stopping somewhere and walking by a river. It was very cold.'

'Was the woman dark-skinned? Indian or Pakistani?'

Tom looked surprised. 'No.'

Susan took her notepad and pen out. 'What did she look like?'

Tom closed his eyes. 'I can see her now,' he said, 'just as clearly as I could then. She was young, much younger than Dad. Probably in her mid-twenties, I'd guess. Not much older than me. She was sitting down, so I couldn't really see her figure properly, but I'd say it was good. I mean, she didn't look fat or anything. She looked nicely proportioned. She was wearing a blouse made of some shiny white material and a scarf sort of thing, more like a shawl, really, over her shoulders, all in blues, whites and reds. It looked like one of those Liberty patterns. She had long fingers. I noticed them for some reason. Am I going too fast?'

'No,' said Susan. 'I've got my own kind of shorthand. Carry on.'

'Long, tapered fingers. No nail varnish, but her nails looked well kept, not bitten or anything. She had blonde hair. No, that's not quite accurate. It was a kind of reddish blonde. It was piled and twisted on top with some strands falling loose over her cheeks and shoulders. You know the kind of look? Sort of messy but ordered.'

Susan nodded. Hairstyles like that cost a fortune.

'She was extraordinarily good-looking,' Tom went on. 'Very fine, pale skin. A flawless complexion, like marble, sort of translucent. The kind where you can just about see the blue veins underneath. And her features could have been cut by a fine sculptor. High cheekbones, small, straight nose. Her eyes were an unusual shade of blue. They may have been contact lenses, but they were sort of light but very bright blue. Cobalt, I guess. Is that it?'

'It'll do. Go on.'

'That's about all really. No beauty spots or anything. She was wearing long dangly earrings, too. Lapis lazuli. No rings, I don't think.'

'That's a very good description, Tom. Do you think you could work with a police artist on this? I think we'd like to have a talk with this woman, and your description might help us find her.'

Tom nodded. 'No problem. I could paint her myself from memory if I had the talent.'

'Good. We'll arrange something, then. Maybe this evening.'

Tom took his watch out again. 'I suppose I'd better be going home. Mum and Alison need my support.'

'Did you ever challenge your father about what you saw?' Susan asked.

Tom shook his head. 'I came close once, when he kept going on about how disappointed he was in me, how sick

I was. I told him I was disappointed in him, too, but I wouldn't tell him why.'

'What did he say?'

'Nothing. Just carried on as if I hadn't spoken.'

'Does your mother know?'

He shook his head. 'No. She doesn't know. I'm sure of it.'

'Do you think she suspects?'

'Maybe. Who knows? She's been living in a bit of a dream world. I'm worried about her, actually. Sometimes I get the feeling that underneath all the lies she knows the truth but she just won't admit it to herself. Do you know what I mean?'

'Yes. What about Alison?'

'Alison's a sweet thing really, but she hasn't got a clue. Lives in her books. She's Brontë mad, is Alison, you know. Reads nothing but. And she's got notebooks full of her own stories, all in tiny handwriting like the Brontës did when they were kids. Made up her own world. I keep thinking she'll grow out of it, but . . . I don't know . . . she seems even worse since . . . since Dad . . .' He shook his head slowly. 'No, she doesn't know. I wouldn't confide in her. I kept it all to myself. Can you imagine that? I still do. You're the first person I've told.' He stood up. 'Look, I really must be off.'

'We'll be in touch about the artist, then.'

'Yes. Okay. And . . .'

'Yes?'

'Thanks,' he said, then turned abruptly and hurried off.

Susan watched him go down the path, hands in pockets, shoulders slumped. She poured herself another cup of tea, stewed though it was, and looked out at the river. A beautiful insect with iridescent wings hovered a few feet above the water. Suddenly, a chaffinch shot out from one of the trees and took the insect in its beak in mid-air. Susan left her lukewarm tea and headed off to meet Sergeant Hatchley. The porn hunt awaited.

THREE

After Banks had gone for a swim in the hotel pool, taken a long sauna, and put away three cups of freshly brewed coffee and a plateful of bacon and eggs, courtesy of room service, he was feeling much better.

As he made a few phone calls, he tried to remember something that had been nagging away at him since the early hours, something he should do, but he failed miserably. At about the same time that Susan Gay was talking to Tom Rothwell, he went out for his first appointment, with Melissa Clegg.

The morning sun had burned off most of the rain, and the pavements had absorbed the rest, leaving them the colour of sandstone, with small puddles catching the light here and there. As wind ruffled the water's surface, golden light danced inside the puddles.

It wasn't as warm as it had been, Banks noticed. He had left his torn sports jacket at the hotel. All he wore on top was a light blue, open-neck shirt. He carried his notebook, wallet, keys and cigarettes in his briefcase.

A cool wind whispered through the streets, and there were plenty of dark, heavy clouds now lurking on the northern horizon behind their town hall. It looked like the region was in for some 'changeable' weather, as the forecasters called it: sunny with cloudy periods, or cloudy with sunny periods.

He could drive to his appointment, he knew, but the one-way system was a nightmare. Besides, the city centre wasn't all that big, and the fresh air would help blow away the cobwebs that still clung to his brain.

Banks had grown quite fond of Leeds since he had been living in Yorkshire. It had an honest, slightly shabby charm about it that appealed to him, despite the new 'Leeds-look' architecture – redbrick revival with royal blue trim – that had sprouted up everywhere, and despite the modern shopping centres and the yuppie developments down by the River Aire. Leeds was a scruff by nature; it wouldn't look comfortable in fancy dress, no matter what the price. And then there was Opera North, of course.

Avoiding City Square and the scene of the previous evening's debacle, he cut up King Street instead, walked past the recently restored Metropole Hotel, all redbrick and gold sandstone masonry, and along East Parade through the business section of banks and insurance buildings in all their jumbled glory. Here, Victorian Gothic rubbed shoulders with Georgian classicism and sixties concrete and glass. As in many cities, you had to look up, above eye level, to see the interesting details on the tops of the buildings: surprising gables where pigeons nested, gargoyles, balconies, caryatids.

As he walked along The Headrow past Stumps and the art gallery, he became aware again of the sharp pain in his knee, with which he had probably chipped a cheekbone or broken a jaw the previous evening.

He arrived at the Merrion Centre a couple of minutes early. Melissa Clegg had told him on the phone that she had a very busy day planned. She was expecting a number of important deliveries and had appointments with her suppliers. She could, however, allow him half an hour.

There was a quiet coffee bar with outside tables, she told him, on the second level, up the steps over the entrance to Le Phonographique. She would meet him there at half past ten.

Banks found the coffee bar, and an empty table, with no trouble. At that time on a Wednesday morning, the Merrion Centre was practically deserted: especially the upper level, which seemed to have nothing but small offices and hairdressers.

Melissa Clegg arrived on time with all the flurry of the busy executive. When she sat down, she tucked her hair behind her ears. Today, she wore a pink dress cut square at her throat and shoulders.

The last thing on earth Banks felt he needed was another cup of coffee, but he took an espresso just to have something in front of him. Also, by the feel of his chest, he didn't need a cigarette, either, but he lit one nonetheless. The first few drags made him a bit dizzy, then it tasted fine.

'You look a bit the worse for wear,' Melissa observed.

'You should have seen the other two,' Banks said. He could tell by the way she laughed that she didn't believe him, just as he had expected. But he had also noticed the angry contusion high on his left cheek, just to the side of his eye, when he shaved that morning. Another result of his crash into the alley wall. He tried to keep his skinned knuckles out of sight, which made drinking coffee difficult.

'What can I do for you this time, Inspector, or Chief Inspector, is it?'

'Chief Inspector. I don't suppose you've heard anything from your husband?'

'Ex. Well, near as. No, I haven't. But he's hardly likely

235

to get in touch with me. I still don't know why you're so worried. I'm sure he'll turn up.'

'I don't think so, Mrs Clegg. Remember last time we met I asked you if you knew a Robert Calvert?'

'Yes. I said I didn't and I still don't.'

'I'd appreciate it if you would keep this quiet for the moment, but we believe that Robert Calvert was also Keith Rothwell.'

'I don't understand. Do you mean he had a false name, an alias?'

'Something like that. More, actually. He lived in Leeds, had a flat in the name of Robert Calvert. A whole other life. Mary Rothwell doesn't know, so—'

'Don't worry, I won't say anything. You've got me puzzled.'

'We were, too. But the reason I'm telling you this is that your husband acted as a reference for Robert Calvert in the matter of his bank account and credit card. Also, ironically enough, Calvert listed his employer as Keith Rothwell.'

'Curiouser and curiouser,' said Melissa. 'Daniel must have known about this double life, then?'

'It looks that way.'

'Well, I certainly knew nothing about it. As I told you before, I haven't seen Keith Rothwell since Danny and I split up two years ago.' She frowned. 'I must say it surprises me that Daniel would risk doing something so obviously dishonest as that. Not that dishonesty is beneath him, but it seems too much of a risk for no return.'

'We don't know what the returns were,' Banks said. 'How close are you and Daniel?'

'What do you mean?'

'Did he ever mention a woman called Marci Lapwing to you?'

236

'God, what a name. No. Who is she? His girlfriend?'

'Someone he's been seeing lately.'

'Well, he wouldn't tell me about her, would he?'

'Why not?'

She shrugged. 'He never does. Maybe he thinks I'd be jealous.'

'Would you?'

'Look, I don't see what it has to do with anything, but no. It's over. O.V.E.R. We made our choices.'

'Is there someone else?'

She blushed a little but met his gaze with steady eyes as she fingered the top of her dress over her freckled collarbone. 'As a matter of fact there is. But I won't tell you anything more. I don't want him dragged into this. It's none of your business, anyway. Danny's probably run off with his bimbo.'

'No. Marci Lapwing is still around. Never mind. Let's move on. How do you explain the two men who visited you?'

'I don't know. Perhaps her husband sent them?'

'Whose husband?'

'The bimbo's. Marci whatever-her-name-is.'

'She's not married. Since we last talked,' Banks said, lowering his voice, 'things have taken several turns for the worse. We're talking about very serious matters indeed. It looks as if your husband might be implicated in murder, money-laundering, theft and fraud, and that he may be partly responsible for the savage beating of a young woman.'

'My God . . . I . . .'

'I know. You didn't take all this seriously. Nor did you want to. Now will you?'

She began to fidget with her coffee-spoon. 'Yes. Yes, of

course. I assume you're talking about Keith Rothwell's murder?'

'Yes.'

'And who has been beaten?'

'A friend of Mr Rothwell's. The way it looks, both Keith Rothwell and your husband were laundering money for a Mr X. We think we know his identity, but I'm afraid I can't reveal it to you. Rothwell was either stealing or threatening to talk, or both, and Mr X asked your husband to get rid of him.'

She shook her head. 'Danny? No. I don't believe it. He couldn't kill anyone.'

'Hear me out, Mrs Clegg. He did as he was asked. Maybe his own life was threatened, we don't know. Immediately after he arranged to get rid of Keith Rothwell, he either became a threat himself, or he made off with a lot of illegal money, so Mr X sent two goons to track him down. Maybe he'd seen it coming and anticipated what they would do. At this point, there's a lot we can only speculate about.'

'And that explains the two men?'

'Yes.' Banks leaned forward and rested his arms on the table. 'They visited your ex-husband's office, they visited you, then they visited a girl they saw me talking to. She was the one they beat up. Now tell me again, Mrs Clegg, have you ever seen or heard of a woman called Pamela Jeffreys? She was born here in Yorkshire, but her family came originally from Pakistan. She's about five foot four, slender figure, with almond eyes and long black hair that she sometimes wears tied back. She has a smooth, dark gold complexion and a gold stud through her left nostril. She's a classical musician, a viola player with the Northern Philharmonia.'

Banks watched Melissa's face as he described Pamela Jeffreys. When he had finished, she shook her head. 'Honestly,' she said, 'I've never seen her, and Danny never mentioned anyone like that. She sounds impressive, but he doesn't go for that type.'

'What type?'

'Bright women. Career women. It scared him to death when I started to make a success of the wine business. At first he could just look down on it as my little hobby. You said she was a classical musician?'

'Yes.'

'He doesn't like classical music. All he likes is that bloody awful trad jazz. A woman like the one you describe would bore Danny to death. Besides, she sounds so gorgeous, I'm sure I'd remember her.'

A gentle gust of wind blew through the centre, carrying the smells of espresso and fried bacon from the café. 'Two more things,' Banks said. 'First, in the time you lived with your husband, did you ever come across any acquaintances, say, or clients of his whom you'd describe as shady?'

She laughed. 'Oh, a tax lawyer has plenty of shady clients, Chief Inspector. That's what keeps him in business. But I assume you mean something other than that?'

'Yes. If Daniel did have anything to do with Keith Rothwell's death, he certainly didn't commit the murder himself, as you pointed out.'

'That's true. The Daniel I know wouldn't have had the stomach for it.'

'So he must have hired someone. You don't usually just walk into your local and say, "Look chaps, I need a couple of killers. Do you think you could help me out?"'

Melissa smiled. 'You might try it at a Law Society

banquet. I'm sure you'd get a few takers. But I see what you mean.'

'So he might have known someone who would consider the task, and it might have been someone he met through his practice. I doubt very much that the two of you socialized with hitmen, but there might be someone who struck you as dangerous, perhaps?'

'Who knows who we socialized with?' Melissa said. 'Who knows anything about anyone, when it comes right down to it? No one immediately springs to mind, but I'll think about it, if I may.'

'Okay.' Banks passed on Alison Rothwell's vague description of the two men, especially the one with the puppy-dog eyes, the only distinguishing feature. 'I'll be at the Holiday Inn here for the next day or so, or you can leave a message with Detective Inspector Blackstone at Millgarth.'

'Is he the one who came over last night with my bodyguard?'

'No, that's Detective Sergeant Waltham. I don't honestly believe you're in any danger, Mrs Clegg – I think they're probably miles from here by now – but it's best to be on the safe side. Are you happy with the arrangement?'

'I didn't really understand all the fuss at first, but after what you've just told me I'll sleep easier tonight for knowing there's someone out there watching over me.' She looked at her watch. 'Sorry, Mr Banks. Time's pressing. You said you had two things to ask.'

'Yes. The other is a bit more personal.'

Melissa raised her eyebrows. 'Yes?'

'I mean personal in the true sense, not necessarily embarrassing.'

She frowned, still looking at him. It was a strong,

attractive face with its reddish tan and freckles over the nose and upper cheeks; every little wrinkle around her grey-blue eyes looked as if it had been earned.

'We think Daniel Clegg has probably done a bunk with a lot of money,' Banks began. 'Enough to set him up for life, otherwise these goons wouldn't be so keen on finding him. But it's a bloody big world if you don't know where to look. The two of you shared your dreams at one stage, I suppose, like most married couples. Where do you think he would go? Where did he dream of living?'

Melissa continued to frown. 'I see what you mean,' she murmured. 'That's an interesting question. Where's Danny's Shangri-la, his Eldorado?'

'Yes. We all have one, don't we?'

'Well, Danny wasn't much of a dreamer, to tell you the truth. He didn't have a lot of imagination. But whenever he talked of winning the pools and packing it all in, it was always Tahiti.'

'Tahiti?'

'Yes. He was a big fan of *Mutiny on the Bounty*. Had every version on video. I think he liked the idea of those bare-breasted native girls serving him long, cool drinks in coconut shells.' She laughed and looked at her watch again. 'Look, Mr Banks, I'm sorry, but I really *do* have to go now. I've got a hell of a day ahead.' She pushed her chair back and stood up.

Banks stood with her. 'Of course,' he said, shaking her hand.

'But if I can be any more help, I'll get in touch. I mean it. I never thought Danny was capable of real evil, but if what you say is true . . .' She shrugged. 'Anyway, I'll give what you said some thought. I . . . just a minute.'

Her brow furrowed and she turned her eyes up, as if

inspecting her eyelashes. She looked at her watch again, bit her lip, then perched on the edge of the chair, knees together, clutching her briefcase to her chest. 'There *was* someone. I really can't stay. I'm going to be late. I can't think of the name, but I might be able to remember if you give me a bit of time. He did have those sort of sad eyes, like a puppy, now I think of it.'

Banks sat forward. 'What were the circumstances?'

'I told you Danny doesn't do criminal work, but he is a solicitor, and apparently he was the only one this chap knew. According to Danny, they met in a pub, had a few drinks, got talking. You know how it is. This chap had been in the army or something, over in Northern Ireland. When he got himself arrested, Danny was the only one he knew to call on.'

'What happened?'

'Danny referred him to someone else. I only remember because he came round to the house once. He wasn't too happy about the solicitor Danny passed him on to for some reason. I think it might have been the fee or something like that. They argued a bit, then Danny managed to calm him down. They had a drink, then the man left. I never saw or heard of him again. I'm sorry, I didn't really hear what was going on. Not that I'd remember now.'

'How long ago was it?'

'A little over two years. Shortly before we separated.'

'And you remember nothing more about this man?'

'No. Not off-hand.'

'What pub did they meet in?'

'I can't remember. Isn't that odd? You mentioning about meeting a killer in a pub? What if it was him?'

'What was he arrested for?'

'It was something to do with assault, I think. A fight. I

242

know it wasn't really serious. Certainly not murder or anything. Look, I really must go. I'll try and remember more, I promise.'

'Just one thing,' Banks said. 'Can you remember the name of the solicitor your husband referred him to? We might be able to trace him through our records.'

She compressed her lips in thought for a moment, then said, 'Atkins. Of course, it would have been Harvey Atkins. He and Danny are good friends, and Harvey does a fair bit of criminal work.'

'Thank you,' Banks said, but she was already dashing away.

'I'll be in touch,' she called over her shoulder.

Banks headed for the staircase. While he had been talking with Melissa Clegg, he had remembered what it was that had been nagging at him all morning. He decided to satisfy his curiosity before meeting Ken Blackstone. Things were moving fast.

12

ONE

'**Take the scenic route,**' said Sergeant Hatchley. 'We're not in a hurry.'

Instead of going east to the A1 at the roundabout by the Red Lion Hotel, Susan headed south-west along the edge of the Dales through Masham, Ripon and Harrogate.

Hatchley didn't smoke at all during the journey, though he insisted she stop once at a café in Harrogate for a cup of coffee, during which he chain-smoked three cigarettes. It was very different from travelling with Banks. For a start, Banks liked to drive, and with him there was always music, sometimes tolerable, sometimes execrable. Hatchley preferred to sit with his arms crossed and look out of the window at the passing scenery, no doubt with visions of bare breasts flashing through what passed for his mind.

She wished she didn't have to work with men all the time. One crying jag or sharp response, and it was PMT; a day off for any reason meant it was 'that time of the month'. She had to put up with it without complaint, just take it all in her stride.

Maybe she was being unfair, though. Hatchley aside, the men she worked with were mostly okay. Phil Richmond, with whom she spent the most time, was a sweetheart. But Phil was leaving soon.

Superintendent Gristhorpe frightened her a little, perhaps because he made her think of her father, and she always felt like a silly little girl when he was around.

Banks, though, was like an older brother. And, like a brother, he teased her too much, especially about music when they were in the car. She was sure he played some terrible things just to make her uncomfortable. Right now, though, as she approached the busy Leeds Ring Road, she would have welcomed something soothing to listen to.

Susan was building up a nice collection of classical music. Every month, she bought a magazine that gave away a free CD of bits and pieces of the works reviewed. It provided a breakdown of what to listen for at what points of time – like '6:25: The warm and sunny feeling of the spring day returns', or '4:57: Second theme emerges from interplay of brass and woodwinds'. Susan found it very helpful, and if she liked the part she heard, she would buy the complete work, unless it was a lengthy and expensive opera. At the moment her favourite piece was Beethoven's Pastoral Symphony. She knew Banks would approve, but she was too embarrassed to tell him.

Susan went on to think about her talk with Tom Rothwell by the river, and about the agonies he must be going through. It was hard enough being homosexual anywhere, she imagined, but it would be especially tough in Yorkshire, where men prided themselves on their masculinity and women were supposed to know their place and stick to it.

There was a prime example of Yorkshire manhood sitting right next to her, she thought, all Rugby League, roast beef and pints of bitter. And she couldn't imagine what he could find offensive about her perfume. It certainly smelled pleasant enough to her, and she used it sparingly.

The traffic snarled up on the Ring Road, and Hatchley sat there with the tattered Leeds and Bradford *A to Z* on his lap squinting at signs. He was the kind of navigator who shouted, 'Turn here!' just as you passed by the turning. After several misdirections and a couple of hair-raising U-turns, they pulled up outside candidate number one, a newsagent's shop at the edge of a rundown council estate in Gipton.

Two scruffy kids swaggered out as Susan and Hatchley went in. The girl behind the counter couldn't have been more than fifteen or sixteen. She was pale as a ghost and skinny as a rake. Her hair, brown streaked with silver, red and green, teetered untidily on top of her head, and unruly strands snaked down over her white neck and face, partly covering one over-mascaraed eye.

She looked as if she had a small, pretty mouth underneath the full and pouting one she had superimposed with brownish-purple lipstick. Susan also noticed a pungent scent, which she immediately classified as cheap, not at all like her own. The girl rested her ring-laden fingers with the long crimson nails on the counter and slanted her bony shoulders towards them, head tilted to one side. She wore a baggy white T-shirt with SCREW YOU written in black across her flat chest.

'Mr Drake around, love?' Hatchley asked.

She moved her head a fraction; the hair danced like Medusa's snakes. 'In the back,' she said, without breaking the rhythm of her chewing.

He moved towards the counter and lifted the flap.

'Hey!' she said. 'You can't just walk through like that.'

'Can't I, love? Do you mean I have to be announced all formally, like?' Hatchley took out his identification and held it close to her eyes. She squinted as she read. 'Maybe you'd like to get out your salver?' he went on. 'Then I can put my calling card on it and you can take it through to Mr Drake and inform him that a gentleman wishes to call on him?'

'Sod off, clever arse,' she said, slouching aside to let them pass. 'You're no fucking gentleman. And don't call me love.'

'Who have we got here, then?' Hatchley stopped and said, 'Glenda Slagg, feminist?'

'Piss off.'

They went through without further ceremony into the back room, an office of sorts, and Susan saw Mr Drake sitting at his desk.

Below the greasy black hair was the lumpiest face Susan had ever seen. He had a bulbous forehead, a potato nose and a carbuncular chin, over all of which his oily, red skin, pitted with blackheads, stretched tight, and out of which looked a pair of beady black eyes, darting about like tiny fish in an aquarium. His belly was so big he could hardly get close enough to the desk to write. A smell of burned bacon hung in the stale air, and Susan noticed a hotplate with a frying-pan on it in one corner.

When they walked in, he pushed his chair back and grunted, 'Who let you in? What do you want?'

'Remember me, Jack?' said Hatchley.

Drake screwed up his eyes. They disappeared into folds of fat. 'Is it . . .? Well, bugger me if it isn't Jim Hatchley.'

He floundered to his feet and stuck out his hand, first wiping it on the side of his trousers. Hatchley leaned forward and shook it.

'Who's the crumpet?' Drake asked, nodding towards Susan.

'The "crumpet", as you so crudely put it, Jack, is Detective Constable Susan Gay. And show a bit of respect.'

'Sorry, lass,' said Drake, executing a little bow for Susan. She found it hard to hold back her laughter. She knew that old-fashioned sexism was alive and well and living in Yorkshire, but it felt strange to have Sergeant Hatchley defending her honour. Drake turned back to Hatchley. 'Now what is it you want, Jim? You're not still working these parts, are you?'

'I am today.'

Drake held his hands out, palms open. 'Well, I've done nowt to be ashamed of.'

'Jack, old lad,' said Hatchley heavily, 'you ought to be ashamed of being born, but we'll leave that aside for now. Girlie magazines.'

'Eh? What about 'em?'

'Still in business?'

Drake shifted from one foot to the other and cast a beady eye on Susan, guilty as the day is long. 'You know I don't go in for owt illegal, Jim.'

'Believe it or not, at the moment I couldn't care less. It's not you I'm after. And it's *Sergeant* Hatchley to you.'

'Sorry. What's up, then?'

Hatchley asked him about the masked killer with the puppy-dog eyes. Drake was shaking his head before he had finished.

'Sure?' Hatchley asked.

'Aye. Swear on my mother's grave.'

Hatchley laughed. 'You'd swear night was day on your mother's grave if you thought it would get me off your back, wouldn't you, Jack? Nonetheless, I'll believe you, this time. Any ideas where we might try?'

'What have you got?'

'Shaved pussies, excited penises. Right up your alley, I'd've thought.'

Drake turned up his misshapen nose in disgust. 'Shaved pussies? Why, that's pretty much straight stuff. Nay, Jim, times have changed. They're all into the arse-bandit stuff or whips and chains these days.'

'I'm not just talking about the local MPs, Jack.'

'Ha ha. Very funny. Even so.'

Hatchley sighed. 'Benny still in business?'

Drake nodded. 'Far as I know. But he deals mostly in body-piercing now. Very specialized taste.' He looked at Susan. 'You know, love – pierced nipples, labia, foreskins, that kind of thing.'

Susan repressed a shudder.

'Bert Oldham?' Hatchley went on. 'Mario Nelson? Henry Talbot?'

'Aye. But you can practically sell the stuff over the counter, these days, Ji – Sergeant.'

'It's the "practically" that interests me, Jack. You know what the law says: no penetration, no oral sex and no hardons. Anyroad, if you get a whiff of him, phone this number.' He handed Drake a card.

'I'll do that,' said Drake, dropping back into his chair again. Susan thought the legs would break, but, miraculously, they held.

The girl didn't look up from her magazine as they went out. 'Better give that reading a rest, love,' said Hatchley. 'It must be hell on your lips.'

'Fuck off,' she said, chewing gum at the same time.

Shit, thought Susan, it's going to be one of those days.

TWO

Banks was right, he saw, as he stood on the threshold of Robert Calvert's flat and surveyed the wreckage. The only difference between this and Pamela Jeffreys's flat was that there had been no human being hurt and no prized possessions utterly destroyed. Stuffing from the sofa lay strewn over the carpet, which had been partly rolled up to expose the bare floorboards. In places, wallpaper had been ripped down, and the television screen had been shattered.

So they had come back. It supported his theory. They obviously didn't know that Banks was a policeman, didn't know that Calvert's flat had already been thoroughly searched by professionals. If they had known, they would never have come here.

It was as he had suspected. They had started following him when he left Clegg's Park Square office on Monday morning. They must have seen the police arrive first, but from their point of view, the police arrived sometime *after* Banks, and he left alone, so there was no reason to make a connection, certainly none to suspect that *he* was a policeman. For all they knew, he could have been a friend of Betty Moorhead's, or a colleague of Clegg's.

Still looking for clues to Clegg's whereabouts, they had trailed him on his lunch date with Pamela and noted where she was rehearsing. One of them must have found out where she lived. They didn't know about the Calvert flat until Banks led them there, and they must have thought the place had something to do with Clegg. Finally, when Banks saw them from the window, they ran off, only to come back later and search the place when the coast was clear.

Where were they now? Already, their descriptions had been sent to other police forces, to the airports and ports. If the men had any sense, they would lie low for a while before trying to leave the country. But criminals don't always have sense, Banks knew. In fact, more often than not, they were plain stupid.

And what about Rothwell's killers? If the man Melissa Clegg remembered was involved – and it was a big if – then he was local. Was he the kind to stay put or run? And what about his partner?

No one else was at home in the building, and there was no point looking over the rest of the flat. From the box at the corner of the street, Banks went through the motions of calling the local police to report the break-in, but he knew there was nothing they could do. He had no doubts as to *who* had done it; he just had to find them. Dirty Dick Burgess knew something, Banks believed, but he would talk only when he wanted and tell only as little as he needed.

When Banks had finished the call, he took a bus to Millgarth at the bottom of Eastgate. Over the road, on the site of the demolished Quarry Hill flats, stood the new West Yorkshire Playhouse with its 'City of Drama' sign. It seemed uncannily appropriate, Banks thought, given the events of the past couple of days. Beyond the theatre, high on a hill, was Quarry House, new home of the Department of Health and Social Security, and already nicknamed 'The Kremlin' by locals.

Ken Blackstone was in his office bent over a stack of paperwork. He pushed the pile aside and gestured for Banks to sit opposite him.

'No earth-shattering developments to report, before you get your hopes up,' he said. 'We're still no closer to finding Clegg or Rothwell's killers, but there's a couple of interesting points. First off, you might like to know that the lab boys say the dirt and gravel on the tyres of Ronald Hamilton's Escort match that around Arkbeck Farm. They said a lot of other things about phosphates and sulphides or whatever, which I didn't understand, but it looks like the car the killers used. Rest of it was clean as a whistle. And airport security at Heathrow have found Clegg's red Jag in the long-stay car park.'

'Surprise, surprise,' said Banks.

'Indeed. Coffee?'

Banks's stomach was already grumbling from too much caffeine, so he declined. Blackstone went and poured himself a mug from a machine in the open-plan office and returned to his screened-off corner. There was a buzz of constant noise around them – telephones, computer printers, fax machines, doors opening and closing and the general banter of a section CID department – but Blackstone seemed to have carved himself a small corner of reasonably quiet calm.

Banks told him about Calvert's flat.

'Interesting,' said Blackstone. 'When do you think that happened?'

'I'd say before they went to Pamela's,' Banks said. 'Finding nothing there would put them in a fine mood for hurting someone. Is there any news from the hospital?'

Blackstone shook his head. 'No change. She's stable, at least.' He frowned at Banks and touched the side of his own cheek. 'What about you? And I noticed you limping a bit when you came in.'

'Slipped in the shower. Look, Ken, I might have a lead on one of Rothwell's killers.' He went on quickly to tell Blackstone what Melissa Clegg had said about the mysterious client with the puppy-dog eyes that Clegg had passed on to Harvey Atkins.

Blackstone put the tip of a yellow pencil to his lower lip. 'Hmm . . .' he said. 'We're already running a check on all Clegg's contacts and clients. We can certainly check the court records. At least we've got the brief's name, which helps a bit. Harvey Atkins is certainly no stranger around here. He's not a bad bloke, as lawyers go. It's a bit vague, though, isn't it? About two years ago, she says, something to do with assault, maybe? Do we know if the bloke was convicted?'

Banks shook his head. 'I'm afraid we'll have to depend on the kindness of microchips.'

Blackstone scowled. 'Hang on a minute.' He made a quick phone call and set the inquiry in motion. 'They say it could take a while,' he said. 'It might be a long list.'

Banks nodded. 'What do you know about Tahiti?' he asked.

'Tahiti? That's where Captain Bligh's men deserted in the film. It's part of French Polynesia now, isn't it?'

'I think so. It's in the South Pacific at any rate. And Gauguin painted there.'

'Why are you interested?'

Banks told him what Melissa Clegg had said.

'Hmm,' said Blackstone. 'It wouldn't do any harm to put a few inquiries in motion, check on flights, would it? Especially now we've found the car at Heathrow. A relative newcomer might stand out there. I'll see what I can do.'

'Thanks. Anything else?'

'We finished the house-to-house in Pamela Jeffreys's street. Nothing really, except I think we've fixed the time. One neighbour remembered hearing some noise at about nine-fifteen Monday evening, which fits with what the doc said, and with Mr Judd's statement.'

Banks nodded.

'The people on the other side were out.'

'These neighbours,' said Banks, 'they said they just heard *some noise*?'

'Yes.'

'Ken, imagine how much noise it must have made when they smashed that stuff. Imagine how Pamela Jeffreys must have screamed for help when she realized what was happening.'

'I know, I know.' Blackstone shook his head and sighed. 'I suppose they would have gagged her.'

'Still . . .'

'Look, Alan, according to DC Hyatt, who talked to them, they said they thought it was the television at first. He asked them if she usually played her television set so loud, and they said no. Then they said they thought she was having a fight with her boyfriend. He asked them if that was a regular occurrence, too, and again they said no. Then they said, or implied, that dark-skinned people have odd forms of entertaining themselves and that we white folks had best leave them to it.'

'They really said that?'

Blackstone nodded. 'Words to that effect. They're the sort of people who wouldn't cross the street to piss on an Asian if she was on fire. And they don't want to get involved.'

'And that's it?'

'Afraid so.' Blackstone looked at his watch. 'I don't know about you, but I'm a bit peckish. What do you say about lunch, on me?'

Banks didn't feel especially hungry, but he knew he

ought to try to eat something if he were to keep going all day. 'All right, you're on,' he said. 'But no curries.'

THREE

The other shops were not much different from the first: usually with the windows barred or covered in mesh, and usually close to dilapidated, graffiti-scarred corporation estates or surviving pre-war terraces of back-to-backs in areas like Hunslet, Holbeck, Beeston and Kirkstall. One moment the sun was out, the next it looked like rain. Around and around they drove, Hatchley flipping through the *A to Z*, which had now become so well thumbed that the pages were falling out, missing turnings, looking for obscure streets. It was all depressing enough to Susan, and a far cry from the nice big semi at the top of the hill in Sheffield where she grew up.

But Hatchley, she noticed, seemed to relish the task, even though after another three visits they had got nowhere. His reputation for laziness, she was beginning to realize, might be unfounded. He certainly didn't like to waste energy, and usually took the line of least resistance, but he was hardly alone in that.

Susan had known truly lazy policemen – some of them had even made detective sergeant – but none of them were like Hatchley. They simply put in the time until the end of their shift, generally trying to stay out of the way of any situation that might generate paperwork. Hatchley was determined. When he was after something, he didn't let go until he got it.

The fifth shop was larger and more modern than the others, a kind of mini-market cum off-licence that sold milk, tinned foods, bread and all sorts of odds and ends as well as booze, newspapers and magazines. It was on Beeston Road, not far from Elland Road, where Leeds United played, and it was run, Hatchley said, by a man called Mario Nelson, who, as his name suggested, had an Italian mother and an English father.

It was immediately clear to Susan that Mario took after his father. She knew there were blond-haired Italians in the north of the country, but they didn't look as downright Nordic as Mario. Tall, slim, wearing a white smock, he looked far too elegant to be running a shop. In his early fifties, Susan guessed, he was handsome in a Robert Redford sort of way, and he looked as if he would be more comfortable being interviewed on a film set than unpacking a box of mushroom soup, which is what he was doing when they entered. When he saw Hatchley, a look of caution came to his ice-blue eyes. There was nobody else in the shop.

'Mario, old mate,' said Hatchley. 'Long time no see.'

'Not long enough for me,' muttered Mario, putting the box aside. 'What can I do for you?'

'No need to be so surly. How's business?' Hatchley took out a cigarette and lit up.

'There's no smoking in here.'

Hatchley ignored him. 'I asked how's business?'

Mario stared at him for a moment, then broke off eye contact. 'Fair to middling.'

'Doing much special trade?'

'Don't know what you mean. Look, if you've just come to chat, I'm a busy man.'

Hatchley looked exaggeratedly around the shop. 'Doesn't look that way to me, Mario.'

'There's more to running a shop than serving customers.'

'Well, soon as you've answered our questions, you can get back to it.' He described the man in the balaclava. 'Ever seen anyone like that in here? Is he on your list?'

'It's a bit of a vague description.'

'True, but concentrate on the eyes. They'd just about come up to your chin. Poor misguided bloke has an appetite for shaved pussy magazines, and I know you supply them.'

'You've never proved that.'

'Come off it! The only reason you're still in business is that you've done me a few favours over the years. Remember that. You're a filth-peddler. You know I don't like filth-peddlers, Mario. You know I rank them a bit below a dollop of dog-shit on my shoe.'

Hatchley made some very interesting distinctions, Susan thought, some delicate moral judgments. Simple display of naked flesh was fine with him, obviously, but anything more was pornographic. Bit of a puritan, really, when it came down to it.

She watched Mario shift from foot to foot, and she saw something in his eyes other than wariness; she saw that he recognized Hatchley's description, or thought he did. Hatchley noticed it, too. And she saw fear.

Hatchley dropped his cigarette on the floor and ground it out. 'Susan,' he said, 'would you go put up the "Closed" sign, please?'

'You can't do that,' said Mario, coming out from behind the counter and moving to stop Susan. Hatchley got in the way. He was about the same height and two stones heavier. Mario stopped. Susan went to the door and turned the sign over.

'Might as well drop the latch and pull the blinds down, too,' said Hatchley, 'seeing as it's such a quiet time.'

257

Susan did as he said.

'Right.' Hatchley turned to face Mario. 'What's his name?'

'Whose name? I don't know what you're on about.'

'We're not gormless, Susan and I. We're detectives. That means we detect. And I detect that you're lying. What's his name?'

Mario looked pale. Beads of sweat formed on his brow. Susan almost felt sorry for him. Almost. 'Honest, Mr Hatchley, I don't know what you mean,' he said. 'I run an honest business here. I—'

But before he could finish, Hatchley had grabbed him by the lapels of his shop-coat and pushed him against the shelves. A jar of instant coffee fell to the floor and smashed; tins dropped and rolled all over; a packet of spaghetti noodles burst open.

'Watch what you're doing!' Mario cried. 'That stuff costs money.'

Hatchley pushed him up harder against the shelving, twisting the lapels. Mario's face turned red. Susan was worried he was going to have a heart attack or something. She wished she hadn't become part of this. Gristhorpe would find out, she knew, and she would be thrown off the force in shame. Outside, she heard somebody rattle the door. Do something, her inner voice screamed. 'Sir,' she said levelly. 'Maybe Mr Nelson wants to tell us something, and he's having difficulty speaking.'

Hatchley looked at Nelson and relaxed his grasp. 'Is that so, Mario?'

Mario nodded as best he could under the circumstances. Hatchley let him go. A jar of pickled onions rolled off the shelf and smashed, infusing the air with the acrid smell of vinegar.

'Who is he?' asked Hatchley.

Mario massaged his throat and gasped for breath. 'You . . . shouldn't . . . have done . . .' he wheezed. 'Could have k-k-killed me. Weak heart. I c-c-could report you.'

'But we both know you won't, don't we? Imagine trying to run an honest business with the local police breathing down your neck day and night. Come on, give us the name, Mario.'

'I . . . I don't know his name. J-just that he's been in occasionally.'

'For your under-the-counter stuff? Shaved pussies?'

Mario nodded.

Hatchley shook his head. 'I wouldn't believe it if I hadn't seen it with my own eyes,' he said, 'but you're lying again. After all this.' He reached out for Mario's lapels.

'No!' Mario jumped back, dislodging a few more tins from the shelf. A bottle of gin fell and smashed. He put his hands out. 'No!'

'Come on, then,' said Hatchley. 'Give.'

'Jameson. Mr Jameson. That's all I know,' said Mario, still rubbing his throat.

'I want his address, too. He's on one of your paper routes, isn't he? I'll bet one of your lads delivers his papers, maybe with a special colour supplement on Sundays, eh? Come on.'

'No. I don't know.'

'Be reasonable, Mario. It's no skin off your nose, is it? And it'll put you in good stead with the local bobbies. What's his address?'

Mario paused a moment, then went behind the counter and looked in the ledger where he kept the addresses for newspaper deliveries. 'Forty-seven Bridgeport Road,' he said. 'But you won't find him there.'

'Oh?'

'Cancelled his papers.'

'How long for?'

'Three weeks.'

'Since when?'

'Last Friday.'

'Where's he gone?'

'I've no idea, have I? Off on his holidays, maybe.'

'Don't come the clever bugger with me.'

'I'm not. Honest.'

'Is that all you know?' Hatchley moved forward and Mario backed off.

'I swear it. We're not mates or anything. He's just a customer. And do me a favour – when you do find him, don't tell him you found out from me.'

'Scared of him?'

'He's got a bit of a reputation for scrapping, that's all. When he's had a few, like. I don't think he'd take kindly.'

'Aye, all right, then,' said Hatchley. 'Susan, would you do the honours?'

Susan went over and unlocked the door. A red-faced old woman bustled in. 'What's going on here? I've been waiting five minutes. My poor Marmaduke is going to starve to death if you—' She stopped talking, looked at the mess on the floor, then back at the three of them.

'Slight accident, Mrs Bagshot,' said Mario, straightening his tie and smiling. 'Nothing serious.'

Hatchley bent down and grabbed a pickled onion. After a cursory check to make sure there was no broken glass clinging to it, he popped it in his mouth, smiled at Mrs Bagshot and left.

FOUR

After a light lunch in the police canteen with Ken Black-stone – a toasted cheese sandwich and a plastic container of orange juice – Banks set off back to the hotel. The weather was the same, fast-moving cloud on the wind, sun in and out casting shadows over the streets and buildings. He would have to do something about his jacket, he realized, as he walked past the Corn Exchange. Maybe he could get it fixed this afternoon. The hotel should be able to help. Or maybe he should buy a new one.

He wasn't looking forward to explaining his adventures to Sandra, either. He hadn't phoned her last night, and she would probably be out until this evening. He could phone the gallery, he knew, but she would be busy. Besides, it would only worry her if he told her about the fight over the telephone. He might get his jacket fixed, but there would be no hiding the skinned knuckles and bruised cheekbone from Sandra, let alone the bruises that would soon show up on his side.

All he had to say was that two kids had tried to mug him, simple as that. It might not be the complete truth, but it certainly wasn't a lie. On the other hand, he wondered who he was trying to fool. If he couldn't talk to Sandra about what had happened, who could he talk to? Right now, he just didn't know.

A local train must have just come in, judging from the hordes issuing from the station and heading for the bus stops around City Square and Boar Lane. Banks picked up a *Yorkshire Evening Post* from the aged vendor, who was shouting out a headline that sounded like 'TURKLE AN HONEST LIAR' but which, on reading, turned out to be

'TWO KILLED IN HUNSLET FIRE.' Banks refused the free packet of Old El Paso Taco Shells he was offered with his newspaper.

At the hotel, he found three messages: one to call Melissa Clegg at the wine shop; one to meet Sergeant Hatchley and Susan Gay at The Victoria, behind the Town Hall, as soon as possible; and one to call Ken Blackstone at Millgarth. First, he went to his room and phoned Melissa Clegg.

'Oh, Mr Banks,' she said. 'I didn't want to get your hopes up, but I've remembered his name, the man Daniel met in the pub.'

'Yes?'

'Well, I knew there was something funny about it. After I left you I just couldn't get it out of my mind. Then I was filling some orders and I saw it written down. It came to me, just like that.'

'Yes?'

'Irish whiskey. Funny how the mind works, isn't it?'

'Irish whiskey?'

'His name. It was Jameson. I'm sure of it.'

Banks thanked her and called Ken Blackstone.

'Alan, we've got some names for you,' Blackstone said. 'Quite a lot, I'm afraid.'

'Never mind,' said Banks. 'Is Jameson among them?'

Banks heard Blackstone muttering to himself as he went through the list. 'Yes. Yes, there he is. Bloke called Arthur Jameson. Alan, what—'

'I can't talk now, Ken. Can you pull his file and meet me at The Victoria in about fifteen minutes? I assume you know where it is?'

'The Vic? Sure. But—'

'Fifteen minutes, then.' Banks hung up.

13

ONE

It was foolish, Susan knew, but she couldn't help feeling butterflies in her stomach as she turned the corner where Courtney Terrace intersected Bridgeport Road at number thirty-five. It was mid-afternoon; there was no one about. She felt completely alone, and the click of her heels, which seemed to echo from every building, was the only sound breaking the blanket of silence. Her instructions were simple: find out what you can about Arthur Jameson and his whereabouts.

In her blue jacket and matching skirt, carrying a briefcase and clipboard, she looked like a market researcher. A light breeze ruffled her tight blonde curls and a sudden burst of sun through the clouds dazzled her. She could smell rain in the air.

We know he's not at home, she repeated to herself. He has cancelled his papers for three weeks and gone on a long holiday on the proceeds earned from killing Keith Rothwell. He doesn't answer his telephone, and the two men observing the house over the past hour or so have seen no signs of occupation. So there's nothing to worry about.

But still she worried. She remembered Keith Rothwell kneeling there on the garage floor in his suit, his head blown to a pulp. She remembered the tattered pieces of the girlie magazine, ripped images of women's bodies, as if the killer had intended some kind of sick joke.

And she remembered what Ken Blackstone had told her about Jameson at the makeshift briefing in The Victoria. He had been kicked out of the army for rushing half-cocked, against orders, into an ambush that had killed two innocent teenage girls as well as one suspected IRA trigger-man. After that, he had drifted around Africa and South America as a mercenary. Then, back home, he had beaten an Irishman senseless in a pub because the man's Belfast accent hit a raw nerve. Since the GBH, he hadn't done much except work on building sites and, perhaps, the occasional hit, though there was no evidence of this. He had four A-levels and an incomplete degree in Engineering from the University of Birmingham.

Susan looked around her as she walked. Bridgeport Road was a drab street of dirty terrace houses with no front gardens. From each house, two small steps led right on to the worn pavement, and the tarmac road surface was in poor repair. At the back, she knew, each house had a small bricked-in backyard, complete with privy, full of weeds, and each row faced an identical row across an alley. A peculiar smell hung in the air, a mix of raw sewage and brewery malt, Susan thought, wrinkling her nose.

Outside one or two houses, lines of washing propped up by high poles hung out to dry right across the street. A woman came out of her house with a bucket and knelt on the pavement to scour her front steps. She glanced at Susan without much interest, then started scrubbing. If Jameson really is our man, Susan thought, he'll probably be looking for somewhere a bit more upmarket to live after he has laid low for a while.

There was nobody at home in the first two houses; the timid woman at number thirty-nine said she knew nothing about anyone else in the street; the man at number forty-one didn't speak English; the West Indian couple at number forty-three had just moved into the area and didn't know anyone. Number forty-five was out. Susan felt her heart beat faster as she lifted the brass lion's head knocker of number forty-seven, Jameson's house. She was sure the whole street could hear her heart and the knocker thumping in concert, echoing from the walls.

She had it all rehearsed. If the man with the puppy-dog eyes answered the door, she was going to lift up her clipboard and tell him she was doing market research on neighbourhood shopping habits: how often did he use the local supermarket, that kind of thing. Under no circumstances, Banks had said, was she to enter the house. As if she would. As her mother used to say, she wasn't as green as she was cabbage-looking.

But the heavy knocks just echoed in the silence. She listened. Nothing stirred inside. All her instincts told her the house was empty. She relaxed and moved on to number forty-nine.

'Yes?' An old lady with dry, wrinkled skin opened the door, but kept it on the chain.

Susan kept her voice down, even though she was sure Jameson wasn't home. She showed her card. 'DC Susan Gay, North Yorkshire Police. I'd like to talk to you about your neighbour Mr Jameson, if I may.'

'He's not at home.'

'I know. Do you know where he is?'

The face looked at Susan for some time. She couldn't help but be reminded of reptile skin with slit lizard eyes peeping out of the dry folds.

The door shut, the chain rattled, and the door opened again. 'Come in,' the woman said.

Susan walked straight into the small living room, which smelled of mothballs and peppermint tea. Everything was in shades of dark brown: the wallpaper, the wood around the fireplace, the three-piece suite. And in the fireplace stood an electric fire with fake coals lit by red bulbs. All three elements blazed away. There might be a chilly breeze outside, but the temperature was still in the mid-teens. The room was stifling, worse than Pratt's office. As the door closed, Susan suddenly felt claustrophobic panic, though she had never suffered from claustrophobia in her life. A heavy brown curtain hung from a brass rail at the top of the door; it swept along the floor with a long hissing sound as the door closed.

'What's Arthur been up to now?' the woman asked.

'Will you tell me your name first?'

'Gardiner. Martha Gardiner. What's he been up to? Here, sit down. Can I get you a cup of tea?'

Susan remained by the door. 'No, thank you,' she said. 'I can't stop. It's very important we find out where Mr Jameson is.'

'He's gone on his holidays, that's where. Has he done anything wrong?'

'Why do you keep asking me that, Mrs Gardiner? Would it surprise you?'

She chuckled. 'Surprise me? Nowt much surprises me these days, lass. That one especially. But he's a good enough neighbour. When my lumbago plays me up he'll go to the shops for me. He keeps an eye on me, too, just in case I drop dead one of these days. It happens with us old folk, you know.' She grabbed Susan's arm with a scrawny talon and hissed in her ear, 'But I know he's been in jail. And I saw him with a gun once.'

'A gun?'

'Oh, aye. A shotgun.' She let go. 'I know a shotgun when I see one, young lady. My Eric used to have one when we lived in the country, bless his soul. Young Arthur doesn't think I know about it, but I saw him cleaning it through the back window once. Still, he's always polite to me. Gives me the odd pint of milk and never asks for owt. Who am I to judge? If he likes to go off shooting God's innocent creatures, then he's no worse than many a gentleman, is he? Ducks, grouse, whatever. Even though he says he's one of that *green* lot.'

'How long ago did you see him with the shotgun?'

'Couldn't say for certain. Time has a funny way of moving when you're my age. Couple of months, perhaps. Are you going to arrest him? What are you going to arrest him for? Who'll do my shopping?'

'Mrs Gardiner, first we've got to find him. Have you any idea where he went?'

'How would I know? On his holidays, that's what he said.'

'Abroad?'

She snorted. 'Shouldn't think so. Doesn't like foreigners, doesn't Arthur. You should hear him go on about the way this country's gone downhill since the war, all because of foreigners taking our jobs, imposing their ways. No, he's been abroad, he said, and had enough of foreigners to last him a lifetime. Hates 'em all. "Foreigners begin at Calais, Mrs Gardiner, just you remember that." That's what he says. As if I needed reminding. My Eric was in the war. In Burma. Never the same, after. England for the English, that's what Mr Jameson always says, and I can't say I disagree.'

Susan gritted her teeth. 'And all he told you was that he was going on holiday?'

'Aye, that's what he told me. Likes to drive around the English countryside. At least that's what he's done before. Sent me a postcard from the Lake District once. He wished me well and asked me to keep an eye on his place. You know, in case somebody broke in. There's a lot of that these days.' She snorted. 'Foreigners again, if you ask me.'

'I don't suppose he left you a key, did he?'

She shook her head. 'Just asked me to keep an eye out. You know, check the windows, try the door every now and then, make sure it's still locked.'

'When did he leave?'

'Late Thursday afternoon.'

'When did you last see him?'

'Just before he went. About four o'clock.'

'Was he driving?'

'Of course he was.'

'What kind of car does he drive?'

'A grey one.'

'Did he take his shotgun with him?'

'I didn't see it, but he might have. I don't know. I imagine he'd want to shoot a few animals if he's on holiday, wouldn't he?'

Susan could feel the sweat itching behind her ears and under her arms. Her breathing was becoming shallow. She couldn't take much more of Mrs Gardiner's hothouse atmosphere. But there were other things she needed to know.

'What make was the car?'

'A Ford Granada. I know because he told me when he bought it.'

'I don't suppose you know the number?'

'No. It's new, though. He only got it last year.'

That would make it an 'M' registration, Susan noted. 'How was he dressed?' she asked.

'Dressed? Just casual. Jeans. A short-sleeved shirt. Green, I think it was. Or blue. I've always been a bit colour blind. One of those anoraks – red or orange, I think it was.'

'And he drove off at about four o'clock on Thursday.'

'Yes, I told you.'

'Was he alone?'

'Aye.'

'Do you have any idea where he was heading first?'

'He didn't say.'

Susan needed to know about any friends Jameson might have entertained, but she knew if she stayed in the house a moment longer she would faint. She opened the door. The welcome draught of fresh air almost made her dizzy. Banks would want to question Mrs Gardiner further, anyway. They would need an official statement. Any other questions could wait. They had enough.

'Thank you, Mrs Gardiner,' she said, edging out of the door. 'Thank you very much. Someone else will be along to see you soon to take a statement.'

And she hurried off down the street, heels clicking in the silence, to where Banks and the rest waited in their cars in the Tesco car park off the main road.

TWO

It took the locksmith all of forty-five seconds to open Arthur Jameson's door for Banks and Blackstone to get in. As it wasn't often that four detectives and two patrol cars appeared in Bridgeport Road, and as it was still a nice enough day, despite the occasional clouds, everyone who happened to be home at the time stood out watching, gathered on doorsteps, swapping explanations. The consensus of opinion very quickly became that Mr Jameson was a child molester, and it just went to show you should never trust anyone with eyes like a dog. And, some added, this kind of thing wouldn't happen if the authorities kept them locked up where they belonged, or fed them bromide with their cornflakes or, better still, castrated them.

Like Mrs Gardiner's, Jameson's front door opened directly into the living room. But unlike the gloomy number forty-nine, this room had cream wallpaper patterned with poppies and cornflowers twined around a trellis. Banks opened the curtains and the daylight gave the place a cheery enough aspect. It smelled a little musty, but that was to be expected of a house that had been empty for almost six days.

Jameson's mug shot and a description of his car had already gone out to police all over the country. They had got the Granada's number quickly enough from the central Driver and Vehicle Licensing Centre in Swansea. Local police were warned *not* to approach him under any circumstances, simply to observe and report.

Hatchley and Susan Gay were taking a statement from the woman next door, whom they had managed to persuade, at Susan's insistence, to accompany them to the local station. Mrs Gardiner had, in fact, been quite thrilled to be asked to 'come down to the station', just like on television, and had managed a regal wave to all the neighbours, who had whistled and whooped their encouragement as she got in the car. Things were on the move.

In the living room, Banks and Blackstone examined a small bookcase filled with books on nature, the English heritage and the environment: rain forests, ozone layers, whaling, oil spills, seal-clubbing, the whole green spectrum. Jameson had a healthy selection on birds, flowers and wildlife in general, including Gilbert White's *Natural History of Selborne* and Kilvert's diaries. There were also a few large picture books on stately homes and listed buildings.

Blackstone whistled. 'Probably a member of Green-peace and the National Trust, as well,' he said. 'There'll be trouble if we arrest this one, Alan. Loves Britain's heritage, likes furry little animals and wants to save the seals. They'll be calling him the Green Killer, just you wait and see.'

Banks laughed. 'It's not every murderer you meet has a social conscience, is it?' he said. 'I suppose we should take it as an encouraging sign. Loves animals and plants but has no regard for human life.' He pulled a girlie magazine from down the side of a battered armchair. 'Yes, it looks like we've got a real nature boy here.'

After the living room, they went into the kitchen. Everything was clean, neat and tidy: dishes washed, dried and put away, surfaces scrubbed clean of grease. The only sign of neglect was a piece of cheddar, well past its sell-by date, going green in the fridge. The six cans of Tetleys Bitter on the shelf above it would last for a long time yet.

As he looked in the oven, Banks remembered a story he had heard from Superintendent Gristhorpe's nephew in Toronto about a Texan who hid his loaded handgun in the oven when he went to Canada to visit his daughter and son-in-law, Canadian gun laws being much stricter than those in the USA. He forgot about it when he got back, until his wife started to heat up the oven for dinner the first night. After that, he always kept it in the fridge. Jameson didn't keep his shotgun in the oven or the fridge.

The first bedroom was practically empty except for a few cardboard boxes of small household appliances: an electric kettle, a Teasmade, a clock radio. They looked too old and well used to be stolen property. More likely things that had broken, things he hadn't got around to fixing or tossing out. There were also an ironing board and a yellow plastic laundry basket.

The other bedroom, clearly the one Jameson slept in, was untidy but basically clean. The sheets lay twisted on the bed, and a pile of clothes lay on the floor under the window. A small television stood on top of the dresser-drawers opposite the bed. All the cupboard held was clothes and shoes. Perhaps the soil expert might be able to find something on the shoes linking Jameson to Arkbeck Farm and its immediate area. After all, he had succeeded with the car. The only reading material on his bedside table was a British National Party pamphlet.

There was a small attic, reached through a hatch in the landing ceiling. Banks stood on a chair and looked around. He saw nothing but rafters and beams; it hadn't been converted for use at all.

Next, they opened the cistern and managed to get the side of the bath off, but Jameson had avoided those common hiding places.

Which left the cellar.

Banks never had liked cellars very much, or any underground places, for that matter. He always expected to find something gruesome in them, and he often had when he worked in London. At their very best, they were dark, dank, dirty and smelly places, and this one was no exception. The chill air gripped them as soon as they got down the winding steps and Banks smelled mould and damp coaldust. It must have been there for years, he thought, because the area was a smoke-free zone now, like most of the country. Thank the lord there was an electric light.

The first thing they saw was a bicycle lying in parts on the floor next to a workbench and a number of planks of wood leaning against the wall. Next to them hung a World War II gas mask and helmet.

Dark, stained brick walls enclosed a number of smaller storage areas, like the ones used for coal in the old days. Now they were empty. The only thing of interest was Jameson's workbench, complete with vice and expensive tool-box. On the bench lay a box of loose shot and a ripped and crumpled page from a magazine. When Banks rubbed his latex-covered index finger over the rough surface wood, he could feel grains of powder. He lifted up the finger and sniffed. Gunpowder.

There was a drawer under the bench and Banks pulled it open. Inside, among a random collection of screws, nails, electrical tape, fuse wire and used sandpaper, he found a half-empty box of ammunition for a 9mm handgun.

'Right, Ken,' he said. 'I think we've got the bastard, National Trust or not. Time to call in the SOCOs.'

THREE

Banks cadged a lift with Blackstone back to Millgarth, where Susan and Hatchley were just about to take Mrs Gardiner home before returning to Eastvale. They had found out nothing more from her, Hatchley said as they stood at the doors ready to leave. It seemed that Jameson was a bit of a loner. He had had no frequent visitors, male or female, and she had seen no one answering the vague description of his partner. Neither had the other neighbours, according to the results of the house-to-house.

Banks asked about Pamela Jeffreys's condition and was told there had been some improvement but that she was still in intensive care.

Christ, Banks thought, as he sat opposite Blackstone, it had been a long day. He felt shagged out, especially given his previous night's folly, which seemed light years ago now. He looked at his watch: ten to six. He wanted to go home, but knew he might not be able to make it tonight, depending on the developments of the next few hours. At least he could go back to the hotel and have a long bath, phone Sandra, listen to Classic FM and read the army and probation officer's reports on Jameson while he waited around. If nothing happened by, say, eight o'clock, then he would perhaps go back to Eastvale for the night.

He slipped the reports into his briefcase and again decided to walk back to the hotel. It was that twilight hour between the evening rush-hour and going-out-on-the-town time. The city centre was practically deserted; the shops had closed, workers had gone home, and only a few people lingered in the few cafés and restaurants still open in the arcades and pedestrian precincts off Vicar Lane and Briggate. The sun had at last won its day-long battle with cloud; it lay in proud gold pools on the dusty streets and pavements, where last night's rain was a dim memory; it cast black shadows that crept slowly up the sides of buildings; it reflected harshly in shop windows and glittered on the specks of quartz embedded in stone surfaces.

Back at the hotel, he picked up his jacket, which he had handed over to be mended before leaving for The Vic. There was one message for him: 'Please come to Room 408 as soon as you get back, where you will find out some useful information.' It wasn't signed.

That was odd. Informers didn't usually operate this

way. They certainly didn't book rooms in hotels to pass along their information.

'Who's staying in room 408?' Banks asked, slipping his jacket on. After the obligatory refusal to give out such information on the part of the clerk, and the showing of a warrant card on the part of Banks, he discovered that the occupant of said room was a Mr Wilson. Very odd indeed. It was a common enough name, but Banks couldn't remember, offhand, any Mr Wilson.

He was tempted to ignore the message and carry on with what he planned, but curiosity got the better of him, as it always did.

When the lift stopped at the fourth floor, he poked his head through the doors first to see if there was anyone in the corridor. It was empty. He followed the arrow to room 408, took a deep breath and knocked. He debated whether to stand aside, but decided it was only in American films that people shot holes through hotel doors. Still, he found himself edging away a little, so he couldn't be seen through the peep-hole.

The door opened abruptly. Banks tensed, then let out his breath. Before him stood Dirty Dick Burgess.

'You again? What the hell?' Banks gasped. But before he could even enter the room Burgess had put on a leather jacket and taken him by the elbow.

'About bloody time, Banks,' he said. 'I'm sick of being cooped up in here. There's been developments. Come on, let's go get a drink.'

14

ONE

Despite Burgess's protest that it would be full of commercial travellers and visiting rugby teams, Banks insisted on their drinking in the Holiday Inn's idea of a traditional English pub, the Wig and Pen. He did this because his car was nearby and he still held hopes of getting back to Eastvale that evening. As it turned out, Burgess seemed to take a shine to the place.

He sat at the table opposite Banks with his pint of McEwan's lager, lit a Tom Thumb and looked around the quiet pub. 'Not bad,' he said, tapping his cigar on the rim of the ashtray. 'Not bad at all. I never did like those places with beams across the ceiling and bedpans on the walls.'

'Bed warmers,' Banks corrected him.

'Whatever. Anyway, what do you think of those two over there as a couple of potential bed warmers? Do you think they fancy us?'

Banks looked over and saw two attractive women in their late twenties or early thirties who, judging by their clothes, had dropped by for a drink after working late at one of the many Wellington Street office buildings. There was no doubt about it, the one with the short black hair and the good legs did give Burgess the eye and whisper something in her friend's ear.

'I think they do,' said Burgess.

'Didn't you say something about developments?'

'What? Oh, yes.' Burgess looked away from the women and leaned forward, lowering his voice. 'For a start, Fraud Squad think they've found definite evidence in Daniel Clegg's books and records that Clegg and Rothwell were laundering money for Martin Churchill.'

'That hardly counts as a development,' Banks said. 'We were already working on that assumption.'

'Ah, but now it's more than an assumption, isn't it? You've got to hand it to those Fraud Squad boys, boring little fuckers that they are, they've been burning the candle at both ends on this one.'

'Have you any idea why Churchill would use a couple of provincials like Rothwell and Clegg?'

'Good point,' said Burgess. 'As it happens, yes, I do know. Daniel Clegg and Martin Churchill were at Cambridge together, reading law. Simple as that. The old boy network. I'd reckon the one knew the other was crooked right from the start.'

'Did they keep in touch over the years?'

'Obviously. Remember, Clegg's a tax lawyer. He's been using St Corona as a tax shelter for his clients for years. It must have seemed a natural step to call on him when Churchill needed expert help. You can launder money from just about anywhere, you know. Baby Doc used a Swiss lawyer and did a lot of his business in Canada. You can take it out or bring it into Heathrow or Gatwick by the suitcase-load, using couriers, or you can run it through foreign exchange wire services, whatever. Governments keep coming up with new restrictive measures, but it's like plugging holes in a sieve. It's easy if you know how, and a tax lawyer and a financial consultant with a strong background in accounting certainly knew how.'

'What made Clegg choose Rothwell as his partner?'

'How would I know? You can't expect me to do your job for you, Banks, now can you? But they clearly knew one another somehow. Clegg must have known that Rothwell was exceptionally good with finances and none too concerned about their source. Takes one to know one, as they say.'

Burgess looked over at the two women, who had got another round of drinks, and smiled. The black-haired one crossed her long legs and smiled back shyly; the other put her hand over her mouth and giggled.

'My lucky night, I think,' Burgess said, clapping his hands and showering cigar ash over his stomach. He had a disconcerting habit of sitting still for ages then making a sudden, jerky movement. 'I'll say one thing for the north,' he went on, 'you've got some damned accommodating women up here. *Damned* accommodating. Look, why don't you get a couple more pints in, then I'll tell you something else that might interest you? And mine's lager, remember, not that pissy real ale stuff.'

Banks thought about it. Two pints. Yes, he would be fine for driving back to Eastvale, if he got the chance. 'All right,' he said, and went to the bar.

'Okay,' said Burgess, after his first sip. 'The two men, the white one and the darkie who were following you around?'

Banks lit a cigarette. 'You know who they are?'

'I've got to admit, I wasn't entirely truthful with you last time we met.'

'When have you ever been?'

'Unfair.'

'So you knew who they were last time we talked?'

'Suspected. Now we've got confirmation. They're

Mickey Lanois and Gregory Jackson, two of Churchill's top enforcers. They came into Heathrow last Friday. The way it looks is that Churchill asked Clegg to get rid of Rothwell, and after he did it he took off with a lot of money, probably figuring that he might be next. Churchill heard about Clegg's scarpering pretty quickly and sent his goons to do some damage control. You know what their favourite torture is, Banks?'

Banks shook his head. He didn't want to know, but he knew Burgess would tell him anyway.

'They get a handful of those little glass tubes the doctors use to keep liquid in. What do you call them, phials, right? Really thin glass, anyway. And they put them in the victim's mouth, lots of them. Then they tape the mouth shut securely and beat him a bit about the face. Or her. Churchill himself thought that up. He likes to watch. Think about it.'

Banks thought, swallowed and felt his throat constrict. 'Been letting you practise it at the Yard, have they?' he asked.

Burgess laughed. 'No, not yet. They're still running tests in Belfast. Anyway, the point is that we know who they are.'

'No, that's not entirely the point,' said Banks. 'The point is where are they now and what are you going to do about them?'

Burgess shook his head. 'That's a whole different ball game. We're talking about international politics here, politically sensitive issues. It's out of your hands, Banks. Accept that. All you need to know is that we know who they are and we're keeping tabs.'

'Don't give me that politically sensitive crap,' said Banks, stabbing out his cigarette so hard that sparks flew out of the ashtray. 'These two men damn near killed a woman here a few days ago. You say they like to go around stuffing people's mouths full of glass, then you tell me to trust you, you're keeping tabs. Well, bollocks, that's what I say.'

Burgess sighed. 'Somehow, I knew you were going to be difficult, Banks, I just knew it. Can't you leave it be? They won't get away with it, don't worry.'

'Do you know where they are now?'

'They won't get away with it,' Burgess repeated.

Banks took a sip of his beer and held back his rage. There was something in Burgess's tone that hinted he had something up his sleeve. 'What are you telling me?' Banks asked.

'That we'll get them. Or somebody will. But they'll go down quietly, no fuss, no publicity.'

Banks thought for a moment. He still didn't trust Burgess. 'Can I talk to them?' he asked, aware he was speaking through clenched teeth, still keeping his anger in check.

Burgess narrowed his eyes. 'Got to you, did it? What they did to the girl? I've seen pictures of her, before and after. Nasty. I'll bet you fancied her, didn't you, Banks? Nice dusky piece of crumpet, touch of the tarbrush, probably knew a lot of those *Kama Sutra* tricks. Just your type. Tasty.'

Banks felt his hand tighten on the pint glass. Why did he always let Burgess get to him this way? The bastard had a knack of touching on exactly the right raw nerve. Did it every time. 'I'd just like to be there when you question them, that's all,' he said quietly.

Burgess shrugged. 'No problem. If it's possible, I'll arrange it. All I'm saying is no publicity on the Churchill matter, okay? Let your liberal humanist sentiments fuck this one up and you'll be in deep doo-doo, Banks, very deep doo-doo indeed.'

'What about the press?'

'They can be dealt with. Have you ever considered that for every scandal you read about there are many that you don't? Do you think it's all left to chance? Don't be so bloody naïve.'

'Come off it. You might be able to tape a few mouths shut, but even you can't guarantee that no hotshot investigative reporters aren't going to be all over this one like flies around shit.'

Burgess shrugged. 'Maybe they'll hear Churchill's been killed in a coup. Maybe they'll even see the body.'

'Maybe it'd be best for everyone if he did get killed in a coup. Less embarrassing all round.'

Burgess remained silent for a moment, glass in hand. Then he said, slowly, 'And maybe he's got life insurance.'

'Well, I suppose you'd know. Let's hope there's a good plastic surgeon on St Corona.'

'Look,' Burgess said, 'let's stop pissing around. What I want from you is a promise that you won't talk to the press about the Churchill angle.'

Banks lit another cigarette. What could he do? If Burgess were telling the truth, Mickey Lanois and Gregory Jackson would be caught and punished for their crimes. He could live with that. He would have to. Burgess certainly had a better chance of catching them than Banks did, by the sound of things. Perhaps they were even in custody already.

Also, with luck, Arthur Jameson and his accomplice would go down for the murder of Keith Rothwell. But was Burgess telling the full truth? Banks didn't know. All he knew was that he couldn't trust the bastard. It all sounded too easy. But what choice did he have?

'All right,' he said.

Burgess reached over and patted his arm. 'Good,' he said. 'Good. I knew I could depend on you to keep mum when it counts.'

Banks jerked his arm away. 'Don't push it. And if I find out you've been buggering me around on this one, my promise is null and void, okay?'

Burgess held up his hands in mock surrender. 'Okay, okay.'

'There is another thing.'

'What's that?'

'Rothwell's killers. Lanois and Jackson didn't do that.'

Burgess shook his head. 'I'm not interested in them. They're not in my brief.'

'So what happens when we catch Jameson, if we catch him?'

'Jameson?'

'Arthur Jameson. One of Rothwell's killers.'

'I don't give a monkey's toss. That's up to you. I'm not interested. It's unlikely that this Jameson, whoever he is, knows anything about Churchill's part in the matter. He was probably just a hired killer working for Clegg, who has conveniently disappeared with a shitload of cash.'

'Any ideas where?'

Burgess shook his head then jabbed his finger in the air close to Banks's chest. 'But I can tell you one thing. Wherever he is, he won't be there for long. Churchill has the memory of an elephant, the reach of a giraffe and the tenacity of a bloody pit bull. He didn't get to bleed an entire country dry for nothing. It takes a special talent. Don't underestimate the man just because he's a butcher.'

'So we write off Clegg?'

'I think he's already written himself off by double-crossing Churchill.'

'And Jameson?'

'*If* he goes to trial, and *if* he talks – both big ifs, by the way – all he can say is that Clegg hired him to kill Rothwell. I doubt that Clegg would tell him the real reason. He might be a crooked lawyer, but I'm sure he still knows the value of confidentiality. He wouldn't want to let his hired killers know exactly how much money was involved, would he? It would make him too vulnerable by half. Anyway, I trust you'll have enough physical evidence to prosecute this Jameson when the time comes. If not, maybe we can fabricate some for you. Always happy to oblige.' He held his hand up. 'Only kidding. My little joke.'

Burgess glanced over at the two women, who had got yet another round of drinks and seemed to be laughing quite tipsily. 'Look,' he said, 'if I don't strike soon they'll be past it. Are you sure you won't join me? It'll be a laugh, and the wife need never know.'

'No,' said Banks. 'No, thanks. I'm going home.'

'Suit yourself.' Burgess stretched back his shoulders and sucked in his gut. 'Anything to liven up a miserable evening in Leeds,' he said. 'Once more unto the breach.' And with that, he strutted over to their table, smiling, pint in hand. Banks watched them make room for him, then shook his head, drank up and left.

TWO

'What on earth happened to you?' asked Sandra when Banks walked into the living room at about ten o'clock that evening.

'I had a slight disagreement with a couple of would-be muggers,' Banks said. 'Don't worry, I'm okay.' And he left it at that. Sandra raised her dark eyebrows but didn't pursue it. He knew she wouldn't. She wasn't the mothering type, and she rarely gave him much sympathy when he whimpered through flu or moaned through a bad cold.

Banks walked over to the cocktail cabinet and poured a stiff shot of Laphroaig single malt whisky. Sandra said she'd have a Drambuie. A good sign. After that, he put on his new CD of Khachaturian's piano concerto and flopped on to the sofa.

As he listened to the music, he looked at Sandra's framed photograph over the fireplace: a misty sunset in Hawes, taken from the daleside above the town, all subdued grey and orange with a couple of thin streaks of vermilion. The unusual church tower, square with a turret attached to one corner, dominated the grey slate roofs, and smoke curled up from some of the chimneys. Banks sipped the peaty malt whisky and smacked his lips.

Sandra sat beside him. 'What are you thinking?' she asked.

Banks told her about his meetings with Dirty Dick Burgess. 'There's always some sort of hidden agenda with him,' he said. 'I'm not sure what he's up to this time, but there's not a hell of a lot I can do about it except wait and see. That's about all we can do now, wait.'

'They also serve . . .'

'I was thinking about the Rothwells on the drive home, too. How could a man lead an entire other life, away from his family, under another name?'

'Is that what happened?'

'Yes.' Banks explained about Robert Calvert and his flat in Leeds, his fondness for gambling, women and dancing.

'And Pamela Jeffreys said she was sure he wasn't a married man. She said she'd have been able to tell.'

'Did she? Who's Pamela Jeffreys?'

'His girlfriend. It doesn't matter.'

Sandra sipped her drink and thought it over. 'It's probably not as difficult as you think for two people who live together on the surface to lead completely separate lives, one unknown to the other. Lord knows, so many couples have drifted so far apart anyway that they don't communicate any more.'

Banks felt his chest tighten. 'Are you talking about us?' he asked, remembering what Ken Blackstone had said about *his* marriage.

'Is that what you think?'

'I don't know.'

Sandra shrugged. 'I don't know, either. It was just a comment. But if the cap fits . . . Think about it, Alan. The amount we see each other, talk to each other, we could both be living other lives. Mostly, we just meet in passing. Let's face it, you could be up to anything most of the time. How would I know?'

'Most of the time I'm working.'

'Just like this Rothwell was?'

'That's different. He was away a lot.'

'What about the last couple of nights? You didn't phone, did you?'

Banks sat forward. 'Oh, come on! I tried. You weren't home.'

'You could have left a message on the machine.'

'You know how I hate those things. Anyway, it's not as if you didn't know where I was. You could easily have checked up on me. And it's not that often I'm away from home for a night or more.'

'Secret lives don't always have to be lived at night.'

'This is ridiculous.'

'Is it? Probably. All I'm saying is we don't talk enough to know.'

Banks slumped back and sipped his drink. 'I suppose so,' he said. 'Is it my fault? You always seemed to handle my absences so well before. You understand the *job* better than any other copper's wife I've met.'

'I don't know,' Sandra said. 'Maybe it just took longer for the strain to work its way through. Or maybe it's just worse because *I'm* busy a lot now, too.'

He put his arm around her. 'I don't know what's been happening to us lately, either,' he said, 'but maybe we'll go away when this is all over.'

He felt Sandra stiffen beside him. 'Promises,' she said. 'You've been saying that for years.'

'Have I?'

'You know you have. We haven't had a bloody holiday since we moved to Eastvale.'

'Well, dust off your camera. I've got a bit of leave due and I might just surprise you this time.'

'How long do you think the case will last?'

'Hard to say.'

'There you are, then.'

He stroked her shoulder. 'Tell me you'll think about it.'

'I'll think about it. Tracy comes back on Sunday.'

'I know.'

'Won't you be pleased to see her? Will you even be around to meet her at the airport?'

'Of course I will.'

Sandra relaxed a little and moved closer. A very good sign. The Drambuie was clearly working. 'You'd better,' she said. '*She* phoned earlier tonight. She sends her love.'

'How's she getting on?'

Sandra laughed. 'She said it's not quite like *A Year in Provence* down there, but she likes it anyway. She hasn't bumped into John Thaw yet.'

'Who?'

'John Thaw. You know, the actor who was in *A Year in Provence* on television? I liked him better as Morse.'

'Who?'

She elbowed him in the ribs. 'You know quite well who I'm talking about. I know you liked Morse. He used to be in *The Sweeney*, too, years ago, and you used to watch that down in London. Remember, in your old macho days? Didn't you even go drinking with him once?'

'What do you mean, "old"?' Banks flexed his biceps.

Sandra laughed and moved closer. 'I don't want to fight,' she said. 'Honest, I don't. Not since we've seen so little of one another.'

'Me neither,' said Banks.

'I just think we've got a few problems to deal with, that's all. We need to communicate better.'

'And we will. How about a truce?' He tightened his arm around her shoulder.

'Mmm. All right.'

'I'll have to call the station and see if there's been any developments,' he said.

But he didn't move. He felt too comfortable. His limbs felt pleasantly heavy and weary, and the warmth of the malt whisky flowed through his veins. The slow second movement started in its haunting, erotic way. Soon, the eerie flexatone entered and sent shivers up and down his spine. A cheap effect, perhaps, but sometimes effective if you happened to be in the right mood.

Banks drained his glass and put it on the table by the

sofa. Sandra let her head rest between his shoulder and chest. Definitely a good sign. 'Remember that silly film we saw on TV a while back?' he said. 'The one where the couple has sex listening to Ravel's *Bolero*?'

'Hmm. It's called *10*. Dudley Moore and Bo Derek. And I don't think they were really listening. More like using it as background music.'

'Well, I've never really liked *Bolero*. It's far too ordered and mechanical. It's got a kind of inevitability about it that's too predictable for my taste. I've always thought this Khachaturian piece would be a lot better to make love to. Much better. Wanders all over the place. You never really know where it's going next. Slow and dreamy at the start, with plenty of great climaxes later on.'

'Sounds good to me. Have you ever tried it?'

'No.'

Sandra moved her head up until she was facing him, her lips about two inches away. He swept back a strand of hair from her cheek and let his fingers rest on her cool skin. 'I thought you had to call the station?' she said.

'Later,' he said, stroking her cheek. 'Later. Are the curtains closed?'

THREE

Boredom. They never told you about that down at the recruitment drives, thought PC Grant Everett as he rolled down the window of the patrol car and lit a cigarette. His partner, PC Barry Miller, was good about the smoking. He didn't indulge, himself, but he understood Grant's need to light up every now and then, especially on a quiet night like this one.

They were parked in a lay-by between Princes Risborough and High Wycombe. To the south, through the rear-view mirror, Grant could see the faint glow of the nearest town, while to the north only isolated lights twinkled from scattered farms and cottages. All around them spread the dark, rolling landscape of the Chilterns. It was an attractive spot on a nice day, especially in spring with the bluebells and cherry blossom out, but in the dark it seemed somehow forbidding, inhospitable.

A light breeze swirled the smoke out of the car. Grant inhaled deeply. It had just stopped raining and he loved the way the scent of rain seemed to blend with the tobacco and make it taste so much better. It was at moments like this when he understood why he smoked, despite all the health warnings. On the other hand, he never quite understood it when he got up after a night's chain-smoking in the pub and coughed his guts up for half an hour.

Next to him, Barry was munching on a Mars bar. Grant smiled to himself. Six foot two and sixteen stone already and the silly bugger still needed to feed his face with chocolate bars. Who am I to talk? Grant thought, sucking on his cigarette again. To each his own poison.

Grant felt sleepy and the cigarette helped keep him awake. He had never got used to shift work; his biological rhythms, or whatever they were, had never adapted. When he lay down his head in the morning as the neighbour's kids were going to school, the postman was doing his rounds and everyone else was off to work, he could never get to sleep. Especially if the sun were shining. And then there was Janet, bless her soul, doing her best, trying hard to be as quiet as she could around the house, and Sarah, only six months, crying for feeding and nappy-changing. And the bills to pay, and . . . Christ, he wasn't going to think about that. At least the job got him out of the house, away from all that for a while.

A lorry rumbled by. Grant flicked the stub of his cigarette out of the window and heard it sizzle as it hit a puddle. Occasionally, voices cut through the static on the police radio, but the messages weren't for them.

'Shall we belt up and bugger off, then?' said Barry. He screwed up the wrapper of his Mars bar and put it in his pocket. Ever the careful one, Grant thought, with an affectionate smile. Wouldn't even be caught littering, wouldn't Barry.

'Might as well.' Grant reached for his belt. Then they heard the squealing sound of rubber on wet tarmac. 'What the fuck was that?'

On the main road, a northbound car skidded as it turned the bend too fast, then righted itself.

'Shall we?' said Barry.

'My pleasure.'

Grant loved it when the lights were flashing and the siren screaming. First he was pushed back in the seat by the force when he put his foot down, and then he felt as if he were taking off, seeming somehow to be magically freed from all the restraints of the road: not just the man-made rules, but the laws of nature. Sometimes, Grant even felt as if they were really taking off, wheels no longer on the ground.

But there was no chase to be had here; it was over before it began. The car was about two hundred yards ahead of them when its driver seemed to realize they meant business. He slowed down as they caught up and pulled over to the side of the road, spraying up water from the hedgerow. His number plate was too muddy to read.

Grant pulled up behind him, and Barry got out to approach the car.

It wasn't likely to be much, Grant thought as he sniffed the fresh night air through the open window – maybe a drunk, maybe a few outstanding parking tickets – but at least it was *something* to relieve the boredom for a few minutes.

He could hear perfectly clearly when Barry asked the driver to turn off his ignition and present his driving documents. The driver did as he was told. Barry looked at the papers and passed them back. Next, he asked the man if he had been drinking. Grant couldn't hear the man's reply, but it seemed to satisfy Barry. Grant knew he would be listening for slurred words and sniffing for booze on the driver's breath.

After that, Barry asked the man where he had been and where he was going. Grant thought he heard the man mention Princes Risborough.

No other cars passed. The night was quiet and Grant caught a whiff of beech leaves and cherry wood on the damp air. He thought he heard some cows low in the distance and, farther still, a nightingale.

Then Barry asked the man to get out of the car and clean off his number plate. Grant heard him explain patiently that it was an offence to drive with a number plate that is 'not easily distinguishable' and smiled to himself at the stilted, textbook phrase. But the man would get off with a caution this time; Barry seemed satisfied with his behaviour.

The man got back in the car and Grant heard Barry speak over his personal radio.

'465 to Control.'

'465 go ahead.'

'Ten nine vehicle check please.'

The voices crackled unnaturally over the country night air.

'Pass your number.'

'Mike four, three, seven, Tango Zulu Delta.'

'Stand by.'

Grant knew it would take three or four minutes for the operator to check the number on the computer, then, all being well, they could be on their way.

Barry and the driver seemed to be chatting amiably enough as they waited. Grant looked at the newly cleaned number plate and reached idly for the briefing-sheet beside him. There seemed to be *something* familiar about it, something he ought to remember.

He ran his finger down the list of stolen cars. No, not there. He wouldn't remember any of those numbers; there were always too many of them. It had to be something more important: a vehicle used in a robbery, perhaps? Then he found it: M437 TZD, grey Granada.

Suddenly, he felt cold. The owner was wanted in connection with a murder in North Yorkshire. Possibly armed and dangerous. Shit. All of a sudden, Barry seemed to be taking a hell of a long time out there.

A number of thoughts passed quickly through Grant's mind, the first of which was regret that they didn't do things the American way. Get the guy out of the vehicle, hands stretched on the roof, legs apart, pat him down. 'Assume the position, asshole!' Why pretend they were still living in a peaceful society where the local bobby was your best friend? Christ, how Grant wished he had a gun.

Should he go out and try to get Barry to the car, use some excuse? He could say they'd been called to an emergency. Could he trust himself to walk without stumbling, to speak without stuttering? His legs felt like jelly and his throat was tight. But he felt so impotent, just watching. All he could hope was that the radio operator would understand Barry's predicament and give the guy a clean bill of health. According to the information on the sheet, the man, Arthur Jameson, didn't even *know* he was wanted.

The radio crackled back into life.

'Control to 465.'

'Go ahead, over.'

'Er . . . Mike four, three, seven, Tango Zulu Delta . . . No reports stolen. Er . . . Do you require keeper details over?'

'Affirmative.'

More static. Grant tensed in his seat, hand on the door-handle. Too many pauses.

'Keeper is Arthur Jameson, 47 Bridgeport Avenue, Leeds. Er . . . is keeper with you, over?'

'Affirmative. Any problem?'

She was blowing it, Grant sensed. Someone, probably the super, was standing over her trying to help her calmly get Barry back to the car and the driver on his way, but she was nervous, halting. It was all taking far too long, and if the suspect couldn't sense there was something wrong over the radio, then he was an idiot.

'No reports stolen.'

'You already told me that, love,' said Barry. 'Is something wrong?'

'Sorry . . . er . . . 465 . . . Stand by.'

Grant tightened his grip on the door-handle. This was it. He wasn't going to stand around and let his partner, who had probably dozed off at the briefing and to whom the number obviously meant bugger-all, just stand there and take it.

But before he got the door half open, he saw Barry, all sixteen stone and six foot two of him, drop to the wet road clutching the side of his neck, from which a dark spray of blood fountained high and arced to the ground. Then he heard the shots, two dull cracks echoing through the dark countryside.

Left foot still in the car, right foot on the road, Grant hesitated. Mistake. His last thought was that it was so bloody unfair and pointless and miserable to die like this by a roadside outside High Wycombe. Then a bullet shattered the windscreen and took him full in the face, scattering blood, teeth and bone fragments all over the car. After its echo had faded, the Granada revved up and sped off into the night, and the nightingale sang again into the vacuum of silence the car left behind.

15

ONE

The sky was a sheet of grey shale, smeared here and there
by dirty rags of cloud fluttering over the wooded hillsides
on a cool wind. Rooks and crows gathered noisily in the
roadside trees like shards of darkness refusing to dispel.
Even the green of the dense beech forests looked black.

Banks and Sergeant Hatchley, who had driven through
the night at breakneck speed from Eastvale, stood and
looked in silence at the patrol car with the shattered windscreen and at the outline of the body on the tarmac about
six or seven feet ahead, near which dark blood had
coagulated in shallow puddles on the road surface. Close
by, Detective Superintendent Jarrell from the Thames
Valley Police paced up and down, shabby beige raincoat
flapping around his legs.

The road had been cordoned off, and several patrol
cars, lights circling like demented lighthouses, guarded the
edges of the scene, where the SOCOs still worked. Local
traffic had been diverted.

'It was a cock-up,' Superintendent Jarrell growled,
glaring at the two men from Yorkshire the minute they got
out of Banks's Cortina and walked over to him. 'A
monumental cock-up.'

Jarrell was clearly looking for somewhere to place
the blame, and it irritated the hell out of him that no

matter how hard he tried, it fell squarely on his own shoulders. The two PCs might have made a mistake in not tattooing the Granada's number on their memories, and the radio operator had certainly screwed up royally, but in the police force, as in other hierarchical structures, when an underling screws up, the responsibility goes to the top. You don't blame the foot-soldiers, you blame the general, and *everybody* gets a good bollocking, from the top down.

Banks knew that Ken Blackstone at West Yorkshire had followed correct procedure in getting a photograph, description and details about Arthur Jameson out to all divisions. And the point he had most emphasized was, 'May be armed. Observe only. UNDER NO CIRCUMSTANCES ATTEMPT TO APPREHEND.'

Jarrell's was one of those unfortunate faces in which the individual features fail to harmonize: long nose, small, beady eyes, bushy brows, a thin slit of a mouth, prominent cheekbones, receding chin, mottled complexion. Somehow, though, it didn't dissolve into total chaos; there was an underlying unity about the man himself that, like a magnetic field, drew it all together.

'Any update on the injured officer, sir?' Banks asked.

'What? Oh.' Jarrell stopped pacing for a moment and faced Banks. He had an erect, military bearing. Suddenly the fury seemed to bleed out of him like air from a tyre. 'Miller was killed outright, as you know.' He gestured at the outline and the surrounding, stained tarmac with his whole arm, as if indicating a cornucopia. 'There's about seven pints of his blood here. Everett's still hanging on. Just. The bullet went in through his upper lip, just under the nose, and it seems to have been slowed down or deflected by cartilage and bone. Anyway, it didn't get a chance to do serious brain damage, so the doc says he's got a good chance. Bloody fool.'

'If you don't mind my saying so, sir,' Banks said, 'it looks like they got into a situation they couldn't get out of. We had no reason to think Jameson knew we were on to him. Nor had we any reason to think he was a likely spree killer. We want him for a job he was hired to do cold-bloodedly. He must have panicked. I know it doesn't help the situation, sir, but the men *were* inexperienced. I doubt they'd handled much but traffic duty, had they?'

Jarrell ran his hand through his hair. 'You're right, of course. They pulled him over on a routine traffic check. When Miller called in the vehicle number, the radio operator called the senior officer on the shift. He tried to talk her through it calmly, but . . . Hell, she was new to the job. She was scared to death. It wasn't her fault.'

Banks nodded and rubbed his eyes. Beside him, Hatchley's gaze seemed fixed on the bloody tarmac. When Banks had got the call close to two a.m. – his first night at home in days – he had first thought of taking Susan Gay, then, not without malice entirely, though affectionate malice, he had decided that it was time Sergeant Hatchley got his feet wet. He knew how Hatchley loved his sleep. Consequently, they hadn't said much on the way down. Banks had played Mitsuko Uchida's live versions of the Mozart piano sonatas, and Hatchley had seemed content to doze in the passenger seat, snoring occasionally.

Most chief inspectors, Banks knew, would have had someone else drive, but he was using his own car, the old Cortina, no longer produced now and practically an antique. And, damn it, he *liked* driving it himself.

'Seen enough here?' Jarrell asked.

'I think so.'

'Me, too. Let's go.'

Jarrell drove them down the road. 'Believe it or not,' he said, 'this is very pretty countryside under the right circumstances.'

About a mile along the road, towards Princes Risborough, Jarrell turned left on to a muddy farm track and bumped along until they got to a gate on the right, where he pulled up. A hedgerow interspersed with hawthorns shielded the field and its fence from view. Cows mooed in the next field.

The gate stood open, and as Banks and Hatchley followed Jarrell through, they both sank almost to their ankles in mud. Too late, Banks realized, he hadn't brought the right gear. He should have known to bring the wellingtons he always carried in the boot of his car. Like most policemen, he took pride in keeping his shoes well polished; now they were covered in mud and probably worse, judging by the prevalence of cows. He cursed and Jarrell laughed. Hatchley stood holding on to the gatepost trying to wipe most of it off on the few tufts of grass there. Banks looked at the muddy field dotted with cowpats and didn't bother. They'd only get dirty again.

In the field, a group of men in white boiler suits and black wellington boots worked around a car that stood bogged down in the mud with its doors open. The air was sharp with the tang of cow-clap.

One of the men had propped a radio on a stone by the hedgerow, and it was tuned to the local breakfast show, at the moment featuring a golden oldie: Cilla Black singing 'Anyone Who Had a Heart'. One of the SOCOs sang along with it as he worked. The cows mooed even louder, demonstrating remarkably good taste, Banks thought. They weren't so far away after all. They were, in fact, all lying down in a group just across the field. Cows lying down. That meant it was going to rain, his mother always said. But it had rained already. Did that mean they'd been in the same position for hours? That it was going to rain again?

Giving up on folk wisdom, Banks turned instead to look at the abandoned Granada, the bottom of its chassis streaked with mud and cow-shit. It had been found, Jarrell said, just over an hour ago, while Banks and Hatchley had been in transit.

'Anything?' Jarrell shouted over to the team.

One of the men in white shook his head. 'Nothing but the usual rubbish, sir,' he said. 'Sweet wrappers, old road maps, that sort of thing. He must have taken everything of use or value. No sign of any weapons.'

Jarrell grunted and turned away.

'He'd hardly have left his guns, would he?' said Banks. 'Not now he's officially on the run. I'd guess he probably had a rucksack or something with him in the car. Look, sir, you know the landscape around here better than I do. If you were him, where would you go?'

Jarrell looked up at the louring sky for a moment, as if for inspiration, then rubbed at the inside corner of his right eye with his index finger. 'He has a couple of choices,' he said. 'Either head immediately for the nearest town, get to London and take the first boat or plane out of the country, or simply lie low.' He pointed towards the hills. 'A man could hide himself there for a good while, if he knew how to survive.'

'We'd better cover both possibilities,' Banks said. 'He's spent time in the army, so he's probably been on survival courses. And if he heads for London, he'll likely know someone who can help him.'

'Whatever he does, I'd say he'll most likely go across country first,' said Jarrell. 'He'd be smart enough to know that stealing a car or walking by the roadside would be too risky.' He looked at his watch. 'The shooting occurred at about half past twelve. It's half past six now. That gives him a six-hour start.'

'How far could he get, do you reckon?'

'I'd give him about three miles an hour in this terrain, under these conditions,' Jarrell went on. 'Maybe a bit less.'

'Where's the nearest station?'

'That's the problem,' said Jarrell slowly. 'This is close to prime commuter country. There's Princes Risborough, Saunderton and High Wycombe on the Chiltern Line, all nearby. If he heads east, he can get to the Northampton Line at Tring, Berkhamsted or Hemel Hempstead. If he heads for Amersham, he can even get on the underground, the Metropolitan Line. Unfortunately for us, there's no shortage of trains to London around here, and they start running early.'

'Let's say he's managed about sixteen or seventeen miles,' said Banks. 'What's his best bet?'

'Probably the Chiltern Line. Plenty of trains and an easy connection with the underground. He could even be in London by now.'

They started walking back to the car. 'I can tell you one thing,' said Banks. 'Wherever he is, his shoes will be bloody muddy.'

TWO

If. If. If. Such were Banks's thoughts as he followed Superintendent Jarrell into Jameson's rented cottage an hour or
so later. *If* Everett and Miller hadn't stopped Jameson last
night. *If* Jameson hadn't panicked and shot them. *If.*

In an ideal world, they would have tracked Jameson to
this cottage through a cheque stub or a circled address in
an accommodation guide. Quietly, they would have surrounded the place when they were certain Jameson was
inside, then arrested him, perhaps as he walked out to his
car, unsuspecting, without a shot being fired. For he
hadn't known. That was the stinger; he hadn't known they
were after him. Now, though, things were different. Now
he was a dangerous man on the run.

As it turned out, they discovered that Jameson was
renting a cottage just to the east of Princes Risborough
through an Aylesbury estate agent shortly after the office
opened at eight-thirty that Friday morning. Policemen
were showing Jameson's photograph around and asking
the same questions in every estate agent's, hotel and bed-
and-breakfast establishment in Buckinghamshire, and the
pair of DCs given the Aylesbury estate agents just happened to get lucky. Like Everett and Miller got unlucky.
Swings and roundabouts. That was often the way things
happened.

Jameson had simply driven off from Leeds on his
holidays. Being a lover of nature, he had headed for the
countryside. Why the Chilterns? It was anyone's guess. It
could just as easily have been the Cotswolds or the
Malverns, Banks supposed.

According to the estate agent, the man had simply

dropped in one afternoon and asked after rental cottages in the area. He had paid a cash deposit and moved in. There was no need for subterfuge or secrecy. Arthur Jameson had nothing to fear from anyone. Or he wouldn't have had, were it not for a weakness for pornography, a fleeting contact with Daniel Clegg's estranged wife, Melissa, and Sergeant Hatchley's network of informers. He had either been careless about the wadding, or he thought it was a joke; they didn't know which yet. It hadn't shown up as a trademark in any other jobs over the past few years.

Last night he had probably gone into High Wycombe for a bite to eat, lingered over his dessert and coffee, maybe celebrated his new-found wealth with a large cognac, then headed back for the rented cottage, taking the bend a little too fast.

The cottage was certainly isolated. It stood just off a winding lane about two miles long, opposite a small, perfectly rounded tor. The lane carried on, passed another farmhouse about a mile further on, then meandered back to the main road.

From the mud on the floor, it looked very much as if Jameson had been there after the shooting. A bit of a risk, maybe, but the cottage wasn't far from his abandoned car. In the kitchen, yesterday's lunch dishes soaked in cold water, and breadcrumbs, cheese shavings and tiny florets of yellowed broccoli dotted the counter.

In the living room, Jameson had left the contents of his suitcase strewn around, including a number of local wild-life guides beside a girlie magazine on the table. Hatchley picked up the magazine and flipped through it quickly, tilting the centrefold to get a better look. Then they all followed the mud trail upstairs.

At the bottom of the wardrobe, hardly hidden at all by the spare blankets Jameson had obviously used to cover them, lay a twelve-gauge shotgun wrapped in an oil-stained cloth, and a small canvas bag. Carefully, Banks leaned forward and opened the flap of the bag with the tip of a Biro. It was empty, but on the floor by the blankets lay a few used ten-pound notes. Banks visualized the hunted man hurriedly stuffing the notes into his pockets until they spilled over on the floor. The shotgun was obviously too big and awkward for him to take with him, but he was still armed with the handgun.

Banks pointed to the shotgun and the canvas bag. 'Can we get this stuff to your lab?' he asked Jarrell. 'That shotgun's probably evidence in a murder case.'

Jarrell nodded. 'No problem.'

As Hatchley bent to pick up the shotgun, careful to handle only the material it was wrapped in, and as Banks reached for the canvas bag, a message for Jarrell crackled through on his personal radio.

'Jarrell here. Over.'

'HQ, sir. Subject, Arthur Jameson, spotted at Aylesbury railway station at nine fifty-three a.m. Subject bought London ticket. Now standing on platform. Locals await instructions. Over.'

'Has he spotted them?'

'They say not, sir.'

'Tell them to keep their distance.' Jarrell looked at his watch. It was ten o'clock. 'When's the next train?' he asked.

'Twelve minutes past ten, sir.'

'Which route?'

'Marylebone via Amersham.'

'Thank you. Stand by.' Jarrell turned to Banks and

Hatchley. 'We can pick up that train at Great Missenden or Amersham if you want,' he said.

Banks looked first at Hatchley, then back at Jarrell. 'Come on, then,' he said. 'Let's do it.'

THREE

Banks and Hatchley boarded the train separately at Amersham at ten thirty-two. Reluctantly, Superintendent Jarrell, being the local man, had agreed to stay behind and co-ordinate the Thames Valley end of the operation.

Neither Banks nor Hatchley looked much like a policeman that morning. Waking miserably to the middle-of-the-night phone call, Banks had put on jeans, a light cotton shirt and a tan sports jacket. Over this, he had thrown on his Columbo raincoat. Even though he had done his best to clean the mud off his shoes with a damp rag, it still showed.

Sergeant Hatchley wore his shiny blue suit, white shirt and no tie; he looked as if he had been dragged through a hedge backwards, but there was nothing unusual in that.

They had been told by the Transport Police, who had spotted Jameson, that the suspect still resembled his photograph except that he had about two days' growth around his chin and cheeks. He looked like a rambler. He was wearing grey trousers of some light material tucked into walking boots at the ankles, a green open-neck shirt and an orange anorak. Nice of him, Banks thought, dressing so easy to spot. He was also carrying a heavy rucksack, which no doubt held his gun and money, amongst other things.

The train rattled out of the station. Banks managed to

find a seat next to a young woman who smiled at him briefly as he sat down, then went back to reading her copy of *PC Magazine*. Banks had his battered brown leather briefcase with him, and its chief contents were his omnibus paperback copy of Waugh's *Sword of Honour* and his Walkman. He opened the book at the marker and started to read, but every so often he glanced at the man in the green short-sleeve shirt who sat about four seats down, over to his left. The rucksack and the orange anorak lay on the luggage rack above.

The train moved in a comforting rhythm, but Banks couldn't help feeling tense. He left the Walkman in his briefcase because he was too distracted to listen to music.

They could probably take Jameson right now, he thought. He and Jim Hatchley. Just approach quietly from behind like anyone going to the toilet and grab an arm each. The gun, surely, was up in the rucksack on the luggage rack.

But it wasn't worth the risk. Something could go wrong. Jameson could hold the entire coach hostage. It didn't bear thinking about. This way was far safer and would, with a little patience, skill and luck, guarantee success.

Banks and Hatchley had got on the train simply to keep an eye on Jameson. At the station, Superintendent Jarrell had talked to the Yard, who promised that there would be a number of plain-clothes officers waiting at Marylebone, mixed in with the crowds. These men were experts at surveillance, and they would keep Jameson in sight, no matter how he travelled, without being spotted, until he arrived at his final destination, be it hotel or house.

Some were posing as taxi-drivers, and, with luck, Jameson would get into one of their cabs. Banks had every intention of trying to keep up with the chase, but it was comforting to know that if he lost sight of Jameson, someone else would have him. There were plain-clothes officers at all the stops on the way, too, in case he got off, but Jameson had bought a ticket for London and it was almost certain that was where he was heading. Given his past, he would likely know someone there who could help get him out of the country. What Banks hoped – and this was one of the main reasons for letting their quarry go to ground – was that Jameson would lead them to his accomplice in the Rothwell murder.

As the train rattled out of Rickmansworth, Jameson got up and walked past Banks on his way to the toilet. Banks looked down at his book, not registering the words his eyes passed over. While Jameson was gone, he stared at the khaki rucksack and held himself back. How easy it would be, he thought, just to take it, then grab Jameson when he came back. But he had to keep thinking like a policeman, not give in to the maverick instinct, however strong. This way, with a little patience, the catch might be bigger.

And there was another reason. The gun might not be in the rucksack. Jameson's trousers were of the bulky, many-pocketed kind favoured by ramblers. Banks had glanced quickly as he went by and hadn't been able to discern the weight or outline of a gun, but it *could* be there, and there were too many civilians present to make the risk worthwhile. Best wait. He thought of how much money there might be in the rucksack and smiled at how ironic it would be if someone snatched it while Jameson was having a piss.

Jameson came back. They passed Harrow and entered a landscape of factory yards, piles of tyres and orange oil drums, pallets, warehouses, school yards full of screaming kids, bleak housing estates, concrete overpasses. Before long, the people in the carriage were standing up to get their jackets and bags as the train rumbled slowly into Marylebone station, all anxious to be first off.

Banks spotted Hatchley ahead of him, his head above most people in the crowd that shuffled through the ticket gate. Jameson had his anorak on now and was easy to keep in sight. Banks noticed him look around and lick his lips every now and then, sad, cruel puppy-dog eyes scanning the station forecourt.

But there was nothing to see. Nothing out of the ordinary. The uniformed Transport Police went about their business as usual, people leafed through magazines at the bookstall or headed for the buffet, checked the schedule displays, ran for trains. Carts of luggage and mail threaded in and out of the crowds, announcements about forthcoming departures came over the public-address system in the usual monotone echoing from the roof, where pigeons nested. To Banks, the station smelled of diesel oil and soot, though the age of steam was long gone.

Jameson made his way through the exit and managed to get a taxi. That was their first stroke of good fortune. If things went according to plan, the driver would be a DC; if not, then a taxi crawling through London traffic was easy enough for even a one-legged septuagenarian on foot to follow.

Banks opened the door of the next taxi, Hatchley beside him now. Banks was dying to jump in and say, 'Follow that taxi!' but the driver didn't want to let them in. He leaned over and tried to pull the door shut, holding up a police ID card. 'Sorry, mate,' he said. 'Police business. There's another one behind.' Just in time, Banks managed to get his own card out. 'Snap,' he said. 'Now open the fucking door.'

'Sorry, sir,' said the driver, eyes on the road, following

Jameson's cab through the thick traffic on Marylebone Road. 'I wasn't to know. They never said to expect a DCI jumping in the cab.'

'Forget it,' said Banks. 'I'm assuming it's one of your men driving in the taxi ahead?'

'Yes, sir. DC Formby. He's a good bloke. Don't worry, we're not going to lose the bastard.'

With excruciating slowness, the taxis edged their way south towards Kensington, along the busy High Street and down a side street of five- or six-storey white buildings with black metal railings at the front. Jameson's taxi stopped outside one that announced itself a HOTEL on the smoked glass over the huge shiny black doors. Across the street came the sound of drilling where workmen stood on scaffolding renovating the building opposite. The air was dry with drifting stone dust and thick with exhaust fumes. Jameson got out, looked around quickly and went into the hotel. His taxi drove off.

'Right,' said Banks. 'Looks like we've run the bastard to earth. Now we wait for the reinforcements.'

FOUR

For grey, the hotel manager could have given John Major a good run for his money. His suit was grey; his hair was grey; his voice was grey. He also had one of those faces – receding chin, goofy teeth, stick-out ears – that attract such abusive and bullying attention at school. At the moment, his face was grey, too.

He reminded Banks of Parkinson, a rather unpleasant large-nosed boy who had been the butt of ridicule and recipient of the occasional thump in the fourth form.

Banks had always felt sorry for Parkinson – had even defended him once or twice – until he had met him later in life, fully transformed into a self-serving, arrogant and humourless Labour MP. Then he felt Parkinson probably hadn't been thumped enough.

The manager had obviously never seen so many rough-looking, badly dressed coppers gathered in one place since they stopped showing repeats of *The Sweeney*. Jeans abounded, as did leather jackets, anoraks, blousons, T-shirts and grubby trainers. There wasn't a uniform, a tie or a well-polished shoe in sight, and the only suit was Sergeant Hatchley's blue polyester one, which was so shiny you could see your face in it.

It was also obvious that a number of the officers were armed and that two of them wore bullet-proof vests over their T-shirts.

Short of the SAS, Police Support Units or half a dozen Armed Response Vehicles, none of which the police authorities wanted the public to see mounting a major offensive on a quiet Kensington hotel on a Thursday lunchtime, these two were probably the best you could get. Vest One, the tallest, was called Spike, probably because of his hair, and his smaller, more hirsute associate was called Shandy. Spike was doing all the talking.

'See, squire,' he said to the wide-eyed hotel manager, 'our boss tells us we don't want a lot of fuss about this. None of this evacuating the area bollocks you see on telly. We go in, we disarm him nice and quiet, then bob's your uncle, we're out of your hair for good. Okay? No problems for us and no bad publicity for the hotel.'

The manager, clearly not used to being called 'squire', swallowed, bobbing an oversize Adam's apple, and nodded.

'But what we do need to do,' Spike went on, 'is to clear the floor. Now, is there anyone else up there apart from this Jameson?'

The manager looked at the keys. 'Only room 316,' he said. 'It's lunchtime. People usually go out for lunch.'

'What about the chambermaids?'

'Finished.'

'Good,' said Spike, then turned to one of the others in trainers, jeans and leather jacket. 'Smiffy, go get number 316 out quietly, okay?'

'Right, boss,' said Smiffy, and headed for the stairs.

Spike tapped his long fingers on the desk and turned to Banks. 'You know this bloke, this Jameson, right, sir?' he said.

Banks was surprised he had remembered the honorific. 'Not personally,' he said, and filled Spike in.

'He's shot a policeman, right?'

'Yes. Two of them. One's dead and the other's still in the operating room waiting to find out if he's got a brain left.'

Spike slipped a stick of Wrigley's spearmint gum from its wrapper and popped it in his mouth. 'What do you suggest?' he asked between chews.

Banks didn't know if Spike was being polite or deferential in asking an opinion, but he didn't get a chance to find out. As Smiffy came down the stairs with a rather dazed old dear clutching a pink dressing gown around her throat, the phone rang at the desk. The manager answered it, turned even more grey as he listened, then said, 'Yes, sir. Of course, sir. At once, sir.'

'Well?' Spike asked when the manager had put the phone down. 'What's put the wind up you?'

'It was *him*. The man in room 324.'

'What's he want?'

'He wants a roast beef sandwich and a bottle of beer sent up to his room.'

'How'd he sound?'

'Sound?'

'Yeah. You know, did he seem suspicious, nervous?'

'Oh. No, just ordinary.'

'Right on,' said Spike, grinning at Banks. 'Opportunity knocks.' He turned back to the manager. 'Do the doors up there have those peep-hole things, so you can see who's knocking?'

'No.'

'Chains?'

'Yes.'

'No problem. Right,' said Spike. 'Come with me, Shandy. The rest of you stay here and make sure no one gets in or out. We got the back covered?'

'Yes, sir,' one of the blousons answered.

'Fire escape?'

'That, too, sir.'

'Good.' Spike looked at Banks. 'I don't suppose you're armed?'

Banks shook his head. 'No time.'

Spike frowned. 'Better stay down here then, sir. Sorry, but I can't take the responsibility. You probably know the rules better than I do.'

Banks nodded. He gave Spike and Shandy a floor's start, then turned to Sergeant Hatchley. 'Stay here, Jim,' he said. 'I don't want to lead you astray.'

Without waiting for an answer, he slipped into the stairwell. One of the Yard men in the lobby noticed but made no move to stop him. At the first-floor landing, Banks heard someone wheezing behind him and turned.

'Don't worry, I'm not deaf,' said Hatchley. 'I just thought you might like some company anyway.'

Banks grinned.

'Mind if I ask you what we're doing this for?' Hatchley whispered, as they climbed the next flight.

'To find out what happens,' said Banks. 'I've got a funny feeling about this. Something Spike said.'

'You know what curiosity did.'

They reached the third floor. Banks peeked around the stairwell and put his arm out to hold Hatchley back.

Glancing again, Banks saw Spike point at his watch and mouth something to Shandy. Shandy nodded. They drew their weapons and walked slowly along the corridor towards Jameson's room.

The worn carpet that covered the floor couldn't stop the old boards creaking with each footstep. Banks saw Spike knock on the door and heard a muffled grunt from inside.

'Room service,' said Spike.

The door rattled open – on a chain, by the sound of it. Someone – Spike or Jameson – swore loudly, then Banks saw Shandy rear back like a wild horse and kick the door open. The chain snapped. Spike and Shandy charged inside and Banks heard two shots in close succession, then, after a pause of three or four seconds, another shot, not quite as loud.

Banks and Hatchley waited where they were for a minute, out of sight. Then, when Banks saw Spike come out of the room and lean against the door jamb, he and Hatchley walked into the corridor. Spike saw them coming and said, 'It's all over. You can go in now, if you like. Silly bugger had to try it on, didn't he?'

They walked into the room. Banks could smell cordite from the gunfire. Jameson had fallen backwards against the wall and slid down into a perfect sitting position on the floor, legs splayed, leaving a thick red snail's trail of blood smeared on the wallpaper. His puppy-dog eyes were open. His face bore no expression. The front of his green shirt, over the heart, was a tangle of dark red rag and tissue, spreading fast, and there was a similar stain slightly above it, near his shoulder. His hands lay at his side, one of them holding his gun. Another dark wet patch spread between his legs. Urine.

Banks thought of the chair at Arkbeck Farm, where this man had scared Alison Rothwell so much that she had wet herself. 'Jesus Christ,' he whispered.

'We'd no choice,' Spike said behind him. 'He had his gun in his hand when he came to the door. You can see for yourself. He fired first.'

Two shots, in close succession, followed by another, sounding slightly different. Two patches of spreading blood. 'Our boss tells us we don't want a lot of fuss about this.'

Banks looked at the two policemen, sighed and said, 'Give my regards to Dirty Dick.'

Shandy came back with a not very convincing, 'Who's that?'

Spike grinned, rubbed the barrel of his gun against his upper thigh, and said, 'Will do, sir.'

16

ONE

Banks had always hated hospitals: the antiseptic smells, the starched uniforms, the mysterious and unsettling pieces of shiny equipment around every corner – things that looked like modern sculpture or instruments of torture made of articulated chrome. They all gave him the creeps. Worst of all, though, was the way the doctors and nurses seemed to huddle in corridors and doorways and whisper about death, or so he imagined.

It was Saturday afternoon, 21 May, just over a week since Rothwell's murder and two days after Jameson's shooting, when Banks walked into Leeds Infirmary.

He had spent Thursday night in London, then headed back to Amersham for his car the next morning. After spending a little time with Superintendent Jarrell, Banks and Hatchley had driven back to Eastvale that Friday evening and arrived a little after nine.

On Saturday morning, he had to go into Leeds to consult with Ken Blackstone and wrap things up. After their pub lunch, he had taken a little time off to go and buy some more compact discs at the Classical Record Shop and pay a sick visit before heading back to Eastvale for Richmond's farewell bash. Sandra was off with the Camera Club photographing rock formations at Brimham Rocks, so he was left to his own devices for the day.

Banks paused and looked at the signs, then turned left. At last, he found the right corridor. Pamela Jeffreys shared a room with one other person, who happened to be down in X-ray when Banks called. He pulled up a chair by the side of the bed and put down the brown paper package he'd brought on the table. Pamela looked at it with her one good eye. The other was covered in bandages.

'Grapes,' said Banks, feeling embarrassed. 'It's what you bring when you visit people in hospital, isn't it?'

Pamela smiled, then decided it hurt too much and let her face relax.

'And,' Banks said, pulling a cassette from his pocket, 'I made you a tape of some Mozart piano concertos. Thought they might cheer you up. Got a Walkman?'

'Wouldn't go anywhere without it,' Pamela said out of the side of her mouth. 'It's a bit difficult to get the headphones on with one hand, though.' She directed his gaze to where her bandaged right hand lay on the sheets.

He set the cassette on the bedside table beside the grapes. 'The doctor says you're going to be okay,' he said.

'Hm-mm,' murmured Pamela. 'So they tell me.' It came out muffled, but Banks could tell what she said.

'He said you'll be playing the viola again in no time.'

'Hmph. It might take a bit longer than that.'

'But you *will* play again.'

She uttered a sound that could have been a laugh or a sob. 'They broke two fingers on my right hand,' she said. 'My bowing hand. It's a good thing they know bugger all about musical technique. If they'd broken my wrist that might really have put an end to my career.'

'People like that aren't chosen for their intelligence, as a rule,' said Banks. 'But the important thing is that there's no permanent damage to your fingers, or to your eye.'

'I know, I know,' she said. 'I ought to think myself lucky.'

'Well?'

'Oh, I'm okay, I suppose. Mostly just bored. There's the tapes and the radio, but you can't listen to music all day. There's nothing else to do but watch telly, and I can stomach even less of that. Reading still hurts too much with just one good eye. And the food's awful.'

'I'm sorry,' Banks said. 'And I'm sorry about that day in the park.'

She moved her head slowly from side to side. 'No. My fault. You had to ask. I overreacted. Is this an official visit? Have you come about the men? The men who hurt me?'

'No. But we know who they are. They won't get away with it.'

'Why have you come?'

'I . . . that's a good question.' Banks laughed nervously and looked away, out of the window at the swaying treetops. 'To see you, I suppose,' he said. 'To bring you some grapes and some Mozart. I just happened to be in the area, you know, buying CDs.'

'What did you get?'

Banks showed her: Keith Jarrett playing Shostakovitch's twenty-four preludes and fugues; Nobuko Imai playing Walton's viola concerto. She raised her eyebrow. 'Interesting.' Then she tapped the Walton. 'It's beautiful if you get it right,' she said. 'But so difficult. She's very good.'

'It says in the notes that the viola is an introvert of an instrument, a poet-philosopher. Does that describe you?'

'My teacher told me I had to be careful not to get overwhelmed by the orchestra. That tends to happen to violas, you know. But I manage to hold my own.'

'How long are they going to keep you here?'

'Who knows? Another week or so. I'd get up and go home right now but I think my leg's broken.'

'It is. The right one.'

'Damn. The prettiest.'

Banks laughed.

'Did you catch the men who killed Robert?' she asked. 'Was it the same ones?'

Banks gave her the gist of what had happened with Jameson, avoiding the more lurid details.

'So one got away?' she said.

'So far.'

'That's not bad going.'

'Not bad,' Banks agreed. 'Fifty per cent success rate. It's better than the police average.'

'Will you get a promotion out of it?'

He laughed. 'I doubt it.'

'Don't look so worried,' she said, resting her bandaged hand on his. 'I'll be all right. And don't blame yourself . . . you know . . . for what happened to me.'

'Right. I'll try not to.' Banks felt his eyes burn. He could see her name bracelet and the tube attached to the vein in her wrist. It made him feel squeamish, even more so than seeing Jameson's body against the wall in the hotel room. It didn't make sense: he could take a murder scene in his stride, but a simple intravenous drip in a hospital made him queasy.

Pamela was right. She would be fine. Her wounds would heal; her beauty would regenerate. In less than a year she would be as good as new. But would she ever recover fully inside? How would she handle being alone in the house? Would she ever again be able to hear someone walking up the garden path without that twinge of fear and panic? He didn't know. The psyche regenerates itself, too, sometimes. We're often a damn sight more resilient than we'd imagine.

'Will you come and see me again?' she asked. 'I mean, when it's all over and I'm home. Will you come and see me?'

'Sure I will,' said Banks, thinking guiltily of the feelings he had had for Pamela, not sure at all.

'Do you mean it?'

He looked into her almond eye and saw the black shape of fear at its centre. He swallowed. 'Of course I mean it,' he said. And he did. He leaned forward and brushed his lips against her good cheek. 'I'd better go now.'

TWO

> Why was he born so beautiful?
> Why was he born so tall?
> He's no bloody use to anyone,
> He's no bloody use at all.

Richmond took the Yorkshire compliment, delivered in shaky harmonies by Sergeant Hatchley and an assorted cats' choir of PCs, very well, Banks thought, especially for someone who listened to music that sounded like Zamfir on Valium.

'Speech! Speech!' Hatchley shouted.

Embarrassed, Richmond gave a sideways glance at Rachel, his fiancée, then stood up, cleared his throat and said, 'Thank you. Thank you all very much. And thanks specially for the CD-ROM. You know I'm not much good at giving speeches like this, but I'd just like to say it's been a pleasure working with you all. I know you all probably think I'm a traitor, going off down south—' Here, a chorus of boos interrupted his speech. 'But as soon as I've got that lot down there sorted out,' he went on, 'I'll be back, and you buggers had better make sure you know a hard drive from a hole in the ground. Thank you.'

He sat down again, and people went over to pat him on the back and say farewell. Everyone cheered when Susan Gay leaned forward and gave him a chaste kiss on the cheek. She blushed when Richmond responded by giving her a bear-hug.

They were in the back room of the Queen's Arms on Saturday night, and Banks leaned against the polished bar, pint of Theakston's in his hand, with Sandra on one side and Gristhorpe on the other. Someone had hung balloons from the ceiling. Cyril had hooked up the old jukebox for the occasion, and Gerry and the Pacemakers were singing 'Ferry Across the Mersey'.

Banks knew he should have been happier to see the end of the Rothwell case, but he just couldn't seem to get rid of a niggling feeling, like an itch he couldn't reach. Jameson had killed Rothwell. True. Now Jameson was dead. Justice had been done, after a fashion. An eye for an eye. So forget it.

But he couldn't. The two men who had beaten Pamela Jeffreys hadn't been caught yet. Along with Jameson's accomplice, that left three on the loose. Only a twenty-five per cent success rate. Not satisfactory at all.

But it wasn't just that. Somehow, it was all too neat. All too neat and ready for Martin Churchill to slip into the country one night with a new face and a clean, colossal bank account and retire quietly to Cornwall, guarding the secrets of those in power to the grave. Which might not be far off. Banks wouldn't be surprised if someone from MI6 or wherever slipped into Cornwall one night and both Mr Churchill *and* his insurance had a nasty accident.

Susan Gay walked over from Richmond's table and indicated she'd like a word. Banks excused himself from Sandra and they found a quiet corner.

'Sorry for dragging you away from the festivities, sir,' Susan said, 'but I haven't had a chance to talk to you since you got back. There's a couple of things you might be interested in.'

'I'm listening.'

Susan told him about her talk with Tom Rothwell after the funeral, about his homosexuality and what he had seen his father do that day he followed him into Leeds. 'The artist came in on Wednesday evening, sir, and we managed to get the impression in the papers on Thursday, while you were down south.'

'Any luck?'

'Well, yes and no.'

'Come on, then. Don't keep me in suspense.'

'We've found out who she is. Her name's Julia Marshall and she lives in Adel. That's in north Leeds. She's a school-teacher. We got a couple of phone calls from colleagues. Apparently, she was a quiet person, shy and private.'

'Was?'

'Well, I shouldn't say that, really, sir, but it's just that she's disappeared. That's all we know so far. I just think we should find her, that's all,' she said. 'Talk to her friends. I don't really know why. It's just a feeling. She might know something.'

'I think you're right,' said Banks. 'It's a loose end I'd like to see tied up as well. There are too many bloody dis-appearances in this case for my liking. Is there anything else?'

'No. But it's not over yet, is it, sir?'

'No, Susan, I don't think it is. Thanks for telling me. We'll follow up on it first thing tomorrow. For now, we'd better get back to the party or Phil will think we don't love him.'

Banks walked back to the bar and lit a cigarette. The music had changed; now it was the Swinging Blue Jeans doing 'Hippy, Hippy Shake' and some of the younger members of the department were dancing.

Banks thought about Tom Rothwell and his father. Susan had been sharp to pick up on that. It didn't make sense, given Rothwell's *other* interests, that he should be so genuinely upset that his son didn't want to be an accountant or a lawyer. On the other hand, perhaps nothing was more of an anathema, an insult, to a confirmed heterosexual philanderer than a gay son.

'Penny for them?' Sandra said.

'What? Oh, nothing. Just thinking, that's all.'

'It's over, Alan. Leave it be. It's another feather in your cap. You can't solve the whole world's problems.'

'It feels more like a lead weight than a feather. I think I'll have another drink.' He turned and ordered another pint. Sandra had a gin and tonic. 'You're right, of course,' he said, standing the drink on the bar. 'We've done the best we can.'

'You've done *all* you can. It's being pipped at the post by Dirty Dick that really gets your goat, isn't it?' Sandra taunted. 'You two have got some kind of macho personal vendetta going, haven't you?'

'Maybe. I don't know. I won't say it's a good feeling, knowing the bastard's got his way.'

'You did what you could, didn't you?'

'Yes.'

'But you still think Burgess has won this time, and it pisses you off, doesn't it?'

'Maybe. Yes. Yes, it bloody well does. Sandra, the man had someone *shot*.'

'A cold-blooded murderer. Besides, you don't know that.'

'You mean I can't prove it. And we're not here to play vigilantes. If Burgess had Jameson shot, you can be damn sure it wasn't just an eye for an eye. He was making certain he didn't talk.'

'*Men*,' said Sandra, turning to her drink with a long-suffering sigh.

Gristhorpe, who had been listening from the other side, laughed and nudged Banks in the ribs. 'Better listen to her,' he said. 'I can understand how you feel, but there's no more you can do, and there's no point making some kind of competition out of it.'

'I know that. It's not that. It's . . . oh, maybe Sandra's right and it is macho stuff. I don't know.'

At that moment, Sergeant Rowe, who had been manning the front desk across the street, pushed through the crowd of drinkers and said to Banks, 'Phone call, sir. He says it's important. Must talk to you in person.'

Banks put his pint glass back on the bar. 'Shit. Did he say who?'

'No.'

'All right.' He turned to Sandra and pointed at his pint. 'Guard that drink with your life. Back in a few minutes.'

He couldn't ignore the call; it might be an informer with important information. Irritated, nonetheless, he crossed Market Street and went into the Tudor-fronted police station.

'You can take it in here, sir,' said Rowe, pointing to an empty ground-floor office.

Banks went in and picked up the receiver. 'Hello. Banks here.'

'Ah, Banks,' said the familiar voice. 'It's Superintendent Burgess here. Remember me? What do you want first, the good news or the bad?'

Speak of the devil. Banks felt his jaw clench and his stomach start to churn. 'Just tell me,' he said as calmly as he could.

'Okay. You know those two goons, the ones that beat up the tart of colour?'

'Yes. Have you got them?'

'We-ell, not exactly.'

'What then?'

'They got away, slipped through our net. That's the bad news.'

'Where did they go?'

'Back home, of course. St Corona. That's the good news.'

'What's so good about that?'

'Seems they didn't realize they'd become *persona non grata* there, or whatever the plural of that is.'

'And?'

'Well, I have it on good authority that they've both been eating glass.'

'They're dead?'

'Of course they're bloody dead. I doubt they'd survive a diet like that.'

'How do you know this?'

'I told you. Good authority. It's the real McCoy. No reason to doubt the source.'

'Why?'

'Ours is not to reason why, Banks. Let's just say that their bungling around England drawing attention to themselves didn't help much. Things are in a delicate balance.'

'Did you know in advance that they were out of favour? Did you let them slip out of the country, knowing what would happen? Did you even try to find them?'

'Oh, Banks. You disappoint me. How could you even think something like that of me?'

'Easy. The same way I think you sent Spike and Shandy down to Kensington to make damn sure Arthur Jameson didn't survive to say anything embarrassing in court.'

'I told you, Jameson wasn't in my brief.'

'I know what you told me. I also know what happened in that hotel room. They shot the bastard down, Burgess, and you're responsible.'

'*Superintendent* Burgess, to you. And he shot first is what I heard. That's the official version, at any rate, and I don't see any reason not to believe it. As our cousins over the pond would say, it was a "righteous shoot".'

'Bollocks. They shot him twice then fired off a round from his gun to make it look like he fired first. Apart from the shots, do you know what gave them away?'

'No, but I'm sure you're going to tell me.'

'They left the gun in his hand for me to see. Procedure is that you disarm a suspect *first thing*, whether you think he's dead or not.'

'Well, hurray for you, Sherlock. Don't you think they might have got careless in the heat of the moment?'

'No. Not with their training.'

'But it doesn't matter, does it? You weren't there, officially, were you? In fact you were ordered to stay on the ground floor. Anyway, I don't think we need to go into all that tiresome stuff, do we? Do you really want me to have to pull rank? Believe it or not, I *like* you, Banks. Life would be a lot duller without you. I wouldn't want to see you throw your career down the tubes over this. Take my word for it, *nobody* will take kindly to your rocking the boat. The official verdict is the only one that counts.'

'Not to me.'

'Leave it alone, Banks. It's over.'

'Why does everyone keep telling me that?'

'Because it's true. One more thing. And don't interrupt me. We found an address book in Jameson's stuff and it led us to an old ex-army crony of his called Donald Pembroke. Ring any bells?'

'No.'

'Anyway, it seems this Pembroke just inherited a lot of money, according to his neighbour. The first thing he did was buy a fast sports car, cash down according to the salesman. Two days later he lost control on a B road in Kent – doing eighty or ninety by all accounts – and ran it into a tree.'

'And?'

'And he's dead, isn't he? What's more, there's no way you can put it down to me. So don't say there's no justice in the world, Banks. Goodbye. Have a good life.' Burgess hung up abruptly, leaving Banks to glare into the receiver. He slammed it down so hard that Sergeant Rowe popped his head around the door. 'Everything all right, sir?'

'Yes, fine,' said Banks. He took a deep breath and ran his hand through his short hair. 'Everything's just bloody fine and dandy.' He sat in the empty office gaining control of his breathing. Susan's words echoed in his mind. *'It's not over yet, is it, sir?'* No, it bloody well wasn't.

17

ONE

Banks sat at a taverna by the quayside sipping an ice-cold Beck's and smoking a duty-free Benson and Hedges Special Mild. When he had finished his cigarette, he popped a dolmas into his mouth and followed it with a black olive. One or two of the locals, mostly mustachioed and sun-leathered fishermen, occasionally glanced his way during a pause in their conversation.

It was a small island, just one village built up the central hillside, and though it got its share of tourists in season, none of the big cruise ships came. Banks had arrived half an hour ago on a regular ferry service from Piraeus and he needed a while to collect his thoughts and get his land-legs back again. He had a difficult interview ahead of him, he suspected. He had already contacted the Greek police. Help had been offered, and the legal machinery was ready to grind into action at a word. But Banks had something else he wanted to try first.

By Christ, it was hot, even in the shade. The sun beat down from a clear sky, a more intense, more saturated blue than Banks had ever seen, especially in contrast to the white houses, shops and tavernas along the quayside. A couple of sailboats and a few fishing craft were moored in the small harbour, bobbing gently on the calm water. It was hard to describe the sea's colour; certainly there were shades of green and blue in it, aquamarine, ultramarine, but in places it was a kind of inky blue, too, almost purple. Maybe Homer was right when he called it 'wine-dark', Banks thought, remembering his conversation with Super-intendent Gristhorpe before the trip. Banks had never read *The Odyssey*, but he probably would when he got back.

He paid for his food and drink and walked out into the sun. On his way, he popped into the local police station in the square near the harbour, as promised, then set off along the dirt track up the hill.

The main street itself was narrow enough, but every few yards a side street branched off, narrower still, all white, cubist, flat-roofed houses with painted shutters, mostly blue. Some of the houses had red pantile roofs, like the ones in Whitby. Many people had put hanging baskets of flowers out on the small balconies, a profusion of purple, pink, red and blue, and lines of washing hung over the narrow streets. By the roadside were poppies and delicate lavender flowers that looked like morning glories.

Mingled with the scents of the flowers were the smells of tobacco and wild herbs. Banks thought he recognized thyme and rosemary. Insects with red bodies and trans-parent wings flew around him. The sun beat relentlessly. Before Banks had walked twenty yards, his white cotton shirt stuck to his back. He wished he had worn shorts instead of jeans.

Banks looked ahead. Where the white houses ended halfway up the hillside, scrub and rocky outcrops took over. The house he wanted, he had been told, was on his right, a large one with a high-gated white wall and a shaded courtyard. It wasn't difficult to spot, now about fifty yards ahead, almost three-quarters of the length of the road.

He finally made it. The ochre gate was unlocked, and beyond it, Banks found a courtyard full of saplings, pots of herbs and hanging plants by a *krokalia* pathway of black and white pebbles winding up to the door. Expensive, definitely. The door was slightly ajar, and he could hear voices inside. By the plummy tones, it sounded like the BBC World Service news. He paused a moment for breath, then walked up to the door and knocked.

He heard a movement inside, the voices stopped, and in a few seconds someone opened the door. Banks looked into the face that he had thought for so long had been blown to smithereens.

'Mr Rothwell?' he said, slipping his card out of his wallet and holding it up. 'Mr Keith Rothwell?'

TWO

'You've come, then?' Rothwell said simply.

'Yes.'

He looked over Banks's shoulder. 'Alone?'

'Yes.'

'You'd better come in.'

Banks followed Rothwell into a bright room where a ceiling fan spun and a light breeze blew through the open blue shutters. It was sparsely furnished. The walls were plastered white, the floor was flagged, covered here and there by rugs, and the ceiling was panelled with dark wood. Outside, he could hear birds singing; he didn't know what kind.

He sat down in the wicker chair Rothwell offered, surprised to be able to see the sea down below through the window. Now he was at the end of his journey, he felt bone-weary and more than a little dizzy. It had been a long way from Eastvale and a long uphill walk in the sun. Sweat dribbled from his eyebrows into his eyes and made them sting. He wiped it away with his forearm. At least it was cooler inside the room.

Rothwell noticed his discomfort. 'Hot, isn't it?' he said. 'Can I get you something?'

Banks nodded. 'Thanks. Anything as long as it's cold.'

Rothwell went to the kitchen door and turned, with a smile, just as he opened it. 'Don't worry,' he said. 'I won't run away.'

'There's nowhere to run,' replied Banks.

A minute or so later he came back with a glass of iced water and a bottle of Grolsch lager. 'I'd drink the water first,' he advised. 'You look a bit dehydrated.'

Banks drained the glass then opened the metal gizmo on the beer. It tasted good. Imported, of course. But Rothwell could afford it. Banks looked at him. The receding sandy hair, forming a slight widow's peak, had bleached in the sun. He had a good tan for such a fair-skinned person. Behind wire-rimmed glasses, his steady grey eyes looked out calmly, not giving away any indication as to his state of mind. He had a slightly prissy mouth, a girl's mouth, and his lips were pale pink. He looked nothing at all like the photograph of Daniel Clegg.

He wore a peach short-sleeve shirt, white shorts and brown leather sandals. His toenails needed cutting. He was an inch or so taller than Banks, slim and in good shape – about all he did have in common with Clegg, apart from the colour of his hair, his blood group and the appendicitis scar. When he went to get the drinks, Banks noticed, he moved with an athlete's grace and economy. There was nothing of the sedentary pen-pusher about his bearing.

'Anyone else here?' Banks asked.

'Julia's gone to the shops,' he said, glancing at his watch. 'She shouldn't be long.'

'I'd like to meet her.'

'How did you find me?' Rothwell asked, sitting opposite, opening a tin of Pepsi. The gas hissed out and liquid frothed over the edge. Rothwell held it at arm's length until it had stopped fizzing, then wiped the tin with a tissue from a box on the table beside him.

'It wasn't that difficult,' said Banks. 'Once I knew who I was looking for. We found you partly through Julia.' He shrugged. 'After that it was a matter of routine police work, mostly boring footwork. We checked travel agents, then we contacted the local police through Interpol. It didn't take that long to get word back about two English strangers who resembled your descriptions taking a lease on a captain's house here. Did you really believe we wouldn't find you eventually?'

'I suppose I must have,' said Rothwell. 'Foolish of me, but there it is. There are always variables, loose ends, but I thought I'd left enough red herrings and covered my tracks pretty well. I planned it all *very* carefully.'

'Do you have any idea what you've done to your family?'

Rothwell's lips tightened. 'It wasn't a family. It was a sham. A lie. A façade. We played at happy families. I couldn't stand it any more. There was no love in the house. Mary and I hadn't slept together in years and Tom . . . well . . .'

Banks let Tom pass for the moment. 'Why not get a divorce like anyone else? Why this elaborate scheme?'

'I assume, seeing as you're here, you know most of it?'

'Humour me.'

Rothwell squinted at Banks. 'Look,' he said. 'I can't see where you'd have any room to hide one, but you're not "wired" as the Americans say, are you?'

Banks shook his head. 'You have my word on that.'

'This is just between you and me? Off the record?'

'For the moment. I am here officially, though.'

Rothwell sipped some Pepsi then rubbed the can between his palms. 'I might have asked Mary for a divorce eventually,' he said, 'but it was still all very new to me, the freedom, the taste of another life. I'm not even sure she would have let me go that easily. The way things turned out, though, I had to appear dead. If he thinks I'm alive, there'll be no peace, no escape anywhere.'

'Martin Churchill?'

'Yes. He found out I was taking rather more than I was entitled to.'

'How did you find out he knew?'

'A close source. When you play the kind of games I did, Mr Banks, it pays to have as much information as you can get. Let's say someone on the island tipped me that Churchill knew and that he was pressuring Daniel Clegg to do something about it.'

'Is that how it happened?'

'Yes. And it made sense. I'd noticed that Daniel had been behaving oddly lately. He was nervous about something. Wouldn't look me in the eye. Now I had an explanation. The bastard was planning to have me executed.'

'So you had him killed instead?'

Rothwell gazed out of the window at the sea and the mountainside in silence for a moment. 'Yes. It was him or me. I beat him to it, that's all. Someone had to die violently, someone who could pass for me under certain circumstances. We looked enough alike.'

'Without a face, you mean?'

'I . . . I didn't look . . . in the garage . . . I couldn't.'

'I'll bet you couldn't. Go on.'

'We were about the same age and build, same hair colour. I knew he'd had his appendix out. I even knew his blood group was "O", the same as mine.'

'How did you know that?'

'He told me. We were talking once about blood tainted by the HIV virus. He wondered if he had a greater chance of catching it from a transfusion because he shared his blood group with over forty per cent of the male population.'

'What did you do once you had the idea of passing him off as you?'

'There was this man we'd both met in the Eagle a couple of times, down there for the Ed O'Donnell Band on a Sunday lunchtime, and he'd boasted about being a mercenary and doing anything for money. Arthur Jameson was his name. He was a walking mass of contradictions. He loved animals and nature, but he liked hunting and duck-shooting, and he didn't seem to give a damn for human life. I found him fascinating. Fascinating and a little frightening.

'It was perfect. Daniel knew him, too, of course, and he told me that Jameson had even approached him for some legal help once, shortly after we met. I thought if you found out anything, that would be it. He might have had something in his files. You know how lawyers hoard every scrap of paper. But there was nothing linking Jameson to *me*. It would only reinforce what you suspected already, that Daniel had had *me* killed instead of the other way round. You weren't to know that I was with Daniel the day we met Jameson, or that I'd chatted with Jameson on a number of subsequent occasions.'

'So you and Clegg were pals? Socialized together, did you?'

Rothwell paused. A muscle by his jaw twitched. 'No. It wasn't quite like that,' he said quietly. 'Daniel had a hold over me, but sometimes he seemed to want to play at being boozing buddies. I didn't understand it, but at least for a while we could bury our differences and have a good time. The next day it would usually be back to cold formality. At bottom, Daniel was a terrible snob. Been to Cambridge, you know.'

'How much did you pay Jameson?'

'Fifty thousand pounds and a plane ticket to Rio. I know it's a lot, but I thought the more I paid him the more likely he'd be to disappear for good with it and not get caught.'

'First mistake.'

'How did it happen?'

Banks told him about the wadding and about Jameson's attitude to the world beyond Calais. Rothwell laughed, then stared at the sea again. 'I knew it was a risk,' he said. 'I suppose I should have known, the way he used to go on about the Irish and the Frogs sometimes. But if you have a dream you have to take risks for it, pay a price, don't you?'

'You needn't try to justify your actions to me,' said Banks, finally feeling steady and cool enough to light a cigarette. He offered one to Rothwell, who accepted. 'I was the one left to clean up your mess. And Jameson killed one policeman and seriously wounded another trying to escape.' The fan drew their smoke up to it, then pushed it towards the windows.

'I'm sorry.'

'I'll bet you are.'

'It wasn't my fault, what Jameson did, was it? You can't blame me.'

'Can't I? Let's get back to your relationship with Daniel Clegg. How did you get involved?'

'We met in the George Hotel, on Great George Street. It was about four years ago. A year or so after I left Hatchard and Pratt, anyway. Expenses were high, what with renovations to Arkbeck and everything else, and business wasn't exactly booming, though I wasn't doing too badly. They have jazz at the George on Thursdays, and as I was in Leeds on business, I thought I'd drop by rather than watch television in the hotel room. It turns out we were both jazz fans. We just got talking, that's all.

'I didn't tell him very much at first, except that I was a freelance financial consultant. He seemed interested. Anyway, we exchanged business cards and he put a bit of work my way, off-shore banking, that sort of thing. Turns out some of it was a bit shady, though I wasn't aware at the time – not that I mightn't have done it, anyway, mind you – and he brought that up later, in conversation.'

'He put pressure on you?'

'Oh, yes.' Rothwell paused and looked Banks in the eye. 'A smooth blackmailer, was Danny-boy. I suppose you know about my bit of bad luck at Hatchard and Pratt's, don't you?'

'Yes.'

'That was five years ago. We'd just moved into Arkbeck then and we couldn't really afford it. Not that the mortgage itself was so high, but the place had been neglected for so long. There was so much needed doing, and I'm no DIY expert. But Mary wanted to live there, so live there we did. The upshot was that I had to pad the expenses a little. If I hadn't been married to the boss's daughter, and if Laurence Pratt hadn't been a good friend, things could have gone very badly for me at the firm then. As it was, after I left I didn't have a lot of work at first, and Mary . . . well, that's another story. Let's just say she doesn't have a forgiving nature. One night, in my cups, I hinted to Daniel about what had happened, how I had parted company with Hatchard and Pratt.

'Anyway, later, Daniel used what he knew about me as leverage to get me involved when his old college friend Martin Churchill first made inquiries about rearranging his finances. That was a little over three years back. See, he knew he couldn't handle the task by himself, that he needed my expertise. He told me he could still report me to the board, that it wasn't too late. Well, maybe they would have listened to him, and maybe they wouldn't. Who knows now? Quite frankly, I didn't care. I already knew a bit about money-laundering, and it looked to me like a licence to print money. Why wouldn't I want in? I think Daniel just enjoyed manipulating people, having power over them, so I didn't spoil his illusion. But he really wasn't terribly bright, wasn't Danny-boy, despite Cambridge.'

'A bit like Frankenstein and the monster, isn't it?'

Rothwell smiled. 'Yes, perhaps. And I suppose you'd have to say that the monster far outstripped his creator, though you could hardly say the good doctor himself was without sin.'

'How did you arrange it all? The murder, the escape?'

Rothwell emptied his tin, put it on the table and leaned back. The chair creaked. Outside, gulls cried as they circled the harbour looking for fish. 'Another Grolsch?' he asked.

There was still an inch left in the bottle. 'No,' said Banks. 'Not yet.'

Rothwell sighed. 'You have to go back about eighteen

months to understand, to when I first started using the Robert Calvert identity. Daniel and I were doing fine laundering Churchill's money, and he allowed us a decent percentage for doing so. I was getting rich quick. I suppose I should have been happy, but I wasn't. I don't know exactly when I first became aware of it, but life just seemed to have lost its savour, its sweetness. Things started to oppress me. I felt like I was shrivelling up inside, dying, old before my time. Call it mid-life crisis, I suppose, but I couldn't see the *point* of all that bloody money.

'All Mary wanted was her bridge club, more renovations, additions to the house, jewellery, expensive holidays. Christ, I should have known better than to marry the boss's daughter, even if I did get her pregnant. One simple mistake, that and my own bloody weakness. What was it the philosopher said about the erect penis knowing no conscience? That may be so, but it certainly understands penitence, regret, remorse. One bloody miserable, uncomfortable screw in the back of an Escort halfway up Crow Scar set me on a course straight to hell. I'm not exaggerating. Twenty-one years. After that long, my wife hated me, my children hated me, and I was beginning to hate myself.'

Banks noticed that Rothwell had picked up the empty Pepsi tin and started to squeeze until it buckled in his grip.

'Then I realized I was handling millions of pounds – literally, millions – and that my job was essentially to clean it and hide it ready for future use. It wasn't difficult to find a few hiding places of my own. Small amounts at first, then, when no one seemed to miss it, more and more. Shell companies, numbered accounts, dummy corporations, property. I liked what I was doing. The manipulation of large sums of money intrigued me and excited me like nothing else, or almost nothing else. Just for the sake of it, much of the time. Like art for art's sake.

'I began to spend more time away from home "on business". Nobody cared one way or another. They never asked me where I'd been. They only asked for more money for a new kitchen or a sun-porch or a bloody gazebo. When I was home, I walked around like a zombie – the dull, boring accountant, I suppose – and mostly kept to my office or nipped out to the pub for a smoke and a jar occasionally. I had plenty of time to look back on my life, and though I didn't like a lot of what I saw, I remembered I hadn't always been so bloody bored or boring. I used to go dancing, believe it or not. I used to like a flutter on the horses now and then. I had friends. Once in a while, I liked to have too much to drink with the lads and stagger home singing, happy as a lark. That was before life came to resemble an accounts ledger – debits and credits, profit and loss, with far too much on the loss side.' He sighed. 'Are you sure you wouldn't like another beer?'

'Go on, then,' Banks said. His bottle was empty now.

Rothwell brought back a Pepsi for himself and another Grolsch for Banks. His glasses had slipped down over the bridge of his nose and he pushed them back.

'So I invented Robert Calvert,' Rothwell said after a sip of Pepsi.

'Where did you get the name?'

'Picked it from a magazine I was reading at the time. With a pin. The *Economist*, I believe.'

'Go on.'

'I rented the flat, bought new clothes, more casual. God, you've no idea how strange it felt at first. Good, but strange. There were moments when I really did believe I was going mad, turning into a split personality. It became a kind of compulsion, an addiction, like smoking. I'd go to the bookie's and put bets on, spend a day at the races, go listen to trad jazz in smoky pubs – the Adelphi, the George, the Duck and Drake – something I hadn't done since my early twenties. I'd go around in jeans and sweat-shirts. And nobody back at Arkbeck Farm ever asked where I'd been, what I'd been doing, as long I turned up every now and then in my business suit and the money kept coming in for a new freezer, a first edition Brontë, a Christmas trip to Hawaii. After a while I realized I wasn't going mad, I was just becoming myself, returning to the way I was before I let life grind me down.

'And, sure enough, the money kept coming in. I had tapped into an endless supply, or so I thought. So I played the family role part of the time, and I started exploring my real self as Robert Calvert. I had no idea where it would lead, not then. I was just trying out ways of escape. I told Daniel Clegg one night when we'd had a few, and he thought it was a wild idea. I had to tell someone and I couldn't tell my family or Pratt or anyone local, so why not tell my blackmailer, my confidant? He helped me get a bank account and credit card as Calvert, which he thought gave him an even stronger hold over me. He could always claim he'd been deceived, you see.'

'What about the escape?'

'You're jumping ahead a bit, but as I'd already created Robert Calvert successfully enough, it wasn't very difficult to go on from there and create a third identity: David Norcliffe. As you no doubt know, seeing as you're here. Rothwell was dead, and I couldn't go as Calvert. I had to leave him behind; that was part of the plan. So I shuffled more money into various bank accounts in various places over a period of several weeks. After all, that's what I do best. I've laundered and hidden millions for Churchill and his wife.'

'How much for yourself?'

'Three or four million,' he said with a shrug. 'I don't know exactly. Enough, anyway, to last us our lifetime. And there was plenty left in Eastvale for my family. They're well provided for in the will and by the life insurance. I made sure of that. Believe me, they'll be better off without me.'

'What about Daniel Clegg? What about Pamela Jeffreys?'

'Pamela? What about her?'

Banks told him.

He put his head in his hands. 'Oh, my God,' he said. 'I would never have hurt Pamela . . . It wasn't meant to be like that.'

'How did you meet her?'

Rothwell sipped some more Pepsi and rubbed the back of his hand across his brow. 'I told you the Calvert thing felt very strange at first. Mostly, I just used to walk around Leeds in my jeans and sweatshirt. I'd drop in at a pub now and then and enjoy being someone else. Occasionally, I got chatting to people, the way you do in pubs. I'll never forget how frightening and how exciting it was the first time someone asked me my name and I said "Robert Calvert". I knew it was still me – you have to understand that – we're not really talking about a split personality here. I was Keith Rothwell, all right, just playing a part, or trying to find himself, perhaps. It gave me an exhilarating sense of freedom.

'Anyway, as I said, I used to drop in at pubs now and then, mostly in the city centre or up in Headingley, near the flat. One night I saw Pamela in The Boulevard – you know, the tarted-up Jubilee Hotel on The Headrow. It seemed a likely place to meet women. They stay open till midnight on weekends and they've got a small dance floor. Pamela was with some friends. They'd been doing something at the Town Hall, a Handel oratorio, or something like that. Anyway, something happened, some spark. We caught one another's eye.

'She wasn't with anyone in particular. I mean, she didn't seem to have a boyfriend with her. The next time she was at the bar, I made sure I got there, too, next to her, and we got chatting. I wasn't a great fan of classical music, but Pamela's a down-to-earth sort of person, not a highbrow snob or anything. I asked her to dance. She said yes. We just got on, that's all. We slept together now and then, but both of us knew it was just a casual relationship really. I don't mean to denigrate it by saying that. We had a wonderful time. I was astounded she fancied me. Flattered. It was the first time in my entire marriage that I'd been with another woman, and the hell of it was that I didn't feel guilty at all. She was fun to be with, and we had a great time, but we weren't in love.'

'What came between you?'

'What? Well, we stayed friends, really. At least, I like to think we did. There was her work, of course. It's very demanding and between us we couldn't always be sure we could make time to get together. And Pamela was more outgoing. She wanted more of a social life. She wanted me to meet her friends, and she wanted to meet mine.'

'But you didn't have any?'

'Exactly. And I didn't want to get too well known around the place. It was a risk, playing Calvert, always a risk.'

'Go on. What happened next?'

'I met Julia.'

'How?'

'We met on a bus, would you believe? It had been raining, one of those sudden showers, and I was out walking without an umbrella. So I jumped on a bus into town. Then the rain stopped and the sun came out. I'd been looking at her out of the corner of my eye. She was so beautiful, like a model, such delicate, fragile, sculpted features. I imagined she was probably stuck-up and wouldn't talk to the likes of me. Anyway, she left her umbrella. I saw it, grabbed it, and dashed after her. When I caught her up she seemed startled at first, then I gave it to her and she blushed. She seemed flustered, so I asked her if she wanted to go for a coffee. She said yes. She was very shy. It was hard to get her talking at first, but slowly I found out she was a teacher and she lived in Adel and she adored Greek history and literature.

'Do you believe in love at first sight, Mr Banks? Do you? Because that's what this is all about, really. It's not just about money. It's not just about leaving my old life behind and seeking novelty. I fell in love with Julia the moment I saw her, and that's the truth. It might sound foolish and sentimental to you, but I have never in my life felt that way before. Bells ringing, earth moving, all the clichés. And it's mutual. She's everything I've ever wanted. When I met Julia, nothing else mattered. I knew we had to get away, find our Eden, if you like, our paradise. I had to get a new life, a new identity. Everything was in such a mess, falling apart. No one was supposed to get hurt.'

'Except Daniel Clegg.'

Rothwell banged on his chair arm with his fist. 'I told you! That wasn't my fault. I had to appear to have been violently murdered. By Daniel himself, or by someone he'd hired. And that's exactly the way it would have been, too, if I hadn't been tipped off and made other plans. But Julia knew nothing of that. She's a complete innocent. She knows nothing of the things we've just been talking about.'

'So you invited Clegg over to the Calvert flat to get his fingerprints there? Am I right?'

'Yes. On the Monday. I said I had some business to discuss that couldn't wait and he came over. I showed him around, had him touch things. I'd cleaned the place thoroughly. Daniel was a touchy-feely kind of person. Anything he saw, he'd pick it up and have a look: compact discs, wallet, credit cards in Calvert's name, coins, books, you name it. He'd even let his fingers rest on surfaces as if he were claiming them or something. He handled just about everything in the place. I was much more careful to make mine blurred.' Rothwell laughed quietly. 'He really was a fool, you know. Every time I got him to help me with something illegal, like setting up the Calvert bank account and credit card, for example, he thought *he* was getting more power over *me*.'

'So you must have known we'd find out about the Calvert identity, about Pamela, about Clegg and the money-laundering?'

'Of course. As I said earlier, I had to leave Calvert behind. It was part of my plan that you should find out about him. Another dead end. But please believe me, Pamela wasn't meant to be a part of it, except maybe to confirm the Calvert identity. I mean, I thought she might get in touch with the police if she saw my picture in the papers. Or someone else might, someone who thought they recognized me. It was meant to confuse you, that's all. I left a careful trail for you. I thought it led the wrong way. I knew the police would be able to unlock and interpret the data on my computer eventually, that they would realize I'd been laundering money for Martin

Churchill. I also left a letter for Daniel Clegg in a locked file. I knew you'd get at that eventually, too.'

'That was one of the things that bothered me,' Banks said. 'In retrospect, it was all too easy. And we never found a copy of the letter among his papers. He could have destroyed it, of course, but it was just one those little niggling details. Lawyers tend to hang on to things.'

'I never sent it,' said Rothwell. 'I just created the file so you'd get on to Daniel if you hadn't already. It was a way of telling you his name, but I couldn't make it *too* easy. Then you'd assume he'd had me killed and disappeared with the money.'

'Oh, we did,' said Banks. 'We did.'

'Then why are you here?'

'Because I'm a persistent bastard, among other things. There were too many loose ends. They worried me. Two different sets of thugs roaming the country, for a start. They could be explained, of course, but it still seemed odd. And we couldn't find any trace of Clegg, no matter how hard we tried. His ex-wife said he fancied Tahiti, but we had no luck there. We had no luck anywhere else, either. Of course we didn't. We were looking for the wrong person. But mostly, I think, it was the connection with Julia that really did you in.'

'How did you find out about her?'

'Pamela Jeffreys mentioned her first. She said she thought you were in love. Just a feeling she had, you understand. Then I began to wonder how it would upset the apple-cart if you fell in love as *Robert Calvert*. How would you handle it? Then Tom came back from America for your funeral.'

'Ah, Tom. My Achilles heel.' .

'Oh, he didn't realize the significance of it. But you

made him angry. He followed you to Leeds once. He saw you have lunch with a woman. Julia Marshall. You didn't know that, did you? But Tom couldn't imagine the scale of your plans. He's just a kid who caught his father with another woman. He was already angry, mixed up and confused at the way you treated him. He was after getting his own back, but what he saw upset him so much that all he could do was keep it to himself.'

'Christ,' he muttered. 'I didn't know that. He didn't tell Mary?'

'No. He wanted to protect her.'

'My God.' Rothwell ran his hand over the side of his face. 'Maybe you think I reacted too harshly, Chief Inspector? I know we're living in liberal times, where anything goes. I know it's old-fashioned of me, but I still happen to believe that homosexuality is an aberration, an abomination of nature, and not just an "alternative lifestyle", as the liberals would have it. And to find out that *my* own son . . .'

'So you decided it would be best to send Tom away?'

'Yes. It seemed best for both of us if he went away, a long way away. He was well provided for. As it turned out, he wanted to go travelling in America and try to get into film school there. By then I knew I had to get away, too, so it seemed best to let him go. At least he had a good chance. I might have abhorred his homosexuality, but I'm not a tyrant. He was still my son, after all.'

'Tom gave us an accurate description of Julia,' Banks went on. 'He's a very observant young man. We ran the artist's impression in the *Yorkshire Post* and a woman called Barbara Ledward came forward, a colleague of Julia's, then Julia's family. Nobody lives in a vacuum. When we followed up on their phone calls, we found out that Julia had resigned from her teaching job suddenly and told everyone she was going away, that she had a once-in-a-lifetime opportunity abroad but couldn't divulge the details. She said she'd be in touch, then she simply disappeared about three days before your apparent murder. Her family and friends were worried about her. She didn't usually behave so irresponsibly. But they didn't report her as a missing person because she had *told* them she was going away.

'We might have been a bit slow on the uptake, but we're not stupid. All Julia's friends and colleagues mentioned how fascinated she was by the ancient Greeks. She even tried to teach the kids about the classics at school, though I'm told it didn't go down well with the head. He wanted them to study computers and car maintenance instead. We had to assume you didn't think we'd find out about Julia. Oh, you might have suspected we'd find out there was *someone*, but you didn't think we'd try to find her, did you?'

'No,' said Rothwell. 'After all, why should you want to? No more than I thought you would waste time and money doing tests to see if it really was *my* body in the garage. Another risk. I was clearly dead, executed because of my involvement in international crime. What did it matter if I, or Calvert, had a girlfriend? I never thought for a moment you'd look very closely at the rest of my private life.'

'Then you shouldn't have revealed the Calvert identity to us,' Banks said. 'If it hadn't been for that, we might have gone on thinking you were a dull, mild-mannered accountant who just happened to get into something beyond his depth. But Calvert showed imagination. Calvert showed a dimension to your character I had to take into account. And I had to ask myself, what if Calvert fell in love?'

'I couldn't get rid of Calvert,' said Rothwell. 'You know that. I didn't have time. Too many people had seen him. I had to figure out a way to make him work to my advantage quickly. I thought he'd be a dead end.'

'Your mistake. Poor judgment.'

'Obviously. But I had no choice. What else could I do?'

'So how did you handle the killing?'

'Another drink?'

'Please.'

Banks stared out over the pink and purple flowers in the window box at the barren hillside and the blue sea below. Rothwell's mention of the forensic tests galled him. He knew they should have tried to establish the identity of the deceased beyond doubt. Forensics should have reconstructed the teeth and checked dental records. That was an oversight. It was understandable, given the way Rothwell had apparently been assassinated, and given the state the teeth were in, but it was an oversight, nevertheless.

Of course, the lab had been as burdened with work as usual, and tests cost money. Then, when the fingerprints at Calvert's flat matched the corpse's, they didn't think they needed to look any further. After all, they had the pasta meal, the appendix scar and the right blood group, and Mary Rothwell had identified the dead man's clothing, watch and pocket contents.

A red flying insect settled on his bare arm. He brushed it off gently. When Rothwell came back with a Grolsch and a Pepsi, he was not moving with quite the same confidence and grace as he had before.

'I gave Jameson instructions to hold Alison until we got back,' he began, 'but *not* to harm her in any way.'

'That's considerate of you. He didn't. What about his accomplice, Donald Pembroke?'

Rothwell shook his head. He held the Pepsi against his shorts. The can was beaded with moisture and Banks watched the damp patch spread through the white cotton. 'I never met him. That was Jameson's business. He said he needed someone to help and I left it to him, getting guarantees of discretion, of course. I never even knew the man's name, and that's the truth. Pembroke, you say? What happened to him?'

Banks told him.

Rothwell sighed. 'I suppose fate catches up with us all in the end, doesn't it? What is it the eastern religions call it? Karma?'

'Back to the murder.'

Rothwell paused a moment, then went on. 'They held Alison, then when Mary and I got home, they tied her up, too, and took me out to the garage. They had instructions to pick Clegg up after dinner. I knew he didn't like to cook for himself and on Thursdays he always dropped by a trattoria near the office for a quick pasta before going home. That's why I chose that day. I knew Mary and I would be going out for the annual anniversary dinner, and I arranged for us to eat at Mario's. You see, I thought of everything. Even the stomach contents would match.

'They'd already knocked Clegg out and secured him earlier. I even made sure to tell Jameson to use loose handcuffs to avoid rope burns on Clegg's wrists. We got him into my clothes as quickly as possible. He was starting to come round. He was on his hands and knees, I remember, shaking his head as if he was groggy, just waking up, then Jameson put the shotgun to the back of his head. I . . . I turned away. There was a terrible explosion and a smell. Then we went through the woods and they drove me to Leeds. I drove Clegg's Jaguar to Heathrow, wearing gloves, of course. Then I left the country as David Norcliffe. I already had a passport and bank accounts set up in that name. I joined Julia here. It was all pre-arranged. It had to be so elaborate because I was supposed to be murdered. I'd read about a similar murder in the papers a while back and it seemed one worth imitating.'

'Well, you know what the poet said. "The best laid plans . . ."'

'But you can't prove anything,' said Rothwell.

'Don't be an idiot. Of course we can. We can prove that you're alive and Daniel Clegg was murdered in your garage.'

'But you can't prove I was there. It's only your word against mine. I could say they were taking me out to kill both of us. I managed to get away and I ran and hid here. They killed Daniel, but I escaped.'

'They killed him in *your* clothes?' Banks shook his head slowly. 'It won't wash, Keith.'

'But it's all circumstantial. Jameson and Pembroke are both dead. A good lawyer could get me off, and you know it.'

'You're dreaming. Say you do beat the murder conspiracy charge, which I think is unlikely, there's still the money-laundering and the rest.'

Rothwell looked around the room, mouth set firmly. 'I'm not going back,' he said. 'You can't make me. I know there are European extradition treaties. Procedures to follow. They take time. You can't just take me in like some bounty hunter.'

'Of course I can't,' said Banks. 'That was never my intention.' He heard the gate open and walked over to the window.

A pale, beautiful woman in a yellow sun-dress, red-blonde hair piled and knotted high on her head, had walked into the courtyard and paused to check on the flowers and potted plants. She carried a basket of fresh bread and other foodstuffs in the crook of her arm. She put out her free hand and bent to hold a purple blossom gently between her fingers for a moment, then inspected the herbs. The sun brought out the blonde highlights in her hair. 'It looks like Julia's back,' Banks said. 'Doesn't tan well, does she?'

Rothwell jumped up and looked out. 'Julia knows nothing,' he said quickly, speaking quietly so she couldn't hear him. 'You have to believe that. I told her I had business problems, that I had to burn a lot of bridges if we were to be together, that we'd be well set up for life but we couldn't go back. Ever. She agreed. I don't know if you can understand this or not, but *I love her*, Banks, more than anyone or anything I've ever loved in my life. I mean it. It's the first time I've ever . . . I already told you. I love her. She knows nothing. You can do what you want with me, but leave her alone.'

Banks kept quiet.

'You'll never be able to prove anything,' Rothwell added.

'Maybe I don't even want to take that risk,' said Banks. By now they could both see Julia and hear her humming softly as she rubbed the leaves on a pot of basil and sniffed her fingers. 'Maybe I'd rather you made a clean breast of it,' he went on, keeping his voice low. 'A confession. It might even go in your favour, you never know. Especially the love bit. Juries love lovers.'

Julia stood up. Some of her piled tresses had come loose and trailed over her cheeks. She was flushed from the walk and some of the hairs stuck to her face, dampened with sweat.

'You must be mad if you think I'd give all this up willingly,' Rothwell said.

'You can't buy paradise with blood, Keith,' said Banks. 'Come on home. Tell us everything about Martin Churchill's finances, everything you know about the bastard. Let's go public, make plenty of noise, sing louder than a male-voice choir. We can make sure he never sets foot in the country even if he turns up looking like Mr Bean. We could offer you protection, then perhaps another identity, another new life. You'd do some time, of course, but I'm willing to bet that by the time you got out, Martin Churchill would be just another of history's unpleasant footnotes, and Julia would be still waiting.'

'You're insane, do you know that? I'd kill you before I'd do what you're suggesting.'

'No, you wouldn't, Keith. Besides, there'd be others after me.'

Rothwell paused on his way to the door and stared at Banks, eyes wide open and wild, no longer calm and steady. 'Do you know what will happen if I go home?'

'It might not be half as bad as what will happen if I let Churchill know you're still alive,' said Banks. 'They say he has a long reach and a nasty line in revenge.' Julia had almost reached the door. 'It wouldn't stop at you,' Banks said.

Rothwell froze. 'You wouldn't. No. Not even *you* would do a thing like that.'

At that moment, Banks hated himself probably more than at any other time in his life. He felt sorry for Rothwell, and he found himself on the verge of relenting.

Then he remembered Mary Rothwell, living in a haze of tranquillizers; Alison, burying her head deep in her books and fast losing touch with the real world; and Tom, flailing around in his own private mire of guilt and confusion. Rothwell could have helped these people. Then he thought of Pamela Jeffreys, just out of hospital, physically okay, but still afraid of every knock at her door and unsure whether she would get back the confidence to play her viola again.

For this man's gamble on paradise, Daniel Clegg lay in his grave with his head blown off, Barry Miller had died on a wet road at midnight and Grant Everett might have to spend the next few years of his life relearning how to walk and talk. Even Arthur Jameson and Donald Pembroke were Rothwell's victims, in a way.

And, much farther away but no less implicated, was a dictator who got fat while his people starved, a man who liked to watch people eat glass, a man who, now, if Banks could help it, would never enjoy a peaceful retirement in the English countryside, no matter what he had on some powerful members of the establishment.

And the more Banks thought about these people, victims and predators alike, the less able he was to feel sorry for the fallen lovers.

'Try me,' he said.

Rothwell glared at him, then all the life seemed to drain out of him until he resembled nothing more than a tired, middle-aged accountant. Banks still felt dirty and miserable, and despite his resolve, he wasn't certain he could go through with his threat. But Rothwell believed him now, and that was all that mattered. This bastard had caused enough trouble already. There was no more room for pity. Banks felt his pulse race, his jaw clench. Then the door opened and Julia drifted in, all blonde and yellow, with a big smile for Rothwell.

'Hello, darling! Oh,' she said, noticing Banks. 'We've got company. How nice.'

ACKNOWLEDGMENTS

My thanks are long overdue to Cynthia Good, my editor from the beginning of the series. I must also thank my agent, Dominick Abel, for his advice and encouragement. This book in particular could not have been completed without the help of many people, all generous with their time and expertise. My thanks go especially to Keith Wright of Nottingham CID, both detective and novelist; Douglas Lucas, Director of the Centre for Forensic Sciences, Toronto; Mario Possamai for his book *Money on the Run*; Ken McFarland, Chartered Accountant; John Picton, journalist; and to Rick Blechta for putting me right about viola players. Any errors are entirely my own and were made purely in the interests of dramatic fiction.

THE HANGING VALLEY

For Jan

PART ONE:

MOTION IN CORRUPTION

1

ONE

It was the most exhilarating feeling in the world. His thighs ached, his calves throbbed and his breath came in short sharp gasps. But he had made it. Neil Fellowes, humble wages clerk from Pontefract, stood at the summit of Swainshead Fell.

Not that it was an achievement comparable to Sir Edmund Hillary's; after all, the fell was only 1,631 feet high. But Neil was not getting any younger, and the crowd at Baxwell's Machine Tools, where he worked, had taken the mickey something cruel when he told them he was going on a fell-walking holiday in the Yorkshire Dales.

'Fell?' taunted Dick Blatchley, one of the mail-room wags. 'Tha'll a fell before tha's got started, Neil.' And they had all laughed.

But now, as he stood there in the thin air, his heart beating deep in his chest like the steam-driven pistons in the factory, he was the one to laugh. He pushed his wire-rimmed glasses back up to the bridge of his nose and wiped off the sweat over which they had slid. Next he adjusted the straps of his rucksack, which were biting into his shoulders.

He had been climbing for well over an hour: nothing too dangerous – no sheer heights, nothing that required special equipment. Fell-walking was a democratic recreation, just plain hard work. And it was an ideal day for walking. The sun danced in and out between plump white clouds and a cool breeze kept the temperature down. Perfect late May weather.

He stood in the rough grass and heather with nothing but a few sheep for company – and they had already turned their backs on him and scuttled a safe distance away. Lord of the whole scene, he sat on a weathered limestone boulder to savour the feeling.

Back down the fell he could just make out the northern tip of Swainshead village, from where he had come. He could easily pick out the whitewashed front of the White Rose across the beck, and the lichen-covered flagstone roof of the Greenock Guest House, where he had spent a comfortable night after the previous day's walking in Wharfedale. He had also enjoyed there a breakfast of sausage, bacon, black pudding, fried bread, grilled mushrooms, tomato, two fried eggs, tea, toast and marmalade before setting off that morning.

He stood up to take in the panorama, starting with the west, where the fells descended and rolled like frozen waves to the sea. To the north-west ranged the old rounded hills of the Lake District. Neil fancied he could see the Striding Edge along Helvellyn and the occasional glint of sun on Windermere or Ullswater. Next he looked south, where the landscape hardened into the Pennines, the backbone of England. The rock was darker there, with outcrops of millstone grit ousting the glinting white limestone. Miles of wild forbidding moorland stretched down as far as Derbyshire. South-east lay Swainsdale itself, its valley bottom hidden from view.

But what astonished Neil most of all was a small wooded valley down the eastern slope just below where he stood. The guidebooks hadn't mentioned anything of particular interest on the route he had chosen; indeed, one of his reasons for taking it was that nobody was likely to spoil his solitude. Most people, it seemed to Neil, would be off in search of stone circles, old lead mines and historic buildings.

In addition to its location and seclusion, the dale also had unusual foliage. It must have been a trick of the light, Neil thought, but whereas the trees everywhere else were fresh and green with spring, the ash, alders and sycamores below him seemed tinged with russet, orange and earth-brown. It seemed to him like a valley out of Tolkien's *Lord of the Rings*.

It would mean an extra mile or two and an unplanned climb back out again, but the sides didn't appear too steep, and Neil thought he might find some interesting wild flowers along the shaded banks of the beck. Balancing his pack, he struck out for the enchanted valley.

Soon, the rough tussocks underfoot gave way to springier grass. When Neil entered the woods, the leaves seemed much greener now the sunlight filtered through them. The smell of wild garlic filled his nostrils and made him feel light-headed. Bluebells swayed in the breeze.

He heard the beck before he saw it between the trees; it made a light bubbling sound, joyful and carefree. From the inside too, the valley clearly had a magical quality. It was more luxuriant than the surrounding area, its ferns and shrubs more lush and abundant as if, Neil thought, God had blessed it with a special grace.

He eased off his rucksack and laid it down on the thick grass by the waterside. Taking off his glasses, he thought he would stay a while and relax, perhaps drink some coffee from his flask before carrying on. He rested his head on the pack and closed his eyes. His mind emptied of everything but the heady scent of the garlic, the song of the beck, the cool fingers of the wind that rustled through wild roses and honeysuckle and the warbling of skylarks as they aimed themselves up at the sun and floated down like feathers, singing.

Refreshed – indeed feeling as if he had been born anew – Neil wiped his eyes and put on his glasses again. Looking around, he noticed a wild flower in the woods across the water. It seemed, from where he was, to be about a foot high, with red-brown sepals and pale yellow petals. Thinking it might be a rare lady's slipper orchis, he decided to cross over and have a closer look. The beck wasn't very wide, and there were plenty of fortuitously placed stepping stones.

As he neared the flower, he became aware of another smell, much more harsh and cloying than the garlic or loam. It clogged his nose and stuck to his bronchial passages. Wondering what it could be, he looked around, but could see nothing unusual. Near the flower, which was definitely a lady's slipper, some branches fallen from a tree lay on the ground and blocked his way. He started to pull them aside to get a better view.

But he didn't get very far. There, under a makeshift cover, lay the source of the smell: a human body. In the instant before he turned to vomit into the shrubs, Neil noticed two things: that it had no face, and that it seemed to be moving – its flesh was literally crawling.

Pausing only to wash his face and rinse out his mouth in the beck, Neil left his rucksack where it was and hurried as fast as he could back to Swainshead.

TWO

Disgusting, thought Katie Greenock, turning up her nose as she emptied the waste bin of room three. You'd think people would be ashamed to leave such things lying around for anyone to see. Thank God they'd left that morning. There always had seemed something unwholesome about them anyway: the way they kissed and canoodled at the breakfast table, how it was always so long before they set off for the day and so early when they returned to their room. She didn't even believe they were married.

Sighing, Katie brushed back a strand of ash-blonde hair and emptied the bin into the black plastic bag she carried with her on her rounds. Already she was tired out. Her day began at six o'clock, and there were no easy rustic mornings of birdsong and dew for her, just sheer hard work.

First she had to cook the breakfasts and coordinate everything so that the eggs weren't cold when the bacon was ready and the tea was fresh for the guests as soon as they decided to come down. They could help themselves to juice and cereal, which she had put out earlier – though not too early, for the milk had to be chilled. The toast could get as cold as it liked – cold toast seemed to be a part of the tradition of an English breakfast – but Katie was pleased when, as sometimes happened, she succeeded in serving it warm at exactly the right time. Not that anyone ever said thank you.

Then, of course, she had to serve the meals and manage a smile for all the guests, whatever their comments about the quality of the food and no matter what their sweet little children saw fit to drop on the floor or throw at the walls. She was also often asked for advice about where to go for the day, but sometimes Sam would help with that part, breaking off from his usual morning monologue on current events with which he entertained the visitors daily whether they liked it or not.

Next, she had to clear the tables and wash the dishes. The machine Sam had finally bought her helped a lot. Indeed, it saved her so much time that she could hurry down to Thetford's Grocery on the Helmthorpe Road and take her pick of the morning's fresh produce. Sam used to do that before he had installed the machine, but now he had more time for the sundry business matters that always seemed to be pressing.

When Katie had planned the menu for the evening meal and bought all the ingredients, it was time to change the sheets and clean the rooms. It was hardly surprising then that by noon she was almost always tired. If she was lucky, she could sometimes find a little time for gardening around mid afternoon.

Putting off the moment when she would have to move on to the next room, Katie walked over to the window and rested her elbows on the sill. It was a fine day in a beautiful part of the world but to her the landscape felt like an enormous trap; the fells were boulders that shut her in, the stretches of moorland like deserts impossible to cross. A chance of freedom had offered itself recently, but there was nothing she could do about it yet. She could only wait patiently and see what developed.

She looked down on the grassy banks at each side of the fledgling River Swain, at the children sitting patiently with their home-made fishing nets, a visiting couple having a picnic, the old men gossiping as usual on the small stone bridge. She could see it all, but not feel the beauty of any of it.

And there, almost dead opposite, was the White Rose, founded in 1605, as its sign proudly proclaimed, where Sam would no doubt be hobnobbing with his upper-class chums. The fool, Katie thought. He thinks he's well in, but they'll never really accept him, ever after all these years and all he's done for them. Their kind never does. She was sure they laughed at him behind his back. And had he noticed the way Nicholas Collier kept looking at her? Did Sam know about the times Nicholas had tried to touch her?

Katie shuddered at the thought. Outside, a sudden movement caught her eye and she saw the old men part like the Red Sea and stare open-mouthed as a slight figure hurried across the bridge.

It was that man who'd set off just a few hours ago, Katie realized, the mild-mannered clerk from Castleford or Featherstone or somewhere like that. Surely he'd said he was heading for the Pennine Way? And he was as white as the pub front. He turned left at the end of the bridge, hurried the last few yards and went running into the White Rose.

Katie felt her chest tighten. What was it that had brought him back in such a state? What was wrong? Surely nothing terrible had happened in Swainshead? Not again.

THREE

'Well,' Sam Greenock was saying about the racial mix in England, 'they have their ways, I suppose, but—'

Then Neil Fellowes burst through the door and looked desperately around the pub for a familiar face.

Seeing Sam at his usual table with the Collier brothers and John Fletcher, Neil hurried over and pulled up a chair.

'We must do something,' he said, gasping for breath and pointing outside. 'There's a body up on the fell. Dead.'

'Calm down, mate,' Sam said. 'Get your breath, then tell us what's happened.' He called over to the barman. 'A brandy for Mr Fellowes, Freddie, if you please. A large one.' Seeing Freddie hesitate, he added, 'Don't worry, you bloody old skinflint, I'll pay. And get a move on.'

Conversation at the table stopped while Freddie Metcalfe carried the drink over. Neil gulped the brandy and it brought on a coughing fit.

'At least that's put a bit of colour back in your cheeks,' Sam said, slapping Neil on the back.

'It was terrible,' Neil said, wiping off the brandy where it had dribbled down his chin. He wasn't used to strong drink, but he did approve of it in emergencies such as this.

'His face was all gone, all eaten away, and the whole thing was moving, like waves.' He put his glass to his thin lips again and drained it. 'We must do something. The police.' He got up and strode over to Freddie Metcalfe. 'Where's the police station in Swainshead?'

Metcalfe scratched his shiny red scalp and answered slowly. 'Let me see. . . There aren't no bobbies in T' Head itself. Nearest's Helmthorpe, I reckon. Sergeant Mullins and young Weaver. That's nigh on ten miles off.'

Neil bought himself another double brandy while Metcalfe screwed up his weather-beaten face and thought.

'They'll be no bloody use, Freddie,' Sam called over. 'Not for something like this. It's CID business, this is.'

'Aye,' Metcalfe agreed, 'I reckon tha's right, Sam. In that case, young feller mi' lad,' he said to Neil, 'it'll be that chap in Eastvale tha'll be after. T' one who were out 'ere

10

last time we 'ad a bit o' bother. Gristhorpe, Chief Inspector Gristhorpe. Years back it was though. Probably dead now. Come on, lad, you can use this phone, seeing as it's an emergency.'

FOUR

'Chief Inspector' Gristhorpe, now Superintendent, was far from dead. When the call came through, he was on another line talking to Redshaw's Quarries about a delivery for the drystone wall he was building. Despite all the care he had put into the endeavour, a section had collapsed during an April frost, and rebuilding seemed a suitable spring project.

The telephone call found its way instead to the office of Detective Chief Inspector Alan Banks, who sat browsing through the *Guardian* arts pages, counting his blessings that crime had been so slack in Eastvale recently. After all, he had been transferred from London almost two years ago for a bit of peace and quiet. He liked detective work and couldn't imagine doing anything else, but the sheer pressure of the job – unpleasant, most of it – and the growing sense of confrontation between police and citizens in the capital had got him down. For his own and his family's sake, he had made the move. Eastvale hadn't been quite as peaceful as he'd expected, but at the moment all he had to deal with were a couple of minor break-ins and the aftermath of a tremendous punch-up in the Oak. It had started when five soldiers from Catterick camp had taunted a group of unemployed miners from Durham. Three people ended up in hospital with injuries ranging from bruised and swollen testicles to a bitten-off earlobe, and the others were cooling off in the cells waiting to appear before the magistrate.

'Someone asking for the super, sir,' said Sergeant Rowe, when Banks picked up the phone. 'His line's busy.'

'It's all right,' Banks said. 'I'll take it.'

A breathless, slightly slurred voice came on the line. 'Hello, is that Inspector Gristhorpe?'

Banks introduced himself and encouraged the caller, who gave his name as Neil Fellowes, to continue.

'There's a body,' Fellowes said. 'Up on the fells. I found it.'

'Where are you now?'

'A pub. The White Rose.'

'Whereabouts?'

'What? Oh, I see. In Swainshead.'

Banks wrote the details down on his scrap pad.

'Are you sure it's a human body?' he asked. There had been mistakes made in the past, and the police had more than once been dragged out to examine piles of old sacks, dead sheep or rotten tree trunks.

'Yes. Yes, I'm sure.'

'Male or female?'

'I . . . I didn't look. It was—'

The next few words were muffled.

'All right, Mr Fellowes,' Banks said. 'Just stay where you are and we'll be along as soon as possible.'

Gristhorpe had finished his call when Banks tapped on the door and entered his office. With its overflowing bookcases and dim lighting, it looked more like a study than part of a police station.

'Ah, Alan,' Gristhorpe said, rubbing his hands together. 'They said they'll deliver before the weekend, so we can

12

make a start on the repairs on Sunday, if you'd care to come?'

Working on the drystone wall, which fenced in nothing and was going nowhere, had become something of a ritual for the superintendent and his chief inspector. Banks had come to look forward to those Sunday afternoons on the north daleside above Lyndgarth, where Gristhorpe lived alone in his farmhouse. Mostly they worked in silence, and the job created a bond between them, a bond that Banks, still an incomer to the Yorkshire Dales, valued greatly.

'Yes,' he answered. 'Very much. Look, I've just had a rather garbled phone call from a chap by the name of Neil Fellowes. Says he's found a body on the fell near Swainshead.'

Gristhorpe leaned back in his chair, linked his hands behind his head and frowned. 'Any details?'

'No. He's still a bit shook up, by the sound of it. Shall I go?'

'We'll both go.' Gristhorpe stood up decisively. 'It's not the first time a body has turned up in The Head.'

'The Head?'

'That's what the locals call it, the whole area around Swainshead village. It's the source of the River Swain, the head of the dale.' He looked at his watch. 'It's about twenty-five miles, but I'm sure we'll make it before closing time if I remember Freddie Metcalfe.'

Banks was puzzled. It was unusual for Gristhorpe to involve himself so much in an actual field investigation. As head of Eastvale CID, the superintendent could use his discretion as regards his role in a case. Theoretically, he could, if he wanted to, take part in searches and house-to-house enquiries, but of course he never did. In part, his job was administrative. He tended to delegate casework and monitor developments from his office. This was not due to laziness, Banks realized, but because his talent was for thinking and planning, not for action or interrogation. He trusted his subordinates and allowed them far greater leeway with their cases than many superintendents did. But this time he wanted to come along.

They made an incongruous couple as they walked to the car park at the back: the tall bulky Gristhorpe with his unruly thatch of grey hair, bristly moustache, pockmarked face and bushy eyebrows; and Banks, lean, slight, with angular features and short almost cropped black hair.

'I can't see why you keep on using your own car, Alan,' Gristhorpe said as he eased into the passenger seat of the white Cortina and grappled with the seat belt. 'You could save a lot of wear and tear if you took a department vehicle.'

'Have they got radio-cassettes?' Banks asked.

'You know damn well they haven't.'

'Well, then.'

'Well, what?'

'I like to listen to music while I'm driving. You know I do. It helps me think.'

'I suppose you're going to inflict some on me, too?'

It had always surprised Banks that so well read and cultured a person as Gristhorpe had absolutely no ear for music at all. The superintendent was tone-deaf, and even the most ethereal Mozart aria was painful to his ears.

'Not if you don't want,' Banks said, smiling to himself. He knew he wouldn't be able to smoke on the way, either. Gristhorpe was a non-smoker of the most rabid kind – reformed after a twenty-year, twenty-a-day habit.

Banks pulled into the cobbled market square, turned

left on to North Market Street, and headed for the main Swainsdale road, which ran by the river along the valley bottom.

Gristhorpe grunted and tapped the apparatus next to the dashboard. 'At least you've had a police radio fitted.'

'What was it you said before?' Banks asked. 'About this not being the first body in Swainshead.'

'It was before your time.'

'Most things were.' Banks made the sharp westward turn, and soon they were out of the town, driving by the river meadows.

Gristhorpe opened his window and gulped in the fresh air. 'A man had his skull fractured,' he said. 'It was murder, no doubt about that. And we never solved it.'

'What happened?'

'Some Boy Scouts found the body dumped in an old mineshaft on the fell side a couple of miles north of the village. The doctor said it had been there about a week.'

'When?'

'Just over five years ago.'

'Was it a local?'

'No. The victim was a private detective from London.'

'A private investigator?'

'That's right. Name of Raymond Addison. A solo operator. One of the last of the breed, I should imagine.'

'Did you find out what he was doing up here?'

'No. We had his office searched, of course, but none of his files had any connection with Swainsdale. The Yard asked around among his friends and acquaintances – not that he had very many – but they turned up nothing. We thought he might have been on holiday, but why choose Yorkshire in February?'

'How long had he been in the village?'

'He'd arrived fairly late in the day and managed to get a room in a guest house run by a chap named Sam Greenock, who told us that Addison said nothing except for some remarks about the cold. He wrapped up well and went out for a walk after the evening meal, and that was the last anyone saw of him. We made enquiries, but nobody had seen or heard him. It was dark when he went out, of course, and even the old men who usually hang about chatting on the bridge come rain or shine had gone in by then.'

'And as far as you could find out he had no connection with the area at all?'

'None. And, believe me, we dug and dug. Either nobody knew or, more likely, someone wasn't talking. He was an ex-serviceman, so we checked up on old army pals, that kind of thing. We ended up doing a house-to-house of the entire village. Nothing. It's still unsolved.'

Banks slowed down as he drove through Helmthorpe, one of the dale's largest villages. Beyond there, the landscape was unfamiliar to him. Though still broader than most of the dales, thanks to a glacier of particularly titanic proportions, the valley seemed to narrow slightly as they got closer to The Head, and the commons sloped more steeply up the fell sides. There were none of the long limestone scars that characterized the eastern part of Swainsdale, but the hills rose to high rounded summits of moorland.

'And that's not all,' Gristhorpe added after a few moments of silence. 'A week before Addison's body was found – the day after he was killed, as far as the doctors could make out – a local woman disappeared. Name of Anne Ralston. Never been seen since.'

'And you think there must have been a connection?'

'Not necessarily. At the time she went, of course, the body hadn't been discovered. The whole thing could have been a coincidence. And the doctor admitted he could have been wrong about the exact day of death, too. It's hard to be accurate after a body's been buried that long. But we've no idea what happened to her. And you've got to admit it's damned odd to get a missing person and a murder in the same village within a week of each other. She could have been killed and buried, or maybe she simply ran off with a fellow somewhere. We'd hardly cause to block all the ports and airports. Besides, she could have been anywhere in the world by the time the body was found. At best we'd have liked her to answer a few questions, just to put our minds at rest. As it was, we did a bit more poking around the landscape but found no traces of another body.'

'Do you think she might have murdered Addison and run off?'

'It's possible. But it didn't look like a woman's job to me. Too much muscle work involved, and Anne Ralston wasn't one of those female bodybuilders. We questioned her boyfriend pretty closely. He's Stephen Collier, managing director of the company she worked for. Comes from a very prominent local family.'

'Yes,' Banks said. 'I've heard of the Colliers. Did he cause any problems?'

'No. He was cooperative. Said they hadn't been getting on all that well lately, but he'd no idea where she'd gone, or why. In the end we'd no reason to think anything had happened to her so we had to assume she'd just left. People do sometimes. And Anne Ralston seemed to be a particularly flighty lass, by all accounts.'

'Still . . .'

'Yes, I know.' Gristhorpe sighed. 'It's not at all satisfactory, is it? We reached nothing but dead ends whichever direction we turned.'

Banks drove on in silence. Obviously failure was hard for Gristhorpe to swallow, as it was for most detectives. But this murder, if that's what it really turned out to be, was a different case, five years old. He wasn't going to let the past clutter up his thinking if he could help it. Still, it would be well to keep Raymond Addison and Anne Ralston in mind.

'This is it,' Gristhorpe said a few minutes later, pointing to the row of houses ahead. 'This is Lower Head, as the locals call it.'

'It hardly seems a big enough place to be split into two parts,' Banks observed.

'It's not a matter of size, Alan. Lower Head is the newest part of the village, the part that's grown since the road's become more widely used. People just stop off here to admire the view over a quick cup of tea or a pint and a pub lunch. Upper Head's older and quieter. A bit more genteel. It's a little north–south dale in itself, wedged between two fells. There's a road goes north up there too, but when it gets past the village and the school it gets pretty bad. You can get to the Lake District if you're willing to ride it out, but most people go from the Lancashire side. Turn right here.'

Banks turned. The base of a triangular village green ran beside the main road, allowing easy access to Swainshead from both directions. The first buildings he passed were a small stone church and a village hall.

Following the minor road north beside the narrow River Swain, Banks could see what Gristhorpe meant. There were two rows of cottages facing each other, set back quite a bit from the river and its grassy banks. Most of them were either semis or terraced, and some had been converted into shops. They were plain sturdy houses built mostly of limestone, discoloured here and there with moss and lichen. Many had individualizing touches, such as mullions or white borders painted around doors and windows. Behind the houses on both sides, the commons sloped up, criss-crossed here and there by drystone walls, and gave way to steep moorland fells.

Banks parked the car outside the whitewashed pub and Gristhorpe pointed to a large house farther up the road.

'That's the Collier place,' he said. 'The old man was one of the richest farmers and landowners around these parts. He also had the sense to invest his money in a food-processing plant just west of here. He's dead now, but young Stephen runs the factory and he shares the house with his brother. They've split it into two halves. Ugly pile of stone, isn't it?'

Banks didn't say so, but he rather admired the Victorian extravagance of the place, so at odds with the utilitarian austerity of most Dales architecture. Certainly it was ugly: oriels and turrets cluttered the upper half, making the whole building look top-heavy, and there was a stone porch at each front entrance. They probably had a gazebo and a folly in the back garden too, he thought.

'And that's where Raymond Addison stayed,' Gristhorpe said, pointing across the beck. The house, made of two knocked-together semis, was separated from the smaller terraced houses on either side by only a few feet. A sign, GREENOCK GUEST HOUSE, hung in the colourful well-tended garden.

''Ey up, lads,' Freddie Metcalfe said as they entered, 't' Sweeney's 'ere.'

'Hello again, Freddie,' Gristhorpe said, leading Banks over to the bar. 'Still serving drinks after hours?'

'Only to the select few, Mr Gristhorpe,' Metcalfe replied proudly. 'What'll you gents be 'aving?' He looked at Banks suspiciously. 'Is 'e over eighteen?'

'Just,' Gristhorpe answered.

Freddie burst into a rasping smoker's laugh.

'What's this about a body?' Gristhorpe asked.

Metcalfe pursed his fleshy lips and nodded towards the only occupied table. 'Bloke there says he found one on t' fell. 'E's not going anywhere, so I might as well pull you gents a pint before you get down to business.'

The superintendent asked for a pint of bitter and Banks, having noticed that the White Rose was a Marston's house, asked for a pint of Pedigree.

''E's got good taste, I'll say that for 'im,' Metcalfe said. 'Is 'e 'ouse-trained an' all?'

Banks observed a prudent silence throughout the exchange and took stock of his surroundings. The walls of the lounge bar were panelled in dark wood up to waist height and above that papered an inoffensive dun colour. Most of the tables were the old round kind with cast-iron knee-capper legs, but a few modern square ones stood in the corner near the dartboard and the silent jukebox.

Banks lit a Silk Cut and sipped his pint. He'd refrained from smoking in the car in deference to Gristhorpe's feelings, but now that he was in a public place he was going to take advantage of it and puff away to his heart's and lungs' content.

Carrying their drinks, they walked over to the table.

'Someone reported a death?' Gristhorpe asked, his innocent baby-blue eyes ranging over the five men who sat there.

Fellowes hiccuped and put his hand in the air. 'I did,' he said, and slid off his chair on to the stone floor.

'Christ, he's pissed as a newt,' Banks said, glaring at Sam Greenock. 'Couldn't you have kept him sober till we got here?'

'Don't blame me,' Sam said. 'He's only had enough to put some colour back in his cheeks. It's not my fault he can't take his drink.'

Two of the others helped Fellowes back into his chair and Freddie Metcalfe rushed over with some smelling salts he kept behind the bar for this and similar exigencies.

Fellowes moaned and waved away the salts, then slumped back and squinted at Gristhorpe. He was clearly in no condition to guide them to the scene of the crime.

'It's all right, Inshpector,' he said. 'Bit of a shock to the syshtem, thass all.'

'Can you tell us where you found this body?' Gristhorpe spoke slowly, as if to a child.

'Over Shwainshead Fell, there's a beautiful valley. All autumn colours. Can't mish it, just down from where the footpath reaches the top. Go shtraight down till you get to the beck, then cross it . . . Easy. Near the lady's slipper.'

'Lady's slipper?'

'Yes. The orchish, not the bird's-foot trefoil. Very rare. Body's near the lady's shlipper.'

Then he half twisted in his chair and stretched his arm up his back.

'I left my rucksack,' he said. 'Thought I did. Just over from my rucksack, then. Ruckshack marks the spot.' Then he hiccuped again and his eyes closed.

'Does anyone know where he's staying?' Banks asked the group.

'He was staying at my guest house,' Sam said. 'But he left this morning.'

'Better get him back there, if there's room. He's in no condition to go anywhere and we'll want to talk to him again later.'

Sam nodded. 'I think we've still got number five empty, unless someone's arrived while I've been out. Stephen?' He looked over to the man next to him, who helped him get Fellowes to his feet.

'It's Stephen Collier, isn't it?' Gristhorpe asked, then turned to the person opposite Greenock. 'And you're Nicholas. Remember, I talked to you both a few years ago about Anne Ralston and that mysterious death?'

'We remember,' Nicholas answered. 'You knew Father too, if I recall rightly?'

'Not well, but yes, we bent elbows together once or twice. Quite a man.'

'He was indeed,' Nicholas said.

Outside, Banks and Gristhorpe watched Sam and Stephen help Neil Fellowes over the bridge. The old men stood by and stared in silence.

Gristhorpe looked up at the fell side. 'We've got a problem,' he said.

'Yes?'

'It's a long climb up there. How the bloody hell are we going to get Glendenning and the scene-of-crime team up if we need them? Come to that, how am _I_ going to get up? I'm not as young as I used to be. And you smoke like a bloody chimney. You'll never get ten yards.'

Banks followed Gristhorpe's gaze and scratched his head. 'Well,' he said, 'I suppose we could give it a try.'

Gristhorpe pulled a face. 'Aye,' he said. 'I was afraid you'd say that.'

2

ONE

'Problem, gentlemen?' Nicholas Collier asked when he walked out of the White Rose and saw Banks and Gristhorpe staring up dejectedly at Swainshead Fell.

'Not at all,' Gristhorpe replied. 'Simply admiring the view.'

'Might I suggest a way you can save yourselves some shoe leather?'

'Certainly.'

'Do you see that narrow line that crosses the fell diagonally?' Nicholas pointed towards the slope and traced the direction of the line with a long finger.

'Yes,' said Gristhorpe. 'It looks like an old track of some kind.'

'That's exactly what it is. There used to be a farmhouse way up on the fell side there. It belonged to Father, but he used to let it to Archie Allen. The place has fallen to ruin now but the road that leads up is still there. It's not in good repair, of course, and you might find it a bit overgrown, but you should be able to get a car well above halfway up, if that's any help.'

'Thank you very much, Mr Collier,' Gristhorpe said. 'For a man of my shape any effort saved is a blessing.'

'You'll have to drive two miles up the road here to the next bridge to get on the track, but you'll see your way easily enough,' said Nicholas, and with a smile he set off for home.

'Odd-looking sort of fellow, isn't he?' Banks remarked. 'Not a bit like his brother.'

Whereas Stephen had the elegant, world-weary look of a *fin de siècle* decadent, Nicholas's sallow complexion, long nose and prominent front teeth made him appear a bit horsy. The only resemblance was in their unusually bright blue eyes.

'Takes after his father, does Nicholas,' Gristhorpe said. 'And Stephen takes after his mother, as handsome a woman as I've seen around these parts. There's many a man drowned his sorrows in drink when Ella Dinsdale married Walter Collier. Didn't last long though, poor lass.'

'What happened?'

'Polio. Before inoculations came in. Come on, let's go and have a look at this body before it gets up and walks away.'

Banks found the bridge and track easily enough, and though the old road was bumpy, they managed to get as far as the ruined farmhouse without any serious damage to the car.

A little to the left, they saw the footpath Neil Fellowes had taken and began to follow it up the fell side. Even though they had been able to drive most of the way, the path was steep and Banks soon found himself gasping for air and wishing he didn't smoke. Gristhorpe, for all his weight, seemed to stride up much more easily, though his face turned scarlet with the effort. Banks guessed he was more used to the landscape. After all, his own cottage was halfway up a daleside, too.

Finally, they stood at the top, where Fellowes had surveyed the scene a few hours earlier. Both were puffing and sweating by then, and after they'd got their breath back Gristhorpe pointed out the autumnal valley below.

'It looks enchanted, doesn't it,' he said as they walked down the slope towards the woods. 'Look, there's the rucksack.'

They crossed the beck as directed and headed for the lady's slipper orchis by the fallen branches. When they smelled the corpse, they exchanged glances. Both had known that stench before; it was unmistakable.

'No wonder Fellowes was in such a state,' Banks said. He took out a handkerchief and held it to his nose. Cautiously, Gristhorpe pulled more branches aside.

'By Christ, Glendenning's going to love this one,' he said, then stood back. 'By the look of that mess below the ribs there, we've got a murder case on our hands. Probably a knife wound. Male, I'd say.'

Banks agreed. Though small animals had been at parts of the body and maggots had made it their breeding ground, the dark stain just below the left ribcage stood out clearly enough against the white shirt the man was wearing. Fellowes had been right about the movement. The way the maggots were wriggling under his clothes made it look as if the body were rippling like water in the breeze.

'"Motion in corruption",' Gristhorpe muttered under his breath. 'I wonder where the rest of his gear is. By the look of those boots he was a walker sure enough.'

Banks peered as closely as he could at the cleated rubber Vibram treads. 'They look new as well,' he said. 'Hardly worn at all.'

'He must have had more stuff,' Gristhorpe said, rubbing his whiskery chin. 'Most walkers carry at least a rucksack with a few dried dates, compass, maps, torch, changes of clothing and what have you. Somebody must have taken it.'

'Or buried it.'

'Aye.'

'He's not wearing waterproofs, either,' Banks observed.

'That could mean he knew what he was doing. Only amateurs wear waterproofs all the time. Experienced walkers put their clothes on and off in layers according to the weather. If this is all he was wearing when he was killed, we might be able to get some idea of the date of death by checking weather records.'

'It's been fairly constant these past few weeks,' Banks pointed out. 'We had a late spring, but now it looks like an early summer.'

'True enough. Still, forensic might be able to come up with something. Better get the team up, Alan.'

'The way we came? It's not going to be easy.'

Gristhorpe thought for a moment. 'There might be a better way,' he said at last. 'If my geography's correct.'

'Yes?'

'Well, if I'm right, this'll be the beck that ends in Rawley Force on the Helmthorpe road about a mile east of Swainshead village. It's a hanging valley.'

'Come again?'

'A hanging valley,' Gristhorpe repeated. 'It's a tributary valley running into Swainsdale at a right angle. The glacier here was too small to deepen it as much as the larger one that carved out the dale itself, so it's left hanging above the main valley floor like a cross-section. The water usually reaches the main river over a waterfall, like Rawley Force. I thought you'd been reading up on local geology, Alan.'

'Haven't got that far yet,' Banks mumbled. In fact, he'd put aside the geology book after reading only two chapters in favour of a new history of Yorkshire that his daughter, Tracy, had recommended. The trouble was that he wanted to know so much but had so little time for learning that he tended to skitter from one subject to another without fully absorbing anything.

'Anyway,' Gristhorpe went on, 'Rawley Force is only about ninety feet high. If we can get in touch with the Mountain Rescue post at Helmthorpe and they're willing to rig up a winch, we'll be able to get the team up and down without much trouble. I can hardly see Glendenning, for one, walking the way we did. There'll be a lot of coming and going. And we'll have to get the body down somehow, too. A winch just might be the answer. It should be easy enough. The Craven and Bradford pothole clubs put one up at Gaping Gill for a few days each year to give the tourists a look, and that's a hell of a lot deeper.'

'It sounds good,' Banks said dubiously. He remembered swinging the three hundred feet down Gaping Gill, which opened into a cavern as huge as the inside of York Minster. It was an experience he had no wish to repeat. 'We'd better get cracking though, or it'll be dark before they all get here. Should we get Sergeant Hatchley in on this, too?'

Gristhorpe nodded.

'DC Richmond?'

'Not just yet. Let's see exactly what we've got on our hands before we bring in all our manpower. Richmond can hold the fort back at the station. I'll stay here while you go back to the car and radio in. You'd better let the doctor know what state the body's in. He might need some special equipment.'

Banks glanced towards the corpse, then back at Gristhorpe.

'Are you sure you want to stay here?'

'It's not a matter of wanting,' Gristhorpe said. 'Somebody should stay.'

'It's been here alone long enough. I doubt that another half-hour will make any difference.'

'Somebody should stay,' Gristhorpe repeated.

Banks knew when to give up. Leaving the superintendent sitting like Buddha under an ash tree by the beck, he set off back through the woods to the car.

TWO

'What's wrong?' Katie Greenock asked as Sam and Stephen staggered in with Fellowes between them.

'He's had a bit too much to drink, that's all,' Sam said. 'Out of the way, woman. Is number five still vacant?'

'Yes, but—'

'Don't worry, he's not going to puke on your precious sheets. He just needs sleep.'

'All right,' Katie said, biting her lip. 'Better take him up.'

Stephen smiled apologetically at her as they passed and struggled up the stairs. Finally, they dumped their burden on the bedspread and left Katie in the room with him. At first she didn't move. She just stood by the window looking at Fellowes in horror. Surely Sam knew how much she hated and feared drunks, how much they disgusted her. And Mr Fellowes had seemed such a nice sober man.

She couldn't really picture her father clearly, for he had died along with her mother in a fire when Katie was only four, but he had certainly been a drunk, and she was sure that he was at the root of her feelings. The only vague image she retained was of a big vulgar man who frightened her with his loud voice, his whiskers and his roughness.

Once, when they hadn't known she was watching, she saw him hurting her mother in the bedroom, making her groan and squirm in a way that sent shivers up Katie's spine. Of course, when she got older, she realized what they must have been doing, but the early memory was as firmly established and as deeply rooted as cancer. She also remembered once when her father fell down and she was afraid that he'd hurt himself. When she went to help him though, he knocked her over and cursed her. She was terrified that he would do the same thing to her as he had done to her mother, but she couldn't remember any more about the incident, no matter how hard she tried.

The fire was a memory she had blocked out too, though strange tongue-like flames sometimes roared and crackled in her nightmares. According to her grandmother, Katie had been in the house at the time, but the firemen had arrived before the blaze reached her room. Katie had been saved by the grace of God, so her granny said, whereas her parents, the sinners, had been consumed by the flames of hell.

The fire had been caused by smoking in bed, and her grandmother had seemed especially satisfied by that, as if the irony somehow marked it as God's special work, an answer to her prayers. It had all been God's will, His justice, and Katie was obliged to spend her life in gratitude and devoted service.

Katie took a deep breath, rolled Fellowes over carefully and pulled back the sheets – they could be washed easily, but not the quilted spread. Then she unlaced his walking boots and put them on some newspaper by the bed. They weren't muddy, but fragments of earth had lodged in the ribbed treads.

'Cleanliness is next to godliness,' her grandmother had

drilled into her. And a lot easier to achieve, Katie might have added if she had dared. Apart from an unusually long list of its attributes – mostly 'thou shalt nots', which seemed to include everything most normal people enjoyed – godliness was an elusive quality as far as Katie was concerned. Lately, she had found herself thinking about it a lot, recalling her grandmother's harsh words and 'necessary' punishments: her mouth washed out with soap for lying; a spell in the coal hole for 'swaying wantonly' to a fragment of music that had drifted in from next door's radio. These had all been preceded by the words, 'This is going to hurt me more than it will hurt you.'

Fellowes stirred and snapped Katie out of her reverie. For a second, his grey eyes opened wide and he grasped her hand. She could feel the fear and confusion flow from his bony fingers through her wrist.

'Moving,' he mumbled, falling back into a drunken sleep again. 'Moving . . .'

Spittle gathered at the edges of his lips and dribbled down his chin. Katie shuddered. Leaving him, she hurried back downstairs. There was still the evening meal to prepare, and the garden needed weeding.

THREE

Banks leaned over the edge of Rawley Force and watched Glendenning coming up in the winch. It was an amusing sight. The tall white-haired doctor sat erect, trying to retain as much dignity as he could. A cigarette dangled from the left corner of his mouth, as usual, and he clutched his brown bag tightly against his stomach.

Luckily there had been hardly any rain over the past

two weeks, so the waterfall to the doctor's right was reduced to a trickle. The staff at the Mountain Rescue post had been only too willing to help and had come out and set up the winch in no time. Now the police team were ready to come up slowly, one at a time, and Glendenning, as befitted his status, was first in line.

Puffing, as he struggled out of the harness, the doctor nodded curtly at Banks and straightened the crease in his suit trousers. Banks led him half a mile along the wooded valley to the scene, where Gristhorpe still sat alone.

'Thanks for coming so quickly,' the superintendent said to Glendenning, getting up and dusting off his seat. Everyone in Eastvale Regional Police Headquarters found it paid to be polite, even deferential, to the doctor. Although he was a crusty old bugger, he was one of the best pathologists in the country and they were lucky he had chosen Eastvale as his home.

Glendenning lit another cigarette from the stub of his old one and asked, 'Where is it, then?'

Gristhorpe pointed towards the pile of branches. The doctor cursed under his breath as he tackled the stepping stones, and Gristhorpe turned to Banks and winked. 'Everyone here, Alan?'

'Looks like it.'

Next the young photographer, Peter Darby, came hurrying towards them, trying to head off Glendenning before the doctor could get to work. To Banks he always looked far too fresh-faced and innocent for his line of work, but he had never been known to bat an eyelid, no matter what they asked him to photograph.

After him came Sergeant Hatchley, red-faced after his short walk from Rawley Force along the hanging valley. The fair-haired sergeant was a big man, like Gristhorpe, and although he was twenty years younger, his muscle was turning quickly to fat. He resembled a rugby prop forward, a position he had indeed played on the local team until cigarettes and beer took their toll on his stamina.

Banks filled him in on the details while Gristhorpe busied himself with the scene-of-crime team.

Glendenning, kneeling by the corpse, kept shooing the others away like flies. At last, he packed his bag and struggled back over the beck, stretching out his arms for balance like a tightrope walker. With one hand he clung on to his brown bag, and in the other he held a test tube.

'Bloody awkward place to go finding a corpse,' he grumbled, as if the superintendent were personally responsible.

'Aye, well,' Gristhorpe replied, 'we don't get to pick and choose in our business. I don't suppose you can tell us much till after the post-mortem?'

Glendenning screwed up his face against the smoke that rose from his cigarette. 'Not much,' he said. 'Looks like a stab wound to me. Probably pierced the heart from under the ribcage.'

'Then someone got very close to him indeed,' Gristhorpe said. 'It must have been someone he knew and trusted.'

Glendenning sniffed. 'I'll leave that kind of speculation to you boys, if you don't mind. There are lacerations and blows to the face, too. Can't say what did it at the moment, or when it was done. Been dead about ten days. Not more than twelve.'

'How can you be certain?' Banks asked, startled by the information.

'I can't be certain, laddie,' Glendenning said, 'that's the problem. Between ten and twelve days doesn't count as

32

accurate with me. I might be able to be more precise after the PM, but no promises. Those chappies over there have got a bag to put him in. He'll need to soak in a Lysol bath for a day or two.' Glendenning smiled and held up his test tube. 'Maggots,' he said. '*Calliphora erythrocephalus*, if I'm not mistaken.'

The three detectives looked at the white, slow-moving blobs and exchanged puzzled glances.

Glendenning sighed and spoke as he would to a group of backward children. 'Simple really. Bluebottle larvae. The bluebottle lays its eggs in daylight, usually when the sun's shining. If the weather's warm, as it has been lately, they hatch on the first day. Then you get what's called the "first instar" maggot. That wee beauty sheds its skin like a snake after eight to fourteen hours, and then the second instar, the one you use for fishing' – and here he glanced at Gristhorpe, a keen angler – 'that one eats like a pig for five or six days before going into its pupa case. Look at these, gentlemen.' He held up the test tube again. 'These, as you can see, are fat maggots. Lazy. Mature. And they're not in their pupa cases yet. Therefore, they must have been laid nine or ten days ago. Add on a day or so for the bluebottles to find the body and lay, and you've got twelve days at the outside.'

It was the most eloquent and lengthy speech Banks had ever heard Glendenning deliver. There was obviously a potential teacher in the brusque chain-smoking Scot with the trail of ash like the Milky Way down his waistcoat.

The doctor smiled at his audience. 'Simpson,' he said.

'Pardon?' Banks asked.

'Simpson. Keith Simpson. I studied under him. Our equivalent of Sherlock Holmes, only Simpson's real.'

'I see,' said Banks, who had learned to tease after so

long in Yorkshire. 'A kind of real-life Quincy, you mean?'
He felt Gristhorpe nudge him in the ribs.

Glendenning scowled and a half-inch of ash fell off the
end of his cigarette. 'Quite,' he said, and put the test tube
in his bag. 'I hope that glorified truss over there can get me
back down safely.'

'Don't worry,' Gristhorpe assured him. 'It will. And
thank you very much.'

'Aye. Now I have first-hand knowledge of what it feels
like to have my arse in a sling,' Glendenning said as he
walked away.

Banks laughed and turned back to watch the experts at
work. The photographs had been taken, and the team
were busy searching the ground around the body.

'We'll need a more thorough search of the area,'
Gristhorpe said to Hatchley. 'Can you get that organized,
Sergeant?'

'Yes, sir.' Hatchley took out his notebook and pen. 'I'll
get some men in from Helmthorpe and Eastvale.'

'Tell them to look particularly for evidence of anything
recently buried or burned. He must have been carrying a
rucksack. We're also looking for the weapon, a knife of
some kind. And I think, Sergeant,' Gristhorpe went on,
'we'd better bring DC Richmond in on this after all. Get
him to check on missing persons with the Police National
Computer.'

Vic Manson, the fingerprint expert, approached them,
shaking his head. 'It'll not be easy,' he complained. 'There
might be prints left on three or four fingers but I can't
promise anything. I'll try wax injections to unwrinkle the
skin, and if they don't work, it'll have to be formaldehyde
and alum.'

'It'll be a devil of a job finding out who he was,'

Banks said. 'Even if we can get prints, there's no guaranteeing they'll be on record. And someone's gone to great lengths to make sure we can't recognize him by his face.'

'There's always the clothes,' Gristhorpe said. 'Or teeth. Though I can't say I've ever had much luck with them myself.'

'Me neither,' Banks agreed. He always thought it amusing when he watched television detectives identify bodies from dental charts. If they really knew how long it would take every dentist in the country to search through every chart in his files . . . Only if the police already had some idea who the body was could dental charts confirm or deny the identity.

'He might even be German,' Hatchley added. 'Or an American. You get a lot of foreigners walking the fells these days.'

Across the beck, two men wearing face masks slid the body into the large zip-up bag they had brought. Banks grimaced as he watched them brush off the maggots, shed in all directions, before they were finally able to secure the zip. They then started to carry their burden along the valley towards the winch.

'Let's go,' Gristhorpe said. 'It's getting late. There's nothing more to be done here till we can start a search. We'd better post a couple of men here for the night though. If the killer knows we've discovered the body and he's buried important evidence nearby, he might come back after dark.'

Hatchley nodded.

'We'll arrange to send someone up,' Gristhorpe went on. 'You'd better stick around till they get here, Sergeant. See if you can persuade the rescue people to wait for them with the winch. If not, they'll just have to come the long way, like we did.'

Banks saw Hatchley glance towards where the corpse had lain and shiver. He didn't envy anyone stuck with the job of staying in this enchanted valley after dark.

FOUR

Sam took Katie as roughly as usual in bed that night. And as usual she lay there and gave the illusion of enjoying herself. At least it didn't hurt any more like it had at first. There were some things you had to do, some sins you had to commit because men were just made that way and you needed a man to take care of you in the world. The important thing, Katie had learned from her grandmother, was that you must not enjoy it. Grit your teeth and give them what they want, yes, even cheat a little and make them think you like it – especially if they treat you badly when you don't seem enthusiastic – but under no circumstances should you find pleasure in it.

It never lasted long. That was one consolation. Soon Sam started breathing quickly, and she clung to him tighter and mouthed the sounds he liked to hear, told him the things he liked to know. At last he grunted and made her all wet. Then he rolled over on his side and quickly began snoring.

But sleep didn't come so easily for Katie that night. She thought about the body on the fell and pulled the sheets up tighter around her chin. Last time it had been awful: all those questions, all the trouble there'd been – especially when the police tried to connect the dead man with the missing girl, Anne Ralston. They'd acted as if Stephen or one of his friends might have killed both of them. And what had they found out? Nothing. Raymond Addison seemed to have come from nowhere.

Katie had hardly known Anne, for she and Sam hadn't been in Swainshead long when all the trouble started five years ago. The only reason they had met her at all was because Sam wanted to seek out the 'best people' in the village. He latched on to the Colliers, and Anne Ralston had been going out with Stephen at the time.

She hadn't been Katie's type though, and they'd never have become good friends. Anne, she remembered, had seemed far too footloose and fancy-free for her taste. She had probably just run off with another man; it would have been typical of her to go off without a word and leave everyone to worry about her.

Katie turned on her side to reach for some Kleenex from the bedside table, dragging the sheets with her. Sam stirred and yanked back his half. Gently, she wiped herself. She hated that warm wetness between her legs. More and more every time she hated it, just as she had come to loathe her life with Sam in Swainshead.

And things had been getting worse lately. She had been under a black depression for a month or more. She knew it was a woman's place to obey her husband, to stay with him for better, for worse, to submit to his demands in bed and slave for him all day in the house. But surely, she thought, life shouldn't be so bleak. If there was any chance of escape from the drudgery that her life had become and from the beatings, would it really be such a sin to take it?

Things hadn't always been so bad. When they had met, Katie had been working as a chambermaid at Queen's Hotel in Leeds, and Sam, an apprentice electrician, had turned up one day to check the wiring. It had hardly been love at first sight; for Katie, love was what happened in the romantic paperbacks she read, the ones that made her blush and look over her shoulder in case her granny could see her reading them. But Sam had been presentable enough – a cocky young bantam with curly chestnut hair and a warm boyish smile. A real charmer.

He had asked her out for a drink three times, and three times she had said no. She had never set foot in a pub. Her granny had taught her that they were all dens of iniquity, and Katie herself held alcohol responsible for her father's wickedness and for the misery of her mother's life. Katie didn't realize at the time that her refusal of a drink was taken as a rejection of Sam himself. If only he would ask her to go for a walk, she had thought, or perhaps to the Kardomah for a coffee and a bite to eat after work.

Finally, in exasperation, he had suggested a Saturday afternoon trip to Otley. Even though Katie was over eighteen, she still had a difficult time persuading her grandmother to let her go, especially as she was to ride pillion on Sam's motorbike. But in the end the old woman had given in, muttering warnings about the Serpent in Eden and wolves in sheep's clothing.

In Otley they had, inevitably, gone for a drink. Sam had practically dragged her into the Red Lion, where she had finally broken down and blurted out why she had refused to go for a drink before. He laughed and touched her shoulder gently. She drank bitter lemon and nothing terrible happened to either of them. After that she went to pubs with him more often, though she always refused alcohol and never felt entirely comfortable.

But now, she thought, turning over again, life had become unbearable. The early days, just after their marriage, had been full of hope after Katie had learned how to tolerate Sam's sexual demands. They had lived with his parents in a little back-to-back in Armley and saved every penny they earned. Sam had a dream, a guest house in the Dales, and together they had brought it about. Those had been happy times, despite the hours of overtime, the cramped living quarters and the lack of privacy, for they had had something to aim towards. Now it was theirs, Katie hated it. Sam had changed; he had become snobbish, callous and cruel.

Like every other night for the past few months, she cried quietly to herself as she tried to shut out Sam's snoring and listen to the breeze hiss through the willows by the nameless stream out at the back. She would wait and keep silent. If nothing happened, if nothing came of her only hope of escape, then one night she would sneak out of the house as quiet as a thief and never come back.

FIVE

In room five, Neil Fellowes knelt by the side of the bed and said his prayers.

He had woken from his drunken stupor in time to be sick in the washbasin, and after that he had felt much better. So much so, in fact, that he had gone down and eaten the lamb chops with mint sauce that Mrs Greenock had cooked so well. Then he spent the rest of the evening in his room reading.

And now, as he tried to match the words to his thoughts and feelings, as he always did in prayer, he found he couldn't. The picture of the body kept coming back, tearing aside the image of God that he had retained from childhood: an old man with a long white beard sitting on a cloud with a ledger on his lap. Suddenly, the smell was in his nostrils again; it was like trying to breathe at the bottom of a warm sewer. And he saw again the bloody maggot-infested pulp that had once been a face, the white shirt rippling with corruption, the whole thing rising and falling in an obscene parody of breathing.

He tried to force his mind back to the prayer but couldn't. Hoping the Lord would understand and give him the comfort he needed, he gave up, put his glasses on the table and got into bed.

On the edge of sleep, he was able to reconstruct the sequence of events in his mind. At the time, he had been too distraught, too confused to notice anything. And very soon his head had been spinning with the drink. But he remembered bursting into the pub and asking for help. He remembered how Sam Greenock and the others at the table had calmed him down and suggested what he should do. But there was something else, something wrong. It was just a vague feeling. He couldn't quite bring it to consciousness before sleep took him.

3

ONE

'**What is it?**' Banks asked, examining the faded slip of
paper that Sergeant Hatchley had dropped on the desk in
front of him.

'Forensic said it's some kind of receipt from a till,'
Hatchley explained. 'You know, one of those bits of paper
they give you when you buy something. People usually
just drop them on the floor or shove them in their pockets
and forget about them. They found it in his right trouser
pocket. It'd been there long enough to go through the
washer once or twice, but you know what bloody wizards
they are in the lab.'

Banks knew. He had little faith in forensic work as a
means of catching criminals, but the boffins knew their
stuff when it came to identification and gathering evidence. Their lab was just outside Wetherby, and Gristhorpe must have put a 'rush' on this job to get the results
back to Eastvale so quickly. The body had been discovered
only the previous afternoon, and it was still soaking in a
Lysol bath.

Banks looked closely again at the slip, then turned to its
accompanying transcription. The original had been too
faint to read, but forensic had treated it with chemicals
and copied out the message exactly:

```
          CHOOSE FRESH
          CHOOSE WENDY'S
           *Store 006308*

          SNGL / CHZ
           WITH . . .
           TOMATO
           BACON          2.69
           FRIES           .89
           SMALL COKE      .85
     Tax                   .35
     Inside               4.78
                    05.26PM 04/25
```

'Wendy's,' Banks said. 'That's a burger chain. There's a few branches in London. Look at those prices, though.'

Hatchley shrugged. 'If it was in London . . .'

'Come on! Even in London you don't pay two pounds sixty-nine just for a bloody hamburger. At least not at Wendy's you don't. You don't pay eighty-five pence for a Coke, either. What does that tax work out at?'

Hatchley took out his pocket calculator and struggled with the figures. 'Eight per cent,' he announced finally.

'Hmm. That's an odd amount. You don't pay eight per cent VAT on food in England.'

'I suppose it's an American company,' Hatchley suggested, 'if they sell hamburgers?'

'You mean our man's an American?'

'Or he could have just come back from a trip there.'

'He could have. But that'd make it a bit soon for another holiday, wouldn't it? Unless he was a business-man. What about the labels on his clothes?'

'Torn off,' Hatchley said. 'Trousers and underpants seem to be ordinary Marks and Sparks cotton and poly-ester. Same with the shirt. The boots were Army and Navy.

They could have been bought at any of their branches.'

Banks tapped his ballpoint on the edge of the desk. 'Why is it that somebody doesn't want us to know who he is or where he's from?'

'Maybe because if we knew that we'd have a good idea who the killer was.'

'So the quicker we identify the body, the better our chances. Whoever did it was obviously counting on no one finding it for months, then being unable to identify it.' Banks sipped some lukewarm coffee and pulled a face. 'But we've got a lead.' He tapped the receipt. 'I want to know where this Wendy's is located. It shouldn't take you long. There's a store code to go on.'

'Where do I go for that kind of information?' Hatchley asked.

'Bloody hell!' Banks said. 'You're a detective. At least I hope you are. Start detecting. First, I'd suggest you call Wendy's UK office. It's going to be a couple of days before we get anything from Glendenning and Vic Manson, so let's use every break we get. Did Richmond come up with anything from missing persons?'

'No, sir.'

'I suppose our corpse is still supposed to be on holiday then, if no one's reported him missing. And if he's not English it could be ages before he gets into the files. Check the hotels and guest houses in the area and see if any Americans have registered there lately. If they have, try and track them down.'

Dismissed, Hatchley went to find Richmond, to whom, Banks knew, he would pass on as much of the load as possible. Still, he reasoned, the sergeant's work was solid enough once he built up a bit of momentum, and the pressure would serve as a test of Richmond's mettle.

Since passing his computer course with flying colours, the young detective constable looked all set for promotion. That would cause problems with Hatchley though. There was no way, Banks reflected, that the sergeant could be expected to work with Richmond at equal rank. Things had been bad enough when Banks came from the Metropolitan force to fill the position Hatchley had set his own sights on. And Hatchley was destined to stay a sergeant; he didn't have the extra edge needed to make inspector, as Richmond did.

Grateful that promotion was not his decision, Banks glanced at his watch and headed for the car. Neil Fellowes was waiting in Swainshead, and the poor sod had already had to arrange for one extra day off work.

TWO

As he drove along the dale, Banks marvelled at how familiar some of its landmarks had become: the small drumlin with its four sick elms all leaning to the right like an image in one of those Chinese watercolours that Sandra, his wife, liked so much; the quiet village of Fortford with the foundations of a Roman fort laid bare on a hillock by the green; the busy main street of Helmthorpe, Swainsdale's largest village; and above Helmthorpe, the long limestone edge of Crow Scar gleaming in the sun.

The Kinks sang 'Lola', and Banks tapped his fingers on the steering wheel in time with the music as he drove. Though he swore to Sandra that he still loved opera, much to her delight he hadn't played any lately. She had approved of his recent flirtation with the blues, and now he seemed to be going through a nostalgic phase for the music he had listened to during his last days at school and first year at London Polytechnic: that idyllic halcyon period when he hadn't known what to do with his life and hadn't much cared.

It was also the year he had met Sandra, and the music brought it all back: winter evenings drinking cheap wine and making love in his draughty Notting Hill bedsit listening to John Martyn or Nick Drake; summer boat trips for picnics in Greenwich Park, lying in the sun below Wren's observatory looking down on the gleaming palace, the Thames and London spread out to the west, the Beatles, Donovan, Bob Dylan and the Rolling Stones on the radio . . . All gone now, or almost all. He had lost interest in pop music shortly after the Beatles split up and the glitter boys took over the scene in the early 1970s, but the old songs still worked their magic on him.

He lit a cigarette and rolled down the window. It felt good to be on his own in his own car again. Much as he loved the superintendent, Banks was glad that Gristhorpe had reverted to his usual role of planner and coordinator. Now he could smoke and listen to music as he drove.

More important still, he liked working alone, without the feeling that someone was always looking over his shoulder. It was easy enough to deal with Hatchley and Richmond, but with a superior heading the field investigation, it was difficult to avoid the sensation of being under constant scrutiny. That had been another reason for leaving London – too many chiefs – and for pinning his hopes on the Eastvale job after a preliminary chat with Superintendent Gristhorpe about the way he liked to run things.

Banks turned right at the Swainshead junction and parked his car in one of the spaces outside the White Rose.

As he crossed the bridge, the old men stopped talking and he felt their eyes boring holes into his back as he walked down to the Greenock Guest House.

Though the door was open, he rang the bell. A young woman came rushing to answer it. She had a slender dancer's body, but Banks also noticed an endearing awkwardness, a lack of self-consciousness about her movements that made her seem even more attractive. She stood before him drying her hands on her pinafore and blushed.

'Sorry,' she said in a soft voice. 'I was just doing some washing. Please come in.'

Though her accent was clearly Yorkshire, it didn't sound like the Swainsdale variety. Banks couldn't immediately place it.

Her eyes were brown – the kind of brown one sees in sunlight filtered through a pint of bitter, thought Banks, amused at just how much of a Yorkshireman he must have become to yoke beer and beauty so audaciously. But her hair was blonde. She wore it tied up at the back of her neck, and it fell in stray wisps around her pale throat and ears. She wore no make-up, and her light complexion was completely smooth, her lips full and strawberry red without any lipstick. Between her lower lip and the curve of her chin was a deep indentation, giving her mouth a look somewhere between a pout and an incipient smile. She reminded him of someone, but he couldn't think who.

Katie, as she introduced herself, led him into a hall that smelled of lemon air-freshener and furniture polish, as clean and fresh as a good guest house should be. Neil Fellowes was waiting for him in room five, she said, and disappeared, head bowed, into the back of the house, where Banks guessed the Greenocks had their own living quarters.

He walked up the thick-pile burgundy carpet, found the room and knocked.

Fellowes answered immediately, as if he had been holding the doorknob on the other side. He looked much better than the previous day. His few remaining strands of colourless hair were combed sideways across his bald head, and thick-lensed wire-rimmed glasses perched on the bump near the bridge of his nose.

'Come in, please er . . .'

Banks introduced himself.

'Yes, come in, Chief Inspector.'

Fellowes was obviously a man who respected rank and title. Most people automatically called Banks 'Inspector', some preferred plain 'Mister', and others called him a lot worse.

Banks glanced out of the window at the wide strips of grass on both sides of the Swain. Beyond the cottages and pub rose the overbearing bulk of a fell. It looked like a sleeping elephant, he thought, remembering a passage from Wainwright, the fell-walking expert. Or was it whale? 'Nice view,' he said, sitting down in the wicker chair by the window.

'Yes,' Fellowes agreed. 'It doesn't really matter which side of the house you stay in. At the back you can see Swainshead Fell, and over there it's Adam's Fell, of course.'

'Adam's Fell?'

Fellowes adjusted his glasses and cleared his throat. 'Yes. After Adam and Eve. The locals do have a sense of humour – of a sort.'

'Do you visit the area often, Mr Fellowes?'

'No, not at all. I just like to research the terrain, so to speak, before I embark. By the way, Chief Inspector, I do apologize sincerely about yesterday. Finding that . . . that corpse was a great shock, and I never take liquor as a rule – or tobacco, I might add. I wouldn't have thought of it myself, but Mr Greenock was kind enough . . .' He slowed and stopped like an old gramophone winding down.

Banks, who had taken note of Fellowes' declaration of abstemiousness and let go of the cigarette packet he'd been toying with in his pocket, smiled and offered a cliché of consolation. Inwardly, he sighed. The world was becoming too full of non-smokers for his comfort, and he hadn't yet succeeded in swelling their ranks. Perhaps it was time to switch brands again. He was getting tired of Silk Cut, anyway. He took out his notebook and went on.

'What made you visit that spot in the first place?' he asked.

'It just looked so inviting,' Fellowes answered. 'So different.'

'Had you ever been there before?'

'No.'

'Did you know of its existence?'

'No. It's certainly not mentioned in my guidebook. Locals would know it, I suppose. I really can't say. Anyone could wander into it. It's on the maps, of course, but it doesn't show up as anything special.'

'But you do have to make quite a diversion from the footpath to get there.'

'Well, yes. Though I'd hardly say it's that much of a haul.'

'Depends on how fit you are,' Banks said, smiling. 'But you reckoned it would be worthwhile?'

'I'm interested in wild flowers, Chief Inspector. I thought I might discover something interesting.'

'When did you arrive in Swainshead?'

'Three days ago. It was only a short break. I'm saving most of my holidays for a bicycle tour of Provence in autumn.'

'I hope you have a less grim time of it there,' Banks said. 'Is there anything else you can remember about the scene, about what happened?'

'It was all such a blur. First there was the orchis, then that awful smell, and . . . No. I turned away and headed back as soon as I'd . . . as soon as I refreshed myself in the beck.'

'There was nobody else in the valley?'

'Not that I was aware of.'

'You didn't get a feeling of being followed, observed?'

'No.'

'And you didn't find anything close to the body? Something you might have thought insignificant, picked up and forgotten about?'

'Nothing, Chief Inspector. Believe me, the feeling of revulsion was sudden and quite overwhelming.'

'Of course. Had you noticed anything else before you found the body?'

'What do you mean?'

'The victim's rucksack was missing. We think he must have been carrying his belongings with him but we can't find them. Did you notice any signs of something being buried, burned, destroyed?'

'I'm sorry, Chief Inspector, but no, I didn't.'

'Any idea who the victim was?'

Fellowes opened his eyes wide. 'How could I have? You must have seen for yourself how . . . how . . .'

'I know what state he was in. I was simply wondering if you'd heard anything about someone missing in the area.'

Fellowes shook his head.

Banks closed his notebook and put it back in the inside pocket of his pale blue sports jacket.

'There is one thing,' Fellowes said hesitantly.

'Yes?'

'I don't like to cast aspersions. It's only a very vague impression.'

'Go on.'

'And I wasn't in full control of my faculties. It was just a feeling.'

'Policemen have feelings like that, too, Mr Fellowes. We call them hunches and they're often very valuable. What was this feeling you had?'

Fellowes leaned forward from the edge of the bed and lowered his voice. 'Well, Chief Inspector, I only really thought about it in bed last night, and it was just a kind of niggling sensation, an itch. It was in the pub, just after I arrived and, you know, told them what I'd seen. I sat at the table, quite out of breath and emotionally distraught . . .'

'And what happened?'

'Nothing happened. It was just a feeling, as I said. I wasn't even looking, but I got the impression that someone there wasn't really surprised.'

'That you'd found a body?'

'Yes.'

'Was that all?'

Fellowes took off his glasses and rubbed the bridge of his nose. Banks noticed how small his eyes looked without the magnifying lenses. 'More than that,' Fellowes went on. 'I was looking away at the time, but I felt an odd sort of silence, the kind of silence in which glances are exchanged. It was very uncomfortable for a moment, though I was too preoccupied to really notice it at the time. I've thought about it a lot since last night, and that's the only way I can put it, as if a kind of understanding look passed between some of the people at the table.'

'Who was there?'

'The same people as when you arrived. There was the landlord over at the bar, then Sam Greenock, Stephen and Nicholas Collier and John Fletcher. I'd met them the previous day when I was enquiring about the best places to search for wild flowers.'

'Did it seem to you as if they were all in on some kind of conspiracy?'

'I'm not paranoid, if that's what you're getting at, Chief Inspector.'

'But you were upset. Sometimes our senses can over-react.'

'Believe what you wish. I simply thought you ought to know. And in answer to your question, no, I didn't sense any gigantic conspiracy, just that someone at the table knew something.'

'But you said you thought a glance was exchanged.'

'That's what it felt like.'

'So more than one person knew?'

'I suppose so. I can't say how many or how I received the impression. It just happened.'

Banks took his notebook out again and wrote down the names.

'I don't want to get anybody into trouble,' Fellowes said. 'I could be wrong. It could have happened just as you said, an overreaction.'

'Let *us* worry about that, Mr Fellowes. We don't usually ask people to stand up in a court of law and swear to their feelings. Is that all you can tell me?'

'Yes. Will I be able to go home now? There'll be trouble at work if I'm not back tomorrow.'

'Better give me your address and phone number in case we need to talk to you again,' Banks said.

Banks made a note of Fellowes' address and left, thinking what a celebrity the man would be at work for a while. He went out of the open door without seeing Katie Greenock and breathed in the fresh air by the beck. A young man dangled his legs over the bank, eating a sandwich from greaseproof paper and reading a thick paperback; the old men still huddled around the eastern end of the stone bridge; and there were three cars parked outside the White Rose. Banks looked at his watch: twenty past one. With a bit of luck the same crowd as yesterday would be there. He read over the names Fellowes had given him again and decided to make a start.

THREE

First things first, Banks thought, and headed for the bar. He ordered Cumberland sausage, beans and chips, then paid, took his numbered receipt, and waited while Freddie Metcalfe poured him a pint of Pedigree.

'Is tha getting anywhere?' Metcalfe asked, his biceps bulging as he pulled down on the pump.

'Early days yet,' Banks answered.

'Aye, an' it got to late days an' all last time, and still tha didn't find owt.'

'That's how it goes sometimes. I wasn't here then.'

'Thinks tha's better than old Gristhorpe, does tha, eh?'

'That's not what I meant.'

'From down sahth, aren't tha?'

'Yes. London.'

'London.' Metcalfe placed the foaming brew on the cloth in front of Banks and scratched his hairy ear. 'Bin there once. Full o' foreigners, London. All them A-rabs.'

'It's a busy place,' Banks said, picking up his beer.

'Don't get many o' them arahnd 'ere. Foreigners, that is. That why tha came up 'ere, to get shut on t' A-rabs, eh? Tha'll find plenty o' Pakis in Bradford, like, but I don't reckon as I've ever seed a darkie in Swainshead. Saw one in Eastvale, once.'

Banks, growing quickly tired of Metcalfe's racist inanities, made to turn away, but the landlord grabbed his elbow.

'Don't tha want to ask me any questions then, lad?' he said, his eyes glittering.

Holding back his temper, Banks lit a cigarette and propped himself up against the bar. He had noticed that the three men he recognized from the previous day were only into the upper thirds of their pints, so he had enough time to banter with Metcalfe. He might just pick up some interesting titbit.

'What do you want me to ask you?' he opened.

'Nay, tha's t' bobby. Tha should know.'

'Do you get many walkers in here?'

'Aye. We don't fuss 'em abaht rucksacks and boo-its and whatnot like that stuck-up pillock on t' main road.'

'But I understand this is the "select" part of town?'

'Aye.' Metcalfe laughed. 'Tha could say that. It's t' oldest, anyroads. And t' Colliers drink 'ere, as did their father before them. Select, if tha likes, but dahn to earth, not stuck up.' He shook his head slowly. 'A right lad, were Walter Collier.' Then he leaned forward and whispered, 'Not like 'is sons, if tha knows what I mean. Wouldn't know a cratch from a gripe, neither on 'em. And they was brought up by a farmer, too.'

Banks, who didn't know a cratch from a gripe either, asked why.

'Eddication,' Metcalfe said, intoning the word as if it were responsible for most of the world's ills. 'Fancy bloody Oxford eddication. Wanted 'em to 'ave a better chance than 'e'd 'ad, did old Walter. Farming don't pay much, tha knows, an' Walter were sharp enough to get out 'imself.' Metcalfe turned up his nose. 'Well, tha can see what eddication does.'

'What are they like, Stephen and Nicholas?' Banks asked.

Metcalfe sniffed and lowered his voice. He was clearly enjoying his role as dispenser of local opinion. 'Right bloody useless pair, if y'ask me. At least yon Nicholas is. Mr Stephen's not so bad. Teks after old Walter, 'e does. Bit of a ladies' man. Not that t' other's queer, or owt.' Metcalfe laughed. 'There were a bit o' trouble wi' a servant lass a few years back, when 'e were still a young lad, living at 'ome, like. Got 'er up t' spout, Master Nicholas did. Old Walter 'ad to see 'er right, o' course, and I've no doubt 'e gave t' lad a right good thrashing. But it's Mr Stephen that's t' ladies man. One after t' other.'

'What's the difference in their ages?'

'Nobbut a couple o' years. Stephen's t' eldest.'

'What happened to the farm land?'

'Old Walter sold some on it,' Metcalfe said, 'and leased t' rest. T' Colliers are still t' biggest landowners in t' dale, mind thee. John Fletcher over there bought a goodly chunk on it.' He wagged his chin in the direction of the table. The drinkers were now into the last thirds of their drinks, and Banks decided it would be a good time to approach them.

'Tha still an't asked me no real questions,' Metcalfe protested.

'Later,' Banks said, turning. 'I'd like to talk to these gentlemen here before they leave.' Of the gentlemen in question, he recognized Nicholas Collier and Sam Greenock from the previous day; therefore, the third had to be John Fletcher.

'Wait on a minute,' Metcalfe said. 'Dun't tha want tha sausage and chips?'

And as if on cue, a freckled little girl in a red dress, her hair in pigtails, appeared from the kitchens and called out, 'Number seventy-five! Sausage, beans and chips.'

Banks gave her his receipt and took the plate, then helped himself to the condiments from the bar.

When he walked over to the table, the three men shifted around, scraping their chair legs on the flagged floor, and made room for him.

'Do you mind if I eat at your table?' he asked.

'Not at all. Freddie been giving you a rough time, Inspector?' Nicholas Collier asked. His smile showed his prominent teeth to great disadvantage; they were discoloured with nicotine and crooked as a badly built drystone wall. His speech, Banks noticed, bore traces of the local accent under its veneer of public school English.

'No,' he said, returning the smile. 'Just entertaining me. Quite a fellow.'

'You can say that again. He's been behind the bar as long as I can remember.' Nicholas leaned forward and lowered his voice. 'Between you and me, I don't think he quite approves of Stephen and myself. Anyway, have you met John, here?'

The squat man with the five o'clock shadow was indeed John Fletcher, gentleman farmer. Stephen Collier, his brother said, was away dealing with some factory business.

'Is this just a social visit or do you have some questions for us?' Sam asked.

'Just one, really,' Banks said, spearing a mouthful of sausage. 'Have you any idea who it was we found up there?'

After a short silence Nicholas said, 'We get quite a lot of visitors in the area, Inspector. Especially when we're blessed with such a fine start to the year. There's nobody local missing, as far as I know, so it must be a stranger. Can't you check?'

'Yes,' Banks said. 'Of course we can. We can go through every name in every hotel and guest house registration book and make sure everyone's accounted for. But, like you I'm sure, we're all for anything that saves extra effort.'

Collier laughed. 'Naturally. But no, I can't think of anyone it might be.'

'Your victim hadn't necessarily come through Swainshead, you know,' Sam pointed out. 'He could have been heading south from Swaledale or beyond. Even from the Lake District. He could have set off from Helmthorpe too, or any number of other villages in the dale. Most of them have at least one or two bed and breakfast places these days.'

'I know,' Banks said. 'Believe me, we're checking.' He turned to Fletcher. 'I hear that you own quite a bit of land?'

'Yes,' Fletcher said, his dark eyes narrowing suspiciously. 'Walter sold it to me when he gave up farming and went into the food business.' He glanced at Nicholas, who nodded. 'Neither Nick here nor his brother Stephen wanted to take over – in fact Walter hadn't wanted them

56

to, he'd been preparing to sell for quite a while – so I thought I'd give it a go.'

'How is it working out?'

'Well enough. I don't know if you understand much about Dales farming, Mr Banks, but it's a hard life. Old Walter himself had had enough, and he was one of those men – rare around these parts – with enough vision to get out and put what he'd got to better use. I'd never blame a farmer for wanting a different life for his sons. I've got no family myself,' he said, and a hard look came into his eyes. 'I'm not complaining, though. I make a living – the EEC and the National Parks Commission notwithstanding.'

Banks turned to Nicholas. 'What do you do?'

'I teach English at Braughtmore, just up the road here. It's only a small public school of course, but it's a start.'

'But you don't actually live there?'

'No. Hardly necessary, really. The house is so close. The pupils live in. They have to; it's so damn far from civilization. And we have housemasters. Some of the teachers live in the grounds, but a couple of others have chosen to settle here in the village. The school's only five miles north, quite isolated. It's a good school, though I say so myself. Do you have any children, Inspector?'

'Yes. A boy and a girl.'

'What school do they attend?'

'Eastvale Comprehensive.'

'Hmm.' The corner of Collier's lip twitched, giving just a fleeting hint of a sneer.

Banks shifted uneasily in his chair. 'Your brother runs the family business, I gather.'

'Yes. Managing director of Collier Food Enterprises. It's over the Lancashire border, about ten miles west, just off the main road. The arrangement suits us both perfectly.

Stephen never had a great deal of academic ambition, despite the excellent education he received, but he's bright and he's put his mind to good enough use – making money. It was one of father's wisest moves, buying up that old mill and setting up the food-processing operation. And as for me, I'm happy with my books and a few pliant young minds to work on.' Again he bared his teeth in a smile.

They had all finished their drinks and Banks was wondering how to edge them gently towards the murder again, when Fletcher stood up and excused himself. Immediately, the others looked at their watches and decided they ought to leave and take care of various tasks.

'There's nothing else, is there, Inspector?' Nicholas asked.

'No,' Banks said. 'Not yet.'

Freddie Metcalfe ambled over to the table to pick up the plate and the empty glasses as Banks was stubbing out his cigarette.

'Find owt aht yet?' he asked.

'No,' Banks said, standing up. 'Nothing.'

'Early days, eh?'

And the deep chortling laughter followed Banks out into the street.

FOUR

Back at Eastvale police station things were quiet. Grabbing a cup of coffee from the filter machine on the way, Banks walked upstairs to his office, a plain room furnished with nothing but filing cabinets, metal desk and a calendar of local scenes. The illustration for May showed the River Wharfe as it flowed among the limestone boulders of

Langstrothdale. More recently Banks had added, next to it, one more decoration: a broken pipe, which he had just rediscovered at the back of his drawer. It represented a vain attempt to project a rural image and wean himself from cigarettes at the same time, but he had cursed it constantly and finally thrown it at that very same wall in frustration over the Steadman case almost a year ago. It hung there like a piece of conceptual art to remind him of the folly of trying to be what one is not.

There were quite a few cars parked in the cobbled market square outside, and visitors walked in and out of the small Norman church and the shops that seemed almost built into its frontage. The gold hands of the clock stood at three thirty against its blue face. Banks looked down on the scene, as he often did, smoking a cigarette and sipping his coffee. The police station itself was a Tudor-fronted building on narrow Market Street across from the Queen's Arms, which curved around the corner so that one of its entrances stood on the side of the square opposite the church. Looking to his right, Banks could see along the street, with its coffee houses, boutiques and tourist shops, and in front was the busy square itself, with the NatWest bank, the El Toro coffee bar and Joplin's newsagent's on the opposite side.

A knock at the door interrupted him. Sergeant Hatchley came in looking very pleased with himself. When he was excited about something he moved much faster than usual and seemed unable to stand still. Banks had come to recognize the signs.

'I've tracked it down, sir,' Hatchley said. 'That bit of paper he had in his pocket.'

The two of them sat down and Banks told the sergeant to carry on.

'Like you said, I tried the London office. They said they'd check and get back to me. Anyway, they found out that that particular branch is in Canada.'

'So our man's a Canadian?'

'Looks that way, sir. Unless, like I said before, he'd just been on holiday there. Anyway, at least we know there's a close connection.'

'Anything else?'

'Yes. Once he'd discovered the outlet was in Canada, the bloke from Wendy's became very helpful.'

Such helpfulness was a common enough occurrence, Banks knew from experience. He'd even invented a term for it: the amateur sleuth syndrome.

'That particular branch is in Toronto, on Yonge Street near Dundas Street, if that means anything.'

Banks shook his head. 'Never been over the Atlantic. You?'

Hatchley grunted. 'Me? I've never been further west than Blackpool. Anyway, that narrows things down quite a bit, I'd say.'

'It does,' Banks agreed. 'But it still doesn't tell us who he was.'

'I got on to the Canadian High Commission and asked a bloke there to check if anyone from Toronto had been reported missing over here lately, but nobody has.'

'Too early yet, I suppose. If he *is* from Toronto, obviously everyone back there still thinks he's on holiday.'

'Aye, but that won't last for ever.'

'We haven't got for ever. Who knows, he might have been a student and come over for the whole bloody summer. How's Richmond doing?'

'He's covered quite a few places already – Lyndgarth, Relton, Helmthorpe, Gratly.'

'Well, his task ought to be a bit easier now we know it's a Canadian we're after.'

'There's been quite a few Canadians staying locally,' Hatchley said. 'It's easy enough to call the B and Bs and make a list from their records, but it's damned hard to trace people's movements after they've left. They don't usually leave forwarding addresses, and it's only once in a while a landlady is able to tell us where they said they were going next.'

'There can't be that many men from Toronto travelling alone,' Banks said. 'I'm sure if he was a member of a group or a family somebody would have reported him missing by now. Better stick at it. At least you've narrowed the field considerably. Heard anything from Dr Glendenning?'

'The super called him a while ago. Still killing off those bloody maggots in disinfectant. Says he won't be able to make a start till tomorrow morning at the earliest.'

Banks sighed. 'All right. You'd better go and help Richmond now. And thanks, Sergeant; you did a good job.'

Hatchley nodded and left the office. They'd been working together for almost two years now, Banks realized, and he still couldn't bring himself to call the sergeant Jim. Maybe one day he would, when it came naturally to his lips. He lit another cigarette and went back to the window, where he watched the people wander about in the square, and drummed a tattoo on the sill.

FIVE

'Sam's not in,' Katie said that evening when she opened the back door to find Stephen Collier standing there. 'He's having a night out with his old mates in Leeds.'

'Can't I come in, anyway?' Stephen asked. 'Just for a cup of tea?'

'All right,' Katie said, and led him through to the spotless kitchen. 'Just five minutes, mind you. I've work to be doing.' She turned away from him and busied herself with the kettle and teapot. She felt her face burning. It wasn't right being alone in the house with a man other than her husband, even if it was someone as pleasant as Stephen. He had a reputation as a womanizer. Everybody knew that. Someone might even have seen him coming in.

'Nick tells me the police were around today,' Stephen said.

Katie glanced at him over her shoulder. 'It's to be expected, isn't it? One of our guests did find a dead body.'

'He still here?'

'No. He left this afternoon.'

'Well,' Stephen said. 'I just thought I'd drop by to see if you were all right. I mean, it can be a bit of a shock to the system, something like that happening right on your doorstep, so to speak. Did the police ask a lot of questions?'

'Not to me, no. Why should they?'

'Just wondering,' Stephen said. 'How are things, anyway?'

'All right, I suppose,' Katie answered. Though she had known him for over five years and certainly preferred him to his brother, Katie hadn't really spent much time alone with Stephen Collier before. Mostly, they had met socially at summer garden parties the Colliers liked to throw, in the pub and at occasional dinners. She liked Stephen. He seemed kind and thoughtful. Often at social functions she had caught him looking at her in an odd way. Not *that* way, not like Nicholas. It was a look she didn't quite understand, and she had never been able to return his gaze for long without lowering her eyes. Now she was alone with him she felt shy and awkward; she didn't really know how to behave. She brought the tea to the table and opened a packet of Fox's Custard Creams.

'Come on, Katie,' Stephen said. 'You're not very convincing. You don't sound all right to me.'

'I don't know what you mean.'

'Yes, you do. I can tell. I've felt some sort of bond with you right from the start. I've been worried about you these past few months.'

'Worried? Why?'

'Because you're not happy.'

'Of course I'm happy. That's silly.'

Stephen sighed. 'I can't make you open up, can I? But you *can* talk to me if you want, if you need to. Everybody needs somebody to talk to now and then.'

Katie bit her lower lip and said nothing. She couldn't talk to him. She couldn't tell anyone the things that went on in her mind, the sins she dreamed of, the desperation she felt. She couldn't tell him about her one chance of escaping from her miserable life, and what it had already cost her.

'Anyway,' Stephen went on, taking a biscuit, 'I might not be around here for much longer.'

'What do you mean?'

'I've had enough of it, Katie. The plant, the house, the village. Lord, I'm nearly thirty. It's about time I got out and about, saw a bit of the world before I get too old.'

'B-but you can't,' Katie said, shocked. 'Surely you can't just up and go like that? What about—'

Stephen slapped the table. 'Oh, responsibilities be hanged,' he said. 'There's plenty of others willing and able to run Collier Foods. I'll take a long holiday, then maybe try something else.'

'Why are you telling me all this?' Katie asked.

Stephen looked at her, and she noticed that he suddenly looked old, much older than his twenty-eight years.

He ran his hand through his short brown hair. 'I don't know,' he said. 'I told you, we're kindred spirits. You're the only person I've told. There's nobody else, really.'

'But your brother . . .'

'Nicky? He wouldn't understand. He's too wrapped up in his own world. And don't think I haven't noticed the way he looks at you, Katie, even if Sam hasn't. I'd stay away from him if I were you.'

'Of course I will,' Katie said, blushing. 'Why shouldn't I?'

'Oh, he can be very persuasive, Nicky can.'

'What about John?' Katie asked. 'Or Sam? Can't you talk to them?'

Stephen laughed. 'Look, Katie,' he said, 'Nicky, Sam and the rest, they're all good drinking friends, but there are things I can't talk to them about.'

'But why me?'

'Because I think it's the same for you. I think you're unhappy with your life and you've nobody to talk to about it. Why are you so afraid of talking to me? You've got all your problems bottled up inside you. Don't you like me?'

Katie traced rings on the table with her forefinger. 'It's not that,' she said. 'I'm fine, really I am.'

Stephen leaned forward. 'Why don't you open up, show some feeling?' he urged her.

'I do.'

'Not for me.'

'It's not right.'

'Oh, Katie, you're such a moralist.' Stephen stood up to leave. 'Would that I had your moral fibre. No, it's all right, there's no need to show me out.'

Katie wanted to call after him, but she couldn't. Deep inside, she felt a thick darkness swirling and building in power, trying to force its way out. But it was evil and she had to keep it locked in. She had to accept her lot, her place in life. She was Sam's wife. That was her duty. There was no point talking about problems. What could she say to Stephen Collier? Or he to her? Why had he come? What did he want from her? 'The thing that all men want,' said a strong harsh voice inside her. 'The same thing his brother wants. Don't be fooled by talk of companionship. Satan has a sweet tongue.'

'But he was reaching out to you,' another, quieter voice said, 'reaching out in friendship, and you turned him away.'

Katie's chest tightened and her hands shook as she tried to bring the teacup to her mouth. 'I'm lost,' she thought. 'I don't know what to do. I don't know what's right any more. Help me, someone, please help me!' And the cup rolled to the floor and smashed as Katie laid her head on the table and wept.

4

ONE

Two days later, on 31 May, forensic information started trickling in. During that time, Richmond and Hatchley had tracked down all but two wandering Canadians who had left local hotels or guest houses between ten and thirteen days ago.

Events were moving too slowly for Banks. Most leads appear during the first twenty-four hours after a murder has taken place, but this body was about two hundred and forty hours old by the time it was found. Still they had very little to go on.

Therefore, when the first report from the forensic lab landed on his desk at ten thirty that morning, Banks drank in the information like a man stranded in a desert without water for three days.

Dr Glendenning had established that death was due to a stab wound from a single-edged blade, probably a sheath knife about six inches long. One upward thrust had penetrated the heart from beneath the ribs. After that, the face had been slashed and then beaten with a rock until it was unrecognizable. The victim was white, in his early thirties, five feet eleven inches tall, ten and a half stone in weight, and in good physical condition. That last part always irritated Banks: how could a corpse ever be in good physical condition? This one, certainly, had been about as far from it as one could get.

Vic Manson had finally managed, through peeling the skin off and treating it with glycerine, to get three clear prints. He had already checked these against the Police National Computer and discovered that they weren't on record. So far no good, Banks thought. The forensic odontologist, a note said, was still working on his reconstruction of the dental chart.

Calling for Sergeant Hatchley on his way out, Banks decided it was time for a discussion over elevenses in the Golden Grill. The two men weaved their way through the local shoppers and parties of tourists that straggled along both pavements and the narrow street, and found a table near the window. Banks gave the order for coffee and toasted teacakes to Peggy, a plump girl with a bright smile, and looked across at the whitewashed front of the police station with its black timber beams. Black and white, he thought. If only life was as simple as that.

As they drank their coffee, Banks and Hatchley tried to add up what they had got so far. It wasn't much: a ten-day-old corpse of a white male, probably Canadian, found stabbed in an isolated hanging valley. At least cause of death had been established, and the coroner's inquest would order a thorough investigation.

'Perhaps he wasn't travelling alone,' Banks said. 'Maybe he was with someone who killed him. That would explain the need to disfigure him – to give the killer plenty of time to get back home.'

'If that's the case,' Hatchley said, 'it'll be for the Canadian police to handle, won't it?'

'The murder happened on our turf. It's still our problem till the man at the top says different.'

'Maybe he stumbled into a coven of witches,' Hatchley suggested.

Banks laughed. 'They're mostly bored accountants and

housewives in it for the orgies. I doubt they'd go as far as to kill someone who walked in on them. And Glendenning didn't mention anything about ritual slaughter. How's the search for the elusive Canadians going?'

Hatchley reached slyly for another cigarette to prolong the break. 'I'm beginning to feel like that bloke who had to roll a rock up a hill over and over again.'

'Sisyphus? Sometimes I feel more like the poor sod who had his liver pecked out day after day.'

Hatchley lit his cigarette.

'Come on then,' Banks said, standing up to leave. 'Better get back.'

Hatchley cursed under his breath and followed Banks across the street.

'Chief Inspector Banks!' Sergeant Rowe called out as they passed the front desk. 'Telephone message. You're to call a Dr Passmore at the lab. He's the odonto . . . the odotol . . . Oh, the bloody tooth fairy, or whatever they call themselves.'

Banks smiled and thanked him. Back in his office, he picked up the phone and dialled.

'Ah, Chief Inspector Banks,' said Passmore. 'We've never met, but Dr Glendenning brought me in on this one. Interesting.'

'You've got something for us?' Banks asked eagerly.

'It's a bit complicated. Would it be a great inconvenience for you to drop into the lab?'

'No, not at all.' Banks looked at his watch. 'If I leave now I can be there in about an hour. Can you give me some idea over the phone?'

'I think we'll be able to trace the identity of your corpse before too long, if I'm not mistaken. I don't think his dentist is too far away.'

'With all due respect, I don't see how that can be, Doctor. We're pretty sure he was a Canadian.'

'That's as may be,' Passmore replied. 'But his dental work's as English as yours or mine.'

'I'm on my way.'

Still puzzled, Banks slipped a cassette into the machine and eased the Cortina out of the car park at the back of the station. At least something was happening. He drove slowly, dodging the tourists and shoppers who seemed to think Market Street was for pedestrians only. The breathy opening of Donovan's 'Hurdy Gurdy Man' started on the tape.

He passed the new estate under construction on the town's southern edge, then he put his foot down once he got out of the built-up area. Leaving the Dales for the plain, he drove through a patchwork landscape of green pasture and fields of bright yellow rape, divided by hawthorn hedgerows. Bluebells and buttercups, about the only wild flowers Banks could put a name to, were in bloom among the long grass by the roadside. A frightened white-throat darted out in front of the car and almost ended up, like so many unfortunate rabbits and hedgehogs, splattered all over the tarmac.

The forensic lab was a square three-storey red-brick building just north of Wetherby. Banks identified himself at reception and climbed up to Passmore's second-floor office.

Dr Passmore gave new meaning to the term 'egghead'. The Lilliputians and the Blefuscudians could have had a fine war indeed over which end to open his egg-shaped skull. His bare shiny dome, combined with circumflex eyebrows, a putty nose and a tiny rosebud of a mouth, made him look more like an android than a human being. His mouth was so small that Banks wondered how there could be room for teeth in it. Perhaps he had chosen his profession out of tooth-envy.

Banks sat down as directed. The office was cluttered with professional journals and its one glassed-in bookcase was full to overflowing. The filing cabinets also bulged too much to close properly. On Passmore's desk, among the papers and pencil stubs, stood a toothless skull and several sets of dentures.

'Glad you could make it, Chief Inspector,' Passmore said, his voice surprisingly rich and deep coming from such a tiny mouth. 'I'm sorry to drag you all the way down here, but it might save time in the long run, and I think you'll find it worth the journey.'

Banks nodded and crossed his legs. He looked around for an ashtray, but couldn't see one; nor could he smell any traces of smoke when he surreptitiously sniffed the air. Bloody hell, another non-smoker, he cursed to himself.

'The victim's teeth were very badly damaged,' Passmore went on. 'Dr Glendenning said that he was hit about the face with a rock of some kind, and I concur.'

'He was found close to a stream,' Banks said. 'There were plenty of rocks in the area.'

'Hmm.' Passmore nodded sagely and made a steeple of his fingers on the desk. 'Anyway, I've managed to make a rudimentary reconstruction for you.' He pushed a brown envelope towards Banks. 'Not that it'll do you much good. You can hardly have every dentist in the country check this against every chart he or she has, can you?'

Banks was beginning to wonder why he'd come when Passmore stood up with surprising energy and walked over to a cabinet by the door. 'But,' he said, pausing dramatically to remove something and bring it back to the table, 'I think I might be able to help you with that.' And he dropped what looked like a fragment of tooth and pink plastic on the desk in front of Banks. 'A denture,' he announced. 'Upper right bicuspid, to be exact.'

Banks stared at the object. 'You got this from the body?'

Passmore nodded. 'It was badly shattered, of course, but I've managed to reassemble most of it. Rather like putting together a broken teacup, really.'

'How does this help us?'

'Well, in the first place,' Passmore said, 'it tells us that the deceased was more likely to be British than Canadian.'

'How?'

Passmore frowned, as if Banks was being purposely obtuse. 'Contrary to what some people believe,' he began, 'British dentists aren't very far behind their North American cousins. Oh, they might instigate new procedures over there before we do, but that's mostly because they have more money. Dentistry's private over there, you know, and it can be very expensive for the patient. But there are differences. Now, if your victim had come from Russia, for example, I could have told you immediately. They use stainless steel for fillings there. But in this case, it's merely an educated guess, or would be if it weren't for something else, which I'll get to in a moment.'

Come on, Banks thought, fidgeting with the cigarette packet in his jacket pocket, get to the bloody point. Putting up with rambling explanations – full of pauses for dramatic effect – seemed to be the price he so often had to pay for information from specialists like Passmore.

'The mere fact that your corpse has denture work leads me to conclude that he's European rather than North American,' the doctor continued. 'The Americans go in for saving teeth rather than replacing them. In fact, they hardly do denture work at all.'

'Very impressive,' Banks said. 'You mentioned some-thing else – something important.'

Passmore nodded. 'This,' he went on, holding up the false tooth, 'is no ordinary denture. Well, it is, but there's one big difference. This is a coded denture.'

'What do you mean?'

'A number of dentists and technicians have taken to signing their work, so to speak, like painters and sculptors. Look here.'

Passmore prodded the denture with a pointed dental instrument, the one that always gave Banks the willies when he was in the chair. He looked closely at the pink plastic and saw a number of dark letters, which he couldn't quite make out.

'The code,' Passmore said. 'It's formed by typing the letters in a small print face on a piece of nylon, which you put between the mould and the plastic. During the manu-facturing process, the nylon becomes incorporated into the denture and the numbers are clearly visible, as you can see.'

'Why do they go to such trouble?' Banks asked.

Passmore shrugged. 'For identification purposes in case of loss, or fire.'

'And what does the code tell us?'

Passmore puckered his mouth into a self-satisfied smile. 'Everything we need to know, Chief Inspector. Everything we need to know. Have a closer look.'

Banks used a pair of tweezers to pick up the denture and looked at the code: 5493BKJLS.

'The last two letters give us the city code, the ones before that are the dentist's initials, and the rest is for identification of the owner.'

'Amazing.' Banks put the false tooth down. 'So this will lead us to the identity of the victim?'

'Eventually. First, it'll lead us to his dentist.'

'How can I find out?'

'You'd consult the directory in the library. But, luckily, I have a copy here and I've done it for you.'

'And?'

Passmore smiled smugly again and held up a school-teacherly finger. 'Patience, Chief Inspector Banks, patience. First, the city. Do you recognize that postcode?'

'Yes. LS is Leeds.'

'Right. So the first thing we discover is that our man's dentist practises in Leeds. Next we look up the initials: BKJ. I found two possibilities there: Brian K. Jarrett and B. K. James.'

'We'll have to check them both,' Banks said. 'Can I use your phone?'

Passmore rubbed his upper lip. 'I, er, I already took the liberty. B. K. James doesn't do denture codes, according to his assistant, so I called Brian K. Jarrett.'

'And?'

Passmore grinned. 'The patient's name is Bernard Allen.'

'Certain?'

'He's the one who was fitted with the denture. It was about four years ago. I'll be sending down the charts for official confirmation, of course, but from what we were able to compare over the phone, I'd say you can be certain, yes.'

'Did you get an address?'

Passmore shook his head. 'Apparently Allen didn't live in Leeds. Mr Jarrett did give me the sister's address, though. Her name's Esther Haines. Is that of any use?'

'It certainly is.' Banks made a note of the first real lead so far. 'You've done a great job, Dr Passmore.' He stood up and shook hands.

Passmore inclined his head modestly. 'If ever you need my help again . . .'

TWO

Katie walked down to the shops in Lower Head later than usual that day. There was no road on her side of the beck, just a narrow path between the houses and the grassy bank. At the junction with the main Helmthorpe road, where the River Swain veered left into the dale proper, a small wooden bridge, painted white, led over to the village green with its trees and benches, and the path continued to the row of shops around the corner from the church.

As she neared the road, a grey Jaguar passed by with Stephen Collier behind the wheel. He slowed down at the intersection, and Katie became flustered. She half raised her hand to wave, but dropped it quickly. Stephen didn't acknowledge her presence at all; he seemed to be looking right through her. At first she told herself he hadn't seen her, but she knew he had. Perhaps he was thinking of something else and hadn't noticed his surroundings. She often walked around in a daze like that herself. The blood ran to her face as she crossed the road and hurried on to the shops.

'Afternoon, Katie love,' Mrs Thetford greeted her. 'A bit late today, aren't you? Still, I've saved you some nice Brussels sprouts.'

Katie thanked her and paid, her mind still on Stephen Collier. Why had he called last night when he knew Sam was out? Katie couldn't understand his desire to talk to her about his problems, or his apparent concern for her.

'Your change, dearie!' Mrs Thetford called after her.

Katie walked back to the counter and held out her hand, smiling. 'I'd forget my head if it was loose.'

She called at the butcher's and bought some pork loin chops, the best he had left, then turned back towards home. Stephen really had sounded as if he needed a friend. He had been tired, burdened. Katie regretted letting him down, but what else could she have done? She couldn't be his friend; she didn't know how. Besides, it wasn't right.

She noticed the speeding Mini just in time to dodge it and crossed the green again. A few people, mostly old women, sat on the benches nattering, and a light breeze rustled the new pale green leaves on the trees. What Stephen had said about her being unhappy was true. Was it so obvious to everyone, or did he really sense a bond between them? Surely with all his money and success he couldn't be unhappy too.

Katie tried to remember when she had last been happy, and thought of the first weeks in Swainshead. It had been hard work, fixing up the house, but they had done it. And what's more, they had done it together. After that though, when everything was ready, Sam left the running of it all to her. It was as if he'd finished his life's work and settled into early retirement.

'Ideas above his station,' her granny had always said of Sam. And sure enough, no sooner were they in residence than he was off to the White Rose ingratiating himself with the locals. As soon as he found out that the Colliers, who owned the big house over the road, were the dale's wealthiest and most powerful family, there was no stopping him. But give him his due, Katie thought, he never fawned or lowered himself; he just seemed to act as if he'd found his natural place in the order at last. Why they accepted him, if indeed they did, she had no idea.

When she wasn't busy running the guest house, Katie became an adornment, something for Sam to hang on his arm at the summer garden parties. She was a kind of Cinderella for whom the ball was always ending. But unlike the fairy-tale character, Katie hated both her roles. She had no love for gowns and glass slippers. Finery, however stylish and expensive, made her feel cheap and sinful. Once, a workmate fortunate enough to go on holiday to Paris had brought her back a pretty green silk scarf. Her granny had snipped it into pieces and scattered them like spring leaves into the fire.

Perhaps, though Katie hated to admit it, she had last been truly happy when her grandmother died. She and Sam hadn't seen much of the old woman after they went to live with his parents in Armley. They visited her in hospital though, where she lay dying of cancer of the colon, bearing all the pain and humiliation with the same hard courage as she had suffered life. She lay there, silver head against the white pillow, and would accept no comfort for what 'God's Will' was gracing her with. It was almost, Katie thought, as if she had found true joy in the final mutiny of the flesh, of its very cells, as if dying was proof to her that life on earth really was nothing but a vale of tears. But that couldn't be true, Katie realized, for her granny had never taken pleasure in anything in her life.

Katie fainted at her funeral and then gagged on the brandy the minister gave her to bring her round. Now all she had left of Granny was the heavy wooden cross on the living-room mantelpiece. A bare dark cross, with no representation of the crucified Christ (for such things smelled too much of popish idolatry for Granny), it symbolized perfectly the harsh arid life the old woman had chosen for herself and her granddaughter. Katie hated the thing, but she hadn't been able to pluck up the courage to throw it out. Outbreaks of boils and plagues of locusts would surely follow such a blasphemous act.

So Stephen Collier was right – she was unhappy. There was nothing anyone could do about it though, except perhaps . . . But no. She had a terrible feeling of apprehension about the future, certain that her only possible escape route was cut off now. Why she should feel that way she didn't know, but everyone was behaving oddly again – Stephen, Sam, John Fletcher. Could it really be a coincidence that Anne Ralston's name had been mentioned to her again so recently? And that so soon after it had come up, there had been another murder in the village?

Shuddering as if someone had just stepped over her grave, Katie walked back up the path and into the house to get on with cleaning the rooms.

THREE

After leaving the lab, Banks first drove into Wetherby and bought an *A to Z* street atlas of Leeds. He knew the city reasonably well, but had never been to Armley, where Allen's sister lived. He studied the area and planned a route over lunch in a small pub off the main street, where he ate a rather soupy lasagne and drank an excellent pint of Samuel Smith's Old Brewery Bitter.

He listened to the Donovan tape as he drove. Those old songs certainly brought back memories. Why did the past always seem so much brighter than the present? Because he had been more innocent then? Surely every childhood summer couldn't have been as sunny as he recalled. There must have been long periods of rain, just as there always seemed to be these days. What the hell, he thought, humming along with 'Teen Angel' as he drove – today's beautiful, enjoy the sun while it's here. Most of all, he wanted to put out of his mind for as long as possible what he would soon have to tell Bernard Allen's sister.

He lit a cigarette and turned on to the Leeds Inner Ring Road, which skirted the city centre by a system of yellow-lit tunnels affording occasional flashes into the open and glimpses of church spires, tower blocks and rows of dark terraced houses. It still felt warm, but the sun was now only a blurred pearl behind a thin grey gauze of cloud.

He came out on to Wellington Road, by the *Yorkshire Post* building, then crossed the River Aire and, immediately afterwards, the Leeds and Liverpool Canal.

There had been a great deal of development in the area, and one or two very colourful red-and-gold barges stood moored by the quay. But the river and canal banks were still very much of a wasteland: overgrown with weeds, littered with the tyres and old prams people had dumped there.

Many of the huge Victorian warehouses still hung on, crumbling and broken-windowed, their red brick blackened by the industrial smoke of a hundred years or more. It was a little like the Thames, Banks thought, where old wharfs and warehouses, like the warrens where Fagin had run his band of child-thieves, were daily being converted into luxury apartment complexes, artists' studios and office space. Because Leeds was in the depressed and abandoned North though, the process of regeneration would probably take quite a bit longer, if indeed it ever happened at all.

Skilfully navigating the lanes of traffic and a huge roundabout, Banks managed to get on Armley Road. Soon he was at the bottom of Town Street, where the road swung right, past the park, to Bramley and Stanningley. He turned left up Crab Lane, a narrow winding one-way street by a small housing estate built on a hill, and parked on the street near the library.

Banks soon found Esther Haines's house. It had a blue door, freshly painted by the look of it. In the garden was an overturned plastic tricycle, green with thick yellow wheels.

Banks pressed the bell and a thin-faced woman answered. She was perhaps in her late twenties, but she seemed haggard and tired. Judging from the noise inside the house, Banks guessed that the cares of motherhood had worn her down. She frowned at him and he showed her his identification card. Immediately, she turned pale and invited him in. For people on estates like this, Banks realized, a visit from the police always means bad news. He felt his stomach muscles tighten as he walked inside.

In the living room, cluttered with children's toys, Mrs Haines had already sat down. Hands clasped in her lap, she perched on the edge of her seat on the sofa. A dark-haired man came through from the kitchen, and she introduced him as her husband, Les. He was wearing only vest and trousers. His shoulders and chest were matted with thick black hair, and he had a tattoo of a butterfly on his right bicep.

'We were just having our tea,' Esther Haines said. 'Les is on the night shift at the yeast factory.'

'Aye,' her husband said, pulling up a chair and facing Banks aggressively. 'What's all this about?'

A child with jam smeared all over his pale grinning face crawled through the open kitchen door and busied himself trying to tear apart a fluffy toy dog.

'I'm sorry,' Banks said, 'but I've got some bad news for you.'

And the rest followed as it always did: disbelief, denial, shock, tears and finally a kind of numb acceptance. Banks was relieved to see that the first thing Mr Haines did was light a cigarette. He followed suit. Esther clutched a handkerchief to her nose. Her husband went to make tea and took the child with him.

After Mr Haines had brought in the teapot and cups, leaving the child to play in the kitchen, Banks leaned forward in his seat and said to Esther, 'There are some questions I've got to ask.'

She nodded. 'Are you sure?' she said. 'Are you sure it's our Bernie?'

'As sure as we can be at this point,' Banks told her. He didn't want to have to tell her what state her brother's corpse had been in. 'Your answers will help us a lot. When did you last see him?'

'It was a couple of weeks ago, now,' she said. 'He stayed with us a week.'

'Can you find out the exact date he left here, Mrs Haines? It's important.'

Her husband walked over to a calendar of Canadian scenes and ran a stubby finger along the squares. 'It was the thirteenth,' he said, then looked over at Esther. 'Remember, love, that morning he went to the dentist's for that filling he needed?'

Mrs Haines nodded.

'Did he leave immediately after his visit to Mr Jarrett's?'

'Yes,' said Les Haines. 'He was heading for the Dales, so he had to be off about eleven. He was after taking one of them trains on the Settle–Carlisle route.'

'And that was the last time either of you saw him, at eleven o'clock on May the thirteenth?'

They both nodded.

'Do you know where he was going?'

'Of course,' Esther said. 'He were off back to Swainshead.'

'Going back? I don't understand. Is that where he was before he came to stay with you?'

'No, it's where he grew up; it's where we used to live.'

Now Banks remembered where he'd heard the name before. Allen. Nicholas Collier had directed Gristhorpe and himself to the ruins of Archie Allen's old farmhouse high on the side of Swainshead Fell.

'Is your father Archie Allen?' he asked.

'Yes, that's right.'

'And you lived on the fell side, worked a farm?'

'Until it went belly up,' Mr Haines cut in.

'Did you live there too?' Banks asked him.

'Me? No. Leeds born and bred. But the missus grew up there.'

'How long ago was this, Mrs Haines?' Banks asked Esther, who had started weeping quietly again.

'It's ten years since we moved, now.'

'And you came straight here?'

'Not until Les and I got married. We lived in an old back-to-back off Tong Road. It's not far away. Dad got a job at Blakey's Castings. It were all he could get. Then they went to Melbourne – Australia, like – to go and live with our Denny after they retired. Oh God, somebody'll have to tell Mum and Dad.' She looked beseechingly at her husband, who patted her arm. 'Don't worry about that, love,' he said. 'It'll keep a while.'

'As far as I can gather,' Banks said when Mrs Haines had regained her composure, 'your brother had some connection with Toronto in Canada. Is that right?'

She nodded. 'He couldn't get a job over here. He was a

bright lad, our Bernie. Got a degree. But there was no jobs. He emigrated eight years ago.'

'What did he do in Toronto?'

'He's a teacher in a college. Teaching English. It's a good job. We was off out to see him next year.'

Banks lit another cigarette as she wiped away the tears and blew her nose.

'Can you give me his address?'

She nodded and said, 'Be a love, Les.' Her husband went to the sideboard and brought out a tattered Woolworth's address book.

'How often did Bernard come home?' Banks asked, writing down the Toronto address.

'Well, he came as often as he could. This was his third trip, but he hadn't been for four years. Proper homesick he was.'

'Why did he stay in Canada, then?'

She shrugged. 'Money. No work for him here, is there? Not with Thatcher running the country.'

'What did he talk about while he was with you?'

'Nothing really. Just family things.'

'Did he say anything odd to you, Mr Haines? Anything that struck you as unusual?'

'No. We didn't talk a lot. We'd not much in common really. I'm not a great reader, never did well at school. And he liked his books, did Bernie. We talked about ale a bit. About what the boozers are like over there. He told me he'd found a nice pub in Toronto where he could get John Smith's and Tartan on draught.'

'Is that all?'

Haines shrugged. 'Like I said, we didn't have much in common.'

Banks turned to Mrs Haines again. 'What state of mind

was he in? Was he upset about anything, depressed?'

'He'd just got divorced about a year ago,' she said, 'and he were a bit upset about that. I think that's what made him homesick. But I wouldn't say he were really depressed, no. He seemed to think he might be able to come back and live here again before too long.'

'Did he say anything about a job?'

'No.'

'How could he manage to move back here then?'

Esther Haines shook her head. 'I don't know. He didn't say. He just hinted. Maybe it were wishful thinking, like, now he didn't have Barbara any more.'

'That was his wife?'

'Yes.'

'What happened between them?'

'She ran off wi' another man.'

'Where had Bernie been before he visited you?'

Esther took a deep breath and dabbed at her red eyes. 'He'd come to England for a month, all told,' she said. 'First off, he spent a week seeing friends in London and Bristol, then he came up here. He'd be due to go back about now, wouldn't he, Les?'

'Do you know how to get in touch with these friends?' Banks asked.

She shook her head. 'Sorry. They were friends of Bernie's from university.'

'Which university?'

'York.'

'And you didn't know them?'

'No. They'd be in his notebook. He always carried a notebook full of names and stuff.'

'We didn't find it. Never mind, we'll find them somehow.' If necessary, Banks knew he could check with the university authorities and track down Bernard Allen's contemporaries. 'Do you know where he was heading after Swainshead?'

'He were going to see another friend in Edinburgh, then fly back from Prestwick. You can do that with Wardair, he said, fly to London and go back from somewhere else.' She put her handkerchief to her nose again and sniffed.

'I don't suppose you have this person's address in Edinburgh?'

She shook her head.

'So,' Banks said, stubbing out his cigarette and reaching for the tea, 'he left here on May the thirteenth to do some fell-walking in the Dales, and then—'

Mrs Haines cut in. 'No, that's not right. That's not the reason he went.'

'Why did he go, then? Sentimental reasons?'

'Partly, I suppose. But he went to stay with friends.'

'What friends?'

'Sam and Katie. They run a guest house – Greenock's. Bernie was going to stay with Sam and Katie.'

Struggling to keep his excitement and surprise to himself, Banks asked how Bernard had got to know Sam and Katie. At first, Mrs Haines seemed unable to concentrate for weeping, but Banks encouraged her gently, and soon she was telling him the whole story, pulling at the handkerchief on her lap as she spoke.

'They knew each other from Armley, from after we came to Leeds. Sam lived there, too. We were neighbours. Bernie was always going on about Swainshead and how wonderful it was, and I think it were him as put the idea into Sam's head. Anyways, Sam and Katie scrimped and saved and that's where they ended up.'

'Did Bernie have any other close friends in Swainshead?'

'Not really,' Esther said. 'Most of his childhood mates had moved away. There weren't any jobs for them up there.'

'How did he get on with the Colliers?'

'A bit above our station,' Esther said. 'Oh, they'd say hello, but they weren't friends of his, not as far as I know. You can't be, can you, not with the sons of the fellow what owns your land?'

'I suppose not,' Banks said. 'Was there any bitterness over losing the farm?'

'I wouldn't say that, no. Sadness, yes, but bitterness? No. It were us own fault. There wasn't much land fit for anything but sheep, and when the flock took sick . . .'

'What was Mr Collier's attitude?'

'Mr Walter?'

'Yes.'

'He were right sorry for us. He helped out as much as he could, but it were no use. He were preparing to sell off to John Fletcher anyway. Getting out of farming, he were.'

'How would that have affected you?'

'What do you mean?'

'The sale.'

'Oh. Mr Walter said he'd write it into the terms that we could stay. John Fletcher didn't mind. He and Dad got on quite well.'

'So there was no ill feeling between your family and John Fletcher or the Colliers?'

'No. Not to speak of. But I didn't think much of them.'

'Oh?'

She pulled harder at the handkerchief on her lap, and it began to tear along one edge. 'I always thought they were a pair of right toffee-nosed gits, but I never said nowt.

Stephen thinks he's God's gift to women, and that Nicholas is a bit doolally, if you ask me.'

'In what way?'

'Have you met him?'

'Yes.'

'He's like a little kid, gets all overexcited. Especially when he's had a drink or two. Practically slavers all over a person, he does. Especially women. He even tried it on with me once, but I sent him away with his tail between his legs.' She shuddered. 'I don't know how they put up with him at that there school, unless they're all a bit that way.'

'What about Stephen?'

Esther shrugged. 'Seems a pleasant enough gent on the outside. Bit of a smoothie, really. Got a lot more class than his brother. Bit two-faced, though.'

'In what way?'

'You know. All friendly one minute, then cuts you dead next time he sees you. But they can afford to do that, can't they?'

'Who can?'

'Rich folks. Don't have to live like ordinary people, like you and me, do they?'

'I don't imagine they have the same priorities, no,' Banks said, unsure whether he approved of being called an ordinary person. 'Did he try it on too?'

'Mr Stephen? No. Oh, he liked the girls, all right, but he was too much of a gentleman, for all his faults.'

Mrs Haines seemed to have forgotten her grief for a few moments, so absorbed had she been in the past, but as soon as silence fell, her tears began to flow again and her husband put his arm around her. In the kitchen, something smashed, and the child ran wailing into the room and buried his jammy face in Esther Haines's lap.

Banks stood up. 'You've been very helpful,' he said. 'I'm sorry to have been the bearer of such bad news.'

Esther nodded, handkerchief pressed to her mouth, and Mr Haines showed him to the door. 'What are we to do about . . . you know . . .'

'The remains?'

'Aye.'

'We'll be in touch soon,' Banks said. 'Don't worry.'

Upstairs, a baby started crying.

The first thing Banks did was look for a phone box to call Sandra and tell her when he'd be back. That didn't prove as easy as it sounded. The first three he came across had been vandalized, and he had to drive almost two miles before he found one that worked.

It was a pleasant drive back to Eastvale through Harrogate and Ripon. In a quiet mood, he slipped in Delius's *North Country Sketches* instead of the 1960s pop he'd been listening to. As he drove, he tried to piece together all the information he'd got that day. Whichever way he looked at it, the trail led back to Swainshead, the Greenocks, the Colliers and John Fletcher.

5

ONE

Only the cry of a distant curlew and the sound of water gurgling over rocks in the stream at the back broke the silence.

Then Sam Greenock echoed the news: 'Bernie? Dead? I can't believe it.'

'I'm afraid so,' Banks said. It was the second time in two days that he had been the bearer of bad news, but this time it was easier. The investigation proper had begun, and he had more on his mind than Sam Greenock's disbelief, real or feigned.

They sat in the living room at the back of the house: the Greenocks, Banks, and Sergeant Hatchley taking notes. Katie gazed out of the window, or sometimes she stared at the huge ugly wooden cross on the mantelpiece. She had said nothing, given no reaction at all.

'It's true he was staying with you then, is it?' Banks asked.

Sam nodded.

'Why didn't his name show up on the register? We went to a lot of trouble checking every place in Swainsdale.'

'It's not my fault,' Sam said. 'He was staying with us as a friend. Besides, you know as well as I do that those guest books aren't legal requirements; they're only for people to write comments in if they want, show they've been here.'

'When our man called and asked if you'd had any Canadians staying recently, why didn't you mention Bernard Allen?'

'He didn't ask me anything. He just looked at the register. Besides, I never thought of Bernie as a Canadian. Oh, I know he lived there, but that's not everything, is it? I've known people who lived in Saudi Arabia for a year working on the oil fields but I don't think of them as Saudis.'

'Come off it, Sam. Bernard Allen had been in Canada for eight years, and you hadn't seen him for four. This was only his third trip back,' said Banks.

'Still . . .'

'Did you have any reason to lie about Bernie being here?'

'No. I told you—'

'Because if you did, we can charge you with concealing information. That's serious, Sam. You could get two years.'

Sam leaned forward. 'Look, I never thought. That policeman who came, he didn't tell us what he was looking for.'

'We can check, you know.'

'Bloody check then. It's true.'

Sam couldn't remember the officer's name, so Banks asked Hatchley to make a note of the time and date. It would be easy enough to find out who had made the visit and what approach he had taken. He still wasn't sure about Sam Greenock, though.

Banks sighed. 'All right. We'll leave that for now. Which room did he stay in?'

Sam looked at Katie. She was staring out on the fell side, so he had to nudge her and repeat the question.

'Five,' she said, as if speaking from a great distance. 'Room five.'

'We'll need to have a look,' Banks told her.

'It was two weeks ago,' Sam said. 'There's been other people in since then. That's where we took Fellowes after he'd found the body.'

'We'll still need to look.'

'Do you think he's hidden some secret message there, Inspector? Taped it to the bottom of the dresser drawer, maybe?'

'You've been reading too many espionage novels. And if I were you, I'd cut the bloody sarcasm. You might start me thinking that there's some reason you don't want me to look in Bernie Allen's room. And while we're at it, he's not the first person to get killed after leaving this guest house, is he, Sam?'

'Now wait a minute,' said Sam. 'If you're trying to imply—'

Banks held his hand up. 'I'm not trying to imply anything. What was it the man said: once is happenstance, twice is coincidence? Let's just hope there's not a third time.'

Sam put his head in his hands and rubbed his eyes. 'I'm sorry,' he said. 'Really, I am. It's the shock. And now all these questions.'

'Look at it from my point of view, Sam. Bernard Allen was killed after he left your guest house. That's given his killer about two whole weeks to cover his tracks, leave the country, arrange for an alibi, whatever. I need everything I can get, and I need it quickly. And the last thing I need is some clever bugger who just might have been withholding information to start playing the comic.'

'Look, I've said I'm sorry. What more do you want?'

'First of all, you can tell us when he left.'

'About two weeks ago.'

'Can you be more specific?'

'Katie?'

Again, with great difficulty, Katie turned her attention to the people in the room. Banks repeated his question.

'It was a Friday,' she said.

Hatchley checked the dates against his diary. 'That'd be the seventeenth, sir,' he said. 'Friday. May the seventeenth.'

'What time?'

'Just after breakfast. About nine thirty. He said he wanted to get an early start,' Sam said.

'Where was he going?'

'He was heading for the Pennine Way, then up to Swaledale.'

'Do you know where he was intending to stay?'

Sam shook his head. 'No. He just said he'd find some where on the way. There are plenty of places; it's a very popular route.'

'Did he say anything to you about visiting the hanging valley on his way?'

'No. I wouldn't have been surprised, though. He used to play there when he was a kid, or so he said.'

'What did you do after he'd gone?'

'I drove to Eastvale to do some shopping. I always do on a Friday morning.'

'What shops did you go to?'

'What is this? Are you trying to tell me I'm a suspect in the murder of my friend?'

'Just answer the bloody question.'

'All right, Inspector, there's no—'

'It's Chief Inspector.' Banks didn't usually pull his rank,

but Sam Greenock had rubbed him up the wrong way.

'Chief Inspector, then. Where did I go? I went to Carter's for some seeds, peat moss and fertilizer. Katie's trying to get a vegetable patch going in the back garden. It'll save us a bit of money in the long run.'

'Is that all?'

'No. But they'll remember me there. I called in at a newsagent's for some magazines – that one on King Street opposite the school road.'

'I know it.'

'I'm a regular there, too.'

'Thanks, that'll do fine for a start. What kind of car do you drive?'

'A Land Rover. It's in the garage.'

'And you, Mrs Greenock, what did you do after Bernard Allen left?'

'Me? Housework. What else?'

Banks turned back to Sam. 'You met Allen in Leeds about ten years ago, is that right?'

'Yes. In Armley. We lived just off Tong Road and the Allens came to live next door after they gave up the farm. Bernie and I were about the same age, so we palled up.'

'What was he doing then?'

'Just finishing at university. It was only York, so he was home most weekends and holidays. We used to go for a jar or two every Saturday night.'

'How did the family take the move?'

Sam shrugged. 'They adapted. At first Mr Allen, Bernie's dad, went around as if he'd been kicked out of paradise. It must have been very hard for him though, swapping farm work for a crummy factory job. Hard on the pride.'

'Is that what he said?'

'Never in so many words, no. You could just tell. He's a tough old bird anyway, so they survived.'

'And Bernard?'

'He tried to fit in. But you know what it's like. He got his degree and all, but he couldn't get the kind of work he wanted. He lived at home and did all kinds of odd jobs – mushroom picking at Greenhill Nurseries, sweeping factory yards, production line . . . all dull routine work.'

'Is that when he decided to go to Canada?'

'After a year or so of it, yes. He'd had enough. Someone he knew from university had already gone over and said it wasn't too hard to get teaching jobs in the colleges. He said they paid well, too.'

'Who was this?'

'His name was Bob Morgan. I think he and Bernie taught at the same place, Toronto Community College.'

'Was Bernie homesick?'

'I suppose so. I mean, you don't forget your roots, do you? But he stayed. One thing leads to another. He made friends over there, got married, divorced.'

'What was his state of mind while he was staying here?'

'He was fine. Cheerful. Happy to be back.'

'Did he talk about coming home to stay?'

Sam shook his head. 'He knew better than that. There aren't any jobs for him.'

'So he didn't seem unusually homesick or depressed, and he didn't say he was planning to come back.'

'No.'

Banks lit a cigarette and studied Katie's profile. She was a blank; he had no idea what she was thinking.

'How long have you been in Swainshead?' he asked Sam.

'Six years.'

'And it's going well?'

Sam nodded. 'Can't complain. We're hardly million-aires, but we like the life.'

'And you, Mrs Greenock?'

Katie turned and focused on him. 'Yes. It's better than cleaning rooms at the Queen's Hotel.'

'Did Bernie have any other friends in the village apart from you?'

'Not really,' Sam answered. 'See, most of the kids he grew up with had moved away. A lot do these days. They see the good life on telly and soon as they're old enough there's no stopping them. Like Denny, Bernie's older brother. Off to Australia like a shot, he was.'

'Was Bernie friendly with the Colliers?' Esther Haines had said not, but Banks thought she might have been prejudiced by her own opinions of Nicholas and Stephen.

'Well, I'd hardly say they were friends. Acquaintances, more like. But we had an evening or two in the White Rose together. I think Bernie was always a bit uncomfortable around Stephen and Nick though, them having been his landlords so to speak, the local gentry and all.'

Banks nodded. 'Can you think of anyone in the village who might have wanted him out of the way?'

'Bernie? Good Lord, no.'

'He had no enemies?'

'None that I know of. Not here.'

'What about in Leeds?'

'Not there either, as far as I know. Maybe somebody followed him over from Canada, an enemy he'd made there?'

'Mrs Greenock,' Banks said, turning to Katie again, 'do you know of anyone with a reason for getting rid of Bernard Allen?'

Katie hesitated before answering. 'No. He was harmless. Just a friendly sort of person. Nobody would want to hurt him.'

'One more thing: what was he carrying when he left here?'

'Carrying?' Sam said. 'Oh, I see. His belongings. A big blue rucksack with his clothes, passport, money, a few books.'

'And what was he wearing?'

'I don't really remember. Do you, Katie?'

Katie shook her head. 'It was a warm day, though,' she said. 'That I do remember. I think he was just wearing an open-necked shirt. White. And trousers, not jeans. It's only the amateurs wear jeans for walking.'

'They're too heavy, you see,' Sam explained. 'Especially if they get wet. We try to give a bit of advice to our guests sometimes, and we always make sure we know where they're going if they're due back in the evening. That way, if they don't return, we can let the Mountain Rescue post know where they were heading.'

Banks nodded. 'Very sensible. Have you any vacancies at the moment?'

'I think so,' Sam said.

'Six and eight,' Katie added.

'Good, we'll take them.'

'You're staying here?'

'There'll be quite a lot of questions to ask in Swainshead,' Banks said, 'and it's fifty miles to Eastvale and back. We'll be staying here tonight at least.'

'One's a single,' Katie said. 'The other's a double.'

Banks smiled at her. 'Fine. Sergeant Hatchley will take the single.' It was patently unfair, Banks knew. He was much more slightly built than the well padded Hatchley, and a good four or five inches shorter. But rank, he reflected, did have its privileges.

'Don't sulk, Sergeant,' he said as they walked over to the car to pick up their overnight bags. 'My room might be bigger, but it's probably right next to the plumbing. What did you think of Mrs Greenock?'

'Not bad if you like those wand-like figures,' Hatchley said. 'Prefer 'em with a bit of meat on their bones, myself.'

'I wasn't asking you to rate her out of ten on looks. What about her attitude?'

'Didn't say much, did she? Seemed in a bit of a daze to me. Think there might be more to her than meets the eye?'

'I think there might indeed,' said Banks. 'In fact, I got the distinct impression that she was holding something back.'

TWO

The Greenocks ate their lunch in silence, then Sam dashed out. Katie, who had lost her appetite and merely played with her food, piled the dishes in the washer, set the controls and turned it on. There was still shopping to do and the evening meal to prepare, but she felt she could afford to relax for a few minutes.

As she lay down on the sofa and looked out on the slopes of Swainshead Fell beyond the back garden, she thought of Bernie helping her clear the dishes, talking about Toronto, watching cricket on the telly. She remembered the little presents he had brought each time – no doubt picked up at the airport at the last minute, for Bernie was like that – jars of pure maple syrup, a box of cigars or a bottle of malt Scotch for Sam, Opium perfume or Chanel

No. 5 for Katie. She'd never had the heart to tell him that she didn't wear perfume, that the one time she had tried she had felt like a tramp, even though it had been White Linen, and had scrubbed it off straight away. Now the three little bottles lay in the dark inside her dresser drawer, untouched.

Bernie had even helped her with the garden sometimes; he might not have had green fingers, but he could wield a trowel or a hoe well enough. Bernie: so considerate, so kind. But the dark images began to crowd out her thoughts. Frowning, she pushed them away. Instead she saw endless prairies of golden wheat swaying in the breeze, heard the sea beating against a rough coastline where redwood forests reared as tall as the sky. Bernie had told her all about Canada, all the places he'd been. She'd never get to see them now, she realized, because Bernie was dead.

Fellowes' words came back to her, what he'd said in his drunken stupor when he grasped her hand by the bed: 'Moving,' he'd said. 'Moving.' And she hadn't understood at the time. Now she did. If Bernie had been lying up there for two weeks he would have been like that dead lamb she had seen on Adam's Fell last year. It didn't bear thinking about.

She'd given a bad impression to the police, she knew that, but at the time she had been unable to help herself. The lean dark one, the one who seemed too short to be a policeman, would want to talk to her again, that was for sure. How could she keep her secret? She pictured her grandmother standing over her, lined face stern and hard, eyes like black pinheads boring into her. 'Secrets, girl, secrets are the devil's doing. God loves a pure and open heart.' But she had to keep this secret.

There were so many things, it seemed, one had to do in

life that went against God's commandments. How could a person live without sinning? She was no longer even sure that she knew what was right or wrong. Sometimes she thought it was a sin to breathe, to be alive. It seemed you had to sin to survive in today's world. It was wrong to keep secrets and tell lies; but was it wrong to keep your word, your promise? And if you had broken it once for a special reason, was it all right to break it again?

Wearily, Katie got up and prepared to go to the shops down in Lower Head. Work and duty, they were the only constants in life. Everything else was a trap, a trick, a temptation to betrayal. The only way to survive was to shun pleasure. She picked up her purse and shopping basket and pulled a face at the nasty soap taste in her mouth as she left the house.

THREE

After Banks and Hatchley had carried their bags to their rooms, they walked over to the White Rose for lunch. The place was busy with Saturday tourists who had let their curiosity lead them to the northern part of Swainshead, but none of the regulars was present. Luckily, Freddie Metcalfe was too busy to chat. They both ordered gammon and chips and carried their pints over to a corner table.

'I want you to get on to Richmond after lunch,' Banks said, 'and have him check to see if anyone in Swainshead has connections with Canada, specifically with Toronto. I know it sounds like a big job, but tell him to start with the people we already know: the Greenocks, Fletcher, the Colliers. You might also add,' he said, lowering his voice, 'Freddie Metcalfe over there, and Neil Fellowes too.'

'The bloke who found the body? But he's from Pontefract.'

'No matter. Remember, we thought Allen was from Canada at first, then from Leeds. And while we're on the subject, have him check on the brother-in-law, Les Haines. I want to know if he's made any trips to this area in the past few weeks. Ask him to get as much background as he can on all of them. I'm sure the superintendent will be able to get him some help from downstairs. And get someone to go to Carter's and that newsagent's to check Greenock's alibi. Tell them to make sure they get the times as exact as possible.'

'Don't you believe him?'

Banks shrugged. 'He could be telling the truth. He could also have driven to a convenient spot along the main road and approached the valley from the other side.'

The little waitress brought over their food and they ate in silence. At the bar they could hear Freddie Metcalfe enthralling visitors with examples of Yorkshire humour filched from *The Dalesman*, and at the next table two middle-aged women from Lancashire were talking about lager louts: 'They get right confident after a few drinks, young 'uns do.'

When they had finished eating, Banks sent Hatchley to radio in to Richmond, then he stood outside the pub for a moment and took a deep breath of fresh air. It was June 1, another fine day. Nobody knew what the Dales had done to deserve such a long stretch of good weather, but according to a radio Banks overheard, it certainly wasn't any thanks to Yorkshire County Cricket Club, currently 74 for 6 at Somerset.

Banks wanted to talk to the Colliers, but first he returned to his room to change his shirt. On his way back down, he spotted Mrs Greenock in the hall, but she seemed to see or hear him coming and scuttled off into the back before he could catch her. Smiling, he walked back out into the street. He knew he could have followed her and confronted her with his suspicions there and then, but decided instead to let her play mouse to his cat until she tired of it.

There were plenty of people on the grassy banks of the River Swain that afternoon. Three children fished for tiddlers with nets at the end of cane rods while their parents sat and watched from deckchairs, dad with a knotted handkerchief over his head reading the *Daily Mail* and mum knitting, glancing up occasionally to make sure the offspring were still in sight.

The Dales were getting as crowded and noisy as the coast, Banks thought as he crossed the bridge. There was even a small group of teenagers farther down, towards Lower Head, wearing cut-off denim jackets with the names of rock bands inked on the back. Two of them, a boy and a girl, Banks assumed, were rolling on the grass in an overtly sexual embrace while tinny music rattled out of a portable stereo placed close to one prostrate youth's ear.

Many of his colleagues, Banks knew, would have gone over and told them to move on, accused them of disturbing the peace and searched them for drugs. But despite his personal distaste for some gangs of youngsters and their music, Banks made it a rule never to use his power as a policeman to force his own will on the general public. After all, they were young, they were enjoying life, and apart from the noise, they were really doing no one any harm.

Banks passed the old men on the bridge and made a

mental note to have a chat with them at some point. They seemed to be permanent fixtures; maybe they had seen something.

He met Sergeant Hatchley at the car and they headed for the Collier house.

'Have you noticed,' Banks said, 'how Allen seemed to have a different story for everyone he talked to? He was upset; he was cheerful. He was coming home; he wasn't.'

'Maybe,' said Hatchley, 'it's just that all the people he talked to have a different story for us.'

Banks gave the sergeant an appreciative glance. Thinking things out wasn't Hatchley's strong point, but there were times when he could be quite surprising.

'Good point,' Banks said. 'Let's see what the Colliers have to add.'

Gristhorpe was right; the Collier house was a Victorian monstrosity. But it had its own grotesque charm, Banks thought as he walked up the crazy paving with Hatchley. Most Dales architecture was practical in nature and plain in style, but this place was for show. It must have been the great-grandfather who had it built, and he must have thought highly indeed of the Collier status.

Banks rang the bell on the panelled door and Stephen Collier answered, a frown on his face. He led them through a high-ceilinged hall into a sitting room at the back of the house. French windows opened on to a patio. In the centre of the large lawn stood an elaborate stone fountain. White dolphins and cherubim curled about the lip of the bowl.

The room itself contrasted sharply with the exterior of the house. Off-white walls created a sense of light and space on which the ultra-modern Swedish pine and chrome and glass furnishings made hardly any encroachment at all. Abstract paintings hung over a blue-tiled mantelpiece:

bold and violent splashes of colour reminiscent, in their effect on Banks's eyes, of the Jackson Pollocks Sandra had insisted he look at in a London gallery years ago.

The three of them sat in white wicker chairs around a table on the patio. Banks half-expected a servant to arrive with a tray of margaritas or martinis, but Collier himself offered them drinks. It was warm, so both men eagerly accepted a cold bottle of Beck's lager.

Before he went to fetch the drinks, Stephen Collier rapped on the French windows of the next room and beckoned to Nicholas. Banks had wanted to talk to them separately, but it wasn't important at this point. Stretching, he got up and walked over as Nicholas emerged on to his half of the patio. He was just in time to catch a glimpse of a much darker room, all oak panelling, leather-bound books and oil paintings of ancestors gleaming on the walls.

Nicholas smiled his horsy yellow smile and held out his hand.

'It's an interesting set-up you've got here,' Banks said.

'Yes. We couldn't bear to get rid of the house, however ugly it might seem from the outside. It's been in the family for years. Lord knows what prompted my great-great-grandfather to build such a folly – ostentatious display of wealth and position, I suppose. And it's so inappropriate for the area.' Despite the deprecating tone, Banks could tell that Nicholas was proud of the house and the status of his family.

'Do you share the place?' Banks asked Nicholas after they had sat down at the table.

'Sort of. It's divided into two halves. We thought at first that one of us could take the upstairs and the other the downstairs, but it's better like this. We've got the equivalent of two completely separate houses. Stephen and I have very different tastes, so the two halves make quite a contrast. You must let me show you round my half one day.'

Stephen returned with the drinks. Dressed all in white, he looked like a cricketer breaking for tea. Nicholas, however, with his slight stoop, pale complexion and comma of black hair over his forehead, looked more like an ageing umpire. It was hard to believe these two were brothers; even harder to accept that Stephen was the elder.

After giving both of them time to register surprise and shock at the news of Bernard Allen's death, of which he was certain they knew already, Banks lit a cigarette and asked, 'Did you see much of him while he was here?'

'Not a lot,' Stephen answered. 'He was in the pub a couple of times with Sam, so naturally we talked, but that's about all.'

'What did you talk about?'

'Oh, just small talk, really. This and that. About Canada, places we'd both been to.'

'You've visited Canada?'

'I travel quite a bit,' Stephen said. 'You might think a small food-freezing plant in the Dales isn't much, but there are other businesses connected. Import, export, that kind of thing. Yes, I've been to Canada a few times.'

'Toronto?'

'No. Montreal, as a matter of fact.'

'Did you ever see Bernard Allen over there?'

'It's a big country, Chief Inspector.'

'Did you get the impression that anything was bothering Allen while he was over here?'

'No.'

'What about you?' he asked Nicholas.

'No, I can't say I did. I've always found it a bit awkward

talking to Bernard, to tell you the truth. One always feels he has a bit of a chip on his shoulder.'

'What do you mean?'

'Oh, come on,' Nicholas said, grinning. 'Surely you know what I mean. His father spent his life working on land rented from my father. They were poor. From where they lived they had a fine enough view of this place, and you can't tell me that Bernard never thought it unfair that we had so much and he had so little. Especially when his father failed.'

'I didn't know Bernard Allen or his father,' Banks said, peeling the foil from the neck of the Beck's, which he preferred to drink straight from the bottle. 'Tell me about him.'

'I'm not saying I knew him well myself, only that he became a bit of a lefty, a socialist. Up the workers and all that.' Nicholas grinned again, showing his stained teeth. His eyes were especially bright.

'Are you saying that Bernard Allen was a communist?'

'I don't know about that. I don't know if he was a party member. All I know is he used to spout his leftist rot in the pub.'

'Is this true?' Banks asked Stephen.

'Partly. My brother exaggerates a bit, Chief Inspector. It's a tendency he has. We sometimes had arguments about politics, yes, and Bernard Allen had left-wing views. But that's as far as it goes. I'd hardly say he was a proselytizer or that he toed some party line.'

'His political opinions weren't particularly strong, then?'

'I wouldn't say so, no. He said he left the country partly because Margaret Thatcher came into office. Well, we all know about unemployment, don't we? Bernard couldn't

find work in England, so he left. You could hardly say he
was running from country to country to escape political
tyranny, could you?'

'He just used to whine about it, that's all,' Nicholas cut
in. 'Expected the government to do everything for him
without him having to lift a finger. Typical socialist.'

'As you can gather, Chief Inspector,' Stephen said with
a strained smile, 'my brother's something of a young
fogey. That hardly gave either of us reason to do away
with Bernard, though.'

'Of course not,' Banks said. 'And I was never suggesting it did. I just want to know as much about the
victim as possible. Would you say that there was any real
animosity between you – political arguments aside – over
the farm?'

'Do you mean did he blame us?' Stephen asked.

'Yes.'

'He blamed everyone but himself,' Nicholas cut in.

Stephen turned on him. 'Oh, shut up, Nicky. You're
being bloody awkward, you know.'

'Did he?' Banks asked Stephen again.

'Not that I ever knew of. It was nothing to do with us,
really. As you know, Father was preparing to give up
farming anyway, and he certainly hadn't groomed us to
take over. Nobody kicked Archie Allen off the land. He
could have stayed there as long as he wanted to. It just
wasn't financially viable any more. Ask any farmer; they'll
tell you how things have changed over the past twenty
years or so. If Bernard was holding a grudge, then it was
a very unreasonable one. He didn't strike me as an
unreasonable person. Does that answer your question?'

'Yes, thank you,' Banks said. He turned to Nicholas
again. 'I understand you knew Mr Allen's sister, Esther.'

Nicholas reddened with anger. 'Who said that?'

'Never mind who said it. Is it true?'

'We all knew her,' Stephen said. 'I mean, we knew who she was.'

'More than that,' Banks said, looking at Nicholas, whose eyes were flashing. 'Nicholas knows what I mean, don't you?'

'Don't be ridiculous,' Nicholas said. 'Are you trying to suggest that there was anything more to it than a landlord–tenant relationship?'

'Was there?'

'Of course not.'

'Didn't you find her attractive?'

'She was hardly my type.'

'Do you mean she was of a lower class?'

Nicholas bared his teeth in a particularly unpleasant smile. 'If you want to put it that way, yes.'

'And what about the servant girl? The one who used to work here.'

'I insist you stop this at once, Chief Inspector,' Stephen said. 'I can't see how it's relevant. And I'm sure I don't have to remind you that the deputy chief constable is a good friend of the family.'

'I'm sure he is,' Banks said. He wasn't at all put out; in fact, he was enjoying their discomfort tremendously. 'Just a couple of minor points, then we'll be on our way. When was the last time you saw Bernard?'

Nicholas said nothing; he appeared to be sulking. Stephen paused for a moment and answered in a business-like manner, 'I'd say it was in the White Rose the evening before he left. Thursday. I remember talking to him about Tan Hill in Swaledale.'

'Is that where he was heading?'

'Not specifically, no, but it's on the Pennine Way.'

'Did he talk about the hanging valley at all, the place where his body was found?'

'No, not that I remember.'

'Did either of you see him set off from Swainshead?'

Both the Colliers shook their heads. 'I'm usually at the office before nine,' Stephen said. 'And my brother would have been at Braughtmore.'

'So you saw nothing of him after that Thursday evening in the White Rose?'

'Nothing.'

'Just one more thing: could you tell us where John Fletcher lives?'

'John? He's a couple of miles north of the village. It's a big farmhouse on the eastern fell side. You can't miss it; it's the only one in sight.'

'Fine, then.' Banks nodded to Hatchley and they stood up to leave. Stephen Collier led them out and Nicholas followed, still sulking. As soon as the door closed, Banks could hear them start arguing.

Hatchley turned up his nose in disgust. 'What a pair of wankers,' he said.

'Aptly put,' said Banks. 'But we did learn a few things.'

'Like what?'

'I never told them what time Allen left Swainshead, so why should Stephen Collier make a point of mentioning nine o'clock?'

'Hmm,' said Hatchley. 'I suppose he could have just been assuming that Allen would leave after breakfast. Or maybe it had been mentioned the night before?'

'It's possible,' Banks said. 'Come to that, Sam Greenock could have told them. Nicholas Collier seemed much more annoyed by my reference to Esther Haines than I thought he'd be. There could be much more to that than even she let on.'

'I thought you were pushing it a bit there,' Hatchley said. 'I mean, the super did say to take it easy on them. They're important.'

Banks sniffed. 'The problem is, Sergeant, that it's all arse backwards, isn't it?'

'What do you mean?'

'Let's say Nicholas Collier might have been messing around with Allen's little sister, or Allen might have been bitter over losing the farm and eventually having to leave England. That gives him a motive for murder, but he's the one who ends up dead. Odd that, don't you think?'

'Aye, when you put it like that,' Hatchley said.

'Get on the radio and see if Richmond has turned up anything yet, will you? I want a word with these blokes here.'

Hatchley carried on to the car. Banks neared the bridge and steeled himself for the encounter with the old men. Three of them stood there silently, two leaning on walking sticks. No flicker of interest or concern showed on their weather-beaten faces when Banks approached them. He leaned against the warm stone and introduced himself, then asked if they had been out as early as nine o'clock a couple of weeks ago.

No one said a word at first, then one of them, a gnarled, misshapen man, turned to face Banks. With his flat cap and dark brown clothing, he looked like some strange plant with the power to uproot itself and walk among people.

He spat in the beck and said, ''Appen.'

'Do you know Bernard Allen?'

'Archie Allen's lad? Aye, o' course.'

'Did you see him that morning?'

The man was silent for a moment; he screwed up his eyes and contemplated Adam's Fell. Banks took out his cigarettes and offered them around. Only one of them, a man with a huge red nose, took one. He grinned toothlessly at Banks, carefully nipped off the filter and put the other end in his mouth.

'Aye,' the spokesman said finally.

'Where did he come from?'

The man pointed towards the Greenock Guest House.

'Did he stop anywhere on his way?'

The man shook his head.

'Where did he go?'

'Up there.' The man pointed with his stick to the footpath up Swainshead Fell.

'And that was the last you saw of him?'

'Aye.'

'What was he wearing?'

'Nay, lad, I don't remember that. 'E was carrying one o' them there 'aversacks on 'is back, that's all I recollect. P'raps 'e was wearing a shirt. I don't remember no jacket.'

'Did you notice anyone go after him?'

The man shook his head.

'Could someone have followed him without you seeing?'

''Appen. There's plenty o' ways to get up t' fell.'

'We know he went to the hanging valley over the fell top,' Banks said. 'Are there many other ways to get there?'

'A few. Tha can go from t' main road, 'bout a mile past Rawley Force, and from further up t' valley.'

'How could anyone know where he was heading?'

'That's tha job, bobby, in't it?'

He was right. Someone could easily have watched Allen

set off up the side of Swainshead Fell and then gone up by another route to head him off somewhere out of sight. And Sam Greenock had said he wouldn't have been surprised if Bernard had visited the hanging valley. Anyone else could have known that too, and gone up earlier to wait for him there.

Typically, as more information came to light the case was becoming more and more frustrating. Clearly it would be necessary to do a house-to-house in the village and ask the people with an eastern view if they had noticed anything that morning. It would also be useful to know if anyone had seen a car parked off the Helmthorpe road near the other access point. The trouble was that 17 May was so long ago most people would have forgotten.

And those were only the most obvious ways in. Someone could surely have approached the hanging valley from almost any direction and lain in wait overnight if necessary, especially if he knew Bernard Allen was bound to pass that way. The break, if it came, didn't look likely to come from establishing opportunity – just about everyone who had no alibi seemed to have had that – but from discovering a motive.

Banks thanked the old men and walked off to find Sergeant Hatchley.

6

ONE

Hatchley started the next day in a bad mood. He grumbled to Banks that not only was his bed too small but the noise of the plumbing had kept him awake.

'I swear there was some bugger in there for a piss every five minutes. Flushed it every time, too. The bloody thing took at least ten minutes to quieten down again.'

Banks, who had slept the sleep of the truly virtuous, overlooked the sergeant's spurious arithmetic. 'Never mind,' he said. 'With a bit of luck you'll be snug and warm in your own bed tonight.'

'Not if I can help it.'

'Carol Ellis?'

'Aye.'

'How long's it been now?'

'Over eighteen months.'

'It'll be wedding bells next, then?'

Hatchley blushed and Banks guessed he wasn't far from the truth.

'Anyway,' Banks went on. 'I'm sorry to keep you away from your love life, but I think we'll be finished here today unless Richmond comes up with anything else.'

Hatchley had been on to the detective constable back in Eastvale, but Richmond had discovered nothing of importance except that Sam Greenock's alibi seemed to hold. There remained, however, some doubt about the exact times he had called at Carter's and the newsagent's, so he wasn't entirely out of the running.

Also, Richmond had spoken to PC Weaver, who had called at the Greenocks' to ask about Canadian visitors. Weaver said that in all cases he had both checked the register and made enquiries. It looked like Sam Greenock was lying. Weaver could have been covering himself, but he was a good officer and Banks tended to believe him.

The previous evening, Banks and Hatchley had gone to interview John Fletcher, but he had been out. On the way back, they called in at the White Rose for a nightcap and had an early night. Mrs Greenock had still been skilfully managing to avoid them.

Breakfast seemed to cheer Hatchley up. Delivered by Katie, who blushed and ran as soon as she put, or almost dropped, the plates in front of them, the main course consisted of two fried eggs, two thick rashers of Yorkshire bacon, Cumberland sausage, grilled mushrooms and tomato, with two slices of fried bread to mop it all up. Before that they had drunk grapefruit juice and eaten cereal, and afterwards came the toast and marmalade. By some oversight, the toast was actually hot, and Hatchley, his equilibrium much restored, recoiled in mock horror.

'What's on after we've talked to Fletcher?' he asked.

'We've got to put it all together, write up the interviews, see what we've got. I'm due for lunch with the super, so as far as I'm concerned you can take the rest of the day off and make an early start in the morning.'

Sergeant Hatchley beamed.

'I'll drop you off at home,' Banks said. 'I've got to go back to Eastvale to pick up Sandra and the kids, anyway.'

They finished their tea and left the room to the quiet

Belgian couple by the window and the young married in the corner who hadn't noticed anyone except each other. The Greenocks themselves were nowhere in sight.

Outside, the three men Banks had spoken to the previous day were on the bridge as usual. The one who had acted as spokesman gave him a curt grudging nod of acknowledgement as he passed.

Hatchley nudged him as they got in the car. 'It usually takes an incomer two generations to get any sign of recognition from those characters. What did you do, slip 'em a tenner each?'

'Southern charm, Sergeant,' Banks said, grinning. 'Sheer charm. That and a lot of luck.'

About two miles up the valley, they crossed the low bridge and took a narrow dirt road up the fell side. Fletcher's farmhouse was a solid dark-stone construction that looked as if it had been extruded from the earth like an outcrop of rock. Around the back were a number of pens and ditches for dipping and shearing. This time, he was at home.

'I'm sorry I wasn't in,' he said when Banks mentioned their previous visit. 'I was doing a bit of business over in Hawes. Anyway, come in, make yourselves comfortable.'

They followed him into the living room, a spartan kind of place with bare plastered walls, stiff-backed chairs and a solid table on which rested an old wireless and precious little else. Whatever money Fletcher had in the bank, he certainly didn't waste any on luxurious living. The small window looked out across the valley. With a view like that, Banks thought, you'd hardly need paintings or television.

One thing in particular caught Banks's eye immediately, partly because it just didn't seem to fit in this overtly masculine environment. Propped on the mantel-piece was a gilt-framed photograph of a woman. On closer inspec-tion, which Banks made while Fletcher went to brew tea, the photo proved doubly incongruous. The woman, with her finely plucked eyebrows, gay smile and long wavy chestnut hair, certainly didn't look as if she belonged in Fletcher's world. Banks could imagine her cutting a fine figure at society cocktail parties, sporting the latest hat at Ascot or posing elegantly at fashion openings, but not living in this godforsaken part of the world with a dark, squat, rough-cheeked sheep farmer.

When Fletcher came back, Banks pointed to the photo-graph and asked who she was.

'My wife,' he said. 'She's been gone two years now.' There was a distinct chill in his tone that harmonized with the lonely brooding atmosphere Banks sensed in the house.

He didn't like to ask, but curiosity, as it often did, got the better of him. 'I'm sorry,' he said. 'Is she dead?'

Fletcher looked sharply at him. 'Not dead, no. If you must know, she left me.'

And you're still in love with her, Banks thought. At least that explained something of the heaviness that Fletcher seemed to carry around inside himself.

'We've come about Bernard Allen,' Banks said, accept-ing a cup of tea and changing tack quickly.

'Aye, I heard,' Fletcher said. 'Poor sod.'

'Did you know him well?'

'Not really, no. Just used to pass an evening or two in the White Rose when he dropped in for a visit.'

'Did you know him before he went to Canada?'

'I met him a few times. Hard not to when I was dealing with Walter Collier. Archie Allen worked some of his land.'

'So I heard. What were you going to do about that?'

Fletcher shrugged. 'I wasn't going to evict them, if that's what you're getting at. They were quite welcome to stay as far as I was concerned.'

'But they couldn't make a go of it?'

'That's right. It's tough, sheep farming, like I said before. I felt sorry for them, but there was nothing I could do.'

'So you only knew Bernard through his father at first?'

'Aye. He was off at university around then, too. And his brother had emigrated to Australia. There was only the young lass left.'

'Esther?'

'Aye. How is she? Have you seen her?'

'Yes,' Banks said. 'She's well. Married. Lives in Leeds. Did you ever hear anything about her and Nicholas Collier?'

Fletcher frowned. 'No, I can't say as I did. Though I wouldn't put it past him. She were a nice lass, young Esther. I've often thought things might've worked out different if the others had stuck around, kept the family together, like.'

'You mean Bernard and Denny going away might have caused their father's problems?'

'Some of them, perhaps. Not all, mind you. But it costs money to hire men. If you've got a family, there might be more mouths to feed, but there's more hands to help, too.'

'Did you have any connection with Bernard other than his father? There can't have been much of an age difference between you.'

'Nay, I'm older than I look,' Fletcher said, and grinned. 'Like I said, we'd pass the time of day in the White Rose now and then. Him and his girlfriend were in there often enough.'

'Girlfriend? Who was that, Mr Fletcher?'

'The one who disappeared. Anne Ralston, her name was.'

Banks felt a tremor of excitement. 'She was Bernard Allen's girlfriend?'

'Aye. Childhood sweethearts. They grew up together. I don't think it was owt serious later, like, or he wouldn't have gone off to Canada and left her. But they were thick as thieves, them two – more like brother and sister, maybe, as they got older.'

'And after he'd gone, she took up with Stephen Collier?'

'Aye. Got a job at Collier Foods and, well . . . Stephen's got a way with the women.'

'Did Bernard Allen ever say anything about this?'

'Not in my hearing he didn't. You're thinking maybe he was jealous?'

'Could be.'

'Then the wrong one got himself killed, didn't he?'

Banks sighed. 'It always seems to look that way in this case. But if Allen thought Stephen Collier had harmed her, he might have been out for revenge.'

'Waited long enough, didn't he?' Fletcher said.

'I'll be frank with you, Mr Fletcher,' Banks said. 'We've no idea why Bernard Allen was murdered, none at all. At the moment I'm gathering as much information as I can. Most of it will probably turn out to be useless. It usually does. But right now there's no way of telling what's of value and what isn't. Can you think of any reason why someone in Swainshead would want him out of the way?'

Fletcher paused to think for a few moments, his dark eyebrows knitting together. 'No,' he said finally. 'It's nothing to do with the farming business, I'm sure of that. There's not enough money in it to make murder worthwhile. And there was no animosity between myself and the Allens. Like I said, I don't think there was bad feeling between Bernard and the Colliers, but I couldn't swear to it. I know he bated them a bit about being capitalist oppressors, but I don't think anyone took that seriously enough to kill for.'

'What was your impression of Bernard Allen?'

'I liked him. As I said, I didn't know him well, and I can't say I agreed with his politics – with him on one side and Nicholas on the other, it was hardly my idea of a peaceful evening's drinking. But he was bright, thoughtful, and he loved the land. He knew he wasn't cut out to be a farmer – few are – but he loved The Head.'

'When was the last time you saw him?'

'The evening before he left. We were all in the White Rose. He was getting quite maudlin about coming home. Said if only he could get a job, however little it paid, or maybe a private income, then he'd be back like a shot. Of course, Nicholas jumped on that one – a socialist wanting a private income!'

'Were there any serious arguments?'

'No. It was all playful. The only serious bit was Bernard's sentimentality. He really seemed to convince himself that he was coming back here to live. But he'd had a few too many, of course. Sam had to help him back to the house. I'm sorry I can't be more useful, Mr Banks. I'd like to, but I don't know anything. I had no reason to harm Bernard and, as far as I know, nor did any of the others. If there are motives, they're hidden from me.'

'Did he mention his divorce at all?'

'Oh aye,' Fletcher said grimly. 'I could sympathize with him over that.'

'Did he seem upset about it?'

'Of course. His wife had run off with another man. Wouldn't you be upset? I think that's what set him thinking about coming back home to stay. You get like that when you lose whatever it is that keeps you away.'

'Did Mr Allen know your wife?'

Fletcher's face hardened. 'What do you mean "know"? "Know" in the biblical sense? Are you suggesting there was something between them and I killed him in a fit of jealousy?'

'No,' said Banks, 'I'm simply trying to get a grasp on the web of relationships.'

Fletcher continued to eye him suspiciously. 'She didn't know him,' he said. 'Oh, I'm not saying their paths never crossed, that they wouldn't say hello if they passed one another in the street, but that's all.'

'Where is your wife?'

Fletcher looked at the picture. 'In Paris,' he said, his voice shaking with grief and anger. 'In Paris with that bastard she ran off with.'

The silence that followed weighed on them all. Finally, Banks gestured to Hatchley and they stood up to leave. 'I'm sorry if I upset you,' he said. 'It wasn't intentional, believe me, but sometimes in a murder investigation . . .'

Fletcher sighed. 'Aye, I know. You've got to ask. It's your job. No offence taken.' And he held out his square callused hand.

Driving down the fell side, Banks and Hatchley said very little. Banks had been impressed by Fletcher's solidity; he seemed a man with great integrity and strong foundations. But such a man, he knew, could kill when pushed too far. It was easier to push an earnest man too far than it was a more frivolous one. Although he was inclined to believe Fletcher, he nonetheless made a mental note of his reservations.

'Ideal place, isn't it?' Hatchley said, looking back at Fletcher's farm as they crossed the bridge.

'In a way,' Banks answered. 'A bit dour and spartan for my tastes, though.'

'I didn't mean that, sir.' Hatchley looked puzzled. 'I meant it's an ideal location for approaching the hanging valley unseen.'

Banks slowed down on the narrow road as Sam Greenock's Land Rover passed them going in the other direction. Sam waved half-heartedly as he drove by.

'Yes,' Banks said absently. 'Yes, I suppose it is. I'd just like to stop off at the Greenocks' before we go back to Eastvale. There's something I'd like to do. You use the radio and get on to Richmond. See if anything's come up.'

TWO

Katie flinched and backed towards the wall when she saw Banks appear in the doorway of the room she was cleaning.

'It's all right, Katie,' he said. 'I'm not going to hurt you. We've got to have a little talk, that's all.'

'Sam's out,' Katie said, clutching the yellow duster tightly over her breast.

'I know he is. I saw him drive off. It's you I want to talk to. Come on, Katie, stop playing games. You've been trying to avoid us ever since we got here. What is it? What are you afraid of?'

'I don't know what you're talking about.'

Banks sighed. 'Yes, you do.' He sat down on the corner of the bed. 'And I'm prepared to wait until you tell me.'

Now, as she stood cringing by the window, Banks

realized who she reminded him of: Hardy's Tess Durbeyfield. Physically, she resembled Nastassja Kinski, who had played Tess in the film version, but the similarity went deeper than that. Banks had a sense of Tess as a child in a woman's body, not fully aware of her own beauty and sexuality, or of the effect she might have on men. It wasn't entirely innocence, but it was close – a kind of innocent sensuality. He made a note to look up the description of Tess in the book when he got home.

'Look,' he went on, 'we can either talk here, or we can go to police headquarters in Eastvale. It's up to you. I don't really mind at all.'

'You can't do that,' Katie said, thrusting out her bottom lip. 'You can't just take a person away like that. I haven't done anything. I've got my work to finish.'

'So have I. You're withholding evidence, Katie. It's a crime.'

'I'm not withholding anything.'

'If you say so.' Banks stood up with exaggerated slowness. 'Let's go, then.'

Katie stepped back until she was flat against the wall. 'No! If you take me away Sam . . . Sam'll . . .'

'Come on, Katie,' Banks said, more gently, 'don't be silly.' He pointed to the chair. 'Sit down. Tell me about it.'

Katie flopped into the chair by the window and looked down at the floor. 'There's nothing to tell,' she muttered.

'Let me try and make it a bit easier for you,' Banks said. 'Judging by the way you behaved when we talked to you and Sam yesterday, I'd guess that something happened between you and Bernard Allen while he was staying here. Maybe it was personal. You might think it's your business and it has nothing to do with his death, but I'm the one to be the judge of that. Do you understand?'

Katie just stared at him.

'You'd known him a long time, hadn't you?'

'Since he came to Leeds. We lived next door.'

'You and Sam?'

'With his parents.'

'What happened to your own parents?'

'They died when I was a little girl. My grandmother brought me up.' Katie lowered her gaze down to her lap, wringing the yellow duster in her hands.

'Did you ever go out with Bernie Allen?'

She looked up sharply, and the blood ran to her cheeks. 'What do you mean? I'm married.'

'Well, something happened between you, that's clear enough. Why won't you tell me what it was?'

'I've told you,' Katie said. 'Nothing happened. We were friends, that's all.' She went back to twisting the duster on her lap. 'I'm thirsty.'

Banks brought her a glass of water from the washbasin.

'Were you lovers, Katie?' he asked. 'Did you sleep with Bernard Allen while he was staying here?'

'No!' Tears blurred Katie's clear brown eyes.

'All right.' Banks held up his hand. 'It's not important. I believe you.' He didn't, but he often found it useful to pretend he believed a lie. It was always clear from the teller's obvious relief that it had been a lie. Afterwards it was easier to get at the information that really mattered. And he had a feeling she was hiding something else.

'But you spent some time together, didn't you? Time alone, like friends do?'

Katie nodded.

'And you must have talked. What did you talk about?'

Katie shrugged. 'I don't know, just things. Life.'

'That's a broad subject. Anything in particular?'

She was chewing on her bottom lip now, and Banks could sense that she was on the verge of talking. He would have to tread carefully to avoid scaring her off again.

'It might be important,' he said. 'If he was a friend of yours, surely you want his killer caught?'

Katie looked at him as if the idea was completely new to her. 'Yes,' she said. 'Yes, of course I do.'

'Will you help me, then?'

'He talked about Canada, his life in Toronto. What it was like there.'

'What about it?'

'How wonderful and exciting it was.'

It was like drawing a confession out of a naughty child. 'Come on,' Banks prompted her. 'There was something special, wasn't there? You'd have no reason to hide any of this from me, and I know you're hiding something.'

'He told me in confidence,' she said. 'I wasn't to tell anyone. Sam'll kill me if he finds out.'

'Why?'

'He doesn't like me talking to people behind his back.'

'Look, Katie. Bernard is dead. Somebody murdered him. You can't keep a secret for a dead man, can you?'

'Life doesn't end with death.'

'Maybe not. But what he said might be important.'

There was a long pause while Katie seemed to struggle with her conscience; each phase of the skirmish flashed across her flawless complexion. Finally, she said, 'Annie was there. That's what he told me. Annie was in Toronto.'

'Annie?'

'Yes. Anne Ralston. She was a friend of Bernie's from years ago. She disappeared when we had all that trouble here five years back.'

'I've heard of her. What exactly did Bernard say?'

'Just that she was living in Toronto now. He'd heard from her about three years ago. She was in Vancouver then. They'd kept in touch, and now she'd moved.'

'Did he say anything else about her?'

Katie looked at him blankly. 'No. She just asked him not to go telling everyone in Swainshead that he'd seen her.'

'This is what Bernard told you?'

'Yes.'

'Why did he tell you, do you think, when Anne had told him not to tell anyone?'

'I . . . I . . . don't know,' Katie stammered. 'He trusted me. He was just talking about people leaving, finding a new life. He said she was happy there.'

'Were you talking about wanting a new life for yourself?'

'I don't know what you mean.'

Her words lacked conviction. Banks knew he was right. Katie had probably been telling Bernard Allen that she wanted to get away from Swainshead. Why she should want to leave he didn't know, but from what he'd seen and heard of Sam so far, she might have one good reason.

'Never mind,' Banks said. 'Did he say anything about coming home to stay?'

Katie seemed surprised. 'No. Why should he? He had a wonderful new life out there.'

'Did he tell you this on the morning he left or before?'

'Before. Just after he arrived.'

'And you were the only one he told?'

'Yes.'

'You're hesitating, Katie. Why?'

'I . . . I don't know. You're confusing me. You're making me nervous.'

123

'Were you the only one he told?'

'As far as I know, yes.'

'And who did you tell?'

'I didn't tell anyone.'

'You're lying, Katie.'

'I'm not. I—'

'Who did you tell? Sam?'

Katie pulled at the duster so hard it tore. 'All right, yes! I told Sam. He's my husband. Wives aren't supposed to keep secrets from their husbands, are they?'

'What did Sam say?'

'Nothing. He just seemed surprised, that's all.'

'Did he know Anne Ralston?'

'Not well. It was only about a year after we arrived that she disappeared. We met her with Bernie, and she was going out with Stephen, but Sam didn't know the Colliers as well then.'

'Are you sure you told no one else?'

'No one,' Katie whispered. 'I swear it.'

Banks believed her.

Sam Greenock, he reflected, was quite a one for passing on news, especially to his cronies in the White Rose, with whom he seemed intent on ingratiating himself. Socially, he was beneath them all. The Colliers were cocks of The Head, and Fletcher owned quite a bit of land. Stephen Collier, as Katie said, had been going out with Anne Ralston around the time she disappeared, which had also been coincidental with the murder of Raymond Addison, the London private detective. Somewhere, somehow, Sam Greenock was involved in it all.

What if Sam had told Stephen that Bernard Allen had been in touch with Anne? And what if she was in a position to tell Allen something incriminating about

Collier, something to do with the Addison murder? That would certainly give Stephen a motive. And if that was what had happened, to what extent was Sam Greenock an accessory? For the first time, there seemed to be the strong possibility of a link between the murders of Raymond Addison and Bernard Allen. This would certainly interest Superintendent Gristhorpe, who had withdrawn into his usual role because the two cases hadn't seemed connected.

'Thank you, Katie,' Banks said, walking to the door. 'You'd better keep our rooms for us. I think we'll be back this evening.'

Katie nodded wearily. Pale, slumped in the chair, she looked used and abused like a discarded mistress.

THREE

'Anne Ralston?' Gristhorpe repeated in disbelief. 'After all these years?'

He and Banks knelt beside the pile of stones. Usually when they worked on the wall together they hardly spoke, but today there was pressing police business to deal with. Sandra had taken Brian and Tracy down into Lyndgarth after lunch to see a local craft exhibition, so they were alone with the twittering larks and the cheeky wagtails on the valley side above the village.

'You can see how it changes things,' Banks said.

'I can indeed – if it had anything to do with Bernard Allen's murder.'

'It must have.'

'We don't even know that Anne Ralston's disappearance was connected with Addison's killing, for a start.'

'It's too much of a coincidence, surely?' Banks said. 'A private detective is killed and a local woman disappears on practically the same day. If it happened in London, or even in Eastvale, I'd be inclined to think there was no link, but in a small village like Swainshead . . .?'

'Aye,' said Gristhorpe. 'Put like that . . . But we need a lot more to go on. No, not that one; it's too flat.' Gristhorpe brushed aside the stone Banks had picked up.

'Sorry.' Banks searched the pile for something better. 'I'm working on the assumption that Anne Ralston knew something about Addison's murder, right?'

'Right. I'll go along with that just for the sake of argument.'

'If she did know something and disappeared without telling us, it means one of two things: either she was paid off, or she was scared for her own life.'

Gristhorpe nodded. 'Or she might have been protecting someone,' he added.

'But then there'd be no need to run.'

'Maybe she didn't trust herself to bear up under pressure. Who knows? Go on.'

'For five years nobody hears any more of her, then suddenly Bernard Allen turns up and tells Katie Greenock he's been seeing the Ralston woman in Toronto. The next thing we know, Allen's dead before he can get back there. Now, Katie said that Bernard had been told not to spread it around about him knowing Anne. Was she protecting him, or herself? Or both? We don't know. What we do know, though, is that she didn't want her whereabouts known. Allen tells Katie, anyway, and she tells her husband. I think we can safely assume that Sam Greenock told everyone else. Allen must have become a threat to someone because he'd met up with Anne Ralston, who might have known something about Addison's murder. Stephen Collier was closely associated with her so he looks like a good suspect, but there's no reason to concentrate on him alone. It could have been any of them – Fletcher, Nicholas, Sam Greenock, even Katie – they were all in Swainshead at the time both Addison and Allen were killed, and we've no idea what or who that private detective was after five years ago.'

'What about opportunity?'

'Same thing. Everybody knew the route Allen was taking out of Swainshead. He'd talked all about it in the White Rose the night before. And most of them also knew how attached he was to that valley. The killer could easily have hidden among the trees up there and watched for him.'

'All right,' Gristhorpe said, placing a through-stone. 'But what about their alibis?'

'We've only got Fletcher's word that he was at home. He could have got to the valley from the north without anyone knowing. He lives alone on the fell side and there are no other houses nearby. As for the Colliers, Stephen says he was at the office and Nicholas was at school. We haven't checked yet, but if Nicholas wasn't actually teaching a class and Stephen wasn't in a meeting, either of them could have slipped out for a while, or turned up later. It would have been easy for Nicholas, again approaching from the north, and Stephen could have got up from half a mile past Rawley Force. It's not much of a climb, and there's plenty of cover to hide the car off the Helmthorpe road. I had a look on my way over here.'

'The Greenocks?'

'Sam could have got there from the road too. He went to Eastvale for supplies, but the shopkeepers can't say exactly what time he got there. Carter's doesn't open till nine, anyway, and the chap in the newsagent's says Sam usually drops in at about eleven. That gives him plenty of time. He might have had another motive, too.'

Gristhorpe raised his bushy eyebrows.

'The woman denies it, but I got a strong impression that something went on between Katie Greenock and Bernard Allen.'

'And you think if Sam got wind of it . . .?'

'Yes.'

'What about Mrs Greenock?'

'She says she was at home cleaning, but all the guests would have gone out by then. Nobody could confirm that she stayed in.'

'Have you checked the Colliers' stories?'

'Sergeant Hatchley's doing it tomorrow morning. There's no one at the factory on a Sunday.'

'Well, maybe we'll be a bit clearer when we get all that sorted out.'

'I'm going back to Swainshead for another night. I'll want to talk to Stephen Collier again, for one.'

Gristhorpe nodded. 'Take it easy though, Alan. I've already had an earful from the DCC about your last visit.'

'He didn't waste any time, did he? Anyway, I could do with a bit of information on the Addison case and the Ralston woman's disappearance. How did the alibis check out?'

Gristhorpe put down the stone he was weighing in his hand and frowned. Banks lit a cigarette – at least smoking was allowed in the open, if not in the house. He looked at the sky and noticed it had clouded over very quickly. He could sniff rain in the air.

'Everyone said they were at home. We couldn't prove

otherwise. It was a cold dark February evening. We
pushed Stephen Collier as hard as we dared, but he had a
perfect alibi for the day of the girl's disappearance: he was
in Carlisle at a business meeting.'

'Was Walter Collier around in those days?'

'No. He was dead by then.'

'What was he like?'

'He was quite an impressive man. Complex. He had a
lot of power and influence in the dale, some of which has
carried over to the sons, as you've already found out.
Now, you know how I feel about privilege and such, but
you had to respect Walter; he never really abused his
position. He was proud, especially of the family and its
achievements, but he managed to be kind and considerate
without being condescending. He was also a regular
churchgoer, a religious man, but he liked the ladies and he
could drink most villagers under the table. Don't ask me
how he managed to square that with himself. It's rare for
a Dales farmer, especially one from a family as long-
established as the Colliers, to sell up. But Walter was a
man of vision. He saw what things were coming to, so he
shifted his interests to food processing and encouraged his
sons to get good educations rather than strong muscles.'

'What was he like as a father?'

'I'd imagine he was a bit of a tyrant,' Gristhorpe
answered, 'though I can't say for certain. Used to being
obeyed, getting his own way. They probably felt the back
of his hand more than once.'

Banks held out his palm and felt the first, hesitant drops
of rain. 'When Anne Ralston disappeared,' he asked, 'were
there no signs at all of what might have happened to her?'

'Nothing. There were a few clothes missing, that's all.'

'What about money, bank accounts?'

'She didn't have one. She got a wage packet every two weeks from Collier Foods. What she did with the cash, I've no idea. Maybe she hid it under the mattress.'

'But you didn't find any in the cottage?'

'Not a brass farthing.'

'So she could have packed a few things, a bit of money, and simply run off?'

'Yes. We never found out what happened to her, until now.' Gristhorpe stood up and scowled at the grey sky. A flock of rooks wheeled above the valley side. 'Better go inside.'

As they walked round to the side door, they saw Sandra and the children come hurrying up the drive with their coats thrown over their heads. Banks waved to them.

'It would be very interesting to have a chat with Anne Ralston, wouldn't it?' he said.

Gristhorpe looked at him and narrowed his eyes. 'Aye, it would. But I'm not sure the department would be able to justify the expense.'

'Still . . .'

'I'll see what I can do,' Gristhorpe said. Then Sandra, Brian and Tracy came racing into the house.

7

ONE

Katie finished her cleaning in a daze when Banks had gone, and she was so distracted she almost forgot to put the roast in on time. The Greenock Guest House always served a traditional Yorkshire Sunday dinner, both for guests and non-residents, at two o'clock. It was Sam's idea. Thank God he was in the pub, his usual Sunday lunch-time haunt, Katie thought. He'd be bending elbows with the wonderful Colliers.

Perhaps Sam needn't know what the policeman had made her tell. But the inspector would be sure to question him, she knew, and he would find out; he was bound to accuse her of betraying him.

With a start, she realized she was in room five, where the talk had taken place on the second morning of Bernie's stay. But it wasn't his words she thought of now. The rush of images almost overwhelmed her at first, but she forced herself to re-examine what had happened. Perhaps it hadn't been such a sin, after all? Of course it was, she told herself; it was a double sin, for she was a married woman. But it had happened, she couldn't deny that. The first time in all her married life.

That morning she had been cleaning the rooms as usual, when Bernie had come back to put on his walking boots. The sky had brightened, he said, and he had decided to go for a good long walk after all. They'd talked for as much time as she dared take off from her chores, then he had sat on the bed while she washed the windows. All the time she had been aware of him watching her. Finally, when she felt his arms around her waist, she told him no. She had her back to him and he bent to kiss her neck where the wisps of blonde hair were swept up and tied while she worked. She struggled, but he held her tightly and his hands found her breasts. She dropped the chamois and it fell in the bucket and splashed water on the carpet.

Why did she let him? She had always liked him, but why this? Why let him do what she hated most? She thought perhaps it was because he offered her a chance to escape, and that this was the price she would have to pay. He was gentler than Sam. His mouth moved over her shoulder and his hands slid down along her stomach and over her thighs. She didn't have the heart or the courage to put up a fight; men were so strong. Surely, she thought, it could do no harm as long as she didn't feel pleasure. She couldn't tell Sam. That would mean she'd have to lie, too. She would have to wash her mouth out with soap.

Then he said he loved her, that he'd always wanted her, as his hands unfastened her skirt. She struggled again, but less violently this time, and he backed her towards the bed. There, he finished undressing her. She was trembling, but so was he; even body language speaks ambiguously at times. She held on to the bedposts tightly as he bore down on her, and she knew he thought her groans were sounds of pleasure. Why did men want her like this? Why did they want to do these things to her?

He kissed her breasts and said he would take her back to Canada with him, and suddenly that seemed like the answer. She wanted to get away, she needed to. Swainshead and Sam were stifling her.

So she didn't struggle any more. Bernard talked of the vast prairie skies and of lakes as boundless as oceans as his hands caressed her still body. Yes, he would take her with him, he said; he had always wanted her. Urgently, he drew himself along the length of her body and entered her. She bit her tongue in loathing and self-disgust, and he looked into her eyes and smiled as she made little strangled cries that must have sounded like pleasure.

After, as they dressed, Katie had tried to hide the shame of her nakedness from his gaze. He had laughed and told her he found her modesty very appealing. She said he'd better go, that Sam would be back, and he reminded her about Canada.

'I'll send for you when I get back,' he promised. 'I'll find a place for us and I'll send for you. Anne's there, too. She wanted to get away, just like you. She's happy now.'

'Yes,' she had said, anxious to get rid of him. 'I'll come with you.' Then he had kissed her and left the room.

After that morning, they had hardly spoken to one another – mostly because Sam had been around or Katie had contrived to avoid Bernie – but he kept giving her meaningful glances whenever nobody was looking. She believed him. He would send for her.

Not any more. All for nothing. All gone. All she had left was the guilt. 'As ye sow, so shall ye reap,' her granny had always said. She had behaved wantonly, like that time she had swayed to the distant music. It didn't matter that she hadn't enjoyed it; now everything was a mess, Bernie was dead, and the police were all over the place. She was reaping what she had sown.

TWO

Stephen Collier was sitting in his spacious living room reading a thick leather-bound report when Banks and Hatchley called that evening. The French windows were open on to the patio and lawn, and the fountain played against a backdrop of drystone-walled fell side. A brief heavy shower had cleansed the landscape and in the gentle evening light the grass was lush and green, the limestone outcrops bright as marble.

Stephen seemed surprised and annoyed at a second visit from the police so close on the heels of the first, but he quickly regained his composure and offered drinks.

'I'll have a Scotch, please,' Banks said.

'Sergeant Hatchley?'

'Don't mind if I do, sir.' Hatchley glanced towards Banks, who nodded his permission. After all, he had spoiled the sergeant's weekend. Hatchley took out his notebook and settled in a corner with his drink.

'What can I do for you this time?' Stephen asked. 'Do you want to see my brother, too?'

'Not at the moment,' Banks said. 'I want to talk to you about Anne Ralston.'

Collier frowned. 'Anne Ralston? What about her? That was years ago.'

'I'd like to know what happened.'

'Aren't I entitled to know why?'

'Will you just bear with me for a while?'

'Very well.'

'As far as I know,' Banks began, 'she disappeared the day after the private detective, Raymond Addison, was killed. Am I right?'

'I wouldn't know when he was killed,' Stephen said. 'Though I do remember Superintendent Gristhorpe saying something about a post-mortem report.'

'But it was around that time she disappeared?'

'Yes.'

'And she was an employee of Collier Foods?'

'Yes. Your superintendent already knows all this. Please get to the point, Chief Inspector.' He tapped the book on his lap. 'I have an important report to study for a meeting in the morning.'

'I won't keep you long, sir,' Banks said, 'if you'll just answer my questions. Were you going out with Anne Ralston at the time of her disappearance?'

'Yes. You know I was. But I don't see—'

Banks held up his hand. 'Let me finish, please. Can you think of any reason why she should disappear?'

'None.'

'What do you think happened to her?'

Collier walked over to the cocktail cabinet and refilled his glass. He offered Banks and Hatchley cigarettes from a box on the glass-topped coffee table.

'I thought she might have gone off to see the world,' he answered. 'It was something she'd often talked about.'

'Didn't it worry you?'

'Didn't what worry me?'

'Her disappearance.'

'I must admit, in some of my darker moments I thought something might have happened to her – a wandering psychopath or something – especially with the Addison business. But I decided it wasn't so out of character for Anne to just up and go.'

'Weren't you bothered that she never got in touch with you? Or did she?'

Collier smiled. 'No, Chief Inspector, she didn't. And, yes, it was a bit of a blow to the ego at first. But I got used to it. It wasn't as if we were engaged or living together.'

'I noticed you mentioned a moment ago that you linked her disappearance with the Addison killing – a wandering psychopath. Did it occur to you to link the two events in any other way?'

'What do you mean?'

'Could Anne Ralston have had something to do with Addison's visit to Swainshead? He was a private detective, after all.'

'Yes, I know. But nobody here had any idea why he was in the area. If it was anything to do with Anne, she certainly kept quiet about it. Maybe he was just on holiday. I'm sure private eyes have holidays too.'

'Would she have been likely to tell you?'

'I don't know. I don't imagine she told me everything about her life. Ours was a casual relationship. I'd never have expected her to bare her soul.'

'Are you sure it wasn't more serious on her part?'

'Not at all. She'd been around.'

'And you?'

Stephen smiled. 'I wasn't new to the wily ways of the fair sex, no. Another drink?'

Hatchley passed his empty glass and Banks nodded. He lit a Silk Cut and looked out on to the lawn. Two sparrows were taking a bath in the fountain. There was plenty of room, but each defended its territory with an angry flapping of wings, splashing water all over the place. A shadow fell over the patio and Nicholas Collier popped his head round the French windows.

'Hello,' he said, stepping into the room. 'I thought I heard voices.'

'If you don't mind, sir . . .' Sergeant Hatchley stood up and blocked the entrance, a task for which he might have been specially designed.

Nicholas tilted his head back and looked down his long nose at Hatchley. 'What's going on?'

'I'm just having a little chat with your brother,' Banks said. 'You're perfectly at liberty to stay, but I'd be obliged if you'd refrain from interrupting.'

Nicholas raised his black eyebrows. He seemed to have forgotten his sulking, but he clearly wasn't used to being told what to do. For a moment, anger flashed in his eyes, then he simply nodded and sat by the windows.

'Look,' Stephen said, frowning at his brother and coming back with the drinks. 'Where on earth is all this leading? Anne Ralston is history now. I haven't seen or heard from her in five years. Quite frankly, it was embarrassing enough at the time having our relationship, such as it was, plastered all over the local papers. I wouldn't like to relive that.'

'You mean you didn't know?' Banks said, sipping his Scotch.

'Didn't know what?'

'About Anne Ralston.'

'Look here. If this is some kind of a game . . .'

Did he or didn't he? Banks couldn't be sure. Sam Greenock would know the answer to that – when he got home, and if he could be persuaded to talk.

'Anne's turned up again.'

'But . . . where?'

'Bernard Allen knew where she was. He told the Greenocks. Surely Sam told you?'

'No. No, I'd no idea. How is she? What happened?'

'I don't know all the details,' Banks said. 'Just that

she's alive and well and living in Canada. Are you sure nobody told you?'

'I've already said so, haven't I? This is a complete surprise to me. Though I was sure she'd turn up somewhere, some day.' He went over and poured himself another drink; his hand was shaking. Banks glanced sideways at Nicholas, who sat impassively in his chair. There was no way of telling what he knew or didn't know.

Banks and Hatchley finished their drinks and stood up.

'I'm sorry it came as such a shock, Mr Collier,' Banks said. 'I just thought you ought to know.'

'Yes, of course,' Stephen said. 'I'm very grateful to you. If you do hear anything else . . .'

'We'll let you know.'

'There is just one thing,' Stephen said, standing in the doorway. 'What has this to do with Bernard Allen's death? Do you see any connection?'

'I don't know, Mr Collier,' Banks said. 'I really don't know. It does seem like a bit of a coincidence though – Anne disappearing the day after Addison's killing, then turning up again, so to speak, around the time of Allen's murder. It makes you wonder, doesn't it?'

And they walked back over the bridge, where the three men stood like shadows in the soft light. On impulse, Banks sent Hatchley on ahead and stopped.

'Do you remember Anne Ralston?' he asked the gnarled spokesman.

As was his custom, the man spat in the fledgling River Swain before answering. 'Aye. Allus in and out o' there.' He nodded over at the Collier house.

'Have you seen her at all over the last few years?'

'Nay. She flitted.'

'And she hasn't been back?'

He shook his head.

'Have you seen either Mr or Mrs Greenock go over to the Collier house this afternoon?'

'Aye,' the man said. 'Sam Greenock went over about three o'clock.'

'To see Stephen or Nicholas?'

'It were Mr Stephen's door he knocked on.'

'And did Stephen Collier answer it?'

The man scowled. 'Aye, course he did.'

'How long was Mr Greenock in there?'

'Baht ten minutes.'

'Thank you,' Banks said, heading for the guest house. 'Thank you very much.'

He heard his reluctant informant hack into the beck again, then the murmur of their voices rose up behind him.

THREE

Katie Greenock hurried away when she saw Banks coming, but he couldn't help noticing that she moved with some difficulty.

'Katie!' he called, hurrying down the hall after her and grasping her elbow.

She spun round and faced him, one hand over her stomach. Her face was white and tense with suppressed pain. 'What do you want?' she asked angrily. 'Haven't you caused enough trouble?'

'There'll be a lot more before this business is over, Katie. I'm sorry, but there it is. You'll just have to learn to face the world. Anyway, that's not why I called you. What's wrong? You look ill.'

'Nothing's wrong.'

'You're white as a ghost. And what's wrong with your stomach? Does it ache?'

'What do you care?' she asked, breaking away.

'Is it Sam? Has he hurt you?'

'I don't know what you mean. I've got a tummy ache, that's all.'

'Did you tell Sam you'd told me about Anne?'

'I had to, didn't I? He knew there was something wrong. I'm not good at hiding things.'

'And what did he do, beat it out of you?'

'I told you, I've just got a tummy ache. Leave me alone, I feel sick.'

'Where is he?'

She gestured with her head. 'In back.'

'Will you stay out here for a few minutes, Katie, while I talk to him?'

Katie nodded and edged into the dining room.

Banks walked down the hall and knocked on the door that separated the Greenocks' part of the house from the rest. Sam let him in.

'Chief Inspector Banks,' he said. 'What a surprise. I hope nothing's wrong?'

'Has your wife told you we had a little talk earlier today?'

Greenock sat down. 'Well, yes. She did right, too. I'm her husband.'

'Why didn't you tell me about the Ralston woman earlier, as soon as we found out it was Bernard Allen feeding the maggots up in the hanging valley? This is the second time you've obstructed our investigation, and I'm having serious thoughts about taking you in.'

'Now hold on a minute.' Sam stood up again and puffed

out his chest. 'You can't come round here making accusations like that.'

'She said she told you that Bernard had met up with Anne Ralston in Canada.'

'So?'

'So you should have told me.'

'You never asked.'

Banks glared at him.

'I didn't think it was relevant. Dammit, Chief Inspector, the woman's been gone for five years.'

'You know bloody well how important she is. She's important enough for you to dash out and tell Stephen Collier that Katie had told me what Bernie said. What's going on, Greenock? Just what is your involvement in all this?'

'Nothing,' Sam said. 'There's nothing going on. I don't know what you're talking about.'

'But you did go over to Stephen Collier's this afternoon?'

'So what? We're friends. I dropped in for a drink.'

'Did you also dash over a few weeks ago and tell him what Bernie said about Anne Ralston turning up?'

'I didn't tell anyone.'

'I think you did. I also think you told him this afternoon that your wife had let the cat out of the bag to me about Anne Ralston. Didn't you?'

'I did no such thing. And you can't prove it either.'

'I will prove it,' Banks said. 'Believe me, I will. And when I do, your feet won't touch the ground.'

'You don't scare me,' Sam said.

Banks drew closer and Greenock backed towards the wall. They were both about the same size, though Sam was heavier.

'I don't?' Banks said. 'Well, I bloody well should. Where I come from, we don't always do things by the book. Do you know what I mean?' It was Hatchley's line, Banks knew, but it wasn't as if he was intimidating some scared kid. Sam was a villain, and Banks knew it. His dark eyes glittered with pent-up energy and Sam flinched as he felt his shoulder blades make contact with the wall.

'Leave me alone!' Sam shouted. 'I'll bloody report you, I will.'

Banks sneered. 'That's a laugh.' Then he backed away. 'Keep out of my sight, Greenock,' he said. 'If I want you, I'll know which rock to look under. And when I do, I'll have proof. And if I see or hear any more evidence – even the merest hint – that you've been hurting your wife again, I'll make you bloody sorry you were ever born.'

FOUR

'Will there be anything else?' the waitress asked, clearing away the empty plate.

'What? Oh, yes. Yes. Another cup of tea, please.' Katie Greenock had to pull herself back from a very long way. It would be her third cup but why not? Let it simply be another part of her little rebellion.

She sat at a table with a red-checked cloth – very clean, she noticed – by the window of the Golden Grill in Eastvale. The narrow street outside was busy with pedestrians, even in the thin drizzle, and almost directly opposite her was the whitewashed building with the black beams and the incongruous white-on-blue sign over the entrance: POLICE.

It was early Monday afternoon, and she didn't know

what she was doing in Eastvale. Already she was beginning to feel guilty. It was simply a minor gesture, she tried
to convince herself, but her conscience invested it with the
magnitude of Satan's revolt.

That morning, at about eleven o'clock, she had felt so
claustrophobic cleaning the rooms that she just had to get
out – not only out of the house, but out of Swainshead
itself for a while. Walking aimlessly down the street, she
had met Beryl Vickers, a neighbour she occasionally talked
gardening with, and accepted her offer of a lift into
Eastvale for a morning's shopping. Beryl was visiting her
sister there, so Katie was left free to wander by herself for
a few hours. After buying some lamb chops and broccoli
at the indoor market for that evening's dinner, she had
found the Golden Grill and decided to rest her feet.

She had only been sitting there for fifteen minutes when
she saw three men come out of the pub next door and
hurry through the rain back into the police station. Two of
them she recognized – the lean dark inspector and his fair
heavy sergeant – but the young athletic-looking one with
the droopy moustache and the curious loping walk was
new to her. For a moment, she thought they were sure
to glance over their shoulders and see her through the
window, so she covered the side of her face with her hand.
They didn't even look.

As soon as she saw the inspector, she felt again the
bruises that Sam had inflicted on her the previous
afternoon. She knew it wasn't the policeman's fault – in
fact, he seemed like a kind man – but she couldn't help the
association any more than she could help feeling one
between room five and what she had let Bernie do to her.

'What's wrong with you?' Sam had asked when he
came home.

Katie had tried to hide her red-rimmed eyes from him, but he grasped her chin between his thumb and forefinger and asked her again. That was when she told him the police had been back and the inspector had interrogated her so hard she couldn't hide it from him any more.

Sam had hit the roof.

'But it's not that important,' Katie protested. 'It can't be!'

'That's not for you to say,' Sam argued. He threw up his hands. 'You stupid bloody bitch, have you any idea what trouble you might have caused?'

Though she was scared, Katie still felt defiant. 'What do you mean, trouble?' she asked, her lower lip trembling. 'Trouble for who?'

'For everyone, that's for who.'

'For your precious Colliers, I'll bet.' As she said it, her image was of Nicholas, not Stephen.

And that was when Sam hit her the first time, a short sharp blow to the stomach. She doubled up in pain, and when she was able to stand again he thumped her left breast. That hurt even more. She collapsed on the sofa and Sam stood over her. His face was red and he was breathing oddly, in short gasps that seemed to catch in his throat. 'If we make something of ourselves in this place,' he said, 'it won't be any thanks to you.'

He didn't hit her any more. He knew when enough was enough. But later that night, in bed, the same cruel hands grasped the same wounded breast. He pulled her roughly to him, and there was nothing she could do about it. Katie shuddered, trying to shake off the memory.

'Will that be all?' the waitress asked, standing over her again.

'Oh, yes. Yes, thank you,' Katie said, paying the bill.

Awkwardly, aware of the ache in her breast and the Black Forest gateau sitting uneasily in her sore stomach, she made her way out into the street. She had one more hour of freedom to wander in the rain before meeting Beryl near the bus station at two thirty. Then she would have to go home and face the music.

FIVE

After a pub lunch in the Queen's Arms and a chat with Hatchley and Richmond about the case, Banks was no further ahead. Back in his office, he sat down, sent for some coffee and put his feet up on the desk to think things out. When PC Craig arrived with the coffee – looking very put out, no doubt because Susan Gay had coerced him into carrying it up – Banks lit a Silk Cut and went over what he'd got.

Richmond had discovered that Les Haines, Bernie Allen's brother-in-law, had done a brief stretch in Armley Prison for receiving stolen goods (i.e. two boxes of Sony E-120 video cassette tapes). It was his second offence, hot on the heels of an assault charge against a man in an alley outside a Leeds bar. But Haines had been at work on the day of Allen's murder, so he would have had no opportunity to get to Swainshead and back, even if there had been some obscure family motive. Besides, as Banks well knew, just because a man has a record as a petty thief, it doesn't make him a murderer. Esther had been at home with the kids, as usual, and Banks could hardly visualize her trailing them up to the hanging valley and knocking off her brother.

Most interesting of all were the Colliers' alibis, or lack

of them. Nicholas never taught classes on Friday mornings, but he usually went in anyway and used the time for paperwork. On the Friday in question, however, the headmaster's administrative assistant remembered seeing him arrive late, at around eleven o'clock. This was nothing unusual – it had happened often enough before – but it did leave him without a valid alibi.

Stephen Collier, it turned out, had no meetings scheduled for that day, again quite normal in itself, and nobody could remember whether he had been in or not. Work days, the world-weary secretary explained to Sergeant Hatchley, are so much the same that most office workers have difficulty remembering one from another. Mr Collier was often off the premises anyway, and the people who actually ran the business never saw much of him.

PC Weaver from Helmthorpe, who had been questioning people in Swainshead that morning, reported that nobody remembered seeing Bernard Allen out there on the morning in question, let alone noticed anyone follow him.

At about two o'clock, Richmond popped his head round the door. He'd been using the computer to check with various business agencies and immigration offices, but so far he'd found no one in Swainshead with Canadian connections. Except for Stephen Collier, who dealt with a Montreal-based food products corporation.

'What's a food product, do you think?' Banks asked Richmond.

'I wouldn't know, sir. Something that's not real food, I'd imagine.'

'And I thought he was trading Wensleydale cheese for maple syrup. That reminds me: what time is it in Toronto?'

Richmond looked at his watch. 'It'll be about nine in the morning.'

'I'd better phone the Mounties.'

'Er . . . they won't be Mounties, sir. Not in Toronto.' Richmond stroked his moustache.

'Oh? What will they be?'

'The Toronto Metropolitan Police, sir. The RCMP's federal. These days they mostly do undercover work and police the more remote areas.'

Banks grinned. 'Well, you learn something new every day.'

When Richmond had left, he lit a cigarette and picked up the phone. There was a lot of messing about with the switchboard, but after a few minutes of clicks and whirrs, the phone started ringing at the other end. It wasn't the harsh and insistent sound of an English telephone though; the rings were longer, as were the pauses between them.

When someone finally answered, it took Banks a while to explain who he was and what he wanted. After a few more clicks, he finally got through to the right man.

'Chief Inspector Banks? Staff Sergeant Gregson here. And how's the old country?'

'Fine,' said Banks, a little perplexed by the question.

'My father was a Brit,' Gregson went on. 'Came from Derbyshire.' He pronounced the e as in clergy, and shire came out as sheer. 'Do you know it?' he asked.

'Oh, yes. It's just down the road.'

'Small country.'

'Right.'

Gregson cleared his throat and Banks could hear papers rustling three thousand miles away. 'I can't say we've got any good news for you,' the Canadian said. 'We've had a look around Allen's apartment, but we didn't find anything unusual.'

'Was there an address book?'

'Address book . . . let me see . . .' More paper rustled. 'No. No address book. No diary.'

'Damn. He must have taken them with him.'

'Makes sense, doesn't it? If he was going on vacation he'd be sure to want to send pretty postcards to all his buddies back home.'

'What about his friends? Have you seen any of them?'

'We talked to his colleagues at work. There's not many of them around. College finishes in early May, so teachers are pretty thin on the ground at this time of year. Nice work if you can get it, eh? Now they're all off swimming in the lake and sunning themselves on the deck up at their fancy summer cottages in Muskoka.'

'Is that like a villa in Majorca?'

'Huh?'

'Never mind. What did they have to say?'

'Said he was a bit aloof, stand-offish. Course, a lot of Brits over here are like that. They think Canada's still part of the Empire, so they come on like someone out of *The Jewel in the Crown*.'

'Did you find his ex-wife?'

'Yup. She's been in Calgary for the past six months, so you can count her out.'

'Apparently, there was a lover,' Banks told him. 'Someone at the college. That's why they got divorced.'

'Have you got a name?'

'Sorry.'

Gregson sighed. 'I'd like to help you, Chief Inspector, I really would,' he said, 'but we can't spare the men to go tracking down some guy who ran off with Allen's wife. We just don't have the manpower.'

'No, of course not.'

'Besides, people don't usually steal a man's wife and then kill him.'

'They might if he was causing them problems. But you're right, it's not likely. Did he have any girlfriends?'

'As I said, his colleagues thought he was a bit stuck-up. One of them even thought he was gay, but I wouldn't pay much mind to that. Sometimes, with their accents and mannerisms and all, Brits do seem a bit that way to us North Americans.'

'Yes,' Banks said, gritting his teeth. 'I think that just about covers it all. I can see now why they say you always get your man.' And he hung up. Nothing. Still nothing. He obviously couldn't expect any help from across the Atlantic.

Still feeling a residue of irrational anger at Gregson's sarcasm, he walked over to the window and lit a cigarette. The drizzle had turned into steady rain now and the square below was bright with open umbrellas. As he gazed down on the scene, one woman caught his eye. She walked in a daze, as if she wasn't sure where she was heading. She looked soaked to the skin, too; her hair was plastered to her head and the thin white blouse she wore was moulded to her form so that the outline of her brassiere stood out in clear relief. It took Banks a few moments to recognize Katie Greenock.

He grabbed his raincoat and made a move to go down and make sure she was all right, but when he looked out for her one last time, she was nowhere in sight. She had disappeared like a phantom. There was no sense in searching the town for her just because she was walking in the rain without an umbrella. Still, he was strangely disturbed by the vision. It worried him. For the rest of the wet afternoon he felt haunted by that slight and sensuous figure staring into an inner distance, walking in the rain.

PART TWO:

THE THOUSAND-DOLLAR CURE

8

ONE

The powerful jet engines roared and Banks felt himself pushed back in his seat. It was his first time in a jumbo. The plane lumbered along the runway at Manchester International Airport, fixtures and fittings shaking and rattling, as if defying anyone to believe that a machine of such bulk could fly. But it did. Soon, Lancashire was a chequerboard of wet fields, then it was lost completely under the clouds. The NO SMOKING sign went off and Banks lit up.

In a few moments, the blue-uniformed stewardess with her shocking pink lipstick and impossibly white teeth – the same one who had managed to put such drama into the routine demonstration of the use of the life jacket – came around with more boiled sweets and personal headphones in plastic bags. Banks took a set, as he knew there would be a film later on, but he gave the designer music a miss and took out his own Walkman. Soon the plane was over Ireland, an occasional flash of green between the clouds, the Beatles were singing 'Dear Prudence', and all was well with the world.

Banks ordered Scotch on the rocks when the trolley came around and relaxed with his miniature Johnnie Walker Red.

Closing his eyes, he settled back to reconsider the events that had led to his present unnatural position – about 35,000 feet above the Atlantic Ocean, hurtling at a speed of roughly 600 miles an hour towards a strange continent.

It was Saturday, 3 July, almost a month since the Bernard Allen case had stalled. Banks had visited Swainshead once or twice and found things relatively quiet. Stephen and Nicholas Collier had remained polite in their arrogant way; Sam Greenock had been surly, as usual; Katie Greenock still seemed troubled and distracted; and John Fletcher had expressed passing interest in the progress of the case.

The problem was that there really wasn't a case any more. Enquiries had turned up neither new witnesses nor motives. A number of people had had the opportunity to kill Bernard Allen, but no one had a clear reason. As long as the suspects stuck to their stories, it didn't matter whether they were lying or telling the truth; there was no solid evidence to break the case. That was why it was vital for Banks to find Anne Ralston – she was the link between the Addison and Allen murders – and he had convinced Gristhorpe he could do it in a week.

'How?' the superintendent had asked. 'Toronto's a strange city to you. A big one, too.'

'Where would you head if you were an Englishman living abroad?'

Gristhorpe rubbed his chin. 'I'd seek out the expatriate community, I suppose. The club. I'd want to be among my own.'

'Right. So, given we're not dealing with the gentry, I'd expect Allen to hang around the English-style pubs. Every big city has them. His brother-in-law, Les Haines, told me Allen liked his ale and had found a pub where he could get imported British beer. There can't be all that many of them in Toronto.'

'But it's Anne Ralston we're looking for, remember that.'

'I know. I'm just assuming that if Allen was a bit stand-offish with his mates at work, he had a crowd of fellow émigrés he hung around with in his spare time. The odds are they'd meet up in a pub and stand at the bar quaffing pints. They might know the Ralston woman.'

'So you want to go on a pub crawl of Toronto?'

'Looks like it, doesn't it?'

'Better not tell Jim Hatchley or you'll get nowt out of him for a month or more. Why can't you get the Toronto police to find her?'

'For a start, I got the impression on the phone that they didn't have time or didn't give a damn, or both. And anyway, they wouldn't know how to question her, what to ask. Someone would have to brief them on two murder investigations, the sociology of the Yorkshire village, the history of—'

Gristhorpe held up his hand. 'All right, all right, I get the point.'

'And I think they'd scare her off, too,' Banks added. 'She was nervous enough about what she knew to warn Allen not to spread it around, so if she thinks the police are after her, the odds are she'll scarper.'

'Have you considered that she might not be using her own name?'

'Yes. But I've got her photograph from our missing persons files – it's a bit old, but it's all we've got – and I think I know where to look. Being English myself gives me an advantage in that kind of environment, too. Do you think it makes sense?'

'It's all a bit iffy, but yes, yes I do, on the whole. If you can track down Allen's drinking companions, there's a good chance he'll have told them about Anne Ralston. She might even drop in at his local herself from time to time, if she's the kind that likes to be among her own.'

'So you'll see what you can do about getting me over there?'

Gristhorpe nodded. 'Aye. I'll see what I can do.'

About a week later, on a Thursday morning, the superintendent had asked Banks to come to his office. Banks stubbed out his cigarette and carried his full coffee mug carefully along the corridor. As usual, Gristhorpe's door was slightly ajar. Banks nudged it open with his shoulder and entered the cosy book-lined room. He took his usual seat and put his coffee on the desk in front of him.

Gristhorpe pushed a long envelope over the blotter.

'You've done it?'

'Open it.'

Inside was a return ticket on a charter flight from Manchester to Toronto.

'There's an important international conference on policing the inner city in London, Ontario. I thought you ought to go.'

'But this ticket's for Toronto.'

'Aye, well, there isn't an international airport in London.'

'And Eastvale doesn't have an inner city.'

Gristhorpe scratched his hooked nose. 'We might have, one day. We did have a riot a few months ago, didn't we? It pays to be prepared.'

'Will you be expecting a report?'

'Oh, a brief verbal account will do.'

Banks grinned.

'There's one catch, though.'

'Oh?'

'Money. All I could scrounge was the ticket and a bit of loose change for meals. You'll have to supply most of your own pocket money.'

'That's all right. I'm not likely to be spending a fortune. What about accommodation, though?'

'You'll be staying with my nephew – at least, you can stay in his apartment. He's off to Banff or some such place for the summer. Anyway, I've been in touch and he says he'll be happy to meet you at the airport. I described you to him, so just stand around and look lost. He's rather a lanky lad, as I remember. His hair's a bit too long and he wears those silly little glasses – granny glasses, I think they're called. He's a nice enough lad – graduate student, organic chemistry or some such thing. He says he lives downtown, whatever that means. You told me a week, Alan. I'm depending on you.'

'I'll do my best,' Banks said, pocketing the ticket.

'Find Anne Ralston and discover what she knows. I don't care how you do it, outside torture. And for Christ's sake, keep away from the local police. They wouldn't appreciate your trespassing on their patch. You're a tourist, remember that.'

'I've been wondering why you're sending me,' Banks said. 'You're very much concerned with this case yourself, especially the connection with the Addison murder. Why don't you go?'

'I would,' Gristhorpe said slowly. 'Believe me, I would.' He looked sideways towards the open window. 'I did my National Service in the RAF. I'd always hero-worshipped fighter pilots in the war and I suppose, in my folly, I wanted to be just like them. First time up one of the engines caught fire. If the pilot hadn't been so damn good we'd have both been dead. Even so . . . I've never fancied the idea since.'

'I can't say I blame you,' Banks said. 'I'll find her, don't worry. At least I've an idea where to look.'

And that was that. Sandra and the children were excited and, of course, disappointed that they couldn't go with him. Sergeant Hatchley acted as if Banks had been given a free holiday in an exotic place. And now here he was, high above the Atlantic Ocean, the pink lips and white teeth leaning over him with a tray of food.

Banks took off his headphones and arranged the tray in front of him. The main course appeared to be a small shrivelled chicken leg with pale wrinkled skin, accompanied by tiny potatoes and carrots covered in gravy. On further inspection, Banks discovered that one half of the meal was piping hot and the other still frozen solid. He called the attendant, who apologized profusely and took it away. When she delivered it again, the frozen side was warm and the other overcooked. Banks took a few mouthfuls and gave up in disgust. He also felt no inclination to investigate the mound of jelly-like substance with a swirl of cream on its top, or the limp lettuce leaves that passed for a salad. Instead, he turned to his cheese and biscuits which, being wrapped in cellophane, were at least fresh, and washed them down with a small plastic bottle of harsh red wine.

Feeling the onset of heartburn, Banks declined the offer of coffee and lit a cigarette. After the trays had been cleared, more drinks came. They really were very generous, Banks thought, and wondered what havoc a plane full of drunks might wreak – especially if the booze ran out. But it didn't. He was kept well supplied with Johnnie Walker Red – a kind of sedation, he supposed, insurance against restless and troublesome passengers – and soon people were asked to pull down their blinds against the blazing sunlight in preparation for the movie. This turned out to be a dreadful cops-and-robbers affair full of car chases and shoot-outs in shopping precincts. After about ten minutes, Banks put his headset aside, closed his eyes and went over in his mind the questions he wanted to ask Anne Ralston. The jet engines were humming, the Scotch warmed his veins, and soon he fell into a deep sleep. The last thing he remembered was the crackly voice of the pilot saying they were soon going to reach the tip of Newfoundland and would then fly along the St Lawrence River.

TWO

While Banks was asleep somewhere over Quebec City, Detective Superintendent Gristhorpe sat hunched over a pint of Theakston's bitter and a veal and egg pie in the Queen's Arms, waiting for Sergeant Hatchley.

Frowning, he looked at his watch. He'd told Hatchley to arrive no later than seven thirty. He glanced out of the window at the market square, but saw no sign of the sergeant. It was still raining. That very morning the clouds had closed in again, draining the valley sides of their lush greens and flattening the majestic perspective of fells and moors.

At last Hatchley burst in and looked anxiously around for the superintendent. His hair was slicked down by the rain, emphasizing the bullet shape of his head, and the shoulders of his beige trench coat were splotched dark with wet patches.

'Sorry, sir,' he apologized, sitting opposite Gristhorpe. 'The damn weather's slowing down traffic all along the dale.'

Gristhorpe could smell the beer on his breath and guessed that he'd probably stopped for a quick one in Helmthorpe on his way, or maybe he had even made a minor diversion to the Black Sheep in Relton, where the landlord brewed his own prize-winning beer on the premises. He said nothing though. Without Banks around, Hatchley and Richmond were all he had, and he had no wish to alienate the sergeant before putting his plan into action.

Gristhorpe accepted Hatchley's offer of another pint and leaned back in his seat to avoid the drift of smoke when the sergeant lit a cigarette.

'Did you tell them?' Gristhorpe asked.

'Aye, sir. Found them all in the White Rose.'

'I hope you weren't too obvious.'

Hatchley looked offended. 'No, sir. I did it just like you said. When Freddie Metcalfe started probing and prodding about why I was there, I just told him it was a few loose ends I had to tie up, that's all.'

'And then?'

'Ah, well. Then, sir, I got myself invited over to the table. It was all very casual, like, chatting about the cricket and the local markets as if we was old mates. Then Sam Greenock asked me where my boss was.'

'What did you say?'

'Just what you told me, sir. I said he'd gone off to Toronto to talk to Anne Ralston.'

'And?'

'And what, sir?'

'What happened next, man? How did they react?'

Hatchley took a long pull at his beer and wiped his lips with the back of his hairy hand. 'Oh, they just looked at one another and raised their eyebrows a bit.'

'Can you be a bit more specific, Sergeant? What did Sam Greenock say?'

'He didn't really say anything. Seemed excited to hear the news. I got the impression it made him a bit angry. And Stephen Collier went distinctly pale. That poncy brother of his just looked down his nose like I was something the cat dragged in.'

'Who else was there?'

'Only John Fletcher.'

'Did he react in any way?'

Hatchley scratched his ear. 'I'd say he got a bit tight-lipped. You wouldn't really say he reacted, but it was as if it rang a bell somewhere and sent him off in his own world. More puzzled and worried than anything else.'

Gristhorpe thought over the information and filed it away in his mind. 'Good work, Sergeant,' he said finally. 'You did well.'

Hatchley nodded and started casually rocking his empty pint glass on the table. 'What now, sir?' he asked.

'We keep an eye on them. Tomorrow I'm going to send DC Richmond to stay at the Greenock Guest House for a few days. I don't think his face is well known in Swainshead.' Gristhorpe turned up his nose and leaned forward to grind out Hatchley's cigarette butt, which still smouldered in the ashtray. 'We keep an eye on them,' he repeated. 'And we watch very carefully for one of them to make a slip or try and make a run for it. All right, Sergeant. You don't have to break the bloody glass on the table. I know it's my round. Same again?'

THREE

Somewhere, with maddening metronomic regularity, a bell was ringing. Banks rubbed his eyes and saw the seatbelt sign was lit up. The NO SMOKING sign was still out, so he lit a cigarette immediately to clear his head. Looking out of the window, he saw a vast urban area below. It was too far down to distinguish details, but he could make out the grid system of roads and fancied he could see cars flash in the sun.

The attendant said something over the PA system about a final descent, and passengers were then asked to extinguish their cigarettes. Banks's ears felt funny. He swallowed and yawned to clear them, and the noise of the plane roared in again. All the way down he had to keep repeating the process every few seconds.

The plane banked to the left and now individual buildings and moving vehicles stood out quite clearly. After a long turn, a great expanse of water came into sight on the right and a cluster of tall buildings appeared on the waterside. The plane was dropping quickly now, and within moments it touched the runway smoothly. The loud retro-jets kicked in. They felt like ropes tied to the back of the plane, dragging it to a halt. Several nervous passengers applauded.

After some delay, the doors slid open and the slow line of people left the aircraft, running a gauntlet of fixed smiles from the attendants. Banks negotiated the stairs and corridors, then found himself in a long queue at Immigration. After that, there was another wait until the baggage came round on the carousel. Clutching his small suitcase, duty-free Scotch and cigarettes, he walked past the customs officers, who paid him no attention, and out into the throng of people waiting to welcome friends and relatives. As Gristhorpe suggested, he stood to one side and looked lost. It was easy.

Soon he noticed an Adam's apple the size of a tennis ball stuck in a long skinny neck below a head covered with long brown hair making its way through the crowd. As the head also wore a pair of ridiculously old-fashioned granny glasses, Banks risked a wave of recognition.

'Gerry Webb,' the man said, shaking hands. 'Are you Chief Inspector Banks?'

'Yes. Just call me Alan. I'm not here officially.'

'I'll bet,' Gerry said. 'Come on, let's get out of here.'

They pushed their way through the crowds of relatives embracing long-lost children or parents, and took a lift to the multi-storey car park.

'This is it,' Gerry said, pointing proudly to a saffron Volkswagen bug. 'I call her Sneezy because she's a bit of a dwarf compared to most of the cars here, and she makes a funny noise when I try to start her in the mornings, especially during winter. Still, she gets me around.' He patted Sneezy on the bonnet and opened the boot at the front. Case and duty-free securely stored, Banks got in the passenger door after a false start on the left.

'It always happens when people visit from England,' Gerry said, laughing. 'Without fail. Just wait until you try and cross the road.'

The first thing Banks noticed as Gerry drove out on to the expressway were the huge cars and the stifling heat. It was like trying to breathe at the bottom of a warm bath. In no time, his shirt was stuck to his skin. He took off his jacket and tossed it on the back seat. Even the draught through the open window was hot and wet.

'You've come in the middle of a heatwave, I'm afraid,' Gerry explained. 'It's been between thirty-three and thirty-six degrees for the past three days now. Above ninety per cent humidity, too.'

'What's a hundred like?'

'Funny, that,' Gerry said. 'We never get a hundred. Not even during a thunderstorm. Summer can be a real bitch here. Toronto's a city of extremes as far as climate is concerned. In winter it's bloody cold, real brass monkey weather, and in summer it's so hot and humid it's unbearable, as you can tell. Pollution count goes way up, too.'

'What about spring?'

'We don't have one. Just a lot of rain and then the sun. Fall's the best. September. October. Warmish days, cool evenings. Beautiful.' He glanced sideways at Banks. 'I suppose you were expecting icicles and snowmen?'

'Not exactly. But I didn't expect the heat to be this bad.'

'You should see the Americans,' Gerry said. 'I lived in Windsor for a while when I was doing my M.Sc., and I worked for customs during summer. They'd come over the border from the Detroit suburbs in the middle of July with skis on top of their cars and fur coats on the back seats. What a laugh that was. Americans know bugger all about Canada.'

'I can't say I know much, myself,' Banks admitted.

'Worry not. Keep your eyes and ears open and all will be revealed.' Gerry had an odd accent, part Yorkshire and part North American, with a mixed vocabulary to match.

They swung eastwards around a bay. For a moment, Banks thought they were on the wrong side of the road. He tensed and the adrenalin prickled in his veins. Then, again, he realized he was in Canada.

On the right was Lake Ontario, a ruffled blue sheet with millions of diamonds dancing on it. The white triangular sails of yachts leaned at sharp angles. There seemed to be at least a cooler breeze coming from the water and Banks envied the idle rich who could spend their days sailing like that.

'Those are the Islands over there,' Gerry said, pointing towards a low hazy blur of green. 'They're just a long sandbar really, but everyone calls them islands. People live on the far ones, Ward's and Algonquin, but the politicians want to chuck them off and make a heliport or a mini golf course.'

'That sounds typical,' Banks said, recalling the various schemes for developing adventure playgrounds and safari parks in the Dales.

'A lot of trouble over it,' Gerry said. 'At first, the islanders even got themselves a home guard organized – hard hats, the lot. They were prepared to fight off an invasion.'

'What happened?'

'It's still going on really. Oh, various bright sparks come up with ideas for long-term leases and whatnot, but there's always trouble brewing. It's jealousy, I think. Most of the people who live there now are academics or artists and a lot of people stuck in the city envy them their lives. They think only the filthy rich ought to be able to afford such a pleasant environment.'

'What about you?'

'I don't envy anyone who survives winter after winter out there in not much more than a wooden shack. Look.' He pointed ahead.

In front of them a cluster of tall buildings shimmered in the heat like a dot matrix block graph. A few were black, others white, and some even reflected the deep gold of the sun. Close to the lake, dominating them all, was a tapering tower with a bulbous head just below its long needle-point summit. It was a phallic symbol of such Olympian proportions that it made the London Post Office Tower look like it had a serious sexual dysfunction.

'The CN Tower,' Gerry said. 'Toronto's pride and joy. Tallest free-standing structure in the world – or at least it will be until the Japanese build a bigger one. See those elevators going up the outside?'

Banks did. The mere thought of being in one made him feel dizzy. He wasn't afraid of heights up to a certain point, but he'd never felt like risking a meal in a revolving restaurant at the top of a tower.

'What's it for?' he asked.

'Well you may ask. For show really.'

'What's at the top?'

'A restaurant, what else? And a disco, of course. This is the height of Western civilization. A feat on a par with the Great Pyramids and Chartres cathedral.'

'A disco?'

'Yes. Honest. Oh, I suppose I'm being flippant. They do use the place as a radio and TV transmitter, but it's basically just one of man's muscle-flexing exercises. This is downtown.'

The expressway, on a kind of elevated ramp, rolled past the backs of warehouses and billboards. Because the buildings were so close, the speed the car was travelling at was exaggerated and Banks felt as if he was on a roller coaster.

Finally, Gerry branched off, drove through an industrial wasteland of dirty old factories with external plumbing, then turned on to a busy street. Most of the buildings seemed quite old and run-down, and Banks soon noticed that nearly all the shop signs were in Chinese. Roast ducks hung by their feet in shop windows and teeming stalls of colourful fruit and vegetables blocked the pavements in front of grocery stores. One shop displayed a handwritten sign offering a mysterious combination of LIVE CRABS & VIDEOS. The street was bustling with people, mostly Chinese, pushing and shoving to get to the best deals, picking up and examining wares. The rich smell of food gone bad in the heat, mingled with the aroma of exotic spices, drifted into the car along with the suffocating air. A red and cream tram rattled along its track beside them.

'Chinatown East,' Gerry said. 'Not far to go now.'

He continued up the street past a prison and a hospital. To the left was a broad green valley. Beside the road, it sloped like a huge lawn down to the broad bottom, where a busy expressway ran beside the brown river. Above the trees on the far side, the downtown towers shimmered, greyish blurs in the heat haze. Gerry turned right into a tree-lined street and pulled up in the driveway of a small brick house with a green and white porch.

'Home,' he announced. 'I've got the bottom floor and there's a young couple upstairs. They're generally pretty quiet, so I wouldn't worry too much about noise.' He put his key in the lock and opened the door. 'Come on in. I'm dying for a cold beer.'

The place was small and sparsely furnished – apparently with cast-offs bought from second-hand shops – but it was clean and comfortable. Books stuffed every possible shelf and cavity. The Gristhorpe clan certainly seemed to be great readers, Banks thought.

Gerry led him into the small kitchen and took two cans of Budweiser from the fridge. Banks pulled the tab and

poured the iced, slightly malty beer down his throat.
When Gerry tipped back his can to drink, his Adam's
apple bobbed wildly.

'That's better,' he said, wiping his lips. 'I'm sorry it's so
hot in here too, but I can't afford an air-conditioner.
Actually, I've lived in worse places. There's a good
through-draught, and it does cool down a bit at night.'

'What's this area of town called?' Banks asked.

'Riverdale. It's gone very yuppie in the past few years.
Property values have shot up like crazy. You'll see the
main drag, the Danforth, if you walk or take a streetcar up
to the corner. It used to be all Greek cafés, restaurants and
twenty-four-hour fruit and vegetable stores. Now it's all
health foods, late-night bookshops, and bistros with long-
stemmed wineglasses and coral-pink tablecloths. All right
if you like that kind of thing, I suppose.'

'And if you don't?'

'There's a few unpretentious places left. You get some
good blues at the Black Swan on Saturday afternoons. And
then there's Quinn's, not a bad pub. Some of the old Greek
places are still around, but I can't say I've ever been fond
of Greek food myself – it's all greasy lamb, eggplant and
sticky desserts as far as I'm concerned.'

They sat down on the sofa, an overstuffed maroon
1950s monstrosity with arms like wings, and finished their
beers.

'Your uncle said you had to go to a conference somewhere,' Banks said. 'I hope I'm not driving you out?'

'Not at all. Actually, the conference isn't so important,
but Banff is a great place – right on the edge of the Rockies
– so I'll get a bit of hiking and partying done too.'

'How are you getting there?'

'Sneezy.'

'How far is it?'

'A couple of thousand miles. But you get used to distances like that here. Sneezy's done it before. She quite likes long journeys. I'll take my tent and camp out on the way. If you need a car . . .'

Banks shook his head. 'No. No, I wouldn't dare drive on the wrong side of the road. What's the public transport like?'

'Very good. There's a subway, buses and the streetcars you've seen. We don't call them trams here.'

'I was surprised,' Banks said. 'I haven't been on one of them since I was a kid.'

'Well, now's your chance to make up for lost time. I use them a lot myself to get around the city. Often it's not worth the bother of parking in town, and the cops can be pretty sticky about drinking and driving. Oops, sorry.'

Banks laughed.

'Anyway,' Gerry went on, delving into a drawer and bringing out a couple of maps, 'this is the city – easy to find your way about as it's mostly an east–west, north–south grid system. And here's the transit map. It's not as complicated as the London Underground, so you shouldn't have much trouble.'

And Gerry went on giving information about subway tokens and free transfers from one mode of transport to another. But after the journey and in the sweltering heat, Banks felt his eyes closing. He could do nothing about it.

'Here,' Gerry said, 'I'm boring you to death. I don't suppose you're taking any of this in.'

'Not much.'

'Do you want to go to bed?'

'I wouldn't mind a nap.'

Gerry showed him the bedroom.

'Isn't this your room?' Banks asked.

'It's OK. I'll bed down on the couch tonight.'

'I can do that.'

'Not necessary. I'm off early in the morning anyway. This'll be your room for the next week.'

Too tired to argue more and, frankly, grateful for a bed, Banks undressed, sank on to the mattress and fell asleep within seconds.

When he woke he was disoriented at finding himself in an unfamiliar bed. It took him a few moments to remember where he was. It was hot and dark, and the sheets felt moist with sweat. Hearing sounds in the front room, Banks rubbed his eyes, pulled on his trousers and walked through. He found Gerry stuffing clothes into a huge backpack. For a moment, it made him think of Bernard Allen.

'Hi,' Gerry said. 'I thought you were out for the count.'

'What time is it?'

'Ten o'clock. Three in the morning, your time.'

'I just woke up suddenly. I don't know why.'

'Jet lag does funny things like that. It's much worse going the other way.'

'Wonderful.'

Gerry grinned. 'Beer?'

'Any chance of a cup of tea?'

'Sure. We're not all coffee-drinking barbarians out here, you know.'

Gerry switched on the television and went into the kitchen. Banks sank into the sofa and put his feet up on a battered pouffe. A pretty woman was talking very intensely about a debate in the House of Commons. Again Banks felt the shock of being in a foreign land. The TV newscaster spoke with an odd accent – less overbearing than the Americans he had heard – and he knew none of the politicians' names.

Gerry brought the tea and sat beside him.

'There might be a couple of things you can help me with,' Banks said.

'Shoot.'

'Where can I find Toronto Community College?'

'Easy. The subway's the quickest.' And Gerry told him how to get to Broadview station by streetcar or on foot, where to change trains, and where to get off.

'There's another thing. Do you know anything about the English-style pubs in town? Somewhere that sells imported beer.'

Gerry laughed. 'You've certainly got your work cut out. There's dozens of them: the Madison, the Sticky Wicket, Paupers, the Hop and Grape, the Artful Dodger, the Jack Russell, the Spotted Dick, the Feathers, Quigley's, not to mention a whole dynasty of Dukes. I'll try and make a list for you. What's it all about, by the way, if that's not top secret?'

'I'm looking for a woman. Her name's Anne Ralston.'

'What's she done?'

'Nothing, as far as I know.'

'How very secretive. You're as bad as Uncle Eb, you are.'

'Who?'

'Uncle Eb. You mean you don't know . . .?'

Banks shook his head. Gristhorpe had never mentioned his first name, and his signature was an indecipherable scrawl.

'Well, maybe I shouldn't tell you. He won't thank me for it, if I know him.'

'I won't tell him I know. Scout's honour. Come on.'

'It's short for Ebenezer, of course.'

Banks whistled through his teeth. 'No wonder he never lets on.'

'Ah, but that's not all. His father was a grand champion of the labouring man, especially the farm workers, so he called his oldest son Ebenezer Elliott – after the "Corn Law Rhymer".'

Banks had never heard of Ebenezer Elliott but made a mental note to look him up. He was always interested in new things to read, look at or listen to.

'Ebenezer Elliott Gristhorpe,' he repeated to himself. 'Bloody hell.'

'Thought you'd like that,' Gerry said, grinning. 'It does have a certain ring to it, doesn't it? My poor mum got lumbered with Mary Wollstonecraft. Very progressive, Grandad was, respected the rights of women, too. But my dad was plain old George Webb, and thank the Lord he'd no hobby horse to tie his kids to.'

On the news, a gang of street kids in Belfast threw stones and tossed Molotov cocktails at police in riot gear. It was night, and orange flames blossomed all along the street. Black smoke rose from burning tyres. The world really was a global village, Banks thought, feeling his attention start to slip. Consciousness was fading away again. He yawned and put down his teacup on the low table.

'You can tell me something now,' Gerry said. 'Where did you get that scar?'

Banks fingered the white scar by his right eye. 'This? I passed out from lack of sleep and hit my head on the corner of a table.'

Gerry laughed. 'I get the point. I'm keeping you up.'

Banks smiled. 'I'm definitely falling asleep again. See you in the morning?'

'Probably not,' Gerry said. 'I've got a long way to go and I'm setting off at the crack of dawn. There's coffee and sugar in the cupboard above the sink. Milk and stuff's in the fridge. Here's a spare door-key. Make yourself at home.'

Banks shook his bony hand. 'Thanks,' he said. 'I will. And if you're ever in England . . .'

'I'll be sure to visit Uncle Ebenezer. I always do. And we'll have a jar or two in the Queen's Arms. Goodnight.'

Banks went back into the bedroom. A light breeze had sprung up to ease the suffocating heat a little, but it was still far from comfortable. He flopped down on the damp sheets. Outside, a short distance away, he heard a street-car rattle by and remembered exciting childhood trips to big cities when the trams were still running. He thought of the Queen's Arms on the edge of sleep, and pictured the pub on the corner of Market Street and the cobbled square. He felt very far from home. The Queen's Arms was a long, long way away, and there was a lot to do if he was to track down Anne Ralston before the week was over.

9

ONE

They were going to church: the women smiling in their wide-brimmed hats and cotton print dresses, the men ill at ease in tight ties and pinching waistcoats.

Every Sunday morning Katie watched them as she cleaned the rooms, and every week she knew she should be with them, dragging Sam along with the promise of an hour in the pub for him later while she cooked dinner. But he went to the pub anyway, and she cooked dinner anyway. The only thing missing was the hour in church. And that she couldn't face.

All through her childhood, Katie had been forced to go to the Gospel with her grandmother, and the icy devotion of the congregation had scared her half to death. Though they were praising God, they hardly dared sing so loud for fear He would think they were taking pleasure in the hymns. Katie could never understand the readings or the lessons, but she understood the passionate menace in the tones of those who spoke; she understood the meanings of the spittle that sometimes dribbled over their lips and the way their eyes glazed over. As she grew older, all her fear affixed itself to the sights, sounds and smells of the church: the chill mustiness rising from worn stone flags; the pews creaking as a bored child shifts position; the unearthly echo of the minister's voice; the wooden board announcing the hymn numbers; the stained glass fragmenting colour like broken souls. Just thirty seconds in a church meant panic for Katie; she couldn't breathe, she started trembling, and her blood turned to stone.

But she knew she should go. It was, after all, God's Mansion on Earth, and she would never escape this vale of tears if she didn't give herself to Him completely. Instead, she watched the rest of the village go off in their finery and listened to the hymns on the radio as she dusted, tidied and swept, humming along very quietly under her breath. Surely, surely, He would approve? She was working, doing her duty. It was the sabbath, of course, but there were still guests to take care of, and she suspected deep in her heart that the sabbath was only meant for men anyway. Surely He would approve. Her work would count in her favour. But it was a sin, she remembered vaguely, to court His favour, to say, 'Look what I've done, Lord.' It was the sin of pride. At least some said it was. She couldn't remember who, or whether she had been told to believe or disbelieve them – there were so many heresies, traps awaiting those impure in body and mind – but words such as faith, works and elect circled one another in her thoughts.

Well, Katie concluded dismally, working on Sundays could only add to the weight of sin she carried already. She picked up the black plastic bag. There were still three more rooms to do, then there was dinner to see to. When, she wondered, was it all going to end?

She went downstairs to put the roast in and immediately recognized the new guest standing over the registration book in the hall. He signed himself in as Philip Richmond, from Bolton, Lancashire, and he told Sam, who was dealing with the details, that he was simply after a few relaxing days in the country. But Katie remembered the moustache and the athletic spring in his step; it was the man she had seen with Chief Inspector Banks and Sergeant Hatchley the day she had run away to Eastvale.

Seeing him there brought back the whole day. Nothing had come of it really, except that she had caught a minor cold. The housework got done. Not on time, but it got done. Sam never even found out, so there was no retribution at his hands. Nor were there any outbreaks of boils, thunderbolts from heaven, plagues of locusts or other such horrors her grandmother had assured her would happen if she strayed from the path.

She felt as if she had lost sight of the path completely now. That was all she really knew about what was happening to her. The conflicting voices in her mind seemed to have merged into one incomprehensible rumble, and much of the time she felt as if she had no control over her thoughts or deeds.

There were clear moments though. Like now. Outside, the landscape was fresh after the previous few days' rain, which was now rising in sun-charmed wraiths of mist from the lower fell sides and the valley bottom. And here, in their hall, stood a man she recognized as having a close association with the police.

She hadn't seen what all the fuss was about the previous evening, when Sam had stumbled home from the White Rose in a very bad mood.

'He's gone to find her,' he had said, scowling. 'All the way to bloody Canada. Just to find her.'

'Who?' Katie had asked quietly, confused and frightened of him. In moods like this he was likely to lash out, and she could still feel the pain in her breast from the last time.

'Anne Ralston, you silly bitch. That copper's taken off to Toronto after her.'

'Well, what does it matter?' Katie had argued cautiously. 'If she killed that man all those years ago, they'll put her in jail, won't they?'

'You don't know nothing, woman, do you? Nothing at all.' Sam hit out at her and knocked the wooden cross off the mantelpiece.

'Leave it,' he snarled, grabbing Katie by the arm as she bent to pick it up. 'Can't you think of anything but bloody cleaning up?'

'But I thought you wanted me—'

'Oh, shut up. You don't know nothing.'

'Well, tell me. What is it? Why does it matter so much that he's gone chasing after Anne Ralston in Canada? You hardly knew her. Why does it matter to us?'

'It doesn't,' Sam said. 'But it might to Stephen. She might make things difficult for him.'

'But Stephen hasn't done anything, has he? How could she harm him?'

'She was his fancy woman, wasn't she? Then she ran off and left him. She could tell lies about his business, about . . . hell, I don't know! All I know is that it's all your bloody fault.'

Katie said nothing. Sam's initial rage was spent, she could tell, and she knew she would remain fairly safe if she kept quiet. It was tricky though, because he might get angry again if she didn't give the proper response to his ranting.

Sam sat heavily on the sofa and turned on the television. There was an old black and white film about gangsters on. James Cagney shot Humphrey Bogart and ran for it.

'Get me a beer,' Sam said.

Katie got him a can of Long Life from the fridge. She knew it was no good telling him he'd had enough already. Besides, on nights like this, when he'd had a bit more than usual, he tended to fall asleep as soon as he got to bed.

'And don't forget the Colliers' party next week,' he added, ripping open the can. 'I want you looking your best.'

Katie had forgotten about the garden party. The Colliers had two or three every summer. She hated them.

In the morning, Sam had a thick head and remembered very little about the night before. He sulked until after breakfast, then managed a welcome for the new guest before disappearing somewhere in the Land Rover. Katie showed Richmond his room, then went to get on with her work.

So there was a policeman in the house. She wondered why he was there. Perhaps he was on holiday. Policemen must have holidays too. But if he was from Eastvale, he was hardly likely to travel only twenty-five miles to Swainshead. Not these days. He'd be off to Torquay, or even the Costa del Sol. Katie didn't know how much policemen got paid, so she couldn't really say. But he wouldn't come to Swainshead, that was for sure. He was a spy, then. He thought nobody would recognize him, so he could keep an eye on their comings and goings while the little one with the scar was in Toronto and the big one was God knows where.

And Katie knew who he was. The problem now was what to do with her knowledge. Should she tell Sam, put him on his guard? He'd spread the word then, like he always did, and maybe he'd be grateful to her. But she couldn't remember anything about Sam's gratitude. It just didn't stand out in her memory like the other things. Did she need it? On the other hand, if Sam had done something wrong – and she didn't know whether he had or not – then the policeman, Richmond, if that was his real name, might find out and take him away. She'd be free then. It was an evil thought, and it made her heart race, but . . .

Katie paused and looked out of the back window at the gauze of mist rising like breath from the bright green slopes of Swainshead Fell. It would take a bit of thinking about, this dilemma of hers. She knew she mustn't make a hasty decision.

TWO

'I'm afraid there's hardly anybody here to talk to, Mr . . . er . . .?'

'Banks. Alan Banks. I was a friend of Bernard Allen's.'

'Yes, well, the only person I can think of who might be able to help you is Marilyn Rosenberg.' Tom Jordan, head of the Communications Department at Toronto Community College, looked at his watch. 'She's got a class right now, but she should be free in about twenty minutes, if you'd like to wait?'

'Certainly.'

Jordan led him out of the office into a staff lounge just big enough to hold a few chairs and a low coffee table littered with papers and teaching journals. At one end stood a fridge and, on a desk beside it, a microwave oven. The coffee machine stood on a table below a connecting window to the secretary's office, beside a rack of pigeon-holes for staff messages. Banks poured himself a coffee and Jordan edged away slowly, mumbling about work to do.

The coffee was strong and bitter, hardly the thing to drink in the thirty-three-degree heat. What he really needed was a cold beer or a gin and tonic. And he'd gone and bought Scotch at the duty-free shop. Still, he could leave it as a gift for Gerry Webb. It would surely come in handy in winter.

It was Monday morning. On Sunday, Banks had slept in and then gone for a walk along the Danforth. He had noticed the signs of yuppification that Gerry had mentioned, but he had found a pleasant little Greek restaurant which had served him a hearty moussaka for lunch. Unlike Gerry, Banks enjoyed Greek food.

After that, he had wandered as far as Quinn's. Over a pint, he had asked around about Bernie Allen and shown Anne Ralston's photograph to the bar staff and waitresses. No luck. One down, two dozen to go. He had wandered back along the residential streets south of Danforth Avenue and noticed that the small brick house with the green and white porch fence and columns was a sort of Toronto trademark.

Too tired to go out again, he had stayed in and watched television that evening. Oddly enough, the non-commercial channel was showing an old BBC historical serial he'd found boring enough the first time around, and – much better – one of the Jeremy Brett *Sherlock Holmes* episodes. The only alternatives were the same American cop shows that plagued British TV.

He had woken at about nine o'clock that Monday morning. Still groggy from travel and culture shock, he had taken a shower and had had orange juice and toast for breakfast. Then it was time to set off. He slipped a 1960s anthology tape of Cream, Traffic and Rolling Stones hits in the Walkman and put it in the right-hand pocket of his light cotton jacket. In the left, he placed cigarettes and Hardy's *Tess of the D'Urbervilles*, the only book he'd brought with him.

Jacket slung over shoulder, he set off, following Gerry's directions. A rolling rattling streetcar ride took him by the valley side, rife with joggers. The downtown towers were hazy in the morning heat. Finding the westbound platform at Broadview subway station was every bit as straightforward as Gerry had said, but changing trains at Yonge and getting out to the street at St Clair proved confusing. All exits seemed to lead to a warren of underground shopping malls – air-conditioned, of course – and finding the right way out wasn't easy.

Still, he'd found St Clair Avenue after only a momentary diversion into a supermarket called Ziggy's, and the college was only a short walk from the station.

Now, from the sixth floor, he looked out for a while on the office buildings opposite and the cream tops of the streetcars passing to and fro below him, then turned to the pile of journals on the table.

Halfway through an article on the teaching of 'critical thinking' he heard muffled voices in the corridor, and a young woman with a puzzled expression on her face popped around the door. Masses of curly brown hair framed her round head. She had a small mouth and her teeth, when she smiled, were tiny, straight and pearly white. The greyish gum she was chewing oozed between them like gum disease. She carried a worn overstuffed leather briefcase under her arm, and wore grey cords and a checked shirt.

She stretched out her hand. 'Marilyn Rosenberg. Tom tells me you wanted to talk to me.'

Banks introduced himself and offered to pour her a cup of coffee.

'No thanks,' she said, grabbing a Diet Coke from the fridge. 'Far too hot for that stuff. You'd think they'd do something about the air-conditioning in this place, wouldn't you?' She pulled the tab and the Diet Coke fizzed. 'What do you want with me?'

'I want to talk about Bernard Allen.'

'I've been through all that with the police. There wasn't really much to say.'

'What did they ask you?'

'Just if I thought anyone had a reason to kill him, where my colleagues were over the last few weeks, that kind of thing.'

'Did they ask you anything about his life here?'

'Only what kind of person he was.'

'And?'

'And I told them he was a bit of a loner, that's all. I wasn't the only one they talked to.'

'You're the only one here now.'

'Yeah, I guess.' She grinned again, flashing her beautiful teeth.

'If Bernard didn't have much to do with his colleagues here, did he have a group of friends somewhere else, away from college?'

'I wouldn't really know. Look, I didn't know Bernie that well . . .' She hesitated. 'Maybe it's none of your business, but I wanted to. We were getting closer. Slowly. He was a hard person to get to know. All that stiff-upper-lip Brit stuff. Me, I'm a simple Irish-Jewish girl from Montreal.' She shrugged. 'I liked him. We did lunch up here a couple of times. I was hoping maybe he'd ask me out sometime but . . .'

'It never happened?'

'No. He was too damn slow. I didn't know how much

clearer I could make it without ripping off my clothes and jumping on him. But now it's too late, even for that.'

'How did he seem emotionally before he went to England?'

Marilyn frowned and bit her bottom lip as she thought. 'He hadn't quite got over his divorce,' she said finally. 'So I guess he might have been off women for a while.'

'Did you know his ex-wife?'

'No, not really.'

'What about her lover?'

'Yeah, I knew him. He used to work here. He's a louse.'

'In what way?'

'Every way. Strutting macho peacock. And she fell for it. I don't blame Bernie for feeling bad, but he'd have been well rid of her anyway. He'd have got over it.'

'But he was still upset?'

'Yeah. Withdrawn, sort of.'

'How did he get on with his students?'

'Well enough, considering.'

'Considering what?'

'He cared about literature, but most of the students don't give a damn about James Joyce or George Orwell. They're here to learn about business or computers or electrical engineering – you know, useful stuff – and then they think they'll walk into top high-paying jobs. They don't like it when they find they all have to do English, so it makes our job a bit tough. Some teachers find it harder than others to adjust and lower their expectations.'

'And Bernie was one?'

'Yeah. He complained a lot about how ignorant they were, how half of them didn't even know when the Second World War was fought or who Hitler was. And, even worse, they didn't care anyway. Bernie couldn't understand that. He had one guy who thought Shakespeare was a small town in Saskatchewan. That really got to him.'

'I don't understand,' Banks said. 'How could someone like that get accepted into a college?'

'We have an open-door policy,' Marilyn said. 'It's a democratic education. None of that elitist bullshit you get in England. We don't send our kids away to boarding schools to learn Latin and take a lot of cold showers. All that Jane Eyre stuff.'

Banks, who had not attended a public school himself, along with the majority of English children, was confused. 'But don't a lot of them fail?' he asked. 'Doesn't it waste time and money?'

'We don't like to fail people,' Marilyn said. 'It gives them a poor self-image.'

'So they don't need to know much to get in, and they aren't expected to know much more when they leave, is that it?'

Marilyn smiled like a nurse with a particularly difficult patient.

'What did Bernie think about that?' Banks hurried on.

She laughed. 'Bernie loved youth, young people, but he didn't have much respect for their intelligence.'

'It doesn't sound like they had much.'

'There, you see. That's exactly the kind of thing he'd say. You're so sarcastic, you Brits.'

'But you liked him?'

'Yeah, I liked him. We might have disagreed on a few things, but he was cute and I'm a sucker for an English accent. What can I say? He was a nice guy, at least as far as I could tell. I mean, he might not have thought much of his students, but he treated them well and did his damnedest to arouse some curiosity in them. He was a good teacher. What are you getting at, anyway? Do you think one of his students might have killed him over a poor grade?'

'It sounds unlikely, doesn't it?'

'Not as much as you think,' Marilyn said. 'We once had a guy come after his English teacher here with a shotgun. Luckily, security stopped him before he got very far. Still,' she went on, 'I shouldn't think an irate student would go to all the trouble of following him over to England and killing him there.'

'What did Bernie do when he went home after work? Did he ever mention any particular place he went to?'

Marilyn shook her head and the curls danced. 'No. He did once say he'd had a few pints too many in the pub the night before.'

'The pub?'

'Yeah.'

'He didn't say which pub?'

'No. He just said he'd had six pints when five was his limit these days. Look, what is all this? What are you after? You're not one of those private eyes, are you?'

Banks laughed. 'No. I told you, I'm a friend of Bernie's from England. Swainsdale, where he grew up. I want to piece together as much of his life as I can. A lot of people over there are hurt and puzzled by what happened.'

'Yeah, well . . . me too. He wasn't the kind of guy who gets himself killed. Know what I mean?'

Banks nodded.

'Swainsdale, you said?' she went on. 'Bernie was always going on about that place. At least the couple of times we talked he was. Like it was some paradise on earth or something. Especially since the divorce, he started to get homesick. He was beginning to feel a bit lost and out of place here. It can happen, you know. So he took the thousand-dollar cure.'

'The what?'

'The thousand-dollar cure. I guess it's gone up now with inflation, but it's when Brits take a trip back home to renew their roots. Used to call it the thousand-dollar cure. For homesickness.'

'Did he ever talk of going back to Swainsdale to stay?'

'Yeah. He said he'd be off like a shot if he had a job, or a private income. He said there was nothing for him here after he split up with Barbara. Poor guy. Like I said, he got withdrawn, dwelled on things too much.'

Banks nodded. 'There's nothing else you can tell me? You're sure he didn't name any specific pub or place he used to hang out?'

'Sorry.' Marilyn grinned. 'I'd remember if he had because I'd have probably dropped in there one evening. Just by chance, you know.'

Banks smiled. 'Yes. I know. Thanks anyway. I won't waste any more of your time.'

'No problem.' Marilyn tossed her empty can into the waste-paper basket. 'Hey!' she called, as Banks left the staff lounge. 'I think your accent's cute, too.'

But Banks didn't have time to appreciate the compliment. Coming along the corridor towards him were two very large police officers.

'Mr Banks?' the taller one asked.

'Yes.'

'We'd like you to come with us, if you don't mind.'

'What for?'

'Just a few questions. This way, please.'

There was hardly room for them to walk three abreast

down the hallway, but they managed it somehow. Banks felt a bit like a sardine in a tin. As they turned the corner, he noticed from the corner of his eye Tom Jordan wringing his hands outside his office.

Banks tried to get more out of the officers in the lift, but they clammed up on him. He felt a wave of irrational fear at the situation. Here he was, in a foreign country, being taken into custody by two enormous uniformed policemen who refused to answer his questions. And the feeling of fear intensified as he was bundled into the back of the yellow car. The air smelled of hot vinyl upholstery; a strong wire mesh separated him from the men in the front; and the back doors had no inside handles.

THREE

'What does tha write, then?' Freddie Metcalfe asked, expertly refilling the empty pint glass with Marston's Pedigree Bitter.

'Science fiction,' said Detective Constable Philip Richmond. In his checked Viyella shirt and light brown cords, he thought he looked the part. Posing as a writer would make him less suspicious, too. He would be expected to spend some time alone in his room writing and a lot of time in the pub, with perhaps the occasional constitutional just to keep the juices flowing.

'I knew a chap used to write books once,' Freddie went on. 'Books about t' Dales, wi' pictures in 'em. Lived down Lower 'Ead.' He placed the foaming pint in front of Richmond, who paid and drained a good half of it in one gulp. 'I reckon one of them there detective writers would 'ave a better time of it round 'ere these days.'

'Why's that?'

Freddie leaned forward and lowered his voice. 'Murder, that's why,' he said, then laughed and picked up a glass to dry. 'Right baffled, t' police are. It's got that southron – little chap wi' a scar by 'is eye – it's got 'im running around like a blue-arsed fly, it has. And t' old man, Gristhorpe – well, we all know he durst hardly show his face around 'ere since t' last one, don't we?'

'Last what?'

'Murder, lad! What's tha think I'm talking about? Sheep-shagging?'

'Sorry.'

'Think nowt on it. I'm forgetting tha's a foreigner. Tha sounds Yorkshire to me. Bit posh, mind you, but Yorkshire.'

'Lancashire, actually,' Richmond lied. 'Bolton.'

'Aye, well, nobody's perfect. Anyroads, as I were saying – blue-arsed flies, t' lot of 'em.'

An impatient customer interrupted Freddie's monologue, and Richmond took the opportunity to sip more beer. It was eight thirty on Monday evening, and the White Rose was about half full.

'Keep your eyes skinned, lad,' Sergeant Hatchley had instructed him. 'Watch out for anybody who looks like doing a bolt.' The orders couldn't have been more vague. What on earth, Richmond wondered, did someone about to do a bolt look like? Would he have to sit up all night and watch for the culprit stealing down by the Swain with his belongings tied in a bag on the end of a stick slung over his shoulder, faithful cat at his heels, like Dick Whittington? Richmond had no idea. All he knew was that all the suspects had been told Banks had gone to Toronto.

Richmond also had strict instructions not to identify

himself and not to push himself forward in any way that might make the locals suspicious. In other words, he wasn't to question anyone, no matter how casually. He could keep his ears open then, he was relieved to hear, especially for anything Sam Greenock might let slip over breakfast, or some titbit he might overhear in the White Rose. At least he'd pack away a few pints of Marston's tonight. Maybe even smoke a panatella.

'Where was I?' Freddie asked, leaning on the bar again.

'Murder.'

'Aye, murder.' He nodded in the direction of the table in the far corner and whispered again. 'And them there's all t' suspects.'

'What makes them suspects?' Richmond asked, hoping he was not exceeding his brief by asking the question.

''Ow would I know? All I know is that t' police 'ave spent a lot of time wi' 'em. An' since yesterday they've all been on hot coals. Look at 'em now. You wouldn't think they 'ad a big party coming up, would you?'

It was true that the group hardly seemed jolly. John Fletcher chewed the stem of his stubby pipe; his dark brows met in a frown. Sam Greenock was staring into space and rocking his glass on the table. Stephen Collier was talking earnestly to Nicholas, who was trying very hard not to listen. Nicholas, in fact, seemed the only unconcerned one among them. He smiled and nodded at customers who came and went, whereas the other three hardly seemed to notice them.

Richmond wished he could get closer and overhear what they were saying, but all the nearby tables were full. It would look too suspicious if he went and stood behind them.

He ordered another pint. 'And I'll have a panatella too,

please,' he said. He felt like indulging in a rare treat: a cigar with his beer. 'What party's this?' he asked.

'A Collier do. Reg'lar as clockwork in summer.'

'Can anyone go?'

'Tha must be joking, lad.'

Richmond shrugged and smiled to show he was, indeed, jesting. 'What's wrong with them all, then?' he asked. 'You're right. They don't look like they're contemplating a booze-up to me.'

Metcalfe scratched his mutton chops. 'I can't be certain, tha knows, but it's summat to do wi' that London copper taking off for Canada. Talk about pale! Ashen, they went. But I'll tell tha summat, it were good for business. Double brandies all round!' Freddie nudged Richmond and laughed. 'Aye, there's nobody drinks like a murder suspect.'

Richmond drew on his cigar and looked over at the table. Outside some enemy back in Toronto, it came down to these four. Come on, he thought to himself, make a bolt. Run for it, you bugger, just try it!

FOUR

'I don't know what people do where you come from, but over here we like a bit of advance warning if some foreigner's come to invade our territory.'

Banks listened. There was nothing he could say; he had been caught fair and square. Fortunately, Staff Sergeant Gregson of the Toronto Homicide Squad was nearing the end of what had been a relatively mild bollocking, and even more fortunately, smoking was allowed – nay, encouraged – in his office.

It was an odd feeling, being on the carpet. Not that this was the first time for Banks. There had been many occasions at school, and even one or two in his early days on the Metropolitan force, and they always brought back those feelings of terror and helplessness in the face of authority he had known as a working-class kid in Peterborough. Perhaps, he thought, that fear of authority might have motivated him to become a policeman in the first place. He knew he didn't join in order to inflict such feelings on others, but it was possible that he did it to surmount them, to conquer them in himself.

And now here he was, tongue-tied, unable to say a word in his own defence, yet inwardly seething with resentment at Gregson for putting him in such a position.

'You've got no power here, you know,' Gregson went on.

Finally, Banks found his voice. Holding his anger in check, he said, 'I wasn't aware that I needed any special power to talk to people – either in England or in Canada.'

'You won't get anywhere being sarcastic with me,' Gregson said, a smile tugging at the corners of his tightly clamped mouth.

He was a round man with a square head. His grey hair was closely cropped, and a brush-like wedge of matching moustache, nicotine-yellow around the ends of the bristles, sprouted under his squashed nose. As he spoke, he had a habit of running his fingers under the collar of his white shirt as if it was too tight. His skin had a pinkish plastic sheen, like a balloon blown up too much. Banks wondered what would happen if he pricked him. Would he explode, or would the air hiss out slowly as his features folded in on themselves?

'What have you got against irony, Sergeant?' Banks

asked. That felt odd, too: being hauled up before a mere sergeant.

'You know what they say about sarcasm being the lowest form of wit, don't you?' Gregson responded.

'Yes. But at least it is a form of wit, which is better than none at all.'

'I didn't bring you here to bandy words.'

'Obviously.'

Banks lit another cigarette and looked at the concrete and glass office blocks out of the window. His shirt was stuck with sweat to the back of the orange plastic chair. He felt his anger ebb into boredom. They were somewhere downtown in a futuristic air-conditioned building, but the office smelt of burning rubber and old cigar smoke. That was all he knew.

'What are you going to do, then?' Banks asked. 'Arrest me?'

Gregson shrugged. 'For what? You haven't done anything wrong.'

Banks leaned forward. 'Then why the bloody hell did you get Laurel and Hardy out there to bundle me in the back of a car and bring me here against my will?'

'Don't be like that,' Gregson said. 'When Jordan phoned me and said there was a suspicious Englishman asking questions about Bernard Allen, what the fuck else could I do? What would you have done? Then it turned out to be you, a goddamn police inspector from England. And I hadn't even been advised of your visit. I considered that an insult, which it is. And I didn't find your remark on the phone about getting my man particularly funny, either. I'm not a Mountie.'

'Well, I'm sorry for any inconvenience I've caused you, Sergeant,' Banks said, standing up, 'but I'd like to enjoy the rest of my holiday in peace, if you don't mind.'

'I don't mind,' Gregson said, making no move to stop him walking over to the door. 'I don't mind at all. But I think you ought to bear a few things in mind before you go storming off.'

'What things?' Banks asked, his palm slippery on the doorknob.

'First of all, that what I said to you on the phone before is true: we don't have the resources to work on this case. Secondly, yes, you can talk to as many people as you wish, providing they want to talk to you. And thirdly, you should have damn well asked for permission before jumping on that fucking jet and flying here half-cocked. What if you find your killer? What are you going to do then? Have you thought about that? Smuggle him out of the country? You could be getting yourself into a damn tricky legal situation if you're not very careful.' Gregson rubbed his moustache with the back of his hand. 'All I'm saying is that there are things you can't do acting alone, without authority.'

'And you don't have the resources. I know. You told me. Look, this is where I came in, so if you don't mind—'

'Wait!' Gregson jumped to his feet and reached for his jacket.

'Wait for what?'

Gregson pushed past him through the door. 'Come on,' he said, half turning. 'Just come with me.'

'Where?'

'You'll see.'

'What for?'

'I'm going to save you from yourself.'

Banks sighed and followed the sergeant down the corridor and down in the lift to the car park.

There was enough room for a football team on the front seat of Gregson's car. With the open windows sucking in what hot wet air they could, the staff sergeant drove up Yonge Street and turned right at the Hudson's Bay building. On the crowded street corner, vendors sold ice-cream, T-shirts and jewellery; one man, surrounded by quite a crowd, was drawing large portraits in coloured chalk on the pavement.

Farther along, Banks recognized the stretch of the Danforth he'd walked the previous day: the Carrot Common shopping centre; the little Greek restaurant where he'd eaten lunch; Quinn's pub. They came to an intersection called Coxwell, and Gregson turned left. A few blocks up, he pulled to a halt outside a small apartment building. Sprinklers hissed on the well kept lawn. Banks was tempted to run under one for a cold shower.

They walked up to the third floor, and Banks followed Gregson along the carpeted corridor to apartment 312.

'Allen's place,' the staff sergeant announced.

'Why are you helping me?' Banks asked, as Gregson fitted the key in the door. 'Why are you bringing me here? You said your department didn't have the resources.'

'That's true. We've got a hunt on for a guy who sodomized a twelve-year-old girl, then cut her throat and dumped her in High Park. Been looking for leads for two months now. Twenty men on the case. But this is personal time. I don't like it that a local guy got killed any more than you do. So I show you where he lived. It's no big deal. Besides, like I said, I'm saving you from yourself. You'd probably have broken in, and then I'd have had to arrest you. Embarrassing all round.'

'Thanks anyway,' Banks said.

They walked into the apartment.

'Building owner's been bugging us to let him rent it out again, but we've been stalling. He knows he's sitting on a gold mine. We've got a zero vacancy rate in Toronto these days. Still, Allen paid first and last month when he moved in, so I figure he's got a bit of time left. To tell you the truth, we don't know who's gonna take care of the guy's stuff.'

There wasn't much: just a lot of books, Swedish assemble-it-yourself furniture, pots and pans, a few withered house plants and a desk and typewriter by the window. Bernard Allen had lived simply.

The room was hot and stuffy. There was no sign of an air conditioner, so Banks went over and opened a window. It didn't make much difference.

'What kind of search did your men do?' Banks asked.

'Routine. We didn't open up every book or read every letter, if that's what you mean. The guy didn't keep much personal stuff around, anyway. It was all in that desk drawer.'

Banks extracted a messy pile of bills and letters from the drawer. First, he put aside the bills then examined the sheaf of personal mail. They were all dated within the last six months or so, which meant that he threw his letters out periodically instead of hoarding them like some people. There were letters from his parents in Australia and one brief note from his sister acknowledging the dates of his proposed visit. Banks read these carefully, but found nothing of significance.

It was a postcard from Vancouver dated about two weeks before Allen set off for England that proved the most revealing, but even that wasn't enough. It read:

Dear Bernie,

Wrapping things up nicely out here. Weather great,
so taking some time for sunbathing on Kitsilano Beach.
It'll be a couple more weeks before I get back, so I'll
miss you. Have a great trip and give my love to the folks
in Swineshead! (Only joking – best not tell anyone you
know me!) See you in the pub when you get back.

   Love,
      Julie

It was perfectly innocent on the surface – just a postcard from a friend – so there was no reason why Gregson
or his men should have been suspicious about it. But it
was definitely from Anne Ralston, and it told Banks that
she was going under the name of Julie now.

'Looks like you've found something,' Gregson said,
looking over Banks's shoulder.

'It's from the woman I'm looking for. I think she knows
something about Allen's murder.'

'Look,' Gregson said, 'are we talking about a criminal
here? Are there charges involved?'

Banks shook his head. He wasn't sure. Anne Ralston
could certainly have murdered Raymond Addison and run
for it, but he didn't want to tell Gregson that and risk the
local police scaring her off.

'No,' he said. 'They used to know each other in
Swainshead, that's all.'

'And now they've met up over here?'

'Yes.'

'So?'

Banks told him about Ralston's disappearance and the
Addison murder, stressing that she wasn't seriously
implicated in any way.

'But she might have known something?' Gregson said.

'And told Allen. You think that's what might have got him killed?'

'It's possible. We know that she asked him to keep quiet about meeting her over here, and we know he didn't.'

'Who did he talk to?'

'That's the problem. Someone who makes it his business to make sure that everyone who counts knows.'

'It won't be easy.'

'What?'

Gregson tapped the postcard. 'Finding her. No address. No phone number. Nothing.'

Banks sighed. 'Believe me, I know. And all we've got is her first name. I'm just hoping I can dig out some of the spots she might turn up. She mentioned the pub, so at least I was right about her drinking with him there.'

'Know how many pubs there are in Toronto?'

'Don't bother to tell me. I'd only get discouraged. It's the kind of job I should have sent my sergeant on.' Banks explained about Hatchley's drinking habits and Gregson laughed.

'Can I have a good look around?' Banks asked.

'Go ahead. I'll be down in the car. Lock up behind you.'

After the staff sergeant left, Banks puzzled over him for a moment. He was beginning to warm to Gregson and get some understanding of Canadians, especially those of distant British origin. They behaved with a strange mixture of patronage and respect towards the English. Perhaps they'd had British history rammed down their throats at school and needed to reject it in order to discover themselves. Or perhaps the English had simply become passé as far as immigrants went, and had been superseded by newer waves of Koreans, East Indians and Vietnamese.

The next item of interest Banks found was an old photograph album dating back to Allen's university days. There were pictures of his parents, his sister, and of the Greenocks standing outside a typical Armley back-to-back. But the most interesting was a picture dated ten years ago, in which Allen stood outside the White Rose with a woman named as Anne in the careful white print under the photo on the black page. The snap was a little blurred, an amateur effort with a Brownie by the look of it, but it was better than the one he'd got from Missing Persons. Anne looked very attractive in a low-cut T-shirt and a full, flowing Paisley skirt. She had long light brown hair, a high forehead and smiling eyes. Her face was heart-shaped and her lips curved up slightly at the corners. That was ten years ago, Banks thought, carefully taking the photo from its silver corners and pocketing it. Would she look like that now?

He went on to make a careful search of the rest of the apartment, and he did take out every book and flip through the leaves, but he came up with nothing else. The postcard signed 'Julie' and the old photograph were all he had to go on. By the time he'd finished, his shirt was stuck to his back.

Outside, Gregson seemed quite at ease smoking in his hot car.

'Find anything?' he asked.

'Only an old photograph. Probably useless. What time is it?'

'Ten after four.'

'I suppose I'd better make my way home.'

'Where are you staying?'

'Riverdale.'

'That's not far. How about a beer first?'

'All right.' It was impossible to resist the thought of an ice-cold beer.

Gregson drove back downtown and pulled into a car park behind a grimy cinder-block building with a satellite dish on the roof.

Despite the warm gold sunlight outside, the bar was dark and it took a while for Banks' eyes to adjust. He did notice though, that it was cold, gloriously cold. There wasn't any sawdust on the floor, but he got the feeling there ought to be. It was a high-ceilinged room as big as a barn, peppered with black plastic tables and chairs. At one end was the bar itself, a feeble glimmer of light in the distance, and at the other was a stage littered with amps and speakers. At the moment a rather flat-chested young girl was dancing half-naked in a spotlight to the Rolling Stones' 'Jumpin' Jack Flash'. The volume was much too high. Against a third wall was a huge TV screen on which a game of baseball was in progress.

A waitress sashayed over, shirt-ends tied in a knot under her ample breasts, and took their orders with a weary smile. Shortly, she returned with the drinks on a tray. As Banks looked around, other figures detached themselves from the gloom and he saw that the place was reasonably full. Smoke swirled and danced in the spot beam. Whatever this bar was, it wasn't one of the English-style pubs where Bernard Allen went for his pint. The four glasses of draught beer in front of them were tiny and tapered to thick heavy stems.

'Cheers.' Gregson clinked glasses and practically downed his in one.

'If you have to order two each at a time,' Banks asked, leaning over and shouting against the music, 'why don't they switch to using bigger glasses?'

Gregson shrugged and licked foam off his moustache. 'Tradition, I guess. It's always been like this as long as I can remember.' He offered Banks a cigarette. It was stronger than the ones he usually smoked.

The music ended and the girl left the stage to a smattering of polite applause.

Gregson nodded towards the TV screen. 'Get baseball back home?'

Banks nodded. 'We do now. My son likes it, but I'm a cricket man myself.'

'Can't figure that game at all.'

'Can't say I know much about baseball, either.' Banks caught the waitress's attention and put in another order, changing his to a bottle of Carlsberg this time. She smiled sweetly at him and made him repeat himself.

'Likes your accent,' Gregson said afterwards. 'She heard you the first time. You'll be all right there, if you're interested.'

'Married man.'

'Ah. Still, while the cat's away . . . And you are in a foreign country, a long way from home.'

Banks laughed. 'The problem is, I have to take myself with me wherever I go.'

Gregson nodded slowly. 'I know what you mean.' He tapped the side of his square head. 'There's a few pictures stuck in here I wish I could throw out, believe me.' He looked back at the screen. 'Baseball. Greatest game in the world.'

'I'll take your word for it.'

'Listen, if you've got a bit of time, how about taking in a game next Saturday? I've got tickets. Jays at home to the Yankees.'

'I'd like that,' Banks said. 'Look, don't get me wrong,

but I got the impression you were distinctly pissed off with me a few hours ago. Now you're inviting me to a baseball game. Any reason?'

'Sure. You were out of line and I did my duty. Now I'm off duty and someone's got to show you there's more to Canada than snow, Mounties, beavers and maple trees.'

'Fair enough. Don't forget the Eskimos.'

'Inuit, we call them now.'

Banks finished his beer and Gregson ordered more. The spot came on again and an attractive young woman with long wavy black hair and brown skin came on to the stage.

Gregson noticed Banks staring. 'Beautiful, eh? She's a full-blooded Indian. Name's Wanda Morningstar.'

She certainly was beautiful, in such an innocent natural way that Banks found himself wondering what the girl was doing taking her clothes off for a bunch of dirty old men in the middle of a summer's afternoon. And, come to think of it, what the hell was he doing among them? Well, blame Gregson for that.

More drinks came, and more strippers walked on and off the stage, but none could hold a candle to Wanda Morningstar. It was after ten when they finally left, and by then Banks felt unusually merry. Because the beer was ice-cold it had very little taste and therefore, he had assumed, little strength. Wrong. It was stronger than what he was used to, and he felt light-headed as he followed Gregson to the car.

Gregson paused as he bent to put his key in the door. 'No,' he said to himself. 'Time to take a cab. You've been leading me astray, Alan. It'd be damned embarrassing if I got done for drunken driving in my own city, wouldn't it?'

They walked out on to the street. It was still busy, and many of the shops were open – all-night groceries and the ubiquitous Mac's Milk. Or was this one Mo's, Mc's or Mick's? You'd never get anything but an off-licence open past five thirty in Eastvale, Banks reflected.

Gregson waved and a cab pulled up. They piled in the back. The driver, an uncommunicative West Indian, nodded when he heard the directions. He dropped Banks off first outside Gerry's house, then drove on with Gregson waving from the back.

Banks walked into the hot room and slumped in front of the TV. A rerun of *Perry Mason* came on. Finally, a little dizzy and unable to keep his eyes open any longer, he went into the bedroom and lay down. The events of the day spun round chaotically in his mind for a while, but the last image, the one that lulled his consciousness to sleep, was of Wanda Morningstar dancing naked, not on a stage in a seedy bar but in a clearing somewhere in the wilderness, her dark skin gleaming in firelight.

But the scene shifted, as it does in dreams, and it was no longer Wanda Morningstar dancing but Anne Ralston running ahead of him in her long Paisley skirt. It was a typical policeman's dream too, for try as he might, he just couldn't run fast enough. His feet felt as if they were glued to the earth. Every so often, she would pause and beckon him, smiling indulgently when she saw him try to drag himself along. He woke at six, covered with sweat. Outside, the birds were singing and an early-morning streetcar clattered by. He got up and took a couple of Gerry's aspirins with a pint of water, then drifted off to sleep again.

10

ONE

The sun had just gone down behind Adam's Fell, silhouetting the steep hillside against its deep crimson glow. The guests milled around in the Colliers' large garden. Doors to both parts of the house were open, allowing access to drinks and a huge table of cheeses, pâtés, smoked salmon and fresh fruit. Music drifted out from Stephen's stereo. Now it was Mozart, but earlier there had been Motown and some ersatz modern pop. The crowd was mostly early to mid thirties, apart from one or two older landowners and friends of the family. There were a couple of bright young teachers from Braughtmore, several members of Stephen's management staff, and a great assortment of entrepreneurs, some with political ambitions, from all over the dale. The parties were a fairly regular affair; they helped maintain the social status of the Colliers and introduce those who had something to those who might be willing and able to pay for it.

Katie stood alone by the fountain, with a glass of white wine in her hand. She had been holding it so long it was warm. Occasionally a well dressed young man would approach her and begin a conversation, but after a few minutes of her averted looks, blushes and monosyllabic answers, he would make an excuse to get away.

As usual, Sam had insisted she come.

'I didn't buy you those bloody expensive dresses for nothing, you know,' he had railed when she told him at the last minute that she didn't want to go.

'I didn't ask you to buy them,' Katie said quietly. 'I don't even want them.' And it was true. She felt uncomfortable in finery, full of pride and vanity.

'You'll damn well do as I say. There'll be some important people there and I want you to make a good impression.'

'Oh, Sam,' she pleaded, 'you know I never do. I can't talk to people at parties. I get all tongue-tied.'

'Have a few drinks like everyone else, for a change. That'll loosen you up. For Christ's sake, can't you let your hair down for once?'

Katie turned away.

Sam grasped her arm. 'Look,' he said, 'you're coming with me and that's that. If you're so worried about talking to people, then just stand around and look decorative. At least you can do that. But you are coming. Got it?'

Katie nodded and Sam let go of her. Rubbing her arm, she went up to her room and picked out a cotton print dress just right for the occasion, gathered at the waist and cut low down the back. It looked particularly good if she tied her hair up. She decided to take a fringed woollen shawl, too; sometimes, even in July, the evenings got chilly. After Sam had approved of her appearance and suggested a bit more eye make-up, they left.

She could see Sam in his white suit talking and laughing with a couple of local businessmen. He had a glass of wine too, though she knew he hated the stuff. He only drank it because that was the thing to do at the Colliers' parties.

Katie looked around for John Fletcher, but she couldn't

see him. John was always kind and, of all of them, she found him the easiest to talk to, or even to be silent with. She liked Stephen Collier, but felt more comfortable with John Fletcher. He was a sad and haunted man since his wife ran off, but at least she hadn't gone because he mistreated her. Maureen Fletcher, Katie remembered, had been beautiful, vain, haughty and foolhardy. The small community of Swainshead couldn't hold her. Katie thought John ought to be glad to be rid of her, but she never said anything to him. They never discussed anything personal, but he seemed, beyond the depths of his sadness, a good man.

Katie shivered. The sunset had faded, leaving the sky above Adam's Fell a deep dark violet colour. Even over the clinking glasses and the Motown music, which had started up again because some people wanted to dance, she could hear the eerie mournful call of a curlew high on the fell. She began to make her way into Nicholas's part of the house to pick up her shawl where Sam had left it, then decided she wanted to go to the bathroom too. Pausing on the way, she admired the oak panelling and the old-fashioned style of his living room, with its watercolours of Nelson and Wellington on the walls, and its rows of leather-bound books. She wondered if he ever read them. On a small teak table by the Adam fireplace stood a bronze bust. Looking closer, Katie saw the name Oscar Wilde scratched into the base. She'd heard the name before somewhere, but it didn't mean very much to her. What a beautiful place for a monster like Nicholas Collier to live. It would be difficult to clean though, she thought, taking in all the nooks and crannies with a professional eye.

Finally, she found the toilet, which was more modern than the rest of the house. There, she poured her drink down the bowl and hid for a while, idly glancing at one of the copies of *Yorkshire Life* so thoughtfully set out by the bath. Then she got worried that Sam might be looking for her.

On her way back down the hall, she met Nicholas coming up. He was walking unsteadily, and his bright eyes were glassy. A stubborn lock of hair near his crown stood straight up. He looked like a naughty schoolboy.

'Ah, Katie my dear,' he said, reaching out and holding her shoulders. His voice was slurred and his cheeks were flushed with drink. 'Come to me, for thy love is better than wine.'

Katie blushed and tried to wriggle free, but Nicholas only tightened his grip. He looked behind him.

'Nobody around,' he whispered. 'Time for a little kiss, my rose of Sharon, my lily of the valley.'

Katie struggled, but he was too strong. He held her head still, brought his mouth closer to hers and seemed to suffocate her with a long wet kiss. His breath tasted rank with wine, garlicky pâté and Stilton cheese. When he stopped, she gulped in the air. But he didn't let her go. One hand was on her bare back now and the other was feeling her breasts.

'Ah, thy breasts are like two young roes that are twins,' he said, breathing hard. 'Come on, Katie. In here. In the bedroom.'

'No!' Katie shouted. 'If you don't let me go I'm going to scream.'

Nicholas laughed. 'I like a girl with a bit of spirit. Come on, I'll make you scream, sure enough. But not yet.' He put one hand over her mouth and started dragging her along the hall. Suddenly, she heard a familiar voice behind them and Nicholas's grip loosened. She shook herself free and turned to hear John Fletcher tell Nicholas to take his hands off her.

'You go to hell!' Nicholas said, clearly too far gone in temper to pull back. 'Who are you to tell me what to do? You're nothing but a jumped-up farm boy.'

And suddenly, John hit him. It was a quick sharp blow to the mouth, and it stopped Nicholas in his tracks. He glared at John as the blood welled to his lips and a thin line trickled down his chin. Out in the garden, a glass smashed and somebody giggled loudly above Mary Wells' 'My Guy'. Nicholas bared his teeth at John, put his hand over his mouth and stalked off to the bathroom.

Fletcher rubbed his knuckles. 'Are you all right, Katie?' he asked.

'Yes, yes, thank you.' Katie stared down at the patterned carpet as she spoke. 'I-I'm sorry . . . I'm so embarrassed. It's not the first time he's tried to touch me, but he's never been that rough before.'

'He's drunk,' Fletcher said, then smiled. 'Don't worry. I've been wanting to do that for a long time.'

'But what will he do? He looked so angry.'

'He'll cool off. Come on, let's get back to the others.'

Katie picked up her shawl, and they walked back into the garden, which was lit now by strategically placed antique lanterns. Katie excused herself, thanking John again, and sneaked around the side of the house into the street. She felt she needed to be out of there for a while, at least until her heart stopped beating so wildly and she could catch her breath again. Her flesh felt numb where Nicholas's hands had touched her. She shuddered.

There was no one in the street. Even the old men had gone from the bridge. The lights were on in the White Rose though, and Katie heard the sound of laughter and talk from inside. She thought the young policeman would be in there, the one nobody knew about but her. He hadn't been invited to the party, of course, so he wouldn't get the chance to spy on them that night. She wondered why he was really in the village. He hadn't asked any searching questions of anyone; he just seemed to be there, somehow, always in sight.

Sighing, Katie crept back into the garden. A slow song was playing and some of the couples held each other close. Suddenly, she felt a hand on her back and flinched.

'It's only me. Dance?'

'B-but I . . . can't . . .'

'Nonsense,' Stephen Collier said. 'It's easy. Just follow what I do.'

Katie had no choice. She saw Sam looking on and smiling with approval from Stephen's doorway. She felt like she had two left feet, and somehow her body just wouldn't respond to the music at all. It felt like wood. Soon, she began to feel dizzy and everything went dark. At the centre of the darkness was a biting, sooty smell. She stumbled.

'Hey, I'm not as bad as all that.' Stephen supported her with one arm and led her to the fountain.

Katie regained her balance. 'I'm sorry,' she said. 'I told you I was no good.'

'If I didn't know better,' Stephen said, 'I'd say you'd had too much to drink.'

Katie smiled. 'About one sip of white wine. It's too much for me.'

'Katie?' Stephen suddenly seemed earnest.

'Yes?'

'I enjoyed our little chat in your kitchen that time. It's good to have someone . . . someone outside to talk to.'

'Outside what?'

'Oh, business, family . . .'

The occasion seemed so long ago that Katie could hardly remember. And Stephen had ignored her ever since. She certainly hadn't imagined it as an enjoyable occasion for either of them. But there was something so little-boyish about Stephen, especially now when he seemed so nervous and serious. The muscle in the corner of his left eye had developed a tic.

'Remember what we talked about?' he went on.

Katie didn't, but she nodded.

He looked around and lowered his voice. 'I think I've made my mind up. I think I'm going to leave Swainshead.'

'But why?'

Stephen noticed a couple of his senior executives heading in their direction. 'We can't talk here, Katie. Not now. Can I see you on Friday?'

'Sam goes to—'

'Yes, I know Sam goes to Eastvale on Fridays. I don't want to see Sam, I want to see you. We'll go for a walk.'

'I-I don't know.'

His tone was urgent and his eyes were pleading with her. The two men had almost reached them. 'All right,' she said. 'A walk. A little one.'

Stephen relaxed. Even the tic in his eye seemed to disappear.

'Ah, Stephen, here you are,' one of the executives, a plump florid man called Teaghe, said. 'Trust you to corner the prettiest filly at the party, eh?' He cast a lecherous glance at Katie, who smiled politely and made an excuse to leave.

She poured herself another glass of wine for appearance's sake and leaned by the side of the French windows, watching the lantern-lit dancers in relief against the huge black mass of Adam's Fell. The garden was a tangled web of shadows, crossing and knotting like an enormous cat's cradle. As the warm light caught their features at certain angles, some of the dancers looked positively satanic.

So, although she had never thought of herself as a sympathetic listener – so bound up in her own shyness and discomfort was she – Stephen had asked her to be his confidante and she had agreed to go for a walk with him, to listen to his problems. It was more than Sam ever asked her to do. There were only two things he wanted from her: work and sex.

She trusted Stephen as far as she could trust any man. He hadn't tried anything last time, when he could have, and he'd been distinctly cool towards her since. But why did he want to leave Swainshead? Why did he seem so on edge? Was he running away from something? Still, she thought, if he was going away, and he really liked her, then there was just a chance he might take her with him.

She suspected that it might be a sin to desert her husband, but she had thought so much about it that she decided it was worth the risk. Surely God would forgive her for leaving a man with such vile and lascivious appetites as Sam Greenock? She could make amends, do good works. She might have to give Stephen her body too, she knew that. If not on Friday, then later, if he took her away with him. But that was one sin nobody could catch her out on. She had learned how to comply with all the things men wanted, but she got no pleasure from them herself. She thought it was just because of Sam, her only lover for years, but when Bernie had forced himself on her and she hadn't had the energy or the power to fight him off, she knew that she could never enjoy the act with any man. Bernie had at least been kind and gentle when he got her where he wanted her, but it made no difference to the way she felt about what he was doing.

She looked at the lantern-lit guests again. Sam was dancing with an attractive brunette, probably from Collier Foods, and Nicholas was back in circulation, talking and laughing by the fountain with a group of commuters who lived in Swainsdale and made their money elsewhere. His lower lip was swollen as if he'd been stung by a bee. When he caught her glance, he glared at her with such lust and hatred that she shivered and pulled her shawl up more tightly around her shoulders.

TWO

In Toronto, Banks combined sightseeing with his search for Anne Ralston in the English-style pubs. The weather remained uncomfortably hot and humid, and a window-rattling thunderstorm one night only seemed to make things worse the next day.

Banks gave the CN Tower a miss, but he walked around the Eaton Centre, a huge shopping mall with a glass roof and a flock of sculptured Canada geese flying in to land at one end, and he visited Yonge and Dundas after dark to watch the hookers and street kids on the neon strip. He took a ferry to Ward's Island and admired the Toronto skyline before walking along the boardwalk on the south side. Lake Ontario glittered in the sun, as vast as an ocean. He went to Harbourfront, where he sipped Carlsberg on a waterfront patio and watched the white sails of the yachts cut slow as knives through treacle in the haze.

One morning he took a bus to Kleinburg to see the

McMichael collection. Sandra, he thought, would love the Lawren Harris mountain-scapes and the native art. Also in the collection was a painting by Emily Carr that he associated with Jenny Fuller, a psychologist friend who sometimes helped with cases in Eastvale. She had a print of it on her living-room wall, and it was at her suggestion that he had made the visit.

Nor could he bear to miss Niagara Falls. If anything, it was even more magnificent than he had expected. He went out on the *Maid of the Mist*, wrapped up in oilskins, and the boat tossed like a cork when it reached the bottom of the falls. From a certain angle, he could see a rainbow cut diagonally across the water. When the boat got closer, the spray filled his eyes like a mist and he could see nothing; he could hear only the primeval roar of the water.

The rest of the time, he visited pubs. Allowing an hour or so in each, he would sit at the bar, show the photographs and ask after Bernard Allen and Anne Ralston of bar staff and customers.

This part of the job was hard on his liver and kidneys, so he tried to slow down his intake and pace himself. To make the task more interesting – for solo pub-crawling is hardly the most exciting pastime in the world – he sampled different kinds of draught beer, both imported and domestic. Most of the Canadian beers tasted the same, and they were uniformly gassy. The English beers, he found, didn't travel well. Double Diamond and Watney's he determinedly ignored, just as he did back home. By far the best were the few local brews that Gerry Webb had told him about: Arkell Bitter, Wellington County Ale, Creemore Springs Lager and Conner Bitter. Smooth and tasty, they had body and, when required, boasted fine heads.

Despite good beer, he was heartily sick of pubs. He was smoking too much, drinking too much and eating too much fried food. On Tuesday, after getting back from Kleinburg, he had tried the Sticky Wicket, the Madison and the Duke of York, all close to the university. No luck. On Wednesday, after his return from Niagara Falls, he had started out at the Spotted Dick, then made his way down busy Yonge Street among the shoppers and pleasure-seekers to the Hop and Grape, via the Artful Dodger and the Jack Russell. He had sat in the Hop and Grape, on the ground floor of an office block near Yonge and College, and watched long-haired heavy metal fans in the street flock towards a rock concert at Maple Leaf Gardens. His clothes were soaked with sweat and his feet hurt. The pub was quiet at that time, as the office workers had gone home and the evening crowds hadn't yet turned up. There were only two days left, and he was very much conscious of time's winged chariot at his rear. Fed up, he had gone back to the house for an early night.

He knew he had to be right though; Bernard Allen had frequented an English-style pub, and he must have had drinking companions who would be mourning his loss.

On Thursday at about three fifteen, Banks got off a streetcar outside the Feathers, in the east end of the city. The inside door opened opposite a small darts area: two boards against a green baize backing, pockmarked with misses. To his left was the pub itself, all darkly gleaming wood, polished brass and deep red velvet upholstery. And it was cool.

The wall opposite the bar was covered with framed photographs, mostly of English and Scottish scenes. Banks recognized a pub he knew in York, Theakston's brewery in Masham, a road sign he'd often passed on the way to

Ripon and, most surprising of all, a photo of the Queen's Arms in Eastvale's cobbled market square. It was an odd sensation, seeing that. He was in a pub over three thousand miles from home looking at a photo of the Queen's Arms. Eerie.

The place was almost empty. Near the door sat a group of four or five people listening to a silver-haired man with a lived-in face and a Lancashire accent complain about income tax.

Banks stood at the bar close to a very tall man with short neat hair. He was smoking a pipe and staring abstractedly into space as if musing about the follies of mankind. Behind the bar, above the till, was a small Union Jack.

'I'll have a pint of Creemore, please,' Banks said, noticing the logo on one of the pumps.

The barmaid smiled. She had curly auburn hair and brown eyes full of humour and mischief. When she walked over to the end of the bar to fill a waitress's order, Banks noticed she was wearing a very short skirt. It did more than justice to a fine pair of legs.

'Quiet,' Banks commented, when she placed the ice-cold pint in front of him.

'It usually is at this time,' she said. 'We get busy around five when people drop in after work.'

Banks took a deep breath and reached for the photographs in his jacket pocket. They were getting dog-eared. He was so used to disappointment that he put hardly any enthusiasm into his question: 'I don't suppose you had a regular here by the name of Bernard Allen, did you?'

'Bernie?' she said. 'Bernie who got killed over in England?'

Banks could hardly believe his ears. 'Yes,' he said. 'Did you know him?'

The barmaid's eyes turned serious as she spoke. 'He was a regular here,' she said. 'I wouldn't say I really knew him, but I talked to him now and then. You know, like you do when you're waitressing. He was a nice guy. Never made any trouble. It was terrible what happened.'

'Did he drink alone?'

'No. There was a group of them – Bernie, Glen, Barry and Ian. They always sat on that corner over there.' She pointed to a round table opposite the far end of the bar.

'Was there ever a woman with them?'

'Sometimes. But I never talked to her. Why do you want to know all this? Are you a cop or something?'

Banks decided on honesty. 'Yes,' he said. 'But I'm here unofficially. We think Bernie met an old friend over here who might have some information for us. It could help us find out who killed him.'

The barmaid rested her elbows on the bar and leaned forward.

Banks showed her the photographs. 'Is this her?'

She looked closely and frowned. 'It could be. The shape of the face is the same, but everything else is different. These must be old photos.'

'They are,' Banks said. 'But it could be her?'

'Yes. Look, I'm sorry, I can't stand here talking. I honestly don't know much more. Jack over there used to talk to Bernie sometimes. He might be able to help.'

She pointed to a man on the periphery of the group near the entrance. He was a solidly built man with a moustache and a fine head of greyish hair, in his mid to late thirties, Banks guessed. At the moment he seemed to be poring over a crossword puzzle.

'Thank you.' Banks picked up his half-finished pint and

walked over to the table. He introduced himself and Jack told him to pull up a chair. The Lancastrian at the next table lit a cigarette and said, 'I'll just have another gin and tonic, then I'll go.'

'We weren't really close friends,' Jack said when Banks had asked about Bernie, 'but we had some decent conversations.' He had a Canadian accent, which surprised Banks. He'd assumed that apart from the bar staff all the regulars were British.

'What did you talk about?'

'Books, mostly. Literature. Bernie was about the only other guy I knew who'd read Proust.'

'Proust?'

Jack gave him a challenging look. 'Greatest writer who ever lived. He wrote *Remembrance of Things Past*.'

'Maybe I'll give him a try,' Banks answered, not sure what he was letting himself in for. He tended to follow through on most of his self-made promises to read or listen to things other people recommended, though time constraints always ensured he had a huge backlog.

'Do that,' said Jack. 'Then I'll have someone to talk to again. Excuse me.' He got up and went to the washroom.

The Lancastrian belched and said to the waitress, 'Gin and tonic please, love. No fruit.'

Banks observed the other people at the table: a small slim youth with an earring and a diamond stud in his left ear; a taller thin-faced man with a crewcut and glasses; a soft-spoken man with a hint of an Irish accent. They were all listening to a Welshman telling jokes.

Jack sat down again and ordered another pint of Black Label. The waitress, a nicely tanned blonde with a beautiful smile, took Banks' order for another Creemore too, and delivered both drinks in no time. Banks paid, leaving her a good tip – one thing he'd soon learned to do on his pub crawl of Toronto.

'Did you know any of Bernie's friends?' he asked.

Jack shook his head. 'Self-important Brits, for the most part. They tend to pontificate a bit too much for my liking. But Bernie seemed to have transcended the parochial barriers of most English teachers.'

Marilyn Rosenberg, at Toronto Community College, had said much the same thing in a different way. Whether it was a plus or a minus in her eyes, Banks hadn't been sure.

'When do they usually come in?'

'About five, most days.'

Banks looked at his watch; it was just after four.

'Thanks a lot,' he said. 'By the way, six across is sculls. "Rows – of heads, we hear!" Head . . . skull. To row . . . to scull.' Jack raised his eyebrows and filled in the answer.

They worked at the crossword together for the next hour as the place filled up. At quarter past five, they were puzzling over 'Take away notoriety and attack someone (6)' when two men in white shirts and business suits walked in.

'That's them over there,' Jack said. 'Excuse me if I don't join you.'

Banks smiled. 'Thanks for your help, anyway.'

'Nice meeting you,' Jack said, and they shook hands. 'Defame. Of course!' he exclaimed just before Banks moved away. '"Take away notoriety and attack someone." Defame. Amazing how you get so much more done when there are two minds working at it.'

Banks agreed. It was the same with police work. He could certainly have done with some help on this trip. Not Sergeant Hatchley – he hadn't the self-control to separate work from a pub crawl – but DC Richmond would have been fine.

When he got to their table, the two men had already taken the opportunity to loosen their ties, take off their suit jackets and roll up their sleeves. One was tall and skinny with a bony face and fine blond hair plastered flat against his skull to cover the receding hairline; the other, who only came up to his friend's shoulders, was pudgy and also balding. What little hair he had stood out like a kind of mist or halo around his head. He wore a fixed smile on his lips, and his dark eyes darted everywhere.

Banks walked over to them and told them why he was in Toronto.

'I'm Ian Grainger,' said the tall blond one. 'Sit down.'

'Barry Clark,' the other said, still smiling and looking everywhere but at Banks.

'Glen should be along in a while,' Ian said. 'How can we help you?'

'I'm not sure if you can. I'm looking for Anne Ralston.'

For a moment, both men frowned and looked puzzled.

'You might know her as Julie.'

'Oh, Julie. Yes, of course,' Barry said. 'You lost me there for a second. Sure we know Julie. But what could she have to do with Bernie's murder?' His accent was English, as was Ian's, but Banks couldn't place either of them exactly.

'I don't honestly know if she had anything to do with it,' Banks said, 'but she's the only real lead we've got.' He explained about her disappearance just after the Addison murder.

The drinks arrived just before Glen Tadworth, a dark-bearded, well padded young man with a pronounced academic stoop and a well developed beer belly, walked over to join them. His red shirt seemed glued to his skin, and there were wet patches under the arms and across the chest. He carried a battered black briefcase stuffed with papers, which he plonked on the floor as he sat down and sighed.

'Bloody students,' he said, running his hand through his greasy black hair. '"Dover Beach" – a simple enough poem, you'd say, wouldn't you?' He looked at Banks as he talked, even though they hadn't been introduced. 'One bright spark came up with the theory that it was about Matthew Arnold's hangover. Quite elaborate, it was too. The "grating roar" was the poet being sick. And as for the "long line of spray" . . . Well, I suppose one should be grateful for their inventiveness, but really . . .' He threw his hands up, then reached over and took a long swig from Ian's pint.

'Don't mind him,' Barry said, managing to keep his eyes on Banks for a split second as he spoke. 'He's always like this. Always complaining.' And he introduced them.

'From Swainsdale, eh?' Glen said. 'A breath of fresh air from the old country. Lord, what I'd give to be able to live back there again. Not Swainsdale in particular, though it'd do. I'm from the West Country myself – Exeter. The accent's flattened out a bit over the years here, I'm afraid.'

'Why can't you go back if you want to?' Banks asked, reaching for another cigarette. 'Surely you weren't sent into permanent exile?'

'Metaphorically, my dear Chief Inspector, metaphorically. You know, some people have got hold of the idea that we expatriates, scattered around the ex-colonies and various watering holes of Europe and Asia, are all pipe-puffing Tories enjoying life without income tax.'

'And aren't you?'

'Far from it. Where is that waitress? Ah, Stella, my dear, a pint of Smithwick's please. Where was I? Exile. Yes. If the government really did seek our proxy votes in the next election, I think they'd bloody well regret it. Most of us feel like exiles. We have skills that no one back home seems to value any more. It's hard enough getting jobs here, but at least it's possible. And they pay well. But I, for one, would be perfectly happy to do the same work back home for less money. There's hardly a day goes by when I don't think about going back.'

'What about Bernie?'

'He was as bad as Glen, if not worse,' Barry said. 'At least recently he was. Full of nostalgia. It's time-travel they're after really, you know, not just a flight across the Atlantic. All of us baby boomers are nostalgic when it comes down to it. That's why we prefer the Beatles to Duran Duran.'

Banks also liked the Beatles better than Duran Duran, a group that his son, Brian, had inflicted on him once or twice before moving on to something new. He thought it was because of the quality of the music, but maybe Barry Clark was right and it was more a matter of nostalgia than anything else. His own father had been just the same, he remembered, going on about Glenn Miller, Nat Gonella and Harry Roy when Banks had wanted to listen to Elvis Presley, The Shadows and Billy Fury.

'The longer you're away, the more you idealize the image of home,' Barry went on, eyes roving the room. The place was packed and noisy now. People stood three deep at the bar. Jack, Banks noticed, had been joined by a small pretty woman with short dark hair laid flat against her skull. The Lancastrian and his friends had left. 'Of course, what people don't realize is that the country's changed beyond all recognition,' Barry continued. 'We'd be foreigners there now, but to us home is still the Queen's Christmas message, the last night of the Proms, Derby Day, a Test Match at Lords, the FA Cup Final – without bloodshed! – leafy lanes, a green and pleasant land. Ordered and changeless. Bloody hell, even the dark Satanic mills have some sort of olde worlde charm for homesick expatriates.'

'Damn right,' Glen said. 'I'd work in a bloody woollen mill in Bingley if it meant being back home. Well, maybe . . . It's the wistfulness of the exile, you see, Chief Inspector. You get it a lot in poetry. Especially the Irish.'

Banks was beginning to see what Jack had meant.

'Bernie was just the same,' Ian said. 'You should have heard him going on about Yorkshire. It was bloody Dales this and bloody Dales that. You'd think he was talking about paradise. You'll never catch me going back to live over there. Canada's a great place as far as I'm concerned.'

'That's because you're in real estate,' Glen said. 'You're making a bloody fortune. Is that all you care about – the material things? What about your soul, your roots?'

'Oh, shut up, Glen. You're getting tiresome.'

'If he could have got a job over there,' Banks asked, 'do you think he would have gone back?'

'Like a shot,' Ian answered. The others agreed.

'Did he ever mention anything about a job?'

'He did say there was a chance of getting back to stay,' Glen said. 'Lucky bastard. But I didn't know whether to believe him or not.'

'What was this chance?'

'He didn't say. Very hush-hush, apparently.'

'Why?'

Glen scratched his shoulder and tried to unstick the shirt from his armpit. 'Dunno. It was just one of those nights when you've had a few too many, if you know what I mean. Bernie said something about a plan he had to get himself back home.'

'But he gave you no details?'

'No. Said he'd let us know after he got back.'

'Was it a job he mentioned?'

'Not specifically, no. Just a chance to get back. I assumed it must have been some possible job offer. How else would he be able to live?'

'How attached was he to teaching?'

'He liked it up to a point,' Glen answered. 'It was something he was good at. He should have been teaching at university. He was good enough, but there aren't any jobs. Like most of us though, he hated the conditions he had to work in and he despised the students' wilful ignorance. They don't know anything and they don't want to know – unless it's in a ballpark or on video. They expect you to spoon-feed them knowledge, then ask them to regurgitate it in a test. For that they expect to be given an A-plus, no matter how bad their writing or how inaccurate their answers. I could go on—'

'You usually do, Glen,' Barry cut in, 'but I don't think Mr Banks wants to hear it.'

Banks smiled. 'Actually, I am running out of time,' he said. 'I need to find Julie as quickly as possible. Do you know where she lives?'

'No,' said Ian. 'She just comes in on a Friday after work for a couple of drinks.'

'It's somewhere near here, I think,' Barry added. 'She mentioned sunbathing in Kew Gardens once.'

'Have you any idea what surname she's using?'

'It's Culver, isn't it?' Barry said. 'Or Cleaver, Carver, something like that.'

None of the others could improve on Barry's contribution.

'Do you know where she works?'

'In one of those towers near King and Bay,' Ian answered. 'The TD Centre or First Canadian Place. She complained that the elevators made her ears go funny.'

'That's a lot of help,' Glen said. 'Do you know how many businesses operate from those places?'

Ian shrugged. 'Well, that's all I know. What about you?'

Glen and Barry both shook their heads.

'She should be in here at about six tomorrow though,' Barry said. 'She hasn't missed a week yet.'

'Fine. Look, would you do me a favour? If she turns up early or if I'm late, please don't tell her I want to see her. It might scare her off. You know how some people react to the police.'

'Are you sure you're not after her for something?' Glen asked suspiciously.

'Information. That's all.'

'All right,' Glen agreed. 'If it's going to help catch Bernie's killer, we'll do whatever you want.' He paused to pick up his pint glass and raise it for a toast. 'There is one good thing in all this, you know. At least Bernie died in the place he wanted to live.'

'Yes,' Banks said. 'There is that.'

And they all drank to dying where they wanted to live.

11

ONE

'**John told** me about Nick's behaviour at the party the other night,' Stephen Collier said. 'I'm sorry. I warned you to stay away from him.'

Katie looked down at the stony path and blushed. 'I didn't go seeking him,' she said. 'He's an animal, a filthy animal.'

'But he is my brother, Katie. He's the only family I've got left. I know he acts outrageously sometimes, but . . . I promise it won't happen again.'

Katie remembered a phrase from the Bible: 'Am I my brother's keeper?' Could Stephen keep Nicholas like an animal in a zoo? He looked strained, she thought. He poked at the stones and sods with his ashplant stick as they walked; his face was pale and the tic in his eye was getting worse.

It was fine walking weather: warm but not hot, with a few high white clouds and no sign of rain. Sam was in Eastvale for the day – not that Katie's walking out with Stephen would have mattered to him, she thought; he practically threw her at the Colliers as if she were his membership ticket to some exclusive club.

They took the diagonal path up the side of Swainshead Fell, heading for the source of the river. The air was clear, and after a few minutes' walking even Stephen's pallid cheeks began to glow like embers.

At last they reached their destination. The source of the River Swain was an unspectacular wet patch on the side of Swainshead Fell. All around it, the grass was greener and grew more abundantly than anywhere else. Only yards away was the source of another river, the Gaiel, which, when it reached the valley below, perversely turned north towards Cumbria.

Stephen had brought a flask of coffee and some dark chocolate. They sat down to eat on the dry grass above the source and looked back on Swainshead. A lapwing went into his extended 'pee-wit' song as he wove through the air, plummeted and levelled out just before hitting the ground. His wings beat like sheets flapping in a gale.

'He must be trying to attract a mate,' Stephen said.

'Or scare us away.'

'Perhaps. Coffee? Chocolate?'

Katie accepted the plastic cup of black coffee. She usually liked hers with plenty of milk and a spoonful of sugar, but she took it as it came without complaint. The dark bitter chocolate puckered her taste buds.

'I shouldn't be here, you know,' she said, pushing back a stray wisp of fair hair behind her ear.

'Relax,' Stephen said. 'Sam's in Eastvale.'

'I know. But that's not the point. People will talk.'

'Why should they? There's nothing to talk about. Everybody knows we're all friends. You're so old-fashioned, Katie.'

Katie flushed. 'I can't help it. I wish I could,' she added in a whisper.

'Look,' Stephen went on in a soothing voice, 'we've just gone for a short walk up the fell side, as many people do.

Where's the harm in that? We're not hiding from anyone, we're not sneaking off. You act as if we're guilty of something terrible.'

'It just feels wrong,' Katie said, managing a brief smile. 'Oh, don't mind me. I'm trying, I really am. I'm just not very good with people.'

'Don't you feel comfortable with me?'

Katie fidgeted with the silver paper from the chocolate wrapper, folding it into a neat shiny square. 'I don't know,' she said. 'I don't feel afraid.'

Stephen laughed. 'At least that's a start. But seriously, Katie, sometimes it's necessary to talk. I told you the other night I've got nobody. Nick's hardly the type to make a good listener, and the people at work are just that: employees, colleagues, not friends.'

'What about all those guests at the party?'

'Nick's people, most of them. Or from work, business acquaintances. Don't you ever need to talk to someone real, Katie? Don't you ever have problems you want to let out and share?'

Katie frowned and stared at him. 'Yes,' she said. 'Yes, of course I do. But I'm no good at it. I don't know where to start.'

'Start with your life, Katie. Are you happy?'

'I don't know. Am I supposed to be?'

'That's what life's for, isn't it, to be enjoyed?'

'Or suffered.'

'Are you suffering?'

'I don't think I'm happy, if that's what you mean.'

'Why don't you do something about it?'

'There's nothing I can do.'

'But there must be. You must be able to change things if you want.'

'I don't see how. What would I do? Without the guest house I've got nothing. Where would I go? I don't know anywhere outside Leeds and Swainsdale.' She toyed with a stray tress of hair. 'I could just see me down in London or somewhere like that. I wouldn't last five minutes.'

'Cities aren't quite as bad as you think they are. You only see the worst on television. Many people live happy lives there.'

'Still,' Katie said, 'I'd be lost.' She finished the coffee and wiped her lips with the back of her hand.

'Perhaps by yourself you would be.'

'What do you mean?'

Suddenly Stephen seemed closer, and somehow he seemed to be holding her hand. Katie tensed. She didn't want to upset him. If he wanted to touch her she would have to let him, but her stomach clenched and the wind roared in her ears. His touch was oddly chaste though; it didn't seem to threaten her at all.

'I don't know, Katie,' he said. 'I'm not sure what I'm saying. But I've got to go away. I can't stay around here any longer.'

'But why not?'

She felt him trembling as he moved even closer and his grip tightened on her hand. 'There are things you don't know anything about, Katie,' he said. 'Dear, sweet Katie.' And he brushed his fingers down her cheek. They felt cold.

Katie wanted to move away, but she didn't dare struggle. 'I don't know what you mean,' she burst out. 'Sam's always telling me I know nothing, too. What is it? Am I so blind or so stupid?' There were tears in her eyes now, blurring her vision of the valley below and the water that bubbled relentlessly from the source.

'No,' Stephen said. 'No, you're not blind or stupid. But

things aren't always what they seem; people aren't what they pretend to be. Listen, let me tell you . . .'

TWO

The woman who sat opposite Banks in the dining section of the Feathers had changed considerably from the one in Bernard Allen's photograph, but it was definitely the same person. She wore her hair cut short and tinted blonde now, and was dressed in a cream business suit. When she sat down and fished in her bag for a cigarette, Banks also noticed that the carefree laughter in her eyes had hardened into a wary, suspicious look. Her long cigarette had a white filter which soon became blotched with lipstick; she had a habit of tapping it on the edge of the ashtray even when there was no ash, and she held it straight out between the V of her first two fingers like an actress in an old movie, pursing her lips to inhale. Her nails were long and painted red.

She had turned up at six, as Glen had said, and she and Banks had left the others to go and talk privately over dinner. There wasn't much separation between the two areas of the pub except for the way the seating was arranged, and they could still hear the conversations at the bar and the tables.

The waitress, a petite brunette with a twinkle in her eye and a cheeky smile, came up and gave them menus. 'Something to drink?' she asked.

Julie ordered a White Russian and Banks a glass of red wine, just for a change.

'I need to know why you left Swainshead in such a hurry,' he said, when the waitress had gone for the drinks.

'Can't a woman do as she pleases? It's not a police state, you know. Or it wasn't when I was last there.'

'Nor is it now. It was your timing that interested us.'

'Oh? Why?'

'We tend to be suspicious of someone who disappears without a trace the day after a murder.'

'That was nothing to do with me.'

'Don't play the innocent. What did you expect us to think? You could have been in danger yourself, or you could have been the killer. For all we knew you could have been buried down a disused mineshaft. You didn't stop to let anyone know what had happened to you.'

'Well, I'm telling you now. That killing had nothing to do with me.'

'How do you know about it? You don't seem at all surprised at my mentioning it, but the body wasn't discovered until after you'd left.'

Julie ground her cigarette into the ashtray. 'Don't try your tricks on me,' she said. 'I read the papers. I know what happened.'

The waitress arrived with the drinks and asked if they were ready to order. Banks asked for a few more minutes and she smiled and went away. Julie turned to her menu.

'What would you recommend?' Banks asked.

She shrugged. 'The food's always good here. It depends what you fancy. The prime-rib roast and Yorkshire pudding on special is excellent, if you don't mind being reminded too much of home.'

Banks looked around at the decor and the photos on the walls. 'Not at all,' he said, smiling.

This time a different waitress came for their orders, an attractive woman with reddish blonde hair and a warm manner. Banks hoped he hadn't offended the other.

'Where did you go?' he asked Julie, as soon as they'd ordered their meals.

'None of your damn business.' She sipped her White Russian.

'A week after you left,' Banks pressed on, 'the body of a London private detective called Raymond Addison was discovered in Swainshead. He'd been murdered. Did you know anything about that?'

'No.'

'We've got good reason to think you did. Listen, if you want to make things difficult, Miss Ralston—'

'It's Culver, Mrs. Mrs Julie Culver. And it's quite legal. Julie's my middle name and Culver is my husband's. Ex-husband's, I should say.'

'Why change your name if you've nothing to hide?'

She shrugged. 'It was a new start. Why not a new name?'

'Not very convincing. But Mrs Culver it is. We're on good terms with the Canadian government. We have extradition arrangements and a mutual help policy. If I wanted to, I could make enough fuss to have you sent back to England to answer my questions. This is the easy way.'

Julie lit another cigarette. 'I don't believe you. I'm a Canadian citizen now. You can't touch me at all.'

'That doesn't matter,' Banks said. 'You're connected to a murder in England. Don't expect your government to protect you from that.'

'But you can't prove I had anything to do with it. It's just a coincidence I went away then.'

'Is it? What about your involvement with Stephen Collier?'

Julie paled. 'What about it? What's he been telling you?'

'Nothing. What does he know?'

'How should I know?'

Banks sighed. 'A few weeks ago a friend of yours, Bernard Allen, was murdered in the hanging valley just over Swainshead Fell.'

'I know the place,' Julie said sadly. 'I've been there with him. It always looked like autumn. But what makes you think his death had anything to do with me? I wasn't even in the country. I was here. It could have been a thief or a psycho . . . or a . . .'

There was something in her tone that let Banks know she was interested now, no longer so hostile. 'In the first place,' he said, 'we know that you told him not to let anyone know he'd met you here, which is suspicious enough in itself. And in the second place, he did tell someone: a woman called Katie Greenock. Her heart seems to be in the right place, but she told her husband, Sam, who soon broadcasted it to the whole White Rose crowd. In the third place, Bernard had been talking about going home to stay, and there's no evidence he had a job lined up. Then Bernard got killed before he had a chance to leave the dale. What does all that indicate to you?'

'You're the sleuth. You tell me.' Julie blew cigarette smoke down her nose.

Banks leaned forward. 'The way I read it,' he said, 'is that you knew something about Raymond Addison's murder. Something incriminating. I'm not sure who else was involved, or why, but it had to be someone with money. I'd guess that Stephen Collier played a large part. I think you told Bernard what you knew and he intended to use that knowledge to blackmail his way to what he wanted most – his return to Swainshead.'

'My God! I . . . Are you trying to say I'm responsible for Bernie's death?'

'I'm not placing any blame, Mrs Culver. I simply want to know what happened. I want to nail Bernie's killer.'

Julie seemed to be thinking fast. Conflicting emotions flashed across her face. 'I'm not guilty of anything,' she said finally. 'I've nothing to be afraid of. And I don't believe you. Bernie could never have been a blackmailer.'

The waitress brought their food. Before she left, they ordered another round of drinks, then Banks tucked into his roast while Julie picked at a Caesar salad. They remained silent while they ate. It wasn't until they both pushed their plates aside and reached for their cigarettes that Julie started to talk again.

'It's been such a long time, you know,' she began. 'A lot's happened. There've been long stretches when I haven't thought about Swainshead at all.'

'Not homesick?'

'Me? I'm at home anywhere. Almost anywhere. Though I can't say I cared for the Middle East much.'

'Bernie was homesick.'

'He was the type though, wasn't he? If you'd known him you'd have understood. The place was in his blood. He couldn't even really settle down in Leeds. Yes, Bernie wanted to go back. Which was a shame. I'd kind of been hoping . . .'

'You and Bernie? Again?'

She raised a thin dark-pencilled eyebrow. 'You know about that?'

'It was hardly a state secret.'

'True. Anyway, why not? We were both free agents again.'

'Tell me what happened five years ago that sent you running off around the world.'

The waitress came to pick up their plates. Banks

ordered a pint of Creemore this time and Julie asked for a coffee and a double cognac. All the spaces were occupied now. Next to them, a group of eight people had pulled two tables together.

'It seems more like a million years ago,' Julie said when she got her drink. 'I suppose I was a naive young thing back then. My education really began after I left.'

She was stalling for time, Banks thought, telling the story her own way. Perhaps she wasn't sure yet whether she was going to tell him the truth or not. The best thing for now, he decided, was to let her go with it and subtly steer her in the right direction. 'Where did you go?' he asked.

'First I went to Europe. I'd been saving up for quite a long time – kept my money under the mattress, believe it or not – just waiting for the day when I knew I would take off and never come back. I took a boat over to Holland and ended up in Amsterdam for a while. Then I bummed around France, Italy, Germany. To cut a long story short, I met a man. A Canadian. This'd be about a year later. He took me back to Vancouver with him and we got married.' Julie blew out a steady stream of smoke. 'Life was fine for a while . . . then he decided I wasn't enough for him. Two can play at that game, I thought . . . Anyway, it ended.'

'When did you first get in touch with Bernie?'

'About eighteen months ago. That was after I split up with Charles. Bernie was having marriage problems of his own, I soon found out, and he seemed happy enough to hear from me. I might have got in touch with him earlier, but I'd been wary about doing so. I knew he was here, of course. He left Swainshead before I did. But I felt that I'd burned all my bridges.'

'What made you contact him, then?'

'Circumstances, really. I'm a freelance publicity agent. I started the business in Vancouver because I liked the idea and it gave me something to do while my husband was . . . not around.' She tapped her cigarette against the glass ashtray. 'It turned out I had a knack, a flair, so I decided to open an office in Toronto as well. I don't know how much you understand about Canada, but Toronto is pretty much the centre of the universe here. I knew Bernie lived in the city, so I thought what the hell. Any trouble I might have caused would have blown over by now anyway.'

'Trouble?'

She narrowed her eyes and looked at him closely. 'I had thought Bernie might not want to see me.'

'I don't understand.'

'I went out with Stephen Collier.'

'But Bernard was over here by then. What was that to him?'

'It's not that. Bernie and I were never much more than childhood sweethearts anyway. But we were close friends, like brother and sister. I was hoping that might change here . . .' She sighed. 'Anyway, it's just that Stephen . . . well . . . he's a Collier.'

'And Bernie was very class conscious?'

'Yes.'

'So he'd feel betrayed.'

'Something like that.'

'And did he?'

'He wrote me some pretty nasty letters at the time. Then, when I went away, we lost touch for a while. But when we met up again here it had all blown over. Bernie was compassionate. He understood. That's why I can't believe he was a blackmailer.'

'He might not have been. I can't be sure. He might just have opened his mouth out of turn.'

Julie smiled. 'That sounds more like him.'

'What about Nicholas Collier?' Banks asked. 'Were you ever involved with him?'

Julie raised her eyebrows. 'What on earth do you think I am?' she asked, smiling. 'I didn't get around that much. And credit me with some taste. Nicky really did nothing for me, though I caught him giving me the eye once or twice.'

'Sorry,' Banks said. 'I'm not trying to insinuate you're a—'

'Tart? Slut? Harlot? Jezebel? Loose woman? Believe me, I've been called much worse.' The old laughter lit up Julie's eyes for a moment. 'Do you know the difference between a slut and a bitch?'

Banks shook his head.

'A slut is a woman who sleeps with anyone; a bitch is a woman who sleeps with anyone but you.'

Banks laughed. 'That's from the man's point of view, of course.'

'Of course.'

'So what happened?' he asked. 'What made you leave when you did?'

'You're a persistent man, Mr Banks,' Julie said, lighting another long white cigarette. 'Even my tasteless jokes don't seem to deflect you for very long. But I'm still not sure I ought to tell you.'

Banks caught her eyes and held them. 'Mrs Culver,' he said quietly, 'Bernard Allen – your childhood sweetheart, as you called him – was murdered. All murders are cruel and vicious, but this one was worse than many. First he was stabbed, and then his face was slashed and beaten in with a rock so nobody could recognize him. When we found him he'd been hidden away in the hanging valley for nearly two weeks and there were maggots crawling out of his eye sockets.'

Julie turned pale and gripped her cognac glass so tightly Banks thought she was going to shatter it. Her jaw was clenched and a muscle just below her ear twitched. 'Bastard,' she whispered.

The silent tension between them seemed to last for hours. Banks could hear the aimless chatter around him as if it were from a distant movie soundtrack: snippets of conversation about marathon running, beer, cricket and teaching native children up north, all in a medley of Canadian, Yorkshire, London and Scottish accents. Julie didn't even seem to realize he was there any more. She was staring at the wall just to the left of him. He half turned and saw a photograph of a wooded valley. The leaves were russet, yellow and orange.

He lit a cigarette. Julie finished her cognac and a little colour returned to her cheeks. The waitress came and they ordered another round.

When they had their drinks, Julie shook her head and regarded Banks with something close to hatred. 'For Bernie, then,' she said, and began: 'The night before I left I was supposed to see Stephen. We'd arranged to go to dinner at the Box Tree in Ilkley. He picked me up about half an hour late and he seemed unusually agitated – so much so that he pulled into a lay-by after we'd not gone more than four or five miles. And then he told me. He said there'd been some trouble and someone had got hurt. He didn't say killed at that time, just hurt. He was in a terrible state. Then he said something about the past catching up, that it was connected with something that had happened in Oxford.'

'When he was at university there?'

'I suppose so. He did go to Oxford. Anyway, this man, a private investigator, had turned up out of the blue and was intent on causing trouble. Stephen told me that Sam Greenock called and said there was someone looking for a Mr Collier. Sam was a bit suspicious about the newcomer asking questions and didn't give anything away. The man said he was going for a short evening walk up the valley. Stephen said he went after him and they talked and the man was going to blackmail the family.'

'About this event that had occurred in Oxford?'

'Yes. According to Stephen, tempers were raised, they fought and the man was hurt, badly hurt. I told Stephen he should call an ambulance.

'He got angry then and told me I didn't understand. That was when he said the man was dead. He went on to say there was nothing to connect them. Sam would keep quiet if they humoured him and let him play the local squire. Stephen just had to tell someone, to unburden himself, and he didn't really have anyone else he felt he could talk to but me.'

'What was your reaction?'

Julie lit a fresh cigarette from the stub of her old one. 'You have to understand Stephen,' she said. 'In many ways he's a kind, considerate, gentle man. But he's also a businessman and he can be ruthless when he feels the need. But more than all that, he's a Collier. There are few things more important to him than the good name of his family and its history. I wouldn't say I was in love with him, but I thought a lot of him and I didn't want to see him suffer. Needless to say, we didn't have dinner that night. We stopped at the nearest pub and had a bit too much to drink, then we—' Julie stopped. 'The rest is of no interest. I never saw him again after that night.'

'Why did you leave the next day? Did he suggest it to you?'

'No. I think he trusted me. He knew I was on his side.'

'So why did you go?'

'For my own reasons. First, and perhaps least, I'd been thinking about making a break for a while. I've no family. My parents died ten years ago and I just kept on the cottage. I had no real ambitions, no plans for my life. I was getting bored with my job and I was realistic enough not to see myself as the future Mrs Stephen Collier. Stephen wasn't going to propose, and I'd had hints from him that Nicholas didn't consider me to be of the right class, as if I wasn't aware of that already. These new events just hurried me along a bit. Secondly, I didn't trust myself. I thought if the police came around and started asking me questions, they'd know something was wrong and they'd keep pressuring me until I gave Stephen away. I didn't want to let that happen. I'm not a good liar, Mr Banks, as you can see.'

'And third?'

'Fear.'

'Of Stephen?'

'Yes. As I said, he's a complex man. There's a dark side to him. He's vulnerable in some ways, but very practical in others. Sentimental and pragmatic. It can sometimes make for a frightening combination. Didn't someone once say that Mafia dons are very sentimental people? Don't they send flowers to the widow when they've killed someone? And weren't the Nazis sentimental too? Anyway, he'd done it before, confided in me one day then cut me dead the next – no pun intended – just pretended we'd never been intimate at all. Basically, Stephen couldn't get close to anyone. He'd try, and one of the ways he did it was by confiding. But then he'd regret it the next day and turn cold. What worried me was the importance of this confidence. It was the kind of thing he might not be able to live with, someone as weak as me knowing his secret.'

'In other words, you were worried you might become his next victim.'

'I know it sounds a horrible thing to say about someone you basically like and respect – even loved, perhaps, once – but yes, it did cross my mind. Much easier to disappear, as I'd been thinking of it anyway. And there was no one to make a fuss about my going.'

'What kind of things did he confide in you about before?'

'Oh, nothing much. Perhaps a slightly shady business deal; he was pleased if he'd put one over on somebody. Or an income tax fiddle. He hated the Inland Revenue.'

'Nothing more?'

'No. Not until that time.'

They sipped their drinks and let the conversations flow around them. Julie seemed more relaxed now she had told her story, and Banks could see no traces of that hateful look left in her eyes.

'Did he say anything else about this incident in Oxford?' he asked.

Julie shook her head. 'Nothing.'

'So you don't know what happened there, or who else might have been involved?'

'No. I'm sorry. At the time I never even thought to ask. It was all hard enough to take in as it was.'

Banks sighed. Still, even if he hadn't uncovered the whole story yet, he'd done well. The trip had been worthwhile. Julie rejoined the others. Banks said his farewells and left. It was about nine o'clock, a hot humid evening. Instead of taking the bus, he crossed Kingston Road and started walking towards the lake. The road sloped steeply at one point, crossed another main street with tram rails, then a hundred yards or so farther on ended at a beach.

Couples walked hand in hand along the boardwalk or sat on benches and stared out at the water. Some people jogged by, sweating, and others ambled along with dogs on leashes. Banks made his way over the soft sand to where a group of rocks stuck out into the lake. He clambered as far forward as he could and sat down on the warm stone. Water slopped around just below his feet. The horizon was a broad mauve band; above it, the sky's pink was tinged with misty grey. Banks lit a cigarette and wondered if it was the United States he could see in the distance or just a low narrow layer of mist.

He'd got what he came for, though he still couldn't put everything together. At least when he got back he would be able to question Stephen Collier more thoroughly, no matter what the man's influence with the deputy chief constable. Collier had killed Raymond Addison, and he might even have killed Bernard Allen too. There was no proof as yet, but Banks would find some if it took him a lifetime. Collier wasn't going to escape justice because of influence or social position, of that Banks would make sure.

By the time he had finished his cigarette, the sun had gone down much lower and the sky had changed. The horizon was now grey and the mauve band much higher in the sky. The lake seemed scattered with pink, as if the colour had transformed itself into raindrops and shattered the ice-blue surface of the water. Carefully, Banks got to his feet on the angled rock and made his way back towards a streetcar stop.

THREE

Earlier that day, back in Swainsdale, Detective Constable Philip Richmond had sat on a knoll high on Adam's Fell and unwrapped his cheese and pickle sandwiches. He flicked away the flies that gathered and poured some coffee from his flask. Up there, the air was pure and sharp; below, the sun glinted on the steel kegs in the back yard of the White Rose and flashed in the fountain playing in the Colliers' huge garden behind the ugly Gothic mansion. The old men stood on the bridge, and the Greenocks' front door was closed.

Sam had driven off on one of his regular jaunts to Leeds or Eastvale, and Katie had gone for a walk with Stephen Collier up Swainshead Fell. He thought he could see them across in the north-east, near a patch of grass that was greener than that around it, but it could have been some-one else.

Sipping the bitter black coffee, Richmond had reminded himself that tomorrow was his last day in Swainshead. He was expected back at the station with a report on Sunday morning. Not that he hadn't enjoyed himself – it had been very much like a week's holiday – but he longed to get back to his Eastvale mates. Tomorrow the rugby team was playing Skipton, a game he would have to miss. There was always a good booze-up and sing-song after the match, and it would be a shame to miss that too. Jim Hatchley was usually there for the booze, of course. An honorary member they called him now he wasn't fit enough to play any more. But even the sergeant's presence didn't spoil Richmond's fun: a few jars, a good sing-song, then, with a bit of luck, a kiss and a cuddle with Doreen on the way home. He prided himself on being a man of simple tastes, yet he also liked to think that nothing else about him was simple.

Finishing his sandwich, he unwrapped a Kit-Kat and picked up *The Three Stigmata of Palmer Eldritch*, the last of the four Philip K. Dick books he'd brought along. But he couldn't concentrate. He began to wonder why nothing had happened during Banks' absence. Was the killer certain that the chief inspector would find out nothing in Toronto? Or was there, perhaps, no connection at all between the Addison and Allen murders?

Certainly there had been a bit of a fuss or flap, as Freddie Metcalfe had said, earlier in the week. But it had soon died down and everyone carried on as normal. Was it a false sense of security? The lull before the storm. Perhaps they knew who Richmond was and were being especially careful? He certainly couldn't keep an eye on all of them.

He stroked his moustache and turned back to his book. Not ours to reason why . . . But still, he thought, an arrest would have helped his career. A thrilling car chase, perhaps, or a cross-country marathon. He pictured himself bringing in the killer, arm twisted up his back, and throwing him in Eastvale nick under Banks' approving smile. Then he laughed at himself, brushed a persistent wasp away and went back to Philip K. Dick.

FOUR

That Saturday, the afternoon of his last day in Toronto, Banks went to his first baseball game. The retractable roof was open and a breeze from the lake relieved some of the humidity at the SkyDome, where the Toronto Blue Jays were playing the New York Yankees, but the temperature was still almost thirty degrees. In England, people would have been fainting from the heat.

Banks and Gregson sat in the stands, ate hot dogs and drank beer out of flimsy plastic cups.

'Lucky to be drinking it at all,' Gregson said when Banks complained. 'It took a lot of doing, getting drinking allowed at ball games.'

A fat boy of about twelve sitting next to Banks stopped shovelling barbecue-flavoured potato crisps into his maw to stand up and hurl obscene death threats at the Yankees' pitcher. His equally obese mother looked embarrassed but made no attempt to control him.

Banks wished his son, Brian, could be there. Unlike Banks, he had watched enough baseball on Channel 4 to be able to understand the game. When Banks first took his seat, the only baseball term he knew was home run, but by the end of the third innings, Gregson had explained all about RBIs, the tops and bottoms of the innings, designated hitters, knuckle balls, the bullpen, bunting, the balk rule, pinch hitters and at least three different kinds of pitches.

The game mounted to an exciting conclusion, and the boy next to him spilled his crisps all over the floor.

Finally, the home crowd went wild. Down five–four at the bottom of the ninth, with two out, the sixth Blue Jay up drove one home with all the bases loaded – a grand slam, Gregson called it. That made the score eight–five, and that was how the game ended.

They pushed their way out of the stadium, and Gregson negotiated the heavy traffic up Spadina to Bloor, where they stopped in at the Madison for a farewell drink.

'Are you planning to do anything about the Culver woman?' Gregson asked.

Banks sipped his pint of Conner bitter. They were out on the patio, and the late afternoon sun beat down on his shoulders.

'No,' he answered. 'What did she do, after all?'

'From the sound of it, she withheld evidence. She was a material witness. If she'd spoken up, this new homicide might never have happened.'

Banks shook his head. 'She didn't have much choice really. I know what you mean, but you've got to understand what things are like around Swainshead. It's not like Toronto. She couldn't tell what she knew. There was loyalty, yes, but there was also fear. The Colliers are a powerful family. If she'd stayed we might have got something out of her, but on the other hand something might have happened to her first.'

'So she left under threat?'

'That's the way I'd put it, yes.'

'And you think this Collier guy killed Allen because he knew too much?'

'I think it was more to do with what Allen intended to do with his knowledge. I can't prove it, but I think he was going to blackmail Stephen Collier. Julie Culver disagrees, but from what one of Allen's boozing buddies told me, he had some plan to get back home to England. I think he asked Collier for the money to come home and live in Swainshead again, or maybe to fix him up with a job. Collier's brother teaches at a small public school, and Allen was a teacher. Maybe he suggested that Stephen tell Nicholas to get him a job there. Instead, Stephen decided to get rid of Allen the same way he did with Addison.'

'Shit,' said Gregson. 'I'd no idea Toronto was so bad

that people would stoop to blackmail to get out of here.'

Banks laughed. 'Maybe it's just that Swainsdale is so beautiful people would do anything to get there. I don't know. Allen was seriously disturbed, I think. A number of things took their toll on him: the divorce, the distance from home, the disappointment of not getting the kind of job that would really challenge his mind. Someone told me that he had gone beyond the parochial barriers of most English teachers, but he found himself in a system that placed no value on the exceptional, a system that almost imposed such barriers. The teaching he was doing was dreary, the students were ignorant and uninterested, and I think he tended to blame it on the local educational system. He thought things would be better in England. He probably remembered his own grammar school days when even poor kids got to learn Latin, and he thought things were still like that. Perhaps he didn't even think he was doing anything really bad when he approached Collier. Or maybe he did. He had plenty of cause to resent him.'

'That old British class system again?'

'Partly. It's hard to figure Allen out. Mostly, he seems like a decent person gone wrong, but he also had a big chip on his shoulder all along. I don't suppose we'll ever know what really motivated him.'

'But you do have your killer.'

'Yes – if he hasn't done a bunk. But we've no proof yet.'

'He knows you're here, on to the girl?'

'The whole village knows. We've got a man there.'

'Well, then . . . What time's your flight?'

'Nine o'clock.' He looked at his watch. 'Christ, it's six now. I'd better get back and pick up my stuff.'

'I'll drive you,' Gregson said. 'I'm off duty all day, and it can be a real hassle getting to the airport.'

'Would you? That's great.'

At the house, Banks packed his meagre belongings and the presents he had bought for his family, then left a thank-you note with the bottle of Scotch for Gerry. In a way, he felt sad to leave the house and neighbourhood that had become familiar to him over the past week: the sound of streetcars rattling by; the valley with its expressway and green slopes; the downtown skyline; the busy overflowing Chinese shops at Broadview and Gerrard.

The traffic along Lakeshore Boulevard to the airport turn-off wasn't too heavy, and they made it with plenty of time to spare. The two policemen swapped addresses and invitations outside the departures area, then Gregson drove straight off home. Banks didn't blame him. He'd always hated hanging around airports himself if he didn't have a plane to catch.

After the queue at the check-in desk, the trip to the duty-free shop and the passage through security and immigration, it was almost time to board the plane. As they took off, Banks looked out of the window and saw the city lit up in the twilight below him: grids and figure eights of light as far as he could see in every direction except south, where he could pick out the curve of the bay and the matt silver-grey of Lake Ontario.

Once in the air, it was on with the Walkman – Kiri te Kanawa's soaring arias seemed most appropriate this time – down the hatch with the Johnnie Walker and away with the food. A seasoned traveller already. This time even the movie was tolerable. A suspense thriller without the car chases and special effects that so often marred that type of film for Banks, it concentrated on the psychology of police-man and victim.

He slept for a while, managed to choke down the coffee

and roll that came for breakfast, and looked out of the window to see the sun shining over Ireland.

It was nearly ten o'clock in the morning, local time, when he cleared customs and reclaimed his baggage. Among the crowd of people waiting to welcome friends and relatives stood Sandra, who threw her arms around him and gave him a long kiss.

'I told Brian and Tracy they should come, too,' she said, breaking away and picking up the duty-free bag, 'but you know what they're like about sleeping in on Sunday mornings.'

'So it's not that they don't love me any more?'

'Don't be silly. They've missed you as much as I have. Almost.'

She kissed him again, and they set off for the car.

'It's a bloody maze, this place,' Sandra complained, 'and they really fleece you for parking. Then there's road-works everywhere on the way. They're still working on Barton bridge, you know. It was misty too, high up in the Pennines. Oh, I am going on, aren't I? I'm just so glad to see you. You must be tired.'

Banks stifled a yawn. 'It's five in the morning where I am. Where I was, rather. And I can't sleep on planes. Anything interesting happen while I was away?'

Sandra frowned and hesitated. 'I wasn't going to tell you,' she said, loading the small case and the duty-free bag into the boot of the white Cortina, 'at least not until we got home. Superintendent Gristhorpe called this morning just before I set off.'

'On a Sunday morning? What about?'

'He said he wants to see you as soon as you get back. I told him what state you'd be in. Oh, he apologized and all that, but you've still got to go in.'

'What is it?' Banks lit cigarettes for both Sandra and himself as she drove down the spiral ramp from the fourth floor of the multi-storey car park out into the sunlit day.

'Bad news,' she said. 'There's been another death in Swainshead.'

PART THREE:

THE DREAMING SPIRES

12

ONE

'**Accidental death!** Don't you think that's just a bit too bloody convenient?'

Sergeant Hatchley shrugged as if to imply that perhaps if Banks didn't go gallivanting off to the New World such things might not happen. 'Doctor says it could have been suicide,' he said.

Banks ran his hand through his close-cropped black hair. It was twelve thirty. He was back in his office only an hour after arriving home, jet-lagged and disoriented. So far, he hadn't even had a chance to admire his favourite view of the cobbled market square. The office was smoky and a cup of black coffee steamed on the desk. Superintendent Gristhorpe was keeping an appointment with the deputy chief constable, whose personal interest in events was a measure of the Colliers' influence in the dale.

'And where the hell was Richmond?' Banks went on. 'Wasn't he supposed to be baby-sitting the lot of them while I was away?'

'Yes, sir.'

'Where was he then?'

'Asleep at the Greenocks', I suppose. He could hardly invite himself to spend the night with the Colliers, could he?'

'That's not the point. He should have known something was wrong. Send him in.'

'He's just gone off duty, sir.'

'Well, bloody well bring him back again!'

'Yes, sir.'

Hatchley stalked out of the office. Banks sighed, stubbed out his cigarette and walked over to the window. The cobbled market square was still there, a bit rain drenched, but still there. Tourists posed for photographs on the worn plinth of the ancient market cross. The church door stood open and Banks could hear the distant sound of the congregation singing 'Jerusalem'.

So he was home. He'd just had time to say hello to Brian and Tracy, then he'd had to hurry down to the station. He hadn't even given them their presents yet: a Blue Jays sweatshirt for Brian, the *Illustrated History of Canada* for his budding historian daughter, Tracy, and a study of the Group of Seven, with plenty of fine reproductions, for Sandra. They were still packed in his suitcase, which stood next to the duty-free cigarettes and Scotch in the hall.

Already Toronto was a memory with the quality of a dream – baseball, the community college, Kleinburg, Niagara Falls, the CN Tower, and the tall downtown buildings in black and white and gold. But Staff Sergeant Gregson, the Feathers crowd and Anne Ralston/Julie Culver weren't a dream. They were what he had gone for. And now he'd come back to find Stephen Collier dead.

There was no suicide note; at least nobody had found one so far. According to Nicholas Collier, John Fletcher and Sam Greenock, who had all been with Stephen on his last night at the White Rose, Stephen, always highly strung and restless, had seemed excessively nervous. He had got much more drunk than usual. Finally, long beyond closing time, they had had to help him home. They had deposited Stephen fully clothed on his bed, then adjourned to Nicholas's half of the house, where they had a nightcap. John and Sam then left, and Nicholas went to bed.

In the morning, when he went to see how his brother was, Nicholas had discovered him dead. The initial findings of Dr Glendenning indicated that he had died of suffocation. It appeared that Stephen Collier had vomited while under the influence of barbiturates and been unable to wake up. Such things often happened when pills and booze were mixed, Glendenning had said. All that had to be determined now was the amount of barbiturate in Stephen's system, and that would have to wait until the post-mortem. He had suffered from insomnia for a long time and had a prescription for Nembutal.

So what had happened? According to Hatchley, Stephen must have got up after the others left and taken his sleeping pills as usual, then gone downstairs and played a record – Mozart's *Jupiter Symphony* was still spinning on the turntable – had another drink or two of Scotch from a tumbler, which was still half full, gone back upstairs, taken some more sleeping pills and passed out. By that time, given how much he'd had to drink, he probably wouldn't have remembered taking the first lot of pills. The only question was, did he do it deliberately or not? And the only person who could answer that was Stephen himself.

It was damned unsatisfactory, Banks thought, but it looked like an end to both the Addison and Allen cases. Stephen Collier had certainly confessed to Anne Ralston. He knew that Banks would find her and that when she heard Bernie had been killed, she would pass on the information. He must have gone through a week of torment trying to decide what to do – make a run for it or stay and brazen it out. After all, it was only her word against his. The strain had finally proved too much for him, and either accidentally or on purpose – or accidentally on purpose – he had put an end to things, perhaps to save himself and the family name the ignominy of a trial and all the publicity it would bring down on them.

Feeling calmer, Banks lit another cigarette. He finished his coffee and determined not to haul Richmond over the coals. After all, as Hatchley had said, the constable couldn't be everywhere at once. He still felt restless though; his nerves were jangling and his eyes ached. He had that strange and disturbing sensation of wanting to sleep but knowing he couldn't even if he tried. When he rubbed his chin, he could feel the bristles. He hadn't even had time for a shave.

When Richmond arrived, they walked over to the Queen's Arms. After the morning sunshine, it had turned cool and rainy; a wonderful relief after the hellish steam bath of Toronto, Banks thought as he looked up and let the rain fall on his face. Cyril, the landlord, rustled them up a couple of ham and tomato sandwiches. They found an empty table in a corner, and Banks got the drinks in.

'Look, I'm sorry for dragging you back, Phil,' he said, 'but I want to hear your version of what happened.'

'In the White Rose, sir?'

'The whole week. Just tell me what you saw and thought.'

'There's not very much to tell, really,' Richmond said, and he gave Banks his version of the week's events in as much detail as he could.

'Katie Greenock went off with Stephen Collier on Friday afternoon, is that right?'

'Yes, sir. They went for a walk up Swainshead Fell. I took a walk up Adam's Fell and I could see them across the dale.'

'Did they go towards the hanging valley?'

'No, sir, they didn't go over the top – just diagonal, as far as the river's source. It's about halfway up and a bit to the north.'

Banks wondered if anything had gone on between Katie and Stephen Collier. It seemed unlikely, given the kind of woman she seemed to be, but he was sure that she had surrendered to Bernard Allen. And in her case, the old-fashioned term 'surrendered' was the right word to use. Banks recalled the image of Katie standing in the market square, soaked to the skin, just before he'd left, and he remembered the eerie feeling he'd had that she was coming apart at the seams. It would certainly be worth talking to her again; at the very least she would be able to tell him something more about Collier's state of mind on the day before he died.

'What about Saturday night in the White Rose? How long were you there?'

'From about nine till closing time, sir. I tried to pace myself, not drink too much.'

Banks grinned, remembering his own nights in the Toronto pubs. 'A tough job, eh? Never mind. Notice anything?'

'Like I told the super and Sergeant Hatchley, sir, it seemed pretty much of a normal night to me.'

'You didn't think Stephen Collier was drinking more than usual?'

'I don't know how much he usually drank, sir. I'd say from the other three nights I saw him in the White Rose during my stay, he did drink more on Saturday. But it was

Saturday night. People do overdo it a bit then, don't they? No work in the morning.'

'Unless you're a copper.'

Cyril called last orders and Banks hurried to the bar for another two pints.

'What was the mood like at the table?' he asked when he got back.

'A bit festive, really.'

'No arguments, no sullen silences?'

'No. Everyone seemed to be enjoying themselves. There was one thing . . .'

'Yes?'

'Well, I couldn't hear anything because Sam and Stephen were talking quite loudly, but I got the impression that at one point John Fletcher and Nicholas Collier were having a bit of a barney.'

'What do you mean?'

'I'm just going by the expressions on their faces, sir. It looked like Nicholas was angry with Fletcher for some reason and Fletcher just brushed him aside.'

'Did the others appear to notice?'

'No. Like I said, sir, they were talking, arguing about politics or something.'

'And this was Nicholas Collier and John Fletcher, not Stephen?'

'Yes, sir.'

'Odd. How did Stephen seem?'

'I'd say he was a fairly happy drunk. Happier than he ever seemed sober.'

'What was he drinking?'

'They were all drinking beer.'

'How many pints would you say Stephen had?'

Richmond flushed and fiddled with his moustache. 'I

wasn't really counting, sir. Perhaps I should have been, but . . .'

'You weren't to know he'd be dead in the morning. Don't worry. It's the bane of our lives. If we all had twenty-twenty hindsight our job'd be a lot easier. Just try and remember. Picture it as clearly as you can.'

Richmond closed his eyes. 'At a guess, I'd say about five or six, sir.'

'Five or six. Not a lot, really, is it? Not for a Yorkshire-man, anyway. And he was practically legless?'

'Yes, sir. Maybe he was drinking the vodka as well.'

'What vodka?'

'I'm not clear on it, but I remember Freddie Metcalfe, the landlord, muttering something about having to change the bottle after one of them had been up and bought a round. It was busy and he said he needed eight hands to do his job.'

'But you never saw Stephen put a shorts glass to his lips?'

'No, sir.'

'Did anyone?'

'Not that I remember.'

'Odd, that, isn't it? What happened to the vodka, then?'

'Perhaps whoever bought it just drank it down at the bar.'

'Hmm. It's possible. But why? Let's leave it for the moment, anyway. Did you hear any mention at all of Oxford during the week?'

'You mean the university, sir?'

'Any mention at all. The name: Oxford.'

Richmond shook his head.

'All right, that'll do for now.' Banks rubbed his eyes.

They drifted out into the street with the others as Cyril

prepared to lock up for the afternoon. There was a lot more to think about now. Nothing that Banks had heard since he got back had been at all convincing. Something was wrong, he felt, and the case was far from over. Sending Richmond back home, he decided on a short walk in the rain to freshen himself up before returning to the station.

TWO

Katie watched the rain swell the becks that rushed down Swainshead Fell as it got dark that night. The rhythmic gurgle of water through the half-open window calmed her. All day she had been agitated. Now it was after ten; Sam was still at the pub, and Katie was brooding over the day's events.

If only she had told Sam that their guest was a policeman, probably sent to spy on them. Then he'd have informed all and sundry, and maybe things would have been different. But now Stephen had to die, too; another escape route cut off. Had the policeman noticed anything? Katie didn't think so. There had been nothing really to notice.

Ever since morning, when Stephen's body had been discovered, Upper Head had been stunned. Women gathered in the street after church and lowered their voices, looking over at the Gothic house and shaking their heads. The Colliers were, when all was said and done, still regarded as lords of the manor.

All the curtains of their spooky Victorian mansion across the river had been drawn since morning, when the police and doctors had finished and taken Stephen's body

away. One or two people had dropped in to offer condolences, including John Fletcher, who'd have got a rude
reception from Nicholas, Katie thought, under any other
circumstances. Sam, of course, had been one of the first,
keen to establish himself with the new squire now that
the more approachable Stephen was gone. Now Sam and
John were no doubt getting maudlin drunk in the White
Rose. Katie hadn't gone across to the house; she couldn't
face Nicholas Collier alone again after the incident at the
party.

Rain spilled in over the window sill. Katie dipped a
finger in it and made patterns on the white paintwork. The
water beaded on the paint no matter what she tried to
make it do. A breeze had sprung up and it brought the
scent of summer rain indoors; shivering, she pulled her
grey lambswool cardigan around her shoulders.

'Be sure your sins will find you out,' another of her
grandmother's favourite maxims, sprang into her mind.
With it came the dim and painful memory of a telltale
boy's hair on her collar when she had come home from her
one and only visit to the church-run youth club. It must
have got there in the cloakroom, somehow, but her grandmother had thrust it forward as irrefutable evidence of
Katie's lewd and lascivious nature before making her
stand 'naked in her shame' in the corner of the cold stone-
flagged kitchen all evening. She had been supposed to
repeat 'Be sure your sins will find you out' under her
breath all the time she stood there, but she hadn't. That
was another sin: disobedience. The vicar had got an earful, too, about running a house of ill repute and corrupting
local youth. That had pleased Katie; she didn't like him
anyway because his breath smelled like the toilet when he
came close, which he always did. Taking pleasure in the

misfortune of others was another sin she had been guilty of that day.

Katie closed the window and turned to get into bed. It was after ten thirty. Sam would probably be back soon. There was a chance that if she pretended to be asleep . . .

But sleep didn't come easily. She thought of Stephen again, of his chaste touch. Life might not have been so bad if he had taken her away with him. She knew he would want to have her eventually – it would be part of the price – but he seemed a gentle person, like Bernard had been, and perhaps he wouldn't be too demanding. The images blurred in her mind as sleep came closer: her grandmother brandishing the hair, black eyes flashing, Bernard breathing hard as he pulled at her clothes . . . She heard the back door open and close noisily. Sam. Quickly, she turned over and pulled the covers up to her ears. Her feet were cold.

THREE

'What do you think, then, Alan?'

Banks and Gristhorpe sat at the dining-room table later that night and sipped duty-free Bell's. The children were in bed and Sandra was leafing through the book Banks had brought her from Toronto. Banks felt better after the short nap he had taken late in the afternoon.

'It stinks. I track down Anne Ralston in Toronto and she tells me Stephen Collier practically confessed to killing Addison because of some scandal he was involved in at Oxford. Then, when I get back, I find Collier's conveniently dead – accidental death. It's too pat.'

'Hmm.' Gristhorpe sipped his Scotch. 'It could be true. But let's suppose it's not. What else could have happened?

I'm sorry, I know you're still tired, Alan. Maybe tomorrow would be better?'

Banks lit a cigarette. 'No, it's all right. What do I think happened? I don't know. I thought I'd got it all worked out but now everything's gone haywire. I know it makes sense that Collier killed himself rather than face the trouble he knew he'd be in when I got back. Maybe the pressure built in him over the week. On the other hand, what if he didn't kill Allen? What if he knew who did, and whoever it was was afraid he'd crack under pressure and give it away. That would have given someone enough motive to get rid of him, wouldn't it? We still don't have a clear connection between Addison and Allen, though.'

'Except the Ralston girl.'

'What if there's something else? An angle we haven't really considered.'

'Such as?'

'That's the trouble. I've no idea.'

Gristhorpe swirled the Bell's in his glass. 'Then it has to be connected with Addison and Ralston.'

'I'd like to go down to Oxford as soon as possible and dig around. Ted Folley's in the local CID there. We were at training school together.'

Gristhorpe nodded. 'That's no problem.'

'Maybe Addison found something out and was going to blackmail Collier.'

'He had a clean record.'

'True. But you know as well as I do what private investigators are like, especially solo operators. We can also assume that Bernard Allen had the same information, or part of it, and that he too was blackmailing Collier.'

Gristhorpe rubbed his whiskery chin. 'Aye. But if Collier did kill Allen for that reason, who killed Collier, and why?'

'That's what we have to find out.'

'So we're still looking at the lot of them?'

'It seems that way. Any one of them could have gone back to the house – the French windows at the back weren't locked – and given him another drink with the barbiturates. Or someone could have mixed a few nembies with his drinks earlier. He was so far gone he probably wouldn't have noticed.'

'Risky, though.'

'Yes. But what murder isn't?'

'Aye.'

'And then there's the matter of the vodka. I want to talk to Freddie Metcalfe about that.'

'What vodka?'

'Someone in the party was buying vodka that night, but Richmond never actually saw anyone drink it.'

'So you think someone was spiking Collier's drinks with vodka, making sure he got really drunk?'

'It's a strong possibility, yes. Vodka's pretty much tasteless in a pint.'

'Aye, in more ways than one,' Gristhorpe said.

'The trouble is,' Banks went on, 'it was such a busy night that I can't rely on anyone remembering. It could have been Sam Greenock, John Fletcher or Nicholas Collier – any one of them. I'm assuming they all bought rounds.'

'What about the Greenock woman?'

Banks saw again in his mind's eye the image of Katie standing soaked to the skin in the market square. 'Katie? I suppose she could play some part in all this. As far as I can tell though, she's in a world of her own. There's something not quite right about her. I thought it was just her marriage. Sam's a real bastard – thrashes her every now and then – but I think there's more to it than that. According to Richmond though, she wasn't in the White Rose that night.'

Gristhorpe looked at his watch and stood up. 'Good Lord, is that the time? I'd better be off. Don't worry about being in early tomorrow.'

'I probably will be,' Banks said. 'I want to go to Swainshead and see a few people. Then I'll go to Oxford. Mind if I take Sergeant Hatchley? There might be a bit of legwork, and I'd rather have Richmond up here taking care of business.'

'Aye, take him. He'll feel like a fish out of water in Oxford. Do him good though. Broaden his horizons.'

Banks laughed. 'I'm afraid Sergeant Hatchley's horizons are firmly fixed on beer, idleness, sport and sex – in that order. But I'll try.'

Gristhorpe drained his glass and left. Banks sat beside Sandra and looked at some of the pictures with her, but his eyes began to feel suddenly prickly and heavy. He'd been wondering whether to let the superintendent know that Gerry Webb had revealed his full name, but decided against it. Names were, after all, a kind of power. He would tell no one at the station, but it was too good to keep to himself.

'Do you know,' he said, slipping his arm around Sandra's shoulders, 'I found out a very interesting thing about Superintendent Gristhorpe in Toronto.'

'It sounds like you discovered a lot of interesting things there,' Sandra said, raising an arched black eyebrow. Her eyebrows contrasted sharply with her natural blonde hair, and that was one of the features Banks found sexy about her. 'Go on,' she urged him. 'Tell me.'

'I've missed you,' Banks said, moving closer. 'I'll tell you in bed, later.'

'I thought you were tired.'

'Only my eyes.'

'Is it worth knowing?'

'It's worth it.'

'Right, then.' Sandra turned towards him. 'Let's not waste time and energy climbing upstairs. It has been a whole week, after all.'

FOUR

It was good to be home, Banks thought, as he drove the white Cortina along the dale. The sun was out, the water glittered silver, the valley sides shone vibrant green, and the Beatles were singing 'And Your Bird Can Sing' on the cassette. He lit a cigarette and slowed down to pass a colourful group of hikers. They clustered together in the deep grass by the drystone wall and waved as he drove by.

Who to visit first? That was the question. It was still only ten thirty, so perhaps he'd best leave Freddie Metcalfe till the White Rose opened at eleven and call on Nicholas Collier – the interview he was least looking forward to.

Accordingly, he carried on past the pub and pulled up on the verge outside the Collier house. Nicholas opened the door at the first ring of the bell.

'Chief Inspector Banks,' he said. 'Long time, no see. Come in.' He looked tired; his usually bright eyes had lost their sparkle and there were dark pouches under them. 'Please, sit down.' He pointed towards a leather uphol-stered armchair by the open French windows. 'I'm not in a mood to sit in the sun today, but I feel I must remind myself of its presence.'

'I'm sorry about what happened,' Banks said. 'I'd been hoping to talk to Stephen when I got back.'

Nicholas turned to look at the fountain outside and said nothing. Banks thought he could see a fading bruise at the side of his mouth.

'I hope you're not going to ask me to go through it all again,' Nicholas said at last, taking a cigarette from the porcelain box on the low table beside him. 'Policemen always seem to be asking people to repeat their stories.'

'There's a good reason for that,' Banks said. 'Sometimes people remember things. Little things they thought insignificant at the time.'

'All the same, I very much doubt that I can help you.'

'I was wondering if you had any knowledge of your brother's problems?'

'Stephen's problems? No, I can't say I did. Though he seemed a bit edgy this past week or two, as if he had something on his mind.'

'Did you ask him what it was?'

'No. Does that surprise you? Well, it shouldn't. Stephen wasn't the most forthcoming of people. If he wanted to talk, he would, to whoever struck his fancy at the moment. But if you asked him, you got nowhere. Certainly I never did.'

'I see. So you've no idea what he was worried about?'

'Not at all. I take no interest in the business, so I wouldn't know about that side of things. Did he have business problems? Trouble at t' mill?'

'Not that I know of, no, Mr Collier. His problem was that we think he may have killed a man over five years ago because of something that happened at Oxford. We also think he might have been responsible for the murder of Bernard Allen more recently.'

'Stephen! You're joking, Chief Inspector, surely?'

Banks shook his head. 'When was Stephen at Oxford?'

'He went there nine years ago. But nothing untoward happened to him in Oxford as far as I know.' He paused and his eyes turned hard. 'You're not joking, are you?'

'I'm afraid not.'

'Well, what can I say? Your wording would seem to indicate that this is mere supposition, that you have no proof.'

'Only the testimony of Anne Ralston.'

'That woman Stephen was seeing all those years ago?'

'Yes. I found her in Toronto.'

'And you'd take a slut's word that Stephen was a murderer?'

'She'd no reason to lie. And I don't believe she's a slut.'

Nicholas shrugged dismissively. 'As you like. She certainly wasn't the type of woman I'd want for a sister-in-law. But haven't you considered that she might have been the guilty party? As I remember, she disappeared the morning after the man was killed.'

'Yes, she did.'

'So she'd have everything to gain by trying to put the blame on Stephen.'

'It's possible, yes. But there's Bernard Allen's murder to take into account, too. She wasn't in Swainshead at the time. She was in Toronto.'

'So?'

'So she couldn't have killed Allen.'

'I'm sorry but I don't see the connection. You admit she could have killed the other man, but not Bernard Allen. What I don't see is why you should even think the same person killed both of them. What had Allen and that private detective chappie got in common?'

'Nothing, as far as we can tell. Except that they were both killed in Swainshead.' Banks lit a cigarette. 'There are too many coincidences, Mr Collier. One of the most interesting ones is that Bernard Allen was friendly with Anne Ralston in Toronto. That would make him the only person from Swainshead to see her since she disappeared. And the whole village was aware of that, thanks to Sam Greenock. It's also a coincidence that Stephen was going out with Anne Ralston at the time she left Swainshead, and that she told me he confessed to her about killing Addison. It's another coincidence that Stephen is dead when I return.'

'I can't argue with your logic, Chief Inspector. There certainly are a lot of coincidences. But they *are* coincidences, aren't they? I mean, you've no real evidence to link them or to back up your suppositions, have you?'

'Are you sure you knew nothing about your brother's problems?' Banks asked.

'I've told you.' Collier sighed. 'We just weren't that close. You can see for yourself how we split the house – into two very different halves, I might add. All we had in common was family. Even if he had been a murderer, which I don't believe for a moment, Stephen would hardly have told me.'

'But he told Anne Ralston.'

'So you say. I can only repeat that the woman must be lying to save her own skin.' He leaned forward to stub out his cigarette but didn't slouch back in the chair again. 'Chief Inspector,' he said, folding his hands on his lap, 'I hope you're not going to spread these accusations about my brother around the dale. After all, you admit you've no proof. You could do untold damage to the family name, not to mention my career.'

'Rest assured, Mr Collier. I'm not in the habit of spreading unfounded accusations.'

'And might I suggest,' Nicholas added, 'that even if Stephen had been guilty, he's certainly suffered adequate penalty for his sin, and no useful purpose would be served by going poking around in his past affairs.'

'Ah, that's where we differ,' Banks said. 'I'm not judge or jury, Mr Collier. I just try to dig out the truth. And until there are answers to a number of questions, Stephen's file remains open – wherever Stephen himself may be.' Nicholas opened his mouth to protest but Banks ignored him and went on. 'I don't care who you are, Mr Collier. You can threaten, you can pull strings, you can do what you bloody well want. But I'm going to get to the bottom of this.' He stood up and walked over to the door. Nicholas sat where he was and stared coldly at him.

'One more question,' Banks said. 'Which one of you was drinking vodka in the White Rose on Saturday night?'

'Vodka?' Nicholas grunted. 'None of us, I shouldn't think. Can't stand the stuff, myself.'

'Did you see your brother drink any?'

Nicholas walked over to the door and grasped the handle. 'No, I didn't. Stephen never drank vodka.' He opened the door. 'Now would you mind leaving? And you can be damn sure you haven't heard the last of this.'

Was he lying? Banks found it hard to tell. People of Nicholas Collier's class had so much self-confidence bred into them that they could carry most things off.

'What was your argument with John Fletcher about?' he asked, leaning against the open door.

'What argument?'

'You didn't have words?'

Nicholas flicked his wrist. 'We may have done, but I can't remember why. A trifle, I should imagine. Now . . .' He nodded towards the path.

Banks set off.

It hadn't been satisfactory at all. Banks swore under his breath as he headed down the path. He should have pushed Nicholas even harder. Still, there would be time later. Plenty of time. There was still Oxford. And Katie Greenock and Freddie Metcalfe. He looked at his watch and walked into the White Rose.

'I understand tha's been globetrotting,' Freddie Metcalfe said, pouring out a pint of Marston's Pedigree.

'That's right,' Banks answered. 'Been to visit the New World.' He counted out the money and put it on the damp bar towel.

'I don't 'old wi' Americans,' Freddie said, screwing up his face. 'Get plenty on 'em in 'ere, tha knows. Allus asking for fancy drinks – bourbon and branch water and t' like. Can't understand none on 'em. And Perrier. Bloody Perrier wi' a twist o' lemon them purple-haired old women want. Mutton dressed up as lamb, if y'ask me.' He sniffed and carried the money to the till.

Banks thought of pointing out that Canada was not the same as the USA, but he didn't want to miss a good opening. 'Not get a lot of fancy drinks orders in here, then? Not many drink shorts?' he asked.

'Nah,' said Freddie, ambling back. 'Most tourists we get's fell-walkers, and they like a good pint, I'll say that for 'em. T' lasses sometimes ask for a brandy and Babycham, like, or a Pony or Cherry B. But mostly it's ale.'

'What about vodka?'

'What about it?'

'Get through much?'

'Nah. Bloody Russkie muck, that is. Can't taste it. We get through a good bit o' single malt Scotch, but vodka . . . nah.'

'I understand you had a vodka drinker on Saturday night?'

'What makes tha think that? Tha weren't 'ere then.'

'Never mind that. Did you?'

Freddie scratched his mutton chop whiskers. 'Aye, come to think on it, I do remember 'aving to change t' bottle, so somebody must've been at it.'

'Who, Freddie, who?'

'I can't rightly say. It might not've been me who served 'im. I don't recollect as I did. Lot o' strangers in last weekend 'cos t' weather brightened up, like. It were a busy night, Sat'day, and that gormless lass from Gratly never showed up. S'posed to give me an 'and behind t' bar. No, I'm sorry, lad. It's no good. I know I changed t' bottle, but I were allus serving four orders at once. Need eight bloody arms on this job, specially on Sat'day night. And I only 'ad young Betty to 'elp me.'

'Were there any arguments in the pub that night?'

Freddie laughed. 'Well, it'd 'ardly be a Sat'day night wi'out a few 'eated words, would it?'

'I suppose not. What about at the Collier table?'

'I don't recollect owt. Billy Black and Les Stott were barneying about whippets, and Wally Grimes – Wally's a local farmer, like – 'ad a little disagreement wi' some walkers about National Trust footpaths. But that's all I can remember.'

'You don't remember anything between Nicholas Collier and John Fletcher?'

'Nah. But that wouldn't be nowt new. Now John and Mr Stephen, they understood each other. But John

Fletcher never did 'ave time for young Nicholas, even when 'e were a lad.'

'But you heard nothing on Saturday?'

'Nay. Too much bloody noise. I only 'eard t' others because they were standing at t' bar right a-front o' me.'

'Did you clear the tables later?'

'Nay, Betty did that.' He pointed towards a buxom rosy-cheeked girl washing glasses.

'Can I talk to her?'

'Aye. Betty, lass, come over 'ere. T' inspector wants a word wi' thee.'

The roses quickly spread over Betty's entire complexion, and down as much of her throat and chest as was exposed. She lowered her big brown eyes and stood in front of Banks like a schoolgirl before the head.

'It's all right, Betty,' Banks said, 'I just want to ask you a couple of questions about Saturday night when you worked here.'

She nodded but still didn't look up.

'Do you remember serving Mr Collier's group at all?'

'Aye,' she said. 'Well . . . no . . . I mean, I did serve them, but it were that busy I don't remember nothing about it.'

'And you collected all the glasses later?'

'Aye.'

'Do you remember picking up any shorts glasses from Mr Collier's table?'

Betty thought for a moment – a process Banks fancied he could almost hear – and then shook her head. 'I remember picking up some shorts glasses off t' bar,' she said, 'but I can't say who drank 'em.'

'Is this the part of the bar the Collier group came to for their orders?'

'Aye, it would've been,' Freddie said.

'But neither of you can say which member of the Collier group was ordering vodka?'

They both shook their heads glumly.

Banks sighed, then finished his pint philosophically and lit a cigarette.

'What's it all about, then?' Freddie asked.

'Eh? Oh, never mind for now,' Banks said. 'Probably nothing.'

'They were all a bit merry, like.'

'The Collier group?'

'Aye. All on 'em. But Mr Stephen were t' worst.'

'Did he drink more than the rest?'

Freddie shook his head. 'I can't say. Shouldn't think so, though. They was drinking rounds. Unless . . .' Then comprehension dawned on his round red face. 'Unless 'e were drinking vodka as well as pints.'

'And was he?'

Again, Freddie shook his head. 'I can't say.'

Suddenly Betty, who had remained standing there as if she were waiting to be dismissed, raised her head. Brown curls bobbed around her chubby cheeks. 'I can tell yer!' she said excitedly. 'I can tell yer!'

'What?' Banks asked.

'It can't've been Mr Stephen buying vodka.'

'Why on earth not, lass?' Freddie said.

'Well, yer know,' Betty spluttered, ''e allus used to say 'ello, like, Mr Stephen. Proper gentleman. And 'e'd ask me 'ow I was. Well, once on Sat'day night 'e were on 'is way to t' loo and 'e nearly bumped into me, and me carrying a trayful o'—'

'Get on wi' it, lass!' Freddie bellowed. 'T' inspector dun't want to know what tha et for breakfast an' all, tha knows.'

Betty cast him a dark glance and announced, ''E'd forgotten 'is wallet.'

''E'd what?'

''E sometimes slips me a quid – a tip, like,' she added proudly. 'But on Sat'day 'e patted 'is pockets and said 'e was sorry 'e 'ad no change and 'e'd left 'is wallet at 'ome. 'E was 'aving to depend on t' generosity of 'is friends.' She turned to Banks. 'Those were 'is very words, "the generosity of my friends". 'E'd 'ad a few, like, when 'e said it . . .'

'Thank you, Betty,' Banks said. 'I don't suppose you overheard Nicholas Collier and John Fletcher having an argument?'

Betty's face dropped. 'No. Not while I were picking t' glasses up. Is it important?'

'It might be. But it's not as important as what you've just told me.'

It wasn't a great help, but if Stephen Collier hadn't been up to the bar to buy rounds, and if Freddie had found empty shorts glasses at the spot where the orders had been placed, then one of the party might have been spiking Stephen's beer with vodka. Of course, he realized, anyone could have left the glasses there, and any member of the group could have tipped back a quick shot while waiting for Freddie to pull the pints. But it was a start.

Betty beamed as if she'd solved the case. Freddie sent her back to her glass cleaning and turned to face Banks.

'There,' he said. 'Any 'elp?'

'I hope so.'

'Well, so do I. Tha's taking tha bloody time, I'll say that about thee. Does tha know, t' last Yankee we 'ad in 'ere . . .'

Banks left Freddie mid-sentence and almost bumped into Katie Greenock as he was leaving the pub.

'Ah,' he said, holding the door for her, 'just the person I want to see.'

But she turned and started to hurry away.

'What is it?' Banks called after her. He could sense her fear; it was more than just the adrenalin produced by a shock.

'It's nothing,' she said, half turning. 'I was just looking for Sam, that's all.' He could see a tear streaking down her flushed cheek.

'Katie, have you got something to tell me?' Banks asked, approaching her.

She carried on walking away. Banks put his hand gently on her shoulder. 'Katie?'

'No!' She recoiled and started running down the empty street. Banks dashed after her and soon she slowed, dazed, to a halt.

'Come on, Katie,' he said. 'Let's talk.' He offered his hand, but she wouldn't take it. Instead, she walked obediently beside him back to the car. She was shaking.

'A drink?' Banks suggested.

She shook her head. Her fair hair was tied back, but a few strands freed themselves and stuck to her damp cheeks.

'Let's go for a ride, then.'

She got in the Cortina beside him and he drove north out of Swainshead. Thinking it might help her relax, he took out the Beatles cassette and put on Vivaldi's *Four Seasons*, turning the volume low.

'I was lying,' Katie blurted out as they passed the bridge to John Fletcher's farmhouse. Then she said something else that Banks didn't quite catch. It sounded like 'wash my mouth out with soap'.

'What about?' he asked.

'I wasn't looking for Sam. I saw you go in there. I saw you leave Nicholas Collier's, too. I was trying to get my courage up.'

'For what? Are you sure a drink wouldn't help?'

'No, I don't take alcohol.'

'What is it, Katie?'

'You've got to help me,' Katie said, staring down into her lap and twisting her hands. 'I did it . . . I killed them . . . I killed them all.'

13

ONE

Looking at the ornate limestone building, Banks realized he had never seen Braughtmore school before. Built in the mid-nineteenth century after the previous building had burned down, it had oriels projecting from the first floor, then two floors of tall sash windows topped by dormers and a red pantile roof. It stood at the mouth of a small valley which a tributary had carved on its way down to the Gaiel, and enough flat ground had been cleared around it for rugby and cricket fields.

Banks pulled into a lay-by across the road, lit a cigarette and turned to Katie.

'Tell me about it,' he said.

'I did it,' Katie repeated. 'I killed them.'

'Who did you kill?'

'Bernie and Stephen.'

'Why?'

'Because I . . . because they . . . It was God's judgement.'

'God's judgement for what, Katie?'

'My sins.'

'Because you made love to them?'

Katie turned and glared at him through her tears. 'Not love,' she said. 'They were going to take me away, take me away from here, from my husband.'

'But you made love with Bernard Allen. Did you sleep with Stephen, too?'

'Bernie took me in his room. It was the price. I found no pleasure in it. He said he'd send for me when he got back.'

Banks didn't have the heart to tell her that Bernie had been bent on returning to Swainshead, not staying in Canada.

'And Stephen?' he asked.

'He . . . he kissed me. I knew I would have to pay, but later. And now . . .'

'Did you kill him so that you wouldn't have to pay?'

Katie shook her head. 'He was going to take me away, like Bernard. He had to die.'

'How did you kill him?'

'Everyone who wants to help me dies.'

'But how did you kill him?'

'I don't know, don't remember.'

'Katie, you didn't kill Stephen Collier or Bernard Allen, did you?'

'They died because of me. The Lord's vengeance. Nicholas was the Lord's vengeance, too. Against me. To show me my vile nature.'

'Nicholas? What happened with Nicholas?'

'He put his hands on me. His filthy hands. The hands of the beast.'

'When was this? Where?'

'At his house. The party Sam made me go to. I didn't want to go, I told him. I knew it would be bad.'

'What happened?'

'John came and they fought.'

'John and Nicholas?'

'Yes.'

At least that explained their argument in the White Rose, Banks thought. 'Did Sam know? Did you tell Sam?'

Katie shook her head. 'Sam doesn't care anyway. Not where his precious Colliers are concerned.'

'But you didn't kill anyone, did you?'

She put her head in her hands and wept. Banks moved to put his arm around her, but she stiffened and jerked away towards the door. She rested her cheek against the window and stared ahead at the dale.

'Are you protecting Sam, Katie? Is that what you're doing? Do you think Sam killed them because they were going to take you away?'

'I killed them. I told you.'

'Maybe you think you're responsible, Katie, but you didn't kill anyone. There's a big difference between feeling guilty and taking someone's life, you know. You haven't done anything wrong.'

'I wanted to escape my husband, didn't I?'

'He beats you. He's not a good man.'

'But he's my husband.' She started to sob again. 'I must serve him. What else can I do? I can't leave him and go away by myself. I don't know how to live.'

Banks wound down his window and tossed out his cigarette end.

'Do you want to walk a while?' he asked.

Katie nodded and opened her door.

There was a pathway worn in the hillside opposite the school, and they set off slowly up towards the ridge. About halfway, they sat on warm grass among limestone boulders and gazed down at the scene. The building glowed like mother-of-pearl, and the red S-shaped tiles shone bright in the sun. Some pupils dressed in whites were practising in the cricket nets by one of the mowed fields, and a group in shorts and vests were running around the cinder track. Plenty of exercise and cold showers, Banks thought. Cross-country runs and Latin unseens to keep their minds off sex – and perhaps a bit of masturbation in the dorms, a little buggery in the bushes, sodomy in the cycle sheds. It was every outsider's version of public-school life. Probably the reality was much more innocent. After all, these people were being groomed to run the country, the government. Still, look how many of them ended up on the front pages of the tabloid press. Perhaps the outsider's version wasn't so far from the truth.

Katie plucked blades of grass and scattered them on the light breeze.

'Tell me what happened with Stephen,' Banks said.

'We walked up to the source. He said he was going away. I thought he would take me with him if I let him kiss me. That's all.'

'What else did he say? You must have talked about things.'

'Oh, yes.' Katie's voice sounded like it was coming from a great distance.

'Why was he going away?'

'He said he'd had enough, he couldn't stand being here any longer. He said something about getting away from the past and from who he was.'

'What did he want to get away from?'

For the first time, Katie looked directly at him. Her eyes were red-rimmed with crying but still shone warm brown in the sunlight. Banks could feel her attraction. The desire to protect her merged with the impulse to touch her. She made him want to reach out and brush the blonde hairs away from her cheeks, then kiss her white throat and explore the gentle curves and mounds of her body. And he also knew that she was largely unaware of the effect she had; it was as if she couldn't understand the natural sexual instinct that draws people to one another. She knew what men wanted, yes, but she didn't know why or what it was all about. She was innocent, a unique and vulnerable wild flower growing here at the edge of the moorland.

'What did he want to get away from?' she echoed, shattering his illusion. 'What we all want to get away from. The traps we make for ourselves. The traps God makes for us.'

'It's not such a terrible thing to want to escape a bad marriage, Katie,' Banks said. But he felt he couldn't get the tone right, couldn't find the way to talk to this woman. What he said came out as patronizing when he didn't intend it to.

'It's a woman's duty,' Katie answered. 'Her cross to bear.'

'What was Stephen running away from? Was it me? Did he mention me?'

Katie seemed surprised. 'No,' she said. 'Not you. His past, the life he led.'

'Did he mention anything in particular?'

'He said he'd been bad.'

'How?'

'I don't know. He just talked. I didn't understand it all. I was thinking about something else. The river bubbling up from the grass, how green and shiny the grass was where the water always flowed over it and in it.'

'Can you remember anything? Anything at all?'

'He talked about Oxford. Something bad happened at Oxford.'

'Did he say what it was?'

'A girl. A girl died.'

'Is that all he said?'

'Yes. That's how it started, he said. The nightmare.'

'With a girl dying at Oxford?'

'Yes.'

'How was he involved with this girl?'

'I don't know. Just that she died and it was bad.'

'And now he'd had enough and he was going away to escape the past, the consequences?'

Katie nodded, then she stared at him sharply. 'But you can't escape consequences, can you? Bernie couldn't. Stephen couldn't. I can't.'

'Was Stephen unhappy?'

'Unhappy? I don't think so. He was worried, but not unhappy.'

'Do you think he would have harmed himself?'

'No. Stephen wouldn't have done that. He had plans for the future. He was going to take me with him. But his future killed him.'

'I thought it was his past?'

'It was me,' she said calmly. 'Whatever you say, I know it was me who killed him.'

'That's not true, Katie. I wish I could get you to believe it.' Banks took out his cigarettes and offered her one. She said no and carried on plucking blades of grass and rubbing them between her fingers.

'Why didn't he go away before?' Banks asked. 'He had plenty of time, plenty of opportunity.'

'I don't know. He said it was hard for him – the family name, the house, the business. He seemed to be trying to find the courage to make a break, like me. I didn't tell him, if that's what you're thinking.'

'Didn't tell him what?'

'About the policeman you sent to spy on everyone. I saw him with you one day in Eastvale, but I didn't tell Stephen.'

'Did you tell Sam?'

Katie shook her head slowly. 'No,' she said. 'Not this time.'

So Stephen had been struggling with himself over whether to run or whether to stay and brazen it out. After all, he probably knew that the police could have no real proof of his guilt, just hearsay. Anne Ralston's word against his.

'If he'd gone,' Katie said, as if she'd been reading Banks' mind, 'it would have been like admitting his guilt, wouldn't it?'

'Perhaps.' Banks stood up and brushed the grass from his trousers. 'Come on.' He held out his hand and Katie took it. As soon as she'd stood up, though, she let go and followed him back to the car in silence.

TWO

'What else did she say?' Sergeant Hatchley asked, as the white Cortina with Banks at the wheel, hurtled down the M1.

'Nothing,' Banks answered. 'I told her to get in touch with us if she remembered anything else at all, then I drove her home. She went in without a word. To tell you the truth, I'm worried about her. She's so bloody fragile and she's close to breaking point. The woman needs help.'

Hatchley shrugged. 'If she doesn't like her nest she can always change it.'

'It's not as easy as that for some people. They get stuck; they don't know where to turn, how to take care of themselves. Katie Greenock's like that.'

They passed Sheffield's cooling towers, shaped like

giant whalebone corsets by the motorway. Even with the windows and many of the factories closed, the sulphurous smells of steelworks seeped into the car.

'What exactly will we be doing in Oxford?' Hatchley asked.

'We'll be trying to track down an incident involving the death of a girl about nine years ago, maybe two or three years later. Undergraduate courses are usually three years long, so that's a welcome limit.'

'Unless Collier wasn't actually a student when it happened.'

'That's bloody helpful,' Banks said. 'We'll deal with that if we draw a blank on the other.'

'What kind of incident?'

'It strikes me we're looking for an unsolved crime, or a freak accident. Could have been hit and run, drug overdose, anything.'

'Then what? Whoever this lass was, she won't be doing much talking now.'

'I don't know,' Banks admitted. 'We try and link her to Stephen Collier.'

'And what if we come up blank?'

Banks sighed and reached for a cigarette. He swerved quickly to avoid a Dutch juggernaut meandering into the centre lane. 'You're being bloody negative today, Sergeant,' he said. 'What's the matter, did you have something planned for tonight? A date with Carol, maybe?'

'No. Carol understands my job. And I like a nice ride out. I'm just trying to cover all the angles, that's all. I find the whole damn thing confusing. I'm not even sure we've got a case. After all, Collier is dead, whether he died accidentally or killed himself.'

'It is confusing,' Banks agreed. 'That's why I don't

believe we're at the bottom of it yet. That's why we're off to Oxford, to try and make it simpler.'

'Oh, I see.' Hatchley wound down his window a couple of inches. With the two of them smoking, the fug in the car was making his eyes water. 'I suppose it's full of silly-looking buggers in caps and gowns, Oxford?'

'Maybe so,' Banks said. 'Never been there, myself. They say it's a working town, though.'

'Aye. It might have been at one time. But there's not many left making cars these days. Some nice buildings there, though. I saw those on telly as well. Christopher Wren, Nicholas Hawksworth.'

'Bloody hell, Jim, have you been watching BBC2 again? We'll not have much time for sightseeing. Except for what you can take in on the job. Anyway, it's Hawksmoor. Nicholas Hawksmoor.'

He realized with a shock that it was the first time he had called Sergeant Hatchley by his first name. It felt strange, but Hatchley said nothing.

Banks drove on in silence and concentrated on the road. It was after five o'clock and the stretches of motor-way that passed close to urban areas were busy with rush-hour traffic. By the time they got to Oxford they wouldn't have time to do much but check in at the police station, say hello to Ted Folley and maybe discuss the case over a pint – which would certainly appeal to Hatchley – before bed. Banks had booked them in at a small hotel recommended by Ted on the phone. In the morning the real work would begin.

Holding the wheel with one hand, Banks sorted through the cassettes. 'Do you like music?' he asked. It was odd; he knew Gristhorpe was tone-deaf – he couldn't tell Bach from the Beatles – but he had no idea what

Hatchley's tastes ran to. Not that it would affect his choice. He knew what he wanted to hear and soon found it – the Small Faces' greatest hits.

'I like a good brass band,' Hatchley mused. 'A bit of country and western now and then.'

Banks smiled. He hated country and western and brass bands. He lit another cigarette and edged up the volume. The swirling chords of 'All or Nothing' filled the car as he turned off near Northampton on to the road for Oxford. The music took him right back to the summer of 1966, just before he started in the sixth form at school. Nostalgia. A sure sign he was pushing forty. He caught Hatchley looking at him as if he were mad.

THREE

There weren't many caps and gowns in evidence on High Street in Oxford the following morning. Most of the people seemed to be ambling along in that lost but purposeful way tourists have. Banks and Hatchley were looking for somewhere to eat a quick breakfast before getting down to work at the station.

Hatchley pointed across the street. 'There's a McDonald's. They do quite nice breakfasts. Maybe . . .' He looked at Banks apprehensively, as if worried that the chief inspector might turn out to be a gourmet as well as a southerner and a lover of 1960s music. Despite all the times they'd enjoyed toasted teacakes and steak pies together, maybe Banks would insist on frogs' legs with anchovy sauce for breakfast.

Banks glanced at his watch and scowled. 'At least they're fast. Come on then. Egg McMuffin it is.'

Astonished, Hatchley followed him through the golden arches. Most of the places Banks had eaten in on his trip to Toronto had provided quick friendly service – so much so that it had been one of the things that had impressed him – but it seemed that even McDonald's could do nothing to alter the innate sloth and surliness of the English catering industry. The look they got from the uniformed girl behind the counter immediately communicated that they were being a bloody nuisance in placing an order, and, of course, they had to wait. Even when she slung the food at them, she didn't say, 'Thank you, please come again.'

Finally, they sat by the window and watched people walk in and out of W. H. Smith's for the morning papers. Hatchley ate heartily, but Banks picked at his food, then abandoned it and settled for black coffee and a cigarette.

'Nice bloke, that Ted Folley,' Hatchley said with his mouth half full of sausage. 'Not what I expected.'

'What did you expect?'

'Oh, some toffee-nosed git, I suppose. He's real down-to-earth, though. Dresses like a toff, mind you. They'd have a bit of a giggle over him in the Oak.'

'Probably in the Queen's Arms, too,' Banks added.

'Aye.'

They had found time for a few drinks with Folley before returning to their hotel for a good night's sleep, and Banks wondered whether it was Ted's generosity that had won Hatchley over, or his store of anecdotes. Either way, the sergeant had managed to down a copious amount of local ale (which he pronounced to be of 'passable' quality) in a very short time.

They had stood at the bar of a noisy Broad Street pub, and Ted – a dapper man with Brylcreemed hair and a penchant for three-piece pinstripe suits and garish bow ties – had regaled them with stories of Oxford's privileged student classes. Hatchley had been particularly amused by the description of a recent raid on an end-of-term party: 'And there she was,' Folley had said, 'deb of the year with her knickers round her ankles and white powder all over her stiff upper lip.' The sergeant had laughed so much he had got hiccups, which kept returning to haunt him for the rest of the evening.

'Come on,' Banks said. 'Hurry up. It can't be so bloody delicious you need to savour every mouthful.'

Reluctantly, Hatchley ate up his food and slurped his coffee. Ten minutes later they were in Ted Folley's office in St Aldates.

'I've got the files out already,' Ted said. 'If you can't find what you're after there, come and see me. I think you will, though. They cover all unsolved crimes, including hit-and-runs, involving women during the three-year period you mentioned.'

'Thank God there aren't many,' Banks said, picking up the slim pile.

'No,' Folley said. 'We're lucky. The students keep us busy enough but we don't get all that many mysterious deaths. They're usually drug-related.'

'These?'

'Some of them. Use that office over there.' Folley pointed across to a small glass-partitioned area. 'Doug's on holiday, so you won't be disturbed.'

Most of the cases were easily dealt with. Banks or Hatchley would phone friends or parents of the deceased, whenever phone numbers appeared in the files, and simply ask if the name Stephen Collier meant anything. On the off chance, they also asked if anyone had hired a private investigator named Raymond Addison to look into the unsolved crime. In the cases where no numbers were given or where people had moved, they made notes to follow up on later. In some of those cases, the phone directory told them what they needed to know, and Ted also proved as helpful as ever.

By mid-afternoon, after a short lunch break, they had only three possibilities left. Folley was able to rule one of those out – the girl's parents had died tragically in a plane crash less than a year after their daughter's death – which left one each for Banks and Hatchley. They tossed for it, and Banks drew the phoneless family in Jericho, Hatchley the paraplegic father in Woodstock.

Wedged between Walton Street and the canal, Jericho is a maze of small nineteenth-century terraced houses, originally built for the foundry workers and navvies of the city. Most of the streets are named after Victorian battles or military heroes. It is as far away in spirit and appearance from the magnificent architectural beauty of the old university city as is Eastvale's East End Estate from its cobbled market square and Norman church.

Banks drove slowly down Great Clarendon Street until he found the turning he wanted. His car attracted the attention of two scruffy children playing jacks on the pavement, and he was manoeuvred into paying them fifty pence to 'protect' it for him.

At first no one answered the cracked blue door, but eventually Banks heard someone move inside and when the door opened an old haggard face stared out. He couldn't tell whether it was male or female until a deep man's voice asked him roughly what he wanted.

'It's about your daughter, Cheryl,' he said. 'May I come in?'

The man blinked and opened the door a bit wider. Banks could smell boiled turnip and stale pipe smoke.

'Our Cheryl's been dead six years or more,' the man said. 'Nobody did anything then; why should they bother now?'

'If I could just come in . . .?'

The man said nothing, but he opened the door wider to admit Banks. There was no hall; the door opened directly into a small living room. The curtains were half closed, cutting out most of the light, and the air felt hot and cloying. From what Banks could see, the place wasn't dirty but it wasn't exactly clean either. A grey-haired old woman with a blanket over her knees sat in a wheelchair by the empty grate. She looked round as he came in and gave him a blank smile.

'It's about our Cheryl,' the man said, reaching for his pipe.

'I heard.'

'Look, Mrs Duggan,' Banks said, perching on the arm of the settee, 'I know it's a long time ago, but something might have come up.'

'You've found out who killed her?'

'It's possible. But I still don't know that she was killed. You'll have to help me.'

The file was still fresh in his mind. Cheryl Duggan had been fished out of the River Cherwell not too far from Magdalen Bridge and St Hilda's College on a foggy November Sunday morning over six years ago. The coroner's inquest said that death was due to drowning, or so it appeared. Several odd bruises indicated that her head may have been held under the water until she drowned. She had had sexual intercourse shortly before death, and the stomach contents indicated that she had been drinking heavily the previous evening. In view of all this, an open verdict was recorded and a police investigation was ordered.

To complicate matters, Cheryl Duggan, according to Folley, had been a well known local prostitute since the age of fifteen. She had been only seventeen when she died. The investigation, Folley admitted, had been cursory. This was due to other pressures, in particular the drug-related death of a peer's daughter in which the heir to a brewery fortune was implicated as a pusher.

'It could have been an accident,' Banks said.

'It warn't no accident, Mr Banks,' Mrs Duggan insisted.

'There was water in the lungs,' Banks countered weakly.

Mr Duggan snorted. 'You'd think she were a mermaid, our Cheryl, the way she took to water.'

'She'd been drinking.'

'Yes, well, nobody's saying she was perfect.'

'Did you ever hear her mention a man by the name of Stephen Collier?'

Mr Duggan shook his head slowly.

There was a sense of defeat about the Duggans that weighed heavily in the dim and stuffy room and made Banks feel sick. Their voices were flat, as if they had repeated their stories a hundred times and nobody had listened; their faces were parchment-dry and drawn, the eyes wide and blank, with plenty of white showing between the lower lashes and the pupils. Dante's words came into Banks' mind: 'Abandon all hope, ye who enter here.' This was a house of defeat, a place without hope.

Banks lit a cigarette, which would at least give him a more concrete reason to feel sick and dizzy, and went on. 'The other thing I'd like to know,' he asked, 'is if you hired anyone to look into Cheryl's death. I know you didn't think much of the police investigation.'

Mr Duggan spat into the grate. His wife frowned at him. 'Why does it matter?' she asked.

'It could be important.'

'We did hire someone,' she said. 'A private investigator from London. We looked him up in the phone book at the library. We were desperate. The police hadn't done anything for more than a year, and they were saying such terrible things about Cheryl. We took out all our savings.'

'What happened?'

'He came from London, this man, and he asked us about Cheryl – who her friends were, where she liked to go out and everything – then he said he'd try and find out what happened.'

'He never came back,' Mr Duggan cut in.

'You mean he ran off with your money?'

'Not all of it, Alf,' Mrs Duggan said. 'Only a retainer, that's all he'd take.'

'He took off with the money, Jessie, let's face it. We were had. He never meant to do anything about our Cheryl; he just took us for what he could get. And we let him.'

'What was his name?'

'Don't remember.'

'Yes you do, Alf,' said Mrs Duggan. 'It was Raymond Addison. I haven't forgotten.'

'So what did you do?'

'What could we do?' she said. 'He'd got most of our money, so we couldn't hire anyone else. The police weren't interested. We just tried to forget, that's all.' She pulled the tartan blanket up higher around her hips.

'Mr Addison didn't report back to you at all then, after the first time you saw him?'

'No,' Mr Duggan said. 'We only saw him the once.'

'Can you remember the date?'

The old man shook his head.

'I can't remember the exact day,' his wife said, 'but it was in February, about fifteen months after Cheryl was killed. The police seemed to have given up and we didn't know where to turn. We found him, and he let us down.'

'If it's any consolation, Mrs Duggan, I don't think Mr Addison did let you down.'

'What?'

'He was found killed himself, probably no more than a day or so after you saw him, up in Yorkshire. That's why you never heard from him again, not because he'd run off with your money.'

'In Yorkshire? What was he doing there?'

'I think he did find out something about Cheryl's death. Something the police had missed. You've got to understand that we don't have enough time or men to devote ourselves full time to every single case, Mrs Duggan. I don't know the circumstances, but maybe the police here weren't as active as you think they should have been. It's only in books that policemen find the killer every time. But Mr Addison had only the one case. He must have visited every possible place Cheryl might have been that night, talked to everyone who knew her, and what he found out led him to a village in Yorkshire, and to his death.'

Mrs Duggan bit her knuckles and began to cry silently. Her husband moved forward to comfort her.

'It never does any good raking up the past,' he snapped at Banks. 'Look how you've upset her.'

'I can understand that you're angry, Mr Duggan,' Banks said, 'but if I'm right, then we know who killed your daughter.'

Duggan looked away. 'What's it matter now?'

'Maybe it doesn't, at least not to you. But I think it ought to mean something that Addison didn't let you down, didn't run off with your money. He found a lead, and instead of reporting in he set off while the trail was hot. I think you owe his memory some kind of apology if you've been blaming him and thinking ill of him all these years.'

'Maybe so,' Duggan admitted. 'But what use is it now? Two people dead. What use?'

'More than two,' Banks said. 'He had to kill again to cover his tracks. First Addison, then someone else.'

'All over our Cheryl?' Mrs Duggan said, wiping her eyes.

Banks nodded. 'It looks like that's where it started. Is there anything else you can tell me? Did Cheryl ever talk about anyone at all she knew from Yorkshire? A student she was seeing, perhaps?'

They both shook their heads, then Mrs Duggan laughed bitterly. 'She said she was going to marry a student one day, a lord's son, or a prime minister's. She was very determined, our Cheryl. But she'd too much imagination. She was too flighty. If only she'd done as I said and stuck to her station.'

'Did she hang around with students much?'

'She went to the same pubs as they did,' Mr Duggan said. 'The police said she was a prostitute, Mr Banks, that she sold herself to men. We didn't know nothing about that. I still can't believe it. I know she liked to tart herself up a bit when she went out, but what girl doesn't? And she wasn't really old enough to drink, but what can you do . . .? You can't keep them prisoners, can you? She was always talking about what fun the students were, how she was sure to meet a nice young man soon. What were we to do? We believed her. Our Cheryl could make you believe she could do anything if she set her mind to it. Every day she woke up with a smile on her face, and that's no lie. Happiest soul I've ever known. What did we do wrong?'

Banks had no answer. He dropped his cigarette in the grate and walked to the door. 'If you think of anything, let the local police know,' he said.

'Wait a minute.' Mrs Duggan turned to him. 'Aren't you going to tell us?'

'Tell you what?'

'Who did it. Who killed our Cheryl?'

'It doesn't matter now,' Banks said. 'It looks like he's dead himself.' And he closed the door on their hopelessness and emptiness.

FOUR

'I'm sorry, Alan,' Ted Folley said when he'd heard the story. 'I told you it wasn't much of an investigation. We looked into it, but we got nowhere. We were sure the girl drowned. She'd been drinking and there was water in her lungs. The bruises could have been caused by a customer; it's a rough trade she was in. She didn't have a ponce, so we'd no one we could jump on right from the start.'

Banks nodded and blew smoke rings. 'We got nowhere with the Addison case, either,' he said. 'There was nothing to link him with Oxford, and we couldn't find out why he was in Swainshead. Not until now, anyway. What on earth could he have found out?'

'Anything,' Folley said. 'Maybe he found the last pub

she'd been in, tracked down a pusher who'd run a mile if he even smelled police.'

'Was she on drugs?'

'Not when she died, no. But there had been trouble. Nothing serious, just pills mostly. If Addison trailed around all her haunts and talked to everyone who knew her, showed a photo, flashed a bit of money . . . You know as well as I do, Alan, these blokes who operate outside the law have a better chance. He must have picked up your man's name somewhere and set off to question him.'

'Yes. It's just a damn shame he wasn't more efficient.'

'What do you mean?'

'If he'd gone back and told the Duggans what he'd found out before rushing off to Yorkshire. If he'd just filed some kind of report . . .'

'He must have been keen,' Folley said. 'Some of them are, you know.'

At that moment, Sergeant Hatchley came in from Woodstock. 'Bloody waste of time,' he grumbled, slouching in a chair and fumbling for a cigarette.

'Nothing?' Banks asked.

'Nowt. But judging by the expression on your face, you're that cat that got the cream. Am I right?'

'You are.' He told Hatchley about his interview with the Duggans.

'So that's it, then?'

'Looks like it. Stephen Collier must've met up with this young girl, Cheryl Duggan, gone drinking with her then taken her to the meadows by the river for sex. It was unusually warm for that time of year. He got a bit rough, they fought, and he drowned her. Or she fell in and he tried to save her. It could have been an accident, but it was a situation he couldn't afford to be associated with. Maybe he was on drugs; we'll never know. He might not even have been responsible for the bruising and the rough sexual treatment she'd received; that could have been a previous customer. Collier might even have been comforting her, trying to persuade her back on to the straight and narrow. I suppose the version will vary according to what kind of person you think Stephen was. One mistake – one terrible mistake – and three deaths have to follow. Christ, it could even have been some silly student prank.'

'Do you think he killed himself?'

Banks shook his head. 'I don't know. In his state of mind, if he'd been carrying the guilt all this time and feeling the pressure build, suicide and accidental death might have been much the same thing. It didn't matter any more, so he just got careless. Katie Greenock said he was planning to leave Swainshead, and I suppose he didn't much mind how he went.'

'What do we do now?' Hatchley asked.

Banks looked at his watch. 'It's three thirty,' he said. 'I suggest we pay Stephen's old tutor a visit and see if we can find out whether he was in the habit of taking up with young prostitutes. We might find some clue as to what really happened, who was responsible for what. Then we'll head back home. We should be able to make it before nine if we're on the road soon.' He turned to Folley and held out his hand. 'Thanks again, Ted. We appreciate all you've done. If I can ever return the favour . . .'

Folley laughed. 'In Swainsdale? You must be joking. But you're welcome. And do pay us a social call sometime. A few days boating in the Thames Valley would be just the ticket for the wife and kids.'

'I will,' Banks said. 'Come on, Jim lad, time to hit the road again.'

Hatchley dragged himself to his feet, said goodbye to Folley and followed Banks out on to St Aldates.

'There you are,' Banks said, near Blackwell's on Broad Street. 'Caps and gowns.'

True enough, students were all over the place: walking, cycling, standing to chat outside the bookshops.

'Bloody poofters,' Hatchley said.

They got past the porter, crossed the quadrangle, and found Dr Barber in his office at Stephen's old college.

'Sherry, gentlemen?' he asked, after they had introduced themselves.

Banks accepted because he liked dry sherry; Hatchley took one because he had never been known to refuse a free drink.

Barber's study was cluttered with books, journals and papers. A student essay entitled 'The Dissolution of the Monasteries: Evidence of Contemporary Accounts' lay on the desk but didn't quite obscure an old green-covered Penguin crime paperback. Banks tilted his head and glanced sideways at the title: *The Moving Toyshop*, by Edmund Crispin. He had never heard of it, but it wasn't quite the reading material he'd have expected to find in the office of an Oxford don.

While Dr Barber poured, Banks stood by the window and looked over the neat clipped quadrangle at the light stone façades of the college.

Barber passed them their drinks and lit his pipe. Its smoke sweetened the air. In deference to his guests, he opened the window a little, and a draught of fresh air sucked the smoke out. In appearance, Barber had the air of an aged cleric, and he smelled of Pears soap. He reminded Banks of the actor Wilfrid Hyde-White.

'It was a long time ago,' Barber said, when Banks had

asked him about Collier. 'Let me check my files. I've got records going back over twenty years, you know. It pays to know whom one has had pass through these hallowed halls. As a historian myself, I place great value on documentation. Now, let me see . . . Stephen Collier, yes. Braughtmore School, Yorkshire. Is that the one? Yes? I remember him. Not terribly distinguished academically, but a pleasant enough fellow. What's he been up to?'

'That's what we're trying to find out,' Banks said. 'He died a few days ago and we want to know why.'

Barber sat down and picked up his sherry. 'Good Lord! He wasn't murdered, was he?'

'Why would you think that?'

Barber shrugged. 'One doesn't usually get a visit from the Yorkshire police over nothing. One doesn't usually get visits from the police at all.'

'We don't know,' Banks said. 'It could have been accidental, or it could have been suicide.'

'Suicide? Oh dear. Collier was a rather serious young man – a bit too much so, if I remember him clearly. But suicide?'

'Possibly.'

'A lot can change in a few years,' Barber said. He frowned and relit his pipe. Banks remembered his own struggles with the infernal engines, and the broken pipe that now hung on his wall in Eastvale Police Headquarters. 'As I said,' Barber went on, 'Collier seemed a sober sensible kind of fellow. Still, who can fathom the mysteries of the human heart? *Fronti nulla fides*.'

'There's no real type for suicide,' Banks said. 'Anyone, pushed far enough—'

'I suppose you're the kind of policeman who thinks anyone can become a murderer too, given the circumstances.'

Banks nodded.

'I'm afraid I can't go along with that,' Barber said. 'I'm no psychologist, but I'd say it takes a special type. Take me, for example, I could never conceive of doing such a thing. The thought of jail, for a start, would deter me. And I should think that everyone would notice my guilt. As a child, I once stole a lemon tart from the school tuck shop while Mrs Wiggins was in the back, and I felt myself turn red from head to toe. No, Chief Inspector, I'd never make a murderer.'

'I'm thankful for that,' Banks said. 'I don't need to ask you for an alibi now, I suppose.'

Barber looked at him for a moment, unsure what to do, then laughed.

'Stephen Collier,' Banks said.

'Yes, yes. Forgive me. I'm getting old; I tend to ramble. But it's coming back. He was the kind who really did have to work hard to do well. So many others have a natural ability – they can dash off a good essay the night before – but you'd always find Collier in the library all week before a major piece of work was due. Conscientious.'

'How did he get on with the other students?'

'Well enough, as far as I know. Collier was a bit of a loner though. Kept himself to himself. I hardly need to tell you, Chief Inspector, that quite a number of young lads around these parts go in for high jinks. It's always been like that, ever since students started coming here in the thirteenth century. And there's always been a bit of a running battle between the university authorities and the people of the city: town and gown, as we say. The students aren't vindictive, you realize, just high-spirited. Sometimes they cause more damage than they intend.'

'And Collier?'

'I'm sure he didn't go in for that kind of thing. If there had been any incidents of an unsavoury nature, they would have appeared in my assessment file.'

'Did he drink much?'

'Never had any trouble with him.'

'Drugs?'

'Chief Inspector Banks,' Barber said slowly, 'I do realize that the university has been getting a bad reputation lately for drugs and the like, and no doubt such things do happen, but if you take the word of the media, you'd be seriously misled. I don't think Stephen Collier was involved in drugs at all. I remember that we did have some trouble with one student selling cannabis around that time – most distressing – but there was a full investigation, and at no point was Stephen Collier implicated.'

'So, as far as you can say, Collier was a model student, if not quite as brilliant as some of his fellows?'

'I know it sounds hard to believe, but yes, he was. Most of the time you'd hardly have known he was here. I'm having great difficulty trying to guess what you're after. You say that Stephen Collier's death might have been suicide or it might have been an accident, but if you don't mind my saying so, the questions you're asking seem preoccupied with unearthing evidence that Collier himself was some kind of hell-raiser.'

Banks frowned and looked out of the window again. The shadow of a cloud passed over the quadrangle. He drained his sherry and lit a cigarette. Sergeant Hatchley, quietly smoking in a chair in the corner, had emptied his glass a while ago and sat fidgeting with it as if he hoped Barber would notice and offer a refill. He did, and both policemen accepted. Banks liked the way the dry liquid puckered his taste buds.

'He's a suspect,' Banks said. 'And I'm afraid that's all I can tell you. We have no proof that Collier was guilty of anything, but there's a strong possibility.'

'Does it matter,' Barber asked, 'now that he's dead?'

'Yes, it does. If he was guilty, then the case is closed. If not, we still have a criminal to catch.'

'Yes. I see. Well, I'm afraid I can't offer you any evidence at all. Seemed a thoroughly pleasant hard-working nondescript fellow to me as far as I can remember.'

'What about six years ago? It would have been his third year, his last. Did anything unusual happen then, around early November?'

Barber frowned and pursed his lips. 'I can't recall anything . . . Wait a minute . . .' He walked back over to his ancient filing cabinet and riffled through the papers. 'Yes, yes, I thought so,' he announced finally. 'Stephen Collier didn't finish his degree.'

'What?'

'He didn't finish. Decided history wasn't for him and left after two years. Went to run a business, as far as I know. I can confirm with the registrar's office, of course, but my own records are quite thorough.'

'Are you saying that Stephen Collier wasn't here, that he wasn't in Oxford in November six years ago?'

'That's right. Could it be you've got him mixed up with his brother, Nicholas? He would have just been starting his second year then, you know, and I certainly remember him, now I cast my mind back. Nicholas Collier was a different kettle of fish, a different kettle of fish entirely.'

14

ONE

Katie stared at her reflection in the dark kitchen window as she washed the crystal glasses she couldn't put in the machine. The radio on the table played soothing classical music, quiet enough that she could even hear the beck at the bottom of the back garden rippling over its stones.

Now that Stephen was dead and she had unburdened herself to Banks, she felt empty. None of her grandmother's maxims floated around her mind, as they had been doing lately, and that tightness in her chest that had seemed to squeeze at her very heart itself had relaxed. She even noticed a half-smile on her face, a very odd one she'd not seen before. Nothing hurt now; she felt numb, just like her mouth always did after an injection at the dentist's.

Chief Inspector Banks had told her that if she remembered anything else, she should get in touch with him. Try as she might though, she couldn't remember a thing. Looking back over the years in Swainshead, she had noticed hints that all wasn't well, that some things were going on about which she knew nothing. But there was no coherent narrative, just a series of unlinked events. She thought of Sam's behaviour when Raymond Addison first appeared. She hadn't heard their conversation, but Sam had immediately left everything to her and gone running off across the street to the Collier house. Later, Addison had gone for a walk and never returned. When they found out the man had been murdered, Sam had been unusually pale and quiet for some days.

She remembered watching Bernie pause and glance towards the Collier house before going on his way the morning he left. She had also seen him call there one evening shortly after he'd arrived and thought it odd because of the way he usually went on about them being so rich and privileged.

None of it had meant very much at the time. Katie wasn't the kind of woman to look for bad in anyone but herself. She had had far more pressing matters to deal with and soon forgot the suspicious little things she'd noticed. Even now, she couldn't put it all together. When she told Banks that she had killed Bernie and Stephen, she meant it. She hadn't physically murdered them, but she knew she was responsible.

The things she remembered often seemed as if they had happened to someone else. She could view again, dispassionately, Bernard Allen sating himself on her impassive body, as if she were watching a silent film from the ceiling. And Stephen's chaste kiss left no trace of ice or fire on her lips. Sam had taken her roughly the previous evening, but instead of fear and loathing she had felt a kind of power in her subservience. It wasn't pleasure; it was something new, and she felt that if she could only be patient enough it would make itself known to her eventually. It was as if he had possessed her body, but not her soul. She had kept her soul pure and untainted, and now it was revealing itself to her. Somehow, these new feelings were all connected with her sense of responsibility for the deaths of

Bernie and Stephen. She had blood on her hands; she had grown up.

The future was still very uncertain. Life would go on, she supposed, much as it had done. She would clean the rooms, cook the meals, submit to Sam in bed, do what she was told, and try to avoid making him angry. Everything would continue just as it had done, except for the new feelings that were growing in her. If she stayed patient, change would come in its own time. She wouldn't have to do anything until she knew exactly *what* to do.

For the moment, nothing touched her; nothing ruffled the calm and glassy surface of her mind. Caught up in her dark reflection, she dropped one of a set of six expensive crystal glasses. It shattered on the linoleum. But even that didn't matter. Katie looked down at the shards with an indulgent pitying expression on her face and went to fetch the brush and dustpan.

As she moved, she heard a sound out at the back. Hurrying to the window, she peered through her own reflection and glimpsed a shadow slipping past her gate. A moment later – before she could get to the unlocked door – she heard a cursory tap. The door opened and Nicholas Collier popped his head round and smiled. 'Hello, Katie. I've come to visit.'

TWO

The sun was a swollen red ball low on the western horizon. It oozed its eerie light over the South Yorkshire landscape, silhouetted motionless pit wheels and made the slag heaps glow. On the cassette, Nick Drake was singing the haunting 'Northern Sky'.

Much of the way, the two had sat in silence, thinking things out and deciding what to do. Finally, Hatchley could stand it no longer. 'How can we nail the bastard?' he asked.

'I don't know,' Banks answered. 'We don't have much of a case.'

Hatchley grunted. 'We might if we hauled him in and you and me had a go at him.'

'He's clever, Jim,' Banks said. The sergeant's first name didn't feel so strange to his lips after the first few times. 'Look how he's kept out of it so long. He's not going to break down just because you and I play good-cop-bad-cop with him. That'll be a sign of our weakness to him. He'll know we need a confession to make anything stick, so it will only strengthen his position. No, Nicholas Collier's a cool one. And don't forget he's got pull around Swainsdale. We'd no sooner get started than some fancy lawyer would waltz in and gum up the works.'

'What I'd give for a bloody good try, though!' Hatchley thumped the dashboard. 'Sorry. No damage done. It just makes me angry, a stuck-up bastard like Nicholas Collier getting away with it. How many people has he killed?'

'Three, maybe four if we count Stephen. And he hasn't got away with it yet. The trouble is, we don't know if he killed anyone apart from the girl, Cheryl Duggan. We can't even prove that he killed her. Just because Dr Barber told us he had a reputation for pestering the town's working girls doesn't make him guilty. It certainly doesn't give us grounds for a conviction.'

'But it was Cheryl Duggan's death that sent Addison up to Swainshead.'

'Yes. But even that's circumstantial.'

'Who do you think killed Addison and Allen?'

'At a guess, I'd say Stephen. He'd do it to protect his little brother and his family's reputation. But we don't know, and we never will if Nicholas doesn't talk. I'll bet, for all his cleverness, Nicholas is weak. I doubt he has the stomach for cold-blooded murder. They might both have been at the scene – certainly neither had a good alibi – but I'd say Stephen did the killing.'

'What do you think happened with the Duggan girl?'

Banks shifted lanes to overtake a lorry. 'I think he picked her up in a pub and took her down by the river. She was just a prostitute, a working-class kid, and he was from a prominent family, so what the hell did it matter to him what he did? I think he got overexcited, hurt her perhaps, and she started to protest, threatened to scream or tell the police. So he panicked and drowned her. Either that or he did it because he enjoyed it.'

The tape finished. Banks lit a cigarette and felt around in the dark for another cassette. Without looking at the title, he slipped in the first one he got hold of. It was the 1960s anthology tape he'd taken to Toronto with him. Traffic came on singing 'No Face, No Name and No Number'.

'I think Addison was a conscientious investigator,' Banks went on. 'He more than earned his money, poor sod. He did all the legwork the police didn't do and found a connection between Cheryl Duggan and Nicholas Collier. Maybe they'd been seen leaving a pub together, or perhaps her friends told him Collier had been with her before. Anyway, Addison prised the name out of someone, or bought the information, and instead of reporting in he set off for Swainshead. That was his first mistake.

'His second was to ask Sam Greenock about Nicholas Collier. Greenock was anxious to get in with the local gentry and he was a bit suspicious of this stranger asking questions, so he stalled Addison and took the first opportunity to run over the bridge and tell Collier about it. There must have been real panic in the Collier house that evening. Remember, it was about fifteen months after the girl's death and the Colliers must've thought all was well. I don't know the details. Maybe Sam arranged for Addison to go over to the house when the village was quiet, or maybe he even arranged for the Colliers to go up to Addison's room and kill him there. I don't know how it happened, but I think it was Stephen who struck the blow. That would explain the state he was in when he met Anne Ralston later that night.'

'What about Bernard Allen?' Hatchley asked.

'At first I thought he was just unlucky,' Banks said. 'He told Katie Greenock that he knew Anne Ralston in Toronto. She told Sam, who did his usual town crier routine. Not that it mattered this time, if Allen was intent on blackmail. Stephen Collier was an odd kind of bloke from what I can make out – a real combination of opposites. When he'd killed Addison, he had to unburden himself to his girlfriend, but I'm sure he soon regretted it. He must have had a few sleepless nights after Anne first disappeared. Anyway, Bernard Allen knew that Stephen was involved in Addison's murder and that it was something to do with an incident back in Oxford. He obviously assumed that if the police knew that they could put the whole thing together. Which we did, rather too late.'

'You said you thought Allen was unlucky at first,' Hatchley said. 'What about now?'

'I think he was going to blackmail the Colliers. I've not had time to tell you much about Toronto, but I met a few people there who said that Bernard Allen really wanted to come home to Swainshead. His sister mentioned it too, but the others all played it down. He'd even let on to Katie Greenock that he'd send for her when he got back to Canada. That was because she wanted to escape Swainsdale and he wanted to get into her pants.

'I wondered why I was getting so many conflicting pictures of Allen's state of mind, so many contradictions. But that was his motive. He was blackmailing the Colliers to get himself home. A job at the school, money in the bank . . . I don't know what he'd asked for, but I'm certain that was his reason. And it got him killed. I don't doubt that whoever said "You can't go home again" meant it as literally as that. Anyway, the Colliers decided they couldn't live with the threat, so one or both of them waited for him in the hanging valley that morning. They knew he'd be there because he'd often talked about it and he was heading that way.'

'And what happened to Stephen? Why would Nicholas kill him, if he did?'

'Stephen was getting too jittery. Nicholas knew it was just a matter of time before his brother broke down completely, and he couldn't allow him to remain alive when I got back from Toronto after talking to Anne Ralston. Stephen must have told his brother that he didn't give anything away to Anne about the Oxford business, but that he'd made a serious mistake in hinting at his own involvement in Addison's killing. Nicholas knew that what Anne had to tell me would give me enough grounds to bring Stephen in, and he couldn't trust his brother to stand up under questioning. If we could discover the motive behind Addison's murder, then we'd know everything. Nicholas couldn't allow that.

'What he did was risky, but there was a lot at stake: not

just the family name now, but Nicholas's own freedom, his home, his career. He had to kill his own brother to survive. And if he succeeded, it would look like the accidental death of a disturbed man or the suicide of a guilty one.'

It was dark when Banks negotiated the tricky connections on to the A1 east of Leeds. Cream were singing 'Strange Brew' on the tape and Hatchley had fallen silent.

Banks still didn't understand it all. Stephen had killed to preserve what was important to him, but Nicholas Collier remained something of an enigma. In all likelihood he had drowned Cheryl Duggan, but what bothered Banks was why. Had he done it from pleasure, accident or desperation? And was he also responsible for the bruising and marks of sexual abuse found on her body? Dr Barber had said that Nicholas had been in trouble once or twice over consorting with prostitutes and offering Oxford factory girls money for sex. Banks wondered why. Nicholas had all the advantages. Why hadn't he hung around with his own set, girls of his own social class?

'Let's call in at the station first,' Banks said. 'Something might have turned up.' They were approaching the turnoff on to a minor road that would take them over the moors to Helmthorpe and the main valley road. 'We can always drive to Swainshead later if there's nothing new.' He looked at his watch. 'It's not late, only nineish.'

Hatchley nodded and Banks drove past the exit ramp and on to the Eastvale road.

The station was quiet. There had been no serious crimes while Banks and Hatchley had been gone. There was, however, a message from John Fletcher timed at five o'clock that evening asking if they would call and see him as soon as possible. He said it was important – something to do with Stephen Collier's death – and he would be at home all evening.

There was also a copy of Dr Glendenning's preliminary post-mortem report on Stephen Collier. The doctor had found the equivalent of about five capsules of Nembutal in Collier's system – not enough in itself to cause death but potentially lethal when mixed with alcohol. And his alcohol level had been far higher than the amount five or six pints would account for. It looked as if Banks was right and Collier had been slipped vodka in the pub and more drinks back at the house.

'Should we go to see Fletcher tonight?' Banks asked Hatchley. 'Or leave it until tomorrow?'

Under normal circumstances he would have expected Hatchley to take any opportunity to get off work for a pint or a session on the sofa with Carol Ellis, but this time the sergeant was angry.

'Let's go,' he said. 'Maybe Fletcher's got the answer. I wouldn't want to leave it till he went and got himself killed, too. And I wouldn't mind paying a call on Nicholas bloody Collier either.'

THREE

'Go away!' Katie said, rushing forward and trying to close the door.

But Nicholas had his foot wedged in. 'Let me in, Katie,' he said. 'I want to talk to you about Stephen. He was very fond of you, you know.'

'He's dead,' Katie said, still pushing at the door with her shoulder. But Nicholas was too strong for her and the door knocked her backwards against the kitchen table as he entered. He shut the door behind him and walked towards her.

'I won't hurt you,' he said. 'I know you were talking to Stephen the day before he died. I just wondered if he'd been saying anything silly. He wasn't well, you know.' He reached out and grabbed Katie's arm as she tried to slip away. 'There's no need to be afraid of me,' he said, relaxing his grip a little. 'No need to run away. I won't hurt you. I just want to talk to you.'

'I don't know what you mean,' Katie said. 'There was nothing wrong with Stephen.'

'He was upset. He might have said things he didn't mean.'

'What things?'

'I don't know. That's what I'm asking you, you stupid bitch,' Nicholas shouted, then lowered his voice again. 'Just tell me what you talked about. Aren't you going to offer me a drink?'

'I don't have anything.'

'Liar.' Nicholas opened Sam's drinks cabinet and poured himself a large gin. 'I've been here before, remember? With Sam.' He held out the glass. 'Go on, have some. You like gin, don't you?'

Katie shook her head. Nicholas hooked the back of her neck with one hand, put the glass to her closed lips and tipped it forward. The vile-smelling spirit spilled down Katie's chin and on to the front of her dress. It burned her throat and made her gag.

'Stop it!' she cried, spluttering and pushing him away.

Nicholas laughed, showing his yellowed teeth, and put the glass down. He went back to the cabinet and poured himself some Scotch.

'What did Stephen tell you?' he asked.

311

'Nothing.' Katie coughed and rubbed at her lips with the back of her hand.

'He must have said something. He was quite a one for confiding in the wrong people, Stephen was, especially women. And I saw you talking to that policeman. Where is he now? What's he doing?'

'I don't know. I haven't seen him since yesterday.'

'What did he ask you? What did you say to him?'

'Nothing. He doesn't know anything.'

'Stop lying, Katie. Did you do it with him too, just like you do with all the others?'

Katie turned pale. 'What do you mean?'

Nicholas grinned. The dark comma of hair had flopped over his brow and his cheeks were flushed. 'You know what I mean. Just like you did with Stephen and everyone else. Did you let him do it to you, Katie, that policeman?'

'No!'

'Oh, don't be shy. You do it with everyone, don't you? You know you're nothing but a slut. A filthy whore. Tell me you're a filthy whore, Katie, say it.'

'I'm not.'

Katie rushed desperately for the connecting door, but Nicholas got there before her.

'There's no way out,' he said. 'All your guests are in the White Rose; I saw them. And Sam's off with his fancy women as usual.'

'He's what?'

'Didn't you know? Oh, don't tell me you didn't know. All those times he goes off to see his friends in Leeds or Eastvale. It's women, Katie. Loose women. Can't you smell them on his skin when he comes home? Or do you like it when he comes straight from another woman and takes you? Do you like to smell other women on your husband's skin?'

Katie put her hands to her ears. 'Stop it! Stop it!' she screamed. 'You're evil!'

Nicholas applauded quietly. 'Oh, Katie, what an act.'

Katie dropped her hands to her sides. 'What are you going to do?'

'Do? Why, I'm going to take you away from here. I don't trust you, Katie. There's no telling what you know and what you might say.'

'I don't know anything.'

'I think you do. Stephen told you, didn't he?'

'Told me what?'

'About Oxford.'

Katie could think of nothing to say.

'Look at you blushing,' Nicholas said, pointing at her. 'You know, don't you? I can tell. Be sure your sins will find you out.'

Suddenly, Katie realized what he meant and a terrible thought dawned on her.

'You killed him,' she said quietly. 'You killed Stephen.'

Nicholas shrugged and spoke in a cold passionless voice. 'I couldn't trust him any more. He was falling apart on me.'

Katie stiffened. She felt like a trapped animal. 'What are you going to do?'

'I'm going to take you away, far away. What did he tell you about Oxford?'

'Nothing.'

'Did he tell you about that girl, that stupid slut?'

Katie shook her head.

'He did, didn't he?'

'No! He told me nothing.'

Nicholas leaned against the table. His bright eyes glittered and his breath came in short sharp gasps. He looked like a madman to Katie. A wild, terrifying madman.

'She was nothing but a prostitute, Katie,' he said. 'A fallen woman. She sold herself to men. And when I . . . when I took her, she didn't . . . She told me I was too rough and she tried to make me stop. Me! Nicholas Collier. But I didn't. I couldn't. I knew that was the way she really wanted it. A common tart like her. Like you.'

'No!' Katie said. 'I'm not.'

'Yes, you are. I've had my eye on you. You do it with everyone. Do they pay you, Katie, or do you do it for nothing? I know you like to struggle. I'll pay you if you want.'

'I don't know what you're talking about.'

'I want you to say it for me. Say you're a filthy whore.'

'I'm not.'

'What's wrong? Why won't you say it? I bet you even let that policeman do it. I'm better than the lot of them, Katie. Say it.'

'No! I won't.'

He spoke very softly, so quiet she could hardly hear. 'I want you to go down on your knees, Katie, and tell me you're a filthy whore and you want me to do it to you like an animal. Like a dog. I want you to lift your dress up and crawl, Katie.'

He was moving towards her now, and his eyes held hers with a power that seemed to sap what little strength she had. She felt her shoulders hit the wall by the mantel-piece. There was nowhere else to go. But Nicholas kept coming closer, and when he was near enough he reached out and grabbed the front of her dress.

FOUR

Banks drove fast along the dark dale by the River Swain, passed through Helmthorpe and into the darker fell-shadowed landscape beyond. He turned sharp right at Swainshead, tyres squealing, and carried on up the valley to Upper Head. He slowed down as they passed the Collier house, but the lights were out.

'I hope the bastard hasn't done a bunk,' Hatchley said.

'No, he's too cool for that. We'll get him, don't worry.'

The glimmer of light high on the fell side about two miles north of the village came from Fletcher's isolated cottage. It was a difficult track to manage in the dark, but they finally pulled up outside the squat solid house with its three-foot-thick walls. Fletcher had heard them coming and stood in the doorway. Again they were ushered into the plain whitewashed room with its oak table and the photograph of Fletcher's glamorous ex-wife.

Fletcher was ill at ease. He avoided looking at them directly and fussed around with glasses of beer. Hatchley stood by the window looking into the darkness. Banks sat at the table.

'What is it?' he asked, when Fletcher had sat down opposite him.

'It's about Stephen's death,' Fletcher began hesitantly. 'He was my friend. It's gone too far now. Too far.'

Banks nodded. 'I know. I understood there was no love lost between you and Nicholas.'

'You've heard about that? Well, it's true enough. I never had much time for him. But old Mr Walter was like a father to me, and I always felt like an older brother to Stephen.'

Banks passed around the cigarettes.

'Saturday night,' Fletcher burst out suddenly. 'I thought nothing of it at the time – it was just the kind of silly trick Nicholas would play – but when he went to buy a round I saw him pour a glass of clear spirits into Stephen's drink. As I said, I thought nothing of it. I knew Stephen was upset about something – what it was, I don't know – and he seemed to want to get drunk and forget his problems anyway. No point causing trouble, I thought, so I kept quiet.

'That family has a secret, Mr Banks, a dark secret. Stephen's hinted at it more than once, and I reckon it's something to do with Nicholas and the ladies, though ladies is too dignified a term. Did you know he once forced himself on Molly Stark from over Relton way?'

'No, I didn't.'

'Aye. Well, it was hushed up, like most things Nicholas got up to. All neat and businesslike.'

'Wasn't there also some trouble with a girl when his father was alive?' Banks asked.

'Aye,' said Fletcher. 'Got her in the family way. But money changed hands and shut mouths. It was all arranged, no expense spared, and she did away with it. He had a lust for lasses below his station, as they used to say. Working-class girls, servants, factory girls, milkmaids . . . I even caught him mauling Katie Greenock at Stephen's party last week.'

At last it made sense to Banks. Nicholas Collier couldn't keep away from women of a lower social class: Cheryl Duggan, Esther Haines, Katie Greenock, Anne Ralston, the servant girl, Molly Stark – they were all beneath him socially. Although the term had lost a lot of its meaning over the past few years, they might still be called working-class women. Obviously it didn't matter who they were as individuals; that didn't interest Collier. He probably had some Victorian image of the working class as a seething, gin-drinking, fornicating, procreating mass. He thrust himself on them and became violent when they objected. No doubt like most perverse sexual practices, his compulsion had a lot to do with power and humiliation.

'I knew something serious was up when we had those two murders here,' Fletcher went on, refilling their beer glasses. 'That detective and young Bernard Allen. I knew it, but I didn't know what. Whenever I asked, Stephen clammed up, told me to leave it be and I'd be better off not knowing.' He took a sip of beer. 'Maybe I should've pushed a bit harder. Maybe Stephen would still be alive . . . But I don't think he killed himself. That's what I wanted to tell you. As I said, I saw Nicholas putting something into his drink, and he was in a hell of a state at closing time, worse than if he'd just had a few jars. And the next thing I hear, he's dead. An overdose, they said. I knew he took sleeping tablets, but an overdose . . .?'

'Yes, barbiturates,' Banks said. 'Usually fatal, mixed with as much alcohol as Stephen Collier had in his system.'

'So it's murder, isn't it? That bastard brother of his murdered him.'

'It looks like it, Mr Fletcher, but we've got to tread carefully. We've got no evidence, no proof.'

'I'll testify to what I saw. I'll help put him away, as God's my witness.'

Banks shook his head. 'It'll help, but it's not enough. What if Nicholas was putting vodka in his brother's beer? As you said, it could have been a simple prank, and that's exactly what he'll say. It's all circumstantial and theoretical. We need more solid evidence or a confession.'

'Then I'll bloody well beat it out of him,' Fletcher said, grasping the table and rising to his feet.

'Sit down,' said Banks. 'That's not going to help at all.'

'Then what are you going to do?'

'I honestly don't know yet,' Banks said. 'We might just be able to put together a case, especially if we bring in Anne Ralston, but I don't want to risk it. Even if we could convince the court it's worth a risk, I don't want to take the chance of him getting off, which he might well do on what we've got so far.'

'I know I should've spoken up earlier,' Fletcher said. 'I knew there was something wrong. If I'd told you before you went to Toronto, you might have had something to push at Stephen with, and he just might have told you the truth. He was on the edge, Mr Banks. That's why Nicholas had to get rid of him, I suppose.'

'I think you're right,' Banks said. 'But we still can't prove it. You shouldn't blame yourself though. You might have thought you were going to get Stephen in trouble. I imagine you were protecting him?'

Fletcher nodded. 'I suppose I was. Him and his father's memory.'

'To get Nicholas, you'd have had to betray Stephen. He was protecting his brother, or his father, like you were.'

'What'll happen to me? Will you prosecute?'

'For what?'

'Withholding evidence? Accessory after the fact?'

Banks laughed. 'You have a very thin grasp of the law, Mr Fletcher. Sure, you could have spoken earlier, as could a number of other people around Stephen Collier. But he kept everyone just enough in the dark so there was nothing, really, to say – nothing but vague fears and suspicions. Believe me, few people come to us with those; they don't want to look silly.'

'So nothing's going to happen to me?'

Banks stood up and gestured to Hatchley that it was time to leave. 'No. You've helped us. It's up to us now to put a case together, or set a trap.'

'I'll do anything to help,' Fletcher said. 'Tell the bastard I know something and let him come and try to bump me off.'

'I hope it doesn't come to that,' Banks said, 'but thanks for the offer.'

They sat in the car for a few minutes and lit cigarettes. It was pitch-black, and far down in the valley below the lights of Swainshead glittered like an alley of stars.

'How hard should we push Collier?' Hatchley asked.

'We don't push,' Banks said. 'At least not the first time. I told you, he's clever. He'll see we're desperate.'

'So what do we do?'

'We confront him with what we've got and try to trip him up. If he's too clever to fall for that, and I suspect he is, then we try again and keep trying.' He started the engine and broke the silence.

'You can't help admiring the bastard's nerve though, can you,' Hatchley said. 'What if Freddie Metcalfe and Richmond had remembered seeing him order vodka and pour it in Stephen's pints?'

'Then all he'd have had to say was that he played a practical joke, like Fletcher said. There's nothing illegal about chasers. As things stand, it's only Fletcher's word against his, and a good defence lawyer would soon prove that John Fletcher had more than just cause to want to incriminate Collier. They'd bring up the incident at the party, for a start. Could you imagine Katie Greenock on the stand?'

Hatchley shook his head. 'That lass never seems to know whether she's coming or going.'

For some reason, Banks began to feel uneasy at the thought of Katie. What if she really did know more than she was telling? And what if Nicholas Collier suspected she knew? He might easily have seen her talking to Stephen. And Katie was exactly the kind of woman to set off his violent sexual behaviour.

He turned on to the road and headed south for Swainshead. There was still no light on in Collier's house. Hatchley hammered at the door but got no answer.

'Let's try the pub,' Banks suggested.

Hatchley brightened up at that. He hadn't completely forgotten his priorities in a burst of professional zeal.

'Well, if it isn't Chief Inspector Banks,' Freddie Metcalfe greeted them. 'And Sergeant Hatchley, isn't it? What can I do for you?'

Banks ordered two pints of Pedigree and lit a Silk Cut. Maybe a pint would calm down his jangling nerves. The hairs at the back of his neck were bristling.

'Seen Nicholas Collier tonight?' he asked.

'No, he's not been in,' Freddie said. 'Has tha got any further wi' t' murder?'

'We're getting there, we're getting there,' Banks said.

'Aye, and pigs can fly,' Freddie said, passing their drinks.

'None of the usual lot been in tonight?'

'Nope. It's been as quiet as this since opening time,' Freddie answered miserably, and loped off to serve a youth in hiking boots.

'You know,' Banks said, 'I've been thinking about what to do next, and there's someone else we might profit from leaning on in this case.'

'Sam Greenock?' Hatchley said.

'Yes. Threaten him with arrest as an accessory, and we might just get him to open up. He's cocky, but I don't think he's as cool as Nicholas. Stephen Collier's dead now. If we can convince Sam that Nicholas will fall from grace with or without his help, we might be able to strike a bargain. After all, without gentry to suck up to, what's Sam going to get out of it? Nicholas might well have sawn off the branch he was sitting on by killing Stephen.'

'It's an idea,' Hatchley said.

'And Greenock's a bully,' Banks said. 'Bullies are the easiest of the lot to lean on, especially men who beat up their wives.'

'I think I might be able to work up a bit of enthusiasm,' Hatchley said, grinning.

'Good. Let's go.'

'What? Now? But we haven't finished our drinks.'

'I've just got a feeling, that's all. We can come back to them. Let's see if Sam's in.'

They left the White Rose and crossed the bridge. There were no lights on in the front lower or upper rooms of the Greenock Guest House.

'He's not in,' Hatchley said. 'Let's go back to the pub and call again later.'

'It looks like there's nobody in at all,' Banks said. 'That's odd.' He couldn't explain why he felt disturbed by the dark silent house, but he couldn't ignore the feeling. 'No,' he said. 'I'm going in.'

Hatchley sighed and followed. 'I'll bet the bloody door's locked.'

Before they could close the gate behind them, they heard a car coming. It was Sam's Land Rover. He parked near the pub across the narrow Swain, as there was no road on the Greenocks' side, and came bounding over the bridge.

'Evening, gents,' he called out. 'And what can I do . . . Oh, it's you.'

'Don't sound so disappointed,' Banks said. 'We might be able to do something for you.'

'Oh?' Sam's boyish face looked puzzled. He patted his curly hair. 'All right. Never turn down a favour from a copper, that's me.'

'Can we go in?'

'Of course. I'll get the missus to brew a pot of tea.' He dug in his pocket for his keys, finally found the right one and stuck it in the lock, where he poked and twisted it for a while, then turned to Banks and frowned. 'That's odd. It was already open. Katie usually locks up at ten sharp and the guests let themselves in with their own keys. And it's not usually as dark as this. She puts the hall light on for the guests. They're probably still in the pub, but I can't imagine where she is.'

Banks and Hatchley followed him through the front door into the dark hall. Sam turned the light on. The guest book lay open on its varnished table by a stack of tourist guides, maps and brochures advertising local businesses and leisure pursuits. Automatically, Sam looked at himself in the mirror over the phone and patted his curly hair again.

'Katie!' Sam called.

No answer.

He went into the dining room and flicked the light switch on. 'Bloody hell!'

Banks followed him inside. 'What is it?' All he could see was the room where he and Hatchley had eaten breakfast. The varnished tables gleamed darkly in the shaded light.

'She's not set the tables for the morning. She's not even

put the bloody cloths on,' Sam said. He sounded more angry than worried about why or where Katie might have gone.

They paused at the foot of the stairs, where Sam called again and got no answer. 'It doesn't look like she's at home,' he said, puzzled. 'I can't imagine where she'd be at this time.'

'Maybe she's left you,' Banks suggested.

'Don't be daft. Where would she go? Why would she do a thing like that anyway?'

They carried on to the door that separated the Greenocks' living quarters from the rest of the house.

'Katie!' Sam called once more, hand on the knob.

Still no reply. The absolute silence in the house made Banks' hackles rise.

Sam opened the door and walked along the short narrow corridor that linked the two parts of the house. Banks and Hatchley followed close behind. Coats on hooks on either side brushed against them as they walked in single file behind Sam. The only faint illumination was at the end of the passage.

'At least she's left this light on,' Sam said.

The light came from the pane of frosted glass on the door that led into the Greenocks' living room. Sam called his wife's name again but got no answer. He walked into the room and stopped dead in his tracks.

'Jesus Christ,' he gasped, then stumbled backwards into Banks and started to slide slowly down the wall, hands over his eyes.

Banks regained his balance, pushed past Sam and went in, Hatchley close behind. They stopped in the doorway, awed and horrified by the scene before them. Banks heard Hatchley mutter a prayer or a curse.

There was blood all over the room: on the carpet, the sofa, the hearth, and even splashed like obscene hieroglyphs over the wall above the mantelpiece. Nothing moved. Nicholas Collier lay awkwardly, half on the sofa and half on the carpet, his head bashed in, his face a bloody pulp. He wouldn't even have been recognizable if it hadn't been for the prominent yellowish teeth splintered and bared in agony and shock.

Katie sat on the arm of the settee still holding the heavy wooden cross of her granny's that had stood on the mantelpiece. Her beautiful brown eyes were looking at things nobody else could see. The front of her dress was ripped open at one side and a few drops of blood glistened against the pale skin of her blue-veined breast.